FORRORROIS
Tears of Many Mothers

Book Four of the Forrorrois Series

Suzanne Y. Snow

authorHOUSE®

AuthorHouse™
1663 Liberty Drive
Bloomington, IN 47403
www.authorhouse.com
Phone: 1-800-839-8640

First published by AuthorHouse   10/5/2011

ISBN: 978-1-4634-4398-6 (sc)
ISBN: 978-1-4634-4399-3 (hc)
ISBN: 978-1-4634-4400-6 (e)

Library of Congress Control Number: 2011914117

Printed in the United States of America

This book is printed on acid-free paper.

Cover Art by Sarah A. LeBlanc

I want to thank my great readers for their kind support. They have made this journey more amazing than I ever expected. Special thanks go to my friends and family for their patient encouragement through the editing phase and cover development of this fourth book in the Forrorrois Series. I also want to give a special nod to my fellow 20 Amundsen-Scott South Pole Station 1990-91 Winter-Over crew members who knew me as "Mom"—especially my fellow beakers: Kathryn, Karen, Kia, Bill, John, Jim, Jerry, and Dr. Matt (who gave his life on May 11, 2009 while in service to his country) for their positive spirit in a starkly beautiful wilderness. The old Dome, Skylab and the arches will live in our polie hearts as they move into history, now decommissioned and replaced by the new station set on stilts.

PROLOGUE

Colonel Jack Stern strolled into the Apache helicopter hangar on the U.S. air force base near Rome, NY. As he stepped into the shadow of the large arched building, he let his steel-gray eyes adjust from the bright sunlight and removed his blue service cap while he smoothed his short military cut salt-n-pepper hair before pulling his cap back into place. He smiled when he spotted his friend, Captain Perkins, heading for the pilots' locker room in his flight suit. The young blond-haired captain grinned back at him with a sparkle in his blue eyes. *For all his mischief, Perkins does have an all-American smile,* Jack thought as he approached him.

"Perkins, I thought you were going up for some air time today?" Jack called out.

Perkin threw up his hands, with a shrug. "Good morning, Colonel. Looks like I'm not going up today, my co-pilot cancelled on me. He says he's sick as a dog with the flu. Personally, I think it's a hangover. And to add insult to injury, the control tower has just put out weather advisory, so everything's grounded. They told us it should pass in about an hour."

"Sounds like the cards are stacked against you," Jack laughed.

"I think they are," Perkins replied, shaking his head. Then he stopped. "Hey, Colonel, if you're not too busy, I could use somebody to ride shotgun when the weather clears. You interested?"

Jack nodded. "Sure, my gear is in the locker room, I need to clock a few hours anyway. You can go over the flight plan with me while we're waiting."

"That's great! I thought I was going to have to scrub," Perkins said. "Let's hope the weather clears up like they said it will."

Jack followed Perkins into the pilot's lounge and to the right for the men's locker room and showers. He stepped up to his locker and began pulling out his gear.

"So, Colonel," Perkins continued, lowering his voice. "Have you heard from Forrorrois recently?"

Jack glanced around to make certain that they wouldn't be overheard. "Not recently, why?"

"It's nothing important," Perkins replied. "I was hoping I could get together with her for another training session. I tried calling her the other day, but she hasn't gotten back to me yet."

Jack looked over at his friend, surprised. "That's not like her. Maybe, after we're done this afternoon, I'll give her a ring, myself."

"Thanks," Perkins replied. "I was hoping I could finally qualify on that pursuit ship of hers. She's been a tough instructor."

"Have you considered what she asked the other day?"

Perkins hesitated for a moment. "You mean getting the zendra injection?"

Jack nodded. "Yes."

"That's a big step, Jack," Perkins admitted. "And the risk that the flight surgeon would find them in my bloodstream would be huge."

"It's been over five years now since I was injected with them and they haven't detected them in my blood during any of my physicals. If they aren't looking for them, then they probably won't find them," Jack replied. "Perkins, without the zendra, flying a Dramudam pursuit ship in a battle situation could become overwhelming. It would be like trying to fly an apache without a copilot."

"Yeah, but Colonel, Forrorrois has programmed the pursuit ship's computer to respond to verbal English commands. I could do this without the zendra link," Perkins insisted.

Jack shook his head. "Take it from someone who knows, Perkins. No offense, even with your enhanced reaction time you're good, but still not good enough. You need to take this to the next level. That pursuit was meant to be flown with the zendra link interface. Its computer can't read your mind, you won't be subvocalizing, you'll have to speak out loud and use Intergaltic so there won't be any translation errors—in a battle, that could be tough. Believe me, I've flown those craft with and without the zendra link and there is a huge difference."

ABOUT THE AUTHOR

Suzanne Y. Snow was born in Upstate New York and holds a BS in Physics and a MS in Secondary Education: Physics & Mathematics. She has worked extensively in both the engineering and educational fields and strives to inspire young women to pursue careers in the technical fields.

Jack watched Perkins shift on his feet.

"I've got to think on this," Perkins finally replied.

Jack nodded as he closed his locker and picked up his bundle. "Take your time, it's a big decision. I've got my gear, hurry up and get yours. I still want to go over your flight plan."

"All right," Perkins said, opening up his locker.

Jack sighed. He knew his friend was at a crossroads. Perkins had adjusted amazingly well after he had been taken by the Utahar commander, Collinar, four years ago and had been subjected to the same modifications that Forrorrois had endured. But Jack was no fool. He knew Perkins would never have survived emotionally without Forrorrois' patient guidance. She was the only one qualified to help Perkins on his journey to accept and master the forced changes to his body and mind. Like Forrorrois, Collinar had experimented on Perkins and enhanced his reflexes, increased his bone and muscle density, as well as endowed him with the ability to reduce his mass to one-twentieth of his size at will. But, Jack also realized that Forrorrois had taken Perkins under her wing not just to help him, but to ease the guilt she harbored inside for not having been able to protect Perkins from being taken by Collinar in the first place—a guilt that Jack knew was unfounded.

Together, Jack and Perkins went back into the main room of the pilot's lounge and took a seat at one of the small square tables.

"I'll stop over and see Forrorrois this afternoon," Jack said quietly.

Perkins took a seat across from him. "Thanks, I'd appreciate that. Oh, and can you take these to Celeste for me, please?"

Jack was surprised when Perkins slipped a small vending machine package from his lightweight jacket and handed it to him.

Jack laughed as he took the package of colorful candy. "Wiggly critters? Of course I'll give them to Celeste. You spoil that little girl, Perkins."

"I spoil her? Oh, and who is her 'Unca' Jack?" Perkins retorted.

The thought of Forrorrois' impish three-and-a-half-year-old daughter warmed Jack's heart. Celeste looked so much like her Eldatek father, Trager, with her chestnut-brown skin, long straight black hair, and large almond-shaped black eyes—a father that the little girl only knew from Trager's brief ghostly visits from the Plane of Deception. Jack closed his eyes and wished once more that there was a way to free him from the place where he was trapped with Guruma, the founder of the Dramudam, so that Forrorrois would have him back again. Jack looked over at Perkins and pulled on a smile as his thoughts returned to Celeste—realizing fully the little girl had plenty of her mother's stubborn resolve as well. "She's my little angel," Jack laughed. "Now, let's get back to your flight plan."

CHAPTER 1

Trager walked through the ever-changing colored mist that made up the Plane of Deception. Exhaustion pulled on his shoulders as he reached out his chestnut-brown hand and waved an entrance into existence once he approached the bluish-black square enclosure that seemed oddly out of place in the mist. After four revolution trapped in this dimension, Trager no longer paused at its peculiar properties that allowed him to convert energy into matter at a thought. Inside, he found Guruma sitting at the table made of the same bluish-black metal as the exterior of the building. The entrance merged back into the wall behind him after he entered. Trager tried to smile, but his frustration won out as he approached the elder Dramudam founder. He studied Guruma's black almond-shaped eyes and wisdom-creased chestnut-brown face and knew that he could not hide his disappointment from his perceptive companion.

"Have a seat, Trager and join me for some mawya," Guruma requested.

Trager nodded and took a seat across from the Eldatek elder with a sigh. He didn't even react as Guruma waved his hand and produced two red stone mugs. Trager stared down at the mug and watched the steam curled up from the brim tempting his nostrils with the cleansing scent of mawya that he had routinely drank in the morning on Elda when he was young and later on the Tollon when he served with the Dramudam. Suddenly, his thoughts shifted back to Earth where Forrorrois had introduced him to a similar ya made with a blend of mint leaves and lemon. His heart grew heavier as he longed for his dear ashwan and young daughter. Guruma had pulled him into the Plane of Deception to save him when the ship he was flying was destroyed by an explosive planted by Collinar. Unfortunately, Guruma's act to save him also trapped him there with him, forever separating him from his family.

Absently, Trager conjured a small plate of lemon slices and

squeezed the juice into his mug. Like Guruma, Trager had also become adept at using the energy-matter conversion talent. The Aethereals, who were the native beings of the dimension, could only draw sustenance from the mist but they were incapable of the more sophisticated energy-to-matter conversions that allowed Guruma and Trager to create the room around them—because of this, the creatures had branded them sorcerers.

Guruma shook his head and gave him a gentle smile when he offered him the plate of lemon slices.

"No luck again, this cycle?" Guruma asked, lightly tracing a finger on the handle of his red stone mug.

Trager brushed back a stray lock of silky black hair that had escaped from his traditional Dramudam single braid. "No. It's been nearly two mol since I've been able to contact Forrorrois. She and Celeste must be growing worried."

"I'm certain they are," Guruma agreed. "This lull in the energy level of this plane is becoming a concern."

Trager looked up at Guruma and studied his salt-n-pepper hair, also tied back in a single loose braid. He smiled at the fact that they both had continued to wear the traditional green and black uniforms worn by all master pilots of the Dramudam, clinging to them for some sort of normalcy. The room they sat in was a mirror of the quarters that Trager had once had on the Dramudam Peace ship Tollon where he had been a subcommander. That was, until Trager had become detached from the Tollon and joined with Forrorrois. Like their uniforms, Trager and Guruma's surroundings were an illusion to keep them from dwelling on the fact that they were trapped in the Plane of Deception without any hope of returning back to their own dimension.

"I'm concerned as well, Guruma," Trager replied, lifting the red stone mug to his nose and sniffed the light citrus scent. The scent calmed his nerves ever so slightly, enticing him to take a sip. He closed his eyes briefly as the warm liquid quenched his parched throat.

"I suspect that the energy drain is being caused from the Aethereals increased aggression against us and each other," Guruma stated. "The delicate balance was tipped when I brought you over into this dimension over four revolution ago. But there has also been an increase in their population. I saw this happen once before."

Trager leaned forward, surprised at the revelation. "Really?"

"Yes, shortly after I arrived here over a hundred revolution ago, there was a steep increase in the Aethereal birthrate which seemed to stress the population. A war broke out as several factions fought for power and resources. I suspect that this may be a way to regulate the population."

Trager considered Guruma's words. "If so, then we may need to relocate to another area to find foci with stronger energy levels."

"I agree, but we'll need to be extremely cautious in our search," Guruma replied. "The Aethereal continue to watch our every move. One careless moment..." Guruma began then shrugged.

Trager shuddered at the constant unspoken threat. The Aethereal were adept hunters and would sooner kill both Guruma and himself with their razor-sharp claws than continue to suffer their presence any longer than they already had. "When you are ready, we can begin our search for a new location," Trager agreed.

"Good," Guruma said as he lifted his mug from the table. "Until then, I suggest that we limit our activities to try and conserve the energy we have remaining in this location."

Trager nodded. His thoughts wander briefly to Forrorrois and his daughter, Celeste, and wished that he could get them a message—but for now any contact would have to wait a bit longer.

✶✶✶✶✶✶✶✶✶✶

Forrorrois sat in an overstuffed chair set in the living room of her base, reading the worn old Eldanese book that had belonged to Trager—her joined one. She missed him terribly, wishing he were there with her and their three-and-a half year old daughter Celeste. Her eyes closed tightly when the flash of the explosion which had taken him from her played in her mind for the millionth time— the explosion from the bomb planted by Collinar that had been meant for her—sending Trager forever into the Plane of Deception. *Sometimes it's worse for two beings to be separated by centimeters than by kilometers,* she thought as she fingered the delicate pages. Forrorrois cherished the fact that Trager had survived and visited them when he could focus enough energy to cross back into her world, except they could never touch without him vanishing from the effort. But for the past month, even his visits had stopped. A tear slid down her cheek, against her wishes, as she tried not to think about what could be preventing him from seeing her.

She returned her attention to the beautifully scripted book of the ancient legends of Elda. The Eldanese text had taken her several months to learn to read—even with the help of her zendra link with the computer. Each word was filled with nuance and intrigue, each sentence an onion to peel back in the tome's multiple layers of wisdom. Trager's culture was rich with subtle lessons, with no single word wasted. But all of the volume's insight was little comfort when she ached to be held by him once more—to feel his warm chestnut-brown hand against her face—to gaze into his deep black eyes and touch his long raven hair—to smile at the tickle of his mustache as they kissed. A book was little comfort when all she wanted was him.

Forrorrois looked up from her thoughts as the base computer's chime in her mind through her zendra link.

'Incoming transmission from the air force base,' the computer stated in her mind in Intergaltic.

She closed the book with a sigh. 'Put it on audio,' she subvocalized in Intergaltic, without uttering a sound.

"This is Tracker five, calling Forrorrois, please respond..." an airman's voice repeated in English.

'Open a channel, computer,' she subvocalized.

'Channel open.'

"Tracker five, this is Forrorrois, what is the nature of this transmission?" she asked aloud in English.

She was surprised to hear the voice replaced by General Caldwell's on the other end.

"Forrorrois, we have a situation here. I need your help."

She heard the controlled panic in the general's voice, but still she hesitated—she could never fully trust the older man after his multiple deceptions in the past. "General, what seems to be the problem?" she said.

"It's Colonel Stern. He's in trouble."

Her heart began to pound at the sound of her friend's name. She jumped to her feet and straightened her black uniform tunic. "Is the colonel all right?!"

"I think so, for the moment. A tornado came through the base. It hit the hangar he was in. He's been pinned down in the rumble. I've got crews working on trying to reach him, but the building is a twisted mass of metal. I've got no equipment that can handle the sheer weight involved. As best as we can determine, Colonel Stern is trapped between two support beams."

Forrorrois' heart thundered in her chest. "I'll be there in thirty minutes, Forrorrois out."

The computer severed the transmission before the general could respond. The sound of small footsteps made her look over to the hall that led from the living room of her base. Her three-and-a-half-year-old daughter, Celeste, stood there.

"Momma," she called out. "Momma, is Unca Jack hurt?"

Forrorrois crossed over to her and smoothed her long black hair. "I don't know yet, honey, but I have to go and find out."

The little girl encircled her mother's leg with her arms and hugged her tightly. "You'll make him better?"

"I'll try. But first I have to take you to Grandma and Grandpa. They've been asking to see you."

"All right," Celeste said with a stubborn sniff. "But you'd better hurry up and fix Unca Jack's boo boo."

Forrorrois crouched down and hugged her daughter tightly. "OK... now go get your things. We've got to leave in two minutes."

Her daughter hugged her back then ran down the hallway to her bedroom. Forrorrois knew she couldn't hide anything from her daughter. They shared the same empathic ability of sensing other people's emotions. It was a gift with a terrible burden. Her little girl was being forced to grow up faster than most. Forrorrois tried to shelter her child from the world's ugly emotions, but her position in the Dramudam made doing so difficult at best. She watched proudly as Celeste ran back with her overnight bag that Forrorrois always kept ready for her, stuffed with clothes and toys. Together, they hurried hand-in-hand to the hangar bay.

Forrorrois' long-distance scout stood waiting for them, already alerted by Forrorrois' subvocalized command. Celeste squealed with excitement when she saw the ramp extend and the side hatch open on sleek bluish-black scout. Her daughter loved to fly with her. Celeste ran up the ramp, dropped her bag next to a crate in the cargo hold, and bounded into the front compartment. By the time Forrorrois reached the cockpit, her daughter had already strapped herself into the jump seat beside her command chair.

The flight to her parents was a quiet one. She could feel her daughter's apprehension for her 'unca' mingled with exhilaration from flying. Unable to shield her own mixed emotions, Forrorrois found she could offer her daughter only modest comfort. At an early age, Celeste was able to tell the difference between words and emotions. Forrorrois' world could be a harsh one and there was very little she could do to soften it for her daughter at times like these. All she could do was to make certain the people around her loved her and protected her until she was old enough to emotionally protect herself.

Her parents smiled with delight when Forrorrois dropped their granddaughter off. Their smiles became strained when they realized she was wearing her modified black Dramudam uniform for a reason. Jack was a friend of the entire family. Forrorrois gave her daughter one more hug, then left.

'Computer, drop the EM warping field,' she subvocalized as she neared the air force base near Rome, New York. The base was crawling with rescue crews using heavy equipment to clear the path of destruction that meandered through the base. Her heart began to beat faster as she followed the carnage to the outer buildings near the air field.

"Forrorrois! This is General Caldwell, you are cleared for landing near the helicopter hangar," the general's voice sounded, breaking the silence of her cockpit. If the matter wasn't so grave, she would have chided him for not following his own strict radio protocol, but for all their differences Forrorrois knew that the general begrudgingly admired Jack. "Captain Perkins had been in the hangar with the colonel. But just before the tornado hit, the captain had gone to another hangar to retrieve something. Fortunately, Captain Perkins was able to pinpoint Colonel Stern's last known location, but we're still unable to reach him."

"Understood, General, Forrorrois out."

As she approached the twisted girders of the once vaulted building, fearful tears welled against her eyelids. 'Computer, scan the debris for life forms,' she subvocalized.

'One human male...identity Colonel Jack Stern...elevated life signs.'

Thank God! she thought as she pushed back the tears and guided her elegant scout beside the rubble. The cargo hatch and ramp had already responded to her silent command by the time she left the cockpit. Footfalls on the ramp's metal plates told her that urgency had overridden polite social graces. She raised the visor of her helmet and stared at the blue uniform of the gray-haired ruddy-faced man. "My sensors have confirmed your assessment, General," she said. "Colonel Stern's vital signs are all exhibiting extreme stress. He's in pain." Her steady voice didn't betray her inner turmoil. Neither did his, only a slight relieved twitch at the corner of his mouth gave him away.

"At least he's alive," the general replied. He straightened and signaled for Captain Perkins to approach. Perkins' disheveled, sage-green flight suit was dirt-smudged. Forrorrois studied his frantic blue eyes. Jack and Perkins had been friends long before she had come into the picture. But she had to be careful, the general wasn't aware that she had been training Perkins over the past four years. As far as the general was concerned Perkins and she only knew each other from the last time Collinar had assaulted the air base.

11

She dismissed the general with a glance and turned to the Apache pilot. "Please report, Captain," she said.

"Yes, ma'am, I approached Colonel Stern's position as best as I could. He was able to speak. He told me his left leg is pinned, but that he could still wiggle his toes. Unfortunately, there was no room to reach him unless you're possibly a mouse. I tried."

Forrorrois nodded at Perkin's subtle meaning. She reached up and placed her hand on Perkins' shoulder. "I know you did, Captain," she replied. Her mind raced with ideas. "General, I'm afraid that if I start hoisting beams with my craft that I will shift debris onto the colonel." She crossed over to her weapons locker and pulled two palm-sized oval objects out. "I have a suggestion...but I will need help."

The general recognized the weapons and leaned forward. "Go on."

Forrorrois slid opened two other long floor level lockers. Two hovercycles rolled out on skids. "I could go in, with a second person, and extract Jack using a reduction weapon. This assumes that his leg isn't holding something up."

Perkins stepped forward before the general could speak. "I want to be that second person."

Forrorrois eyed the general.

The general gave her a quick nod. "Do it, Captain."

"Thank you, sir," Perkins replied with a curt nod.

"General, I'm going to have to ask you to leave, while I brief Captain Perkins."

The computer broke into her concentration via her zendra link. She raised her hand to her helmet to focus on the message.

"What is it?" the general said.

"There isn't much time, General. The colonel's vital signs have shifted. He's going into shock. If we wait much longer his body won't be strong enough to endure the stress of the reduction weapon," Forrorrois stated as she placed one of the reduction weapons on the seat of the closest hovercycles, along with an emergency bio kit. Before the general could reply, she aimed and fired at the two personal transports.

Caldwell took an involuntary step backwards from the bluish-green flash. "What do you need me to do?" he asked.

"Have the ambulance ready with a crash cart just in case. I'll keep in contact through my ship," Forrorrois continued, "but I need you to get everyone away from the building. I don't want any witnesses. Now go, General!"

General Caldwell stiffened at her abruptness, then turned and hurried down the ramp.

Relieved, she brought up a force shield just in case he changed his mind. Forrorrois placed the full-sized reduction weapon back in the weapons locker. It was time.

"OK, Perkins, the coast is clear, you know what to do," Forrorrois ordered.

Perkins nodded and then concentrated, transforming his mass into energy until he stood just a little over nine centimeters tall at her feet. The air in the long-distance scout's cargo hold warmed slightly from his transformation. Clearing her own mind, she concentrated. The room swirled as she shifted in size, her molecules contracting to her will. In a flash, she stood at eight centimeters next to Perkins.

"You're getting good at that, Captain," Forrorrois remarked, looking up at him.

"I had a good teacher," Perkins replied, with a wink.

Forrorrois smiled at his veiled complement. "Do you remember how to fly one of these?"

"Yes, ma'am."

Forrorrois winced. "Perkins, drop the ma'am and let's mount up."

Perkins nodded without a word and did as she asked, lightly fingering the controls.

Relieved, Forrorrois slung the strap of the bio kit over her head onto her shoulder, then scooped up the reduction weapon and secured the oval to her waist. She straddled the seat of her hovercycle and waved towards Perkins.

"Follow me," she said as she swung her hovercycle around, then out the door. He caught up to her by the time they approached the monumental twisted remains of the hangar. At regular size, the scrapped building was disheartening, but reduced to the size of a mouse the devastation was like attempting to scale Mount Everest. She was relieved to see that the last of the rescue workers were pulling away from the debris. "Computer, continue to monitor Colonel Sterns' vitals, alert me to any changes through my helmet comm," she said aloud in her adopted singsong tongue, Intergaltic. "I've ordered the computer to pinpoint Jack's position for us. The path is plotted through the debris on your screen."

"The detail is incredible...it's like a video game," Perkin's gasped.

Another time, Forrorrois would have found humor in his observations, but now was a time for action. "Follow me," she urged. "We can talk later."

He nodded and fell in behind her.

Together, they cautiously slipped between a flattened beam and the torn corrugated steel skin of the hangar. The sounds of straining metal settling in the distance sent shivers up her spine. The emotions of the emergency crews that stood outside flooded into her mind, making it difficult for her to concentrate. Forrorrois sensed their nervous tension, impotent at being ordered to pull back from the building without explanation. She pushed their emotions from her mind and pressed forward. The reminiscent sound of a whale song made her head snap up.

"Perkins! Left! Go left!" she cried out, nearly sideswiping him.

Without question, he swerved his hovercycle at her order. The enormous beam crashed down in the middle of their path, throwing up dust and debris.

"Go up!" Perkins suddenly yelled.

She couldn't hear him over the roar of the crash, but she followed his action. Together, they weaved upward, finally breaking free from the wreckage into the dust shrouded sunlight, both visibly shaken.

"Let's try a different approach," Forrorrois said, after she caught her breath.

"All right," Perkins replied.

"We'd better drop straight down from above Jack's position," she said.

Perkins brushed the dust from his already dirty flight suit. "That sounds better," he replied.

They followed the contour of the wreckage for several minutes until the computer signaled her.

"What's the matter?" Perkins asked.

"Jack's floating in and out of consciousness," she answered. "We don't have any time to waste. We're just above him. The computer's plotting a new course. We'll enter just under that sheet of steel in front of us."

"Computer, patch me into the general's frequency," she ordered in Intergaltic.

"Frequency open," her scout's computer echoed in her helmet.

"General, do you read me?" Forrorrois asked in English.

"Yes...yes I do," his impatient voice replied in her ears.

"Good. We're above Colonel Stern's position and we've begun to make our way down through the wreckage," she said.

"I have a medic with me. Do you know what Colonel Stern's condition is?"

"My sensors show he's beginning to lose consciousness. His heart is slow, but still strong."

"I see. Keep us posted."

"Understood—Forrorrois out."

Perkins remained silent for several minutes while they descended through the tangled lattice of metal. Forrorrois could feel his controlled concern for their mutual friend.

Finally, Perkins spoke. "We're close to his position. I can see a filing cabinet from the office area I had left him in."

"I see it!" She nudged forward though the barely fifteen centimeter crack between two jumbled girders. The whine of straining metal made her tense.

"We're almost there," Perkins said. He urged the hovercycle forward and then downward into the shadowy abyss below.

"Careful!" she warned. "We need to stay together."

"I can see him!" Perkins called back.

Forrorrois moaned when he ducked under a remnant of a wooden door. She followed, barely able to see in the filtered light. A loud cough made her heart skip a beat. Her hovercycle dipped easily between two pipes that were bigger around than her cycle and her combined. She pulled back suddenly, feeling electricity in the air, surprised that the ship's sensors hadn't picked up the live conductors. With a quick glance around, she spotted frayed wires in front of them. "Perkins, hold your position!"

"But I can see him just past those wires," he called back.

"I said stop! Those wires are live!"

"What?!" Perkins veered hard to the right and pulled in beside her. "But that's the only way in!"

"I know!" she said, switching on her helmet comm. "General..."

"Yes, Forrorrois?" his voice replied.

"We're blocked by live wires. All the power to the building needs to be cut."

"That's impossible! I ordered the power cut an hour ago."

She just rolled her eyes. "Well, somebody missed something and we can't proceed any further," she said.

"I'm on it...Caldwell out."

"What did the general say?" Perkins asked.

"He said he's on it," she replied, chaffing at the delay. The sound of falling debris made her look up. A chunk of metal dropped from above onto the bare cable in front of them. They both shielded their eyes from the brilliant flash. A second round of coughing made her strain to see passed the deadly barrier. "Jack...can you hear me?!" she hollered as loud as she could.

A moan echoed up from the debris below.

"Colonel, we're almost there, buddy. Hang tight!" Perkins yelled.

"Perkins...is that you?" Jack called out weakly from the jumbled heap below.

"Yes! Yes, it's me...Forrorrois is with me too!"

"Forrorrois...thank goodness," Jack said. His voice began to drift.

"Stay with us, Jack, you can't sleep right now," Forrorrois called out. She could feel his consciousness slip back into gray. "Perkins, keep him talking, we can't let him fall asleep!"

"OK," Perkins said. "Ah, Colonel...tell me about the time you shot down that MiG in 'Nam."

"No...I've told you that one over a hundred times," Jack mumbled back.

"No, only ten times," Perkins joked. "Tell it to me again."

"All right," Jack said.

She gave him a nod. "Good job, Perkins."

"It was a cloudy day..." Jack began in a distant voice. Forrorrois smiled to herself, having heard the story at least twice before. She eased her way to one side and tried to get a better look while Perkins kept him talking. The charged air near the cable made her skin crawl. She peered past the wires down at Jack. He was wedge between a desk and a file cabinet. A metal shelf had deflected a girder from his position, but several layers of corrugated steel were piled haphazardly above him. Forrorrois followed Jack's leg down to his foot and spotted a bar of metal over his ankle. Heaving a sigh of relief, she was glad to see his ankle wasn't crushed. She moved back to Perkins' side.

"I think his foot is just wedged, once we reduce him, we should be able to slide him out without too much difficulty, but I'll have to scan him for other injuries before we move him. You just keep him talking," she said.

"That shouldn't be too difficult," Perkins replied with a strained grin. "You still with me, Colonel?" he called out.

"Yeah...You sound so far away..." Jack answered back.

"So what happen next?" Perkins called out.

Forrorrois nodded with approval. "That's the spirit," she said to Perkins. The transmission in her helmet made her move away.

"Forrorrois...they've found the problem. It was a stray line brought in on a different transformer. The power should be off now," the general's voice sounded over her helmet comm.

She scanned the wires then nodded. "That did the trick, General, it's off."

"Good. How's Colonel Stern?"

"Captain Perkins is keeping him talking," she answered.

"That's good," the general replied.

"Yes, I suspect the colonel might have a mild concussion," she said. "We're heading in."

She turned to Perkins and waved towards the cable. The captain fell in behind her while she threaded her way between the frayed conductors. She heaved a sigh as they cleared the pipes and descended to Jack's position.

"Forrorrois!" Jack gasped as he tried to rise but quickly gave up at the futility.

She hovered over his chest and looked down at her giant friend. "Stay still until I check you out," she ordered.

"Anything for my little Dramudam angel," the salt-n-pepper colonel teased through the pain.

"Little Dramudam Angel?" Perkins said with a sideways stare.

"Don't start, Perkins," she warned while she pulled her bioscanner from her pouch and made a few adjustments.

"Perkins! The general didn't see you like that, did he?" Jack continued when he caught a glimpse of the captain's tiny hovercycle.

"No, I let him think Forrorrois was going to use her reduction weapon on me," Perkins replied.

Jack began to chuckle, but it quickly turned into a grimace.

Forrorrois glanced at Perkins while she continued her scan. She hovered over the complete length of the colonel twice before she spoke.

"Well, Jack, except for being extremely ornery, you'll live. You've got a fracture in your left arm, a badly sprained ankle, and a good old bang on the head. But I'm not too worried about any permanent damage, especially since you've got such a thick skull," Forrorrois said as she put the scanner back in her pouch.

Jack's gray eyes sparkled at her teasing. "Ha ha," he replied with a wince. "So how do you think you're going to get me out of here?"

"The same way Perkins and I got in," she replied.

Colonel Stern's humor melted swiftly replaced by a look of horror.

"Oh...no.... You're not doing that to me again!" he stammered.

"Come on, Colonel, it's the only way out of here," Perkins said. "And really, it's not that bad."

"Oh, that's comforting coming from you," Jack scoffed, "especially since you can do that at will!"

Perkins hovered his cycle just in front of Jack's face. "Ah, you're just chicken," Perkins said.

"If I could move, I'd swat you like a bug, you little..."

"Boys...boys...play nice," Forrorrois said. "Jack settle down. We don't have a choice. What's left of this building isn't stable enough for us to wait for them to dig you out. It's settled, I'm not going to argue with you."

"Forrorrois, you know how I feel...." Jack began, but he cut himself short as the metal groaned above them. Moments later the roof supports of the collapsed hangar shifted to the right of their position, sending a cloud of dust in their direction.

When the dust settled, Forrorrois glanced over at Perkins. His eyes were large from the near miss. Forrorrois could feel Jack's genuine anxiety at the thought of being reduced, but time was running out.

"There isn't time to debate this, Jack," she said. "Now, just relax."

He clenched his eyes shut when she pulled the weapon from her waist. In a flash he was unconscious, barely nine centimeters in length. Perkins and she landed their hovercycles beside him. Forrorrois jumped off her seat and pulled a thin thermal blanket from the seat compartment. She crossed over to Jack and tucked the silver fabric around him while Perkins helped.

"Do you think you can handle him on your hovercycle?" she asked while she passed the bioknitter over Jack's badly bruised ankle.

"I think so," Perkins said.

She could sense his nervousness even without her heightened abilities. With her free hand, she slipped the strap of the pouch over her head and handed the bag to Perkins. "See if you can find the hypo while I finish up his ankle. Jack's going to need something for the pain when he comes around."

Perkins rummaged inside the bag then pulled a cylinder out triumphantly. "Found it."

"Good," she said while she moved from Jack's ankle to his right arm. She widened the tear in his sleeve and saw multiple shades of purple and yellow above and below his elbow. "We'd better let the medics set this. Give me the hypo and find the splint."

She took the hypo from Perkins' outstretched hand and dialed in a low dose. Jack's face relaxed slightly as she hissed the cylinder against his neck.

"Here you go," Perkins said as he handed her the splint.

"Thanks," she replied.

He took the hypo from her and dropped the cylinder back inside the bag. In a few moments, Forrorrois had Jack's fractured arm immobilized against his waist. A moan escaped from the older man's lips.

She slipped the equipment back into her pouch. "He's coming around," she said.

"Thank goodness," Perkins breathed.

"We'll move him when he's fully awake. It'll be easier for you to balance him on the hovercycle," Forrorrois said as she stood up and walked over to her own transport. As she stashed the pouch inside the seat compartment, a horrible creak of failing metal emanated from above, without a second thought, Forrorrois concentrated. Her enlarging body pitched forward above the two miniaturized men as Perkins gasped beneath her. The debris shifted and rained down onto her back. She bit her lip to keep from crying out as a jagged piece sliced through her side and cracked a rib. Metal girders settled on the desk and filing cabinet to either side of her, pressing her down. She strained to keep the shards from harming her tiny charges huddled beneath her. With tremendous effort, Forrorrois maintained her position for several moments until she was certain the mass above her had come to rest once more.

Wet rivulets trickled down her sides. Her back had been cut in several places by ragged pieces of metal. She sucked for air between clenched teeth in shallow breaths and rested her head against her fingers. Attempting a deeper breath, Forrorrois shuddered, unable to get more than a superficial gasp from the fractured ribs. *I have to get them out,* Forrorrois thought as she pushed through the pain. Composure regained, Forrorrois peered under her belly. There, beneath her straddled frame, crouched Perkins, wide-eyed. "Are you all right?" she whispered.

"Yeah," he said. "Thanks."

"Don't mention it," Forrorrois replied as she rolled the debris off her back to one side. Then she concentrated once more and reduced herself back down to eight centimeters in height. The effort left her crumpled on the debris-strewn cement floor.

"You're hurt!" Perkins stammered.

"I'll survive," she replied, curled up on her side. "There's an opening above for you to fly out with Jack. I'll follow."

"Let me help you onto your cycle," he insisted.

Forrorrois wasn't in any shape to argue. "Careful," she said when his arm brushed her shredded back.

"Oh my God, you're bleeding," he said, shifting his hand.

"Don't worry about that," she bristled.

Suddenly, she was assaulted by the general's frantic transmission.

"Forrorrois, respond!"

"We're all right, General. Have the ambulance ready, we'll be out in ten more minutes," she growled into her comm link.

"Acknowledged…"

Forrorrois watched Perkins walk back over to Jack. He was coming around.

"You're not all right, Forrorrois," Perkins said, checking the older man's pulse. "You're bleeding."

"Never mind that—get the colonel on your hovercycle," she ordered, pointing up at the now visible patch of blue sky above them. "That desk isn't going to hold much longer."

Jack opened his eyes and stared up at Perkins. "She did it, didn't she?" he moaned. "She turned me into an elf."

Perkins pulled on a smile. "She said she would. Now, come on old man, get onto your feet, this place isn't going to wait any longer."

Jack hobbled to his good foot and looked down at his arm trussed up in a sling.

"You're lucky," Perkins commented as he shifted Jack onto the seat.

"Yeah, right, I feel like somebody dropped a house on me," Jack said, while Perkins settle in behind him.

Forrorrois smiled at his sour humor and engaged her engine. "After you, gentlemen."

She watched as Perkins held Jack close to him with his left hand and maneuvered the hovercycle straight up. When they cleared the debris, the smell of the fresh breeze greeted them. Perkins searched the horizon then headed for the ambulance. Forrorrois paced him for a while but she soon felt the world begin to swirl before her. *Just a little further,* she kept telling herself, when they made their final approach towards the olive drab emergency vehicle with a red cross painted on the roof and sides.

"General, we're approaching the ambulance. Have them open the rear doors and move the medics from the back. Remember, no witnesses," she said over her helmet comm.

"I'm clearing them out now," he said.

Forrorrois watched the general approach the back, alone, and open the double doors. Perkins flew in and landed on the gurney. She followed him in but remained hovering off to one side of the stretcher while Perkins eased Jack onto the white sheet.

"How's he doing?" the general said, towering behind her.

"He'll be fine, once the medics set his arm and watch him for a few days," she replied. "Perkins, clear out so I can return him back to full size."

"You take it easy, Jack," Perkins said as he returned to his hovercycle.

"I will," Jack replied with a grimace.

She waited for Perkins to move away then in a greenish-blue flash, she enlarged Jack.

"Come on Perkins—let's not hold up the medics," Forrorrois ordered as she placed the reduction weapon back on her waist. The throbbing pain from her cracked ribs and inability to take a deep breath was beginning to blur her vision as she turned her hovercycle from the gurney.

Perkins maneuvered his transport next to her and shook his head. "You need a medic, too," he whispered.

"Not here," she warned in a low voice.

Caldwell turned towards their miniature forms. "What was that?"

She threw a damning stare at Perkins. "Nothing, General," she said. "I was just saying we should leave so that the medics could get in here."

"You're absolutely right. I'll debrief you later," the general replied, returning his attention back to Jack.

Forrorrois turned her hovercycle away and headed out the ambulance rear door towards her shrouded long-distance scout ship. Perkins chased after her. She struggled to maintain a straight course, but the weave of her hovercycle was magnified by the time she approached the shimmering hatchway of her scout. As she passed through the opening, her resolve failed. Her hovercycle hit the floor plates and skittered sideways until the transport hit the far wall. She slid with the craft, nearly blacking out from the agony of her ribs. The world swirled around her when she tried to focus. She gasped for air but her body rebelled, racked in pain, making her wish she'd never gotten out of bed that morning. An odd warm sensation trickled down her back as she rolled over and stared up into Perkins' eyes. Forrorrois reached out and touched his face. Then, without warning, she concentrated, forcing them both to enlarge. Perkins stumbled backwards in surprise to the floor plates—enlarged and unconscious.

"Sorry, Perkins," Forrorrois said as she stumbled to her knees. She peeled off her helmet then attempted to get up. The attempt failed as she stumbled forward and passed out.

When she opened her eyes, Forrorrois was alarmed to find herself in the back of an ambulance with Perkins staring down at her. "Oh great," she mumbled. "I should have locked the hatch."

"Very funny," Perkins replied. "And I didn't appreciate that little stunt you pulled."

"You shouldn't have brought me here," Forrorrois insisted as she became aware of the medic bent over her.

"You're lucky he found you, miss," the medic said, shining a light in her eyes.

"That's Mrs. and where did he say he found me?" she said, annoyed at the light.

"The rubble of the building," the medic replied. "From what I can see, you've got a few fractured ribs, a deep puncture wound to your side, several lacerations, and blood loss—other than that you're in pretty good shape."

She sensed there was more to his words than just an aside when he moved his hand to the side of her face. "You can remove your hand from my person, before I break it," she warned in a low tone.

The man stepped back when she struggled to get up. Perkins stepped forward and rested his hand on her shoulder. His modified strength pinned her down firmly. Forrorrois covered her mouth with her free hand when a coughing fit overtook her. There were flecks of blood on her fingers as she pulled her hand away. "That's not good," she said.

The medic pushed past Perkins and took her hand to examine the blood specks.

"I think you've got a punctured lung," he announced.

"Perkins...where's my bio kit?" Forrorrois growled, pulling her hand away from the medic. The effort made her grab her side in pain.

"On your ship..." Perkins stated then cut off looking at the medic.

"Get it and bring it to me," she gasped.

"I can't, its back on the tarmac and the defense shield went up around it when I carried you off the scout," he replied, lowering his voice.

Forrorrois glanced at the medic and could sense the man's peaking curiosity.

"Stop this vehicle now!" she gasped. The back of the ambulance swam in her head. "Guruma guide me," she continued in Intergaltic. Her vision blurred with increased streaks of black.

"What did she just say?!" the medic asked.

"You don't want to know," Perkins replied.

Forrorrois' head throbbed as her panic only magnified her pain. Finally, the cool cradle of unconsciousness took her.

****

Perkins paced the halls nervously, waiting for word on Jack and Forrorrois' condition. He sensed odd looks from the medical personnel in emergency. He objected when they sent him to the waiting room, but the nurses refused to make an exception for him. Finally, Perkins sat in a chair that was grouped in a line with several others against the wall in the hallway. His flight suit and face were still smudged with dirt from digging through the rubble of the hangar. Perkins ran his fingers through his short blond hair and hung his head as he waited for someone to tell him how Forrorrois and Colonel Stern were doing.

The sound of approaching footsteps made him look up. He tensed when he saw General Caldwell. Immediately, Perkins rose to his feet in attention and snapped a salute.

Caldwell saluted him back.

"At ease, Captain. Any word on Colonel Stern?" the general asked.

"Only that they have stabilized him and set his arm, sir," Perkins replied, lowering his hand to his side.

"And have you been given any word on Forrorrois?"

"Not much, sir," Perkins replied. "They are monitoring her for a collapsed lung caused by a puncture wound."

"I see," the general said with a nod. "She was lucky you brought her back to the medics when you did. Where did you actually find her, Captain?"

Perkins glanced around to make certain that no one was in earshot. "We had returned to the cargo hold of her ship and Forrorrois re-enlarged me. Then, without warning, she collapsed. She had been hurt during the extraction, but I didn't realize how badly until then. When we were retrieving Colonel Stern, the rubble shifted above us and several chunks of debris rained down. Forrorrois shoved me and Jack out of the way and took the brunt of the force."

"She has a special fondness for Colonel Stern," the general commented. "You did the right thing bringing her back to the medics, Captain. I understand that both the colonel and Forrorrois will be taken to rooms soon. I'll have them notify you once the colonel can take visitors. As for Forrorrois, her visitors will be a bit more restricted."

He tensed at Caldwell's unspoken exclusion of him from being able to see Forrorrois. "I understand, sir," Perkins replied.

"In the meantime, Captain, I want you to report to the flight surgeon for a complete physical, just as a precaution, you understand. He's waiting for you in his office," the general said, pointing down the hallway.

Perkins shoulders slumped. "Yes, sir." He saluted and waited for the general to salute back before he dropped his hand to his side. The general nodded then turned in the opposite direction and headed down the hallway. Reluctant to leave, Perkins knew he had to follow orders. Any resistance would get him grounded.

✶✶✶✶✶✶✶✶✶✶✶

As Forrorrois came to, she found herself in a hospital room. A voice sounded from the other side of a blue curtain divider. She moved to get up but abruptly found restraints on her wrists and ankles. Her uniform had been removed and replaced with a pale blue hospital gown. A sharp pain in her side prevented her from any further attempts to move. The curtain was brushed aside by General Caldwell.

"Glad to see you're awake," he said.

She looked at him, suspiciously. "How's Jack?"

"He's recovering nicely. It'll be a few days bed rest for him, though."

Forrorrois breathed a sigh of relief. "That's good." She raised her wrist slightly. "Why am I restrained?" she asked.

"You became violent when the doctors tried to help you. I'll have them removed, if you promise not to try to leave," he said.

"And how long do I have to promise not to leave?" she asked.

"A few days...a week at most," he said. "Perkins told me that you took quite a blow when a piece of debris came down. He said you did it to prevent the debris from hitting Jack and him."

She looked away at his words. "It was purely instinct," she said. "Look General, I can't stay...I have commitments. People will be worried."

The general smiled at her words. "You needn't worry. I've already called your parents to let them know where you are. I assured them that you were all right. I even told them that they could come and visit you here at the base hospital."

The color drained from her pale face. "General...I've told you before to leave my family out of this."

"Forrorrois, your family was worried about you. They were also worried about Colonel Stern. I just wanted them to know where you were going to be for possibly the next week," he said with a shrug.

"Thank you," she replied, a chill in her voice.

"Well, I'd better go now and let you rest. The doctors asked me not to excite you," he said.

She watched him go, still furious inside. Only a few minutes had passed when the curtain parted again. It was Perkins. He was a sight with his disheveled blond hair and rumpled flight suit. Relief was evident in his blue eyes.

"I only have a few minutes, is it safe?" he asked, glancing around.

"Yes, my ship is monitoring the room," she replied.

"That's a relief," Perkins sighed. "The doctors don't even know I'm here. The general didn't put me on your visitor list."

Frustrated by the restraints, she motioned him closer with a nod of her chin. "What did you tell the general?!"

"Nothing, honest," Perkins said.

She scanned his emotions, he was telling the truth. "Good. What about the hovercycles and equipment?"

"All back on your ship. When I carried you out to the ambulance, a few soldiers tried to approach the ramp, but the hatch closed and the ship vanished," he replied, stunned.

She leaned back, relieved. "You did the right thing...maybe not bringing me here...but leaving everything else on the ship. How's Jack?"

Perkins brightened. "Jack's doing fine. They're keeping him for a few days to watch his concussion. His arm set real nice, but he'll be on crutches for a while with his ankle."

Forrorrois leaned her head back against the pillow. Perkins was a good man. "Thank you for getting Jack out. I don't know if I would have been able to do it by myself," she said.

Perkins approached the side of her gurney and rested his hands on the railing. "I should be thanking you. Neither Jack, nor I, would have left there alive if you hadn't done...what you did."

She smiled up at him. "No problem."

His eyes darted towards the curtain. "I'll let the colonel know that you're doing OK," he said.

She watched him reduce his size and dash under the nightstand by her bed. "Thanks," she whispered after him.

Suddenly, a brunette nurse came in and took her wrist, then looked at her watch. "I'm told you can have the restraints removed," the nurse stated after she recorded the vitals on Forrorrois' chart.

Forrorrois glanced up in surprise when the woman proceeded to unfasten the straps from her wrists and ankles. "Thank you," she said to the young woman.

"You have some visitors waiting outside."

Forrorrois reached out with her mind and suddenly felt the familiar sensation of her parents—and daughter. Panic raced in her heart. Why did they bring Celeste? Nobody at the base knew about her, except Jack and Perkins.

"You're still wobbly, so don't get out of bed," the nurse continued while she raised the head of the hospital bed so Forrorrois could sit up. Then she pulled back the curtain.

She waited until the nurse left before she spoke.

"Mom...Dad..." she said, glancing down at her daughter.

"It's all right, Danica. We told them that we were watching a friend's child while they were out of town," her mother informed her.

Forrorrois could feel her daughter's fear at being in the strange place. She motioned her forward. Celeste came closer and stared up at the side of her bed. "Dad, set her up here with me."

"But Danica...your ribs," her mother said.

"They're not that bad, besides, I want to hold my little peanut," she said. Her daughter beamed at her words.

Her father lowered the bed railing and set Celeste next to her. Forrorrois pulled her into a gentle hug and smoothed her hair, ignoring the sharp pain in her ribs. Unfortunately, her daughter could not.

"Momma, I feel your boo boo," her daughter said, pulling back.

"It's all right, peanut, when you're here with me it feels much better," she whispered.

"Grandma says you're going to stay here for awhile...till you get better."

Forrorrois paused then brushed a lock of Celeste's raven-black hair from her reddish-brown cherub face. "Just for a while, then I'll be able to come home."

"Momma...what do you want me to tell Poppa?"

Forrorrois smiled at her daughter. "If Poppa stops by, you can tell him that I'll be home in a few days when I'm feeling better and not to worry. Now, don't forget to practice with your meditation sphere before you go to bed and say your prayers with Grandma and Grandpa."

"I will, Momma," her daughter said.

Forrorrois stared into her almond-shaped black eyes. "That's my good girl. Now, give me a kiss."

Her daughter smiled at her praise and kissed her on the cheek.

Forrorrois looked up when her father collected Celeste in his arms and set her back on the floor.

"You're looking tired," he said as he raised the railing back up.

"It's been a long day," Forrorrois said. "Thanks for watching her."

"It's no trouble at all," her mother said.

Forrorrois looked over at her dad. Without a spoken word he nodded.

"Celeste, I saw a machine just down the hall that had your favorite candy inside," he said while he took her hand.

"Sour Wiggly Critters?!" she squealed. Then she stopped and looked at Forrorrois.

"Yes, you can have some," Forrorrois said with a grin at her little daughter.

Celeste bounced excitedly while her grandfather led her back into the hall.

"Mom...please...stay for a minute," Forrorrois said when her mother turned to go.

Her mother turned back towards her.

"Mom, it's all right. I'm going to be fine," she whispered.

Her mother stepped forward and rested her hands on the railing. Forrorrois reached out and touched her fingers with hers.

"Please don't hold back the words, Mom. I can feel your emotions and so can Celeste," she said.

Her mother looked up at the ceiling then bit her lip. When she looked back at her, tears pressed for release.

"Oh, Danica, I know you're special. I know your job puts you in danger, but it doesn't mean I have to like it. What kind of a life are you raising Celeste in? It's bad enough as your mother, wondering if this is the time you're not coming back, but what about Celeste? Without Trager here—who's going to protect her? She needs to be a child—without secrets."

"Oh, Mom, she has you and Dad. And if you need help, the Dramudam will protect her, like they protected me. She doesn't look that different, besides she is half-Human. This is her world too."

"But what about the other half—Trager's half? Someday she'll need to understand that too," her mother insisted.

Forrorrois looked away for a moment to collect her thoughts. Since Celeste was born, Neeha, Trager's mother on Elda, had refused any contact with either of them. Forrorrois pulled on a smile and looked back at her mother. "Mom, Celeste is learning about the Eldatek. Trager is teaching her what she needs to know. I even read her stories from his world in Eldanese so that she will be able to communicate with Trager's mother, when the time comes and Neeha finally agrees to meet her. She'll be OK."

"I'm sorry, Danica, it's just so difficult to accept everything," her mother said. "It's very unnerving when Trager appears to her like that—like a ghost. And that other one, Guruma, you call him. Both of them just appearing to Celeste without warning—I'm sorry, but it's just not normal. Nothing in your life is normal. Sometimes I just wonder if you put yourself at risk as a cry for help."

Forrorrois looked up at her mother and sighed as she closed her fingers around her mother's hand. "Oh, Mom, put that thought right out of your head," Forrorrois said. "So Trager and I don't have an ideal marriage..."

"Trager's trapped in another dimension, Danica! The only time the two of you get to spend together is when he can focus enough energy to partially cross over to see you, which seems to be getting less and less lately. You can't even touch him when he's here or he vanishes!"

The old argument was making Forrorrois' already aching head hurt worse. She pulled her mother's hand to her lips and kissed her fingers then rested them against her cheek. "Mom, we've been through this before. I can't change it. I'm lucky Trager's alive. Yes, I'd like to see him more, touch him even, but for now I have to be happy with what I've got. Celeste still has her father, that's all we need. As for Guruma, he comforts Trager and guides me when I need advice, just like he guides all the Dramudam. Please try to understand."

Her mother's face softened. "I'm sorry...I had promised your father I wouldn't get into this with you today. But we do need to talk about this," she insisted.

"I know...I know, Mom," Forrorrois said. "When the doctors release me, you and I'll sit down and thrash this whole thing out. Until then, I want you to know I still love you and I'm glad Celeste feels so secure with Dad and you."

Her mother squeezed her fingers then slipped her hands back to the railing. "I love you too, dear. Now, get some rest. You look tired. Your dad and I'll come back in the morning with Celeste."

"Thank you, Mom," Forrorrois said. She watched her go then closed her eyes.

Forrorrois had almost drifted off to sleep when the clearing of a throat made her look up. It was the general. "What do you want?" she mumbled.

"A word about your family," he said, stepping closer.

She peered up at him through heavy lids. Suspicion played at the back of both their minds. "What about them?" she asked.

"The little girl—she resembles Trager," he said.

"She's a neighbor's child. My parents are watching her while the little girl's mother is out of town," she replied.

"Forrorrois, it wouldn't take me more than a few hours to confirm if you are telling me the truth," he said. "No, I think there's more. You disappeared for over a year after that business with Collinar was cleared up. I think she's your daughter. She's the right age. You can't deny that."

Forrorrois studied him closely. Her worst nightmare was unfolding before her. "General, I've warned you before that I will not tolerate you interfering with my family. That little girl will not be harassed in any way. I'll do anything to protect her...and I mean anything," she warned in a low voice.

The general stood for several heartbeats before he shifted his weight on his feet. "I believe you would," he said in a hushed voice.

"Good. Now, if you'll be so kind as to leave, I'd like to get some rest," she said. He nodded to her then left. Between the pain and the general's words, Forrorrois closed her eyes and let the tears slide down her cheeks. She barely looked away when the nurse returned to lower the head of her bed.

"Is everything all right?" the nurse asked, concerned.

"No...Yes...I don't know," she confessed.

"Are you in pain?"

"Yes...I would like to be left alone please," Forrorrois said.

"Let me get you something for the pain," the nurse offered as she headed for the door.

"Thank you," Forrorrois said. She stared up at the ceiling while the woman left the room. The general's words weighted heavily on her mind, she couldn't stay here any longer than she had too.

The scrap of a boot on the floor tile told her she wasn't alone.

"I thought you were going to see the colonel," Forrorrois stated, glancing over towards her bed stand. Perkins was standing full-sized once more beside her bed.

"There was too much traffic, in-and-out of the room for me to leave," Perkins replied, sheepishly. "I didn't mean to eavesdrop."

"Probably just as well," Forrorrois said. "Contact my parents later and tell them it's not safe to return to the base—especially not safe for Celeste. I'm afraid the general is up to his old tricks."

Perkins nodded. "The general is. I was ordered to see the flight surgeon while you and Jack were in the emergency. The flight surgeon gave me a very through checkup including blood work. Afterward, he said I seemed fine, but that I was relieved from duty for the next week until all the test reports were back."

Forrorrois looked up at him, now concerned. "Be very careful, Perkins."

"I will. I'm going to see the colonel, then head home."

"Smart idea—keep a low profile for the next twenty-four hours until the general is distracted," Forrorrois warned.

"I'll stop by tomorrow," Perkins replied, with a twinkle in his blue eyes.

"Thanks," Forrorrois said. Without warning, Perkins reduced his size once more. Forrorrois looked up at the ceiling as she considered Caldwell's next move.

****

Collinar's Utahar golden feline eyes flashed as he piloted the stolen Dramudam one-seat long-distance scout ship toward Earth—back to Forrorrois so he could exact his revenge. His forced incarceration at the Dramudam rehabilitation station for the past four revolution was finally over. For all his plotting and early failed attempts at bribery, it was a fluke which had given him the opportunity to escape. The Dramudam were so overconfident in their belief that he would meekly sit out his sentence in their pathetic prison disguised as a social realignment center! After resisting at first, he played their games and mouthed the words they wanted to hear, but it was just a matter of time before his chance at freedom presented itself. A lax moment in security during a power fluctuation had allowed him to slip from his cell during a guard change—a vacant corridor which led him to an unoccupied hangar bay—a ship fueled and waiting for the taking. *What luck for my chance at freedom to present itself as a fully supplied long-distance scout with hyperfold capability!* he gloated to himself.

Collinar knew he couldn't approach the Utahar directly to regain his position as a commander—he'd have to prove himself first. Killing Forrorrois wouldn't be enough, but he knew that he would thoroughly enjoy the moment. But first he needed a place to regroup—*and what better place than the scene of my supposed crime?* he reveled to himself. *And if Forrorrois just happen to present me with the opportunity of her own demise then why not oblige her?*

Collinar's golden-tan lips curled into a sneer at the sight of the approaching solar system on his medium-range sensors. He would be in communications range of Earth within the hur. *It will be simple to persuade General Caldwell with an opportunity to gain some advanced technology after four tiresome revolution of Forrorrois denying it to him,* Collinar thought as he made an adjustment to the controls. He had grown accustomed to the Dramudam craft—after a few false starts. The thought of allowing zendra to be injected into his body for the sake of communicating with a ship disgusted him. So he was relieved when he found that at least this ship's computer was capable of taking verbal commands. *I shouldn't have any problem passing through the sensor grid around the planet in this craft since its Dramudam. By the time I've reached the general's base, Forrorrois won't have time to react,* he calculated.

Irritated, he reached up and brushed the stray lock of blond hair that fell into his eyes. His hair had grown long during his imprisonment. Something he would remedy once he reached Earth—along with the bland light-green incarceration overalls they had forced him to wear.

CHAPTER 2

The next morning Forrorrois awoke, stiff from Jack's rescue the day before. She was surprised to find Perkins watching her from the curtain. He was dressed in faded blue jeans, a faded plaid shirt and a light denim jacket. In his hand was a large brown paper bag.

"I didn't wake you, did I?" he asked, uncertain.

She smiled at his school boy manners. He was a likable guy. "No...No you didn't," she said with a grimace when she tried to sit up. "Perkins, you shouldn't be here. If the general finds out you'll be in trouble."

Perkins gave her a wink. "Don't worry—no one even knows I'm on the base. I'm supposed to be back at my apartment on medical leave. You're not the only one that can sneak around."

"Perkins, what about the nurse?" she insisted.

"I told you, don't worry. I slipped past the nurse. He was at the desk looking at a chart," Perkins said in a low voice.

Forrorrois shook her head and sighed. "How's Jack doing?" she asked while he set the paper bag on the bed stand next to her.

"Good...but he's worried about you being in here. I told him about the general's visit yesterday." Perkins glanced at the door. "I also heard that the general received a message last night—a long distance message. A friend of mine is a comms officer. The transmission came in on that frequency that they use to contact you. Then it switched to a different one. That's all my friend would say."

Forrorrois forced herself to sit up. *This can't be good,* she worried.

"Oh, I brought you these," Perkins said, pushing the brown paper bag toward her.

Curious, she picked up the bag from the bed stand and looked inside. A smile spread across her face when she realized the paper bag contained her black uniform and boots. "How did you get these?"

He shrugged. A grin tugged at his lips. "I happened to be in a certain room at the right moment."

"Thank you!" She grabbed his arm and pulled him close, kissing him on the cheek.

The captain's eyes grew wide. He touched his fingers to his cheek, stunned by her actions. "I…ah...you're welcome. I'd better go before the nurse finds me in here."

Forrorrois grinned at his reaction, but her mind raced ahead formulating her plan. "Don't go yet," she replied.

"OK," he said, nervously. "I don't have to rush out."

Forrorrois grew serious. "I'm worried about Jack and my family. I don't trust the general—especially since he saw Celeste with my parents yesterday. I have to get out of here and I need to get Jack out, too. If that message was really long distance, then whoever contacted the general is breaking the Isolation Treaty. The general may decide I'm more useful as a prisoner than an ally and begin leveraging the people close to me."

Perkins eyes widened. "You've got to get out of here, Forrorrois!"

"I will, but not without Jack," she insisted. "I need your help."

"You name it," Perkins replied.

"I need you to get Jack out of here. The long-distance scout is on the roof. Get Jack on board and be ready for me. When I know you're on board, I'll head for the ship when I get a break. If things go badly, head directly for my parents—get them and Celeste back to my base. Jack can recuperate at my base if he thinks his cabin is too risky. Just don't let anyone see you or you might end up on a wanted list as well."

Perkins flashed her one of his all American smiles. "Don't worry about me—I can take care of myself. I had a good teacher," he said with a wink.

Forrorrois smiled. "I know you can, that's why I'm asking for your help. Now, get out of here! I've informed the scout that you're coming. Get a personal transport from the ship, I don't think Jack's in any shape to walk. And use a reduction weapon on him if he resists."

"Please, don't tempt me!" Perkins grinned. "Don't fret, I'll take care of getting the colonel out and I'll see you on the roof."

Forrorrois nodded when he turned and left. Then she changed as swiftly as her stiff body would allow. Perkins' comment about a long distance message still rang in her mind. *It could only mean a message from space, but from whom?* With a grunt, she pulled on her boots. Her body protested from her decisive action. Forrorrois gave into her body, realizing she had to wait a little while longer before she could leave. Grabbing the blanket, she pulled the bedding up around her neck and lay back. She needed to be certain that Jack and Perkins were aboard her scout before she left her room.

****

Jack looked up at the sound of the curtain being shifted and was surprised to see Perkins dressed in civilian clothes in his hospital room before visiting hours. He shifted to sit up, but flinched when his arm began to throb in its cast.

"Perkins, what are you doing here this early?" he asked.

"Forrorrois sent me," Perkins whispered. "She wants me to get you out of here, pronto. She's afraid that Celeste and her family might be in danger and she wants them moved to her base."

Jack studied the young captain. "Did something happen since yesterday?"

"Yes, there was a very long distance call that came into comms for the general."

Jack's eyes widened. "Oh, crap," he muttered. "I'm going to draw some attention with my bare butt hanging out in this hospital gown. They cut off my flight suit, so I don't have anything to wear."

Perkin's smiled and grabbed a bundle of clothes from behind the curtain. "I figured you'd need something. I grabbed some scrubs from the doctors' lounge. Here, put them on. And here's a white lab coat, too."

Jack grinned. "I knew there was a reason I let you hang around," Jack said as he took the bundle with his good hand.

Perkins turned around and peeked past the curtain. "I'll keep watch while you change."

Jack changed into the scrubs as quickly as he could with his broken arm.

"So what's the plan?" Jack asked, as he shimmied into the blue pants then clumsily pulled the drawstring tighter with one hand.

"We get to the roof and wait for Forrorrois in her scout."

Jack nodded. "Good plan."

"Shh, someone's coming," Perkins warned.

"Hide," Jack ordered, pulling his blanket to his chin. Perkins dropped from sight as the curtain was shifted to one side. Jack looked at the intruder and wasn't surprise to see it was General Caldwell.

"Glad to see you're awake, Colonel," Caldwell remarked, staring at him.

"It's hard to sleep in a hospital," Jack replied. "People keep coming in the room at all hours of the day to poke at me."

"How's your arm?" the general said, ignoring his barb.

"Broken," Jack said, keeping it under the blanket.

"You're lucky that's all that was broken," Caldwell said. "How's your ankle?"

"Pretty tender, I still can't put my full weight on it yet," Jack replied, conscious that the Caldwell was eyeing him.

"Are you cold, Colonel?" Caldwell asked.

Jack pulled the blanket a bit higher. "Ah, actually, yes, I am. On the last shift I asked them to turn down the air conditioning in here, but they told me it's all in my head. That's bedside manners for you," Jack said, rolling his eyes.

"I'll ask the nurse to bring you another blanket," Caldwell said, still watching him.

"I'd appreciate that," Jack replied with a smile. "So when do you think they'll release me? The doctor isn't telling me anything."

Caldwell shrugged. "I'm certain that the doctor is being cautious, Colonel. You had a hangar collapse on you when that tornado passed through. You'll probably be here for a week at least."

Jack tried not to react. Caldwell was lying—a few hours earlier, the doctor had told him he'd be released by this afternoon. "Well, you're probably right, General," he replied.

"Of course, I am," Caldwell said with a nod. "I've got to go and check on Forrorrois. Try and get some rest before they come back in to poke at you some more."

"Let me know how she's doing. I owe her and Captain Perkins my life," Jack said, nodding back.

"I'll do that, we can talk later this afternoon," Caldwell said as he turned and left the room.

Jack breathed after the general left. He almost jumped when Perkins appeared on the other side of his bed, away from the door. "Jeez, Perkins, it's bad enough when Forrorrois sneaks up on me like that!" he swore in a low voice.

Perkins grinned. "Funny, Colonel."

"We'd better move out, Perkins, I have a feeling that Forrorrois is not going to like seeing the general this morning."

"That's a no-brainer," Perkins replied as he circled Jack's bed and helped him to his feet.

Jack stumbled when he tried to put weight on his ankle. "Damn it," Jack cursed from the pain. "It's no use—I can't step on my foot." He sat back on the bed, frustrated.

"No problem," Perkins replied with a glint in his eye as he held out a miniature transport.

Jack looked down in horror as he spied the reduction weapon in Perkins other hand. Before he could argue, there was a flash of bluish-green. He felt Perkins catch him before he passed out.

****

Jack woke up lying on the bunk in the rear cabin of Forrorrois' long-distance scout. He was relieved to find himself full-sized once more. Perkins was watching him from a chair at the small table.

"You're smart to be out of reach," Jack grumbled, rubbing his throbbing temple with his good hand.

"I thought so," Perkins replied, with a half-smile. "Besides the headache, how are you feeling?"

"Glad to be on the scout, now maybe I can use the bioknitter on my arm and get rid of this cast."

Jack watched as Perkins got to his feet and began to cross over towards him. About halfway across the room, he heard the side hatch shut. 'Computer, what's happening?' Jack subvocalized.

'Forrorrois has ordered the ship to approach her position,' the computer replied in his mind through his zendra link.

"Perkins, hold on!" Jack ordered, grabbing the bunk with his good hand. "Forrorrois is bringing the ship to her!"

He watched as Perkins dove for the table when the ship suddenly moved straight up then to the left. There was no doubt in his mind it was going to be a wild ride.

****

Forrorrois heard the ship confirm in her mind that Perkins and Jack were on board. She moved to climb out of bed when she heard a male voice outside her door.

"General...I wasn't expecting you here this morning," the male voice sounded outside her room.

"Good morning, nurse. I've come to see the patient," General Caldwell's voice replied. "How is she doing today?"

"She was sleeping quietly the last time I looked in on her about a half-an-hour ago," the nurse replied.

Forrorrois looked around the room and saw little cover. Instinctively, she grabbed the blankets and pulled them up to her chin.

"I'll see if she's awake," the nurse continued.

"You needn't bother, I'll see for myself," the general replied.

"General...please...this is still a hospital!" the man insisted.

Forrorrois closed her eyes as the sound of the curtain around the bed was moved roughly aside. She slit her eyes open and stared at the intruder.

"Ah, good, you're awake," the general said as he walked up to her bed.

"And you're annoying," Forrorrois replied.

"General Caldwell, I must protest," the nurse stated with his hands on his hips.

"It's all right," Forrorrois said. "The general only wants to gloat about something. He'll leave soon."

The nurse shook his head and left.

Forrorrois looked back at the general and found him staring at her.

A smug grin tugged at Caldwell's lips. "As a matter-of-fact I do have a little something to speak with you about."

"And what might that be?" Forrorrois said, rolling her eyes in mock disinterest.

"I spoke with a mutual acquaintance last night..."

Forrorrois stared silently at him, feeling the confidence ooze from him.

"I spoke with Collinar."

The name floored her. "What!? That's not possible! He's in a Dramudam rehabilitation station for breaking the Isolation Treaty!" she gasped.

A Cheshire grin now stretched across General Caldwell's lips. "Not anymore. He's heading for Earth and he's asked for asylum. Oh, by the way, he sends his regards."

"What kind of insanity is this, Caldwell? He's a criminal! You're not thinking about giving him asylum?! Are you?!" His unswerving grin told her everything. "You're as insane as he is! Why are you even telling me this?"

"Because, Forrorrois, you're going to be extending your stay here on the base."

Forrorrois scowled at him when he punctuated his words with the barrel of his pistol. "You're a fool," she replied. 'Computer, descend from the roof and position the ship at the window of this room,' she subvocalized.

'Acknowledged,' the computer sounded in her mind.

"Forrorrois, you are a threat to national security and it is my duty to detain you until the threat is over," he stated as he approached her, his weapon leveled at her.

"General, don't come any closer. I won't be coerced. Besides, I'd look out the window first, if I were you. My ship's a bit overprotective—I wouldn't want it to overreact."

"What?!"

She grinned when Caldwell glanced towards the window just as she ordered the computer to drop the EM warping field on her long-distance scout. His jaw dropped at the sight. The glass began to rattle in a sympathetic resonance with the ship's engines.

"You don't think I'd allow myself to be brought here without protection, do you?" Forrorrois jested.

The nurse raced into the room, only to freeze at the sight of the large craft hovering just outside the third-story window.

Forrorrois stiffly tossed the blanket aside. "It's time for me to leave, General. Don't move—my ship has orders to shoot to kill."

Caldwell glanced back at her then snorted when he saw her fully dressed. "I thought the Dramudam didn't kill?"

"They don't, but if you come anywhere near my family I'll make an exception—just for you," she warned. Before either the general or the nurse could react, Forrorrois lurched out the door into the corridor. Outside, two MPs were coming down the hall.

"Halt or we'll shoot!" one of them cried out.

Forrorrois dove for cover behind the nurses' station. Her fractured ribs screamed out as she rolled behind the counter. 'Computer, I need a distraction. Fire a 1/20th power laser pulse at the window. Don't aim directly at the occupants of the room.'

'Firing laser,' the computer replied.

Both the general and the nurse dove from her room at the sound of shattering glass. Smoke rolled into the hallway. Within moments a fire alarm peeled.

Forrorrois was flabbergasted at the unintended force of the blast. "Oops, maybe that was a bit much," she murmured to herself. Glancing about, she looked for a way out.

"Get her!" the general barked.

Forrorrois rolled to her feet and ran for the exit. A bullet ricocheted off the wall above her head. In front of her a woman screamed and ran back into a patient's room.

"Stop her!" one of the MPs shouted.

Forrorrois slammed into the exit door and bowled over two more MPs in the stairwell that were answering the alarm. She vaulted over them and pounded down the stairs. The futile cries for her to stop rang out behind her, spurring her on. Adrenaline surged in her blood, blocking the pain that grated in her ravaged ribs and back.

"She's down there!"

'Computer, raise the EM warping shield and track on my location,' she subvocalized. The sound of heavy boots coming up the stairs made her hesitate, but more people were descending on her position. She grabbed the railing and leapt over the edge to the stairs below. The MP barely had a chance to raise his hand before she caught him square in the chest with her boots. He fell backwards hard against the wall of the landing. Forrorrois gasped as she rolled to her feet and kept on running down the last flight of stairs. As she hit the outside door, the crack of a fractured rib shuddered through her body. Blinded by the pain, she barely realized that she'd stumbled to her feet. A cough racked her chest. When she wiped her mouth, she looked down and was taken aback by the flecks of fresh blood on her hand. 'Computer, emergency pickup, now!' she subvocalized.

The grass swirled in front of her. In the blink of an eye, the hatch yawned before her, ramp extended. Forrorrois stumbled up the incline and fell onto the cool floor plates of the cargo hold. Outside she could hear the frustrated shouts of her pursuers as their weapons fire was defeated by her craft's shields. The shouts faded away when the ramp snicked shut and her ship began to ascend. Her battered body melted against the metal plates in peaceful resignation. Abruptly, the cough returned. She curled herself into ball and rode out the stabbing agony in her chest. When the pain subsided, Forrorrois rolled to her knees.

"Computer," she called out in her adopted tongue. "Plot a course to my parents' house."

"Acknowledged," her ship replied aloud in Intergaltic.

Forrorrois struggled to her knees and clawed open the weapons locker. The cool smooth oval of the reduction weapon slipped easily into her palm. She aimed at the two miniature transports forgotten on the floor near the lockers from when she and Perkins had rescued Jack. She flipped open the seat and pulled out the emergency bio kit. Unable to catch her breath, Forrorrois dropped the seat back down and leaned heavily against the padding. The sound of the rear cabin door sliding open made her look up.

"Forrorrois!" Perkins yelled out as he rushed into the cargo hold.

Forrorrois straightened slightly as she circled the bioknitter over her ribs. "Perkins…How's Jack?"

"He's fine—he's in the back on the bunk."

Heaving a sigh she continued to administer to her ribs. "Thank goodness. Perkins could you put the hovercycles away for me."

"Not a problem. Let me help you up…" Perkins began, but she waved him off.

"I'm fine," Forrorrois stated then flinched as she pulled herself to her feet.

'Approaching coordinates,' the computer announced in her mind.

Forrorrois returned the bioknitter to her med kit and set the bag on the floor next to wall lockers of the cargo hold.

'Computer, land in back of the structure and stand ready. Alert me if anyone approaches,' she subvocalized.

'Standing ready,' the computer replied.

"We're at my parents, Perkins. Stay on the ship until I signal you," she whispered. "I need to speak with my parents alone first."

"Forrorrois, I can get them," Perkins offered, but she cut him short with a look.

"They'll come quicker if I tell them," she replied.

She was glad when he didn't argue with her.

'Open hatch,' she subvocalized. Forrorrois tried to take a deep breath to clear her head, but her sore ribs protested and she began to cough once more. The amount of damage she'd inflicted on herself in the last twenty-four hours would take her more than a few minutes with the bioknitter to repair. Forrorrois stumbled down the ramp to the back door of her parents' white split-level ranch set in the middle of a quiet suburban neighborhood. Through the window she could see her daughter, Celeste, having breakfast with her parents. Forrorrois didn't even knock before Celeste sensed her and jumped from her chair. Her mother chased after her granddaughter, then saw her through the window.

"Danica!" her mother cried out, throwing open the door. Forrorrois fell to her knees and hugged Celeste tightly.

"Momma, you're bleeding!" her daughter cried out touching Forrorrois' face when she pulled back.

Forrorrois tasted her lips and realized she'd coughed up more blood. She wiped her mouth with the cuff of her sleeve. "I'll be all right, peanut, just give me a second to get back on my feet." Forrorrois moved to get back up, but found she didn't have the energy. Her father slipped his arm under hers and helped her up without a word.

"Frank, put her in the chair over there," her mother ordered. "Danica, you shouldn't be out of the hospital!"

"I had to go, Mom," Forrorrois said as she clutched her ribs and took a seat. "Caldwell knows Celeste is my daughter—she's not safe here, and neither are you and Dad."

"Perkins warned us last night," her father replied. "We're prepared. I've already called into work to tell them I'm not coming in for a few days."

"It's worse than that, Dad. Caldwell has double-crossed me. Collinar is returning to Earth!"

"Oh my goodness," her mother gasped. "It's all my fault. I shouldn't have brought her to the base."

"No, it's not, Mom," Forrorrois said, taking her mother's hand. "Please...you both need to come with me and Celeste now. Pack some clothes and anything else you might need. I don't know how long it'll be, but I need to know you're safe."

'Several enforcement vehicles are approaching this location. Estimated time of arrival, 27 tol,' the computer echoed in her mind.

Forrorrois touched her hand to her temple then looked up. She felt their fear. "They're coming. We've only got fifteen minutes. Perkins is in the scout with Jack, Dad. He can help you carry stuff to the cargo hold."

"How's Jack doing?" her father pressed. "We weren't allowed in to see him."

"He's OK, just banged up—he's lying down in the rear cabin of my scout right now. Perkins helped me get him out of the hospital when I escaped. I'll tend to Jack once we get to my base."

"Frank, we can ask questions later. We've got to hurry," her mother urged. "I'll pack the clothes, while you get the extra food you bought last night. There are cardboard boxes in the basement to pack everything in."

"All right," her father replied.

"Celeste, go get your bag," Forrorrois said, attempting to get to her feet. "I'll tell Perkins to come in and help you carry things, Dad."

"Whoa, you stay right there," her father ordered. "Catch your breath. I'll get Perkins."

Forrorrois nodded, relieved by her family's quick action. Their fear was strong in her mind, but they didn't let the insanity of the moment cloud the immediate need to react. She didn't know what she'd do if they were harmed in any way.

Within ten minutes, her mother hurried down the stairs with two large suitcases. Celeste followed her down with her own little knapsack. Her father had already filled two boxes with canned goods and baking supplies and carried them to the cargo hold of her ship with Perkins' help by the time her mother stepped into the kitchen.

"Let me help you with those, Danny," her father said, taking the suitcases from her mother.

Her mother handed them over then ran back up the stairs.

"Mom! We've got to go!" Forrorrois cried out to her.

"I'll be right down, I have to get something I forgot," she called back.

"Perkins, get Danica and Celeste on the ship," her father urged, helping Forrorrois to her feet. "I'll get your mother."

"Yes, sir," Perkins replied, moving to Forrorrois' side.

Forrorrois slipped an arm around his waist for support and then took Celeste by the hand. "Come on, peanut, be a big girl and help me get the ship ready for take off."

Celeste clutched her hand. "Momma...I'm scared."

"It's all right to be scared...but I'll keep you safe." Forrorrois smiled down at her daughter and felt Celeste's fears subside in her mind. *Such a brave little girl, her father would be so proud*, she thought as they hurried up the ramp of the scout ship. "Perkins, help me to the command seat."

"Are you sure? I could fly?" Perkins offered.

Forrorrois felt the world around her becoming unfocused. She stumbled as they cleared the ramp into the cargo hold when the ship's computer broke into her thoughts.

'The vehicles have increased their speed and will arrive in fifteen fol.'

Less than thirty seconds, Forrorrois thought as Perkins guided her to a crate. She sat down and she stared at the back door through the hatch opening.

The sound of sirens in the distance made her tense. Celeste ran to the hatch and peered out at the house.

"Grandma and Grandpa are coming!" Celeste called out, pointing at the back door.

The sound of screeching tires in front of the house made Forrorrois' heart stop. She finally breathed when her parents ran from the house and up the ramp carrying two more boxes.

"Danica, we have to leave—now! The police are out front!" her father called out.

"Did you engage the defense shield on the house?" Forrorrois gasped, holding her ribs.

"Yes, hopefully it'll keep them from entering the house," her father replied.

"It will," Forrorrois stated, trying to push the pain from her mind. "Computer, close the hatch and re-engage the EM warping shield. Return to base," she ordered out loud in Intergaltic.

She felt her father stare at her before she realized what she had done. "Perkins, I've ordered the ship on autopilot," she continued switching to English. "Go in the back and check on Jack and make certain that he's OK."

"Yes, ma'am," Perkins replied, running to the rear cabin before she could scold him for calling her ma'am.

"What are we going to do, Danica?" her mother asked, sitting down beside her on the crate.

"First we're going to go to my base—it's the only place I'm certain that I can protect you," Forrorrois said. "After that, I've got to prepare to face Collinar." The pain in her side and back were increasing. Celeste took her hand.

"Momma, are you all right?"

"I will be as soon as we get home, peanut, but you could do me a favor and get me my med kit. It's over there by the wall locker—on the floor."

Celeste dashed for the bag. "Sure, Momma."

Forrorrois began to cough once more—the metallic taste of blood fouled her tongue. Any healing the puncture wound to her lung had accomplished was failing.

"Oh, Danica," her mother said, resting her arm around her shoulder, protectively. "You should be in a hospital."

Forrorrois wiped the blood from her lips and grimaced. "I have better equipment. When we land, I want you and Dad to take your bags into my bedroom. I'll stay in the cabin of my scout...closer to my diagnostic equipment."

Her mother hugged her shoulders. "No...I need you closer so that I can take care of you."

Forrorrois smiled, she had no energy to argue. "All right," she said. Her vision began to narrow to a tunnel as she found herself lurching forward from the crate. Her father barely caught her before she hit the floor.

"Honey...Honey, stay awake!" her mother called out.

"The ship will take us home," Forrorrois mumbled, unable to focus.

"Danica! Frank, Perkins, help!" her mother insisted.

Forrorrois felt her head swim then she nodded forward. Unable to stay awake anymore—she gave in. Her mother called her name once more, but she couldn't react as her father lowered her to the cool floor plates.

✳✳✳✳✳✳✳✳✳✳✳

Forrorrois opened her eyes and stared up at her mother and father from the floor of her cargo hold of her long-distance scout. A silver thermal blanket was draped over her. The slight hum of the ship was cutting back. *The ship must have just landed,* she thought. She spotted Perkins watching her from the one side, relief evident on his face. Forrorrois turned her head slightly when she heard Celeste sniff back her tears. She smiled when she felt her daughter's little hand petting her hair. Once more, the insanity of her life had turned her family's lives upside down. Forrorrois' mind flooded with guilt.

"She's awake," her father whispered.

"Yes, I am," Forrorrois whispered back. "Where's my bio kit?"

"Right here, Momma," Celeste replied, bravely. "I got it, just like you asked."

Forrorrois smiled at her cherub face and black eyes. "Good job, peanut. Now, could you hand Grandma the bioknitter?"

"Yes, Momma," Celeste said as she set the kit on the floor panel then opened the bag near her head and rummaged inside. Triumphantly, her daughter pulled out the bioknitter and handed the cylinder to her grandmother.

"What do I do with it?" her mother asked.

Forrorrois could sense her uncertainty as she held out the alien medical equipment. "I need you to heal me, Mom. I will try to stay as still as possible while you repair my ribs."

"But, how?!" her mother stammered, kneeling down beside her.

Forrorrois reached out and gently caught her mother's shaking hand. Forrorrois triggered the bioknitter with her zendra link.

"What happened? Its starting to glow?!" her mother gasped, almost dropping the cylinder.

"It's all right, Mom, I just turned it on. I want you to move the bioknitter slowly in a circle over my ribs...that's it."

"How? You didn't touch it," her mother said, holding the cylinder at arms length.

"I used my zendra link," Forrorrois replied. She took her mother's extended hand and lowered the cylinder closer to her ribs then began to move the bioknitter in a circle.

Forrorrois released her mother's hand once her mother slowly took over the circular motion. The regeneration of the cells and bones of her ribs and muscles warmed the area from the bioknitter's field.

"Keep circling until I tell you to move to a different location," Forrorrois encouraged, lowering her hand to her side. "Oh...that's good..."

"Danica, what is it doing?" her father asked from behind her mother.

Forrorrois smiled as the engineer in her father overcame his worry. "It's increasing the blood flow to the injured tissue and bone, stimulating the cells to regenerate," she answered. "Luckily, my lung had only collapsed partially when I re-cracked my rib during my escape. In a few days, I should be as good as new."

Her answer snapped her father back to the immediate situation. "How can you be so casual about this?!" her father retorted. "You almost died!"

"Dad...Celeste," Forrorrois said with a nod towards her daughter.

He followed her glance and looked into his granddaughter's eyes. "We'll talk later," he replied, looking back at Forrorrois. Celeste crossed over to him and slipped her small hand into his.

"Grandpa, Momma's gonna be OK...I can feel it. She's just tired."

Forrorrois watched her father crouch down and hug her daughter tightly.

"You're right, peanut—your momma's going to be fine. She just had us all scared for a moment."

Celeste pulled away and looked up at him. "Yes, she did," she replied.

"Celeste...could you take Grandpa and Uncle Perkins into the house and show them where they can put the groceries while Grandma finishes fixing my boo boos?"

Celeste grabbed her grandfather's hand and grinned. "Sure! Come on, Grandpa! Come on Unca Perkins!"

Her father moved to object, but a warning glance from her mother changed his mind.

Perkins glanced over at her, uncertain.

"I'll be all right, Perkins. Go help my dad and Celeste," Forrorrois urged. "And set up the guest bedroom for Jack."

"Yes, ma'am," Perkins replied with a nod.

"All right, peanut, lead the way," her father said, taking a box and handing it to Perkins.

The gnawing pain in her side was finally easing as her mother made a few more passes with the bioknitter. Forrorrois closed her eyes, grateful for a moment to think. She sensed her mother's stare and looked up at her.

"Your color's better," her mother said, still circling the bioknitter over her ribs.

"You're doing fine, Mom," Forrorrois said, barely able to hold her tired eyes open. "You're a natural med tech." She took a tentative breath relieved at the lack of pain. When she took a deeper breath, a giddy smile tugged at the corners of her mouth. "Oh, that's so much better," she said. Forrorrois unfastened the lower half of her tunic and let the fabric fall open revealing the roughly stitched gash on her side.

"Oh, Danica, you've ripped your stitches," her mother whispered.

"You can fix it. Just pull out the old stitches then pinch the wound together and circle the bioknitter over it." Forrorrois fumbled inside the med kit and pulled out a pair of forceps and a thin knife then handed them to her mother while she lay on her side.

Nervously, her mother took them and slowly began to remove the worthless stitches. Forrorrois controlled her breathing and stared at the wall lockers to keep from wincing. As her mother finished, she retrieved the bioknitter and began to circle the spot above her sliced side. With each pass, Forrorrois felt the pain ease. At last her mother set the bioknitter on the floor panel and breathed.

"This is amazing, there's barely a scar," she whispered.

"You're doing great, Mom. Now, please get my back," Forrorrois replied, rolling on her side.

Her mother brushed back the silky fabric of her black tunic and guided the bioknitter over the torn skin on her back.

"Danica, these stitches are torn as well," her mother whispered. "It's directly inline with the wounded in the front. What exactly happened?"

Forrorrois stared at the crate she was now facing to block out the pinching tug of each stitch. "A section of the hangar fell on me while we were extracting Jack. It impaled me," she gasped. "Luckily, it only nicked my lung and missed the major organs. I was able to pull free and make my way back to my ship before I collapsed. It was then that Perkins took me to the base doctors. I really wish he hadn't."

"He did the right thing, Danica. With all the technology on this ship, you still needed help using it in your condition," her mother scolded her.

Too tired to argue, Forrorrois nodded. "You're right, Mom, at that moment Perkins did the right thing." She was surprised when her mother fell quiet while she applied the bioknitter to the entrance wound and bruising on her back, half expecting another speech about the hazards of her job. She took a tentative breath, relieved at the deeper healing that reconstructed her damaged lung.

"I'm so sorry. This whole thing's my fault..." her mother suddenly gasped, choking back tears.

Forrorrois sighed and looked over her shoulder at her mother. "Mom, get that out of your head. You didn't cause the tornado that pinned Jack in that hangar, or start the argument between me and General Caldwell—or Collinar for that matter. You're a great mom who's been repeatedly asked to cope with the insanity that her daughter has dragged into her life and you've done it with grace and acceptance. If anyone should be sorry, it should be me for having pulled both you and Dad into this mess. I should never have contacted you when I returned to Earth. It would have been easier for you to believe I was dead."

Her mother abruptly set the bioknitter on the floor panel next to her and shook her head. "No...I couldn't go back to not knowing what had happened to you. The countless nights of wondering if you were dead or alive—no—don't ever wish that on your father or me ever again. That was too painful."

Forrorrois rolled over and slipped her hand into her mother's and squeezed her fingers lightly. "I love you, Mom. Never forget that."

Her mom squeezed back. "I love you too. Now, let's get you well so you can stop this Collinar person." With determination, her mother retrieved the bioknitter from the floor panel where she had set the cylinder and circled Forrorrois' ribs once more.

Forrorrois snorted at her mother's grasp of the situation. "Good thinking," she said with a slight nod.

CHAPTER 3

Jack leaned back in the chair in front of the comms station of Forrorrois' base and smiled when Forrorrois' long-distance scout returned on autopilot. Forrorrois had ordered Perkins back to his apartment with the hope that the general wouldn't suspect that he was involved with her and Jack's disappearance from the base hospital that morning. He adjusted his newly-healed ankle on the stool he had placed in front of him to reduce the chance of swelling. Even with the advanced medical equipment at Forrorrois' disposal, his body still needed time to deal with the trauma of the bad sprain he had sustained during the collapse of the hangar. He looked down when his cell phone rang in his pants pocket. Jack pulled it out and wasn't surprised to see the general's number. With a sigh, he accepted the call and placed the phone to his ear.

"Colonel Stern," he stated.

"Colonel! Am I glad to hear your voice!" Caldwell exclaimed. "Where are you?"

"I'm not sure," Jack lied. "One moment I was asleep in my hospital room and the next thing I know I found myself in a room with a bed and some food and water. Where, I don't know. Later on, Forrorrois came in and healed my ankle and arm."

"Are you alone?" the general asked in a hushed voice that made Jack almost smile.

"For the moment," Jack replied. "Forrorrois left the room about an hour ago. I was surprised to hear my cell phone ring. I hadn't realized she had left it with me."

"Lucky she did, maybe we can triangulate on your position."

Jack tried not to snicker. "You can give that a try, sir, but I suspect that she might have done something to my phone to scramble the signal."

"I'll get my people on it immediately, in the meantime, sit tight. Now, Colonel, did she explain why she took you with her?" the general pressed.

"No. She only told me that she wanted to make certain that I was all right and that she would take me back to my cabin once I could walk without crutches," Jack said as he wove his story.

"So you don't feel like you're in any danger?" Caldwell asked.

"Not at the moment, sir," Jack replied, trying to remain serious. "General, can I ask you what provoked Forrorrois to leave the base so suddenly?"

There was a long pause before the general replied. "For security reasons I can't answer that over the phone, Colonel. I'll get comms to assist with tracing your phone. I'll give you a call back when we're ready."

"Sounds good, General—oh, I think I hear her coming. I've got to go," Jack insisted. "I'll wait for your call."

Before the general could answer, Jack terminated the call and began to chuckle as he slipped the phone back into his pants pocket. Danielle knocked on the open door and looked in.

"Were you talking with someone, Jack?" she asked.

Jack looked up at her inquiring hazel eyes and chuckled. "Yes, General Caldwell just called me. He wanted to know if I was all right and where I was."

Danielle's face paled at the mention of Caldwell's name. "Do you want me to get Danica?"

"No, that's all right, she's busy at the moment making last minutes preparations in the hangar bay," Jack replied.

"What did you tell him?" Danielle pressed.

He smiled. "I told him that Forrorrois assured me that she would return me to my cabin once I was back on my feet and that I didn't have a clue where I was," Jack replied.

"Do you think he believed you?"

Jack shrugged. "Maybe, I'm not sure. He did tell me that he would call back later and try to triangulate the signal of my cell phone."

Danielle's hazel eyes widened. "Can he do that?"

Jack nodded. "The technology exists, but don't worry, Danica made a few enhancements to my phone. He'll never pinpoint me."

Forrorrois' mother breathed a sigh of relief. "Thank goodness. I would hate to think he could find us here—especially now that he knows about Celeste."

"Don't worry, your daughter is more than capable of keeping a few steps ahead of the general," Jack reassured her. "Celeste is safe from him. Speaking of Celeste, where is she?"

Danielle smiled for the first time since she had come into the room. "She's out in the hangar bay with Danica."

Jack laughed. "She definitely is her mother's daughter."

"I'm afraid so," Danielle sighed.

"Do I smell a fresh pot of coffee brewing?" Jack asked.

Danielle nodded. "As a matter-of-fact, yes, you do. That was why I came in here in the first place. I wanted to know if you would like a cup."

Jack grinned. "I'd love a cup—I'll be in the kitchen in a few minutes."

"You keep your foot up, I'll bring you a cup," she stated.

"You're an angel of mercy, Danielle," Jack replied as she turned and left the room. His mind turned back to Forrorrois once he was alone again. The thought that she was going to confront Collinar by herself, didn't sit well with him, but he didn't see any other alternative. She needed to stop him before he reached General Caldwell.

✶✶✶✶✶✶✶✶✶✶✶

Perkins was very disappointed when Forrorrois ordered him back to his apartment. The last place he wanted was to be sitting alone, wondering how Forrorrois' confrontation with Collinar went, especially since he knew she should be resting in bed recovering from her injuries. He unlocked his door and stepped inside. His place wasn't much—a one-bedroom with an eat-in kitchen and a living room, but then again he didn't need much. He barely closed the door when a knock sounded on the other side. Perkins opened the door once more, he found three men in blue Air Force uniforms, waiting in the hallway—two were MPs with their hands resting on the butts of their sidearms, their holsters unsecured for quick access.

"Can I help you, sir?" Perkins asked, cautiously, studying the major who stood in front of the two MPs.

"Captain Perceval Perkins?" the major asked.

Perkins winced at the use of his first name. "Yes, sir," Perkins replied.

"Captain Perkins, we need to ask you a few questions about your whereabouts this morning,"

"I was running some errands," Perkins replied.

"I see. Captain, please come with us," the major stated.

"If you think that's necessary, sir," Perkins answered.

"We do, Captain."

Perkins glanced at the two MPs and saw that their hands had now slipped to their pistol grips. This was not a request. "No problem, sir," Perkins said as he stepped into the hallway and locked his apartment door. "If I may ask, sir, where are we heading?"

"Back to the base, Captain," the major replied.

Perkins fell in behind the major while the two MPs stepped in behind them. His mind raced as he tried to figure out a way to get a message to Forrorrois, but for now he had to wait and see where they were taking him.

✸✸✸✸✸✸✸✸✸✸✸

Forrorrois sat down at the comm center at her base and sent a message to the Tollon alerting them of Collinar's contact with General Caldwell. She moved to get up when the base computer announced an incoming message.

"Computer, where is the message originating?" she asked aloud in Intergaltic, half expecting it to be from General Caldwell.

"Incoming message is from the Tollon," the computer replied in Intergaltic.

Forrorrois' heart began to pound. "Play message."

Subcommander Yonofinon's face appeared in a hologram above the counter. His familiar chestnut-brown face and almond-shaped black eyes made her smile as she studied his mouth framed by his silky black mustache that traced down the sides of his mouth. He reminded her so much of Trager.

"Forrorrois, we have received your message. The Tollon has been in pursuit of Collinar since he escaped from the rehabilitation station ten cycle ago. We had hoped to intercept him before he reached your solar system, but his craft is equipped with a more advanced hyperfold drive than our original intelligence indicated. Therefore, we will need you to prevent Collinar from entering the planet's atmosphere and seeking asylum with Earth's authorities. Commander Thoren requests that you take Collinar into custody so that he may be returned to the rehabilitation station to complete his sentence. You will also need to retrieve the single-seat long-distance Dramudam scout that Collinar stole during his escape. The Tollon will achieve orbit in seven kel. We will establish communications once we are within range of audio transmission, Yononnon, out."

Twenty-eight hours, Forrorrois thought, an eternity with the likes of Collinar. "Computer, forward the following response to the Tollon's transmission," she replied. "Tollon, this is Forrorrois. Message received. I am monitoring Collinar's approach and expect interception within the next half kel. Base communications will be monitored by Colonel Stern. I'm looking forward to meeting the Tollon in orbit with Collinar in custody, Forrorrois, out."

"Message sent," the computer replied.

Forrorrois sat back in her chair and tapped her finger on the armrest. She looked up when she realized that Jack was standing behind her.

"Sounds like you need me to hold down the fort," Jack said as he hobbled into the room and leaned against the wall.

"Yes, please keep an eye on everyone for me," she replied, coming to her feet.

"Are you sure you don't want me to fly with you?"

Forrorrois shook her head. "No, I'll bring Collinar in one way or another."

Jack took a deep breath then exhaled slowly. "Commander Thoren wants him brought back to serve the rest of his sentence."

Forrorrois gave her friend an irritated look. "I'll do my best," she grumbled.

"Uh huh," Jack replied.

"OK, I'll find a way to bring him back alive," she answered. "Happy?"

Jack smiled and nodded. "Yes, now go get ready."

Forrorrois left comms and found her father and mother in the living room. They both looked up as she entered. Celeste was sitting on the couch next to her mother.

"Mom, Dad, I've got to head out now. I just got my orders from the Tollon to intercept Collinar," she said as she looked at them.

Her parents were silent for a moment. Forrorrois looked over at Celeste and felt her uncertainty.

"Jack's going to stay at the base with you and monitor the situation," she continued. "If I can stop Collinar in orbit, I'll be able to wrap this up quickly. Then I'll head for the Tollon for a few days. I won't be gone long."

"You go get him, tiger," her father replied, squaring his shoulders. "Your mother and I will keep an eye on Celeste for you. And Jack will keep us company."

"Yes, you go get him, Danica," her mother added, pulling Celeste closer to her in a hug. "We'll be just fine."

When her mother loosened her hold on Celeste, Forrorrois' daughter jumped down from the couch and ran over to her. Forrorrois could feel her fear as she crouched down and caught Celeste in a tight hug.

"I need you to be my brave little girl, all right, peanut?" Forrorrois whispered.

Celeste sniffed back her threatening tears. "Yes, Momma."

"Will you take care of everyone while I'm gone and help them find things?" Forrorrois asked as she pulled away from her daughter and stared into her big almond-shaped black eyes, her hands still resting on her small shoulders.

Celeste brightened. "Yes, Momma, I'll be your big helper," she replied.

"Good, and if you see Poppa, tell him I'll be back soon."

"I will, Momma," Celeste replied, straightening her shoulders and raising her chin.

"That's my little peanut," Forrorrois said with a smile. She gave her daughter's little shoulders a squeeze then she stood back up.

Forrorrois looked around at her parents and nodded. "I'll see you in a few days." Before they could respond, she turned and headed back down the hallway to the hangar bay of her base. Her one-seat pursuit was waiting with the ladder extended for her by the time she reached the craft's side.

****

Forrorrois sat in silence in the command chair of her one-seat pursuit ship and stared off into space while her ship's computer charted Collinar's progress. General Caldwell had made a mistake gloating to her that Collinar was on his way. She had reset the defense grid that the Dramudam installed around her unsuspecting world to detect his arrival. The thought of Collinar returning to Earth made her stomach tense. *When will it end? Oh Trager, I need you so much. Our daughter needs you*, she thought in frustration.

"Duty," she reminded herself out loud—duty to the Dramudam and their training. The muscles in her jaw tensed when the computer sounded in her mind. Collinar's ship was drawing near. Her eyes searched the blackness until they fell on the distant glint of his ship's dull bluish-black metal. *So predictable.* Collinar was quite mad—a cold calculating kind of mad that drove him along his own deviant course. She wished she had never crossed his path, but she had, and now they were eternal enemies. A shudder ran through her while she felt the same coldness inside herself. His madness was infecting her.

'An unidentified Dramudam ship has just crossed the defense grid,' her ship's computer echoed in her mind.

She smiled. *Let the game begin.*

"You are approaching an undeveloped world. Any further movement towards it will place you in direct violation of the Isolation Treaty, enforced by the Dramudam," Forrorrois stated calmly in Intergaltic.

Collinar drew his ship to a defensive halt in a long dramatic pause. She could feel his intense emotions ebbing towards her across the emptiness between their two ships. He couldn't see her yet—her ship was shrouded against his sensors. His agitation grew in her mind, much to her satisfaction. She had no doubt that after she had spoken to Caldwell the night before that Collinar was expecting her to be in custody.

"Ah, Forrorrois," Collinar's silken voice replied aloud in Intergaltic in her cockpit. "So good to hear from you again. Although it would be so much more sociable if I could see you."

"Then it is you, Collinar," she said, exchanging her ship's EM warping field for its defense shields. Forrorrois smiled when she felt Collinar mentally flinch at the sudden appearance of her ship just three hundred meters in front of him. "Why have you returned to Earth?" she asked.

"To seek asylum on your world," he purred back.

"How can you even say that?" she replied. "It's because of this world that you were imprisoned in the first place?!"

"Ah, my little spitfire," he cooed, "I'm not asking asylum from you—I'm asking it from General Caldwell."

"In exchange for technology, I suppose," she stated.

"Of course, I've already sent the message. He's expecting me," he replied.

"That communication was in direct violation of the Isolation Treaty," she answered. "That will compound the fact that you are presently wanted for escaping from a Dramudam rehabilitation station. As a Dramudam it is my duty to detain you until the Tollon arrives."

"I'm going to have to decline this time," he replied. "I'm expected in less than a quarter kel...maybe another time, Forrorrois—when you're not in uniform." The transmission came to an abrupt end.

Bringing up her lasers, Forrorrois pushed her ship forward after his fleeing ship and released a warning burst across his bow. The chase was on. Collinar veered toward the southern hemisphere of the planet, turning briefly to return fire. His frustration oozed into her mind. A wry smile crossed her full lips. The two ships plunged into atmosphere just south of the equator.

She pulled the nose of her craft up and slowed her steep descent to preserve her shields for battle. But Collinar was sloppy—half his shields were peeled away from the friction of the ever thickening air of the lower atmosphere. His rawness at flying the stolen single-seat Dramudam long-distance scout ship, without the assistance of a zendra link, was evident. With practice, Collinar could have flown circles around her older model scout—reinforcing her foresight in choosing her pursuit ship instead of her larger long-distance scout for this encounter. Forrorrois goaded him with a second volley, counting on his bloodlust to overcome his senses. Collinar rotated to face her, striking her shields squarely with a powerful hail of laser fire. She turned and ran, allowing him to follow—his homicidal emotions clouded his mind and gave her the advantage.

With a manic grin, Forrorrois raced down the length of South American towards the frigid waters near the continent's southern tip. Her ship shuddered from his relentless rain of laser fire weakening her shields with every strike, and yet she allowed his deadly firestorm to connect, enticing him to continue his chase.

They raced past the ever-thickening ice flows towards the frozen ice shelf of Antarctica. The Austral winter embraced them in frosty perpetual darkness. She drew him headlong down the Antarctic Peninsula, along the length of the majestic Trans-Antarctic Mountains. The bony spine of the mountains' peaks jutted through the glaciers, encouraging her to play cat-n-mouse with him as she lead him on a treacherous chase toward the continent's interior. In the gasp of a breath, Forrorrois burst across the vast open Antarctic plateau. Breaking her maddening pace, she spun around to face him, lasers flashing.

Collinar's stolen ship staggered from the force of her assault. She felt no mercy for him, striking twice more, dissolving his shields to nothing. Duty stayed her hand from the killing blow. Both ships hung in the icy darkness above the carved sasstrugi below—each waiting for the other to act.

Collinar released a sudden burst of laser fire against her tenuous shields. She sighted on his wing, about to fire, when the computer pressed for her attention. Alarm spread across her face. She hailed his ship.

"Collinar! Ground that ship immediately, the weapons system is overloading!"

"What kind of a trick is this?" he growled.

"It's no trick, believe me, Collinar! Now, land that scout!" she ordered.

Predictably, Collinar fired at her, but the kill shot went wild and only crippled the controls of Forrorrois' pursuit. Forrorrois swore under her breath, while she fought for control of her craft. The strain on Collinar's weapons system was too much and the weapons turret in the nose of his craft fractured from the explosion. Unable to stop his craft, Forrorrois watched as his ship streaked into the hard-packed ice crystals below. Every fiber of her wanted him to die in the crash, but she needed him alive. She ordered a scan of the area. Her dying sensors echoed what she already suspected—they were twenty kilometers from the nearest U.S. station. One-by-one her ship's systems began to fail. She brought her pursuit ship down hard next to Collinar's wreck. Her zendra link to the ship's computer became erratic, then ceased, moments after the swirling crystals settled around her ship. With a sigh, she looked down at the monitor in front of her. It was going to be a cold walk. Forrorrois reached out with her mind and sensed Collinar pain—*at least he lived,* she conceded.

Her insulated uniform wouldn't be enough against the frigid temperatures outside. She pulled the emergency kit from the side of her command chair and extracted the silver environmental suit. With tremendous effort, she slipped the shiny metallic jumper over her uniform inside the tight cockpit. Forrorrois took off her helmet and set it on the floor beside her. Until the Tollon was in range, the comm link would be useless. Instead, she opted for the small hand transmitter from the emergency kit, along with a bioscanner and bioknitter, slipping them into the insulated outer pant's pockets of her low-temp suit. From what she was sensing from Collinar, he was going to need them. With her stun and reduction weapons secured on the waist of her suit, she took the last two items from the emergency kit—a directional finder and large shoulder pack filled part way with supplies. One more glance around, she decided there was nothing more she would need. Fastening her insulated face mask in place, Forrorrois released the canopy of her cockpit.

The thin icy air took the breath away from her respirator while the moist air of the cockpit flashed into frost over the interior. A stiff wind buffeted her, forcing her to steady herself with gloved hands against the rim of the exposed cockpit as the canopy vibrated against the gusts. An involuntary shiver ran down her spine. Forrorrois dropped over the edge to the snow below. As she began to walk, the subzero temperatures caused the snowpack to squeaked beneath her insulated boots. The canopy lowered and closed as she triggered the manual lever. She turned back towards the craft and pulled the reduction weapon from her belt. In a single fluid motion, she fired. The ship glowed briefly in the bluish-green beam. Forrorrois allowed her eyes to adjust to the darkness then she crossed over to her now miniaturized pursuit ship. Dropping the knapsack from her back, she stuffed the now half-meter ship inside. The fit was tight, but she managed to re-close the pack. Slinging the bag up onto her shoulders, she headed for the shadow of Collinar's downed craft. The long-distance scout was half again larger than her pursuit and obviously meant for long haul journeys.

The side of Collinar's one-seat scout was crushed inwards from his hard crash landing. Forrorrois searched the smooth metal panels of the craft's exterior for the manual hatch release. After several moments, she located the lever just under the stubby delta wing. A cloud of moisture was released from the pressure difference. The water droplets froze in a puff then settle to the ground about her. She scrambled through the side hatch located just behind the command chair inside the small cargo hold then closed the hatch swiftly behind her with her stun weapon ready. Entering the cockpit, she found herself face-to-face with her sworn enemy. His proud golden-tan face and lion eyes were filled with pain. She glanced down and saw shrapnel embedded in his right leg from the explosion. A pool of his dark yellow blood was forming on the floor panel below. Collinar's eyes were glazing over from shock by the time she looked up. Without a second thought Forrorrois pulled the med kit from the leg pocket of her silver environmental suit and drew out a hypo. Uncertain what setting to use, she went low and hissed the cylinder against his leg. All thoughts of hatred went from her mind while she worked to repair his lacerated limb.

Collinar's pain eased with each pass of the bioknitter, along with his tense posture. Without the support of the zendra to speedup his healing, Forrorrois knew Collinar would be lame for several days—but at least he would live. Suddenly, her mind screamed out. Instinctively, she twisted away from his reach, barely avoiding the jagged knife he arced towards her turned shoulder. Anger rose inside her at his insane act. Without a second thought, Forrorrois balled her fist and connected a right cross soundly against his firm square jaw, while her left hand caught his wrist and twisted it forcefully until the knife clattered to the deck.

"You're a fool, Collinar," she spat, tossing his brutalized wrist away. "If you kill me now, you'll never live to see another cycle!"

He pulled his wrist from her and rubbed it—eyes burning with loathing.

"Do you even know were we are, Collinar?! We're in Antarctica! The most inhospitable continent on this planet! It's the butt-end of this world where the sun won't shine for another three or four mol!"

Collinar stared at her and sneered. His action enraged Forrorrois.

"You haven't got a clue! Even if you could even begin to repair the damage done to this ship, you'd still have no way to power your emergency cells. You'd be dead from exposure in less than three kel after all the heat has been sucked from the hull of this wreck!"

Collinar's eyes widened slightly when her words slowly sunk in, but his defensive posture remained. He shifted forward and grinned defiantly at her. "I'd just take yours," he growled.

"It's in no better shape than yours," she snorted in lopsided humor. "The only chance you've got is keeping me alive. You're in no shape to make the seven-and-a-half bul to the nearest ice station on your own."

"I'll just wait until they find me," he replied smugly.

"They'll never come," she shot back, enjoying the shock she felt from his mind. "Their station wouldn't be equipped for an extensive search for this season. At the present outside temperature, the hydraulics on their equipment would seize before they were even a hur from their station. No, they'll wait until sunrise in three or four mol and collect the corpses—if they can find them in the drifting snow. They don't have any other choice—besides neither one of us had clearance to be over this continent to begin with. No skin off their noses."

Collinar's shoulders slumped slightly from her words, while he shifted painfully in his command chair.

Forrorrois was surprised when he spoke.

"Then what do you suggest?" he stated calmly, his tawny lion-like eyes meeting hers.

For the moment, she felt his resignation, and decided not to dismiss it lightly. "We don't have any other alternative. We must head out towards the ice station as soon as possible. At this altitude, traveling will be difficult—even without your injuries—but I can't leave you behind. You'd be dead before I could make it back."

"Why are you doing this, Forrorrois?" he asked, narrowing his eyes. "Why are helping me when I know you want me as dead as I want you?"

Forrorrois hesitated before she spoke. "I was ordered to bring you back alive," she replied in a low voice. "I told Commander Thoren that I'd try my best."

He sat back at her backhanded threat. Then a smile curled at the corners of his tanned face while he burst into laughter. "I knew

I could depend on you not to change. If we were on the same side..." he offered with a lusty raise of an eyebrow.

"You disgust me," she growled back. "All I want right now is a truce until we reach that station. If you know what's good for you, you'll continue our truce until I can reach a communication device and contact a ship to pick us up. I have no idea what kind of a reception we're going to get once we arrive at that ice station, so I suggest that we keep a low profile once we get there. Now, get into an environmental suit and we'll head out," she ordered, pointing to the emergency kit by his seat.

"A truce then," Collinar replied, with a smug look. She watched as he took the kit from the holder and opened the case.

Forrorrois shook her head as she watched her enemy struggle into the large silver environmental suit, uncertain how long he would cooperate.

****

Collinar leaned heavily on Forrorrois' shoulder while she helped him out into the frigid dark night, buffeted by the sharp wind that was starting to pick up. The chill cut through her silvered environmental suit. She dismissed the bitterness as an illusion, knowing full well that the coveralls that Collinar and she wore could withstand the near absolute zero temperatures of space, but still a shiver ran through her when she lowered Collinar to the ground. Without a word, she fired her reduction weapon at his crippled ship. The bluish-green glow faded before her, leaving Collinar's scout in miniature on the broken hard-packed snow.

Taking the large knapsack from Collinar's shoulders, she crossed over to miniaturized scout and stuffed the bulk inside. The nose of the craft peeked out from the top of the sack. She wasn't taking any chances that his would be found later. In silence, she returned to Collinar's side, and slipped the pack onto his back.

"Why don't you just reduce me too?" Collinar offered through his full face mask with a shrug. "You'd make better time to the station."

"Sorry, Collinar," Forrorrois replied. "You'll have to walk, same as me. I'm not about to carry both ships and you. Besides, if I become disoriented from altitude sickness, you'd rather not be trapped in my pocket until you froze to death." She smiled when he didn't reply. Securing both her weapons inside her environmental suit—away from his reach, the bitter wind forced her to refasten her suit swiftly. "Come on, it's time for us to start out," she hastened, offering her hand. He struggled to his over two meter height and loomed beside her. Forrorrois resisted the urge to pull away from his touch when he leaned on her shoulder. Distaste burned in her mouth at his closeness. Suppressing her discomfort, she took the directional finder from the leg pocket of her environmental suit and began scanning for the ice station. "This way," she stated with a nod towards the horizon.

The two of them struggled out across the barren, windblown plateau, with only reflected star light guiding their way. They were silent except for the squeak of their boots against the hard packed snow.

✱✱✱✱✱✱✱✱✱✱✱

Perkins sat in a chair at a metal table and waited in the small interrogation room on the base. He glanced up at the small camera in the corner and saw the green light. The MPs were recording everything even though they had left him alone. They had questioned him repeatedly for about an hour about his whereabouts that morning, but Perkins was careful not to give them too much.

They had taken his cell phone so he wasn't even able to get a message to Jack. He prayed that Jack didn't try to call him.

The door suddenly opened to the room and General Caldwell stepped inside.

Perkins moved to stand up and salute, but the general waved him down.

"At ease, Captain," Caldwell stated, taking a seat across from him at the table.

"Permission to speak, sir," Perkins said.

"Permission granted," Caldwell stated.

"Why am I being held here, sir?"

"Forrorrois escaped from the hospital this morning, Captain."

Perkins tried not to react. "Pardon me for asking, sir, but I don't see how that happens to pertain to me. Besides, I wasn't aware that Forrorrois was a prisoner. I thought she came here to help extract Colonel Stern from that collapsed hangar yesterday per your request," Perkins replied.

"She did, but when she disappeared from the hospital, Colonel Stern came up missing as well.

Perkins sat up in his chair. "The colonel is missing?"

"Yes, I've been able to establish contact with him by cell phone, but he's unable to give us his location. We were hoping that you might have a clue to his whereabouts."

"The last time I saw him was yesterday, in his room during visiting hours, but that's it," Perkins replied.

"I see," the general said. "Captain, I just finished speaking with the flight surgeon. It seems that some unique characteristics have shown up in some of your tissue and blood samples that are similar to what we've found in Forrorrois. I find that quite interesting, don't you?"

Perkins mouth went dry. "I don't understand, sir?"

"Captain Perkins, I want you to think back to when you were taken onto that Utahar ship four years ago and I want you to tell me what happened to you," the general replied. "Take your time—I wouldn't want you to omit anything by accident."

Perkins cleared his throat, nervously. "There's not much to say, sir. I was placed in a cell, where I stayed until Forrorrois freed me."

"So why were you gone for more than a week?"

"When the Dramudam arrived and captured the Utahar ship, I was taken to the Dramudam ship for an examination to make certain that I wasn't harmed. Then Forrorrois brought me back to Earth after they had finished securing the personnel on the Utahar ship."

"And that took a week?"

"The Utahar ship was a very big ship, sir."

"I see," the general replied. "When you returned, we didn't have any blood nor tissue samples from Forrorrois to compare with yours. If we had, we might have found this sooner."

"Found what, sir?" Perkins asked, hesitantly.

"Captain, how long have you been hiding these modifications from us?"

"I don't understand, sir," Perkins insisted. "What modifications?'

Caldwell shook his head. "Don't play dumb with me, Captain. You know what modifications I'm talking about. My only question is who made the modifications to you—the Utahar or the Dramudam?"

Perkins felt his heart begin to race. His worse nightmare was unfolding before him. "Please, General, I don't understand what you are talking about."

"It doesn't matter, Captain, I'll have my answer one way or another. Consider yourself under arrest. I'll be turning you over to a team of scientists who will explore these modifications more thoroughly. Things might go smoother if you cooperate with them."

Perkins heart was now pounding. "You can't do this to me, general! I haven't done anything!" he insisted.

"They did something to you four years ago and we need to find out what. Until then we need to isolate you from the general population," the general replied.

Perkins looked up when two MPs stepped into the interrogation room. He came to his feet as they circled the table and each took one of his arms. Perkins tensed at their touch and stared at the open door. If he didn't escape now, he might never get another chance.

One of the MPs took out handcuffs and began to pull one of his hands behind his back. Perkins turned at blinding speed and tossed the two men into the wall with his enhanced reflexes and strength. Stunned, they both slid to the floor.

Perkins looked down at the men astonished at what he had done, then at the general.

The general stared at him in awe. "I knew it! You're as strong as Forrorrois."

Perkins dismissed his superior officer and ran through the open door. General Caldwell was right behind him calling for the alarm. His secret was out and he didn't have a choice but to run. Only Jack and Forrorrois could help him now. Perkins ran down the hallway to the stairwell that led up to the ground floor two levels above. The sound of running feet told him he couldn't stop. In his mind all he could do was curse Collinar for having done this to him.

Footfalls thundered from the stairs above him as he burst though the doors that led to the exit. An MP turned to face him—he looked like a kid—maybe twenty at best. Before the MP could react, Perkins knocked him to the ground and ran for the exit. He crashed into the push bar and freedom beyond, but there wasn't any cover between the building and the parking lot ahead. Perkins dashed for the cars and prayed he'd make it.

The door behind him slammed open and MPs swarmed out after him.

"Halt or we'll shoot!" one of them called out.

Perkins ignored them and redoubled his speed. He dove between two cars as a bullet shattered the rear widow of the one to his right. The shooting stopped while somebody cursed.

"You, idiot, that's my car!"

Perkins scrambled for the next row of cars and the neat rows of base housing beyond. The base was going into lockdown. *I'll have to wait for dark and slip off the base and get to a telephone*, he thought as he wove between the buildings. The sound of a helicopter taking off from the hangar told him that they were stepping up the search. Perkins dove into some shrubs and concentrated. The air around him warmed as he contracted his mass down to nine centimeters. He gasped for air, trying to calm himself. There was no choice now, he would have to wait.

****

Forrorrois looked down at the directional finder, discouraged. In the past two hours they had barely covered four-and-a-half kilometers. The rough snowpack was littered with drifts and sasstrugi, making the going difficult. She looked up at Collinar and sensed he was nearly spent, drained from the sparse atmosphere and his injuries. If he didn't rest soon, he wouldn't be able to continue.

"Time for a break," she ordered, shifting his weight from her tired shoulder. Collinar didn't protest, as he slipped to a snow drift without a word. Forrorrois shrugged of her pack and took out an insulated thermos. "Drink this," she urged, holding the cap of warm water towards him.

"No...That's all right," he refused. "I'd rather save it for later."

"It wasn't a request," she replied. "You need to keep your fluid level up. The lack of humidity coupled with the altitude here will begin to wear you down. I'm not going to carry you!"

He lifted his weary head in surprise. After a moment he reached out for the cap of water. "If you insist," he stated, pulling his mask away just enough to make room for the cap.

She watched to make sure he drank all the water then took the cap from him and did the same. Cautiously, Forrorrois reached out and touched his mind lightly with hers as she snapped the cap back on the thermos and redeposited the bottle inside her knapsack. The water had refreshed him slightly, but she could sense he remained uncomfortable from his newly healed wounds.

"I feel you're still in pain. Would you care for another hypo to take the edge off," she offered.

"I'm doing fine," he stiffly replied. "That won't be necessary."

She shrugged her shoulders then pulled her knapsack onto her back. "Suit yourself. Break's over. We've got a long ways to go still," she answered, presenting him with her shoulder.

He struggled to his feet with a grunt. "How much further?"

"A little over five-and-a-half bul. We're making slower progress than I hoped we would," she admitted, consulting her instrument.

"I still think you'd make better time if you carried me," he quipped.

"And I've already told you, I'm not going to carry you and your ship," she growled. "If something happened to me, you wouldn't stand a snowball's chance in the sun of making it to that station alive."

"I seriously doubt anything could happen to you," he goaded. "Not with all those modifications my scientists made to you."

She stopped dead in her tracks then shoved him from her in disgust. Collinar lost his precarious balance and sat down hard onto a sasstrugi.

"Hit a nerve, didn't I?" he stated smugly. "You can't stand the fact that most of what you are now is because of me...because of the Utahar. Even you're joining the Dramudam was because of me. Face it, Forrorrois—I created what you are this cycle. You wouldn't be the ultimate pilot you are now without the reflexes I gave you. Your strength, your endurance, your modified memory—you were nothing before I came across you."

Her blood boiled at his words, she hated him for the fact that part of what he said was true. Clenching and unclenching her fist, Forrorrois gazed down at him, loathing his very existence. Finally, she turned her back and walked away.

"Where are you going?!" he called out.

She could hear the snow squeak while he struggled to his feet. "I'm going to that station," she replied coldly, not turning back.

"You're not leaving me, are you?! What about your word as a Dramudam? What will you tell Commander Thoren?!"

"I'll tell him you died in the crash. I'll tell him that your ship slipped into a crevasse," she called back, still refusing to look at him. "I don't care what I tell him, just as long as I don't have to listen to your self-serving monologue!"

"Forrorrois...Forrorrois!" Collinar cried out in panic, "You wouldn't let me die like this, not without a fight?!"

She heard him stumble onto the snow. His pathetic whining grated on her ears. Walking a little further, she finally stopped and turned. The pain oozed from his mind, he had re-injured his leg in his attempt to follow her. Forrorrois cursed herself under her breath. For now, her sense of duty was stronger than her vow of revenge. Crossing back to where he sat in the snow, she stood at arms length from him.

"You're right, Collinar," she stated in disgust. "I can't leave you here to die—we've been enemies too long for me to get any satisfaction from that. Now, get on you're feet," she ordered, freeing the hypo from one of her many insulated pockets. Before he could react, she pulled back the base of his face mask and injected him in the throat.

He jerked back from her sudden assault. "What did you just do?!"

"It's just a pain killer. Relax," she replied darkly. "Now, let's get going before I change my mind and leave you here permanently."

For the moment she could feel his resignation. Without a word, Collinar leaned against her shoulder and they continued for the ice base.

****

Jack limped from the guest bedroom at Forrorrois' base to the communication room and shook his head. Seven hours had passed since he had lost contact with Forrorrois' ship over Antarctica. His only consolation was that Collinar's craft disappeared at the same time. He chaffed at her last instruction to wait until she contacted him. Jack looked up when Frank stepped into the room.

"Any word yet from Danica?" Frank asked.

"Not yet," Jack replied. "There's been comm traffic between the air base and an ice station near the pole though. The crew at the ice station has orders to provide them with shelter until the air force can arrange pickup, if they show up. The station has people searching for them."

"But Jack, you have an idea where they are, why don't you go down and get them?"

"I would, but Danica ordered me to wait for her instructions," Jack said, shaking his head.

"Jack, that's insane, she could be hurt!" Frank insisted.

"Yes, but she gave me orders to wait for at least twenty-four hours before I came after her, unless she contacted me to go in sooner."

Frank shook his head, stubbornly.

"Frank, listen carefully. Your daughter can take care of herself. She'll get word to us and then I'll head in and pick her up, but we have to give her time to recapture Collinar. This world's in danger as long as he's free."

Frank's shoulders sagged. "You're right, but I hate this waiting."

Jack nodded. "It's hard, I know, but this is her mission right now. Once Collinar's back in custody on the Tollon, we can refocus on getting you and Danielle's life back. I'll contact Agent Aster at the F.B.I. and see if he can help. Have you been able to contact George yet?"

"Yeah, he said he's OK, but he's staying alert. He's got a few more shows this week and after that he has a break for about a month."

"Good, then maybe we can pick him up and bring him here for a visit just to make certain he's safe," Jack offered.

Frank looked over at Jack and almost smiled. "Danielle would like that," he replied. "We haven't seen him in nearly a year."

"Good, then it's settled. Next time you talk with him, ask him when he wants a ride home and I'll go get him for you."

"Thank you for being such a good friend, Jack," Frank said with a nod. "Knowing that you and Perkins are working with Danica makes it easier for Danielle and me to sleep at night. With it being so quiet the last few years and having Celeste in our lives, it's been almost normal—well, except when Trager pops in like a ghost from that other dimension, but even that's been OK."

Jack chuckled. "Yeah, but it's been good knowing the big guy is still around for your daughter. Danica would have gone down a very dark path of revenge if Collinar had actually killed him in that explosion instead of just tossing him into the Plane of Deception. As you're always reminding me, God works in mysterious ways."

"Yes, he does," Frank replied.

"Go see how Danielle is doing with Celeste and try not to worry. Remember your granddaughter is an empath like your daughter and she's a bit too young to understand everything you're feeling right now. Try to think happy thoughts."

"I'll try," Frank sighed. "Come into the living room and have a cup of coffee once you're done in here."

"I will," Jack replied. He watched Forrorrois' father leave the room, then brought up a holographic map showing the Antarctica continent above the counter of the comm station. He zoomed in on the last known position he had of Forrorrois and Collinar's ships and correlated them with the nearest ice station—less than twenty kilometers. She should have made it there by now even at that altitude, but his sensors showed the weather had degraded over the past two hours. *She'll contact me,* he thought to himself. *And when she does, I'll be ready.*

CHAPTER 4

The wind picked up to a stiff thirty knots making the visibility drop to less than a few kilometers and fading fast. Razor-sharp ice crystals scraped across their silver environmental suits like sand on metal. Exhausted by the forced march, Forrorrois finally stumbled to the snow, growing disoriented by the lack of oxygen in the thin atmosphere. Collinar melted from her shoulder to the ground, grateful for the break, although he didn't say a word. Both of them greedily gulped the air through their masks, trying to fill their starved lungs. After several minutes, she finally pulled out the thermos from her pack and poured herself a cap full of water. Taking a long drink she refilled the cap and offered the water to Collinar. He accepted the top without an argument this time.

"How much farther?" he asked, handing back the cap.

"Two-and-a-half bul, but if this storm keeps up we may have to take shelter and ride it out," she replied, stuffing the thermos back into her pack.

"A shelter? Where?!" Collinar stated looking at the wind swept plateau around them.

"Snow blocks, all we'd need is a wall to block the wind. Our suits would protect us from the chill," she offered with a shrug.

"No...I say we press on towards the station. We're not that far," he countered.

"It's taken us over two kel to go this far," she reminded him impatiently. "Besides, if you haven't noticed, you're getting heavier by the moment. I may be strong, but my endurance can only be pushed so far."

"No," Collinar replied, now more determined. "I'm not about to end up frozen to death in this forsaken wasteland!—Not this close to that station!"

Forrorrois looked up at him in frustration while he struggled lamely to his feet. Her mind was foggy from her body's struggle to absorb the low levels of oxygen around her. Unable to come up with a sound argument, she struggled to her feet as well. The wind buffeted her while she gained her bearings with the directional finder.

"Let's go," she replied, allowing him to sag against her shoulder in relief.

"Thank you," he said in a quiet voice.

Surprised at his contrition, Forrorrois shifted his weight on her shoulder to ease the pressure off of his tender leg. "Don't mention it," she murmured back.

They stumbled forward into the driving snow crystals, following only the glimmer of the directional finder.

****

Trager forged ahead of Guruma as they trekked through the ever-shifting colored mist that was the basic fabric of the Plane of Deception. Guruma had taught him how to read the color patterns to determine their location, but this was an area where the patterns were unfamiliar. He looked over at the Dramudam founder and saw his shoulders were beginning to sag.

Trager slowed his pace. Guruma looked up at him, surprised.

"Guruma," Trager began, "We've been walking now for about a kel. Forgive me, but I need to rest."

Guruma moved to object then he smiled. "You're right, Trager, we should rest. We're in unfamiliar territory and we need to remain sharp."

Relieved, Trager waved his hand and constructed a shelter around them.

Guruma conjured a bluish-black metal table and chairs and sat down heavily. With a second wave of his hand two red stone mugs appeared.

Trager sat across from him and warmed his hands against the sides of his mug. The pleasant sent of mawya filled his nose as he drew the mug closer. "Thank you for agreeing to take a break," Trager said as he lifted the mug to his lips.

"And thank you for allowing an elder being to save face," Guruma replied.

Trager paused as Guruma called him on his actions. Then he saw Guruma's sly smile and realized that the graying Eldatek was teasing him. Trager shrugged and sipped his mawya.

Guruma chuckled. "It's been a long time since I've been in this location. The energy levels here are beginning to increase as we move away from the foci I've been using for so long."

Trager set his mug down and smiled. "Then we can try and contact Forrorrois?"

Guruma shook his head. "Not yet, the energy levels haven't strengthened enough, but we may be able to view Elda. There's a foci nearby that I've used in the past to observe activities there. We'll reach it in another cycle."

Trager looked down at his mug. "I guess it would be good to check on my family on Elda. It's been a half revolution since I've had any word on things there."

"Don't sound so enthusiastic," Guruma jested. "Your mother, Neeha, has been busy positioning herself on the council."

Trager shook his head. "Yes, she has been busy...so busy that she refuses to acknowledge her granddaughter, Celeste. Her second granddaughter I might add, after my sister Ralana's daughter Hesthra."

Guruma sighed. "Yes, but your brother Talman and his joined one, Bohata, continue to remain childless—it's becoming a stigma between Neeha's family and Bohata's. It's good that you are here instead of on Earth."

Trager looked up at Guruma, surprised. "Why is that?"

"Trager...if Bohata decides to terminate her joining with Talman then Neeha must compensate her family. If you were accessible, then Neeha would attempt to force you back to Elda to serve as a second. You've already demonstrated that you can produce a female child—a very desirable commodity at the moment for a barren couple. Believe me, that fact has not gone unnoticed among certain members of Eldatek society—especially since Neeha has refused to sanction the joining between you and Forrorrois."

Trager felt a knot forming in the pit of his stomach. The threat—no matter how remote—of being torn from Forrorrois and Celeste and thrown into a loveless joining for the sole purpose of re-securing his mother's power base made him ill. "You've been watching the Council of Elda closer than I suspected, Guruma."

Guruma shrugged. "Elda's council intrigue never fails to remind me how much this galaxy needs organizations like the Dramudam… but even the Dramudam can't shield a male Eldatek from being forced back if their family is faced with a crisis such as this. Most of the time, these males resign out of their sense of duty to their family, but unfortunately, there have been known cases of kidnapping when they have resisted. When this has happened the relationship between the council and the Dramudam have become strained—to say the very least."

Trager rubbed his thumb along the rim of his mug. Finally, he spoke. "Then I agree that at the present my being trapped here is a good thing. Let's hope that Monomay blesses Talman and Bohata with a child soon so that Neeha will keep peace between her family and Bohata's."

"Yes, may Monomay bless them with a child," Guruma agreed. "We'll start again next cycle after we get some rest," he continued. "We'll be able to reach the foci to view Elda by third kel."

Trager sipped his mawya and thought on Guruma's words. After he enlisted in the Dramudam he had thought he was free of the antiquated laws that had bound his elder brother, Talman. But now, his ill-fate at being thrown into the Plane of Deception may have been a blessing in disguise.

✳✳✳✳✳✳✳✳✳✳✳

Forrorrois shifted Collinar's arm on her shoulder as they shuffled through the snow. She tried repeatedly to hold a conversation with him, but his sentences were beginning to make less and less sense. Certain that his thermo suit was functioning properly, she became increasingly concerned that he was being overcome by altitude sickness. An hour had passed since she had forced him to take more water. Exhausted, Forrorrois looked down at her directional finder and gratefully acknowledged the fact that the dim glow she saw before her wasn't a mirage. They were less than a kilometer to the base. The wind had let up only slightly, still masking the drifts and sasstrugi before them.

"Come On, Collinar," she urged stiffly. "Help me out here. Use your feet and walk, you're dead weight!"

He moaned slightly as he tried to do what she asked.

With a sigh, she struggled forward with his hulking frame barely responding, only to stumble over a snowdrift sending them both to the ground. Her freshly healed ribs protested as she hit the ground. Laying on the hard pack for several minutes to ride out the pain, Forrorrois brought her exhausted mind back into focus. The thought of falling asleep and never waking up embraced her with its images of warmth—so peaceful and inviting as the pain subsided. Then the thought of her daughter being left alone slipped rudely in.

"Not so close," she whispered hoarsely to herself. "Get up, Collinar. Come on and move it!" He didn't move or make a sound. Panic rose in her mind. She reached out empathically and realized he had slipped into light unconsciousness. "You're not dying on me! Not after I dragged you this far!" she swore as she stumbled to her feet and roughly rolled him into a slumped sitting position. Grabbing the scruff of his knapsack, Forrorrois began to drag him across the uneven snow. The packed ice crystals squeaked against his smooth-metallic fabric. She shoved the directional finder into a leg pocket of her suit and focused her attention on the dim light before her.

✱✱✱✱✱✱✱✱✱✱✱

The uneven snowpack gave way to chewed-up powder when Forrorrois stumbled into the recent trail of a tracked vehicle. Her boots slid in the greasy, talc-like mix, making the going even more difficult. Her arms ached from dragging Collinar's limp form behind her. Suddenly, she realized she was moving down a ramp out of the cutting wind. The incline took her by surprise and sent her sprawling for several meters down to the bottom. With a shake of her head, she picked herself up. Before her was a large opening, over six meters high and close to nine meters wide. Enormous wooden doors were swung inwards, waiting in silence for one of the behemoth tracked vehicles to return. An orange building stood twenty meters past the large wooden doors, sheltered inside the corrugated steel arch against the frigid cold. Seeing no one, she doubled back for Collinar.

He groaned slightly when she forced him back onto his feet. She sensed nothing but confusion from his mind. The snow crystals were slick under her boots, turned to talc from hundreds of passes of tracked vehicles. After several minutes, she found more solid footing on the path between the building and the great arch of corrugated steel that curved close to two stories above her head.

The sound of voices startled her. Instinctively, she pressed both Collinar and herself between two storage shelves filled with heavy equipment parts and the outer wall of the orange building. Two men in bulky red parkas, smudged with oil and grease, came walking towards her position. Her heart pounded when she overheard their conversation.

"I still can't believe that station meeting this morning," one remarked in a deep voice.

"Yeah. I wish I knew the whole story. The idea of going out and performing a search and rescue in this weather is just plain stupid. Even if those pilots did survive until we could reach them, short of locking them up in a room, where would we hold them? We're not prison guards! Besides, we're thirteen hundred kilometers from nowhere," the second exclaimed in a slightly higher pitched voice.

"I don't know," the first replied. "It just sounds like the Air Force has got a bug up its nose about the two jets."

Forrorrois pressed harder against the building, trying not to be seen while the two men came closer and closer. She held her breath when they stopped and turned towards some steps just one meter from the shelf she and Collinar were hiding behind.

"Well, I don't know about you, but that wasted my morning," the second stated in disgust. "Old Katie's giving me trouble again. I won't have her up and running until midnight. She's the only one not being used for the search and I still have to do a snow run. The station is running low on water."

"I'd hate to go back on water rations again, I've got laundry to do," the deeper voice replied. "Let me give you a hand getting her back on line."

"Sounds good," the second voice replied.

Forrorrois breathed a sigh of relief when the two men climbed the steps up into the orange metal-clad building. Collinar stirred against her shoulder. She knew she needed to find a location where she could begin recharging the emergency cells of her ship—some place with a light source that was private so they wouldn't be discovered. She needed to re-pressurize the cockpit and give Collinar relief from the disorienting altitude.

A loud stereo began to blast from the building she was leaning against. She looked up in surprise and spotted the overhead flood lights that lit the path and part of the top of the orange building. Collinar slid to the ground against the wall as she pulled off his knapsack and slung the heavy sack over her shoulder along with her own. Testing the strength of the shelf next to her, she smiled when the rack didn't sway. In a matter of moments, Forrorrois climbed to the top. She brushed away a circle of the frost that had formed from the humidity that had escaped from the building and laid the two knapsacks down on the flat roof of the orange building. Within a few moments she had her ship pulled out and positioned under the floodlight that hung above her from the corrugated steel archway that shielded the interior builds from the raging storm outside.

Reluctantly, Forrorrois removed the head covering of her silver environmental suit and shivered when the frigid air kissed her bare face. Her nose hairs froze as she took her first tentative breath through her nostrils. She concentrated then stumbled to her knees. Consciousness threatened to leave her while she forced her form to contract to five percent of its mass. At times like this she didn't regret some of the changes the Utahar had made to her molecular structure. Placing a silver-gloved hand on the side of her damaged ship, she steadied herself. *No more time to waste*, she thought as she triggered the manual release for the ladder. The rungs extended easily, powered by the craft's reserve energy cells. She climbed up to the cockpit and forced open the hatch. Leaning inside, Forrorrois grabbed a black face mask from a small locker next to her command chair and pulled the knit fabric over her head to protect her exposed skin from frostbite. Keying in a manual code, Forrorrois began the emergency energy cells charging sequence—to her relief a few indicator lights signaled that they were taking a charge from the light above. Her relief was short lived when she heard voices sound from the pathway below.

"Hey, come quick," a woman's voice called out. "There's somebody out here!"

Her heart turned cold. *They've found Collinar!* Forrorrois scrambled down the ladder of her miniature pursuit, closing the hatch on the way, and hit the roof at a dead run for the edge of the building. By the time she slid to her stomach to look over the edge several red parka-clad figures were leaning over Collinar's slumped form. She cursed herself for not trying to bring him up with her when she first climbed up the shelves, or even using the reduction weapon to make it easier to carry him, but that would have been too dangerous in his present condition. Abruptly, Forrorrois pulled back as she realized she was casting a shadow with her tiny form.

Stupid—stupid—stupid! she berated herself. *The last thing I need right now is for someone to suspect that there are two of us.* Unconsciously, she rubbed her arms shivering at the thought of being discovered.

"He must be one of the pilots from the crash," a deeper male voice stated in concern. "Help me get him to Bio Med!"

Cautiously, Forrorrois looked down in time to see four people lift Collinar onto a white banana sled. They dragged him down the narrow path between the building and the arch. Then she concentrated quickly and returned to her full 1.6 meter height. She scrambled down the shelves and peered along the long ice-packed passage after them.

There was no time to waste. Reaching out with her mind, she scanned the area for more people, but no one was nearby. Relieved, Forrorrois glanced at the door the two men had gone through earlier and saw a plaque marked 'heavy shop' and stored the location in her mind. Then she carefully began to shadow the quartet's progress, ducking into the cover of storage shelves whenever they looked up from their charge. The corridor narrowed briefly when the arch seemed to end, only to widen again exposing another interior building. A low thrum filled her ears. She glanced at the sign above the door and realized the building housed the power plant. The archway narrowed once more past the building. Forrorrois halted when she realized that the passage opened up to a main intersection. Unable to go any further, she watched helplessly while the four crossed the main corridor into a second archway—an orange building with a red cross on a square of white stood just on the other side. They hoisted the white banana sled holding Collinar's large frame up the steel-grated steps and shoved open the freezer-like white door at the top. Suddenly, the door slammed shut behind them, cutting her off from her old enemy.

Forrorrois glanced both ways then darted for the steps, unseen. The distant sound of footsteps alerted her that more people were on their way. Concentrating once more, she reduced herself to less than eight centimeters tall once more—a shiver ran through her as the temperature of the air around her warmed from her exothermic transformation. Forrorrois steadied herself against the base of the four metal-grated steps and regained her bearings while she waited to see who was coming. A woman, followed by two men, stepped into view. The woman stormed up the steps, leaving the two men outside.

"We should begin searching the rest of the base in case the second pilot also made it inside as well," the taller of the two men stated.

"Maybe the second pilot didn't make it," the second man remarked, casting a glance around.

"There's always that possibility," the first replied, "but I still say we keep our eyes peeled. That second message from the Air Force was pretty specific about apprehending both pilots...and to consider them both highly dangerous."

"I know," the shorter of the two replied. "I don't want the rest of the station panicked over this. As far as they know it's just two hotshot pilots that are now facing a court marital because of an unauthorized flight in top secret jets."

The taller one nodded his head secretly. "Agreed, that's why you get the big bucks as the station manager, Bill."

Forrorrois stiffened at his words. Cautiously, she judged the distance between the station manager's oversized white rubber boots and her position. The hems of his black windpants were low enough on his boots for her to catch a ride. Without hesitation, she sprinted the short distance and pulled herself up inside.

"And don't you forget that, Mr. Science Officer," the station manager chided. "I'm going inside to make a positive ID on this guy. I want you to head over to Comms and radio that we found one of their people," the station manager added.

The science officer grunted something back, but Forrorrois didn't catch his reply. She tightened her grip on the threads of the windpants' interior seam while the station manager marched up the metal steps. Her ears popped from the change in air pressure when the heavy insulated door closed behind them. She held on firmly while he walked through a second door. The sound of a woman giving orders filled her ears. Peering out from under the station manager's hem, she found herself inside of an emergency/exam room. The station manager moved over towards a cabinet, out of the way of the well organized trauma team. Forrorrois dropped from her perch to the worn gray carpeted floor then slipped behind one of the metal legs of the cabinet.

Forrorrois looked up at the stretcher and spotted Collinar's boot. The authoritative voice of the woman sounded once more.

"Give me his stats every five minutes."

"He's beginning to respond to the oxygen," a second woman replied. Forrorrois recognized her voice from the icy path near the storage shelves.

"That's good to hear, Cynthia," the first women answered, relief evident in her voice. "Strip him down and get him into a gown then wrap him in heated blankets. I want to make sure he doesn't go into shock."

"You got it, doc," one of the men replied. "Hey, the scissors won't cut this material…"

"Then find the fasteners and strip it off of him," the doctor shot back. "I can't examine him with it on."

Forrorrois listened to them struggle for a moment while they peeled the silver environmental suit off of Collinar's two-meter frame. Finally, the suit was dropped in a corner by the wall.

"Hey, Doc, take a look at his pant leg. It's soaked with some dried yellow stuff," a male voice remarked.

"It probably happened in the crash. I'll examine his leg after you finish getting him stripped down. Don't worry about it right now, John, we need to stabilize him first," the doctor replied.

"Well, well, he definitely works out," the second woman's voice admired.

"Enough of that, Cynthia, just help John get him into a gown and cover him with those heated blankets," the doctor's voice admonished.

Forrorrois looked up and suddenly felt guilty that she wanted a closer look while Cynthia and John finished stripping the green incarceration uniform from Collinar's well-toned golden-tan body. John quickly replaced Collinar's clothes with a blue-on-white print hospital gown. She smiled to herself when she imaged how Collinar was going to react when he regained consciousness. It wasn't a long wait. In her mind, she could already feel him stirring.

"He's coming around, Doc," the women reported, draping the gray wool blankets over Collinar's legs and torso.

The doctor moved to Collinar's face and quickly began checking his eyes.

"Oh, my goodness, his pupils," the doctor gasped.

"*Get that light out of my eyes,*" Collinar growled groggily in Intergaltic, pushing the light away from his face.

Forrorrois sensed the doctor's uncertainty at Collinar's strange sounds. Finally, the woman regained her composure and continued her examination. "Sir, hold still while I examine you..." the doctor ordered firmly in English. "Are you wearing any contacts?"

"Where is Forrorrois?" Collinar started again, this time in English. He raised his arm to block her light from his face. "I said—get that light out of my face!"

"Restrain him! He's disoriented," the doctor ordered as she stepped back from Collinar's outstretched arm. "You need to calm down, sir— you've been through quite an ordeal in the past eight hours!"

"Let go of me!" Collinar bellowed angrily. "Where is she?! Where is Forrorrois?!"

"Please calm down, sir, I don't know who you're talking about. Was she the other pilot?"

Suddenly, Forrorrois felt Collinar's anger shift to suspicion. He grew silent as he reassessed the situation. "Who's in charge here?" Collinar asked, cautiously.

"I'm in charge here. I'm the station manager, Bill Anderson," the medium-height man with a heavy black beard stated. "I've received a message from General Caldwell. You must be Commander Collinar. The general told us to take good care of you."

Forrorrois felt Collinar relax completely, he had fallen for the station manager's lie. If she didn't have to take him back to the Tollon, she would have laughed at his misguided trust. In less than two days her emergency power would be charged enough to get them back to her base. *It would be so easy to just leave you behind, Collinar, but what would I tell Commander Thoren?* Forrorrois thought.

"He also mentioned a second pilot," the man continued, rubbing the four-day old scruff on his chin. "The one you're calling Forrorrois, you wouldn't happen to know where she is right now, would you? I want to make sure she's all right."

Collinar looked at him carefully, before he spoke. "I'm not certain. I don't remember how I got here. I was injured during the crash."

"What caused it?" the manager asked with interest.

The room grew silent. All eyes focused on Collinar. Forrorrois felt his guard begin to rise at the manager's unusual interest.

"That is something I only wish to discuss with General Caldwell," Collinar replied, evasively. "Now, I suggest you begin your search for the other pilot. I'm certain that I wouldn't have made it here with out her help," he added darkly.

Before Anderson could comment, the doctor impatiently broke in. "If you two don't mind, we can discuss that later. Right now, I'd like to finish your exam, Commander Collinar. Bill will have the rest of the station looking for the other pilot. If she's anywhere near the station, they'll find her. In the meantime, just relax and let the oxygen do its job. You're not use to the thin atmosphere at this altitude—you're overexerting yourself."

Forrorrois looked over at the doctor, surprised at Collinar's sudden change of heart. His lusty emotions trickled into her mind. The doctor was definitely a handsome middle-aged woman from what Forrorrois could see from her position under the cabinet. Her features were oddly similar to Subcommander Ma'Kelda who had served Collinar years ago, except that the doctor's hair was a dark brown, not Ma'Kelda's golden-blonde. Forrorrois knew in some strange way Collinar had loved Ma'Kelda, even after he executed her for treason for helping her and Trager escape seven years ago. At least the lady doctor would keep his mind occupied for the moment. Moving deeper under the cabinet Forrorrois leaned against the wall and sat down to wait.

✳✳✳✳✳✳✳✳✳✳

Forrorrois started awake, suddenly realizing she had fallen asleep. The room was darkened. Cautiously, she got to her feet and peered out from under the metal cabinet of the at the ice station's Bio Med. Collinar was alone, asleep on the gurney in the middle of the room. The curtain was drawn, separating the examination room from the hallway. Stepping out into the middle of the room, she concentrated for a brief moment, enlarging herself to her full 1.6 meter height. Forrorrois reached out and covered Collinar's mouth with her silver-gloved hand. He started awake, but she motioned for him to remain silent.

"Just listen," she whispered in Intergaltic. Collinar narrowed his eyes at her then finally nodded in agreement. "The general has double-crossed both of us. I heard the station manager talking to the science officer when they brought you here. They've been told to hold us prisoner until planes can come in several mol from now. I don't know about you, but I'm not going to wait that long."

"That's ridiculous," Collinar whispered back as she removed her hand. "They haven't said a word about that. In fact, they were informed by the general to take care of our needs!"

"Collinar, I've learned over the revolution that I've known the general that he can't be trusted," she warned. "Without technology to exchange, you have nothing to barter with. When the general gets bored of your overbearing personality, he'll turn you over to his scientists and they'll probably dissect you to see what an alien looks like from the inside out!"

"That's absurd!" he shot back in a low growl. "You're just trying to get me to go back with you to the Tollon. Well, I'm not going!"

"Shh. Someone's coming," she whispered back. "Just remember what I said, Collinar. The general has double-crossed you, so watch your back."

The curtain pulled back, revealing the doctor as she peered into the darken room. Forrorrois crouched behind the gurney and concentrated. In the space of a heartbeat, she reduced her size and rolled under the gurney out of harms way. The doctor crossed over to where Forrorrois had just stood.

"I thought I heard voices," the woman stated, quietly.

"It must have been your imagination," Collinar replied.

"How are you feeling, Commander Collinar?" she asked with more than a passing interest.

"Just Collinar," he replied, a bit more warmly. "Much better, thank you. Have you heard anything about the other pilot?"

"No...Not yet...but the station is still out looking for her," she reassured him.

"I'm sure she's around somewhere," Collinar replied.

"You seem so certain about that," the doctor said in surprise. "Have you remembered something?"

"No, but I've known her for a long time. She always shows up when you least expect it," he snorted more to himself than to the doctor.

"I see," the women replied, uncertain.

"I'm still exhausted, so if you don't mind, I need to rest," he stated, dismissing her.

"No, not at all," the doctor replied.

Forrorrois felt the woman pull back emotionally from Collinar's affront. When the doctor left to go back to her room, Forrorrois waited a few seconds then returned to full size next to the gurney. Collinar started at her sudden reappearance. "You sure know how to make friends," Forrorrois stated in disgust. "I have to go check on a few things, but I'll be back. Keep your ears open. You might be surprised at what you'll find out."

"Oh, I'll be listening," he stated, "and if I find out that it's just you they're looking for, I'll tell them where to look."

"They'll never find me," Forrorrois laughed, "I'll be back for you." She flashed him a smile then headed out the airlock door into the frigid polar night.

✶✶✶✶✶✶✶✶✶✶

"Computer, can you hear me?" Forrorrois asked again—frustrated by the silence from her ship's computer. The energy level of the miniaturized pursuit ship was barely registering on the panel before her. "Damn it, I need to contact Jack and let him know where I am," she cursed to herself. "I guess I have no choice, I have to get inside the radio room."

Reluctantly, Forrorrois opened the hatch manually. The cutting air chilled her face—freezing the moisture in her nostrils. Still clad in her silver environmental suit, she shivered slightly as she pulled her black balaclava over her exposed face and climbed out of the cockpit. She dropped lightly to the roof of the heavy shop and peered over the edge to the ground. The coast was clear. Enlarging herself, Forrorrois scrambled down the shelf of the storage rack and reached out with her mind for anyone nearby.

Beneath her feet, the snow was compressed to patches of ice from the hundreds of boots that had traversed the narrow passage between the orange rectangular interior building and the exterior corrugated steel archway that protected it and the other buildings from the harsh Antarctic winds outside. She stepped cautiously forward, making her way through the frosted corridors. The path widened as she reached the major junction before Bio Med. Hesitating, she glanced around. The corridor to her right was half again as high as the one she was in and led into the main section of the snow-buried station—cover in the corridor was sparse. Sensing no one nearby, Forrorrois headed towards the cluster of buildings at the end of the arched corridor. The passage ended abruptly, giving way to a multi-story domed enclosure that sheltered a cluster of orange two-storied buildings inside. Each building was labeled in typical military efficiency. She smiled to herself. *This is going to be easier than I thought.*

Taking in her surroundings, she noted that the only building that had any windows was on her right and was marked as the galley. The stairwells to the second floor of each building were metal grates that were mounted on the outside. She edged to the right-hand side of the dome, away from the windows that pointed toward the center of the circle of buildings, and followed the curve of the large geodesic structure. Pallets of frozen food towered on either side of her, while she made her way around the back next to the metal plates of the exterior dome.

No sense wasting energy on free freezer space, she thought to herself. A sudden noise made her halt. Reaching out with her mind, she felt the soggy mind of a man who had been imbibing. As she looked up, she was surprised to see a small walkway that connected the second floor of the galley to two other buildings. The man's red parka was loosely pulled around his shoulders. He wasn't going far, except down the stairs—the hard way. She watched in disbelief when the man slipped on the top step and tumbled the rest of the way down to the metal landing below.

The door from the upper level swung open seconds later, pouring out several men and women dressed in tan canvas overalls and red parkas. Forrorrois raced to the other side of a small building labeled 'Freshies' and peered towards the building she was trying to reach. Shouts for help brought a man and a woman from the communications shack. Forrorrois reached out and felt no one else was inside. Moving to the corner of the building, she watched for a moment more to make certain they were all absorbed with their drunken friend then she bolted onto the metal grating and through the door, into the airlock of the communications shack, before anyone noticed.

As she left the airlock through a second door into the hallway, there was a small room on either side. The hallway opened up to a large room filled with communications equipment. She headed straight for the desk with a microphone resting on the counter in front of a rack of equipment with glowing numbers. Resetting the readout to match her base's emergency frequency, she began to broadcast, praying that she could reach Jack.

"Jack, this is Forrorrois, do you copy?" She released the mic button and allowed the soft static hiss fill her ears. "Jack, this is Forrorrois, do you read me?!"

The empty static continued to sound from the small speaker. *Damn it! The ice station must have limited satellite coverage*, she thought to herself. Trying again, she waited, still nothing. Voices alerted her she was running out of time. Redialing the original frequency, Forrorrois turned at the sound of the airlock door opening. A cold blast of air crawled across the floor in a misty fog. It was too late—a man and women in red parkas and black windpants had spotted her.

"Whoa now," a man with a black mustache and couple days of growth on his chin demanded. "Now, I suggest that you step away from the counter and keep your hands in full view."

Forrorrois did as she was told, mindful of any quick movements. She didn't see any weapons, but she decided not to take any chances.

"Joanie, go get Bill and bring him here right away," he ordered the women, without taking his eyes off Forrorrois. Joanie turned immediately and ran out the door. "Take a seat and remove your balaclava," he stated, cautiously.

Forrorrois pulled one of the wheeled chairs away from the table and sat down. She sized up the man and concluded she could take him easily, but decided against a fight. If she was going to be stuck here for a while, a hot meal would be nice. She pulled off her knit face mask. Her braided auburn hair came loose and fell about her silver-clad shoulders. The man liked what he saw. A fresh face at a remote station always could get a reaction.

"What's your name?" he asked, nervous.

"Suppose you tell me?" she replied. "I'm certain you've already met the other pilot."

"Why are you hiding?" the man insisted.

"Why are you looking for me?" she responded back, evasively.

Before he could respond, the door opened and closed with a billow of cold air from the airlock. The station manager had arrived. Forrorrois could feel his anxiousness. She smiled at him confidently—unnerving him.

"I want to speak with her alone," the station manager stated, dismissing the two comms personnel. He waited until they left before he spoke again. "You and your partner have put this station in a rather unusual position. We don't normally get visitors this time of year. It'll be months before a plane will even be able to land to take you back."

"I apologize for the inconvenience, Mr. Anderson," she replied. He stiffen when she mention his last name.

"How did you know my name???"

"It's not important, what is important is that you tell me why General Caldwell has given orders for you to restrain Collinar and myself?" she stated, pointedly.

"I'm not the one in trouble here, young lady," he stated, "and I suggest you remember that. It's going to be a long couple of months and I'm not going to start them off by playing twenty questions with you!"

"In other words, you don't know why. You're just following orders," Forrorrois replied, caustically. "Well, I think you'd better get all the facts before you blindly lock me up. I know the general and I have never gotten along too well, but I think you'd better let him know someone higher up is coming to take Collinar back. They're not going to be too happy when they find out the general had you obstruct me from my duty."

"I don't know what you're talking about, but I sure know that you're under arrest by the order of the U. S. Air Force," he gruffly stated. "Now, you're coming with me over to the infirmary. I'm certain that you're partner will be glad to know you're alive."

"Oh, I'm sure he knows that all ready. I can't wait until you tell him he's under arrest," she stated with a wicked grin. She stood to her feet and smoothed her silver environmental suit. He looked her up and down then dismissed her as a threat and pointed towards the door.

"This way," he ordered, grabbing her arm.

Forrorrois stood her ground, burning a gaze into his hand. He released his grip without a word. Nodding tersely at him, she walked out the door.

****

Forrorrois sensed the unseen eyes that followed her to the ice station's Bio Med. The entire facility was now aware of her capture. *Innocent bystanders,* she reminded herself. The time wasn't right for her to show her hand. She followed Bill Anderson's directions and climbed the four metal steps of Bio Med. She reached out with her silver-gloved hand, pulled the lever of the freezer door then stepped into the air lock. Anderson closed the door behind them, for a brief moment they were alone.

"I believe I know the way," Forrorrois remarked while she opened the second door.

Anderson gave her a look as he waved her inside.

Forrorrois looked to her right then smiled at Collinar. He rolled to his side on the gurney covered by a couple grey wool blankets and chuckled under his breath at the sight of her being led in. The doctor greeted them and pointed her towards a chair.

"Sit down, I'd like to have a look at you," the doctor stated.

Forrorrois acquiesced without a word. The women approached her with a thermometer.

"Here, stick this under your tongue," she continued as she placed her fingers against her throat to take her pulse. After a few moments the doctor took the thermometer from her month and read it. "Temperature is slightly below normal, but that's to be expected, I'd like to examine you closer—just to make sure you're all right after the crash." When the woman reached over to unfasten her environmental suit, Forrorrois pulled away, aggravating her banged-up ribs. The woman didn't miss her hand reflexively move to protect her right side.

"I'm fine," Forrorrois said, straightening in her chair.

"I disagree," the doctor remarked.

"I assure you, I am fine," Forrorrois insisted, shaking her head no. "I just want to know why Collinar and I are being held prisoner." She felt Collinar's jovial mood change to suspicion at her words, sitting up from his place on the gurney.

Anderson tensed at Collinar's sudden movement. The station manager glanced quickly toward the doctor then Forrorrois. "You are both under arrest for unauthorized usage and destruction of classified aircraft," he stated cautiously.

"What!" Collinar bellowed, swinging his legs over the edge of the stretcher. "By whose orders?!"

"By the order of General Caldwell," Anderson sputtered, taking a step back when Collinar slid down from the stretcher, towering above him by over a good head in his short hospital gown.

Forrorrois felt Collinar's pain when he put his full weight onto his newly repaired leg. She quickly stood up and blocked the Utahar commander from advancing on the hapless station manager. Collinar leaned heavily on her shoulder while Forrorrois allowed him to save face instead of crumpling to the ground.

"Collinar," she warned. "The man's just following orders! He's not the one you want! Now, just relax and sit back down."

She felt the pressure of Collinar's hand on her shoulder while he steadied himself. His mind was seething with anger from the general's betrayal.

"It won't do you any good to try and escape," the rattled manager stated. "As you probably already know, this base is thirteen hundred kilometers away from anywhere. You'd freeze to death before you could reach the nearest base!"

"Get him out of my sight," Collinar growled in a dangerous low tone. "Get him out of my sight before I kill him with my bare hands!"

"Relax, Collinar," Forrorrois said carefully. "He's just a pawn. You really want Caldwell. Who knows, maybe you'll get your chance—that is if I don't take him out first."

"Take them to the isolation room," Anderson ordered the doctor. "They'll be easier to watch in there."

Forrorrois didn't resist, letting Collinar lean on her shoulder as they led them down the narrow corridor, glad to be heading for a more remote location. *They'll relax as soon as they think Collinar and I are secured*, she thought, wryly.

CHAPTER 5

Perkins made his way in the darkness to the perimeter of the air force base and slipped through a hole in the fence that had been there since before he'd been stationed there—sort of a shortcut to the convenience store that nobody ever thought to report. He smiled about the lack of security, relieved that he'd never mentioned it. The entire base had been looking for him well into the night and he wasn't about to let the general turn him into a lab rat. He made his way into some scrub brush towards the light of a housing tract not far away. Beyond that, there was the small convenience store and gas station that still had a payphone outside. Perkins walked through the brush to an ATV trail. His mind kept mulling over the consequences of the general's discovery. They all pointed back to the fact that his career in the Air Force was at an end.

The dirt trail emptied to the back parking lot of the small poorly lit convenience store. Perkins glanced through the windows and saw the place was deserted except the bored clerk sitting at the counter staring at the fuel pumps. The phone booth was mounted on the side of the building, just out of view from the clerk. Perkins approached the phone and pulled some change out of his pants' pocket. Glancing around once more, he quickly dialed Jack's cell number.

There was a distant ring on the other end. It rang twice more, before there was an answer.

"Colonel Stern."

"Jack! It's me!"

"Perkins? What's the matter?" Jack's voice asked.

"Jack, I need your help. General Caldwell had me arrested when I went back to my apartment. I was able to escape, but I don't know how much longer I can elude them."

"Where are you now?"

"I'm behind the convenience store just off the base. You know— the one that has those mega burritos."

"Yeah, I know the one. Stay down, I'm coming for you. You can tell me the details then."

"Thanks, Jack, I owe you one," Perkins said as he hung up. Looking around once more, Perkins headed back into the scrub brush to wait.

✶✶✶✶✶✶✶✶✶✶

Hours had passed since the station manager had locked up Forrorrois and Collinar in the small isolation room of Bio Med. Forrorrois sat quietly on the stiff mattress of her bed still clad in her silver environmental suit. She leaned against the wall while she considered her next move. Collinar lay propped up on his bed set against the opposite side of the narrow room. He'd changed back into the green incarceration uniform and boots he'd been wearing when she had shot him down, but the station manager hadn't given him back his environmental suit. She felt his gaze on her and turned to look at him, sensing his discomfort by the proximity they were forced to share.

"What's on your mind, Collinar?" she asked in Intergaltic, with a little less bite than she normal showered on him.

"I was just thinking about how you tried to warn me about Caldwell," he admitted in a low tone in the singsong language. "I realize you had other reasons for telling me...but the fact that you did can't be dismissed."

"Don't get sentimental on me. I did it because I have to bring you back to the Tollon so you can finish your sentence," she stated bluntly, looking down at her hands. "Besides, no matter how much I hate you...I could never let you go through what you did to me," she continued, bitterly. "And you're my worst enemy..."

She started when she felt the thin thread of compassion filter towards her. Glancing over at him she saw his hard golden feline eyes soften—ever so slightly.

Collinar snorted. "You're too soft," he replied in a husky voice, looking away. "There is nothing they could do to me that I haven't done already to another being. Death doesn't frighten me."

"I wasn't talking about death," she whispered, distantly. "You don't know how many times I prayed for death while your scientist carved away at my soul. Each time I felt death's icy fingers, they'd drag me back. Of course, General Caldwell's scientists aren't so skilled. Your prayers might be answered." He tensed at her words. Another time she would have grinned at his shudder. "How's your leg?" she asked, changing the subject. Collinar's relaxed slightly.

"It's felt better. Times like these I wish the Utahar were less resistant to the use of free-willed zendra," he stated, shifting his position.

"They would have had you up and walking by now," Forrorrois mused. "It's amazing how attached I've become to mine. Why, the last few times you almost killed me, they had me up and about in less than seven cycle. So, when do you think you'll be ready to travel?"

He looked over at her in surprise. "I don't recall either of our ships being in any condition to fly?"

"Mine might. You just severed one of the power lines. I was able to patch it before they brought me in. At the moment its emergency cells are recharging," she calmly stated.

Collinar's eyes brightened. "It's good to hear you haven't lost your touch with repairs. Ahzell spoke highly of your skill," he replied.

Forrorrois froze at the mention of her dead friend's name. She turned away from him towards the wall afraid that she might overreact.

"I'm sorry, I forgot she was a sore subject with you," he apologized.

"I know you don't understand the concept, but she was a dear friend. You could have let her live," she whispered still looking at the wall as she forced down her anger.

"Ahzell made her choices," he stated. "Let's not dredge up the past."

Forrorrois remained silent for several minutes before she could look back at him and trust herself to speak. "Look, I just need to know if you're whole enough to walk out of this place."

Collinar thought for a moment then shook his head. "No... They'd be on us before I could reach the door, even if you helped me."

"I suspected as much," she replied in frustration. "At least they gave you your clothes back, although they still have your low temp suit. You'll need something to survive outside."

"I can't believe you're that easily stumped," he shot back.

Before she could speak, footsteps sounded in the hallway outside. They both looked up to see who was coming. She grew intrigued when she spotted a lanky man with dark hair and glasses staring through the window of the door.

The man pushed the door open enough to poke his head through. "May I come in?" he asked, nervously in English.

Collinar moved to object, but Forrorrois waved him silent. She recognized the voice as the station's science officer, who she had heard speaking to Anderson when Collinar was first brought to Bio Med. "Yes, please do," she agreed, swinging her boots off the bed to the floor. "Have a seat," she offered, patting a spot on the mattress next to her.

He sat down cautiously on the edge of her bed. An odd smile tugged at the corner of his lips. "My name is Dorian. I'm here to speak to you as a scientist," he began. "I have some questions about you."

"What kind of questions?" she asked, gingerly, uncertain which direction he was going to go in.

"The general hinted at a few things...I just wanted to know if they are true," he posed, tensely. When she didn't speak, he continued. "He implied that you both are not from around here."

Forrorrois hesitated at first then she snorted a laugh. "Of course we're not from around here," she jested. "No one's from here! It's a frozen wasteland."

Dorian shifted uncomfortably. "No...I mean...not from Earth," he whispered.

"Oh...I see," she replied, maintaining her smile. "Well, I think the general's pulling your leg, Dorian."

The tall man fidgeted on the bunk next to her. She could sense his hesitation. He didn't accept what she was telling him. "Maybe you're right, but that still doesn't explain how you both got here and why General Caldwell is the one personally sending the message all the way from New York state."

"Honest, I couldn't tell you why, except that the three of us go back a few years. The general can be quite the jokester at times," she replied with a sly smile.

The science officer mulled over her words once more, but she could still sense he didn't accept the answer. "If you don't mind, I'd like to verify this for myself. I'm going to ask the doctor to perform some simple blood tests. They should confirm whether my information is false or not."

She felt Collinar's emotions run cold, as did her own.

"I will not submit to a blood test," Collinar stated in a dark tone, raising himself onto his elbow and staring the man down.

Forrorrois knew she couldn't let that happen either. "You must forgive Collinar—he has strict religious beliefs which do not permit removal or injection of bodily fluids." She threw a warning glance at him to be quiet. "To ask him to submit would be like asking him to damn his soul to Hell," she continued. "But if you feel the need for a blood test, I will be more than willing to offer it."

Dorian looked at her, then at Collinar. "I don't want to have to take anything by force, but I am prepared to do so. The blood test will proceed with or without your consent."

"Excuse me, Dorian, but unless I am mistaken this is still a U.S. base, and I am a U.S. citizen. That entitles me to proper due process of law. What you are suggesting is a complete violation of our civil rights. If you think that either one of us are going to allow you to do as you please with us then you have another thing coming. We both accepted being incarcerated for whatever crime you feel we've committed, but we will not stand by and have our heritage questioned."

"I'm sorry you feel that way," the lanky man replied, coming to his feet. "The doctor will be in shortly, along with some assistants. Please don't make this anymore difficult than it needs to be."

Forrorrois watched him leave, unable to speak from anger.

"We can't let them do this," Collinar stated firmly in Intergaltic, swinging his legs over the edge of the bunk uncomfortably. "We've got to get out of this room!"

"You're right. I'll take care of the guard outside," she replied calmly in the singsong language. "I haven't seen any weapons since we got here. I don't think they allow them for psychological reasons. When they brought us here, I saw an exit just down the hall. There were parkas hanging on the wall next to it. You'll need one for outside."

"How are you going to get the doors open?" he began.

Forrorrois just smiled. "How else?" Concentrating, she reduced herself to eight centimeters. Taking a moment to regain her senses, she slipped under the heavy door. The woman guard was sitting in a chair reading a book next to the doorway. Forrorrois felt a twinge of guilt just before she enlarged herself next to her and put her into a sleeper hold. The woman didn't make a sound as she slid to the gray carpeted floor—unconscious. Forrorrois grabbed a large parka from the rack by the exterior door, and then returned quickly to the room that still held Collinar and unbolted the latch. To her surprise, an argument had erupted from the other end of the hall between Dorian and the doctor.

"Put this on," she urged Collinar, pulling the large red down jacket around his shoulders.

"I can dress myself," he growled in irritation.

"Then do it, quickly," she spat. "And put these mittens on. I don't want you to get frostbite from touching any metal." He glared at her, while he zipped up the parka. She crouched down, to allow him to support himself on her shoulder.

"You sound like a doting mother," he retorted, coming to his feet.

"I am," she shot back, hustling him through the door. "Now move it, before the doctor stops arguing with Dorian." She sensed his shocked silence, suddenly wishing she hadn't spoken so rashly. The sound of shouting filled her ears, they had been spotted. She forced the door of the building open and dragged Collinar through into the frigid archway. *Escape would be simpler if I didn't have him slowing me down!* She pushed the thought from her mind and looked around for a route of escape. There were exterior storage shelves against the wall before them and a worn icy path that lead in either direction. She turned to the right and spied a small opening into another archway.

Dorian's voice sounded over the all-call. "The two pilots have escaped. All available station personnel report to Bio Med immediately!"

Collinar looked at her and tried to pick up his speed.

"This way," she urged. "We don't have much time."

"I agree," Collinar growled, leaning heavily against her shoulder while she darted into the narrow passage. The path opened up into a cavernous poorly-lit archway. The pungent smell of high-altitude jet fuel permeated the crisp air. She nearly stumbled over a hose that crossed the path and ran along the edge of the deeply ribbed steel walls on her left. Following the tube with her eyes to the right, she focused on an enormous pillow-shaped object that sat in the middle of the long archway. All of a sudden she realized there was seven other fuel bladders just like the one before her—side by side in an arched space larger than a football field.

"What is this place?" Collinar asked, casting his eyes about.

"Their fuel supply," she replied. "Come on, there's a stairwell at the end leading up. It must be the way out!"

"We could ignite the fuel!" Collinar exclaimed, hobbling after her as quickly as he could.

Forrorrois gave him a dark look. "Are you nuts? With this much fuel all that would be left of this base would be a crater," she shot back. "Besides, even if they did survive the explosion, they probably wouldn't be able to make it until rescue planes could arrive to get them out. I couldn't live with that."

"You always were too soft-hearted," he replied, shaking his head.

"It's a good thing too, or I would have left your sorry butt back in that crash," she warned, stopping at the foot of the long steep wooden stairway. "Now, start climbing these stairs..."

"They're in the fuel arch!" a voice called out behind them.

"Oh, great! Move it, Collinar—they've spotted us!" she ordered.

He hauled himself up the wooden steps, leaning heavily on the railing. Without a word, Forrorrois eased the weight from his leg with her shoulder. At the top of the stairway, she helped him into the wooden enclosure at the top.

"Can you climb the ladder?" she asked Collinar, pointing to the wooden rungs that ascended up the square chute through the peak of the structure.

"Yes, go ahead of me to make sure no one has blocked our path," he insisted.

Forrorrois didn't argue with his logic and began the five-meter ascent to the wooden hatch above. Hesitating for a moment, she reached out with her mind. *No one—so far,* she thought and shouldered the lid open. The wooden door flipped open, caught by a gust of bitter wind. The stars shone dully above her, obscured by the ice crystals caught in the fast moving wind. Bitter subzero temperatures cut against her bare face. Forrorrois tumbled from the opening to the ground three feet below, turning her face away from the wind. She tugged her black balaclava from her belt and covered her head and face from the brutal gusts. Looking up, she spotted Collinar. She rolled to one side to avoid him when he dropped to the ground beside her.

"What a harsh place this is," he gasped from the frigid wind.

She patted his bulging pockets and pulled out a knit face mask. "Put this on," she ordered. He did as he was told. Forrorrois pulled his hood into place and zipped his parka all the way, ignoring his protests. Coming to her feet, she forced the hatch cover back in place. "They'll be here any moment. We need to get to the other side of the station."

"I'll try, but it's difficult for me to catch my breath in this thin atmosphere."

"Shut up and breathe through your nose or you'll freeze your lungs. We don't have time for you to catch your breath," she stated bluntly. "I'll drag you if I have too, but we have to keep moving!"

"That won't be necessary," he replied, indignantly.

"Then let's go—the wind has sculpted the drifting snow that surrounds the dome. We can follow the hollow around," she said.

"That's a sheer drop off!" he gasped.

"It's not that sheer," she pressed. The sound of people climbing up the hatch grated at her nerves. There was no time for hesitation. She body-blocked Collinar over the side of the three story drift. The two of them slid down to the bottom into the hollow on the slickness of Collinar's red parka. His eyes glowed from displeasure when she looked down at him from her position on top of his chest. Before he could speak, she rolled him face first into the base of the drift. "Be quiet," she whispered.

"I don't see them," a male voice stated in puzzlement from above.

"They couldn't just disappear," Dorian's voice replied in disgust. "Tell the others to spread out and begin searching all the outbuildings. They couldn't have gotten very far—not with the big guy being injured."

"You got it, Dorian," the other voice replied.

Forrorrois waited for several moments until she couldn't sense them any longer, then she relaxed her hold. Her body began to shiver slightly from the heat loss of her poorly covered head—her newly healed ribs and lungs protested her rough treatment of them. Without warning, she began to cough. Forrorrois tried to muffle the sound as she rolled off Collinar's chest and clutched her side. The frigid air made it difficult to catch her breath even through her face mask.

"We have to get back inside," Collinar said softly, when she struggled to sit up.

"We will," she agreed, looking around in the darkness—only the starlight reflecting off the snow provided any light. Gradually, her eyes focused on a white rectangle at the base of the tall orange structure attached to the dome about four-meters away from their position. Forrorrois got to her feet and extended her free hand to Collinar. "There's a door into this building. Let's try it."

Collinar leaned against her shoulder and together they made

their way to the heavy steel door. Forrorrois pulled on the freezer-style latch then gave the door a good shove with her shoulder. The metal door gave way inward—stubbornly—forcing her ribs to protest even louder. Forrorrois suppressed a groan and pushed Collinar forward. The sound of voices behind them made her turn quickly and close the door. She pulled off her face mask to try and see in the pitch darkness. Unable to see a thing, she fumbled for a switch on her right and turned on the lights. A low-wattage bulb revealed the landing they were on gave way to a raised platform that housed a low storage room directly in front of her and a narrow set of stairs leading downward to her right.

The exertion at the high altitude left her gasping to catch her breath. She began to cough once more. As she took her hand away, she realized that there were flecks of pink froth on her silver gloved fingertips. Collinar did not miss her reaction.

"You still have blood on you lips," he commented.

Subconsciously, Forrorrois wiped her mouth with the back of her gloved hands—fully aware he was studying her.

"I didn't say anything earlier, but you've been favoring your right side. Were you injured during the crash?" he asked.

"No," Forrorrois replied as she glanced around to assess where they were. The storage room had a low ceiling—even for her—and the small area looked like a dead-end. She dismissed the raised platform and looked down the stairs. The narrow stairwell curved slightly and ended at a wooden door. Forrorrois reached out with her empathic ability and didn't sense anyone on the other side. She started when Collinar reached out and placed his gloved hands on her shoulders.

"You're shivering," he stated, rubbing her upper arms.

"It'll pass," she stated, defensively, pulling away. "We can't stay in one place, they'll find us."

Apologetically, he removed his hands from her and leaned against the wall. "After you."

She nodded then headed down the narrow stairs. "I don't feel anyone on the other side of the door. Careful on the steps, they might be slippery," she said, mechanically. He hobbled after her, without a word, leaning against the wall for support.

Forrorrois opened the door slowly at the bottom of the stairs and peered inside hearing only a low hum of energized power supplies. The room was dark—lit only by a multitude of indicator lights from a wall of equipment racks. She squeezed past the end of the racks then crossed to the door on the other side of the room and listened. "Collinar, turn off the light and close the door. I don't want to leave any clues that we've been here."

Collinar fumbled with the antiquated switch by the door and moved into the darken room.

Forrorrois listened to the soft click of the door and nodded. As she moved to the next door, she nearly doubled over in another coughing fit.

"Take a moment and catch your breath," Collinar said quietly.

"No, we've got to keep moving," Forrorrois insisted, as she recovered herself.

"No. Catch your breath. You will draw attention if you keep coughing like that."

Forrorrois glared at him then grudgingly leaned against the door. Her strength was waning and he was too big to carry. "Fine, I'll take a moment," she replied.

Collinar leaned against the wall as well—Forrorrois could see that the high altitude was taking its toll on both of them.

"Good," Collinar said. "So, if you didn't get hurt in the crash, then how did you get hurt?"

Forrorrois stared at him hard then shook her head in resignation. "If you must know, a storm came through the air base and collapsed a building. I went inside to extract a trapped pilot when the debris shifted and there was a cave-in. I received a couple of fractured ribs and a punctured lung. To add insult to injury, Caldwell tried to take me prisoner when I pulled out the pilot."

She felt surprise filter into her mind which soon shifted to amusement.

"General Caldwell would have made a fine Utahar," Collinar growled in a laugh. "And you constantly astound me."

Irritated, Forrorrois narrowed her eyes. "And why is that?"

"You know that General Caldwell will betray you…and yet…you offer to assist his pilots even at your own personal risk. Why?"

Forrorrois rolled her eyes. "I didn't do it for the general, Collinar. I did it for the pilot that was trapped in the collapsed building."

"I see," Collinar replied, visibly trying to catch his breath. "And is that the same logic you use to justify helping me?"

Forrorrois shook her head and tried not to laugh. "Don't flatter yourself. I do have to admit that I get a small bit of pleasure knowing how irritated the general is going to be once he finds out that I got to you before he did. But, we both know that I'm taking you into custody so that you can finish your term at that Dramudam rehabilitation center for violating the Isolation Treaty. And before you even think of fighting me on this point, just remember that if I don't get you out of here really soon your symptoms are going to grow even worse and you'll die from the effects of high altitude sickness. My getting you away from this ice station is your only chance for survival—and deep down inside you know that."

Collinar looked away, his mirth gone.

"Now, give me your arm, we've got to get moving," Forrorrois offered.

Stubbornly, Collinar limped over to her and leaned against her shoulder in silence.

She opened the door and peered out. In front of her was a steel door, to her right was a set of stairs that led upward, and much to her surprise, on her left was an elevator style door. Her breath hung in the air before her in the unheated enclosed stairwell. She looked above the steel door and signaled towards the exit sign. Collinar nodded and let her help him over the lip of the door towards the one on the other side. Reaching out once more, she felt stillness. "The path is clear."

They stepped through the exit into a long narrow oval tube of corrugated steel that was about two-and-a-half meters tall at the highest point. At the other end, she spotted an orange building. The passage was slippery from the snow being compressed into ice by hundreds of past footfalls, forcing her to steady Collinar. The tube ended abruptly and opened up into the dome she had been in earlier. Forrorrois looked around as she tried to get her bearings. Finally, she urged him to go to the left behind the Communications building.

"This way," she gasped, feeling the effects of the lack of oxygen from the high altitude sapping her strength. Collinar nodded, unable to waste his breath on the effort of words. The sound of voices nearby made her freeze. She looked quickly around and saw no one. Sheepishly, she realized she was being deceived by the parabolic acoustic nature of the dome. Pressing harder, she forced Collinar to stumble onward towards the backside of the comms building and the galley along the dome's outer perimeter.

"I've got to stop," Collinar insisted, leaning against a stack of boxed frozen meats, behind the galley.

"We're close," she implored. "I know you're leg is throbbing, and you can hardly catch your breath, but we have to keep moving!"

"Where are we going from here?" he gasped.

"Through there," she pointed towards the large rectangular opening of the dome that lead back into the archway towards Bio Med and the power plant. "Then we'll turn left down another corridor. After that it won't be much further, I promise. But we have to take advantage of the fact that they are looking for us outside."

"All right," he agreed, pushing away from the stack of boxes.

Relieved, she shouldered his weight once more. "That's the spirit," she encouraged him.

They followed the curve of the dome to the large opening. Their feet slid in the greasy powder of the dirty snow, where the tracked vehicles had chewed it up, while they navigated the wide passage. At last, they came to the end.

She glanced briefly at the opposing opening at Bio Med then turned Collinar towards the power plant arch. The distant thrum of the generator filled her ears, muffled by the walls of the building. She felt Collinar's mind begin to wander again from the effects of the altitude. Only by getting to her ship on top of the heavy shop could she hope to revive him with oxygen in her re-pressurized cockpit. The passage narrowed once more, briefly, before opening up to the final arch. She stumbled through the icy passage to the edge of the orange rectangular building. Her mind was fogging from exhaustion and her poorly healed punctured lung was making the final steps agony. Forcing her feet to go the last few meters, Forrorrois finally let Collinar slip to the ground between the storage racks next to the heavy shop. With little time to waste, she climbed the rack next to the building then rolled onto the top of the building—her energy spent.

The cold was making it harder and harder for her to think. Forrorrois rolled over and grabbed one of the duffels she had left next to the ship—she fumbled in the bag until she found both her weapons. With stiff, gloved, fingers she placed them onto her belt then closed the duffel.

'Computer,' she subvocalized to the tiny ship via her zendra mind link. 'Computer can you hear me?'

'Yes,' ship's computer replied in her mind.

She closed her eyes in gratitude. 'Do you have enough power stored to lift off and land at the base of this building?'

'Yes,' the ship's computer replied through her zendra link.

'Then do it,' she ordered. 'I'll follow you down.'

The miniaturized ship hovered from the metal plates of the roof then glided to the edge of the roof. Forrorrois gathered up the duffels and slung them over her shoulder before she scurried back down the side of the shelves to Collinar's crumpled form. The ship landed further down the path towards the large opening to the outside.

"Wake up, Collinar," she stated. When he didn't respond she shook him slightly, and then peeled back his knit mask.

"He's suffering from the altitude," a voice stated calmly in English behind her.

"Dorian," Forrorrois exclaimed, turning to facing the tall thin man. She cursed herself for being so tired that she hadn't sensed him.

"I suspected you'd come back to this spot," he continued. "Rather like a murder mystery. I see you stashed quite a few things up there before you came looking for your friend," Dorian added, glancing up as he stepped closer.

Forrorrois narrowed her eyes and pulled out her stun weapon from her belt. "Don't come any closer," she warned.

He stopped in his tracks. "I'm not armed," he offered, beginning to walk towards her once more.

"I am and I'll use it," she hissed impatiently, aiming her stun weapon. "I don't have any time to waste on you. I need to attend to Collinar."

"The doctor could help you," Dorian offered, standing still.

"That won't be necessary. Now, I suggest you turn around and leave. Oh, and you can give the general this message. Tell him don't ever double-cross me again or I'll settle the score personally," she warned.

"I can't do that. I can't let you leave," he stubbornly replied.

"Don't be stupid, Dorian, this isn't your fight." She lowered her weapon and pulled Collinar to his feet, shouldering his weight. "He needs to be re-pressurized to sea level. That's something you can't do for him. If you had the equipment, you would have done it already."

"I admit our equipment must seem primitive to you, but we can help him," Dorian insisted.

Forrorrois began to edge backwards towards the end of the archway where the two large exterior doors stood open—a gust of frigid air buffeted her as she drew nearer. The miniature ship maneuvered at her silent command and landed pointing towards the opening. "I have to go now. Don't try to stop me." She switched weapons with her free hand and pointed the reduction weapon at the tiny ship,

Nothing happened when she fired.

Taken aback, Forrorrois looked down at the weapon and realized that the energy cell was depleted from the long exposure to the extreme cold.

Dorian regained his composure and stepped forward. "Having some technical difficulties?"

Forrorrois returned the reduction weapon to her waist and pulled out her stun weapon and aimed at the science officer. "Step back, Dorian."

"If that weapon's powered the same way, I can only guess, but that it might have the same problem," Dorian replied and continued to advance.

Frustrated, Forrorrois confirmed that the energy cell was drained from the cold as well. She slipped the weapon back onto her belt.

Don't make me hurt you, Dorian," Forrorrois warned, still shouldering Collinar while she faced the lanky man.

"The others will be here soon. You don't have anyplace left to run," Dorian laughed as he stopped less than arms length from her.

The sound of running feet made her look up confirming his assertion.

"I see them by the Heavy shop!" a voice called out.

Forrorrois felt the weight of Collinar slumped against her and the duffels hanging on her shoulders. Her small ship waited just down the path near the enormous yawning doors to the outside at the end of the arch. Defeated, she looked back at Dorian. She could escape, but not with Collinar. Dorian reached out for her arm.

"Don't touch me," Forrorrois warned, pulling away—nearly losing her balance.

"Nobody needs to get hurt," Dorian offered. "Just come with me."

Forrorrois glared at him. "I said don't make me hurt you!"

Dorian laughed and moved to take her arm as the others arrived behind him.

Suddenly, the whine of a stun rifle charging behind Forrorrois made Dorian hesitate.

"I'd listen to the lady. She really doesn't need a weapon to inflict damage," a familiar male voice sounded. "And by the way, my energy cells are just fine."

Forrorrois grinned when she spotted the silver-clad figure with his stun rifle leveled at Dorian.

"Glad to see you, Captain," she called out to Perkins. Then she turned back towards the lanky man and shrugged. "I'm sorry Dorian, and all of you here," she added with a nod to the station personnel standing behind the science officer. "But, like I said, Collinar needs immediate medical attention and you're not equipped to help him."

"No!" the station manager bellowed as he rushed forward from the crowd towards her.

Perkins dropped him with his stun rifle in mid-stride, before he could reach Forrorrois. "Let her go peacefully or I'll stun the bunch of you," he warned.

Dorian dropped to his knees and checked the station manager's pulse. Relieved, he looked up. "He's alive."

"Of course he is, he's only stunned, but at this temperature, I wouldn't want to be unconscious long," Forrorrois warned. "Now, if you'll excuse me, I've got to get Collinar to some proper medical attention," she stated. "Come on, Collinar, work with me," she urged quietly. He groaned back to consciousness and stumbled with her passed Perkins.

Perkins backed up with his stun rifle still pointed at the small crowd of red parka-clad personnel.

Forrorrois heaved a sigh when her long-distance scout appeared just outside the open doors of the arch. She guided Collinar's large frame up the ramp, Perkins was right behind her scooping up her pursuit as he passed the miniature craft. Balancing Collinar carefully against her shoulder, Forrorrois guided the large Utahar to the rear cabin and dumped him onto the bunk. Then she let the heavy duffle bags slide from her shoulder to the floor plates as she sat down at a seat by the small table—exhausted.

The cabin filled with oxygen-rich air, flushing the fogginess from her mind. Collinar stirred on the bunk when the cabin had re-pressurized to near sea level.

"My head," he moaned in English, raising his hand to his forehead.

"It'll pass," she replied. "Just remain still."

"Where are we heading?" Collinar asked, distantly.

"To the Tollon," Perkins answered, stepping into the rear cabin with his stun rifle ready. "It will be in orbit soon."

"Don't take me there," Collinar stated in a hushed voice.

Forrorrois looked at Collinar then at Perkins. "I've got this under control, Perkins. Who's flying?"

Perkins glanced at Collinar. "Jack is."

"Good, go see if you can help him out," she ordered.

Perkins hesitated, then turned and left. When the door closed, Forrorrois looked back at Collinar. He was studying Perkins as he left the rear cabin.

"You know I have to take you back to the Tollon, Collinar," she stated.

"Yes, I know, it's your duty—spare me," Collinar said as the door slid shut. "I see you recruited him."

Forrorrois glanced at the closed door where Perkins had just stood and felt the anger rise inside her. "You left me no choice, he needed protection from the general until he understood what you had done to him," Forrorrois replied. "How many more lives do you intend on destroying for your own personal gain?"

Collinar shook his head and looked away. "It's who I am. Why did you risk your life back at that ice station to get me out?"

Forrorrois studied him, cautiously. "For the same reason you do what you do, Collinar. I kept you alive because of what I've become," she answered. "Because of your actions, I became a Dramudam. Maybe not one of the best ones," she snorted to herself, "but I became one all the same."

"I still think you're a fool for being one," he scoffed.

She sensed him gathering his strength to resist her, but she just smiled, palming the small hypo in her hand from the duffel bag at her feet. "Maybe I am, Collinar, but I was never your fool," she stated as she crossed over to his bunk and pressed the cylinder against his leg. The hypo hissed through the thin material of his green incarceration uniform. He slumped back against the bunk without further resistance. Forrorrois settled back in her seat at the small table. The pain in her side was becoming more than an annoyance. She covered her mouth as she began to cough once more. As she took her hand away she spotted the flecks of red. She leaned back and shook her head. *Leenon's going to be busy patching everybody up*, she thought, wincing when she tried to take a deep breath.

****

Forrorrois entered the cockpit of her long-distance scout ship as Jack piloted the craft away from Earth. They approached the enormous bluish-black Dramudam peace ship which blacked out the stars and replaced them with tiny regularly spaced lights that grew into port windows along the rectangular sides. Mixed emotions filled her while she stood behind Jack as he sat in the commander chair of her long-distance scout. She inhaled then released her breath slowly. Four years had passed since she'd set foot on the Tollon's decks—four years since Trager had been thrown into the Plane of Deception by the explosion of the booby-trapped ship Collinar had left with General Caldwell. The thought made her look away in pain.

With out a word, Jack rose from the command chair and waved her to sit down. She smiled and accepted his gesture, taking her place at the helm of her scout. Butterflies danced in her stomach while she cleared her throat. Jack waved Perkins to join him in the cargo hold.

'Computer, please open audio communications to the Tollon,' she subvocalized.

'Channel open,' the computer replied via her zendra link.

"Pilot Forrorrois to the Peace Ship Tollon, requesting permission to land," she stated aloud in Intergaltic.

"The Tollon reads you and welcomes you to come aboard, Master Pilot Forrorrois. It's good to hear your voice again."

She smiled when she heard Yononnon's voice. "By the hand of Guruma, Subcommander, it's good to hear yours again too. Tell the commander I will need an escort from security, I have Collinar with me. He's in need of medical attention."

There was a pause. "I see," Yononnon replied. "Jack told me you had been successful, but he hadn't supplied any details. I will meet you in the hangar bay with a team of med techs and a security detail, Yononnon out."

She smiled at the concern in Yononnon's voice, but her amusement faded when a signal flickered on the perimeter sensor on her control panel. 'Computer, what was that?' she subvocalized.

'A small ship has just left the defense grid,' her ship's computer replied in her mind.

'Why wasn't I informed of its presence?'

'It displayed a friendly signature...'

'Computer, no ship is considered friendly except mine...how long was it in the atmosphere?'

'One kel.'

"By Guruma's hand! Forrorrois to Tollon! Forrorrois to Tollon!" she called out, but static hissed in her ears. "Computer, the transmission is being jammed. Find an alternate frequency immediately," she stated aloud. Pressing her scout forward, she raced towards the opening of the hangar bay. 'Computer, calculate the craft's trajectory. I want to know where it was and where it's headed!'

Forrorrois pulled her craft into a tight turn and decelerated suddenly for her final approach. The shimmering wall of the atmospheric force shield wavered before her. A chill ran through her heart when the computer gave her an update. The ship had been at her base.

Her mind was churning by the time she landed. She barely read the confusion that radiated from the Dramudam hangar crew that circled her craft. Forrorrois leapt from her command chair and ran into cargo hold as the side hatch hissed open and the ramp extended—startling Jack and Perkins. Her ears filled with the thrum of the Tollon's hangar bay. The familiar smells of metal and lubricants filtered into her nostrils. Searching the crew below her, she focused on Yononnon's chestnut-brown face and mouth framed by his black mustache.

"What just happened? We lost contact with you!" the Dramudam subcommander called up.

"There's trouble," she stammered as she ran down the ramp of her scout to the hangar deck plates. "A ship just left Earth..."

"What!" Yononnon exclaimed, moving out of her way.

"Track it! It was on the surface, near my base!" Forrorrois cried out.

"You heard her, get on it!" Yononnon ordered one of the security officers. "You two, secure the prisoner!"

"He's in the rear cabin," Forrorrois stated, pointing up the ramp. "Jack, show them. Perkins, bring the duffel bags, Subcommander Peldor will want to examine the ship Collinar stole for evidence."

The security officers headed up the ramp followed by med techs with a hover litter. In short order they had Collinar secured and left back down the ramp. Jack and Perkins followed after them.

"Forrorrois...the commander is waiting for your report," Yononnon stated.

An overwhelming sense of dread seeped deep into her soul. "I can't, Yononnon—I've got to go, something's terribly wrong," she replied. "Jack, you and Perkins give Yononnon the report. I've got to go!"

"Forrorrois, wait!" Yononnon yelled, but she blocked him out as she ran back up the ramp and shouted orders for her scout to lift off immediately. The hangar crew scattered when the ramp of her ship retracted and the hatch abruptly closed. Her stomach trembled anxiously while she pitched forward through the atmospheric barrier back into the darkness of space.

✶✶✶✶✶✶✶✶✶✶✶

Jack watched as Forrorrois' long-distance scout abruptly left the Tollon's hangar bay for Earth, leaving him and Perkins standing beside a very frustrated Subcommander Yononnon. He motioned for Perkins to remain quiet, while he assessed the situation, still uncertain what had just happened. His friend did what he was told—still holding the two duffel bags and Forrorrois' miniaturized pursuit.

"What am I going to do with her?" Yononnon exclaimed in Intergaltic, turning to Jack.

Jack shrugged. "Be patient, Subcommander. You should know that her parents and her daughter are staying at her base. If she thinks they might be in danger, there's no way that you could have stopped her."

Yononnon's black eyes widened. "By Guruma's hand, this is bad."

Jack looked up and struggled to mask his surprise when a boar-like creature with curved tusks protruding from his lower jaw approached Yononnon. Perkins glanced at Jack for assurance, but remained silent.

"I'm afraid the ship engaged its hyperfold drive before we could identify it, Yononnon," the creature reported.

"I see," Yononnon replied, smoothing his black mustache. "Thank you, Peldor, I appreciate you trying. Forgive my manners. Subcommander Peldor, may I introduce Colonel Jack Stern and..."

"Captain Perkins," Jack volunteered.

"Yes, Captain Perkins. They arrived with Forrorrois from Earth and aided in the recapture of Collinar," Yononnon said, motioning towards them.

"It is a pleasure to finally meet you both," Peldor said with a slight bow. "Yononnon has mentioned you both fondly from Forrorrois' reports."

"The pleasure is ours," Jack replied with a nod. Perkins smiled and nodded as well.

"Now, you must forgive me, but I must head to Bio Med and make certain that the prisoner is secure," Peldor said with an odd grin that showed his small lower chewing teeth between his tusks.

"Peldor, let me know when Collinar has been moved to security," Yononnon said as Peldor turned to leave.

"Of course, Yononnon. Colonel Jack Stern, Captain Perkins," he replied, gruffly.

Peldor turned and left before Jack could speak.

Yononnon heaved a sigh and looked at Jack. "I need to make a report to the commander..."

"Go ahead, Yononnon, I'll take care of our guests," a voice rasped from behind Yononnon. "Besides, it looks like Forrorrois has left me a challenge."

Jack looked up at the voice and was surprised to see Goren, the master pilot instructor approach, wearing the same green and black uniform as the rest of the pilots on the hangar deck. He had met the gruff Silmanon briefly four years before, but Perkins had been occupied in Bio Med and hadn't had the pleasure. Before Perkins could react, the tall slim creature reached out his velvety black furred hand and took Forrorrois' damaged miniaturized one-seat scout from Perkins. Perkins let him take the craft without a word. Goren was about the same height as the young captain, but his face was covered with the same fine black velvet fur as his hands and his eyes were ink black with no whites to them. He had small round ears and for some odd reason his face reminded Jack of a pug-nosed mule.

"Thank you, Goren. Jack, Captain Perkins, I will see you after I am finished with Commander Thoren," Yononnon said as he turned quickly and left the hangar bay.

"It's good to meet you again, Master Pilot Instructor Goren," Jack said with a nod after Yononnon had departed.

"You as well, Jack," Goren replied. "And you must be Captain Perkins. I've been interested in meeting you."

Perkins' eyes widened much to Goren's amusement.

"You must forgive the captain, he doesn't speak Intergaltic," Jack replied. He does have a translator that Forrorrois provided him. And from what I understand the Tollon's computer can provide you with a translation from English to Intergaltic."

"Yes, it will. Captain Perkins, I am told you are able to fly multiple types of Dramudam craft," Goren remarked, directly to Perkins. "This must be a challenge without a zendra link."

"Forrorrois was concerned that the presence of zendra in my bloodstream would be detected," Perkins replied, carefully in English.

"I see," Goren said as he studied Perkins. "On a nonspacefaring world, yes, that would be a problem." Goren returned his focus on the miniature craft in his hands. "I need to get a reduction weapon to re-enlarge this…"

"I have one here," Jack offered, taking it from his belt and showing the weapon to the Silmanon.

Goren nodded his head in approval. "Let's take the ship over to the repair bay and see what Forrorrois has done to this ship of hers."

"I have a second one in this duffel bag. I think it was Collinar's," Perkins offered.

"Excellent, we'll look at them both," Goren replied. "I'm interested to see how Forrorrois disabled Collinar's ship. The fact that Collinar is still alive is a good sign that she might have remembered at least a few of my lessons."

Jack smiled at Goren's jest and looked over at Perkins, but the young captain was still overwhelmed from Goren's presence. His thoughts wandered back to the glimmering atmospheric barrier that stretched across the enormous hangar bay doors and the space beyond. Forrorrois wouldn't have disobeyed Yononnon and left them there without being certain that something was wrong at her base. He had learned to trust her instinct over the years he had known her. Jack prayed that everything was all right.

✶✶✶✶✶✶✶✶✶✶✶

Forrorrois landed her shrouded long-distance scout ship back in the hangar bay of her base. She had ignored all messages from the Tollon to return over the past hour. Barely waiting for the ramp to extend, Forrorrois leapt to the floor of the hangar bay with her helmet still on and ran into the living quarters. The lights burning in the living room made her heart race. She burst from the hallway to see her mother sobbing in her father's arms, clutching Celeste's small yellow blanket. Forrorrois reached out with her mind and searched the shelter, but she couldn't feel the one small essence she craved for.

"Oh, Danica," her mother wailed. "She's gone…they took Celeste… we couldn't stop them!"

Forrorrois' heart froze at her distraught mother's words. The grief in her father's eyes burned into her soul. "Who?" she whispered, leaning heavily against the wall.

"Two women," her father replied, still rocking her mother.

"All we found was her blanket," her mother sobbed.

Shaking, Forrorrois stepped over to her parents and touched the soft yellow knit blanket. An image flashed in her mind, driving her to her knees, as two Eldatek females dressed in dark red robes burst into the living quarters and cornered her parents. They began shouting orders in Eldanese demanding Celeste. Her parents shielded her daughter when the robed females stepped forward and fired a stun weapon. Forrorrois gasped as her parents fell to the floor. Celeste screamed when one of the Eldatek grabbed her. Suddenly, Forrorrois fainted as the image faded in her mind.

She came to as her father shook her.

"Danica!" he called out.

Forrorrois opened her eyes and sat up abruptly. Her father steadied her.

"What just happened?" her mother gasped.

Forrorrois looked at both of them and realized they had just shared the same vision. "I saw what you went through," Forrorrois whispered, tears streaming down her face. "It wasn't your fault," she replied, coming to her feet. Her parents stood with her. She wrapped her arms around them, still trembling from the shared vision.

"Oh, Danica, why?" her mother demanded.

"I spotted a ship leaving the atmosphere about an hour ago," Forrorrois replied. "When I tried to get a fix on them, they jammed my sensors—as well as those of the Tollon's. Whoever took Celeste went to a lot of trouble and had a lot of inside information."

"You've got to find her, Danica!" her father pressed.

"I will," Forrorrois said, pulling them both into a hug, once more. "I'm sorry you were put through this...I'm so sorry," she repeated over and over. After several moments she pulled back, touching her hand to her helmet when another message was received from the Tollon. "I've got to go. I've got to return to the Tollon. I don't know when I'll be back, but I won't come back until I've found her. I'll send Jack to stay with you while I hunt them down."

Her mother paled at her words. "Keep safe..."

Forrorrois opened her mouth to speak but the words failed her. She nodded her head and turned to leave. The touch of her father's hand on her shoulder made her look back.

"God speed," he whispered.

"Thank you. I'll send a message when I've found something. I love you both, don't ever forget that," she replied, pulling them both into a final hug. Wiping the tears from her eyes, Forrorrois turned. "I'll find the beings who took her."

"Oh, Danica, please find her," her mother begged.

"I will, Mom, don't worry. And when I do, the beings responsible will pay."

Forrorrois raced out of the living quarters back to her long-distance scout. The thought that the Eldatek might have had something to do with her daughter's abduction still swirled in her mind. If ever she needed to speak to Trager, it was now.

✳✳✳✳✳✳✳✳✳✳

Jack was surprised when Subcommander Yononnon asked him to report to Commander Thoren's briefing room. Goren had assured him that Perkins could remain on the hangar deck so Jack left the master pilot instructor and joined Yononnon to provide his report. He didn't need Forrorrois' empathic senses to read the concern written across Yononnon's chestnut-brown face as they walked the bluish-black metal wall paneled corridors of the Tollon. Jack's ankle was still tender from the hangar collapse, but he managed to keep pace with the tall subcommander, limping only slightly.

Finally, Yononnon broke his silence.

"Jack, I'm hoping you can provide me with some insight on Forrorrois' emotional state these past few revolution. I've only been visited by Trager a few times since he was trapped in the Plane of Deception and Forrorrois' reports offer me only routine information."

Jack looked up at Yononnon sensing he was asking as Forrorrois' Dramudam foster parent and Trager's friend—not her subcommander. "It's been difficult for both of them," Jack admitted. "But neither will admit it. As for Celeste, she's never known anything different, so she accepts that this is normal."

Yononnon closed his eyes briefly and nodded. "The innocence of a child. We could learn so much from her."

"Will you have time to see Celeste before you leave orbit?" Jack asked. "I'm sure she would love to see her 'Unca' Yononnon."

Yononnon looked at him and smiled for the first time since they had left the hangar bay. "I'll have to ask the commander if he would allow me to make planet fall."

"We can always say that you are bringing supplies for Forrorrois' base."

"Yes," Yononnon replied, with a twinkle in his almond-shaped black eyes. He wave towards a door as they stopped in the corridor. "We're here, Jack."

Jack looked up as the panel slid open. He waited as Yononnon stepped through then he followed. Inside, he found Commander Thoren sitting at a desk at the far end of the room. There were chairs along the walls on either side with two more placed directly in front of the desk. The Dramudam commander stood as they entered and waved to the chairs in front of him. To Jack's left he spotted Subcommander Peldor standing to one side. Yononnon stepped forward and saluted then took the chair to the right. Uncertain, Jack bowed to the commander and took the empty seat beside Yononnon. Jack had seen Commander Thoren only briefly the last time he had been on the Tollon four years before. Like Yononnon and Trager, Thoren was Eldatek with chestnut-brown skin and black almond-shaped eyes, but his black hair was more salt than pepper in contrast to Yononnon's raven black—both had their hair tied back in the traditional Dramudam single loose braid.

"Thank you for coming here to report on Collinar's capture, Colonel Jack Stern," Thoren began. "Your assistance to Forrorrois on Earth has continued to be of great value to her mission there."

"You're welcome, Commander Thoren," Jack replied.

Thoren nodded his head slightly in approval, easing Jack's uncertainty.

"Subcommander Peldor is here as head of security and is investigating Collinar's escape from the rehabilitation station. Anything you have witnessed or have been told by Forrorrois will be of great assistance."

"Of course, Commander," Jack replied. "Forrorrois learned of Collinar's intent to contact Earth for asylum while she was in the Bio Med at the air base."

At the mention of Bio Med, Jack could feel the businesslike air in the room shift to concern.

"Why was she in Bio Med?" Thoren asked.

Jack forced himself not to shift in his seat. "A storm had hit the air base and the hangar I was in collapsed. Forrorrois and Captain Perkins pulled me out, but Forrorrois was injured during my extraction. General Caldwell had her taken to Bio Med for treatment."

Yononnon studied Jack carefully. "That's why you were limping as we walked here. Forgive me, Jack for not having asked why sooner," the subcommander commented.

"I'm fine, Subcommander. Forrorrois provided me care and my zendra are strong," Jack replied.

"All the same, after you've finished here, I want you to report to Bio Med and see Med Tech Leenon," Thoren stated.

"Yes, Commander," Jack replied. "As I was saying, Forrorrois was informed by General Caldwell that Collinar had requested asylum. General Caldwell then placed Forrorrois under arrest and informed her that he also had learned about Celeste being her daughter. Forrorrois and I escaped from the air base with Captain Perkins' help and we immediately went to her parents' home to retrieve them and Celeste. Her family is now at her base."

Commander Thoren held up his hand and Jack paused. "I have an incoming message from Forrorrois," Thoren announced. Jack watched in wonder as Forrorrois' image appeared as a hologram above Thoren's desk, but his heart nearly stopped as he saw the frantic look on her face.

"Commander, my base has been breached by two unidentified females wearing red robes," Forrorrois' image reported. "From the description my parents provided I believe that they are Eldatek. They stunned my parents and took Celeste—" her voice broke into a sob as she spoke her daughter's name.

Yononnon jumped from his chair as Jack's jaw dropped at her words.

"We'll find her, Forrorrois," Thoren replied. "Return to the Tollon, we'll make better time."

"Commander, please send Jack back with a pursuit ship to defend my base and protect my parents," Forrorrois requested.

"Consider it done, Forrorrois. Guruma be with you," Thoren replied.

"Thank you, sir," Forrorrois answered. The transmission ended abruptly, leaving all in the briefing room on edge.

"Yononnon, prepare a fully armed pursuit for Colonel Jack Stern. He will be returning to Earth immediately with Captain Perkins."

Jack came to his feet. "Commander Thoren, I have a request."

"Speak," Thoren urged.

"I would like to humbly request that Captain Perkins remain on the Tollon and complete his pilot training with Master Pilot Instructor Goren," Jack stated.

Thoren studied him for a moment.

"You are his superior?" Thoren asked.

"Yes," Jack replied. "General Caldwell has discovered that Captain Perkins has been modified like Forrorrois. Captain Perkins is not safe on Earth...at least not without completing his training."

"Yononnon, speak with Goren and make arrangements for Captain Perkins to stay."

Jack bowed to Commander Thoren. "Thank you, sir. I am in your debt."

"You've paid this debt many times already, Colonel Jack Stern,"

Thoren replied with a deeper bow. "It is I who am in your debt. Protect Forrorrois' parents and her base."

"Yes, sir," Jack answered with a second bow.

"Come, Jack," Yononnon stated, taking Jack's arm. "Goren is preparing a ship in the hangar bay."

"Guruma be with you," Commander Thoren said with a formal Dramudam salute.

"And he with you, sir," Jack replied, straightening and raising his hand to his temple in a crisp salute. Then he turned with Yononnon and hurried into the corridor, he stepped gingerly on his lame ankle. His chest tightened at the thought of little Celeste being torn from her grandparents. *Why would two Eldatek females take her?*

CHAPTER 6

Forrorrois hadn't spoken a word since she had arrived back on the Tollon. She had informed Commander Thoren of what had occurred enroute to the peace ship, but when she landed she refused to let anyone onboard her long-distance scout. She just lay on her bunk in her rear cabin and stared at the ceiling plates.

She looked over in surprise when she heard the side hatch of her cargo hold open without her orders. Still, she didn't get out of her bunk, sensing Goren's familiar presence

"I've brought you something to eat," the Silmanon rasped as the door of her rear cabin opened.

She looked up to see her old friend and former pilot instructor standing in the doorway with a tray. His familiar mulish black velvety face almost brought a smile to her lips. "Goren...I knew I should have changed the override codes," she muttered.

He chuckled as he stepped inside the rear cabin and set the tray on the small table. "I heard you might need an ear," he stated, twitching his small round ones towards her. "You need to keep your strength up if you're to find your daughter."

Forrorrois looked over at Goren and felt her lower lip begin to quiver. She forced herself to sit up. He crossed over to her and placed his hand on her shoulder without a word. His simple action crushed the remaining resolve left inside her. "Oh, Goren," she cried, coming to her feet and wrapping her arms around his large chest. The familiar smell of ship lubricant clung to his uniform. He touched her cheek with his black velvety finger, and brushed the tear that rolled down it aside. "They took her...they took my daughter, Celeste. They broke into my base, assaulted my parents, and took her! Why?"

"I don't know...but I'll help you find Celeste anyway I can," he rasped.

"Things have all gone wrong, Goren," she sobbed. "Jack was hurt in an accident and when I went to help him, the general found out that Celeste was my daughter and that Captain Perkins was modified by Collinar and had him arrested."

"Yes, I know. That's why Jack asked Commander Thoren to let Perkins stay on the Tollon for a while."

Forrorrois pulled away and looked at him—stunned. "Perkins is still here? On the Tollon?"

"Yes, I'm going to accept him as an intermediate pilot—with your permission," Goren replied.

"But he's not ready yet," Forrorrois insisted. "I've offered the zendra to him, but he won't accept them. He's afraid that the general would find them in his bloodstream and arrest him…"

"That seems like a moot point now," Goren said, finishing her sentence.

"This has to be his choice, Goren," she persisted.

"And it will be. From what you have told me, this Human male holds a lot of promise, much like you did when you first arrived on the Tollon," the old Silmanon stated. "But more importantly, I also think you need a friend right now."

"But I have friends—here on the Tollon."

"Yes, but they only know you as a pilot and a Dramudam—not as a mother worried about her missing child."

Forrorrois looked at the master pilot instructor and knew she wasn't going to win. "Thank you, Goren."

"Don't thank me, thank Jack. He was the one that made the request to Commander Thoren. Now, eat something. You will need your strength," Goren replied. "And from what I understand from Perkins, you should probably be in Bio Med being checkout by Leenon."

Forrorrois sniffed back the tears. "Not right now, Goren. I can't explain it, but at the moment I don't know who I can trust. I had a vision when I touched my daughter's blanket. The assailants were two female Eldatek. Why would the Eldatek take my daughter?"

Goren studied her for a moment then he shook his head. "I don't know, Forrorrois. But we'll find out. Why don't you call Kela, she can come down to the hangar bay and give you a physical here on your scout."

Forrorrois almost smiled at the mentioned of her friend's name. The reptilian female had taught her everything she knew about emergency medicine. "You're right. If I can trust anyone from Bio Med at the moment, it would be Kela," Forrorrois replied with a nod.

"Good. Then, when you feel strong enough, maybe the being you ought to be asking these questions is Collinar."

Forrorrois looked at the floor and tried to keep her rising anger in check. "I've thought of that," she admitted. "I just don't understand. How was he hiding this from me? Why didn't I sense that he was there to distract me?"

Goren shook his head. "Maybe he's become more devious in the four revolution he's spent in the rehabilitation station. Or maybe he didn't know he was being used."

Forrorrois looked up with a start at Goren's suggestion then nodded. "I'll speak to Peldor after first kel and see if he will allow me to speak with him."

"Good. I've got some errands to run. In the meantime, eat, and then speak with Captain Perkins. I think he's feeling a bit confused at the moment at being left behind on the Tollon by Jack."

Concerned, Forrorrois looked over at Goren. "Where's Perkins now?"

"He's working on repairs to your pursuit. He seems to know his way around the tools, no doubt you've given him many challenges over the past few revolution," Goren replied with a twinkle in his eye.

Appalled, Forrorrois squared her shoulders. "I'll have you know he created a few of those challenges himself when he was practicing takeoffs and landings," she objected.

"I don't doubt it, with him trying to fly without zendra," Goren scoffed. "I'll be ready to teach him when you release him to me. Now, eat something before I'm forced to have Leenon admit you to Bio Med," he insisted.

"Yes, Goren," she replied as he walked out the door into the cargo hold. Left alone, Forrorrois looked at the tray the Silmanon had brought her and sat down. Her stomach growled reminding her she hadn't eaten since the ice station with Collinar. The thought of the former Utahar Commander made her blood begin to boil. *How did he keep me from knowing it was all a diversion? Unless...Goren is right and he wasn't aware that he was being used,* she considered as she picked up a piece of bread from the tray deep in thought and took a bite.

✸✸✸✸✸✸✸✸✸✸✸

Jack landed the Dramudam pursuit ship that Commander Thoren had issued him in the hangar bay of Forrorrois' base. He removed his helmet and subvocalized to the ship's computer to shut down the engines. As the canopy of the ship rose above his head, he spotted Frank Jolan watching him from the entrance to the living quarters. Relief was evident on Frank's face once Jack climbed out of the cockpit and hobbled, still favoring his tender ankle, down the ladder that had extended along the side of the sleek bluish-black craft.

"Am I glad to see you, Jack," Forrorrois' father said as he met Jack halfway across the floor of the hangar. "When I heard the ship, I wasn't sure who it was."

Jack nodded. "Commander Thoren sent me back as soon as we got word from Danica about Celeste. Frank, I'm so sorry."

Frank looked down without a word.

"Danica will find her," Jack added, placing a hand on Frank's shoulder.

Frank nodded his head, unable to speak.

Jack pulled him into a firm hug. "Everyone on the Tollon is dedicated to finding her. They'll turn this galaxy upside-down to help Danica find your granddaughter."

Frank sniffed back his tears as he hugged Jack back. "Thank you," was all Frank could say as he slowly pulled away.

"Let's head inside and get a cup of coffee," Jack continued. "For all the wonders on that enormous Dramudam ship, they don't have anything to match a cup of Danielle's coffee."

"Danny does make a good cup of coffee," Frank snorted at Jack's comment. "She just made a fresh pot before you landed."

"Great, you can tell me about what happen once I've gotten off this bum ankle of mine," Jack replied.

The two walked through the winding passage to the living quarters and found Danielle waiting just on the other side. Jack could see the pain in her eyes. The ordeal of having Celeste forcibly kidnapped from them had taken a toll on both of Forrorrois' parents.

"Jack, thank God it's you," Danielle said as she spotted him.

"Danielle, I'm sorry I wasn't here," Jack said.

"It was horrible," Danielle replied, visibly shaken. "Those two women were ruthless. Why did they take our little Celeste?"

"I don't know, Danielle," Jack answered, "but your daughter is going to find her, don't ever doubt that—either of you."

"There was nothing we could do to stop them…" Danielle continued, breaking down in tears.

Frank crossed over to her and pulled her into a gentle embrace. "Hush, Danny, it'll be OK, Danica's gone after them. She'll find her. And Jack told me that all the Dramudam are looking for our granddaughter."

"That's right, Danielle," Jack replied. "Now, why don't we have a seat in the living room and I'll get us all some coffee."

"Jack, you get that ankle up," Frank ordered. "You go in and sit with Danny."

Danielle sniffed back the tears and looked up at Jack. "Frank's right, Jack, you're favoring your ankle," she fussed.

Jack sighed then nodded and let Danielle lead him into the living room.

"Now you sit right down, Jack," she ordered, pointing to the overstuffed chair and hassock. She didn't take a seat on the matching overstuffed couch until he obliged her.

He moved to tell her to stop mothering him, but then he realized she was fussing to distract herself from worrying about Celeste.

Frank soon joined them with the fresh brewed pot of coffee on a tray that also contained sugar and creamer and three mugs. He set the tray on the coffee table in front of the couch and filled each of the mugs. Jack moved to retrieve his cup but Danielle waved him off and added cream then set his coffee on the end table beside him. Frank was adding some sugar to Danielle's mug and stirred it for her as he took a seat beside her.

For a moment an oppressive silence hung in the room, broken by the slight clink of Danielle's spoon as she stirred her coffee. She stopped abruptly and looked at Jack.

"Where's Perkins?" Danielle suddenly asked.

Jack looked up in surprise. "I, ah, asked him to remain on the Tollon with Danica. I thought it was best for now with the general finding out about the modifications that were made to him. Besides, he needs to finish his training."

Danielle gave Jack a fragile smile and reached over and touched his arm. "Thank you, Jack. I feel better that Danica isn't on her own up there while she looks for Celeste."

Jack nodded. "I kind of thought so, too," he confessed.

"You're a good friend, Jack," Frank said as he picked up his mug. "I don't know how we'd get through all this without you."

Jack smiled. "We will get through this, don't you worry," he assured them. Then he sat back in his chair and sipped his coffee. Inside, he prayed that he was right.

****

Perkins was glad that Goren had shown him the tools in the repair section of the enormous hangar bay and then left him alone to work on repairing Forrorrois' pursuit ship. He needed something to keep his mind off of Jack ordering him to stay on the Tollon with Forrorrois. Nervously, he had averted his eyes and had tried to avoid all the strange creatures that made up the Tollon's crew. Perkins inspected the hull that he had just patched from the top of a ladder he was standing on when the sound of a throat clearing behind him made him tense. He turned slowly and looked down—relieved to find Forrorrois standing below him.

"Goren told me I'd find you here," Forrorrois said in English as she stepped a bit closer.

"Thank goodness it's you, Forrorrois," Perkins replied back in English, climbing down the ladder.

"Who did you think it was, Peldor?" she teased.

"Oh, please, don't even get me started," Perkins admitted, looking around as he wiped his hands off on a rag. "How did you get your head around all this?"

Forrorrois smiled. "I admit that it took me some time. Have you eaten yet?

"Yes, Goren brought me a tray. It was kind of weird looking, but it tasted pretty good," Perkins answered.

"Yeah, it took me a while to get use to the food as well. Just be careful if somebody offers you some towan paste," she replied.

"Towan paste?"

"Oh yeah—the Eldatek spread it on bread like peanut butter. It's red and about ten times hotter than wasabi and habaneras combined. The only thing that puts out the fire is yahwa fruit. Trust me, I know."

Perkins' eyes widened. "Thanks for the heads up."

"No problem. Now, I have to ask you, Perkins, do you know why Jack asked you to stay?"

Perkins looked up at her, uncertain. "No, he just ordered me to stay and then jumped into a pursuit ship that Subcommander Yononnon had waiting for him."

Forrorrois took a deep breath. "Then you haven't heard about Celeste."

Perkins set the rag onto the rung of the ladder and studied Forrorrois. "No, has something happened?"

"She's been kidnapped," Forrorrois replied, her voice dropping to a whisper.

Perkins took a quick breath. "Forrorrois...when did this happen?"

"Just after you and Jack picked me and Collinar up at the ice station…two non-Human women raided my base and stunned my parents. When my parents came to, Celeste was gone."

Perkins eyes widened as he thought of little Celeste. Without thinking he reached out and took her hand. "We'll find her."

Forrorrois straightened and released his hand, then nodded her head. "We will," she agreed. "I know it's not your choice to be here, Perkins, but I'm glad that Jack had you stay."

Perkins nodded as he dropped his hand to his side, embarrassed by her rebuff. "Me too."

"Perkins, now that the general knows about your modifications, maybe it's time for you to accept the zendra," Forrorrois offered.

Perkins shuddered. "I don't know."

"It's your choice, but I've taught you everything I can without them."

He looked at her, uncertain. "I know…I just need to think. This is all happening too fast."

"I understand, Perkins," Forrorrois replied. "But Earth could use another pilot right now."

Perkins' shoulders slumped. He hated to admit that she was right. "If I do this, will you let me qualify with weapons?"

Forrorrois nodded. "Yes, I'll even be your sponsor to have you accepted as an intermediate pilot with Goren here on the Tollon."

Perkins hesitated. "Can't you teach me?"

Forrorrois smiled and shook her head. "Perkins, Goren taught me. Who better than the best?"

Perkins looked at her, uncertain. Heaving a sigh, he nodded his head. "All right, I'll do it."

"Thank you, Perkins. I'm contacting Kela and asking her to come down to the hangar bay," Forrorrois replied.

"Who's Kela?" Perkins asked, nervously.

"An old friend," Forrorrois replied. "Kela's a Serban, she taught me emergency medicine."

"A Serban?"

"Yes, the Serban are a warm-blooded reptilian race. Kela has the most unusual shade of green scales—in the right light her scales are almost iridescent—quite stunning, actually."

Perkins' eyes widened. "OK, now you're just trying to freak me out."

Forrorrois shook her head and took his hand. "Believe me, Perkins—I don't need to freak you out. This place does it for me," she teased.

Perkins gave her a look.

"Now, come with me," Forrorrois continued. "Kela will meet us in my scout. Leenon has agreed to allow her to stay with you for the first twenty hours until the zendra establish themselves. After that, your mind will begin to acclimate to the Tollon's language files. Before you know it, you'll be speaking Intergaltic like a native."

Perkins swallowed hard and let her lead him back to her long-distance scout. He couldn't believe the insanity he had just agreed to—all he felt was numb.

****

Forrorrois folded down the spare bunk on the right side of her long-distance scout's rear cabin and motioned for Perkins to take a seat. The sound of footfalls on the ramp of her scout made her reach out with her empathic senses. She smiled when Perkins spotted Kela as she lumbered into the rear cabin on her well-muscled haunches. The reptilian female's figure became more slender from the waist to her shoulders. She smoothed her traditional beige tunic and black pants worn by Dramudam med techs with her free three-fingered claw as she clutched a bio kit in her other. Kela's tongue flitted briefly between the fine scales of her lips as she studied her patient.

"Perkins, this is my dear friend, Kela. She is here to administer the zendra," Forrorrois stated in English.

"It's a pleasure to meet you, Kela," Perkins replied in English, nervously, extending his hand. He pulled it back slowly when Forrorrois shook her head.

Kela glanced at his hand and then nodded her head. "The

pleasssure isss mine, Perkinsss," she stated in Intergaltic. "Thank you for allowing me to obssserve a male of your speccciess. Now, if you would be ssso kind, pleassse remove your garmentsss and lay down on the bunk."

As the translator deciphered Kela's words in Perkins' ear, his jaw nearly dropped. He glanced nervously towards Forrorrois and moved to object.

Forrorrois struggled to hide her amusement. "Please, Perkins, Kela's a full med tech. She's only asking for medical reasons. If it makes you feel better you can keep your briefs on."

"Yes, it would," Perkins replied. "Now, if you don't mind, please turn around."

Kela and she turned their backs. She could sense Kela's amusement mirroring her own.

"Are all Human malesss ssso modessst?" Kela whispered in Intergaltic to Forrorrois.

"Only when they feel vulnerable," Forrorrois whispered back.

"Ah. Isss he a good ssspecccimen of a Human male?"

Forrorrois blushed. "Yes, he's a very good specimen."

"Excccellent, then my time here will be well ssspent."

"I'm ready," Perkins called out.

Forrorrois smiled when she noticed that Perkins had pulled the sheet on the bunk over himself.

Kela approached Perkins as he lay on the bunk. Perkins swallowed nervously when the slender Serban lean over him and pulled out a hypo from her med kit.

"You will feel a brief ssssting from the injectsssion. Then you will feel warmth in your arm, thisss will ssspread into your body. After that you will feel tired. I will give you a sssedative to help you relaxsss. It will be take three full cccycle for the zendra to complete their network," Kela said as she placed the cylinder against Perkins exposed upper arm and began the injection.

"Please be gentle," Perkins replied, but the words became a mumble as he drifted off to sleep.

Kela pulled back the sheet to expose Perkins' chest and observed his breathing.

"Ssso far ssso good," Kela stated as she covered him again with the sheet. Then she turned to Forrorrois and motioned towards the bunk on the left side of the rear cabin. "Now, it isss your turn. Remove your tunic and lie back on the bunk, while I ssscan you. I don't like the sssound of your breathing."

Forrorrois unfastened her tunic and slipped off the silky material and lay back on the bunk with only her bra covering her upper body. Kela's practiced eye immediately focused on the newly healed scar on her right side.

"Turn on your ssstomach," Kela ordered. "Ah, yesss. Your lung isss ssstill weak from a recent puncture wound. And I detect a low grade infection. You need ressst."

Before Forrorrois realized what Kela was doing, she felt a hypo against her arm. Her muscles relaxed as she too fell into a deep sleep.

****

Forrorrois stirred awake and realized that she was on her bunk in the rear cabin of her scout ship. The lights were dimmed and she was covered with a blanket. A rhythmic breathing sounded from the other side of the cabin. Forrorrois reached out empathically and sensed Perkins still sleeping, although his mind was agitated. Her concern waned when she realized that his brain was struggling to process the language files from the Tollon through his newly forming zendra link. The sudden awareness of a third person in the room made her turn and strain to see in the gray shadows. Her mind trembled when she sensed the familiar emotions she had missed for so long.

"Trager…is that you?" she whispered.

"Yes, my ashwan," Trager's warm hushed voice filled her ears.

"It's been so long since I saw you last. Where have you been?" she whispered.

"It's difficult to explain, but there has been an energy drain in the Plane of Deception. I can only stay briefly."

"Do you know about Celeste?" Forrorrois asked, desperately.

"Guruma and I have only just learned about her kidnapping. Have you discovered anything?" Trager pressed.

"Only that I suspect two Eldatek females…"

"What? How can that be?" Trager exclaimed in a hushed voice.

"I don't understand either, Trager, but I was able to get a vision from Celeste's blanket when I reached our base and I saw two Eldatek females in red robes. They spoke Eldanese to Celeste just before they stunned my parents and took her."

Trager shook his head. "It doesn't make any sense. Red robes are only worn by Council High Guard. They are an elite unit that takes their direction solely from the council. The regular guard wears turquoise robes. Forrorrois, you must limit who you speak with about this until you've gathered more information. If the council has any involvements then use caution dealing with any Eldatek you are not familiar with on board the Tollon."

Forrorrois nodded. "I agree, Trager."

"Ashwan, you must forgive me, but I'm losing my intersection with your plane," Trager gasped. "I promise that Guruma and I will look for her. Please be careful."

"Help me find her, Trager!" Forrorrois whispered, but she already knew that his tenuous connection was broken. He was gone once more like a spirit on the wind. She clutched at the hope that he would find their daughter, but the brief encounter only made her grief deepen.

"Forrorrois," Perkins voice sounded on the other side of the room.

She sat up in the darkness and pulled on her tunic that Kela had left next to the pillow of her bunk. Fastening her uniform quickly, she was surprised to hear him awake. "I'm here, Perkins, what's the matter?"

"I thought I heard voices."

Forrorrois crossed over to Perkins' bunk and sat on the edge. "That's normal, Perkins. You're hearing the ship's computer."

"No…I heard Trager's voice," Perkins insisted.

Forrorrois reached out and touched his forehead. He was drenched in sweat. "You did, Trager was just here. You're fever has broke. Let me get you some water."

"Does he know about Celeste?"

"Yes. He said he would look for her."

"That's good," Perkins stated. "Forrorrois, I don't feel so good. Is this normal?"

Forrorrois reached out and gave his hand a squeeze. "I'm afraid so, Perkins. Initially, your body fights the zendra as a foreign body, but then the zendra establishes a symbiotic relationship with your body's defenses—the breaking fever means that the zendra are now established. The fight is over. Relax while I get you some water."

"Thanks," Perkins replied.

Forrorrois poured him a cup of water from the faucet of the small sink next to the door panel and returned to Perkins side. She lifted his head and placed the cup to his lips. Perkins took a couple of swallows. Forrorrois reached out with her mind for Kela and was surprised that the med tech was still in the cargo hold of her scout. Perkins shivered as she lowered his head back onto his sweat soaked pillow. She touched his sheets and realized they were damp as well.

"Let me get you some fresh blankets, I don't want you to catch a chill," Forrorrois stated. In the darken room she went to the wall locker at the rear of the cabin and pulled out a fresh sheet, pillow, and blanket then returned to Perkins bunk. She pulled the damp sheet off of him and quickly replaced it with the fresh one. Then she draped a thick blanket over him and tucked it tightly around his legs and arms. He smiled up at her as she swapped out his pillow as well.

"Do you feel a bit warmer?" she asked, rubbing his arms.

"Yes, thank you. Forrorrois, my head feels like it's going to explode from all the information."

"I know the feeling, but what I need you to do is focus on remembering. As much as you hate what Collinar did to you, he did expand your memory. When you reduce yourself, your zendra link will not function. So you won't have access to the computer's language files and other records. It will be important for you to remember as much as you can."

"I'll try," Perkins replied.

"That's my good captain," Forrorrois said with a smile. "Now, try to sleep and let your mind relax."

Perkins nodded and closed his eyes. Within a few moments his shivering had stopped and he drifted off to sleep. Forrorrois touched his forehead and was relieved to feel his skin was cooler. She reached out with her mind once more and sensed Kela was agitated—she was not alone in the cargo hold. Forrorrois crossed over to the door and ordered it open. To her surprise, she found Kela squared off with Leenon.

"Kela, is there a problem?" Forrorrois asked, glancing over at Leenon.

"No, I wass jussst telling Leenon that you needed to ressst and that thisss could wait until firssst kel," Kela replied.

Forrorrois studied Leenon's face and felt her conflicted—but urgent—emotions. Leenon wouldn't wait. "Kela, Perkins' fever has broken, could you check on him and make certain that he's resting comfortably?"

Kela glanced at Leenon, and then her and finally nodded her head. "That isss good to hear, I'll be in the rear cabin if you need me."

"Thank you, Kela," Forrorrois replied. She waited until Kela had closed the door panel to the rear cabin before she continued. "What is so important that you can't wait until first kel, Leenon? I can feel your urgency."

"I never could fool you," Leenon said with a shake of her head. "You sense my emotions too well. I've been sent as a messenger by the Council on Elda."

Forrorrois froze. After speaking with Trager, the mere mention of the council sent a shiver down her spine.

"You have been summoned to stand before them without delay," Leenon continued. "I'm sorry Forrorrois, but you have no choice."

"What is this about?" she stated. "I've never been to Elda. What would the council want with me?"

"Neeha, Trager's mother, is on the council. She's the one who summons you," Leenon replied.

Forrorrois studied the Eldatek female's clay-brown face for a moment. "Leenon, I don't need this right now," Forrorrois replied, turning her back on her at the mention of Neeha's name. "I'm trying to find my daughter! You'd think since Neeha is Celeste's grandmother that she'd be at least a bit worried too. And if you didn't notice Captain Perkins is recovering from an initial zendra injection."

"I don't think you understand," Leenon continued. "Neeha is commanding your presence. Trager's mother has grown very powerful."

"So powerful that she can command a Dramudam?" Forrorrois parried as she turned to face her once more. She was surprised when Leenon dropped her gaze.

"Indirectly...Yes," Leenon conceded. "Yononnon has already taken a leave of absence from his post as subcommander and left for Earth. He will act on your behalf and work with Colonel Jack Stern until Captain Perkins can rejoin the colonel back on Earth."

"Hold it!" Forrorrois stated, barely in control of her temper. "What about the Isolation Treaty? Yononnon's presence would violate it, or has the Council of Elda and the Dramudam conveniently forgotten that?!"

"He will remain at your base to limit his exposure to other Humans," Leenon replied. "Forrorrois, I implore you in the name of your joining with Trager to go to Elda. Listen to what Neeha and the council have to say."

Forrorrois bristled at her words.

"Time is of the essence," Leenon continued. "Please, if nothing else, do it to honor Trager. I am certain Colonel Jack Stern will be able to fill Yononnon in on all the pertinent information about your base."

Forrorrois chaffed at Leenon's condescending tone. "Jack knows the systems as well as I do," she replied. "I will go only because of my obligation by joining...and because I know that Trager cares a great deal for Neeha and tradition."

"Then it's settled," Leenon stated, "the Tollon has already changed course for Elda and initiated the hyperfold drive for multiple folds. We will arrive in less than a cycle."

Forrorrois was stunned that the Tollon was already on its way to Elda. "Who will care for Captain Perkins until he's back on his feet?"

"Kela will. After that, Goren will arrange for his quarters while Captain Perkins is training with him," Leenon stated.

Forrorrois nodded stiffly to Leenon. "My parents are staying at my base. They are there for protection against the general who was trying to grant Collinar asylum. If anything happens to them, so help me."

Leenon bowed deeply towards her. "Yononnon is aware of their presence and has promised to guard them with his life."

"I see," Forrorrois said. "All right, I'm ready, Leenon, but I refuse to stay any longer than I have to—Celeste is still missing and the trail to find her is growing cold."

"I understand," Leenon replied, stiffly. "I'll have Captain Perkins moved to bio med…"

Forrorrois shook her head and cut her off. "No, Perkins stays right here in the hangar deck."

"Be reasonable," Leenon insisted.

Forrorrois moved to speak, but stopped as she spotted Goren coming up the ramp of her scout.

"Forrorrois is right, Captain Perkins will remain here on the hangar deck while he recovers," Goren stated. "He's been assigned to me as an intermediate student by Commander Thoren."

Forrorrois could sense Leenon was frustrated by Goren's sudden appearance.

"But Goren, he's still recovering from his initial zendra injection," Leenon persisted.

Goren shook his head. "And Kela will continue to watch him until he's back on his feet, just like we had originally arranged. I'll just move him to my quarters a little sooner than I had planned. I hardly use them anyways so he won't be bothered."

"Very well," Leenon replied. "Forrorrois, be prepared to leave for Elda in a quarter kel. The Tollon will meet you in orbit."

"Understood," Forrorrois said with a stiff bow. Leenon nodded to her then glanced at Goren before she turned and left down the ramp. After she was gone, Forrorrois shook her head and looked up at Goren with a sigh. "Thank you."

"You're welcome, Forrorrois," Goren answered.

"Goren, why does Neeha want to see me?" Forrorrois asked.

Goren hesitated then glanced at the door panel to the rear cabin. "A lot has happened on Elda in the past few mol. I did some checking after our last discussion and I just found out that Trager's brother, Talman, has died."

Forrorrois looked up at Goren in surprise. "Oh, Goren, that's horrible. I don't think that Trager knows about this or he would have said something to me. How did it happen?"

Goren shook his head. "I don't know—the details have been very sketchy on that point—but his death occurred about two mol ago. One thing that I did find out was that Talman died without producing any children in his joining to Bohata. Neeha's power on the council is now slipping because of this."

"Well, it seems she still has enough power to order a Dramudam peace ship to deliver me halfway across the galaxy," Forrorrois scoffed.

"Be careful, Forrorrois, there are forces here at work that we aren't aware of yet," Goren warned.

Forrorrois thought hard on his words then shook her head. "I don't understand, Goren. How could Neeha's power be slipping? Doesn't her first-born daughter, Ralana, have children already from her joining?"

Goren nodded. "Yes, but that just secures her line, but on Elda power also comes from strategic alliances with other families that are also secured through their lines. First-born heirs are crucial."

Forrorrois sighed. All she wanted to do was search for her daughter. "It's so complicated," she admitted.

Goren gave her a gentle smile. "Go get your scout ready to leave immediately. I'll help Kela move Captain Perkins."

"Thank you, Goren. It's good to know that Perkins will be safer with you watching over him," she replied.

"I enjoy a challenge," Goren rasped. "Oh, Forrorrois, is there anything I should know about the modifications that Collinar made to Captain Perkins?"

"No, just that they are the same as the ones he made to me," Forrorrois replied.

Goren paused for a moment. "All the modifications?"

Forrorrois smiled up at the tall Silmanon. "Yes. He could be quite useful if you needed to retrieve a small fastener from a tight space."

Goren began to chuckle. "I'll have to keep a close eye on him."

Forrorrois nodded. "That you will," she replied as she left him and stepped into her cockpit to begin her preflight check. She was taken aback to see the coordinates for Elda had already been fed into her ship's computer. At her present coordinates she calculated three hyperfolds to reach the edge of the Eldatek solar system and another kel to reach Elda. When she heard the door to the rear cabin open, Forrorrois walked back to her cargo hold. Perkins was dressed and on his feet, leaning heavily against Goren's side. Kela was watching him carefully, shaking her head, with her tongue flitting in and out, very concerned.

Perkins looked over at her and tried to pull on one of his smiles, but it was more of a grimace.

"I'll be back soon, Captain. In the meantime, listen to Kela and Goren," Forrorrois said as she stopped in front of him.

"I will, Forrorrois," Perkins replied in stiff Intergaltic.

Forrorrois smiled. "You're Intergaltic is improving."

"We will have him speaking fluently in no time," Goren stated. "Come, Kela, we need to go now. Forrorrois has a long trip ahead of her and I'm certain that she wants to get it over as soon as possible."

"Yesss, Massster Pilot Insssstructor," Kela replied, following him and Perkins down the ramp.

Forrorrois watched as they left and suddenly felt very alone. Heaving a sigh, she subvocalized to the scout's computer to close the hatch. Her heart was heavy as she sat in her command chair and initiated her final preparations. Elda was the last place she wanted to be heading. She glanced at the empty jump seat beside her—frustrated that the trail for Celeste was growing cold.

****

Jack looked up in alarm when the computer alerted him that a ship had crossed the defense net. He was even more surprised when he received a hail from Yononnon. He hobbled into the Comms room of Forrorrois' base and opened communications immediately. Subcommander Yononnon's chestnut-brown face appeared in a hologram above the counter. His thin black mustache traced down the sides of his mouth, framing his lips.

"Jack, this is Yononnon," he stated in Intergaltic.

"Yononnon, I'm surprised to see you. Do you have any word on Celeste?" Jack replied back in Intergaltic, taking a seat at the comms station.

Yononnon dropped his gaze and shook his head. "Alas, no, Jack," Yononnon replied then he looked back up. "I have requested a leave of absence from the Tollon so that I might offer my assistance in defending Forrorrois' base and parents while she is away. I'll stay until Captain Perkins can return."

Jack's eyes widened. "Your assistance is welcome, Subcommander. I'll be waiting for your arrival in the hangar bay."

"Thank you, Jack," Yononnon replied. The hologram dissipated, leaving Jack still stunned. He heard a shoe scuff the floor and spotted Frank at the doorway.

"I heard you rush in here," Frank said nervously, "is there any news?"

Jack smiled. "Yes, Subcommander Yononnon is coming to stay temporarily here at the base while Forrorrois is away—just until Perkins can come back to offer protection to you and Danielle."

Frank gave him an uncertain look. "Who's Subcommander Yononnon?"

"A very special person," Jack replied. "I think both you and Danielle are going to like him. When Danica was first brought to the Tollon, Yononnon, and his sister, Leenon, were assigned by Commander Thoren to watch over her while she was in training. Danica even lived in their quarters. You could almost say they were her foster parents."

He watched as his words sunk in. "Foster parents?" Frank replied—a bit stunned.

"Yes," Jack answered.

"You'll have to forgive me," Frank said. "Danica rarely talks about what happened while she was away. I just thought that she was in a barracks or something. I guess I knew she had friends, and of course Trager was more than a friend, but the idea that they placed her with foster parents is a surprise. I just always thought of the Dramudam as more military."

Jack nodded. "I understand what you mean, Frank. But four years ago, when I went on board the Tollon for the first time, I realized that the crew also acts as an extended family. Since Yononnon and Leenon don't have children of their own, they grew to think of Danica as their adopted daughter. They even witnessed Danica's joining with Trager. You should know that Yononnon personally requested a leave of absence from his post to come and stay here to help provide protection for you."

Frank leaned heavily against the door jamb. "Wow," he replied. "I don't know what to say."

"Well, for right now, why don't you inform Danielle that we have a guest arriving so that she'll be ready to meet him? We can figure out the rest later."

"I'll go tell her," Frank replied, still stunned.

Jack rose from his chair and smiled. "Sounds good. I'm heading for the hangar bay to meet Yononnon when he arrives. You and Danielle can join me if you like."

"Of course," Frank said as he headed for the living room. "I'll go get Danielle at once."

Jack turned in the other direction and stepped through the winding passage that was carved in the granite of the hill to the hangar bay—all the while hoping that Yononnon might have more news when he arrived.

He didn't have to wait long. Yononnon's sleek single-seat scout cut through the barrier that camouflaged the mouth of the base's hangar bay. Jack watched while Yononnon landed the craft beside the pursuit that Commander Thoren had issued him. The canopy hinged open as the ladder extended from the side of the bluish-black scout. Silently, the large Eldatek male removed his helmet and smoothed his black braid before he rose from his command chair. He climbed down the ladder then straightened the tunic of his forest green uniform as Jack approached him.

"It's good of you to come and assist me while Forrorrois is looking for Celeste, Subcommander," Jack said in Intergaltic as he came to a stop in front of the tall Dramudam.

"It was the least I could do for Forrorrois during these trying times," Yononnon replied in Intergaltic. He hesitated and looked past Jack.

Jack turned and spotted Forrorrois' parents standing near the door to the living quarters. He waved for them to approach.

"Yononnon, I wish to introduce Frank Jolan and his joined one Danielle Jolan, they are Forrorrois' parents," Jack said in Intergaltic as they came closer.

Yononnon bowed deeply. "It is an honor to meet the parents of Forrorrois," he replied carefully in English.

"The honor is ours, Subcommander Yononnon," Frank replied. "I should be thanking you. Jack tells me that you and your sister welcomed Danica into your home while she trained on the Tollon."

Yononnon smiled warmly. "Yes, Danica was assigned to us by Commander Thoren."

"Yononnon, pardon me, but I didn't know that you could speak, English," Jack said.

Yononnon shrugged. "I must confess to speak very little English. I have been studying the language records and am using the ship's computer to assist me."

Danielle smiled up at him warmly. "You're doing fine, Subcommander."

Yononnon looked down shyly. "Thank you, Danielle Jolan. You are very kind."

"Please, Subcommander Yononnon, call me Danielle," she insisted.

"Thank you, Danielle. Please call me Yononnon," he replied.

"And you can call me Frank," Forrorrois' father added.

"Thank you, sir," Yononnon replied.

"You must be exhausted from your trip," Danielle said as she took his arm, flustering the subcommander with her attention, much to Jack's amusement. "I have a fresh pot of coffee on. We can all have a cup while you tell us about the progress being made on the search for our granddaughter."

"Of course," Yononnon replied, allowing the petite Danielle to lead him into the living quarters. "May I ask, what is 'coffee'?"

"It's like ya," Jack replied, following them into the winding passage. "Don't worry—Trager liked it."

"Oh?" Yononnon replied.

Jack grinned. "Honest, you'll like it," he commented as they reached the hallway of the living quarters.

CHAPTER 7

Alone, Forrorrois touched down her long-distance scout on the landing pad outside of Lor'Koria, the capital city of Elda which was set on a large plateau. This was her first time visiting Trager's homeworld. She wasn't certain what to expect since Neeha had never recognized the joining between Trager and her. The planet's orange-red sun had just risen over the mountains to the east of her position with the harsh sunlight spreading across the arid sandstone barrens between the city and the jagged crags. Suddenly, she understood why Trager had fallen so deeply in love with her world—Earth was the opposite of this place—it was filled with such diversity, open water, and forests.

After giving silent orders to her ship's computer, Forrorrois stepped onto the ramp of her scout. The atmosphere was thinner and drier than she was accustomed, forcing her to catch her breath. She was surprised at the chill in the air, but reminded herself that the sun was just coming up and the temperature would soon rise to a searing heat. Descending to the bottom of the ramp, she was immediately greeted by two statuesque female Eldateks in long loose-fitting robes of turquoise. Their clay-brown faces and black almond-shaped eyes were impassive. They said little while they escorted her along the broad black-and-gray tiled sidewalks of Lor'Koria. Forrorrois surreptitiously glanced about as her escort hastened towards the center of the city and the enormous domed building that she quickly learned housed the council chambers. The ornately-arched airy buildings towered above her, as they entered the heart of the city. The majority of them were formed of reddish-gray granite, while others were of smoother black basalt. Another time, Forrorrois would have delighted in the carvings of the alien animals and birds that adorned the doors and archways that faced the wide streets, but her mind kept straying to Celeste.

Her escorts finally stopped in front of a grandly carved portal. They began to climb the steep tall steps to the recessed doors. She felt the ham strings of her thighs stretch when she placed her foot on the first step. The two females guarded their amusement while they continued up the stairs without slowing down. *So very different from the Eldatek I have known on the Tollon*, she thought to herself. Their actions were obvious. As an off-worlder, they were intentionally trying her patience.

At the top of the steps, she moved quickly to catch up to them.

The two turquoise-robed females finally halted before a set of enormous doors. They glided open at the merest touch of each of their hands. Forrorrois looked past them into the large chamber. Inside, the hall was constructed in a circle with a raised dais off to the right side. The empty seats filled three-quarters of the outer diameter, offering room for hundreds. Opposite the door, on the other end of the hall, was an imposing raised platform in the shape of a wedge. From the floor, one was forced to look up at the long red stone table that was set near the edge of the platform.

"Proceed down the ramp and take your place in the petitioner's stand," the guard to her right ordered in Eldanese.

Forrorrois translated their orders quickly in her mind then nodded. She moved down the ramped aisle towards the raised dais in the center of the empty hall. As she reached the floor, she immediately climbed up the steep stairs of the raised circular platform to her right and found that the top was ringed with a gray stone railing—the image of a trial popped into her mind. To the back of the circle was a shallow bench. The two guards dressed in turquoise followed her to the top. Forrorrois resisted the urge to sit, instead took her place at the railing.

A door opened in the wall of the raised wedged platform before her and three older Eldatek females in golden robes emerged. Forrorrois watched as they took their places at the great red stone table. Each had three locks of their long salt-and-pepper hair braided on the left side—intertwined with a gold cord denoting their rank as Eldatek councilors. The protracted silence gnawed at Forrorrois as they studied her with disdain.

"You are the one the Dramudam call Forrorrois?" the wizened councilor to her left eventually asked.

Suddenly, she realized that it was her Dramudam uniform that fed their displeasure. "Yes, I am, Councilor," she replied.

"You have been summoned here to face the questions of Neeha, Mother of Haator," she continued.

Forrorrois was mildly surprised at the use of Trager's Eldatek name, another confirmation that the Eldatek did not embrace the Dramudam. Her gaze fell to the female in the center. Her black eyes were cold and steady against her clay-brown face. Forrorrois had seen images of Neeha, but she was even more formidable in person.

"You have a daughter?" Neeha stated, never breaking her stare.

"Yes, Celeste, the joyous product of Trager's and my joining, but she has been..."

"His name is Haator—please refer to him by his given name," Neeha warned.

Forrorrois bowed her head slightly in respect. Neeha's bitterness radiated from her like the harsh sun of Elda. "My apologies, Councilor Neeha, yes, Celeste is the daughter of your son, Haator and..."

"It is unusual for two Dramudam to join," Neeha cut her off. "Especially two who are still active in their duties!"

Forrorrois steeled herself for the pointed question. "At the time of our joining Haator and I were detached from the Peace ship, Tollon. We continued to function as Dramudam in order to protect my world from contamination of its technology by the Utahar. That was our only Dramudam function."

"That function was enough to cost Haator his existence in this plane!" Neeha spat. "And to keep him from returning to Elda to accept a proper joining with an Eldatek partner, not some off-worlder who bears an illegitimate child and is ignorant to our ways!"

The two elder councilors turned in surprised at Neeha's vehement verbal attack.

"I did not come here to reopen old wounds," Forrorrois declared, fighting for control. "Nor did I come for your open cruelty towards Haator's daughter, whom he loves very deeply. I came here because you summoned me! Obviously, we are done here. I have a more pressing issue of looking for my daughter—your granddaughter, if you haven't forgotten. If you don't already know, she was kidnapped from my parents and all my leads are growing cold while I waste my time standing here!" Forrorrois stated, turning on her heels and moving to descend the stairs.

The two older councilors gasped at Forrorrois' abrupt action while Neeha narrowed her almond-shaped black eyes. The slight wrinkles feathered from them across her strong cheekbones, creasing her clay-brown skin. The three small braids, denoting her rank of councilor, fell across her left cheek.

"Stand where you are!" she ordered.

Two females in turquoise blocked Forrorrois' path, plunging the room into a deep silence. Forrorrois turned back towards the bitter female's stare and held it.

Finally, Neeha broke the silence. "I've called you here to inform you that Haator's brother Talman has died."

Forrorrois softened her stance, seeing the pain in Neeha's eyes. "I just heard about your loss, please accept my condolence," she replied.

"Do you also know that he didn't sire any children for Bohata, his Joined one?" Neeha asked.

Forrorrois hesitated. "I had heard that," she answered.

"As an off-worlder I don't expect you to understand the ways of Elda, but Bohata must be compensated for her loss. Therefore, I have no choice, but to claim Mo'yuto for Bohata," Neeha continued.

Suddenly, Forrorrois felt a coldness form in the pit of her stomach. She spun at Neeha's words to see the door to the council chamber open behind her. A high council guard in red robes entered with a small child holding her hand.

"Momma!" the three-and-a-half year old child screamed, wrestling to break the female guard's hold.

"Celeste!" Forrorrois cried out, moving for the stairs, but she halted when the guards pointed a weapon at her, forcing her to turn back towards the council. Anger and disgust roiled inside her as she stared into Neeha's eyes. "How could you?! How could you tear

Celeste from the only home she has ever known? How could you order my parents assaulted in front of her?"

"Silence!" the head councilor ordered to Neeha's left. When order was restored to the chamber, Neeha continued.

"Your parents were not injured, only stunned. You have my word that Celeste will not be harmed," Neeha stated. "She will be given to Bohata to be raise as her own. There is much she can learn here. Me'Hal has spoken highly of her intelligence. As for her talents as an empath she will receive special attention. It is a rare gift among the Eldatek."

Forrorrois started at the use of Leenon's Eldatek name then stared at Neeha, appalled at her callous disregard for her family. "Neeha! This is unforgivable," she spat. "You've insulted my family and you are frightening Celeste! You're her grandmother, for pity's sake! By the hand of Guruma, there is no honor in this action. You show the deceit of an Utahar in your actions!"

The two other councilors at the table gasped at her inadvertent affront. "How dare you question my actions and how dare you invoke that Dramudam's name here!" Neeha howled.

"If it weren't for that Dramudam, your son would be dead right now!" Forrorrois growled back. "As a mother, let me go to my daughter!" she demanded, heading for the stairs towards Celeste, but one of the two large female guards blocked her way once more.

"Momma!" Celeste cried out. Abruptly, her daughter squirmed from the guard's hold and ran down the aisle towards the raised dais she was on.

Seeing her daughter approaching the stairs, Forrorrois dove at the guards and knocked them to the surface of the petitioner's stand. Then she jumped over the prostrate guards and ran down the stairs. Merely centimeters from her daughter, the whine of a stun weapon sounded in her ears—the reddish beam hit her as she reached out for Celeste's small hand. "I love, you," she whispered in English as her daughter reached her side. The last sound she heard was Celeste's screams for her as she slipped into unconscious on the cool smooth gray stone floor.

****

Trager staggered backwards as the foci he was using to observe the Council of Elda chamber lost its attenuation and dissolved. Guruma caught him before he fell to his knees in the swirling colorful mist of the Plane of Deception. The shock of what he just witnessed had dumbfounded him.

"Trager! Are you all right?" Guruma asked, still holding him upright.

Trager covered his face with his hand as he struggled to compose himself. "Neeha has Celeste," was all he could say.

"Come, let's head back to the shelter," Guruma urged. "It's not safe to linger here any longer."

Trager allowed the elder Dramudam founder to lead him back to the structure they had conjured near the foci. Unable to hide his emotions any longer, Trager felt the tears begin to stream down his face unchecked.

Guruma led him to the square bluish-black metal table and eased him into a chair.

"What else did you see?" Guruma asked, conjuring two red stone mugs steaming with mawya.

Trager looked upward at the ceiling of the room and gasped as he tried once more to compose himself. After a deep breath, he exhaled. "I saw the Council of Elda's chamber. Neeha and two other councilors were seated at the great red table. I saw Forrorrois standing in the petitioner's stand. There were two guards in turquoise robes standing behind her."

Guruma listened intently.

"Neeha told Forrorrois that Talman had passed away two mol ago," Trager continued.

Guruma gasped. "Trager, I'm so sorry about your brother."

Trager tightened his grip on his mug, grief heavy in his heart. "It's worse than that, Guruma. Neeha is claiming Mo'yuto for Bohata."

Guruma's eye's widened. "But to come all the way to Earth…"

Trager nodded. "I agree—Neeha told Forrorrois that Bohata had to be compensated since Talman had not provided her with a child and that she was giving Celeste to be raised by Bohata. My mother kidnapped Celeste!"

Guruma closed his eyes and shook his head. "They did the same to my son. The council can be so callous in matters of the heart."

"Guruma, I should be there to stop this! Forrorrois tried to reach Celeste when Neeha had one of the Council High Guards bring her out. The guards stunned Forrorrois—right in front of Celeste! My little daughter was screaming for her mother, and they tore her away from Forrorrois' unconscious body! How can this be happening?"

"Forrorrois is resourceful, she will find a way to get Celeste back," Guruma replied, softly.

"Guruma, how can Monomay allow her innocent children to be harmed like this?" Trager whispered. "Neeha didn't even acknowledge Celeste when she was born. She's never asked Forrorrois to bring her to Elda for a visit. How could she do this to her own granddaughter?"

"In Neeha's eyes, Celeste is just a pawn that she can use to re-secure her bond with Bohata's family. If you had been on Earth, Neeha would have found a way to take you instead and force you to take the role as second to replace your brother."

"I'd give my life if it meant Celeste was safe," Trager vowed.

"Trager, be careful, if it was you instead of Celeste, Forrorrois would still be heartbroken and she would do everything she could to free you. Neeha will never allow her powerbase to be diminished, especially not for the happiness of an off-worlder."

Trager covered his face once more with his hand. "There has to be a way to free Celeste," he moaned.

"We will find a way, Trager, but that means we must remain vigilant and gather as much information as we possibly can," Guruma urged. "You must stay strong for Forrorrois' sake. When the energy of the foci has re-strengthened you must let her know that you will help her."

Trager nodded his head. "You're right, I must be ready," Trager replied. He took a deep breath, and then exhaled slowly to clear his mind. "I'll be ready."

****

Forrorrois awoke in the rear cabin of her long-distance scout. She was surprised to see both Commander Thoren and Leenon hovering over her. Her head ached when she sat up too quickly on her bunk. Suddenly, she looked around wildly when her memory of the events in the council chambers returned.

"Where's Celeste?! Oh, no…Leenon, they've still got her!" she cried out.

"What do you mean they've still got her? Who has her?" Thoren asked.

"Hush, Forrorrois," Leenon soothed.

"Don't you tell me to hush! I just found out that Neeha took my daughter!" Forrorrois exclaimed.

"I'm certain that Neeha wouldn't harm Celeste," Leenon offered.

Forrorrois stared at Leenon hard and felt Thoren's suspicions shift toward Leenon as well.

"Then tell me, Leenon, tell me how a child isn't harmed when she is taken by force by her own paternal grandmother and then witnesses her mother being shot with a stun weapon?! Tell me that?!!" Forrorrois insisted.

Leenon looked away at her stinging words.

Forrorrois looked up at Thoren—still angry. "I trusted you, Commander! I trusted both of you! And where did it get me? It was Neeha who took my daughter!" The tears began to stream down her pale face.

She felt Leenon's arm slide around her shoulder, but Forrorrois stiffened at her touch.

"Leenon, this is a horrendous accusation," Commander Thoren stated, his jaw set. "The Dramudam and the Council of Elda have never been forced into this kind posture before. Neeha had no right to break trust like this!"

"I…agree," Leenon confessed. "Believe me—I didn't know she did this. Please believe me, Forrorrois, I didn't know!"

Forrorrois pulled away from Leenon's gentle hold. She was sincere, she sensed that, but there was more. Leenon knew more, but how much more? *Think! Think! Overreacting won't get Celeste back*, she thought. Forrorrois looked at Leenon and relaxed her posture. "I know...I'm not blaming you, Leenon. Or you either, sir," she added, looking up at the Dramudam commander beside her bunk. "It's just now I have to do something about it...I have to get Celeste back!"

"No, I can't let you do that," Thoren replied. "This can't be handled by force."

Forrorrois stared back at him, stunned at his words. "What do you mean?"

"It would start an interplanetary incident..."

"Commander, it already is an interplanetary incident! Neeha made it one the moment she sent Council High Guards to Earth, assaulted my parents, and took Celeste by force—violating the Isolation Treaty!" she shot back.

Leenon looked her in the eyes. "Forrorrois, do you remember what basis Neeha used for why she took Celeste?" she pressed.

Forrorrois closed her eyes for a moment and thought back to the council chamber. As she opened them again, she looked at Leenon. "She claimed something called Mo'yuto... Mo'yuto for Bohata."

Both Commander Thoren and Leenon tensed. Forrorrois glanced at the two of them as the cabin fell silent.

"This isn't good," Thoren finally stated in a hushed voice.

"No," Leenon replied, composing herself. "Forrorrois, you need to move forward with cautioned. Neeha is powerful...and she's grieving for not one, but two sons. Her feelings wouldn't be the same as she would for the loss of a daughter, but Tallman was her connection to Bohata's family. Without children this connection is dissolved. I realize that Neeha may not be thinking straight right now, but know that what she has done is sanctioned by Eldatek law."

"You can't be serious," Forrorrois scoffed.

Leenon nodded. "Forrorrois, please, it is within Neeha's right to claim Mo'yuto and remove a child from a second born male who is in an unsanctioned joining. She could even claim this right if she had agreed to the joining of the second-born male—if the council agrees that it is in the best interest of the child and the families involved. This child would suddenly be inline to inherit the wealth, properties, and position of the first born mother. Her status would be greatly enhanced. Her birth parents would see this as opportunity that they themselves would never be able to afford her. They would agree that it would be in their daughter's best interest."

Forrorrois' jaw dropped at Leenon's defense of Neeha's action. "Kidnapping Celeste and giving her to Bohata to be raised isn't in my daughter's best interest. She's an empath—she can feel the emotions of everyone around her. And the minute those Council high guards entered Earth's solar system they were violating the Isolation Treaty and violating Earth's laws—which includes breaking and entering, assault, and kidnapping to name just a few—so, tell me Leenon, how can you think that this is right?"

Leenon looked away as if she'd been slapped. "Right or wrong, it's the will of the Council of Elda," she whispered.

"Forrorrois is right, Leenon," Thoren stated. "More than one law has been broken here. Just because Celeste is now on Elda doesn't erase the fact that the method of how Neeha gained custody of her was illegal. Forrorrois' family must also be compensated for the loss of their grandchild."

Still angry, Forrorrois shook her head as she stared at the head med tech. Then she looked at Thoren. Her guard went up as she gathered her wits. "Hold it! How did you both get on board my scout?"

"It returned to the Tollon on autopilot," Thoren replied. "I asked Goren to let us onboard when you didn't answer our hail."

Forrorrois squared her jaw. *Goren would have done that*, she thought. "Computer," she called aloud in Intergaltic, "by whose order did you return me back to the Tollon."

"By the order of Councilor Neeha," the computer replied in its monotone. "She left you a message."

Forrorrois stiffened at her name. "Computer, repeat it for me aloud," she order.

"Forrorrois, I have given you my word to keep Celeste from harm," Neeha's voice sounded in Eldanese. "Bohata will raise her as her own and give her a respectable place in Eldatek society. Do not attempt to return to Elda. She is no longer your concern." The message ended abruptly, leaving the three of them speechless.

"Forrorrois, for now, please heed Neeha's words. We will find a way to make this right," Thoren insisted.

"Commander, the council has spoken," Leenon countered.

"And they are wrong in this decision," Thoren replied.

Leenon moved to speak then stopped when Thoren gave her a warning stare.

The tension in the room was thick. Forrorrois looked at Leenon, then Thoren, astounded when Leenon backed down on an Eldatek issue.

Forrorrois glanced between the two then cleared her throat. "All right, Commander, I will heed Neeha's words for now, but we will make this right."

Thoren nodded while Leenon glanced between the two of them, conflicted.

Forrorrois looked up at Thoren and nodded back.

"Commander, I have a request," she began.

Thoren looked at her carefully. "Speak it."

"I wish to talk with Collinar."

Thoren hesitated. "Why do you want to talk to him?"

"I want to know more about how he escaped from that rehabilitation station. But I need to ask him alone—without any room recorders."

Leenon shook her head. "No, that's a bad idea, Forrorrois. You're not thinking straight at the moment. I won't patch him up again."

Forrorrois snorted. "If he tells me what I want, I won't harm him."

Thoren glanced between Leenon and her for a moment. "I'll tell Peldor that you are coming down to security," Thoren stated.

"Commander, I strongly recommend against this!" Leenon began, but Thoren cut her off.

"And your protest has been duly noted, Leenon."

"Commander!" Leenon started again.

Thoren stopped her with a stare then turned to Forrorrois. "I'll allow Peldor to turn off the room recorder, but the security force shield remains in place. It will be up to his discretion if he feels that his presence is needed during your question. Do you understand, Forrorrois?"

Forrorrois stiffened at the restriction then nodded. "Yes, sir, I understand. Thank you, sir. Now, if you'll excuse me I have a prisoner to interrogate," Forrorrois replied, rising from her bunk. Thoren and Leenon moved aside and let her pass without another word.

Leenon's actions in front of Thoren were highly uncommon and Forrorrois was certain that the two would have a lengthy discussion once she was out of earshot.

****

Forrorrois stared at Collinar sitting on the bunk of his holding cell inside the Tollon's security corridor. The only barrier between them was the iridescent-purple glow of the security force shield. Thoren had insisted that the shield remain in place—at least her commander had allowed the room recorder to be switched off—but even that made Forrorrois uneasy. Peldor was kind enough to remain down the corridor, just out of earshot. Even so, this needed to be between Collinar and her alone.

Collinar rose from his bunk and stepped to the middle of the holding cell when she stepped into his field of vision.

"And what do I owe the great honor of your presence?" Collinar asked sarcastically, staring back at her.

"I just returned from Elda," Forrorrois replied as she reached into Collinar's mind for a reaction.

Collinar gave her a confused look. "And this is important because?"

His non-reaction surprised her. She shifted on her feet for a moment.

"I was summoned there," she continued.

Collinar stepped closer, his interest peaked.

"Summoned by who?" he asked.

"By the council," she replied.

"Really? That must have been a treat. Is Neeha still a councilor?"

"Why, yes," Forrorrois replied as she stepped closer. "It turns out that she was the one that summoned me."

Collinar's golden-feline eyes opened slightly wider. "Fascinating, but pardon me for asking, why are you telling this to me? Don't get me wrong, I do so enjoy court intrigue, and the entertainment here in this cell is so limited, but what reason do you think I would care?"

Forrorrois reached empathically deeper into his mind and still she felt nothing that would connect him to Neeha. "You're right, why should I tell you about this? Actually, I wanted to ask you about how you escaped from the rehabilitation station."

Collinar sighed and turned away from the force shield. "Oh, please, Forrorrois, as I've already told Subcommander Peldor, I simply walked out of my cell during a power failure, made my way to the hangar bay and took the first available craft."

Forrorrois smiled. He was actually telling her the truth—at least as much of the truth that he was aware of. She chuckled to herself. "So, you're telling me that it was all just dumb luck that allowed you to escape from a high security Dramudam rehabilitation station?"

Collinar turned quickly as she bust into laughter and scowled at her. "The power failure may have been dumb luck, but my using the opportunity certainly wasn't," he growled.

Forrorrois struggled to maintain a more serious composure as he stepped closer to the force shield. "You know, Collinar, I was curious about your account. So, I looked up the records of the rehabilitation station and found some odd things about the cycle you escaped. For instance, yours was the only cell that had its lock malfunction. All the other cells immediately were secured by the failsafe device that's in place. That's standard protocol in a power failure."

Collinar narrowed his eyes while she continued.

"Second, all the corridor recording devices also failed on the exact path that you took to the hangar bay. And did you realize that the single-seat long-distance scout that you so conveniently stole for your escape had already been reported as stolen only a few kel before from a nearby Dramudam repair station?"

"What are you implying?" Collinar demanded as he stepped dangerously close to the force shield that separated them.

Forrorrois snorted while she savored his uncertainty. She lowered her voice to a whisper. "I'm implying that someone used you as a diversion and you obliged them."

"What? That's absurd!" Collinar replied. "What are you talking about?!"

Again, Forrorrois searched his mind for any trace of deceit, but all she found was his wounded pride.

"I'm talking about a being that knew you so well that they predicted exactly where you would go if you escaped. Don't you find it highly convenient that the craft that you found waiting for you was fueled and stocked for a long journey?"

Collinar growled at her and turned away from the opening with his arms folded across his chest.

"This being knew you would head straight for Earth because you couldn't go back to the Utahar—not yet anyway," she goaded. Forrorrois felt his anger rise inside him and relished his indignation. "You've lost your power in the Utahar and without some type of leverage—you'll never get it back. Groveling to General Caldwell was your only chance."

Collinar turned towards her and charged the opening. He slammed his hands on either side of the doorway before he reached the electrified space. Forrorrois stood her ground, almost disappointed that he hadn't run into the force shield instead.

"Get to your point," Collinar growled.

"The point is this being knew you so well that they used you as a diversion to get me away from my base."

Collinar snorted at her. "And why would a being go through all of that just to break into your base?"

"Simple, Collinar. They did it to kidnap my daughter," Forrorrois replied in a low dangerous voice.

Stunned disbelief radiated from Collinar's large frame. "Your what?"

"My daughter," Forrorrois repeated. Her enemy's reaction was plain—he didn't even suspect she had a child.

"You have a daughter?" Collinar stammered. Then he glanced at the ceiling as the reality struck him. "Of course, how could I be so blind?! When you fastened my jacket and I told you to stop acting like a mother—you are a mother!" he laughed as he stared back at her.

"Yes, Collinar," Forrorrois replied, impatiently. "And now my daughter has been kidnapped and they used you as a diversion."

The amusement in Collinar eyes darkened. "They wouldn't dare!" he snarled.

"Yes, they did, Collinar, and you fell for it," she replied. "And now you're heading right back to the rehabilitation station with a few more revolution tacked onto your sentence for your bad behavior."

"You're enjoying this," Collinar snapped as he crossed his arms and began to pace in the small cell.

"Actually, no, I'm not," Forrorrois replied. "I just want my daughter back."

Collinar stopped dead in his tracks and threw his arms up in the air. "And what does that have to do with me?" he demanded.

"I can give you the name of the being that used you," Forrorrois offered.

Collinar crossed his arms once more. "And why would you give me this being's name?"

"Because I want some information that I think you might know."

Collinar's golden-feline eyes sparkled as he began to smirk. "A trade…I like that."

"I thought so," Forrorrois replied. "Four revolution ago, you said something to me about how I could get Trager back. Were you lying or were you telling me the truth?"

The larger Utahar's smirk grew into a grin. "You finally want to know about the Beliespeir. Whatever changed your mind?"

Forrorrois glanced down the corridor at Peldor then lowered her voice. "I think Trager can help me get Celeste back."

"Forrorrois, he's just a male puppet on a female dominated world. What makes you think that he can get Celeste back for you?" Collinar purred.

She shook her head. "Look, Collinar, I don't have time to waste here. The last time I saw Trager, he said that the energy levels were dropping in the Plane of Deception…"

"And you're worried that you'll lose him as well," Collinar baited.

Forrorrois clenched her jaw trying not to let him rattle her.

"And you were wondering if I knew where to find the Beliespeir so that you could use them to contact him?" Collinar continued.

"Yes," she replied, sensing Collinar grow bolder.

"And what do you offer me in return?" he asked.

Forrorrois narrowed her eyes. "I've already told you—the name of the being that used you," she replied.

Collinar shook his head. "Not enough."

Forrorrois sighed. "The name is what I offer for the information. If the information you provide me helps free Trager, then I will personally speak on your behalf at the rehabilitation station hearing and argue for a reduction of your sentence."

Collinar raised a blond eyebrow at her offer. "Tempting…I'll have to think about it."

"Don't push me, Collinar," she warned.

"Oh, all right," Collinar replied. "First, give me the name."

Forrorrois hesitated.

"Oh, come on, Forrorrois. What can I do with a name if I'm stuck in here? Your testifying on my behalf, now that is definitely worth the information that I have to offer."

Forrorrois stepped closer to the force shield and waited for

Collinar to do the same. Then she dropped her voice to an inaudible whisper. "Neeha," was all she uttered.

Stunned, Collinar stepped away. "You're right not to speak her name too loudly in this place," he replied, glancing around cautiously. "You've got yourself a formidable foe."

Forrorrois stared at him, impatiently. "All right, Collinar, it's your turn," she replied.

Collinar smiled. "Don't forget our bargain."

"Oh, I won't," Forrorrois replied.

"Good," Collinar said. He dropped his voice to a whisper. "Take your long-distance scout to the coordinates that I'm about to tell you. You will find a planet where one shouldn't be, in area of space where your navigation systems won't work. On this planet you will find a large grassy plateau with a large outcropping of rock at its center. In the outcropping is the mouth of a cave. Land your ship outside of this cave and open your side hatch then wait. It may take several cycle, but you will be contacted. I'm told that they can read minds so be careful with any stray thoughts."

Forrorrois leaned closer to the purple hue of the force shield as Collinar dropped his voice even lower.

"Go alone," Collinar continued. "Once you've been contacted, send your scout back to the Tollon. Erase the flight plan from your scout's computer so that the Dramudam can't trace its way back to the Beliespeir's homeworld."

"That's absurd," Forrorrois scoffed. "How will I get back?"

"Where you're going, you won't need your ship," he insisted.

Forrorrois searched her enemy's golden-feline eyes and knew he was telling the truth. When he moved to speak, she shook her head.

"Don't say the coordinates aloud," Forrorrois whispered.

Collinar gave her a strange look. "What?"

"Ma'Kelda did something for me before she let me escape," Forrorrois whispered. She could feel Collinar's emotions shift briefly to sadness at the mention of his former subcommander's name.

"And I killed her for letting you escape," Collinar growled, regaining his composure.

"Yes…but before she let me go, she gave me a gift. She called it 'opening' my mind," Forrorrois said, leaning within a hair's breath from the field.

Collinar gave her a strange look. "Why are you telling me this?"

"I'm telling you because I suspect that Ma'Kelda may have done the same for you and you'll know what to do," she replied. Before he could object, Forrorrois lifted her hand and lightly touched the field. The energy tingled against her skin. Her breathing became rapid as she pressed her hand slowly forward. She fixed his eyes with hers and refused to let him lower his gaze.

Collinar's eyes widened at her action. He clenched his fist then relaxed his fingers. His breathing matched hers as he raised his large golden-tan hand and touched the force shield opposite her smaller one.

The edge of the shield prickled at first then the intensity increased as they slowly forced their outstretched hands together, confirming to her that Ma'Kelda had shared more than a bed with him. Forrorrois' eyes widened as the image of the coordinates flooded into her mind the moment their palms touched. She gasped as more images of the planet inundated her. Then the image shifted to a tender moment between Ma'Kelda and Collinar. Forrorrois' eyes grew large when she realized that Ma'Kelda knew Collinar would kill her when she freed her, but the image was not a condemnation—the message was forgiveness. Ma'Kelda had planted the image in Forrorrois' mind to one day deliver to Collinar. Forrorrois gasped as she saw the tears well in Collinar's eyes. As suddenly as the images started, they stopped. The force shield strengthened, throwing both Forrorrois and Collinar backwards from each other. When she opened her eyes, she saw Collinar on the floor of his cell staring at her—his emotions mixed. Tears stained his golden-tan face. He turned away and wiped his face when Subcommander Peldor lumbered down the corridor towards her.

"Are you all right?" Peldor cried out as he grabbed her arm. Before she could answer, the Gintzer yanked her up onto her feet. "What were you thinking?"

"I'm all right," Forrorrois replied when he let go of her arm. She looked over at Collinar as he picked himself off the floor of his cell. "I'm done here," she stated.

Peldor glanced between the two of them and shook his head. "I hope you got the information you were looking for," he remarked.

"I did," Forrorrois said with a nod towards Collinar then turned and headed out of the security corridor. The images and coordinates were burned into her memory—as well as the image of Collinar and Ma'Kelda in a brief moment of happiness. Forrorrois steadied herself against the corridor wall panel when she was out of Peldor's view. She couldn't let the revelation distract her. All she knew was that she had to leave the Tollon immediately.

* * * * * * * * * * *

Forrorrois had reduced herself down to eight centimeters and slipped inside the air vent located in the corridor. After several minutes, she made her way through the shaft to a vent that emptied into Commander Thoren's office. She spotted the large Eldatek male at his desk, studying a report on his monitor. His black hair was sprinkled with grey and his chestnut-brown face was beginning to show the creases of wisdom. Even after all the insanity Forrorrois had put him through over the years; Thoren had always dealt with her fairly and with an even hand—as he did with his entire crew. If there was one Eldatek on board the Tollon that she knew she could still trust, it would be Thoren. She climbed over the lip of the slatted vent cover and dropped to the floor panel. When she enlarged, Commander Thoren started by her sudden appearance.

"Forrorrois!" he gasped.

"Forgive my intrusion, Commander," Forrorrois said with a respectful bow. "I needed to speak with you—without anyone knowing."

Thoren considered her words and motioned her to the chair in front of his desk. "Please take a seat."

"Thank you, sir," she replied with a second bow then she approached the chair and sat down.

"Have you spoken with Collinar?" he asked, leaning back in his chair as he watched her from behind his desk.

"Yes, sir, I just came from there," she answered.

"Did he give you the answer you were looking for?"

"Yes, sir," Forrorrois began. "I must go on a journey, but I can't let anyone onboard know the coordinates where I'm going, including you, sir. Trager appeared to me briefly before I left for Elda. He told me that the energy levels in the Plane of Deception are ebbing. I'm afraid that Guruma and he may be in danger."

Thoren nodded. "Guruma mentioned this a few mol ago the last time he appeared to me."

"Commander, if what Collinar suggests is true, then there is a chance of finding a way to crossover to the Plan of Deception and contact Trager and Guruma directly."

Thoren sat up in his chair and leaned forward. "If this is true, Forrorrois, I wish to go with you."

Forrorrois gently shook her head. "Commander, as much as I would find comfort in having another travel with me, the Tollon needs you here. I believe that there is a spy on board, possibly Eldatek."

Thoren leaned back slightly and closed his eyes for a moment. "I've been suspecting the same thing," he admitted.

Forrorrois looked up at him, surprised by his admission. She reached out with her empathic abilities and sensed he was sincere. "For how long?"

Thoren sighed. "The moment you reported Celeste was taken by females in red robes matching the description of members of the council's high guard. My suspicions were reinforced when you returned from Elda and told me that Neeha was behind Celeste's abduction. From Peldor's report about the medium-range sensor failure when Celeste was taken, it was becoming increasingly obvious that that Tollon's sensors were jammed in a manner that needed internal access to this ship's systems."

Forrorrois leaned forward. "Commander, I believe that Collinar's escape from the rehabilitation station was meant as a diversion to separate me from my daughter."

"I agree," Thoren said replied. "Collinar's accomplice also provided him with that pursuit…"

"Commander," Forrorrois interrupted. "When I spoke with Collinar, it was apparent that he was unaware that his escape was a setup. As much as I hate to admit this, Collinar was used."

Thoren narrowed his eyes. "Are you certain?"

"Yes, Commander," Forrorrois admitted. "He was genuinely surprised to realize that he had been manipulated—and a bit angry as well. I'm so certain that I have promised Collinar that I will speak on his behalf when we return him to the rehabilitation station—if the information he provided helps me get to the Plane of Deception."

Thoren sat back in his chair. "I'm impressed."

"Sir?" Forrorrois questioned as she studied him.

"Peldor contacted me just after you had left security. He said that you actually reached through the energy field and made physical contact with Collinar before the two of you were throw in opposite directions. I thought you had lost your temper, but I was wrong. You would help Collinar when he is faced with an unjust situation even though he is your enemy. You've grown," Thoren replied with a gentle smile.

Forrorrois looked down, embarrassed. "I didn't think of it that way, sir."

Her commander chuckled. "Go and talk with Goren. He'll arrange a distraction that will allow you to slip off the ship. Hopefully, no one will notice you've left the ship for at least a half a kel. While you're gone, I'll continue to search for the traitor."

"Thank you, sir," Forrorrois breathed. "Sir, I have one more favor to ask."

"Speak it."

"If something should happen to me, please make certain that Captain Perkins makes it back to Earth after he finishes his training with Goren."

"You will return," Thoren replied. "And I assure you that Captain Perkins will be protected until then and that he will make it back to Earth safely."

Forrorrois fought to maintain her composure from his perceptive response. "Thank you, sir. I'm in your debt."

"May Guruma guide you," Thoren replied. "Leave the same way you came in, I don't want anyone to speculate on this meeting. It's disturbing to confirm my suspicions that a member of this crew is suspect."

Forrorrois rose from her chair. She knew Commander Thoren wouldn't rest until he identified the spy among his crew. With a nod, she reduced herself then walked towards the vent. In moments she was heading down the air vent, her mind racing to solidify her plan.

CHAPTER 8

Perkins looked up from his work on Forrorrois' single-seat pursuit in the repair bay when he heard footsteps approaching. He smiled when he saw Forrorrois, but his smile soon melted into concern when she didn't smile back. Nervously, he smoothed the brown work overalls he was wearing.

"I saw your scout come back earlier from Elda," he said in English as Forrorrois stopped in front of him. "I was worried when Commander Thoren asked Goren to open your ship. Is everything all right?"

Forrorrois reached up and ran her hand over the recent repairs he'd made on the nose of her pursuit. She nodded her silent approval then dropped her hand to her side. "No, but I've found out who has Celeste," she replied back in English.

Perkins studied her for a moment. "Is Celeste all right?"

Forrorrois' shoulders sagged. "She's on Elda. Trager's mother, Neeha, has her. I felt her mind…my little peanut is afraid, Perkins. Neeha was the one who ordered her taken."

Perkins mind tumbled at Forrorrois' words. Without thinking, he reached out and pulled her into a gentle hug. To his surprise, the strong petite woman began to sob uncontrollably. "It'll be all right, Forrorrois. I'll help you anyway I can. You just name it!"

Forrorrois pulled away slowly and sniffed back her tears. "Thank you, Perkins."

He reached out and brushed the tears from her cheeks. "Now, tell me what you need."

Forrorrois collected herself with a deep breath then exhaled slowly. "How far are you on the repairs of this pursuit?"

Perkins glanced at the ship and shrugged. "She's ready to fly. I've just been puttering with her because Goren didn't want me to repair Collinar's scout—something to do with it being evidence."

"Good. I need a diversion."

Perkins drew on a cautious smile. "Like what?"

"Tell Goren that you'd like to give my pursuit a test flight to ensure that all repairs are sound," she replied.

"You think he'll let me?" Perkins asked. "I mean, I haven't clocked that many hours in space."

Forrorrois smiled. "Flying in an atmosphere is tougher than open space. You'll do fine, now that the zendra are established. Have you been practicing your subvocalization?"

Uncertain, Perkins nodded. "Yes."

"Good. Goren told me that you've been doing well in the simulators. He'll let you go into open space. In a few more hours, the Tollon will be out of the Eldatek solar system. Once we are out, I want you to make your request to Goren. I can't tell you anymore then that in case they question you. Just know that it might take me some time before I return. While I'm gone, stay close to Goren and pay attention to his training. He's going to push you hard, but he does it to help keep you alive."

Perkins sobered. "I understand."

"Thank you," Forrorrois said. Then she glanced around and continued. "Perkins, because of the situation with Celeste, I don't know who I can trust. I'm sorry that I've put you in this situation, but I'm glad you're here. Please know that you can trust Goren. He will guide you to others that you will be able to trust while I am gone."

Perkins drew on a confident smile. "Forrorrois, I've got your six. You do what you have to do and I'll take care of myself until you get back." He could tell that Forrorrois only half bought his show of bravado.

"One more thing before I go," Forrorrois said.

Perkins studied at her carefully. "What's that?"

"Remember that you have an advantage. You've been in battle situations before as an Apache pilot. You know how to keep your head when you are under fire—that's something most intermediate pilots have never experienced outside a simulator. I've only taught you how to fly a Dramudam craft, but you already had the skill of being a pilot. When Goren has finished the final leg of your training and you return to Earth, I will be proud to have you flying by my side as a fellow pilot."

Perkins straightened at her unexpected praise. "Thank you, ma'am," he replied with a salute.

Forrorrois straightened and returned his salute with a Dramudam salute, her fist clenched over her heart with her thumb and pinkie extended to either side and bowed slightly towards him. "May Guruma be with you," she replied.

As she dropped her hand to her side, Perkins dropped his own hand and watched as she turned and left.

Perkins prayed that she would return soon with Celeste. As she reached her scout, he glanced over at the door of Goren's office. He would make his request in one hour and hoped that the master pilot instructor would agree to the test flight.

****

Perkins was surprised when Goren agreed to allow him to perform a test flight on Forrorrois' pursuit. Within minutes of his request, Goren ordered the enormous doors of the hangar bay opened. The Silmanon master pilot instructor told him to begin his preflight immediately. Butterflies danced in Perkins gut as he climbed up the ladder on the side of Forrorrois' one-seat pursuit and took his seat in the cockpit. Pulling on his helmet, he quickly went through the pre-launch sequence then maneuvered the craft from the repair bay into the launching area. There was an odd silence as the work in the cavernous hangar bay came to a halt. He felt an odd anticipation from several Dramudam master pilots on deck as they watched him make his final preparations—the word had gone out that he was Forrorrois' student and the weight of doing her proud rested on the next few moments. Perkins closed his blue eyes and said a short prayer. Then he pulled on his helmet and subvocalized in broken Intergaltic for the visor fall into place.

'Computer, prepare for lift-off,' he silently ordered the craft.

'Lift-off preparations complete,' the computer echoed in his mind.

"Captain Perkins, you have been cleared to leave the hangar bay," Goren's voice sounded over his comm link in Intergaltic. "Please follow the maneuvers that I have instructed you on so that I can observe your repairs."

"Thank you, sir," Perkins replied aloud in Intergaltic, still surprised how easily the sing-song language rolled off his tongue.

He stared out at the shimmering atmospheric barrier while he reached out for the colored controls on the panel before him. 'Computer, engage lift-off and take the pursuit out on impulse thrusters,' he subvocalized.

'Lift-off initiated and ahead on impulse thrusters,' the computer replied.

Perkins' heart beat faster as he cleared the barrier into open space. His hands steadied as he pulled away from the Tollon and began the test maneuvers. First, he banked left, then right. As he straightened the craft out, he paced the speed of the Tollon. Then he increased his speed and entered into a sideways roll. A grin spread across his lips by the time he completed his third barrel roll.

"Captain Perkins," Goren's voice sounded, "my sensors show that all your repairs are holding. I want you to perform one more maneuver. I want you to manually pull up into a steep climb, flip over the top in a complete circle, nose-to-tail, and then level out and return to the hangar bay."

"Yes, sir," Perkins replied, a bit relieved as he shifted to the more familiar manual controls and began the steep climb. He grinned like a school boy when he felt the sudden increase in g-forces against his restraints while he guided the pursuit over the top of the circle in a belly-up position. Head-over-tea-kettle he ended the maneuver upright once more and headed for the Tollon, pulling back his speed as he approached the shimmering atmospheric barrier across the mouth of the rectangular opening of the hangar bay.

The moment he sliced through the barrier, the craft's autopilot engaged and guided the ship into the pursuit arch of the Tollon then touched down in an empty slot next to a line of other pursuits. Adrenaline pumped in his veins as he pulled off his helmet. In his ears, the sound of the engines cut back then the craft came to a full stop. He exhaled slowly while the canopy lifted above his head.

When he stood from his command chair, he was surprised by the small crowd of Dramudam master pilots wearing green tunics and black pants and boots who stepped forward and began to clap. Goren stepped forward from the group and nodded.

Perkins dropped his helmet into the holder by his command chair and stared at the mix of Gintzers, Eldatek, Serban, Bevitch—and other races that he didn't even have names for—applauding him. His gaze fell on Goren when he approached his pursuit.

"Congratulations, Captain Perkins, on your very successful first flight. You have shown yourself worthy of the instruction that Forrorrois has given you," Goren said with a sly smile. "Now come down and meet your fellow pilots. It will take time before you are a master pilot, but you are well on your way."

Perkins looked at the menagerie before him and suddenly saw them as comrades. He grinned as he climbed down the ladder that had automatically extended from the side of the craft when he had landed. Goren waved a few of the master pilots forward, while the rest dispersed.

"Captain Perkins, I wish to introduce to you some of the pilots that were intermediate pilots with Forrorrois. This is Kelcore," Goren began.

Perkins watched as the tall slim Bevitch, with short gray fur covering its exposed face and hands, stepped forward. The creature had dark blue eyes with no whites to them, and lemur-like facial features. Kelcore bowed slightly in greeting then stepped to one side as Goren pointed towards two muscular reptilian Serbans. Perkins noticed that their heads were squarer than Kela's.

"This is Ronnon and Venue—they are brothers," Goren continued.

Perkins returned their bows and then looked over at the burley Gintzer that Goren waved forward.

"This is Grogon."

Again, Perkins bowed, trying not to stare at the heavy tusks that protruded from Grogon's boar-like lower jaw. He looked over at Goren as he waved forward one more pilot. Perkins' heart skipped a beat as he found himself staring at the most stunning Eldatek woman he'd yet seen. He tried not to react as she stepped forward, but he was enchanted by her black almond-shaped eyes and clay-brown skin. Her glossy black hair was tied back in the traditional single braid worn by the Dramudam.

"And this is Alham."

Perkins bowed towards her. His heart rate increased as she smiled and returned the bow.

"These master pilots have agreed to be available to you while you train with me here on the Tollon. If you have questions and you see them on the hangar deck, you may approach them," Goren stated.

Perkins looked around at the group. "Thank you in advance for your assistance. Forrorrois will be pleased to know that you have taken her lowly student under your wing," he replied in Intergaltic.

"Yes, she will," Goren said. "Now, please excuse me. I have some things to attend to, but I'm certain that these master pilots would like to help you celebrate your successful repairs and flight. I leave you in their capable hands."

Perkins turned to object as Goren left the group, but Alham took his arm and guided him out of the pursuit wing towards the double doors that lead into the Tollon's corridors. The others followed after them.

"So, Captain Perkins," Alham began, in Intergaltic. "What do you prefer to be called?"

Perkins glanced at her, surprised to realize that she was the same height as him then he swallowed hard. "Ah…Just Perkins. Captain is my rank on Earth."

"Captain…Hmmm. Is this a military rank?" she continued.

"Yes," Perkins replied. "I'm a captain in the U.S. Air Force. I fly Apache helicopters," he continued, slipping into English for the words that had no translations.

"Have you ever flown in battle?" Alham asked.

Perkins nodded, suddenly realizing that the other pilots were listening very intently to his answers. "Yes, I've fought in a couple of war zones," he replied.

"Experience, that's good!" Grogon stated, slapping him on the shoulder. Perkins staggered from the well intended gesture. "Forrorrois has good instinct bringing you to Goren."

They continued down several corridors before stopping in front of a door panel. Perkins was surprised when the door slid open to reveal a room with round tables and what seemed like a small bar near the back. He grinned as they passed gaming type equipment and quickly realized that this was a recreational facility. Alham guided him to a table and sat down beside him to his left while Grogon took the seat to his right. The rest joined them around the table. A large Gintzer approached the table with two trays. One filled with slices of orange pulpy fruit and a second tray of small shot glasses filled with a red liquid.

"Perkins, to celebrate your first official flight, please join us in a traditional round of fermented towan root juice and yahwa fruit," Alham announced as the large Gintzer left the table.

Perkins' eyes widened as she mentioned the word 'towan'. He'd been a U.S. Air Force pilot long enough to know that certain hazing rituals existed in the majority of military organizations. He steeled himself as the others each reached out and took a glass. Perkins only hoped that Forrorrois' advice about the yahwa fruit was true. Nervously, he reached out and took the last shot from the tray. He forced himself not to react to the unexpected warmth that radiated from the liquid through the glass.

Alham smiled as he took the drink. "May your ship never fail you and your repairs always hold," she exclaimed. Perkins raised his glass to the toast and then watched as they all downed the small glasses of thick red liquid. He took a deep breath then threw back his own. The thick drink slid over his tongue and down his throat, coating them. The fermented liquid tasted sweet at first, with a slight tang of exotic fruit—then the fire hit. Perkins struggled not to react, but the burn was incredible. He glanced around the table and saw them all begin to perspire—all except Alham. Perkins looked at the fruit and then back at the group. He soon realized that everyone was waiting for the first one to flinch and reach for the yahwa. His face felt hot as he held out as long as he could while trying not to breathe. Finally, the intensity of the burn in his stomach became too much and Perkins reached out for the chilled sliced fruit. As soon as he popped the cool salvation into his mouth the others also grabbed a piece. The cool pulp of the yahwa immediately soothed the flames in his mouth. As he swallowed, the relief followed down his throat and into his stomach. Grogon laughed and slapped him on the back, knocking him forward.

"You did well, Perkins," he gruffly stated, still chuckling.

Perkins looked over at Alham in amazement as she took the last piece of fruit and slowly bit into the orange pulp—long after the others had given in.

"How can you stand that?" Perkins gasped, staring at her.

"Never mind her," Kelcore, the Bevitch, stated. "The Eldatek spread towan paste on their toast for first kel."

"Really?" Perkins replied.

Alham smiled as she licked the juice from her fingers. Perkins looked away quickly when he realized he was staring at her full lips.

"So how long have you known Forrorrois, Perkins?" Grogon asked.

Perkins composed himself quickly then looked at the group as he gave a shrug. "I've known her for about six revolution, but we actually met the first time seven revolution ago."

"Intriguing," Alham remarked. "That would have been shortly after she had returned to Earth to fight against Collinar."

Perkins looked over at Alham in surprise. "Ah, yes."

"So, tell us about the first time you saw her," Kelcore encouraged.

"Sure," Perkins began. "I was flying a prototype craft with Colonel Stern...."

"Wasss he the other Human that arrived with you?" Ronnon asked.

Perkins looked over at the reptilian Serban, still unaccustomed to hearing himself being referred to as a Human. "Ah…Yes," Perkins replied.

"Please, go on," Alham pressed.

"Well, we were inspecting the site where Forrorrois had originally landed when we were ambushed by an Utahar pursuit ship. Before I had time to react, the Utahar had fired on my craft and hit my tail rotor. The controls went dead and I went down. The next thing I knew the colonel and I were heading back to the base in the cargo hold of her long-distance scout. I probably would have died from my injuries if she hadn't shot down the Utahar craft and then risked being exposed to the U.S. Air Force to get me and the colonel back to the base for medical treatment," Perkins confessed.

He was surprised to see tears glistening in Alham's eyes.

"Guruma knew her path and she followed it well," she stated quietly. "Tell me, Perkins, what have you heard of her daughter, Celeste? Is there any news on where she might be and who took her?"

Perkins glanced down at his hands, uncertain what to say. Finally, he looked at the group and studied their faces. "Celeste has been found on Elda with her grandmother, Neeha. That's all I know," he said quietly.

A silence fell on the group as they surreptitiously glanced towards Alham. At last, Grogon spoke.

"At least she's safe," he whispered.

"Yes," Alham replied, obviously uncomfortable with his revelation. "Please, Perkins, tell us about Forrorrois' daughter," Alham pressed. "Forrorrois has kept to herself since this whole ordeal began and we want to support her in anyway we can."

Perkins could see the pain on Alham's face at the unspoken concerns that were mirrored with the other pilots. He nodded. "Of course," he replied. "Celeste is a bit over three-and-a-half revolution. She takes after Trager in her looks, but she has Forrorrois' empathic abilities and spirit. She has a smile that could make you forgive almost anything." Perkins paused with a grin as he thought of her. "She calls me 'Unca' Perkins. And the colonel, she calls him 'Unca' Jack."

"Oh, how sweet," Alham whispered with a maternal smile.

Perkins looked around the table surprised to see that all the pilots were eager to hear more. Like many of the soldiers he had know when he was stationed far from home, the mention of children melted the hearts of even the most harden warrior. Encouraged, he continued. "She is. Forrorrois' parents spoil her every chance they get, but Celeste is never a trouble. Her favorite thing is to fly with Forrorrois in the cockpit of her long-distance scout."

"With two of the bessst Dramudam pilotsss asss her parentsss, of courssse Cccelessste lovesss to fly," Venue, Ronnon's brother, remarked.

Venue's unguarded observation of Forrorrois and Trager's skill as pilots reinforced Perkins' own belief in them. "Yes," Perkins replied. He looked around at the beings sitting with him and suddenly he understood. Goren was a sly fox. These were Forrorrois' friends and allies on the Tollon—and now they were his.

****

Trager stood in the ever-changing colorful mist of the Plane of Deception and reached out with his mind to focus the energy so that he could open a portal to Forrorrois' base. He had overheard Leenon telling Forrorrois that Yononnon had been sent to Earth to protect her parents. Trager realized that the energy in the area was still low from his effort to reach Forrorrois on Elda, but he needed to warn Yononnon about the unfolding events. He had to try, even against Guruma's wishes. Closing his eyes, Trager willed his mind to see the hangar bay of the base he had once shared with Forrorrois. Slowly the image of the cavernous hangar appeared before him. Relief washed over him when he spotted Yononnon inspecting his single-seat scout. Suddenly, Trager felt the barrier between the two dimensions weaken, allowing him to partially step through. Now suspended between the Plane of Deception and Earth—he stood behind Yononnon in the hangar bay.

"Yononnon," Trager spoke aloud in Intergaltic.

His friend turned quickly at the sound of his voice and froze—stunned at seeing him standing there.

"Trager! Is that really you?" Yononnon gasped.

"Yes, my old friend," Trager replied. "I don't have much time, but I need to warn you about events I've just witnessed on Elda."

Yononnon stepped forward, anxious. "Did you see Forrorrois? She was summoned there by the council."

"Yes. My mother, Neeha was the one that had summoned her," Trager replied. "Neeha has Celeste."

Yononnon breathed a sigh of relief. "Forrorrois must be ecstatic…"

Trager shook his head, sadly. "No, Yononnon, she's not. My brother, Talman has died without giving Bohata a child. It was Neeha who had Celeste kidnapped. She's claimed Mo'yuto for Bohata to justify her actions."

He watched as Yononnon leaned heavily against the side of his scout, stunned.

"What! Then why did Neeha summon Forrorrois to Elda?!" Yononnon gasped.

Frustrated, Trager shook his head. "I don't know. I can only guess that she did it to prevent Forrorrois from continuing her search for Celeste."

"How can the council let this happen?" Yononnon demanded. "I haven't heard of the council permitting Mo'yuto in over a hundred revolution!"

Trager sighed. "It's Elda, Yononnon. If I had been within Neeha's grasp, she would have sent the Council High Guard and had me taken instead to serve as a second to Bohata," Trager confessed.

"I've been away from Elda too long, I've forgotten how truly oppressive it can be," Yononnon whispered. "Being in the Dramudam has insulated us from the daily exposure of being second class citizens as males."

Trager nodded. "When I saw Forrorrois confronted by Neeha, I was reminded how we've been lulled into the illusion of personal freedom on the Tollon, but Elda's reach is far. Neeha brought Celeste into the council chamber for Forrorrois to see her power. When Forrorrois broke from the guards and tried to reach Celeste, the guards stunned her. Celeste's screams still echo in my ears as she was dragged from Forrorrois' still form. Then Neeha ordered Forrorrois unconscious body to be sent back to the Tollon in her long-distance scout. I fear that Forrorrois will return back to Elda and try to take Celeste back by force. Neeha has gone too far and she must be stopped."

"Trager...what do I tell Forrorrois' parents?" Yononnon pressed.

"The truth," Trager replied. "They must know that Celeste is alive, but as for the rest, I'm at a loss for words. I will continue to gather information, but the reduced energy levels here in the Plane of Deception are making it difficult."

"I'm so sorry, Trager," Yononnon said as he reached out to touch his shoulder.

Trager nodded when he felt the brief contact of his friend's hand, then the hangar bay faded from his view and was replaced by the swirling mist of the Plane of Deception—his tenuous focus broken by the physical contact. He bit his lip to keep the tears from falling as he thought of his daughter's heart-wrenching cries for her mother. Calming his nerves, Trager began to make his way back to the shelter.

The sudden rustle of dry leaves where there were no trees alerted him that he was not alone. Glancing around, he quickened his pace. The glowing red eyes of an Aethereal appeared out of nowhere blocking his path. Before Trager could conjure a protective field, the Aethereal's great claws slashed him across his chest. Trager covered his face with his arms and staggered backwards as a second Aethereal attacked him from behind. Their claws were razor sharp, cutting though his uniform and skin with ease. Trager forced his mind past the pain and focused the energy around him into an electrifying burst of energy that tossed his assailants away from him. Then Trager staggered forward towards the shelter.

The pair picked themselves up from the mist and pursued him—this time more cautiously. One grew bold and half leapt-half flew over him, blocking his path once more, baring its teeth as they dripped with silver saliva. Desperately, Trager dropped his personal shield and materialized a stun weapon, leveling the small oval at the Aethereal. In a flash of a red, the creature crumpled unconscious to the ground. The second creature howled its banshee wail and charged him from behind. Trager turned in time to feel the Aethereal's claw pierce his abdomen, unable to reestablish his personal field in time. He fired his stun weapon and dropped the creature. The Aethereal's long claws pulled slowly from his stomach as the creature crumpled into the mist.

Trager groaned, grasping his abdomen. He reached out toward the wall of the structure and forced the smooth surface to dissipate as he stumbled forward.

"Trager!" Guruma called out and rushed to his side.

"Help me inside," Trager gasped. "I was ambushed by two Aethereals."

He felt Guruma grab his arm and drag him through the opening. The conjured room faded from his view when unconsciousness mercifully embraced him.

✶✶✶✶✶✶✶✶✶✶✶

Jack looked up from his overstuffed chair in the living room of Forrorrois' base. He had been talking with Frank and Danielle Jolan when Yononnon entered the room. The Dramudam subcommander was visibly shaken.

"Forgive my intrusion," Yononnon began in English.

"You're not interrupting anything, Yononnon," Danielle said as she waved him in from her place beside Frank on the couch. "Please join us."

"Thank you, Danielle," Yononnon said as he stepped into the room, but then the Eldatek subcommander stopped by the wooden dining room table and rested his hand on back of one of the wooden chairs. "I have just received a visit from Trager…"

Jack straightened in his chair as everyone in the room grew silent.

"Does he have any word on Celeste?" Frank asked, leaning forward.

"Yes," Yononnon replied. "He saw Celeste on Elda. She is with Neeha, Trager's mother."

Jack tensed. Neeha had never recognized Forrorrois' joining with Trager or acknowledging their daughter.

Danielle grabbed Frank's hand. "Is she all right? How did she get there? Does Danica know yet?" Danielle pressed.

Yononnon nodded. "Yes, Danica knows—Neeha summoned her to Elda."

"When will she be bringing Celeste home?" Frank asked.

Yononnon hesitated. "Danica will not be bringing Celeste home—at least not yet."

Jack felt a weight in the pit of his stomach as he glanced over at Danielle.

"What do you mean?" Danielle pressed harder.

Yononnon dropped his gaze to the floor. "Trager's brother, Talman, died about an Earth month ago."

"That's terrible," Danielle exclaimed.

Yononnon nodded. "Yes, his brother's death was sudden. I'm certain that his loss has affected Trager deeply. They were very close before Talman joined with Bohata."

"Trager must be devastated, but what does this have to do with Celeste coming home?" Danielle asked.

Yononnon shifted on his feet. "Talman was Neeha's first-born male. He died without providing his joined one, Bohata, with a child. There is a very old custom on Elda that permits Neeha to take a female child from her second-born male and give the child to her first-born's widow to foster as compensation and provide the widow an heir."

Shock enveloped the room as Yononnon's words sunk in.

Danielle jumped to her feet, followed by Frank. "What?!" Danielle challenged. "Jack, what is he talking about? Neeha can't just take Celeste! She didn't even want anything to do with her!"

Jack's eyes widened as the large subcommander stepped back from the small auburn-haired woman advancing on his position and came to his feet to prevent Danielle from stepping any closer. "Hold on, Danielle, we don't have all the facts yet," he cautioned, glancing back at Yononnon.

"Yononnon, how is this possible?" Frank demanded. "What is the Dramudam going to do about this!?"

Yononnon glanced over at Jack then back at Frank and Danielle. "I assure you that the Dramudam are doing everything they can, but this is a very delicate situation. Neeha did this with the sanction of the Elda Council."

Danielle gave Frank a horrified look.

"What about our laws here on Earth?" Frank countered. "Who protects the rights of the people of this world?"

Yononnon dropped his graze—visibly ashamed. Jack waited as the subcommander regained his composure then look back up. "I give you my word that Commander Thoren will pursue this. He will offer Danica every assistance he can to help her regain custody of Celeste."

Danielle dropped her face into her hands and collapsed in Frank's arms, sobbing uncontrollably. Frank eased her back onto the couch as he tried to console her.

Jack stepped from the living room area toward the visibly shaken subcommander. "Thank you, Yononnon," Jack said. "Could you please come with me?"

"Yes, Jack. Again, Mr. and Mrs. Jolan, forgive me for bearing such news," Yononnon said with a deep bow towards Frank and Danielle.

Frank glanced at him and gave him a curt nod, then turned his attention back to his wife.

Jack touched Yononnon's arm and nodded towards the hallway. The large subcommander followed him back to the hangar bay in silence. Jack didn't need Forrorrois' empathic ability to sense the pain he saw in Yononnon's almond-shaped black eyes. He motioned the subcommander to take a seat at the repair bench. Yononnon slumped on the stool and leaned forward on the bench.

"I could really use a strong drink right now," Jack murmured in Intergaltic, slumping next to him onto his own stool.

Yononnon turned towards him. "How strong?"

Jack looked over at him with a raised eyebrow. "Very strong," he replied.

Without a word, Yononnon slipped off his stool and climbed the ladder of his single-seat long-distance scout. A few moments later he reappeared with a bottle of green liquid and two red stone mugs. The Eldatek male placed the bottle and mugs on the bench and resumed his slump on his stool. Jack watched as the subcommander poured a shot into each of the mugs then pushed one toward Jack.

Uncertain, Jack lifted the mug and sniffed the contents. The pleasant slightly spicy scent seemed harmless enough.

Yononnon raised his mug to Jack. "May your ship never fail you and may your repairs always hold," he toasted then he sipped from his mug.

Jack nodded and raised the mug to own his lips. The green liquor slid across his tongue and vaporized into a mist of very strong alcohol at the back of his throat. Jack choked back a cough from the effect. "Good stuff," he replied.

Yononnon almost smiled. "Forrorrois did the same thing the first time she drank this."

"When was that?" Jack queried, still clearing his throat.

"Just after her first flight in space," Yononnon reminisced. "My sister, Leenon, brought out a bottle of this Unyah to celebrate. She was still Danica then and what a handful she was."

Jack chuckled at the subcommander's unguarded comment. "Yes, she still can be," he replied, taking a second, better prepared, sip, as a ghost of a smile played on Yononnon's lips.

"The whole intermediate pilot class was making their first flights," Yononnon continued. "I stood with Trager and Commander Thoren and watched as Goren ran them through their paces. When it was Forrorrois' turn, inside I thought I was going to burst with pride while I watched her. She performed one of the tightest barrel rolls that I had ever seen on a first flight. Of course, I wasn't allowed to tell her how proud I was—I would have seemed biased since she was assigned to me and Leenon, but I was very proud. She was one of the best intermediate pilots I'd ever seen."

Jack studied Yononnon's proud chestnut face and smiled. "You really think of her as your adopted daughter, don't you?" Jack observed.

Yononnon hesitated then he nodded. "Yes, I do," he admitted. "I hurt for her right now. What Neeha has done is so cruel."

Jack watched as the subcommander drained his mug then poured himself another shot. Before Jack could object, Yononnon poured a second shot into his mug as well.

"So, where do you get this Unyah from?" Jack said, with a glance at the bottle.

Yononnon pulled on a mischievous grin. "Actually, Leenon gets it. I swiped it from her room before I left the Tollon to come here."

Jack gave Yononnon a surprised look then he shook his head and snorted a laugh. "I've met your sister—you certainly like to live on the edge, messing with her."

Yononnon looked over at Jack and burst out laughing. "I have to do something to entertain myself on the Tollon. It's been boring without Trager or Forrorrois to liven things up."

"It certainly has been less boring with the two of them around here—even with Trager being stuck in the Plane of Deception for the past four revolution," Jack replied.

Yononnon nodded then he grew serious once more.

"Thank you, Jack," Yononnon said.

"For what?"

"Thank you for being here for Forrorrois and her parents. I don't know how this will all be resolved, but knowing that you are here helps me realize that they have a good friend in you."

"It's the least I could do for them—and for Forrorrois," Jack replied.

Yononnon gave him a gentle smile then sipped from his mug.

Jack sipped his own and let the pungent liquor dull the pain in his chest. A desperate prayer rose in his heart for Celeste to be returned back to those who loved her.

CHAPTER 9

Forrorrois approached the brown planet in her long-distance scout. She had slipped off the Tollon while Perkins tested his repairs on her pursuit with Goren's permission—a ruse to cover her departure. If Commander Thoren had sent anyone after her, he had delayed them long enough not to let them find her trail. Alone, she engaged her hyperfold drive several times and crossed the vast stretch of space to reach this lonely world so far removed from the bustle of activity that thrummed at the center of the galaxy. She had spent her solitude, contemplating her insane mission, and sorting through ancient records for any additional clues that might aid her. Each night she tried to reach out to Trager using the meditation sphere he had given her at their joining, but, each failed attempt left her more drained and hopeless.

Collinar hadn't lied about the world being 'where a planet shouldn't be'. She had traveled through a magnetic storm into a heart of dark space. In the center of the dark space was a single yellow star similar to that of Earth's. Her sensors reached out towards the planet, but the gravity well that should have existed from the sphere's mass didn't register. Forrorrois shook her head at the strange anomaly that shrouded this world from the rest of the galaxy and orbited the average-sized planet—beginning a visual search of the brown terrain that was occasionally veined with blue rivers and streams. Her sensors still gave no indication that there was even a world below her ship. At last she spotted a plateau that fit Collinar's description and headed for a large rock outcropping.

The final distance to the brown world's lush plains left her uneasy. No known contact had been made with this world. There were no treaties or protocol. When she brought her scout to rest on the vast plain, there was an eerie silence broken only by the light rustle of the drying grass lapping at the side of her ship in the slight breeze.

To the north were mountains that struck upward violently. To the west an abyss of a canyon that cradled a trickling stream. To the east was a second endless plain. And to the south a great ocean that wove its way over a third of the planet. There were no signs of civilization here. No markers to tell her where to start, except that the mouth of the cave was where Collinar said it would be.

Alone, on the strange world, Forrorrois watched from her command chair as the night descended, filling the sky with weak shades of red and purple. She smoothed her black uniform while she rose from her seat. Without any sensor information, her computer was useless. Uncertain, Forrorrois decided not to open the hatch just yet until she confirmed that the atmosphere was safe to breath. She headed back through the small cargo hold to her scout's rear cabin. The door hissed open quietly at her silent command. Glancing into the mirror, she grimaced at the dark circles of exhaustion under her bloodshot golden-brown eyes. She pulled the band from her loose single braid and slowly combed out her long auburn hair. A gentle smile tugged at her lips when she thought of how much Trager used to love combing her hair. Lost in thought, she started when the intruder alarm sounded.

Reaching out with her mind, she felt the alien emotions on the other side of the door. Forrorrois drew her stun weapon from her belt and signaled the door to open. Her own nervousness was amplified by that of the creature which greeted her on the other side. She stepped back in shock. The cargo hold was filled with snorting black fur and large red leathery wings that were unable to unfold in the cramped space. Glossy black hoofs pranced in a frantic clatter as they struck the floor panels. At the swish of the door, the creature reared in fright then struck its equine head soundly against the metal panels of the ceiling, forcing it back down in front of her, stunned, shaking its fiery red mane.

She was astonished at the range of emotions that ran through her mind from the creature before her, but all she could think of was one word...*Beliespeir!* The creature froze before her as the thought crossed her mind. Its silky black fur quivered tensely, watching her while she placed the weapon back on her belt. Forrorrois offered both hands open—empty. The words formed on her lips as she stepped forward. "Beliespeir...I need your help...Please!"

The creature twisted nervously at her advance. Without warning the black and red figure swerved away from her and lunged towards the closed hatch with a flash of fire red tail against its silky black hide. Before she could cry out, the creature vanished into nothing. Stunned, she gaped at the closed door. Cursing to herself for not having done so earlier, she ordered the hatch to open. Impatient, she leapt into the darkness of the windswept plain without extending the ramp. The grass was well over a meter high, making walking difficult as the blades clung to her body with every step. Before her was nothing. Frustration welled up inside her when her sanity returned. She wouldn't find anything in the pitch of night. Resigned, she struggled back to the hatch and hauled herself aboard—there was nothing she could do until morning.

****

Forrorrois sat in the command chair of her long-distance scout and contemplated what she had seen the night before. She hadn't had much sleep, uncertain when, and if, the creature would return. The creature fit the description of the mythical beasts, but still, she questioned her own mental health. A sudden clatter in her cargo hold made her jump from her seat. She subvocalized immediately to the computer to silence the intruder alarm that had sounded. The ship fell silent. Cautiously, she edged into the hold. Her mind filled with confusion, excitement, and concern. She peered into the cargo area and found herself staring into the black-velvety muzzle of the intruder. They both tensed, but remained still, each waiting for the other to make the first move.

Forrorrois flinched first when she felt something in her mind, the feelings morphed into disjointed images. Then she gasped when the disjointed images became words.

You seek Beliespeir?

The words formed in her mind without a sound. Nervously,

Forrorrois nodded her head. *Yes,* she thought back, `I do seek Beliespeir`. She felt the tension in the air begin to melt when the equine creature uttered a whinny-like nervous laugh.

`You're a strange creature,` the creature thought to her. `No hoofs, no wings?!`

Forrorrois cracked a strained smile while she cautiously moved to one of the storage containers and took a seat. `I agree I must look strange,` she offered. `You must have seen creatures like me before...maybe a Beliespeir saw one like me a long time ago?`

The four-legged creature shifted on its feet in thought. `Yes, I remember stories,` the Beliespeir replied mentally, `but I never believed until now!`

She relaxed at the honest answer. The creature hid nothing from her.

`Why do you seek Beliespeir?`

She smiled at the Beliespeir's directness. `I seek Beliespeir to help me find another creature like me,` she thought back. `You can cross into other dimensions?`

`Dimensions?` the creature puzzled. `What are they?`

Forrorrois studied its liquid dark eyes. `The first time we met, when you left the ship, you didn't use the hatch. How did you do that?`

`I moved in time to a point when the door was open,` the Beliespeir thought back, fluttering its leathery red wings in a slight shrug. `How else would I do it?`

She sat back at the innocent statement. `When you are moving in time, you are in a partial or other dimension,` she thought quickly—as much to herself as to the creature. `You could do this to go to another dimension, maybe you could take me?`

The creature bobbed its head in understanding. `You want me to take you to this other creature that looks like you? Tell me more!`

She was taken aback by the creature's forwardness. The Beliespeir was definitely reading her mind more deeply than she first thought. She smiled cautiously. *We haven't been introduced*, she thought, *my name is Forrorrois, what's yours?*

Mine is Nur, it half thought, half whinnied aloud its name. *I'm the son of Merus and Seena. Forrorrois, what a musical name! Are you male or female?*

Forrorrois blushed. *Female*, she thought back.

This Beliespeir will help you find the other creature, if it can be found. May I see into your mind? I need to know where this creature is lost.

Yes, Nur, you may, but you have to lead me. I don't know how to let you in, she replied.

She froze where she sat, while Nur's mind brushed into hers. Images welled up from the depths of her soul of Trager, her beloved ashwan. The retrieval of the Utahar ship, the explosion of the bomb planted on Utahar craft by her enemy, Collinar. Her pain while she watched, unable to save him. Finally, her bitter joy when he reached out to her in the briefest of contacts to let her know he was still alive. Her face was wet with tears when Nur finally released her mind. She could sense he was deeply disturbed by the images he had just witnessed.

I know of this dimension, his thoughts whispered to her after a long pause. *It is a very dangerous place. You are right to be concerned for this other creature you call Trager.*

Will you help me? she asked, holding her breath.

Nur looked down at the floor plates. His wings fluttered nervously with indecision. Forrorrois sensed his reservations, unable to say anything that would sway him either way. At last he thought back to her.

There's more. You feel pain about something else. I saw a little one...where is this little one?

Forrorrois struggled to stifle the threatening tears. He had sensed Celeste. For once she was glad she didn't have to say it in words. She flooded her mind with her confrontation with Neeha, feeling a moment of peace at sharing it fully with someone else. Once again,

Nur became a tomb while he contemplated her thoughts. Forrorrois found herself holding her breath—slowly she exhaled, trying to calm herself while he mulled the images.

This other you call Neeha, why would she take your little one? he asked cautiously.

Forrorrois felt his confusion. *Neeha is very sad and is grieving for her little ones. I think your mother would feel the same*, she replied.

Maybe you're right, Nur answered. *Family is strongest when it is together. I must consult with others before I give you my answer. The wise ones will tell me more of this other dimension. They will give me guidance. I will return with my answer, Forrorrois.*

Thank you, Nur, she replied filled with cautious hope, *that's all that I can ask.*

He nodded his proud head and leapt through the closed hatch.

She watched him leave, wondering when he would return.

****

Forrorrois sat quietly in the command chair of her long-distance scout, studying the colorful panels on the console before her. Three days had passed since her last encounter with Nur. Hope was quickly turning into despair while she considered the possibility that he wasn't going to return at all. Sadly, she walked over to the side hatch and opened the portal. The sky was melting into shades of purple of another sunset. She watched wistfully, clinging to the slimmest hope. The dry grass rustled lightly against the ship in a lonely song. Turning away from the finally rays of sunset, she moved to close the hatch. The sudden flutter of wind against leather made her whirl in defense. A tentative smile tugged at her lips at the sight of Nur diving through the opening, nearly bowling her over.

Nur! I thought something had happened, she thought to him.

I said I'd return, he replied, slightly confused.

So what is your decision? she asked, with reservation.

The wise ones were very concerned about my questions about the other dimension, he replied. *They told me many things—frightening things. I began to doubt. Then they told me one must not turn their back on an honest request. They know much. That's why I returned. I offer my assistance.*

"Thank you," she whispered aloud. *Thank you,* she repeated in her mind. *You know of this dimension, Nur. You must lead the way.*

He turned his head, eyeing her. *You place so much trust...* He looked away in thought, taking a steadying deep breath. Forrorrois waited, hopeful for his words, sensing his uncertainty at being thrust into the forefront. *We won't need this craft...I will take you on my back.*

She nodded gratefully. *I will send it back into space. Will I need provisions?*

No. We travel light. All you need is something that reminds you of the one you called Trager, he replied.

She nodded in understanding and quickly retrieved the small meditation sphere from her rear cabin. *This is something we both shared,* she stated when she reappeared.

Yes, he replied with a glimmer of hope. *Yes, I feel the strong bond between you. This will be all we need. Carry it close to you at all times. Its energy will guide us to him!*

****

Perkins stood on the access ladder he had placed beside Forrorrois' pursuit ship and checked the fuel pellet supply one more time. Concerned, he shook his head. He could have sworn he had more than what he was counting now. His test flight shouldn't have used that many. *Wherever they've gone, they aren't where they should be*, he thought, with a frustrated glance upward at the high ceiling of the Tollon's hangar bay.

He heaved a sigh and closed up the fuel feed access panel behind the weapons turret. There wasn't anything more he could do but see Goren about them. Perkins climbed down the ladder, then straightened the dark brown coveralls he was wearing to work on the pursuit ship, and headed for Goren's office. He was surprised to run into Alham just leaving it. The sight of the beautiful Eldatek woman in her forest green and black pilot uniform made his heart pound a little faster.

"Alham, are you getting ready to go out on patrol?" Perkins asked in Intergaltic.

"No, I just finished one, Perkins," she replied back in Intergaltic. "If you are looking for Goren, he's in."

"Thanks," Perkins said. He stepped to the open door and knocked.

"Enter, Perkins," Goren rasped. "What can I do for you?"

Perkins stepped inside and stood in front of Goren's desk. "I was inspecting the fuel pellets in Forrorrois' pursuit ship and I've discovered that they are low. Would it be possible for me to get more pellets for her ship?"

Goren nodded. "Yes, of course. If you catch up with Alham, she can show you where they are stored."

"Thank you, Goren," Perkins replied and hurried out of his office. He glanced around the hangar bay and spotted her heading for the pilot's equipment room. "Alham!" he called out.

She turned and smiled warmly while he ran over to her.

"What can I help you with, Perkins?" she said as he approached.

"Goren told me that you could show me where the fuel pellets are stored. I need to restock Forrorrois' pursuit ship," he replied.

"Certainly," Alham said as she began to walk away from the pilot's equipment room. Perkins followed after her. "They are stored in this corridor down a ways," she continued. "As you already know, pellets themselves are not volatile, but under certain conditions and mixed with the right materials they can be explosive. Therefore they are stored away from the main hangar bay."

Perkins followed her down the long corridor and was surprised when they passed through several open air locks before they reached the area where the pellets were stored. Alham moved to subvocalize for the door lock to open when she turned and spotted a second door, across the corridor, sitting wide open.

"That's odd," she murmured.

"What's odd?" Perkins asked as he followed her over to the open door and looked inside. The storage cell was empty. On the side wall there were three long shelves that were deep enough that a person could lay on them.

"This door shouldn't be left open," Alham stated. She stepped inside the narrow storage room and then back out. "It's empty."

Perkins moved to speak when a loud explosion sounded from the direction they had just come. The door panel of the airlock, two sections down, abruptly slid shut, cutting them off from the hangar bay. An alarm began to sound as a second explosion ignited just one airlock down. Perkins looked toward the sound at the airlock they had just passed through sliding shut. His eyes grew big as he spotted a black disc mounted beside the controls of the airlock. Without another thought, Perkins grabbed Alham's arm and shoved her through the open door of the storage room that she had just inspected.

"Take cover!" he cried out.

They hit the floor and rolled into the small cell as the explosive ignited just outside. An alarm continued to drone as the light flickered then failed. Without warning, the door to the room that Alham and he took cover in slid shut. A few moments later the emergency lights flickered on in the storage compartment. "Are you all right, Alham?" he asked as he rolled over and found her still on the floor with him.

"Yes, I'm unharmed. What about you?" she replied, glancing towards the closed door.

"I'm good. Why would someone plant an explosive down here?" Perkins asked, moving to a sitting position.

"I don't know, but whoever did, they knew that it would trigger the airlock shut to quarantine this area," Alham replied.

Perkins looked at her carefully. "Why would someone do this?"

"I'm not certain, yet," Alham said as she stood to her feet and examined the door. "Computer, open the door," she ordered.

"Unable to open door lock until airlock integrity has been restored," the computer replied aloud.

"Computer, please establish contact with Goren. I need to speak with him immediately," she ordered.

"Communications established."

"Goren, this is Alham," she began.

"Alham, what happened? Are you and Perkins all right?" Goren's raspy voice sounded from the comm in the storage cell.

"For the moment, yes, Goren," she replied. "We're locked in a storage cell across from the fuel pellets chamber. At least three air locks have been triggered by explosives."

"I heard the explosions. I'm pulling up the schematics now," Goren stated. There was a pause before he continued to speak. "Alham, that storage cell you both are in is airtight. Locate the emergency air supply. It should be near the door behind a panel."

Perkins watched Alham open a panel next to the door. She turned abruptly towards him and shook her head. "Goren, the emergency oxygen supply is missing," she reported.

"This isn't good," Goren rasped. "Alham, describe what you and Perkins remember before the explosion."

"We were coming down to get a supply of fuel pellets," Alham began. "When we reached the fuel pellet storage locker, we noticed that the storage cell across from the fuel storage locker was left open."

"That's very odd," Goren replied.

"That's what I thought," Alham agreed. "When I looked inside, I found the cell was empty. Moments later, Perkins and I heard the first of three explosions. Perkins spotted something just before the third explosion and shoved me inside the empty storage cell. He saved my life," she added.

Perkins looked at her in surprise.

"Perkins, what did you see that made you react?" Goren asked.

"Well, it was a black disc mounted beside the airlock door, sir," Perkins replied. "It looked out of place."

"You're right," Goren replied. "It sounds like a disc explosive with remote detonation capabilities. Perkins, was there anything else that seemed out of place in the past half kel?"

Perkins thought back to the hangar bay. "Yes, I could have sworn that there were plenty of fuel pellets in Forrorrois' pursuit a few cycle ago before my first flight, but when I inspected the fuel system, I found that it was reading nearly depleted. That's when I came to ask you if I could get more."

Alham shook her head. "This was a trap," she announced.

Perkins eyes widened at her words.

"I'd have to agree," Goren voice rasped. "If my calculations are right, it will take the repair crews at least a kel to repair all three of those airlocks. Once that is complete, the lock of the storage cell you're in should release automatically. Unfortunately, without the emergency air supply and with two of you locked in there, you only have enough air for a half a kel before the carbon dioxide levels become toxic and you both suffocate."

Perkins straightened and looked at Alham. His mind began to race for a solution. When Alham began to speak, he waved her to be quiet. "Goren," he called out, "what if one of us doesn't use as much air?"

Alham gave him a strange look, but Perkins just stared up at the ceiling waiting for Goren to speak.

After a pause, Goren responded. "Yes. Yes that just might work, Perkins," Goren voice rasped. "But if I understand what you are suggesting, that also means that you will have to be careful about hypothermia."

"What are you two talking about?" Alham interrupted.

"Perkins can explain, Alham," Goren cut in. "But, Master Pilot, you must keep him alive, no matter what you need to do."

Alham glanced towards Perkins then nodded her head. "Understood, Master Pilot Instructor."

Perkins was surprised by her formal response when Goren used her rank. He had given her an order, not a request.

"Good, I have to coordinate the emergency repair crew. I'll contact you periodically to make certain that you're all right. If it's possible, try to get to a higher position in the storage cell. Carbon dioxide is heavy and will settle towards the floor. You'll be able to breathe longer."

"There are storage shelves we can utilize, Goren," Alham replied.

"Good, I'll keep you apprised of the repairs, Goren, out."

Perkins crossed over to the shelves and tested one with his weight. It was firmly secured. He looked up to the top shelf and figured that there was enough space for Alham to lie down and still be a half-meter from the ceiling. He turned to find Alham standing directly behind him.

"Perkins, tell me what you and Goren were talking about," Alham demanded.

Perkins studied her for a moment then swallowed nervously. He had never allowed anyone but Forrorrois and Jack to see him in miniature before, but there wasn't much he could do or say that would prepare someone to witness what he was about to do. Sharing this with another person was terrifying to him and he'd never attempted to stay reduced for more that fifteen or twenty minutes at a time before—by then he would begin to feel chilled. Without Alham's assistance—four hours could be deadly. He needed her to accept what he was about to do.

"Sit down, Alham, I have to tell you something," he began.

Alham stared at him hard before she did as he asked and sat on the lower shelf. "All right, for Goren's sake, I'm sitting."

"Alham, did Forrorrois ever talk to you about the changes that Collinar had made to her when she was held on that Utahar experimental station?"

Alham shrugged. "Not really, she was kind of quiet about it," Alham replied.

"I see," Perkins said, uncertain what he should tell her. "Well, Collinar performed these same changes on me about four revolution ago."

Alham narrowed her eyes, but remained silent.

Perkins shifted on his feet then continued. "One of the changes allows me to reduce my mass in a kind of mass-to-energy exchange—sort of the same effect as the Utahar's reduction weapon, except that I can do it at will."

The tall Eldatek woman's clay-brown face softened. "I'd heard of rumors about Forrorrois being able to do that, but I never asked her about it," Alham confessed. "When a Dramudam doesn't wish to speak about personal matters, other Dramudam don't press. But that doesn't matter right now. Goren said I needed to keep you alive, what did he mean by that?"

Perkins shrugged, apologetically. "One of the side effects of this reduction talent is that if I stay reduced for a long period of time I have an accelerated rate of body heat loss which makes me susceptible to hypothermia. I've never stayed reduced for a more than a hur before. I don't even know if I can," he confessed. "But if I do, I won't be using as much oxygen."

He held his breath as Alham studied him for several heartbeats before she spoke. "Well, I guess we're going to find out," she finally replied.

Perkins exhaled, relieved that the idea didn't disturb her. "One other thing."

"What's that?"

"My zendra link will be broken with the ship's computer. "I may have trouble remembering enough Intergaltic to communicate with you."

"We'll work something out," Alham replied. "By Guruma's hand, I will keep you alive. I owe you my life." Perkins moved to object, but she shook her head. "I also do it for our mutual friend, Forrorrois."

"Thank you," Perkins replied. He took a deep breath then exhaled slowly. "All right, here it goes," Perkins said as he concentrated. The air in the room warmed as he began to contract down to 9.4 centimeters. The effort left him drained and slightly chilled as he looked up at the now towering Alham sitting on the shelf before him. He stepped back when she leaned forward and offered her hand.

Nervously, Perkins stepped onto her clay brown palm then steadied himself while she gently curled her fingers around him and raised him up to eyelevel for a better look at him.

"I guess you truly are a handful," she jested.

Perkins struggled to translate her words then grinned when he realized she had just made a joke.

"Here, let me put you up on the top shelf and I'll climb up there with you," Alham said as she lifted him up.

Perkins jumped off her hand and moved back against the wall. He watched Alham pull herself up and slide into the tight space. Before Perkins could object, Alham scooped him up and deposited him on her abdomen. She covered him with her hand protectively.

"Are you warm enough?" she asked.

"Yes, for now," Perkins replied, trying not to squirm against the firm, but gentle, pressure she applied with her palm against his prone miniature body.

"Good, I'll keep an ear out for Goren's next contact."

"Thank you," Perkins answered. He closed his eyes to remain focused, but the smell of her skin was slightly spicy, intoxicating him with her closeness.

****

Forrorrois sat astride Nur's strong silky black back, balanced behind his folded red bat-like wings. Together, they watched while her scout ascended towards open space. Nur shifted nervously at the odd sight, causing the tall brown grass to brush against her black boots. She felt the link between her and her ship's computer sever as the craft exceeded the range of her zendra link, leaving her empty in its absence. The weight of the small pouch containing her personal meditation sphere on her waist made her look away from her scout. She adjusted the emergency med kit over her shoulder and looked down at Nur's velvety withers. Anxious butterflies danced in her stomach as she gathered a handful of silky fire-red mane in her small pale hand and tightened her legs against his sides. In her wildest dreams, she never thought she would be this close to seeing Trager again.

I'm ready, Nur, she thought to him.

The Beliespeir unfurled his magnificent leathery wings in the pitch black and lunged forward into the night. Forrorrois gasped as the darkness liquefied into a spiral of shifting colors and shapes. Consciousnesses threatened to leave her while her mind fought to comprehend what she was witnessing. Forrorrois tightened her grip, afraid she'd fall from his rippling back.

Accept it for what it is, Nur offered, *don't try to force it to make sense.*

She nodded as she tightly closed her eyes. Clearing her mind, Forrorrois centered on the steady stride of Nur's movements and the thrum of his wings—slowly, the fear subsided inside her. She reopened her eyes—awe had replaced fear. The colors swirled about her in a mist that was gentle and calm. Nur's motion had slowed to a steady pace, gliding through vapor.

Where are we? she thought in astonishment.

We are in the other dimension, he thought back. *We must stop and gain our bearings.*

Forrorrois shivered at his words. *Tell me what to do*, she said, while he landed on the misty surface.

You must guard your thoughts, he warned. *What you think can become real here. There are also creatures that call themselves Aethereals. They are very dangerous and attack without warning. Their wings rustle like dry grass in the soft wind. They will claw you to death if they catch you.*

By the hand of Guruma! she thought back desperately. *What has Trager been living with these past four revolution? He said nothing of this to me!*

Nur glanced back at her. *You have strange images...is there another here?*

Yes, Guruma...I forgot about him in my selfishness, she admitted. *He's a great peacemaker. He founded the Dramudam many seasons ago. Trager told me Guruma pulled him through to this dimension when the ship exploded.*

Then we must focus our thoughts on both of them, he assured her. *They will be together. You must help me find the direction.*

She pulled the clear smoky sphere from her pouch and peered into the orb between her fingertips. Concentrating on her lover's face, she visualized his strong features. His gentle smile and full long black hair tied back in the traditional loose Dramudam braid—his mustache framing his mouth as it flowed into a trim goatee. Tears glided down her face when his image formed in the center of the orb. His tender almond-shaped black eyes looked back at her unseeing. She ached to touch his chestnut-brown cheek, to kiss his lips, so long denied her. Reality came back to her when she felt Nur shifting uncomfortable beneath her. Collecting her thoughts, she slowly turned in her seat and dowsed for direction. Time seemed endless while she panned the horizon with the sphere. The orb warmed in her hands with a gentle glow. She stopped and looked into the distant swirling colors of the mist.

This way, she urged, *they are this way!*

✱✱✱✱✱✱✱✱✱✱✱

Perkins lay in miniature on Alham's abdomen with her hand covering him for warmth while they waited for Goren's team to extract them from the storage compartment. Together, they had taken refuge on the tight upper shelf of the compartment to slow their exposure to the carbon dioxide buildup in the sealed room. In the distance, he could hear the team working to release the airlocks that had triggered closed from the explosives set by a saboteur and silently prayed that they would reach them in time.

Reflexively, he rubbed his arms against a chill and wished he had something heavier on than the brown coveralls he had been wearing to work on Forrorrois' pursuit ship. The heat from Alham's hand was no longer enough to fight off hyperthermia in his reduced state. He fought a shiver and looked into the concerned clay-brown face of the Eldatek master pilot when she lifted her fingers to peer at him from her position resting flat on the shelf. Her black eyes softened as she drew him closer to her face to examine him.

"You're shivering," she remarked.

"Yes. Unfortunately, I'm growing colder," he admitted.

"I'll put you in my tunic pocket," she stated.

Before he could object, she unbuttoned her breast pocket and slipped him inside—feet-first. Stunned, Perkins suddenly found himself reclined against the curve of her body. Then it registered that he was resting on her left breast with only the silky fabric of her forest green tunic between him and her skin.

"Are you warmer?" she asked, peering at him from the top of her pocket.

Perkins swallowed hard as he felt his throat go dry. "Ah, yes."

"Good," Alham replied, from her prone position.

Another time, this would have been a fantasy come true for him, but Perkins found the sudden reality unsettling. He curled against her curved softness and tried not to think about the intimacy of the situation. The rhythm of her breathing slowly lulled him to a light sleep as his body began to warm.

****

Excitement shifted to monotony while Nur carried Forrorrois through the disorienting mist of the Plane of Deception. Glancing around, Forrorrois felt thirst forming in her throat from the long journey. She leaned forward and tapped Nur on the black fur covered withers. *Nur, maybe we should rest, we've been traveling for a long time since we arrived, surely you must be tired.*

Yes, he admitted, coming to a halt. *Maybe we should eat something to keep up our strength.*

But Nur, she asked, *we have no provisions?*

Just think about what you need, concentrate on it and it will appear, he replied, dipping his head down into a pile of hay that suddenly appeared from nowhere.

She sat back in astonishment, unable to believe her eyes. *How did you..?*

Just concentrate, he thought back while he munched his hay. A bowl of water popped into view next to the hay.

Just concentrate, she thought uncomfortably to herself. *Well, I guess I really could use a glass of water right now.* She glanced down at the cool water in the bowl below wistfully. The image of the glass was cold to the touch in her hand, wet going down her throat. The thought almost tortured her. She licked her dry lips at the thought. Her fingers spread slightly when the glass appeared in her hand, causing her to nearly drop the chilled container in shock. *It worked!* she gasped.

Of course, Nur replied in her mind, continuing to eat.

She lifted the glass to her nose and sniffed. *Nothing odd about the smell.* Cautiously tipping the glass to her lips, she tasted the clear liquid. The cool sweet flavor of spring water trickled down her parched throat, invigorating her. The idea boggled her mind that such magic could exist. Her thoughts fell to her brother. *George would go wild in a place like this! What magic he could conjure at the merest whim.* Forrorrois thought for a second with her other hand stretched out. In the blink of an eye a falafel appeared in warm pita bread. She bit into it eagerly, savoring the creamy cucumber dressing that covered the crisp lettuce.

This is fantastic! she thought while she chewed. *And to think nobody will tell me not to talk with my mouth full*, she mentally laughed.

You find humor in the strangest things, Nur replied,

shaking his large head. *We must be going before we lose our direction.*

Whenever you're ready, she thought back, finishing her sandwich. Taking one last sip she wished the glass away. *This is wild! No dishes!*

Forrorrois, you must concentrate, he urged. *Which way?*

Pulling out the meditation sphere from the small pouch on her waist, she calmed herself. Forrorrois held the orb out and swept a slow arc. The orb brightened when she pointed it ahead. *Forward,* she replied pointing into the mist.

Forward it is, he agreed.

****

Perkins started awake when Alham peeked down at his miniature form inside her tunic pocket. His mind was foggy when he looked up at her beautiful almond-shaped black eyes. A chill ran through him when the cooler air seeped in.

"I feel you shivering again, Perkins," Alham said as she stared at him, from her horizontal position on the shelf.

"I'm all right," Perkins replied, repressing another shiver. "How much longer?

"Another quarter of a kel."

Perkins shook his head, he wasn't going to last another hour. "Alham, I'm losing heat too fast," he confessed.

"I spoke to Kela while you were resting," Alham said as she shifted slightly to her right side forcing Perkins to steady himself. "She suggested I try a different way to keep you warm. Please climb onto my fingers so that I can lift you out of my pocket."

Perkins instinctively pulled away when the pocket opening darkened and she reached in with her slender fingers. Forcing the fear from his mind, he shifted his weight onto her fingers, and then let her draw him out into the chilled air. His shivering grew worse causing his teeth to begin to chatter. He was barely aware that Alham had pulled back the flap of her tunic before she lowered him directly against her skin between her breasts. The brief flash of her Dramudam mark against her clay-brown skin was all that registered in his mind as the heat of her body began to re-warm him, then the light was extinguished when she moved her tunic flap back into place. Perkins curled into a ball, cradled between her breasts, shivering. As he slowly warmed, he breathed in the spicy musk of her skin. The fog began to lift in his mind, allowing him to relax his body. Without thinking, he reached out and brushed his hand against the curve of her right breast—the softness of her skin surprised him.

"That tickles," Alham whispered, moving the flap slightly aside to peer at him.

"I'm sorry," Perkins sputtered as he pulled his hand back. "I…I…"

"Hush," Alham replied. "Kela suggests that skin-to-skin contact would offer you more warmth."

The image of what she was suggesting, hit Perkins like a stone. "I don't think so," he stammered. "I think I'll keep my coveralls on, thank you."

"As you wish," she replied, disappointment hinted in her voice. "I offer as a mother would offer to warm a newborn."

Perkins rolled over onto his back and stared up at the cloth of her tunic suspended above him. "Thank you, but I'm afraid that I wouldn't react like a newborn," he confessed.

"And I'm afraid I wouldn't react as a mother," she admitted and reclosed her tunic flap to keep the cooler air out.

Her comment made him smile slightly as he felt his eyelids slide shut. His breathing fell into a calm rhythm while silence fell between them. Perkins slowly became very aware that he could feel her heartbeat against his back. The rate increased when Alham shifted her position slightly under him. Perkins opened his eyes once more in the shadows and stared up at the silky cloth that was suspended above his bosom cradle.

"Perkins, do human males have physical relations with more than one female?" she suddenly asked.

He took a quick breath, surprised at her question. "Sometimes, but generally only one at a time," he called back.

"On Elda, we remain celibate until we are joined and then we only know our joined one."

Uncertain where she was going with the conversation, Perkins cleared his throat. "Do you have a joined one?" he asked.

"No, I am a second born daughter of a poor family. My sister has had a successful joining and has two children. It is doubtful that I will ever be allowed to be joined."

Perkins felt the sorrow in her voice. "Is that why you enlisted with the Dramudam?" he called out.

"Yes," she whispered. "But when I saw how happy Trager and Forrorrois were, I realized that maybe the ways of Elda or the Dramudam are not the only paths. How about you, Perkins, are you joined?"

"No, I've never met the right female," he confessed. "I guess that's why I'm in the military."

"We are not so different then," Alham said quietly. "You must tell me more about Earth when we get out of here. I understand it is very beautiful and green with great oceans."

Perkins smiled. His body was warmed again and for a moment he had almost forgotten that he was cradled between her ample breasts. "Where I live it is very green—except in the winter when ice crystals fall instead of rain—then it's white and grey."

"It does sound beautiful," Alham whispered. "If I could get permission to go to the surface, would you show me?"

Perkins smiled at her innocent request. "Of course I would." Suddenly, he fought off a yawn.

"I would enjoy that very much," she whispered. "Perkins, I am feeling very tired. I don't think I'm going to be able to stay awake much longer."

Perkins' eyes widened. His yawn was not an accident. The air must be getting stale faster than they expected. "How much more time before the repair crews finish?"

"Maybe another hur," she replied, distantly.

"Hold on Alham," Perkins called out as he sat up.

Alham didn't answer. Perkins felt her breathing become shallower.

Suddenly, Goren's voice sounded from the comms. "Alham is everything all right?" he rasped urgently. "Your bio signs are shifting."

"Yes, Goren, but the air is getting very thin in here," she gasped.

"Are the two of you staying warm?"

"We're working on that, Goren, but I'm more worried about breathing at the moment," Perkins shouted. "How much time before you can get us out of here?"

"I'm afraid it will be at least another half a hur. The last airlock was badly damaged. Stay awake for a bit longer," Goren replied.

"We'll do our best," Perkins gasped as he struggled to keep his eyes focused. "Hang on, Alham," he whispered as he felt her go limp beneath him. He struggled to keep his own eyes open, but it was getting more difficult by the moment.

The smell of her spicy skin intoxicated him. He listened to the sounds of repairs on the third airlock, just outside the door, but his eyes drooped as he struggled to stay conscious.

The abrupt clang of a door lock releasing made his eyes open briefly then he drifted off once more letting unconsciousness embrace him while the sounds of voices rang in the distance.

****

Forrorrois looked up as Nur came to a halt in the ever-changing mist that made up the Plane of Deception. She shifted her position on his broad back. They had been traveling for hours. In her mind she could hear Nur speak.

We'll stop here, Nur stated. *We'll need to keep watch while we rest.*

I'll take the first watch, Forrorrois volunteered. *You've been carrying me since we've arrived, you must be tired.*

You're not a burden, little creature, he replied, *but I am tired. The air seems chilly.*

Let me start a small fire, she replied with the wave of her hand. The sound of crackling wood along with the pleasant scent of smoke filled the air. Nur stepped back nervously from the sight.

What have you conjured? his thoughts stammered.

Something to keep us warm, she assured him. *It will not harm you, if you don't touch it.*

Nur cautiously stared at it. *It is warm*, he admitted. *I've never seen it so contained, only in terrible firestorms that blacken the plains!*

I promise this will not become a firestorm, she reassured in his mind. Patting him lightly, she slipped from his back. Her legs felt unsteady from sitting astride for so long. She eased herself to the ground near the small camp fire. *Rest while I take watch.*

He nodded, still remaining several paces from the flickering light. *Wake me when you feel tired.*

I will, she replied, *now get some sleep.*

She sat for several hours and listened for sounds in the quiet mist. The crackle of the fire was her only companion. Sipping on a mug of conjured mawya, she gazed into the small meditation sphere, wishing Trager would answer her. His last brief contact had her concerned.

"Trager, I know you're near," she whispered aloud. "Help me find you in this insane place. Give me hope." The distant sound of dead leaves in autumn murmured in her mind. She shook the stray sound from her head, but the noise persisted, growing louder. Abruptly, she realized the sound wasn't in her mind. Jumping to her feet, Forrorrois rushed over to Nur's motionless form and tugged at his mane. *Wake up Nur*, she thought loudly, *something's coming!*

He started awake. She sensed his panic immediately.

Quick, climb up onto my back, he urged, kneeling down so she could mount.

She wasted no time scrambling behind his muscular red leather wings onto his broad back. *What is it?*

Aethereals! They've sensed us, he replied. *We must run before they catch us!*

Forrorrois doused the fire with the wave of one hand while she held on tightly to his mane with the other. Nur spread his wings and soared upward into the mist. The sound of the Aethereals grew louder in her ears. She spotted one in the distance and looked away in horror. The creature's eyes glowed like red coals, locking onto them in their flight. When the Aethereal opened its mouth, a soul-wrenching banshee wail emanated after them, chilling her to her very bones. *Nur, it's so hideous,* she thought, clutching his mane, frantically. *From what hell did it come from?*

The hell of this place, he replied. *Hang on, I can out fly it...I hope.*

The haste of his great wings swirled the mist into jumbled disorder, leaving a trail that a blind man could have followed. She shook her head in frustration. *This is no good. Even if we out distance the Aethereal, it will just be a matter of time before it follows in our wake. We've got to land. We'll disturb the mist less if you walk!*

But it will catch us for certain if I land, Nur countered frantically. *We have no choice!*

Yes, we do, she replied, as she pulled her stun weapon from her belt. *If we confront the Aethereal, I'll be able to stop it. It will gain us time to walk away in the mist before it recovers!*

I don't understand, he replied, turning to face the wailing demon, *but I'll do what you ask.*

Thank you, my friend, she thought back, taking aim at the closing creature. The intensity of its piercing scream rose to a maddening pitch. She shuddered as its grasping claws reached out for her flesh. Nur landed on the mist covered ground and tensed for the oncoming assault. The hideous creature rushed towards them hungrily. She counted the seconds, steadying her hand. *Now,* she thought firing the weapon. The reddish beam lanced forward, bathing the confused creature in its light. The Aethereal dropped to the ground, motionless.

What did you do? Nur cried out in her mind.

It's still alive, she reassured him, *but it won't remain unconscious for long. Start walking that way before he wakes up!*

She felt his confusion while he headed where she pointed. His pace skittish in the swirling mist. She could only hope they would distance themselves before the Aethereal regained its senses.

∗∗∗∗∗∗∗∗∗∗∗

Perkins stirred as he heard the hiss of air in his ears. He opened his eyes and tried to focus, but everything seemed to be bent and curved around him. Suddenly, the distortion lifted away and he found himself starting up at Kela towering over him—her slim tongue flitting between her scaly lips in concern as she studied him. Goren moved into view beside her. From the scale of everything, he realized he was still in miniature—wrapped in a thick cloth.

"We ssshould take them both to Bio Med," Kela stated in Intergaltic.

"No, they'll be safer here," Goren rasped.

"Where's Alham?" Perkin's called out. The effort of speaking caused him to fall into a coughing fit.

"She's in the other bunk," Goren replied. "Over there," he pointed.

Perkins looked over and spotted her resting on the bunk across from him. There was a clear oxygen mask covering her nose and mouth. He looked around and realized that Goren had moved them to the rear cabin of Forrorrois' long-distance scout.

"Is Alham all right?" he asked.

"Yesss," Kela replied. "Thanksss to your reduction talent. Ssshe will have a bit of a headache, but ssshe will recover fully."

"I'm glad," Perkins replied. "Where's Forrorrois?"

Goren shook his head. "She's not back yet. She sent her ship back to the Tollon on autopilot. Unfortunately, she wiped the flight plan out of the computer so we don't know where she is right now."

Perkins looked up at Goren and saw his concern. "She'll be back," Perkins replied.

Goren nodded his head. "Of course she will. Now, if you're strong enough, I'd like you to return to full size so Kela can tend to you."

Perkins nodded. He closed his eyes and concentrated. The room grew colder as he drew the energy from the air. He looked up at Goren when he reached full size. The effort was too much as his head rolled to one side and he lost consciousness once more.

CHAPTER 10

The tension in Forrorrois' shoulders relaxed. Several hours had passed since Nur and she had lost the Aethereal in the mist of the Plane of Deception. The Beliespeir's slow pace was maddening, but safer, leaving little disturbance in the slowly shifting mist. Forrorrois sensed Nur's questions and knew full well she should answer them soon. Rubbing her hand against his velvety soft withers she gave a sigh.

What's on your mind? Nur, she thought gently.

He hesitated. *I still don't understand what you did to stop the Aethereal. All I saw was a flash.*

I used a weapon. But I assure you it only stunned the creature, she replied.

I realize that now, he said, *I felt its mind in the distance. It was just so unexpected...*

I'm sorry. I should have told you I was carrying it. I was wrong not to, she answered.

You're kind is so different, he stated. *The Wise Ones were right to caution me...but I'm glad that you brought it. I may not have been able to outrun the Aethereal without leaving this dimension. Then we would have had to start all over looking for the one called Trager.*

Thank you for understanding, Nur, you're a good friend, she replied patting him gently. Suddenly, the glow of the sphere increased in her hand, she lifted the sphere and glanced around. *Nur, I don't think it's much further!*

She felt his excitement grow with hers. In the distance, she spied a building wavering in the shifting fog. The square structure seemed so out of place in the featureless surroundings of colored mist. Her thighs tighten against the sides of the Beliespeir, urging him forward. He quickened his pace beneath her, sensing the end of their quest. She reached out with her mind, grasping for any sign of life inside the shimmering walls. The closer they came, the stronger the emotions grew from inside.

Trager is inside! And he is there with another, Nur thought to her.

Something's wrong, she thought nervously when she slipped to the ground as Nur came to a halt outside the shimmering large box.

I sense something also, he thought back. *Someone is hurt!*

Frantically, Forrorrois circled the box, but there were no openings anywhere. *How do we get in?* She reached out to touch the wall but pulled back when the tips of her fingers began to tingle. *Stay away from the walls—they're electrified,* she warned Nur. "Trager," she called out loud. "Trager please let me in!" The sound of her voice echoed into the distance, but nothing happened. The walls remained. *Why can't he hear me?* she cried out in her mind to Nur. *He's so close but I can't reach him!*

You must stop and think, he urged. *Use this dimension as they have learned to use it!*

She looked at the box wishing harder and harder she could find a way inside. Suddenly the air filled with the distant rustle of wings. Without looking—she knew the Aethereal were coming. Focusing on the wall, she cried out once more. "Trager! See me!"

The banshee wail behind her made her turn in defense. She pulled her weapon, only to be bowled over by the frightful creature. Her shoulder burned as her flesh was grazed by the Aethereal's claw. The stun weapon skittered into the fog beyond her reach. Rolling defensively to her feet, Forrorrois stepped back as the Aethereal charged her once more. Instinctively, she waved her hand before her. A wall of flames encircled Nur and herself. The smell of scorched leather filtered through while the Aethereal screamed in pain and fury.

Forrorrois, you've conjured such horror, Nur cried out in her mind.

She waved the flames away, watching the hideous creature sulk away in frustration. *I'm sorry, Nur, there was barely time to react,* Forrorrois replied, retrieving her weapon from the mist. Turning back to the shimmering wall, she concentrated once more. A portion began to waver then fall in the shape of a large door. Reaching out, she pulled back, stunned, painfully shaking her hand.

What's wrong, Nur asked.

It's still electrified, she replied. Hot wet tears slipped down her cheeks in frustration. "Trager! I can feel you in my mind...I can feel your pain! I share it!" Touching her hand to her shoulder, its sticky ooze warmed her fingers.

Focus you mind away from your wound. Focus on the sphere! Nur echoed in her mind.

Forrorrois fumbled her hand in the pouch, and withdrew the smoky orb she had slipped inside. Falling to her knees, she gazed deeply into it. Trager's ashen face was beaded with sweat. Guruma bent over him, his strong aging hands clenched in frustration.

You cannot reach him, his consciousness is slipping, Nur stated. *Contact the other!*

Tearfully, she focused on Guruma's wizened face. "Guruma hear me! Open the door," she cried aloud. "For Trager's sake open the door!"

The air began to vibrate in sympathetic resonance of her sobs. Soon, the ground trembled in her wake. Clutching the sphere to herself, she rocked in a trance. Behind her, the rustle of dry leaves magnified by ten.

Forrorrois...Forrorrois, they are coming!

She blocked his words, seeing only the sphere before her. Forrorrois formed a sphere of liquid metal above Trager, startling Guruma. The Elder Dramudam's eyes widened when he saw her image reflected inside. He jumped to his feet when he saw the door she had conjured. She trembled from the strain, collapsing forward as the light poured over her from the room.

Guruma grabbed her arm. "Forrorrois!"

She stumbled to her feet, feeling Nur nosing her other arm.

"He's with me," she gasped when she felt the elder Dramudam pull back at the sight of Nur.

"Quickly then," he urged.

She grasped Nur's mane and struggled through the door. The door melted back into the wall when they were through. All fatigue faded when her gaze fell to her ashwan. His uniform was tattered and stained with his pinkish-red blood. Forrorrois dropped to her knees and draped her body over his, smoothing his matted hair from his face.

"Oh Trager...stay with me...be strong," she cried. Frantically, she pulled her bioscanner from her pouch and scanned him. As she read the results, she looked up at Guruma. "He needs blood and he's suffering from infection."

"I know," Guruma replied, resting his hand on her shoulder. "But neither of us can produce it. It's far more complicated than just an illusion."

"Then we must get him back to the Tollon! Nur, help us!"

I need an image to focus...a place in time. This plane is omni-directional, he replied in her mind.

Guruma started from Nur's voice in his head, another time Forrorrois would have just smiled—instead she grabbed the older being's arm. "Trager told me you watch over the Tollon...show us how!"

"I usually need a focal point. They exist in several places in the mist. There's one not far from here, but the Aethereals are on the warpath. We'll never make it."

Forrorrois pulled the stun weapon from her waist. "We can make it. Just show Nur!"

Guruma eyed her cautiously then Nur, hope glimmered in his eyes for the first time since she arrived. "I believe we can," he whispered.

Nur, can you carry both of them?

Yes...but what about you?

I'll worry about me, she replied with a determined nod. "*Guruma, climb onto Nur's back and steady Trager in front of you. There's no time to argue. He's slipping with each passing moment!*"

Guruma froze his objection and followed her lead. Forrorrois struggled to roll Trager onto her shoulders and staggered to her feet, she heaved Trager up in front of the older Dramudam already on the Beliespeir's back. Nur ducked his head and wing while she threw his leg over.

"I've got him," Guruma stated, encircling Trager's waist with his arms.

"Take the med kit, use it if you have to—just keep him alive," she ordered. "Now open a door and I'll clear the way," she replied, holding her weapon ready.

The wall faded before them. Banshee wails shattered the silence. Stepping forward, Forrorrois blanketed their path with a brilliant flash. Several Aethereals dropped unconscious from her onslaught. The others fell back in confusion and fear. "Guruma, tell Nur where to go," she cried out, shifting nervously at every sound.

Nur began to walk into the mist, shying at the glowing red eyes that surrounded them. Suddenly, their path was blocked by a single wiry silhouette. The creature raised its tattered leathery winged arms. Forrorrois took aim.

"Don't fire, Forrorrois," Guruma ordered.

Forrorrois hesitated, glancing between Guruma and the ominous looking creature before her.

"You have brought another sorcerer to plague us," the Aethereal rattled in a rustle of dry leaves. "It has caused pain!"

"As your kind has caused pain," Guruma darkly replied looking down at Trager. "She is his mate."

Forrorrois felt its glowing eyes burn into her. Defiantly, she glowered back.

"She has great power, yet she chooses not to kill," the Aethereal replied. "As a mate, it is her right."

"My mate still lives, but barely. I will kill if you do not let us pass," she hissed.

All fell silent at her words, no one moved. Seconds ticked in her head, each one brought Trager closer to death. In frustration, Forrorrois grabbed a handful of Nur's mane and stepped forward towards the Aethereal. Nur trembled from her touch, but followed. The creature's burning eyes locked with hers, but she held the Aethereal's gaze and felt its foul breath as she led them past. Dismissing the red glowing eyes, she felt the creature's mind tense. Releasing Nur's mane, Forrorrois turned quickly to meet his assault. Her weapon flashed, dropping the horror as it swung its claw. The remaining Aethereals erupted in anger at her action and descended on them like locust. Gathering her senses, Forrorrois conjured a flaming sphere about her companions for protection. Nur reared in fright, nearly unseating his two charges. Howls of frustration sounded all around them from the creatures.

Go forward, it will move with you, she urged Nur. "Guruma lead us!"

"It's just ahead," Guruma called back. "But it's hard to tell without seeing the mist. I have to see the patterns."

"All right," she cried above the din. Concentrating, Forrorrois widened the sphere and allowed the mist to filter through. The colored pattern shifted at their feet. "How's that?"

"Perfect," the elder replied. "We're almost there!"

She trembled from the effort. "I can't hold this much longer," she gasped.

"Just a little longer," Guruma ordered. "We're here!"

Forrorrois caught her breath when a large liquid mirror appeared before them. Its image distorted and wavered. The great hall of the Tollon appeared dimly lit before them—the first place she had ever seen Guruma.

I can't take you all, Nur stammered.

"I'll stay behind," she replied.

"No! Reduce yourself," Guruma ordered. "Take my hand and do it!"

Spent, Forrorrois handed him her weapon and dropped the illusion of fire. Then she reached for his chestnut-brown hand and concentrated. Too weak, she shook her head. "I can't!"

"Do it!" Guruma commanded.

Forrorrois bit her lip as she tightened her hold on his hand. He pulled her upward while the black comets overwhelmed her consciousness. As her body contracted at her mental command she felt her grip slip from his growing fingertips. Exhaustion dulled the panic that should have overtaken her mind when she suddenly found herself tumbling freely in the air. Guruma's firm grip returned, enveloping her entirely in his palm as he caught her tiny form.

"Get us out of here, Nur!" Guruma ordered.

Her stomach lurched forward with the shifting planes of existence. The sound of hoofs against metal floor plates clanged painfully in her ears. Peering between Guruma's fingers, she flinched when Nur pulled his wings back and charged through the seemingly closed door into the corridor. Several Dramudam scattered from his path, flattening themselves against the walls. Forrorrois pictured the ship in her mind for Nur to follow. In moments, he skidded to a halt in front of Bio Med. Leenon rushed from her office into the corridor.

"What is going on out here?!" Leenon demanded then she froze in mid-sentence. "Guruma!" she gasped, stunned by the Dramudam founder sitting on the back of what must have seemed like a strange four-legged creature with folded red leather wings, then her eyes fell to his arms. "Trager! I need a med team now! Emergency triage!"

The sound of running feet echoed everywhere. Nur shied from the sudden swarm of beings flexing his red leathery wings in warning.

Steady Nur, Forrorrois soothed in his mind.

"Take him," Guruma ordered, slipping Trager's torn body into the waiting arms of the female med techs.

"Let me down," Forrorrois begged as she strained to see between Guruma's fingers.

"He's in good hands, Forrorrois, let them do their job," Guruma urged, cupping her tiny form close to him as he slid from Nur's back.

A voice from behind them made Guruma turn. Forrorrois moved to speak but stopped, sensing Guruma's attention shift to one being in particular.

"Is that you, Guruma? In the flesh?" Commander Thoren gasped.

Guruma rested his free hand on the commander's shoulder then pulled him into a tight hug, guarding Forrorrois with his other hand. "Yes, I've missed you, Thoren," Guruma whispered.

Thoren closed his arms around the older Eldatek in a frantic hug. "It's been too long, dear friend."

Forrorrois looked up from Guruma's cupped hand at her commander, when the two Eldatek males separated.

"Yes, it has," Guruma replied, holding her up for Thoren to see. "Forrorrois found a way to cross into the Plane of Deception," as he rested his free hand on the Beliespeir's withers. "Nur was the key."

Thoren bowed deeply towards Nur. "Thank you, Nur, for the risk you took. You've returned three fine Dramudam—I'm forever in your debt."

Forrorrois smiled when Nur mimicked Thoren's action and bowed his head back towards Thoren.

"Where are my manners?" Thoren exclaimed. "You must all be exhausted."

"Thank you, Thoren. Nur and I would like a place where we won't be such a spectacle. If I recall, there are a few isolation rooms right in Bio Med that will do just fine. And Forrorrois really should have someone tend to her shoulder once Leenon can spare a med tech from the team working on Trager—he's been dreadfully mauled."

Thoren grew more serious. "Of course, Leenon informed me on the way here," he replied. "Med Tech," Thoren called to the nearest free crewmember who had been staring at them, "those isolation rooms will be fine. Please make them ready for our guests. And have Forrorrois tended to immediately."

The Eldatek female shook herself out of her daze at seeing Guruma standing in the flesh before her and bowed deeply. "Yes, sir, please come with me, Guruma," she said with a wave as she headed into Bio Med.

Forrorrois smiled as Guruma carried her protectively from the corridor and placed her onto the center of a stretcher not far from where they were working on Trager.

"Nur and I won't be far away," Guruma said as he glanced towards

Leenon's team working frantically on Trager. "Enlarge yourself, then rest. Let Leenon do her job and Trager will be fine."

"Thank you, Guruma," Forrorrois replied then she closed her eyes and concentrated. The air grew chilled as she enlarged, but the effort was more than the reserves she had left. Heaving a sigh, Forrorrois embraced unconsciousness, comforted by Trager's essence nearby.

****

Jack stepped into the hangar bay of Forrorrois' base and spotted Yononnon tinkering with his one-seat long-distance scout. He stepped over to the large Eldatek male and nodded to him when he turned to face him.

"How is Danielle doing this cycle?" Yononnon asked in Intergaltic.

"She's still upset by the turn of events. Frank is keeping an eye on her. I wish George was here to help her stay positive," Jack replied.

"Yes, Forrorrois' brother would be a great comfort for Danielle and Frank," Yononnon said with a nod. "They must know that Forrorrois will bring Celeste back home again, but she must do it with the consent of the council or Celeste will never be safe."

Jack heaved a sigh. He hated to admit what Yononnon was suggesting was correct. "I agree."

Yononnon gave him an odd look. "Jack, I sense something else is troubling you."

Jack pulled on a smile. "Is it that obvious?"

Yononnon shrugged. "You've been agitated since you last communicated with General Caldwell."

He couldn't fool the perceptive subcommander. "I have to report to the base after second kel. General Caldwell has insisted that I am examined by the flight med tech, before I can resume my duties. I'm concerned that his request may be a trap," Jack admitted.

Yononnon hesitated. "You think this because of what happened with Captain Perkins?"

"Yes," Jack replied. "But if I don't go, then the general will have me arrested for disobeying a direct order."

Yononnon traced his silky mustache with his fingertips as he shook his head. "This is very serious, Jack."

"Yes, it is," Jack agreed.

"Jack, I must insist on monitoring your encounter with this flight med tech and General Caldwell," Yononnon stated. "If it is a trap, as you suspect, then Forrorrois would never forgive me if I allowed you to be harmed."

Jack studied Yononnon for a moment. What the Dramudam subcommander suggested could place him in direct violation of the Isolation Treaty, but the risk for a double-cross by the general was greater. He took a deep breath and let it out slowly. "All right," he finally answered, "but you must remain on your scout. The security on the base has been heightened since Forrorrois' escape."

Yononnon nodded. "I will remain shrouded unless you are in danger. Then I will proceed with caution to extract you."

Jack paused. He knew Yononnon wouldn't sit quietly by if he was in danger, but it was comforting to know that he had backup if he needed it. "All right. I'll tell Frank and Danielle that we'll be gone for the rest of the cycle."

"I'll prepare my scout," Yononnon replied.

Jack walked back into the living quarters, uncertain how the day was going to go.

✵✵✵✵✵✵✵✵✵✵

Jack pulled his truck up to the gate at the base and nodded to the airman that waved him through. He knew that Yononnon was just above him in his shrouded one-seat long-distance scout. Jack signaled as he turned towards the infirmary and drove to the parking lot just outside the building. When he got out of his truck, he spotted the general approaching him.

"It's a relief to see you, Colonel," General Caldwell said as Jack shut the door of his truck and stepped onto the sidewalk.

Jack saluted then waited for the general to salute back before he dropped his hand to his side. He limped slightly from his still tender ankle as he approached his superior officer. "It's good to be seen, sir," Jack replied.

"I see you are still recovering," Caldwell observed.

"It'll be a few more weeks before my ankle is completely healed," Jack said. "But my arm is doing pretty good," he added, flexing his arm.

"Amazing," Caldwell remarked as they walked into the building. "So, Forrorrois finally let you go back to your cabin?"

"Yes," Jack lied. "I got back there last night."

"She is very enigmatic," Caldwell said as they turned down the corridor towards the flight surgeon's office.

"Why do you say that, sir?" Jack asked.

"I had personnel all over the hospital. Forrorrois was covered from the moment I informed her that I wanted to extend her stay on the base to the moment she got onto her craft. I still don't understand how she managed to get you off the base."

Jack paused. "I don't know," he confessed. "Like I told you earlier on the phone, I was knocked unconscious—probably by a stun weapon—and woke up in the room that she held me in until last night."

"She must have had an accomplice," Caldwell stated. He stopped in front of the flight surgeon's office and opened the door. "Well, we're here, Colonel. Hopefully, the flight surgeon can shed some light on what happened to you while you were in Forrorrois' custody.

Jack had an uneasy feeling as he stepped inside the office and spotted the two chairs in front of the flight surgeon's desk.

The flight surgeon looked up from a chart he'd been studying on his desk. He immediately came to his feet and saluted. "General, Colonel, please come in," the uniformed doctor stated.

Jack and the general saluted him back then took seats in front of the desk. The flight surgeon resumed his seat and looked back down at the chart—Jack saw his name on the tab.

"You seem to be recovering nicely, Colonel," the man stated. "I suspect that you will be limping for a few more weeks, but your arm seems to have made remarkable progress. From my report it states that your arm was broken."

Jack flexed his arm and smiled. "Yes, Forrorrois used what she called a bioknitter on it—quite a remarkable device."

"I agree, we could use one of those around here," the flight surgeon replied. "I suppose you're wondering why I asked the general to sit in on this conversation."

Jack glanced at the general then back at the doctor. "Actually, yes."

"Colonel, I've found a strange anomaly in your blood," the flight surgeon announced.

Jack stiffened, very aware that the general was studying him closely. "What do you mean by strange anomaly?"

"Well, the anomaly seems to be organic in nature, but I was concerned that I found the same anomaly in Forrorrois' blood as well. Do you happen to know what this might be?"

Jack could feel the general's stare intensify. His answer would be critical.

"I'm not one-hundred percent sure," Jack replied, slowly. "Forrorrois had injected me with something when I was shot by the leader of that terrorist group which attacked the base a few years back. Forrorrois told me that it would help me recover faster."

"May I ask why you didn't report this when it happened?" the flight surgeon asked, leaning forward.

Jack shrugged. "I thought they were like an antibiotic. I didn't realize that they would remain in my blood this long."

Before the flight surgeon could comment, General Caldwell broke his silence. "Colonel, that answer isn't acceptable. You knowingly withheld information."

Before Jack could reply, the general continued. "Colonel, have you had contact with Captain Perkins since the hangar collapse?"

Jack pulled on his best poker face, not surprised by the sudden change in the direction of the conversation. "No, why do you ask?"

"I'm asking because I believe that Captain Perkins was instrumental in extracting you from the hospital during Forrorrois' escape," the general stated. "I also believe that Captain Perkins has had the same physical modifications performed on him as Forrorrois had by Commander Collinar of the Utahar. Blood and tissue tests showed identical genetic anomalies in both Forrorrois and Captain Perkins—although we didn't find evidence of the anomaly that we found in your blood. Until now, we'd never had a reason to make the comparison."

"General, where's Captain Perkins now?" Jack asked, cautiously, knowing full well he was safe on the Tollon.

"The captain escaped when we tried to take him into custody. He's been AWOL ever since. We won't be making that mistake with you, Colonel," the general replied. Jack watched as his commanding officer rose from his chair and opened the door to the corridor.

Jack didn't say a word as the general waved in two MPs. He just looked down and closed his eyes as he subvocalized. 'Computer, alert Yononnon to prepare to extract me when I exit the building.' When he reopened his eyes, the MPs were positioned on either side of him.

"Please, come with us, sir," the MP to his right requested.

Jack sighed and rose from his chair. "General, please reconsider. I've always put the best interest of this country first in all my decisions."

Caldwell just shook his head. "Colonel, I've humored you long enough. You've become a liability to the security of this base. You'll be examined more thoroughly to uncover any other anomalies. In the meantime, I'm having you taken into custody. Take him away."

Jack stepped towards the MPs. "I'm sorry you feel that way, General."

"I'm sorry, sir," one of the MPs began as he pulled out handcuffs from a holder on his belt.

Jack heaved a sigh and offered his wrists in front of him to allow the man to cuff him without resisting. He was grateful that the security officer cuffed him in front to make it less obvious—a courtesy offered to him as an officer.

He allowed the MPs to lead him out of the flight surgeon's office and down the hallway to the front entrance of the building. General

Caldwell followed after them, and then paused as they reached the front steps.

Outside, in the parking lot, Jack spotted the MPs' squat vehicle parked next to his truck. Suddenly, the whine of a stun rifle charging made Jack look up. He glanced over towards the sound in time to see a flash of red. A second flash immediately followed the first. The two MPs crumpled to the ground on either side of him. Jack scooped the keys for his handcuffs from the belt of one of the MPs then quickly inserted the key and unlocked them. A flash of bluish-green lanced past Jack towards his truck, reducing the vehicle down to a toy. Jack dropped the cuffs and keys to the ground then ran over and scooped up his miniaturized truck.

Jack grinned as Yononnon dropped the EM warping shield on his scout. He had landed the craft just meters away in the grass between the building and the parking lot. Yononnon stood with the visor down on his helmet in a defensive position from the cockpit with the canopy hinged open—his stun rifle poised. The ladder was extended on the side of the craft waiting for Jack.

"Stop him!" the general's voice sounded from the door of the building.

A shot rang out behind him, but the aim was wild.

"Come quickly, Jack," Yononnon stated in Intergaltic.

"You don't have to tell me twice," Jack replied back, in Intergaltic, running towards the scout with his truck in the crux of his arm like a football.

A second shot rang out behind him, as Jack grabbed the rung of the ladder with one hand while he held his truck close with his other hand. The bullet rang off the side of the ship, barely missing him. Spurred on by adrenaline, Jack was up the ladder and over the lip of the cockpit in a heartbeat. Yononnon blanketed the area with a broad stun beam dropping everyone with weapons as they emerged from the building.

Jack looked back and saw the general glaring at him.

"We must leave, Jack. Reinforcements are coming. For your safety, please go into the rear cabin below," Yononnon stated.

Jack turned away from the general's stare and did as he was told. He barely reached the bunk when he heard the canopy snick shut over the cockpit. The scout lifted straight up—dropping Jack onto the bunk face first. He exhaled as the craft leveled out and looked over at his truck, still cradled in his arm. With a sigh, he closed his eyes and resigned himself to the fact he was now a wanted man. His career was over—along with any chance of retaining his retirement.

He heard the computer respond to Yononnon's request to bring up the EM warping shield. The sudden ring of his cell phone made him open his eyes. Jack glanced around then patted his pants pocket and pulled the phone out to look at the screen. His eyes widened when he saw the call was from none other than the general himself.

Hesitantly, Jack answered the call. "Stern, here."

"Colonel, I don't know what your game is, but if I catch you on this base again, be forewarned that I am giving orders to shoot you on sight," the general stated.

"Understood, sir," Jack replied, calmly. "And you should also be aware that Collinar is back in the custody of the Dramudam."

"Why are you doing this, Colonel? Why are you betraying this country like this?"

"General, I'm not betraying anyone. I'm protecting this planet. And if it means that I have to resign from the Air Force to do it, then consider this my resignation," Jack stated.

"Resignation accepted, Colonel," General Caldwell growled. "Your covert activities have been reported and you have been listed as an enemy combatant. I was hoping to bring you in peacefully."

Jack shook his head. "I appreciate the heads up, General—I wish that this could have gone a better way."

"Me too," the general replied, his tone slightly softened.

Jack's heart pounded in his chest as he terminated the call and stared up at the ceiling panels above the bunk. The general had been busy. His eyes widened when he thought about the general's threat. Panic sliced though him when he hit the speed dial on his phone. The phone rang twice before there was an answer.

"Agent Aster," the voice replied with a slight British accent.

"Aster, this is Colonel Stern…well just Stern. Can you talk right now?"

"Jack! What a coincidence. Bloody hell is breaking loose down here, what have you been doing? I just saw your name listed as an enemy combatant five minutes ago."

"Long story, Aster," Jack replied. "I just need to know if it's more than just me."

"No. Frank and Danielle have been named as well, along with George. And tell Forrorrois to keep her head down."

Jack sat up quickly on the bunk. "Frank and Danielle are safe, Aster. Have they picked up George yet?"

"Thank goodness Forrorrois' parents are safe," Aster breathed. "So far, I don't have any word that they've picked up George yet. The paperwork said he's scheduled for pickup this afternoon in Las Vegas."

"Not if I can help it," Jack stammered.

"Brilliant," Aster replied. "I've only got a few minutes before I have to report to my director's office. Is there anything else I should know?"

"At the moment, the less you know the better," Jack shot back. "I've got to go."

"Good luck, Jack, keep them safe," Aster replied.

"I'll do my best," Jack replied then he terminated the call and limped up the three short steps to the cockpit of Yononnon's small scout.

"Yononnon, we're not heading back to the base yet. We've got to get George."

Yononnon glanced over at him. "What happened?"

"He's going to be arrested. We have to reach him before the authorities do."

"Give me coordinates and I'll take you to him," Yononnon replied.

"Thank you. Start heading for the far coast of this continent," Jack stated as he hit the speed dial on his cell phone. Three rings sounded before there was an answer.

"Hello?" George's voice answered.

"George, this is Jack," he began in English.

"Jack, is there something wrong?" George replied, concerned.

"Yes, where are you?"

"I'm in my hotel room in Vegas, why?"

"I'm coming to pick you up. Hold on a moment," Jack ordered. He switched to Intergaltic. "Yononnon, get George's coordinates from this signal."

"I've got his position," Yononnon replied in Intergaltic.

"George, the F.B.I. is coming to arrest you," Jack stated, switching back to English.

"What?! Crap! What did Danica do this time?" George stammered.

Jack took a deep breath then let it out slowly. "Believe me, George, it wasn't her fault this time," Jack answered.

"No, it was probably that general's fault," George shot back.

Normally, Jack would have laughed at his sarcasm, but time was running out. "George, you've been listed as an enemy combatant, so have your parents. Your parents are safe, but I need to pick you up, as soon as possible. Pack your bags—I'll be there in twenty minutes. Keep your phone on so we can track it. Can you get to an open area?"

"Ah, yeah," George stammered. "There's a heliport on the roof of the hotel."

"Perfect. Do you still have that stun weapon your sister gave you?"

"Yeah..." George replied, hesitantly.

"Good, be prepared to use it if someone tries to stop you. Now, get packing, I'll see you on the roof."

"OK," George replied.

Jack looked over at Yononnon. "How long?"

"I'll get us there in fewer than nine tol," Yononnon answered. "Hang on."

Less than 6 minutes! Jack thought as his eyes widened. He gripped the back of Yononnon's command chair to keep his footing as the subcommander pushed the craft to the atmospheric limit and thundered towards Nevada.

****

Jack spotted the heliport on the roof of the Vegas strip hotel that George had been staying in and pointed. Yononnon nodded and guided his shrouded long-distance scout towards the circle. As they approached for a landing they were surprised when a helicopter suddenly headed for the same landing pad. Yononnon swerved to one side as Jack gripped the back of his command chair.

"There are armed Humans on that craft," Yononnon announced.

"Do you have a fix on George, yet?" Jack asked, looking at the holograph of the 3D building schematic floating between them and the controls.

"Yes, he's in the stairwell two floors from the roof," Yononnon stated, pointing at the moving point in the holograph. "There are two armed Humans one-flight below and gaining on his position.

Jack watched the side door of the helicopter slide open and six men with weapons drawn jumped down to the ground. All were wearing body armor and the letters F.B.I. were printed across their backs.

"Land on the roof and block their way to the stairwell. As soon as you're down, stun them," Jack ordered.

"By Guruma's hand," Yononnon replied, dropping his EM warping shield.

The F.B.I. agents came to an abrupt stop as the Dramudam one-seat scout abruptly appeared in front of them. Yononnon was out of his seat with his stun rifle leveled on the group before they could recover their senses. In a flash, the subcommander blanketed the area with a flash of red. With a second flash, Yononnon stunned the pilot. The air fell silent except for the slowly turning blades of the helicopter coming to a halt. The six men were crumpled on the ground and the pilot was slumped in his seat.

Jack turned at the sound of the door slamming open. He spotted George as he ran out of the door with two bags over his shoulder. George was almost 30 years old, but he had a youthful face that normally shone with a boyish smile—at the moment his brown eyes were wide with panic.

"George, this way!" Jack called out. "Up the ladder!"

"They're right behind me!" George yelled back.

"You're covered!" Jack replied.

Yononnon shifted his sights to the door and waited.

George was scrambling up the ladder when the door slammed open once more and two men with F.B.I. printed on their jackets poured out. He flinched when Yononnon fired just above his head at the men, dropping them just short of the roof access door. George hesitated as he reached the cockpit and spotted the large Eldatek male. Nervously, he glanced at the extended chestnut-brown hand much to Jack amusement.

"George, this is Subcommander Yononnon, he's with me," Jack stated, in English.

George cautiously took Yononnon's hand and climbed into the cockpit.

"Come below," Jack continued.

Yononnon nodded to them and resumed his seat as Jack guided George down the short steps into the rear cabin. George stumbled and fell onto the bunk. When he looked up at Jack, he was shaking. Jack steadied himself against the wall panel when the craft lifted off.

"Are you all right?" Jack asked.

George nodded. "Yeah, I barely left my room when I heard these guys coming down the hall. One of them called out my name. When I turned to look at them, they pulled their guns and told me halt or they'd shoot. I was next to the door for the stairs so I dove into the stairwell and just started running up. I didn't even have a chance to pull out the stun weapon Danica had given me."

Jack walked over to him and studied his brown eyes set against his pale face. Then he placed his hand on his shoulder. "You did fine,

George. Luckily, Yononnon got to the helicopter on the roof before they reached you."

George looked up at him, stunned. A lock of light brown hair was hanging in his eyes. "I think that Yononnon guy is bigger than Trager. Who is he?"

Jack smiled. "Yononnon is a subcommander from the Tollon—he requested a leave of absence to stay with your parents while your sister is off-world."

"Wow, I'm glad he's here."

"Me too," Jack admitted. "Your parents have been anxious to see you."

"Any word yet on Celeste?" George asked as he slipped the shoulder strap of one of his bags from his shoulder and set it on the bunk beside him.

Jack sat down beside George and heaved a sigh. "It's complicated, but we've found out that Celeste is on Elda."

George hesitated. "Isn't that where Trager's from? That's good news, right?"

"Yes, that's where Trager is from," Jack replied then he shook his head. "As for being good news, unfortunately, no it's not. Neeha, Trager's mother was the one that ordered Celeste's kidnapping."

George's brown eyes widened. "What?!"

"It was a political move," Jack explained. "Believe me, George, your sister is doing everything she can to fight this and get Celeste back. But in the meantime, we have to take care of ourselves until she can return."

"Jack, this is totally crazy! I still don't understand what's happened. And I definitely don't understand why my parents and I have been listed as enemy combatants."

"I agree. I've been listed as well," Jack confessed.

"You too?"

Jack nodded. "Yes, I was almost arrested on the base this afternoon. Luckily, Yononnon came with me as backup and got me out. They've discovered the zendra in my blood. General Caldwell felt that this compromised me and has declared me a security risk."

"Jack…doesn't the general know that you and my sister risk your lives for this planet?"

Jack shrugged. "It depends on your perspective. At least I don't have to hide anymore."

"Yeah, but what about my parents? What about me? What are we suppose to do? We can't go back to our lives, not with the F.B.I. after us."

"Well, for now, we go to your sister's base. She's got plenty of supplies for us so we'll be fine for the time being."

George shook his head. "I never understood why Danica chose to live in secret—until now. I can't believe I'm fugitive."

Jack rested his hand on the young man's shoulder. "We'll figure something out, George. Now, when you see your parents, keep it positive. Your mom is very upset about Celeste being taken by Neeha. She needs you to be strong right now."

George nodded. "I'll do my best."

"Good, man," Jack replied.

Suddenly, George panicked. "Jack, what about my props? I just finished packing them last night—I had them shipped into storage this morning. I was getting ready to go see my parents."

Jack smiled as he pulled the reduction weapon from the weapons locker in the cabin. "Let me ask Yononnon if we can make a side trip and get your props. We'll take them with us."

George's eyes widened. "That would be great…" he stammered.

Jack nodded as he climbed back up into the cockpit. It was the least he could do for George. Outwardly, he remained calm, but Jack's mind was churning as he calculated the ramifications of the day's events. He could only pray that he would hear from Forrorrois soon and that her news would be good.

CHAPTER 11

Forrorrois dozed lightly in the chair next to Trager's bed in Bio Med. When she awoke, she found him watching her. "Trager," she gasped, unfolding herself stiffly from her seat. "Trager...you're awake!"

Tears began to stream down his face when she touched his cheek. "You're real—" he whispered. "This is real!"

"Yes! This is all real," she replied, kissing his tears. "I thought I'd lost you forever this time."

With effort, Trager raised a hand and caught hers. She trembled when he brushed his fingertips along her cheek and lips. Then he slipped his hand under her hair and drew her closer. She didn't resist, allowing him to lightly taste her lips. When he pulled her closer, she thrilled at his new found strength while he hungrily ravaged her mouth with frantic kisses.

"Help me up so that I can hold you," he gasped. "I need to know this is real!"

Forrorrois pulled back slightly and shook her head. "Stay still, Trager, you need to be careful. You just had surgery..."

"Then lie with me, just don't leave me," he urged.

Forrorrois looked at the narrow bed and hesitated. Then she saw the need in his eyes and gently traced her hand along the side of his face. "Oh, ashwan, I would never do that," she whispered and slipped into the hollow of his arm beside him. How her body thrilled to his touch...his spicy scent...his taste. Gingerly, she laid her head on his shoulder and melted into his side as if she had never been separated from him.

"I've missed this so much," he whispered, lightly stroking her temple with his free hand.

She smiled when his breathing slowed. The steady rhythm lulled her mind peacefully back to sleep.

****

Trager breathed deeply as he held Forrorrois while she dozed in his arms on the narrow bunk in Bio Med. It was still hard for him to believe that after four revolution he was back on the Tollon. Forrorrois had found a way to rescue him and Guruma from the Plane of Deception. He couldn't love her more than he did that moment as she lay sleeping against his side. At the sound of the door panel sliding open he looked over and spotted Leenon as she stepped into the room.

"Ah, you're awake," Leenon whispered.

"Yes," Trager whispered back.

Forrorrois stirred as they spoke and opened her eyes. "I must have fallen asleep," she murmured.

"Forrorrois, could you step out while I examine Trager?" Leenon asked.

Trager panicked, pulling a protective arm around her. "No—she stays!"

Leenon moved to object, but Forrorrois shook her head. "Hush, Trager. I won't leave the room if you want me here, but I agree with Leenon that it would be easier to examine you if I wasn't in the way."

His anxiety intensified as he struggled with the decision. Forrorrois reached back and lightly touched his face with her fingertips and gave him a gentle smile. The tension in his body eased.

He watched as she sat up slowly and reluctantly pulled away from his warm touch. "I love you," she whispered in English, leaning over and giving him a longing kiss. "I'll be right here." Then she slipped out of the bed and stood over by the chair.

"You were extremely lucky Forrorrois found you when she did. A half a kel or more and you wouldn't have made it," Leenon stated, examining her bioscanner. "You've kept yourself fit these past four revolution...." She set down the scanner on the bunk and steadied her hand. "We've all missed you..." she said, unable to keep the tremor from her voice.

Trager reached up and touched his old shipmate's hand. "I've missed all of you as well. Everything's going to be fine once I finally see my daughter, Celeste, then Forrorrois and I will be a family once more."

Leenon looked away, distraught.

He watched as Forrorrois stepped forward and slipped her arm around Leenon's waist. "Trager and I will get Celeste back, Leenon. Everything will be fine."

"Forrorrois is right, I've been watching," Trager continued. "I know now what part my mother, Neeha, has played. She is the one to blame!"

Leenon tensed at Trager's words. Forrorrois reached out and placed her hand on Trager's shoulder.

"You mustn't get excited, ashwan," Forrorrois urged. "As soon as you are healthy, we'll head back to Elda and face Neeha. Together, we'll find a way to negotiate for Celeste's release, but not until. Our daughter is a strong little girl. No matter how angry your mother is about our joining, she won't harm her as long as she sees Celeste as a way to keep her relationship with Bohata. Besides, Trager, if it hadn't been for her actions, I never would have sought out the Beliespeir, Nur. I never would have found you in time."

Trager thought on her words and wished he could find forgiveness in his heart for his mother's actions. Finally, he nodded. Forrorrois was right. Once he was healed they would face Neeha together and find a way to get Celeste back.

****

Jack sat in his room at Forrorrois' base. He had originally gone back to his cabin, but his home had already been invaded by the F.B.I. and searched very thoroughly. Luckily, he hadn't kept anything there of value for several years—shortly after he had been shot by that crazy Hartcourt woman. Ever since Forrorrois had injected him with zendra to save his life, Jack had always known in the back of his mind, that this day would come. He glanced over at the picture of Jenny and

Carrie smiling at him on his nightstand. They had been gone for so long. The sound of a knock on his door made him look up.

Jack cleared his throat. "Come in," he answered. He was surprised when the door opened and he found Yononnon standing just outside.

"Jack, I just received word from the Tollon," the large Eldatek male announced in Intergaltic.

Jack straightened. "And?" he answered back in Intergaltic.

"Forrorrois found a way to reach Trager and Guruma. She has brought them back to the Tollon."

Jack jumped to his feet from the edge of his bed. "That's great news!"

Yononnon hesitated. Jack looked at him, growing concern. "Tell me the rest."

"Trager was wounded just before Forrorrois reached them. Trager's now in Bio Med, but Commander Thoren has assured me that he is recovering."

Jack closed his eyes for a moment as he exhaled the breath he suddenly realized he been holding. "Thank goodness. I don't think Forrorrois could take much more heartache."

Yononnon nodded. "I agree. The commander also told me that there seems to be a saboteur on board the Tollon."

Jack grew concerned. "What happened?"

"There were several explosions in a supply wing off of the hangar bay, near a secure storeroom that is used for fuel pellet storage."

"Was anyone hurt?" Jack asked.

"Two injuries were reported but they are recovering. I should tell you that Captain Perkins was one of the injured, as well as Alham, one of the master pilots."

Jack's eyes widened. "I thought he'd be safer there," he whispered.

Yononnon's eyes softened. "He's recovering. Master Pilot Instructor Goren is watching over him—he won't let anyone near him. You should know he saved Alham's life."

Jack straightened his shoulders and nodded stiffly. "I could always trust Perkins to make good decisions." Then he paused as he reflected on the other pilot's name. "Alham, isn't she a friend of Forrorrois?"

"Yes, she's also my niece," Yononnon admitted.

Jack looked up at the large subcommander—surprise at the revelation.

Yononnon smiled. "Both Goren and Commander Thoren speak highly of Captain Perkins and from this point forward I will as well. He'll be back to training in a few cycle. And Alham will resume her duties as a master pilot."

"I'm sorry that your family has been pulled into this," Jack confessed.

"No path is safe, especially the path of a Dramudam," Yononnon replied.

Jack nodded. "Does Commander Thoren know who the saboteurs are?"

"No, but he has his suspicions that a member of the Elda high guard has infiltrated his crew. Perkins was targeted to send a message to Forrorrois. I can only assume that Alham just happened to be in the wrong place at the wrong time."

"But Forrorrois wasn't on the Tollon," Jack objected.

"True, but when her ship returned a few cycle ago, Commander Thoren kept the fact that Forrorrois was not on board a secret. Everyone thought she had returned, when in fact she had made her way to the Plane of Deception to rescue Trager and Guruma."

"Amazing, the Council of Elda must really see Forrorrois as a threat if they would send a message like that. Yononnon, we need step up our vigilance to ensure that Forrorrois' family remains safe. We can't afford to have this base compromised a second time."

"I agree," Yononnon replied. Suddenly, the large Eldatek male looked around and backed towards the door. "Forgive me for intruding on you private quarters. I should return back to the hangar bay. A few of the projectiles grazed the skin of my ship this cycle. The damage is cosmetic...."

"Yononnon, relax, please come in and sit down. You're not intruding," Jack assured him, pointing to the chair next to his bed.

Yononnon pulled on a tentative smile as he approached the chair and took a seat. "Thank you."

"You're welcome," Jack replied. He watched as Yononnon glanced around the room and realized that he hadn't had many opportunities to observe American/Earth culture since he had arrived. Yononnon's gaze fell on the picture on his nightstand. Without a word, Jack picked up the simple frame and handed the picture to the subcommander.

Yononnon took the picture and stared at the photograph for a moment before he looked up at Jack, uncertain. "Who are they?"

Jack sighed. "They were my joined one, Carrie, and my daughter, Jenny."

Yononnon looked up, surprised. "I didn't know that you were joined?"

A melancholy smile crossed Jack's lips. "It was a long time ago. We were coming home from her parents' house when we were struck by another vehicle. I was the only one that survived."

Yononnon's face softened. "I'm so sorry, Jack," he said as he gingerly handed the picture back to him.

Jack took the frame and touched the glass that covered the photo lightly before he placed the picture back on his nightstand. "If my daughter, Jenny, was still alive, she'd be the same age as Forrorrois. They are a lot alike—both smart and stubborn."

Yononnon nodded. "It sounds like if they had known each other they would have been friends."

Jack grinned. "Oh, I'm certain of that." He took a cleansing breath and let it out slowly. "Enough of this depressing talk," he continued. "Why don't we go tell George and Forrorrois' parents the good news about Trager? We can gloss over his being wounded for now. They could use some cheering up."

"I agree," Yononnon said as he rose to his feet.

Jack looked up at the large Dramudam and smiled at how much he reminded him of Trager. His heart warmed at the thought that Forrorrois had found a way to bring Trager back from the Plane of Deception. *Maybe now she can find a way to bring Celeste home as well,* he thought.

****

Collinar looked up from the bunk of his cell in the security corridor of the Tollon when he heard footfalls. He almost smiled when he saw Forrorrois stop in front of the purple hue of the force shield that hummed in the doorway of his cell. Several cycle had passed since she had last graced him with her presence. He straightened his green incarceration uniform and nonchalantly glanced at her.

"So, did you find him?" he asked.

"Yes, the information you gave me was very accurate," Forrorrois replied.

"Good," Collinar commented. "It will be a pleasure to have you testify on my behalf when we reach the rehabilitation station."

"It's the least I can do," Forrorrois answered.

Collinar hesitated—surprised that she didn't have the usual challenge in her voice.

"So when will the Tollon reach the rehabilitation station?"

"I'm not sure," Forrorrois replied. "I'll let you know once Commander Thoren has laid in a course."

Collinar raised an inquisitive eyebrow. "I see. So, tell me about the Beliespeir," he asked, changing the topic.

Forrorrois gave him a curious look. "Didn't you ever go there?"

Collinar snorted a laugh. "Come now, what do you think?"

She almost smiled. "You did go there…but they wouldn't reveal themselves to you."

Collinar sobered. "I hear that they can read minds. My thoughts must not have been pure enough."

Forrorrois started to laugh. "You're probably right. Nur didn't offer his assistance until he was certain he could trust me, and even then he went away and consulted with others before he agreed to take me to the Plane of Deception."

"Nur?" Collinar replied, puzzled by the odd name.

"Yes, Nur, he's the Beliespeir that helped me," Forrorrois stated. "He guided me to Trager and Guruma."

"So, Guruma was there?" Collinar asked in amazement.

"Yes, he came back with me and Trager."

"Very interesting," Collinar remarked with an odd smile, regaining his composure. "I bet that will get the Council on Elda all in a stir once they hear that the old Dramudam founder himself has returned."

Forrorrois didn't hide her smile. "They don't know yet, but I'm certain that they will shortly."

"I can only assume that you and Trager have made up for some lost time," he leered. Again, she surprised him and looked away. "What? You could barely keep your eyes off each other when I took you both hostages. Has the fire cooled?"

Forrorrois shook her head.

Collinar was surprised when her shoulders sagged slightly. For a moment she seemed vulnerable. Whatever had happened was still fresh in her mind.

"No...there are beings called the Aethereals that live in the Plane of Deception. Very primitive. Trager had been attacked just before I reached him. He's in Bio Med recovering."

Collinar suddenly felt a disconcerting twinge of concern, surprised at her uncommon candor with him. "He wasn't...permanently injured, was he?"

Forrorrois looked up quickly then shook her head. "I don't know why I bother to tell you anything. He'll be fine," she replied, defensively.

"Well and good then," Collinar remarked, recovering his bravado. "The two of you will be physical in no time."

She rolled her eyes. "You never cease to amaze me, Collinar. You can be so base," she spat. "I've got to go."

"Enjoy Trager while you can," Collinar warned with a sneer.

Forrorrois turned and stared at him. "What do you mean by that?"

Collinar's lips curled smugly. "Only that you're still underestimating your enemy."

Forrorrois clenched her fists. "Why do I even try with you!" she hissed and turned her back on him.

Collinar sat back down on his bunk and grinned. "Come down

and visit me again," he called out as she stormed down the security corridor. His grin melted when she was gone. He leaned back against the wall, bored. Disappointment gnawed at the pit of his stomach that she didn't take his bait to prolong the conversation. *She's just a pawn to be used...not just by me, but by Neeha,* he reminded himself.

****

Forrorrois entered the Tollon's hangar bay and glanced around. Her long-distance scout was parked not far from the repair bay. The side hatch was open and the ramp was extended, but she could see the shimmer of a force shield across the mouth of the opening suggesting that access was being kept to a minimum. With Trager recovering in Bio Med, and Guruma and Nur occupying one of the isolation rooms there as well to keep their arrival known to only key personnel, she felt alone. Maybe speaking with Perkins would help her shake the uncertainty that gnawed inside her. Forrorrois stepped up the ramp to her long-distance scout and was relieved to sense Perkins was onboard. She ordered the rear cabin open and found Perkins sleeping in her bunk. Curious, she looked to her right and found the other bunk down and Alham sleeping in it. At first she smiled then Forrorrois grew concerned when she noticed that her friend and fellow pilot had an oxygen mask over her nose and mouth.

Forrorrois dropped to her knees beside Alham's side and reached over to take her pulse. Alham's eyes opened slowly then she smiled up at her.

"Forrorrois, you're back," she whispered.

"Yes. What happened, Alham?" Forrorrois asked, touching her hand to her friend's clay-brown forehead.

"Perkins and I had a bit of bad luck in a storage cell off of the hangar bay. We were trapped for over a kel before the maintenance crew could reach us," Alham whispered.

Forrorrois looked back at Perkins and was relieved to see him waking up.

245

"Perkins, how did this happen?" she asked.

But before Perkins could answer, Goren stepped into the cabin.

"Forrorrois, I'm sorry I was unable to speak with you before you came in here," he said as the door slide shut. "There's a spy on board the Tollon and they had set a trap for Perkins. Luckily, Alham and he were able to escape from serious harm with some quick thinking on Perkins' part. Still, they did suffer from carbon dioxide poisoning while they were locked for a period of time in the unventilated storage cell. But, Kela assures me that they will fully recover after some rest. At my request, she's been checking on them regularly."

Forrorrois exhaled as she shook her head. So much had happen while she was away. "Have they caught the spy yet?"

"Not yet, but whomever they are, they seem to have access to the security systems," Goren answered. "Key moments in the corridor surveillance recordings have been blanked out. Peldor is investigating every being onboard that would have that level of access."

Forrorrois got to her feet and brushed a hand against Alham's cheek. "Get well, my dear friend," she whispered.

"I will, Forrorrois," Alham whispered back. "I'm just glad that Perkins is unharmed."

"Me too, I promised Jack I'd get him home in one piece," Forrorrois said as she glanced over at Perkins. "How are you feeling, Perkins?"

"I'm doing fine," Perkins replied. "I'm just glad to see that you're back."

When Perkins moved to get out of bed, Goren stopped him. "Yes, Perkins is doing well, but Kela has ordered bed rest for both of them for at least another cycle."

Forrorrois grinned when she felt Perkins surprise at the older Silmanon's firm hand. "You heard Goren, Perkins, lay back down," Forrorrois laughed as she took a seat at the small table.

Perkins' shoulder slumped as he glanced at Goren then did as he was told.

"So, is it true, Forrorrois? Did you bring back Trager and Guruma back from the Plane of Deception?" Goren asked.

Forrorrois felt all eyes in the cabin on her. Any hope she might have of containing such news was dwindling fast. She nodded. "Yes… Trager is recovering from surgery."

Alarmed, Perkins sat up, before Goren could stop him a second time. "What happened?"

Forrorrois looked over at Perkins and then at Goren and Alham. The tears pressed as the fatigue began to overtake her. "Trager was attacked by a savage creature that inhabits the Plane of Deception just before Nur and I arrived—he was badly injured."

The room grew quiet as Goren took a seat at the table with her.

"He's going to be all right though, right?" Perkins insisted.

Forrorrois felt their sympathy and concern—it was more than she could handle at the moment. She sniffed back the tears and straightened her shoulders. "Yes, Leenon assured me that Trager will recover fully."

"That's good to hear," Goren replied.

Everyone remained silent as they waited for Forrorrois to say more. The refuge she was hoping for was no longer onboard her ship. She looked around and rose from her chair. "I should get back to Bio Med and check on things. I'm glad that you both are all right," she stammered. "Goren, please keep an eye on things for me."

"Of course," Goren replied, rising with her. "Let me know how Trager's doing."

"I will. Perkins, Alham, get healthy. Peldor will find out who did this," she said as she headed for the door.

"We'll be fine," Perkins called out to her when she left the cabin and down the ramp of the cargo hold. Her worst fear had been realized. They were trying to get to her through Perkins and because of that, two of her friends were hurt. All she wanted was a private place to think, but for now she needed to go back and see if Trager was awake after Leenon had sedated him to make him rest.

✳✳✳✳✳✳✳✳✳✳✳

Forrorrois was disappointed when she arrived in Bio Med to find that Trager was still unconscious from a second round of surgery to repair the damage inflicted by the Aethereal's attack. She turned to leave when she was surprised by Guruma motioning for her to come into the isolation room that he and Nur were sharing while they were aboard the Tollon.

"Forrorrois please come and sit with Nur and me. I wish to speak with you," he said as he stood just inside the door of the large rectangular room.

Even though she was exhausted and wanted only to find a place to be alone, she nodded respectfully. "Certainly, Guruma." She smiled at Nur as she entered the isolation room.

Guruma motioned toward the table against the wall. "Please take a seat and have something to eat. Nur told me that you seem hungry."

Forrorrois looked over at the large black furred equine-shaped creature with its slightly unfurled red bat-like wings and nodded. "Actually, I am," she admitted, taking a seat and looking down at the plate of yahwa fruit and bread spread with red towan paste. The spicy scent filled her nose as she raised a slice to her lips. It had been a while since she had the condiment and was pleasantly surprised at how much she had missed the hot spicy flavor. She chased it down with a slice of the orange pulpy fruit. Embarrassed, she quickly dabbed the juice that ran down her chin.

Guruma averted his eyes as he raised a slice of bread and towan paste up in his hand and took a bit. He sighed as he savored the taste. After he swallowed, a blissful smile spread across his lips.

"I'd almost forgotten what the real thing tasted like," he commented as he leaned back in his chair. "Somehow, I could never quite conjure up the unique flavor and fire of a well aged towan paste. Nur, are you certain that you don't want to try some?" he offered to the large Beliespeir standing near the table.

No, thank you, Nur's response echoed in her mind.

"Your loss," Guruma replied with a shrug.

She tried to suppress her amusement from Nur's aversions to the thought of eating such a thing then she glanced over at the Dramudam founder. "Pardon my observation, Guruma, but I was unaware that you were a telepath."

Guruma snorted a laugh. "I'm not by any stretch of the imagination, but my time in the Plane of Deception has…how did Ma'Kelda put it…'opened my mind'. Let's just say that I'm more empathetic than I was before my prolonged stay there."

Forrorrois grew quiet at the mention of Ma'Kelda's name.

"I'm sorry, I didn't mean to open old wounds," Guruma said as he put down his partially eaten slice of bread.

Forrorrois tried to pull on a smile. "No, it's all right. Ma'Kelda was a brave being that risked everything to help me escape."

"And it cost her life, at Collinar's hands," Guruma replied.

"Yes," Forrorrois said as she looked down at her hands.

Nur stepped forward, nervously pulling his red leather wings closer to his silky black equine sides. *You're conflicted by this Collinar's action*, the Beliespeir thought in her mind. *You believe that he cared for her…yet he ended her life? Why did he do such a thing?*

Forrorrois looked up into Nur's liquid black eyes and gently reached out and touched the side of his equine nose.

"Collinar lashed out at her because he thought she had betrayed him, but inside he is deeply filled with remorse for his action because he actually loved her," Forrorrois answered. "Now, he lives with the burden of what he has done."

She was surprised when she felt Guruma studying her and withdrew her hand from Nur.

How very sad, Nur replied. *If you'll excuse me, I wish to find some forage. I will return shortly.*

Forrorrois started when the Beliespeir casually stepped toward the door then vanished as he slipped into another dimension.

"If I didn't know better I would almost say that you feel sympathy for him," Guruma said quietly.

Forrorrois looked away, uncomfortable from his observation. "Collinar is a cruel immoral being."

"If you believe that, then why are you going to testify on his behalf?"

"How do you know that?" Forrorrois stated.

"Thoren told me," Guruma replied.

Forrorrois glanced away. "I agreed to testify on his behalf if he would tell me how to bring Trager back from the Plane of Deception," she confessed.

"I see," Guruma said, still studying her.

"He gave the information—I'm honor bound to keep my word."

"Really? But you know in your heart that Collinar would never feel compelled to keep such a promise," Guruma said with a shrug.

Exhaustion and frustration boiled up inside her. "Whether he would or wouldn't, isn't the point, Guruma. I gave my word," she insisted.

Guruma sat quietly for a moment. "Fair enough," he finally replied.

"I'm glad," Forrorrois said tersely, rising to her feet. "Now, if you don't mind, I need to find a place to get some rest."

"Forrorrois," Guruma said as he rose with her. "Before you go, I want to thank you for finding Nur, no matter who provided you with the information. Freeing Trager and me from the Plane of Deception took a tremendous amount of courage and faith."

"You're welcome," she replied.

"You should know that Thoren has changed course and is now heading for Elda. Goren is aware of this, but he has been sworn to secrecy."

Forrorrois' caught her breath as Guruma continued.

"But I must warn you to be cautious around Leenon. Thoren is not certain where her loyalties rest at the moment. The pull of Elda is strong," he warned.

"I must admit, I've been getting conflicting emotions from her lately," Forrorrois began. "But, Leenon has always treated me as her adopted daughter. She would never harm me or Trager. And she definitely wouldn't harm Celeste. She's not a traitor."

"I agree she would never intentionally cause any of you harm," Guruma said, "but until her motives are revealed, we need to proceed with caution. Going forward, I will need to resume working covertly. Nur has agreed to help me to find some of the answers. We will be leaving the Tollon shortly. It's not safe for me now that the word is out that I have returned. Things will become very difficult soon, but please trust that what I'm doing will all work out in the end."

Forrorrois looked up at Guruma and felt he wanted to tell her more, but continued to hold back. She sighed, knowing he would never give her a straight answer, even if she asked him for one.

"Good rest, Guruma," she replied. "I hope to see both you and Nur, before you leave."

"Of course," Guruma answered.

She turned and left the room, more confused by his underlying remorse, then his cryptic request for her to trust him. Inside, a foreboding rose up. She wanted answers, but knew he wouldn't give them to her—at least not yet.

****

Perkins smiled when he spotted Alham in the hangar bay heading for the pilot's equipment room. Kela had released both of them back to duty several days ago and he missed not seeing her around. He hurried from the repair bay and approached her.

"Alham," he called out in Intergaltic.

She turned and smiled as she saw him. "Captain Perkins, it's good to see you."

"I can say the same for you," Perkins replied. "I haven't seen you around."

"I've been busy getting back into the routine of inspecting my ship and going on patrol," she answered. "What have you been up to?"

"I've been qualifying on weapon systems with Goren," Perkins replied.

"When you finish your training with Goren, will you be joining the Dramudam?"

Perkins shook his head. "No, Forrorrois needs me to return to Earth and help with patrols there."

He was surprised when she glanced away briefly at his answer.

"It's a shame. I was almost hoping that you would be assigned to my squadron," she said. "Perkins, could you come with me for a moment."

"Ah, sure," Perkins said as he followed her into the equipment room. No one was there except the two of them. When the door slid shut Alham turned to face him. A nervous feeling formed in his stomach as he felt her appraise him with her eyes.

"I never properly thanked you for the risk you took," Alham said as she closed the space between them.

Perkins backed up clanging into the wall lockers. He was eye-to-eye with the tall Eldatek female—close enough to smell the spiciness of her clay-brown skin. Nervously, he swallowed. "Knowing you're healthy is thanks enough, Alham."

She reached out and traced his cheek bone with her fingertips.

Perkins felt his body react—before he realized what he was doing he leaned forward and kissed her on the lips. To his relief, Alham returned the kiss. Then his eyes widened as she aggressively pressed him against the wall lockers and prolonged the kiss. He glanced down at her hand when she brushed her palm against his stomach, then down his outer thigh.

As she released his lips, Perkins looked around, nervous that someone would walk in on them. When he glimpsed back into her coal black eyes, he was confused by her demure smile.

"Thank you, Captain Perkins," she whispered. "I'm in your debt."

Perkins watched as she pulled away and straightened her uniform. His mouth ached for her lips, but he didn't stop her—still confused. "You're welcome," he whispered back. "Any time."

Alham tasted her lips. "I should prepare for my patrol."

"Of course," Perkins stammered. "And I should get back to the repair bay."

She smiled and turned away while Perkins stumbled towards the door. He barely breathed until he reached the side of Forrorrois' pursuit ship. His body still tingled from the brief encounter. He licked his lips and wished for the moment to continue. "Wow," was all he could say as he caught his breath.

****

Forrorrois walked over to the repair bay and ran her hand along the fresh repairs on the hull of her pursuit ship. She smiled when she sensed Perkins was nearby. He started when she slipped under the wing and surprised him.

"Forrorrois, I didn't see you come over," he stammered in Intergaltic. "How's Trager doing?" he added.

"Trager's doing well, although Leenon is being very cautious with his recovery," she replied in Intergaltic.

"You don't know how glad I am to hear that he's back," Perkins said as he rested his hand on the side of her pursuit, recovering his composure. "So what do you think of her?"

Forrorrois glanced at her ship and nodded. "She looks great—you took real good care of her while I was gone. Goren said that your maiden flight went flawless."

Perkins gave her a wry look. "Very sneaky, Forrorrois. You should have warned me that was going to be a test."

"I wanted to make certain that it was a valid reason for you to be flying in open space for anyone that was watching. Beside, Goren agreed that you were ready," she replied. "Goren also told me that you are ready to qualify on weapons."

Perkins straightened. "That's right. He said he wants me to be ready for full power target practice in a few cycle."

"I remember my first time out," Forrorrois said with a grin. "Of course it was a bit more exciting than yours should be."

Perkins gave her an odd look. "Why, what happened?"

"A squadron of Utahar showed up," she replied with a shrug.

Perkins eyes widened. "You're kidding me, right?"

Forrorrois sighed. "Nope, Goren had sent me out with my friend, Ahzell...she saved my butt—more than once." The thought of her friend still caused her heart to ache.

"I don't think I've met an Ahzell," Perkins replied. "Is she on the Tollon?"

Forrorrois shook her head, sadly. "No, she was killed helping Trager and I escape from Collinar's ship."

Perkins shoulders drooped. "I'm sorry, I didn't know."

"It was a long time ago," Forrorrois dismissed. "So how's Alham doing? I haven't seen her since she recovered," she said, changing the topic.

Intrigued at Perkins' hesitation, Forrorrois reached out with her empathic abilities and sensed he was nervous from the mention of her name.

"She's all right, isn't she?" Forrorrois pressed.

"Ah, yes," Perkins replied. "I just saw her in the equipment room, she was...um...preparing for a patrol."

Forrorrois forced herself not to grin as he shifted on his feet.

"All right, Captain," Forrorrois said. "Is there a reason that you're blushing?"

Perkins gave her a horrified look. "No...yes...I don't know," Perkins stammered.

His emotions were confused in her mind, making her change her tact.

"Perkins, you know I'm an empath, I can sense that you're troubled by something. Do you want to talk about it?" Forrorrois offered.

Perkins glanced around then lowered his voice. "I need some advice."

Forrorrois studied him for a moment before she spoke.

"On?"

"On what an Eldatek female means when she kisses a male on the lips," Perkins whispered.

Stunned, Forrorrois looked up at Perkins, uncertain what to say.

"You're talking about Alham?" she ventured.

"Yes..."

Alham's actions were highly irregular. The rules for relationships in the Dramudam were very explicit...but Perkins wasn't a Dramudam...or an Eldatek.

"Did she say why she kissed you?" she asked, cautiously.

"Ah, she said it was to thank me for helping her out when we were caught by that explosion," Perkins replied.

Forrorrois relaxed slightly, now confused by the emotions she was feeling from him. She shrugged her shoulders. "That seems harmless enough."

Perkins shifted on his feet. "I don't think it was just a kiss. Ummm, when she was kissing me, she brushed her hand across my stomach and along my thigh…"

Forrorrois' eyes grew large. After a moment she composed herself. "Was there anything else that you remember that she said before this occurred?"

"We were just catching up. I told her I was preparing to qualify and then she asked me if I was going to be joining the Dramudam when I finished my training with Goren. I told her, no, that I was going to return back to Earth."

Forrorrois shook her head, now more anxious. "Ah, I think you're right, Perkins. I think that was more than a 'thank you' kiss. I should go speak with Alham."

Alarmed, Perkins shook his head. "No—it's all right, I don't want to cause any trouble," he began.

Forrorrois smiled. "No, it's not that Perkins. If you had told her you were becoming a Dramudam, then she wouldn't have been so forward. There's a fraternization rule in the Dramudam."

"Oh? Oh!" he gasped. "What should I do?"

Forrorrois softened her stance and shrugged her shoulders. "I don't know, Perkins. Do you like Alham?"

"Well, yes," he admitted.

"Do you want me to talk to her?"

"Ah, no, I mean, I just don't know how to read her signals," he confessed. "I'm new at this alien relations thing."

Forrorrois struggled not to smile. "Then I suggest you read up on the Eldatek culture. It's matrilineal and the females are definitely used to being dominant—even the second and third-born females," she replied.

Perkins' eyes widened.

Forrorrois patted him on the arm. "Take it slow and if you want me to talk with her, I will."

"Thanks…"

"I've got to head back to Bio Med. You can reach me by comm if you need to talk some more. Think of me as your little sister."

Perkins grinned. "I've never had a sister before. I'd appreciate that," Perkins replied.

"Well, I did promise Jack that I'd keep you out of trouble. But on this matter I'm going to need your help," Forrorrois said with a smirk as she turned and walked away. She shook her head as she thought of Alham's advances towards Perkins. *Maybe Alham and I need to share a cup of vaya together,* she thought as she continued to walk toward the double doors out of the hangar bay.

**✦✦✦✦✦✦✦✦✦✦

Ten cycle had passed since Trager had returned to the Tollon from the Plane of Deception after his near fatal attack by an Aethereal. The creature had pierced his abdomen with its claws and it had taken Leenon half that time to completely treat the stubborn secondary infection that had set in from the vicious wound. His only highlight was Forrorrois' frequent visits, but he was growing concerned by their inability to become closer because of Leenon's refusal to release him from Bio Med.

"How are you feeling, old friend?" Goren rasped, stepping into his room.

"A bit restless," he admitted to his former master pilot instructor. "I want to be free of this place. I need to…be alone with Forrorrois."

Goren gave him a sly smile. "How alone?"

"Very alone," he replied. "I've prayed to Monomay for the time the two of us could become one once more, but instead I am cheated by an Aethereal's claws."

"You weren't—permanently injured, were you?" Goren asked, a bit uncomfortable.

"No…No!" Trager replied, embarrassed by Goren's implication.

"Leenon has made me an invalid—I'm trapped in this room. Forrorrois is afraid to touch me—unwilling to risk slowing my recovery. Goren, I'm going out of my mind being so close to Forrorrois and yet I'm denied by the confines of this room," he whispered.

"What if I could smuggle you out of this room and arranged for the two of you to have fifth kel alone?" his friend suggested.

Trager felt his heart begin to beat faster at the thought. Tentatively, he glanced up at Goren. "Could you? Oh, Goren, don't trifle with my affection for Forrorrois," Trager insisted.

"Four revolution is a long time," his old friend replied with a knowing look. "Believe me, Trager, this is no trifling matter."

"It's becoming unbearable, now that she's so close," Trager confessed.

"I have an idea, but I'm going to need your skill with the ship's security system."

"I don't know, it's been four revolution since I was the ship's security officer," Trager stated.

"Ah, but I have the security overrides," Goren rasped.

"I won't ask how," Trager said with a grin. "I can set up a loop, with everything on it—body sensors, everything!"

"That's the Trager I used to know," his friend replied, placing a velvety black hand on his shoulder.

"Now, I'll need to block the ship's sensors since they'd give me away…unless I'm too small to notice—that's it! Ask Forrorrois for her reduction weapon."

Goren stared at him for a moment. "What!?"

"You heard me, I want you to reduce me and take me to her scout."

Goren gave Trager a confused look. "That's an odd request for someone who hates being reduced." Then the Silmanon's liquid black eyes lit with hidden delight. "Maybe not so odd…but wouldn't it be better in a meditation chamber."

"Goren—that's perfect!" Trager exclaimed. "Go to Forrorrois and tell her how to prepare for the Renewal Ceremony."

Goren suddenly shifted on his feet. "Ahhh…wouldn't that discussion be better from another female?"

Trager glanced at him and realized that his request was a bit forward. "I'm sorry, Goren. You've got to help me on this. There's no one else we can trust."

"I can get you a meditation chamber, what more do you need?" Goren rasped.

"Please, Goren, as a mutual friend, Forrorrois and I need your help. The Renewal ceremony will help us break down any barriers from my long absence," Trager pleaded.

"What if I just point her to some reference files?" Goren suggested.

"I know you'll do what's right," Trager replied. "I trust you."

Goren looked up at the ceiling panels and heaved a sigh. "All right, but don't ever tell me I never did anything for you."

"Thank you, Goren, I'm in your debt," Trager answered.

"Yes, I know," Goren rasped. "Don't forget you'll still need to fix the sensors in here first. Oh, and by the way, your original access to the ship's computer has already been reestablished. You just need to make the final configuration changes."

Trager narrowed his eyes. "How did you do that? Only the head of security would have that level of access."

Goren smiled. "What can I say—Peldor is a hopeless romantic under that gruff exterior. Consider it his gift to you and Forrorrois."

Trager shook his head in awe. "Why that old Gintzer, I don't know what to say, Goren."

"Then say nothing. Make the changes to the sensors in here and I'll come back just before fifth kel," Goren rasped.

Trager looked up at his old pilot instructor and suddenly grinned. "Thank you, Goren, now go see Forrorrois. And don't forget the reduction weapon."

Goren snorted. "I don't know how you talked me into this."

"I'll see you shortly," Trager stated.

Trager watch him leave the room and felt hope surge inside him. He reached out with his zendra link and felt the familiar connection to the security systems. Before long, the images of the security links for bio med unfolded in his mind. The thought that

Peldor had arranged this with Goren made him pause. The strong bonds of friendship he and Forrorrois had formed with their fellow Dramudam transcended the politics for the moment. Monomay had truly blessed them.

****

Forrorrois looked up from her repairs to the control panel of her long-distance scout when the ship's computer alerted her that Alham's patrol had returned. By the time she cleaned herself up—Alham was leaving the pilot's equipment room and heading for the double doors out of the hangar. Forrorrois walked down the ramp of her scout and intercepted the tall Eldatek female.

"Alham, do you have a moment?" Forrorrois began.

Alham turned and smiled as she crossed over to the edge of the scout's ramp. "Forrorrois, it's good to see you. How's Trager doing?"

Forrorrois smiled back. "Trager is recovering wonderfully. How are you feeling?"

"Much better," Alham replied. "This cycle was my first time back on patrol."

"I'm so relieved you're well. Do you have a moment for a cup of ya?" Forrorrois offered, motioning up the ramp towards the cargo hold of her scout.

"That would be very nice," Alham said as she strode past her into the craft.

Forrorrois subvocalized to the door of the rear cabin and the panel slid open. When Alham spotted the already steaming cups of ya that she had place on the small table her friend clucked her tongue.

"I assumed that you would say yes," Forrorrois said with a shrug as she took a seat at the table.

Alham sat across from her and laughed. "Thank you," she said as she lifted the red stone mug of steaming ya to her nose. Then she looked at her a bit surprised as she sniffed the hot liquid. "Vaya?"

Forrorrois nodded her head. "Yes, I enjoy a cup to calm my nerves...and other emotions," she replied.

She waited while Alham dropped her gaze and ran her finger along the rim of the red stone mug.

"Perkins told you what I did…" Alham confessed in a whisper.

"Yes," Forrorrois replied as she lifted her mug from the table and took a sip of the vaya. She let the tart viscous hot drink slip down her throat.

"Was he upset?"

"No," Forrorrois said. She set the mug back onto the table. "Just confused."

Alham looked up. "Confused?"

Forrorrois studied her for a moment. "He doesn't understand what your actions meant. On Earth, what you did…and how you did it…suggests openness to a serious relationship. Is that what you wanted him to think?"

Alham took a sip of the strong vaya. "Before I answer, Forrorrois, can I ask you something?"

Forrorrois nodded.

"Your joining with Trager—even with all the insanity of him being thrown into the Plane of Deception—do you have regrets?"

Forrorrois softened her gaze. "No, even with all the insanity."

"Then a joining with an Eldatek and a Human can be successful?"

"If there's love…yes," Forrorrois replied, softly. "Alham, are you having these feelings towards Perkins?"

She was surprised when her normally confident friend struggled for words.

"Forrorrois, I'm a second born female. My first born sister has a successful joining. Her line is secured with children. On Elda, I have no opportunity to succeed any further than I have already succeeded as a master pilot in the Dramudam. I want more. I want what you and Trager have. I want a family of my own—children. On Elda I can never have this, nor can I have this in the Dramudam."

Forrorrois watched as her friend lowered her mug to the table. An uncommon tear slid down her clay-brown cheek. Without hesitation, Forrorrois reached out and brushed the tear aside with her finger tips.

"Alham, the choice that Trager and I made has come at a very high price. The Elda council has allowed Neeha to kidnap Celeste. Neeha never accepted our joining because I am an off-worlder. Would you be willing to risk being an outcast? Would you be willing to become detached from the Tollon—possibly lose your position in the Dramudam?"

Alham looked over at her. "I don't know," she whispered. "All I know is that with Perkins I see a chance for a new life. A life I can never have on Elda—or in the Dramudam. Am I wrong to want this?"

"My dear sweet Dramudam sister," Forrorrois replied. "All I want is for you to be happy. If spending time with Perkins makes you happy, then spend time with him. Just be careful—if you cross the line of duty, then the commander will have to make a decision like he made with me and Trager. Be certain that you know what you really want before that happens."

Alham's relief washed over her.

"Forrorrois, I know you can sense emotions," Alham said, cautiously. "I need to know if Perkins can feel the same way for me. I know nothing about Human males."

Her friend's trepidation made Forrorrois nod. "To be honest, Alham, Human females don't know much about Human males— except that they can be emotionally fragile. I can tell that Perkins really likes you. But you must understand that he and I come from a patrilineal society. If you are too aggressive, it might cause him some uncertainty, since innately he will feel that this forward behavior is his responsibility—not the females. You need to allow him to feel it's his idea."

Alham nodded her head. "Ahhh. I understand. So my forwardness might put him off...this is going to be more complicated than I thought. How will I know I'm sending him the right message?"

Forrorrois patted her arm. "There's no manual for this. Just talk to him. Ask him what he wants, then, more importantly, listen to what he says."

Alham reached out and caught Forrorrois' fingers, then gently squeezed them. "You're a good friend, Forrorrois. Thank you for not judging me."

Forrorrois gave her a gentle smile. "There's nothing to judge. Just remember, I brought Perkins here to finish his training. I need him to come back to Earth and help me defend it. Jack and I have been able to manage so far, but it would be better to have another pilot to help if Earth is attacked again."

"But you'll have Trager again," Alham replied with a sparkle in her eyes.

Forrorrois almost blushed. "Yes, I'll have Trager again. And once I have Celeste back, we can return to Earth and be a real family."

"Then Perkins could stay here and join the Dramudam," Alham insisted.

"True, but I don't think that's what he wants," Forrorrois replied. "Besides, being a Human he isn't breaking the Isolation Treaty."

She was surprised when Alham's shoulder's sagged at the mention of the treaty.

"But I'm not Human…"Alham whispered. "The only way I could ever go to Earth is the way Trager has gone."

Forrorrois closed her eyes for a moment and sighed. "You're getting ahead of yourself, Alham," Forrorrois whispered back. "You don't have to make any of these choices at this moment. Just remember to talk to Perkins and fully understand what he wants. He's like a brother to me, so don't break his heart."

Alham looked at her, surprised. "Then I come to you as his sister and ask for permission to approach him."

Forrorrois' eyes widened at Alham's formal request. "Ummm… wow…Alham, you really are serious."

"Yes, I am, Forrorrois," Alham replied. "I don't understand why, but I don't feel like he is an inferior male. He has proven his worth to me. I've never felt this way with an Eldatek male, or any male for that matter."

"I see," Forrorrois said as she sensed her sincerity. "If you truly feel that way, then I give you my permission. But be certain to listen to what Perkins wants before you find yourself in an isolation cell for fraternization. Now, drink your vaya. I may be heading out again soon and I want you on your toes. Protect Perkins while I'm gone."

"I will make it my personal responsibility to watch over him," Alham replied, solemnly.

Forrorrois smiled. Alham's word was enough. The fact that she could feel Alham's growing emotions for the captain made her all the more certain that Perkins would be kept from harm until she was able to take Perkins back to Earth.

CHAPTER 12

Forrorrois looked up from her work on the main control panel of her long-distance scout when she heard footsteps in her cargo hold. She smiled when she spied her old pilot instructor and pulled herself to her feet.

"Hello stranger," she said. Suddenly, she sensed his agitation. "Is there something wrong?"

"Ah...yes and no," Goren began, glancing out the hatch.

"Is it Trager?" she asked, searching his mulish velvety-black face.

"Trager's fine for the moment...but he wants to see you," he began.

"Not a problem, I can go right now, just let me clean up a bit," she replied, starting towards the cargo hold of her craft, but he stopped her with a touch of his hand on her shoulder. Forrorrois glanced at the fine velvety black fur on his fingers then into his liquid black eyes. "Goren, you're confusing me. Stop being so mysterious and tell me what this is all about."

"Ah...could we step into your rear cabin. It's of a personal nature," he said, averting his eyes.

His uncommon action alerted her empathic senses. "I do believe you're blushing underneath that velvety fur of yours, Master Pilot Instructor," she teased. His embarrassment heightened at her words, forcing Forrorrois to wipe the smile from her face. "I didn't mean to offend, dear friend. Please, come this way," she offered, heading to the door of her rear cabin. The door panel slid open as they approached. Forrorrois led him inside. Then subvocalized for the door to close and waved her hand towards the small table. "Take a seat and tell me what Trager wants," she said as she took a seat across from him.

"Ah...he wants the two of you to have some time alone...to get to know one another again," Goren replied.

Forrorrois sat back in her seat, at a loss for words. She sensed this request was a painfully sensitive thing for Goren to even mention. It was an even more awkward thing for Forrorrois to even begin to discuss with her old master pilot instructor—male or female. She struggled for the right words, watching the large being before her shift in his seat—uncomfortable at her silence.

"Forgive me for my hesitation, but you took me by surprise," she replied. "It's just, if I understand correctly, you're here because Trager wants to be intimate?"

Goren looked down at the table and nodded. "That is correct."

He looked up when she fell silent.

"You do want to be intimate again with Trager?"

"Of course, Goren," she stammered. "I've been waiting for Leenon to give me a sign that he was strong enough, but she continues to have reservations."

Goren searched her eyes. "He is strong enough, regardless of what Leenon has told you. He needs reassurance from you."

"Are you certain, Goren? When I visit with him, I feel his uncertainty."

"Forrorrois, please, I want you to review the Renewal Ceremony. In the Eldatek culture, when a joined couple has suffered a long forced separation—such as in your case—this ceremony is performed in order to peel away your fears and anxieties. I've taken the liberty of downloading the details onto your scout's computer."

She studied him for a moment. "But what about Leenon? She hasn't released him from Bio Med yet. If Trager comes up missing from his room, my scout will be the first place that she will come looking for him."

"Don't worry. I've made arrangements for a mediation chamber for the two of you," Goren replied, lowered his voice. "But Forrorrois, you mustn't tell anyone—especially Leenon—what you are about to do."

Forrorrois felt her heart thunder against her chest. *The chance to be alone with my dear ashwan—away from prying eyes!*

"But Trager's under her direct care, Goren. How can Trager even think he could leave Bio Med undetected?"

"He's fixing that as we speak—he used to be head of security—remember?"

A thrill went up her spine at her ashwan's defiance. "But what about Leenon?"

"Leave her to me. I'll distract her and leave strict orders that Trager's not to be disturbed with the rest of Bio Med," he replied.

"But there's still the ship's sensor..." Forrorrois voiced, still not convinced.

"It's being taken care of...calm yourself. Trager asked me to borrow a reduction weapon from you."

Forrorrois stared into his liquid black eyes in awe. "He would do that for me?"

"Yes...he would," Goren whispered. "Now, review the information I've left for you on your scout's computer. I will leave the required items for the ceremony in the meditation chamber before you arrive."

"Thank you," she replied with a shy smile. "Let me get you that reduction weapon."

Forrorrois led him back into the cargo hold and opened the weapons locker. Lifting out the small weapon, she smiled at its cool touch. "Here, when do I meet you?" she asked as she handed the small weapon to Goren.

He took the oval shaped weapon and gave her a gentle smile. "In three-quarter's of a kel, after Leenon's shift is over. I've arranged for her to meet with Commander Thoren for third kel so I know she'll be occupied until I've secured the two of you inside the chamber."

Forrorrois' eyes widened. "The commander is involved?"

Goren shrugged. "The commander doesn't know all the details, but he is sympathetic to you and Trager having some time together, outside of Bio Med."

Forrorrois stopped him when he turned to go and stood on her toes to kiss him lightly on the cheek. "Thank you again, Goren," she said as he slowly pulled away.

Goren touched his cheek where she had just kissed him. "Trager is a lucky being," he whispered. "The chamber is reserved in your name for the next cycle, but I'll only be able keep Leenon unaware until her next shift."

"I understand," Forrorrois said as she watched him go. Her heart pounded with anticipation and fear of the unknown when she thought of Trager being with her once more.

****

Trager sat on his bed and stared up at the ceiling of his room in Bio Med. He had his arm slipped out of his gown while Leenon finished examining the healed wounds on his shoulder and reviewed his vital signs.

"You can barely see the scars from that Aethereal's attack, Trager. You're making very good progress, but I'm concerned—you're heart rate is up—are you anxious about something?" Leenon asked, still inspecting his shoulder.

Trager looked at her, suddenly nervous she might suspect he was going to meet with Forrorrois. He pushed the thought from his mind then pulled on his best charming smile and laughed. "Of course I am, I can't wait to be out of this room," he teased.

Leenon gave him a sympathetic look. "Well, that will be a bit longer. I want to observe you for seven more cycle, just to make certain you're completely in tiptop form. I know you think I'm being overly cautious, but better safe than sorry."

"Of course," Trager replied, relieved Leenon wasn't suspicious. He slipped his arm back into the sleeve of his gown when she finished her inspection.

"All of your scars will be gone in no time," she stated with approval. "For now, I want you to get some sleep—and please—stay in bed. I know you must feel freer without all those tubes, but you've been bedridden for over a half a mol and you still haven't regained all your strength."

"I do, thank you for removing them. And yes, I'll get some sleep," Trager replied. "Enjoy third kel with Commander Thoren."

"I will," she said with a smile, "I'll see you around first kel."

He watched her leave and then subvocalized to the security recorder to start the loop he had recorded earlier to begin playing. Lying back, he smiled while he waited for Goren. Within twenty-seven tol, his old friend came into his room, smiling. "Everything ready?" Trager asked, as he raised himself up on his elbow.

"Ready and willing," the Silmanon replied, with a grin. "The med techs have switched your room monitors to privacy mode at you previous request."

"Great!" Trager exclaimed as he sat up on his bunk. "Did you get the weapon?"

"Right here, throw your sheet back, so I can get a clean shot at you."

Tossing the covering from his bare legs, Trager closed his eyes.

"Don't worry, Trager, you'll come around before I arrive at the meditation chamber," Goren continued.

The brilliant flash registered even through Trager's closed eyelids. His head swam from the sensation of falling, finally, his mind blacken as he crumpled into a tiny mass in the folds of his bedding.

✶✶✶✶✶✶✶✶✶✶

Trager's head ached as he shifted inside the restrictive folds of cloth. Suddenly, the low light filtered through an opening above his head. Dark strong fingers reached for him, enveloping his tiny form.

"Are you all right?" Goren whispered, while he pulled Trager out of his tunic pocket and set his miniaturized form on the low table in the darken room.

Trager slide from Goren's hand. "Yes...where is she?" he asked straightening his beige infirmary gown.

"Changing behind the screen, here's your wrap and robes," he replied.

The thought of Forrorrois being so near sent a thrill though Trager. "Thank you," he replied. He pulled off the infirmary gown and slipped into the silky white robes. "Where are we going to sit?"

Goren pointed towards the middle of the room. "I've set up a large pillow on the floor, Forrorrois has all ready placed the mediation sphere in the center."

Trager nervously fastened his robes and loosened the clip that held his long black hair in the traditional Dramudam braid. He shook his hair out feeling free of the restrictive bond. Then he took a breath and let it out slowly to calm himself. He reached down and collected the large rectangle of white cloth and draped the fabric over his head and shoulders. "It's like a hot desert night in here," he commented.

"Forrorrois wanted to make certain you wouldn't become chilled at your present size. Drink your ya...it's almost time," his friend urged.

Trager took the tiny cup from the table top and drained the contents. The potency of the hot liquid hit him like a ton of bricks. He stumbled forward. Goren steadied him with two fingers.

"Careful, it has a strong effect."

"That's an understatement," Trager gasped, losing his balance and falling back into his friend's cupped hand.

"Relax, I'll take you to the pillow where you can compose yourself," Goren chuckled.

Trager gave in to the swimming vision, feeling safe in Goren's protective grip.

"Here you go, Trager, it's time for me to get Forrorrois, then I'll be going."

"Wait, Goren," he gasped. His old friend paused, towering above him in a crouched position.

"Yes?"

"Thank you..."

The master pilot instructor smiled down at him and nodded. Straightening, he moved towards the screen at the back of the room.

Trager leaned forward and touched the smoke swirled glass sphere before him. The miniaturized orb was cradled halfway into the center of the pillow. He looked up when he heard Goren's returning footsteps and smiled when the Silmanon lowered Forrorrois' tiny form onto the pillow, opposite him. Trager adjusted the white cloth to cover himself completely, except for his eyes, and waited while Goren dimmed the lights of the room further then left.

He glanced up as Forrorrois' robed form moved forward then settled on the opposite side of the sphere. Without a word, she drew the white outer cloth over her head and draped the material around her body until all he could see was her eyes framed in a triangle of folded material. She reached out and pressed her fingertips against the meditation sphere's surface. Clearing his mind, Trager called forth his emotions and slowly offered them to her. The sphere began to glow—slight at first—then growing in intensity as the psychic bound that had been forged between their minds during their joining ceremony strengthened. He gasped when he felt her acceptance of every flaw he held up to her. Her warmth caused his heart to soar in her inner light—protecting and strengthening him.

Trager gasped as Forrorrois finally allowed the outer cloth to slip from her head and shoulders to the pillow top in a circle of white.

Tilting his head back, Trager let his own outer covering fall. The adoration in her eyes as he revealed his face and robed form filled him with hope.

Reluctantly, Trager allowed his fingers to slip from the sphere's surface, releasing the link between them. He slowly unfolded his legs suddenly aware that he had been kneeling for over a quarter kel. His prolonged stay in Bio Med was catching up to him. Taking a breath, Trager felt giddy while he peered at her silent form—still wrapped in the white outer covering. He rose to his feet—a patient hunger inside. Circling the glass orb, he stopped behind her. She dropped her hands from the sphere, but didn't turn around.

His heart pounded when he finally drew the courage to touch the white silky cloth that covered her. Wishing his heart silent, lest she hear its pounding, he knelt behind her strong back. Trager reached out—then hesitated, clenching his hands into fists to stop them from trembling. When his tremors calmed, he reached out once more and brushed his hands lightly against her thinly-robed shoulders. He smiled as she gasped slightly, but remained still. Trager looked forward and spied her reflection on the glossy surface in front of her. Her face was beautiful. Oh, how he longed to taste her lips once more, but he resigned himself to lightly caressing her arms. He progressed to her back and neck—deliberately touching with only his fingertips. His ardor pulled at his restraint as he ached to touch her pale skin. The heat of the room made him gasp from the lurid passion that stirred inside him. Beads of perspiration began to trickle down his spine. How he wanted to pull his ashwan against him and press his lips to hers—to taste the sweetness of her skin and make her tremble with delight. Trager bit his lip as he resisted once more and traced his fingers down the curve of Forrorrois' back. He increased the pressure of his fingertips and let his palm become part of his touch. He smiled when she swallowed, struggling to maintain the ceremonial resistive posture and lightened the pressure.

Slowly, her body began to tremble—her breathing more rhythmic with each deliberate stroke of his fingertips and palms. She gasped from his intensity and finally arched back into his chest—encircling his head with her arms. He slid his hands along her forearms until he grasped her wrists with one hand. Turning her towards him, he kissed Forrorrois' welcoming lips and neck. She twisted from his grip and for a moment they stopped and breathed in the other's passion. Silently, she shed her robes from her shoulders, never taking her eyes from him. Trager took in her beautiful pale form—he had nothing to fear. She was his and he was hers and there was nothing that could ever drive them apart again. He let his own robes slid from his shoulders and together, they melted into each others arms in desperate passion.

****

Forrorrois smiled as she slipped into Bio Med undetected in miniature on her shrouded hovercycle with Trager straddled on the seat behind her. His strong arms wrapped around her waist, exciting her senses with his closeness. She slowed near his room and looked around. Certain no one was near—she triggered the door lock then guided the craft onto the sheets of his waiting bed. She gasped when he began to nuzzle her neck and ear. His passion was infectious. Turning to face him, she pulled him closer. He arched at her touch, chuckling.

"I never want to let you go," he said with a grin, guiding her leg over the seat so she could curl up in his arms.

"I'm not going anywhere," she purred, "but I do have to get you back to full size before the shift change. Besides, you're shivering already from heat loss."

"All I need is your warmth, my ashwan," he replied slowly, unfastening her black tunic, starting at her neck then following her shoulder and down her left side as he teased her with release of each fastener.

Forrorrois giggled when he slid the fabric aside, exposing her to his eager lips. His mustache and short chin hair tickled the sensitive skin of her throat. She rolled her head back, allowing him to support her neck and shoulders—inviting him forward. Trager suddenly scooped her up in his arms and lifted her from the hovercycle. She wrapped her arms around his neck while he carried her to the center of the expansive bed.

"If I had known you enjoyed being this size, I would have reduced you more often," she giggled while he laid her down in the folds of the canvas-like sheets.

"I would endure any size as long as I'm with you," he whispered, lying down next to her. "Besides, this bed is too small for the two of us full-sized."

Her body thrilled as he lightly traced her Dramudam mark with his chestnut-brown finger. "You always were such a tease," she whispered back.

"I want you all to myself," he replied, attempting to peel away her uniform.

"Trager...the shift change..." she began, stopping his hand, but he silenced her with a long seductive kiss.

"I love you so much," he whispered.

Forrorrois looked up at him, feeling like she did the night of their joining. "I love you, too," she replied. Suddenly tears began to flow down her cheeks. She pulled him closer to her. "Trager, don't ever leave me like that ever again," she whispered.

"Hush...ashwan...hush. I won't...never ever again," he cooed, smoothing her hair as he tightened his grip.

"I was so lost without you...I wanted to die. If it hadn't been for Celeste…Trager, we have to get her back!"

"We will," he replied. "We'll leave in a few cycle with, or without, leave of Leenon or the commander."

Forrorrois pulled him closer and kissed his neck gently then curled against him. A shiver ran through her from the coolness of the room. The reality of hypothermia forced her to pull back. "I should return you back to full size," she stated.

"So soon?" he asked, disappointed.

"It's later than you think," she said with a reluctant smile. "Just stay there while I get the reduction weapon from the transport."

"If I have to," he sighed.

Taking the oval weapon from the compartment under the seat— she changed the setting and aimed it at his prone form near the middle of the bunk. In a flash of bluish-green light, Trager returned to his two-meter frame before her—unconscious. His breathing was relaxed and regular. Placing the weapon back into the seat compartment of her hovercycle, Forrorrois walk down the side of his body and approached his hand. She climbed up into his palm, letting the warmth of his skin chase away the chill that had begun to sink into her body. Eagerly, she climb from his palm up his arm to his chest and curled up against his warm, spicy-scented skin. With a sigh, she pulled the thick fabric of his gown over her. Within moments, the rise and fall of his chest lulled her to sleep.

****

Trager took a deep breath as he stirred awake. The intensity of the lights in his room in bio med had brightened for first kel. He moved to sit up when he felt something stir on his chest. Glancing down, he spotted the tiny pale face and auburn spray of loose hair against his chestnut-brown chest. Lying back, he smiled, not wishing to wake his dear Forrorrois. A knock on the door, made him look up. Suddenly he panicked. Glancing around, he pulled the bed sheet higher to cover them both and the miniature hovercycle beside his pillow. Forrorrois stirred awake from his actions, but he held her down with his hand and shook his head when she moved to object.

"Trager, its Leenon, please release the door lock," she called through the door.

"Quick, Trager, answer her before she becomes suspicious," Forrorrois urged.

'Computer, release the privacy lock,' he subvocalized.

"Trager..." Leenon called again as the door slid open. "You had me worried for a moment."

"I'm sorry, Leenon, I just wanted a fifth kel rest without someone coming in to disturb me."

"I understand," she replied. "I just wanted to make certain you slept all right."

"Best rest in over four revolution," he replied, trying not to grin.

"Well, that's good to hear. Let me come in and check your shoulder..."

"Can it wait?" he asked when she stepped forward, but before she could answer him, Goren burst into the room.

"Leenon," he rasped, catching his breath, "I thought we were going to have first kel together?"

"We are, I just wanted to check on Trager before I joined you," she replied, shaking her head. "Now, do you mind? I was just about to examine him, so, could you please step outside?"

Trager shook his head at the Silmanon while Leenon's head was turned and lifted his sheet slightly so he could see the tiny transport next to his pillow. Goren's solid black eyes grew large.

"Ah, Leenon...before you begin...I need to ask Trager a question... alone, if you don't mind," Goren stammered.

"You mean about that item you wanted me to think about last

cycle?" Trager asked. "I do need to get it off my chest." He glanced downward, trying to get Goren to understand.

"So do I—Oh, yes!" Goren replied, eyes widening even more when he spotted Forrorrois while Leenon's head was turned.

"What are you two talking about?" Leenon broke in, glancing back and forth at the two of them. "I'm certain it can wait. Now, Goren if you would just step outside, I'll be done in a few moments and you can..."

"No, Leenon, I really must unburden myself of this or I won't be able to concentrate a moment longer," Trager replied.

"Alone..." Goren added.

Lennon heaved a sigh and threw up her hands. "Oh, all right," Leenon replied, "five tol and not a moment longer."

They both held their breath until the door slid shut behind the head med tech.

"You're both going to drive her crazy," Forrorrois called out from under the sheet. "Finally, I can breathe again," she continued as Trager lifted the blanket to reveal her lying on his chest. Trager watched her shift to a sitting position and looked up at Goren.

"I can't believe you both came back here!" Goren began.

"I wanted to make certain Leenon wasn't going to find him missing," Forrorrois replied.

"So instead you wanted her to find you here—in his room?" he stammered.

"I'm sorry, I fell asleep," she replied, fastening her tunic flap.

"Well, we're almost out of time," he rasped.

Trager and Goren watched as Forrorrois slid down onto the sheet and crossed over to her transport.

"Don't worry, I can find my own way back to the hangar bay," she said with a grin. "I'll be back for second kel, Trager."

He smiled when Forrorrois blinked from sight then adjusted his gown.

"She's got more tricks up her sleeve..." Goren sputtered, staring at the empty spot.

Suddenly, the door slid open and Leenon strode in.

"Times up, I hope you two have cleared the air of whatever was so pressing. Now, if you'll excuse us Goren, but I'd like to complete Trager's examine so we can go to first kel."

"By all means," Goren rasped, glancing towards Trager. "I'll wait for you outside."

Trager grinned as he left and looked back at Leenon. "Thank you for letting me and Goren talk for a moment," he said, still smiling to himself.

"Well, you're definitely less tense than you were when I first came in," she stated, pulling his gown off his shoulder to begin her exam.

"Goren had me worried about something, but it's all cleared up now," he replied, looking up at the ceiling.

Leenon shifted his sleeve back into place as she finished her exam. "Whatever it was, you definitely needed to discuss it," she stated.

Trager smiled to himself without a word.

"I haven't seen Forrorrois for the last few cycle," Leenon continued, "have you?"

"Yes...in fact she's stopping by around second kel," he replied with a distant smile.

"That's good," Leenon said with a smile. "Your shoulder is looking much better."

"When can I leave bio med?" he asked, hoping.

"In about six more cycle," she replied.

Trager sat up in his bed and threw his legs over the edge. "Please, Leenon, I can't stay here much longer, I'm losing time," he stated. "I can't regain my strength in this room."

Leenon sighed. "All right, maybe I can let you out for some exercise a kel each cycle for the next six cycle."

Trager studied her for a moment. "Thank you, now all I need is a uniform."

"You're rushing yourself," she clucked.

"Leenon, please, I can't walk around the ship like this," he stated, looking down at the short beige infirmary gown with a teasing grin.

She rolled her eyes and shook her head. "Well, at least you've regained your sense of humor. The uniform you were wearing when you were brought in was badly torn. I'll have a new one made up for you by second kel...that way Forrorrois and you can take that walk together to the galley."

Trager brightened. "Could you do something for me, Leenon?" he asked, pausing as she looked at him. "Could you make the tunic like Forrorrois'...black?"

"Whatever for, Trager?" she asked, taken aback.

"Forrorrois is still mourning for Celeste," he insisted, "and so am I!"

Leenon looked at him—appalled. "Celeste isn't dead, Trager, she's with your mother!"

"Exactly," he replied, unable to disguise his anger any longer. "Celeste is only four, Leenon—she barely understands that Neeha is her grandmother. Even worse, Celeste can sense the emotions around her—the hate. She's my child. I renounce Neeha as my life bringer, as my father renounced her after she cast him aside! Neeha is a poison to her own happiness and the happiness of those around her."

"Trager...you don't mean that!" Leenon gasped.

"Yes, Leenon, I do," he replied. "I've watched her rise in rank in the council from the Plane of Deception. She's more cunning than I ever remembered—and even more bitter against the Dramudam then when I left to become one. A time will come when she will destroy everything to serve her bitter end."

"You mustn't talk like that about your mother," Leenon admonished. "She gave you life, you owe her honor!"

"I did—until she took Celeste to give her to Bohata and threatened Forrorrois to never to come back for her," he whispered, barely able to control his anger. "My biggest fear is that Neeha will harm our daughter, deciding she's a threat to Elda because she's half Human."

Leenon placed her hand over her mouth. "Neeha wouldn't harm her only granddaughter, Trager. If you returned to her then things would be different."

"Oh, I will," he replied, looking into her black eyes darkly, "and when I do it won't be Forrorrois she should be worried about."

"Trager, such words," she gasped. "Your time in the Plane of Deception has changed you."

"No, they've opened my eyes to what Forrorrois has been saying for several revolution. She's right to be cautious of the motives of others. I was like a child with my trust until I watched as Neeha bided her time until she could strong-arm the council to do her bidding. They let her take Celeste. I've mourned many things, Leenon, and I will continue to mourn them even after Celeste is returned safely to Forrorrois. I will mourn the loss of my heritage because of the deception of my own world, but I will also celebrate the renewal of my own family and the return in my duties to my adopted homeworld."

Leenon looked away from him, wiping a tear from her eye. "Then you must hate me for what I must tell you. I was the one who gave the council the coordinates to your base on Earth."

Trager stared at her—stunned. "What!?"

"I was following the wishes of the council," she stammered.

Trager leapt to his feet. "What about your vows to the Dramudam?" he shouted. "What about the impartial judgment you must give by renouncing your homeworld?"

"Oh, and what about you?" she returned hotly. "You're one to talk—living on a world protected by the Isolation Treaty joined to another Dramudam!"

He sat back as if he'd been slapped. Suddenly, he didn't know this being in front of him whom he'd served with for more than twenty-eight revolution. "Leenon, you know what I gave up to join with Forrorrois! Without attachment to a ship a Dramudam loses their identity. I was fortunate that Commander Thoren allowed us a loose association with the Tollon and gave us supplies to protect Earth from the Utahar in the name of the Isolation Treaty—a treaty that you broke when you gave the council the coordinates to Forrorrois' base. They sent High Guard who used stun weapons on Forrorrois' parents when they forcefully took Celeste. How could you!?"

Leenon covered her face with her hands. "Forgive me," she wept. "Forgive me!"

He was stunned when she fell to her knees and wrapped her arms around his bare legs. His defenses weakened, Trager reached out and touched her silky black hair. "Leenon, please, this isn't right."

"Please forgive me, Trager, I've brought dishonor by my actions."

"I...I"

"Trager, please, in the name of our friendship," she continued, looking up into his eyes. "Forgive me."

"Leenon please rise to your feet, there's nothing for me to say," he replied, slipping his hand under her arm to assist her. "You have fallen to the will of the council under the machinations of my grieving mother. Even after all these revolution, you are still an Eldatek. It's nothing I can change."

She stood to her feet and searched his face. "Neeha never told me that she would take Celeste. I thought she was going to finally reach out to Forrorrois...I did it because I love you...I always have...but our vows as a Dramudam forbade me to speak it openly."

Trager's jaw dropped at her words, the implications tumbled in his head. "You risked my daughter and Forrorrois..." He turned away from her, repulsed by the words he couldn't speak. "Please leave me, Leenon, right now."

"Trager...please...I never did any of this to gain you as a lover. I did it as a friend to both you and Forrorrois. I knew that the moment I witnessed your joining—it was strong and beautiful. There was nothing I could do that would ever change that. I shelved my feelings for you, holding only to our friendship. But when Neeha contacted me and said she wanted to contact Forrorrois, I was overjoyed at the prospect. I never dreamed she would do what she did. I thought that Neeha wanted to finally meet her and accept Celeste as your daughter. I didn't know about Talman when she contacted me. I only learned about his death later. You must believe me—I acted only as a friend," she pleaded.

Trager turned towards her, studying the delicate clay-brown skin of her elegant cheekbones. "I believe you acted as a friend," he confessed, "but didn't you ever try to reason with Neeha when you realized what was really happening?"

"Yes...at first she tried to reassure me that everything would be fine, but once I saw how devastated Forrorrois was I began to doubt. When Forrorrois returned to the ship without Celeste, I knew I had been used as a pathetic pawn. By then there was little I could do but remain silent and offer Forrorrois any assistance that I could. But she didn't want it—she just barricaded herself in her scout ship and refused to talk with anyone except Goren. Then Neeha severed all communications with the Tollon—there was nothing more I could do."

"But there is something you can do, Leenon," Trager whispered, "you can release me from bio med and get me that modified uniform I asked for."

Leenon looked at him, biting her lip. "All right," she whimpered. "I'll be able to have the uniform by second kel, so that you and Forrorrois can take a walk to the galley, but you must take it slow— you're still recovering. In good conscience I can't release you fully from bio med for at least two more cycle."

Trager weighed what she offered then nodded his head. "Thank you, Leenon," he replied softly. "I'm sorry Neeha put you through this...she must have sensed your feelings for me and played them against you."

Leenon started when he pulled her into a gentle hug, but he smiled.

"Then you forgive me?" she whispered.

"How can I not?" he replied, "You only wanted to offer Neeha a chance to reconcile with Forrorrois, and as for the idea of loving me, maybe in another life time, but not now."

"Thank you," she whispered. After a few heartbeats she bit her lower lip as she pulled away. "I'll go see about that uniform."

Trager watched her leave. When the door closed he sat back down on his bed. The sound of a throat clearing behind him made Trager turn quickly. He was shocked to see Forrorrois standing behind him— full sized. "You heard everything?" he stated, more than asked.

"Yes," she replied.

He waited for her to say more, but she just stood there staring at the door.

"Then you know I can leave bio med for a walk by second kel," he continued.

"Yes," she replied again, this time glancing back at him.

"Don't blame her for her mistake," he stated. "It's difficult to resist the instincts of thousands of revolution."

"I don't...anymore," she replied, "You know, Leenon would have made you a good joined one."

Trager stared at her for a moment. "What!?"

"Just an observation," Forrorrois replied with a slight smile. "Neeha is cunning in her manipulations, but she has played her last hand with me."

"I agree," he stated.

"I'll go back to the scout and make final preparations—we're three kel away from Elda at maximum speed."

He looked up at her in surprise. "How?"

"Commander Thoren changed course the moment you were brought on board. Goren knew but he was sworn to secrecy against Leenon. Thoren suspected that she had played a part in this for sometime now," she stated, crossing towards the door.

"What's going to happen to her?" Trager asked suddenly afraid for her.

"It all depends on what happens when we reach Elda," she replied.

Trager's eyes widened. "You don't think she was involved with the explosion in storage wing?"

Forrorrois shook her head. "No, I still suspect that there is a second being on board that is feeding information to the council," she stated, looking back at him.

"Do you think it's a member of the high guard?" Trager asked in a hushed voice.

"Yes," Forrorrois replied. "Please don't leave here alone until I've returned at second kel. For now this is the only safe place for you—but only as long as they think that you are still recovering."

Trager stiffened. "What do you mean?"

"I mean exactly what I said," she replied. "They tried to harm

Perkins while I was gone. If the council thinks that you and I are going to try and get Celeste back then they will try to stop us. I don't want them to know when we're coming—until we're there. Continue to agree with Leenon that you'll stay in bio med for a while longer. When we head for the galley for second kel, we'll actually be heading for the hangar bay. If something delays me, I'll send Goren, Guruma, or Thoren."

Trager glanced away briefly and nodded. She was right—every move they made was being monitored and reported back to Neeha. "All right."

Forrorrois crossed over to him and stretched up and gave him a kiss. He held her close then let her go. She nodded to him then reduced herself and climbed onto her miniature transport. The door opened and closed without Trager saying a word.

As the door panel slid shut Trager suddenly felt very alone. His world was being blown apart and he wasn't certain what his life was going to look like when the pieces all fell back to the ground. Clearing his head, he concentrated on his little Celeste. His arms ached to hold her for the first time. "Soon, my little one, soon," he whispered.

✶✶✶✶✶✶✶✶✶✶✶

Trager looked up from his bunk in bio med when the door opened, expecting to see Leenon with his new uniform—instead he saw Guruma. The Dramudam founder stood at the door and studied him a moment with his black eyes before speaking.

"May I come in, Trager?"

"Yes, old friend, please," Trager said as he sat up and dropped his legs over the edge of the bunk with his blanket covering his lap and legs.

Guruma came into the room and let the door slide shut before he spoke. "Thank you. I heard that you're preparing to leave for Elda with Forrorrois," he said as he took a seat in the chair next to Trager's bunk.

Trager looked over at him in surprise.

"Who told you this?"

"Thoren did. Don't worry, Leenon doesn't know. Only Forrorrois, Captain Perkins, and Goren know at the moment," Guruma said with a sly smile. "As far as Leenon knows you are just going to go for a walk to help regain your strength. Besides, we don't want to alert the spy onboard of your actions."

Trager's shoulders slumped. "Of course, Forrorrois would have gone to Thoren about the flight plan. We're going to confront Neeha about getting Celeste back."

Guruma's forehead wrinkled. "Trager, have you thought this through?"

Trager sighed. "Yes. I know the risk if I return to Elda, but if I don't, Forrorrois won't get Celeste back."

"Have you talked to Forrorrois about what could happen?" Guruma pressed.

"Not all of it, if she knew what might happen then she won't let me go. Celeste needs her mother. She needs to be raised away from Elda…away from Neeha's influence. I would risk anything to make that happen," Trager confessed.

"Even your happiness with Forrorrois?" Guruma whispered.

Trager nodded then dropped his graze to the floor. "Yes."

"Trager…"

He looked back up into Guruma's sad eyes and shook his head. "I'm not going to argue. If anyone could understand my decision it should be you, Guruma. You gave up your relationship with your son, Thoren. To this cycle, you've never told Thoren that you are his father. You did this because of your duty to Elda. How is what I am doing any different?"

Guruma looked away for a moment then shook his head. When he looked back at Trager, resolve had replaced sadness. "If you choose to do this, you'll break Forrorrois' heart."

Trager shook his head. "If I don't do this, Forrorrois will still have a broken heart because Celeste will remain on Elda."

Guruma sighed. "Trager, please, there's a change happening on Elda. They've held on to the old ways for far too long. The second and third born females are as unhappy as the males. Very soon, the council will be forced to face this unhappiness with forward action—or there will be a revolt."

"I can't wait for a revolt, Guruma. I need to free Celeste now! And if that means that I have to trade places with my daughter so that Forrorrois can get her back—then that's what must be done. Now, please, don't speak with Forrorrois about this. She mustn't know, or she will refuse to go to Elda—or worse—she'll attempt to free Celeste by force and start an interplanetary incident. The solution must be a diplomatic one—otherwise beings on both sides will get hurt."

Guruma moved to object, but the door slide open revealing Leenon carrying a bundle of clothes.

"Pardon me, Trager—Guruma!" she stammered when she spotted the Dramudam founder.

Guruma stood and nodded to her. "I was just leaving, Leenon," Guruma replied. "Trager, I will be back shortly to join you for your walk. Forrorrois said that she will meet us in the galley for second kel. It will do you some good to get some fresh air."

"Thank you, Guruma," Trager said as he watched Guruma leave the room.

"I'm so sorry for not knocking," Leenon said, handing Trager the pile of clothes and a fresh pair of boots.

Trager reached out and took them—remaining seated on his bunk. "You didn't interrupt anything, Leenon. Thank you for making the tunic like I requested," he said, fingering the silky black material. "It will be good to be back in uniform."

"Well, remember not to over do it when Guruma takes you out for a walk to the galley to meet Forrorrois. I'll expect you back here in a quarter kel. You don't want any set backs on your first time out of bio med," Leenon fussed.

Trager smiled when he thought of the fifth kel he had just spent with Forrorrois. Then he struggled to keep his smile when he realized that sweet moment might be his last with her. "Guruma has watched over me for the past four revolution. He'll make certain that I don't over do," he replied.

"I'm glad to hear that," Leenon answered. "Now, you'll have to excuse me, I have some reports to complete."

"Of course, Leenon," Trager said as he watched her turn and leave the room. He looked down at the black silky tunic and closed his eyes briefly. *I am doing the right thing*, he thought as he reopened his eyes.

CHAPTER 13

Collinar looked up from his bunk in his cell on the Tollon. He was surprised to see an older Eldatek male staring at him through the purple haze of the forced shield that stretched across the opening of his cell. He studied the mostly gray hair that was tied back framing his weathered chestnut-brown face and unwavering black eyes. Suddenly, he recognized the elder being before him. He rose to his feet and advanced towards to opening.

"To what do I owe the honor of a visit from none other then the great Guruma himself?" Collinar sneered as he stopped just short of the force shield.

The elder being smiled slightly as he studied him, refusing to react to his taunt.

Finally, the Dramudam founder spoke. "I've come to see you. I've been watching you over many revolution and decided to take a moment to actually speak with you."

Collinar narrowed his eyes. "And how have you been watching me? You've been trapped in the Plane of Deception."

Guruma's eyes twinkled. "The Plane of Deception is an amazing place. With practice, one can learn to open viewing portals into this plane of existence. I've watched many events while I was trapped there for more than one hundred revolution, but your machinations have provided me with the most intrigue."

Collinar shook the weight of the revelation from his mind and shrugged his shoulders. "I'm glad that I provided entertainment in your otherwise tedious existence."

He was surprise when Guruma chuckled at his barb.

"I'm here to inform you that you have an opportunity coming up that might change your situation for the better—if you take advantage of it," Guruma offered.

Collinar paused. "And who might this offer come from?"

"Forrorrois," Guruma, replied.

Collinar raised an eyebrow. "Now you're the one that's providing intrigue," he stated. "But I must admit that being held in this cell offers me little incentive."

"This could change, if you agree to assist Forrorrois—in the very near future. I am certain that it will work in your favor—if you follow the agreement to the letter. It may even mean your freedom and the opportunity to re-secure your status in the Utahar," Guruma replied.

At the mention of the Utahar, Collinar masked his face. "Quite an offer coming from the great Guruma," Collinar answered casually, hiding the uncertainty he felt deep inside.

"The offer is a humble one," Guruma said with a slight tip of his head. "Just be prepared to act on it when it is offered."

Before Collinar could reply, Guruma turned and walked away. Collinar returned to his bunk and puzzled at the Dramudam founder's words. He would have preferred a less cryptic message, but from the rumors he'd heard of Guruma's visitations from the Plane of Deception, he had learned that the founder never gave a straight answer.

****

Forrorrois looked up from her preparations at the sound of Guruma's voice just outside her cargo hold. Closing the locker that she had reorganized three times in the past hour, she ran to the hatch. Her only thoughts were of Trager. She stopped as she caught her breath, taking in Trager's noble air, while he too paused just at the bottom of the ramp. Forrorrois was surprised at the black of his tunic patterned after her own unorthodox uniform. She admired the crisp top edge of the short stiff collar contrasted against the chestnut glow of his chiseled jaw and short black goatee and mustache.

"Black becomes you," she whispered, her heart fluttering as he stepped up the ramp with Guruma's steadying hand at his elbow.

Trager smiled down at her when he reached the top of the ramp and entered the cargo hold of her long-distance scout. Guruma released his elbow as Trager straightened to his full height.

"I felt it was appropriate," Trager replied. "I spoke with Commander Thoren—he would like to come with us, to Elda."

"Yes," she replied with a nod, "I've sensed the commander's been considering this for the past half a mol. We'll be leaving within the quarter kel."

"I'll go get him. He's speaking with Goren," Guruma said, turning away from Trager.

Forrorrois reached out a hand and shivered when he slipped his into hers. Guiding him to a crate, she eased him down.

"Save your strength, Ashwan, you'll need everything when we get to Elda," she whispered.

"I'll be ready," he assured her, pulling her towards him, for a light lingering kiss.

She caught her breath, tracing his temples with her fingers.

"Soon, you'll have Celeste back and I will hold her in my arms for the first time, Forrorrois," he whispered. "Our little daughter will be returned to her true family."

"Oh, Trager, you don't know what it means to me to hear those words," she wept. "She was so frightened when they forced her from me. I can't bear knowing she is alone at the mercy of Neeha..."

Trager looked away.

"Oh, Trager, forgive me, I realize this is...."

"No...Neeha selected the path she's taken," he replied, looking back up at her.

She felt the pain she saw in his eyes.

"Forrorrois...when we arrive on Elda...please let me confront Neeha. You must promise not to interfere with what I must say to her."

"Of course, Trager," she replied, pulling back slightly, "of course."

The sound of footsteps on the ramp, made them release each other. Thoren had arrived.

"Commander! I'm so glad you could make it," Forrorrois glowed.

"Then may I suggest we begin," Thoren stated. "Trager, maybe you should conserve your strength so you'll be ready to meet your daughter in two kel?"

"Maybe you're right," Trager admitted, rising to his feet.

"Make yourself comfortable in the rear cabin," Forrorrois smiled. "I'll have us in deep space before you know it." His warm smile was all she needed to keep her going. As she turned away, a voice called out from the hangar bay.

"What do you mean, they're leaving? Goren, I told you he wasn't ready to go to Elda yet!"

She looked down the ramp to see Leenon trying to push past the master pilot instructor.

"Forrorrois! Be reasonable, he's not ready yet, surely you must sense this?!" Leenon insisted.

Forrorrois shook her head. "His heart is ready, Leenon, and so is mine," she replied. "We're not waiting any longer to get Celeste. Now, step back while I take off." She turned from the hatch and ordered it closed. Leenon's voice grew muffled then there was only silence when the hatch sealed shut. Forrorrois felt Thoren's gaze while she strode to the cockpit and took her seat, but he said nothing.

"Computer, prepare for take off," she ordered. In her heart, it was time for action.

****

Forrorrois knew her long-distance scout ship's computer had the course completely under control, but still she sat in her command chair staring into the blackness before her. She barely looked up when Thoren stepped forward and flipped down the jump seat next to her.

"Trager's still asleep," her commander said, sitting back in his seat.

Forrorrois continued to look forward out into space. "Good, he'll need his strength," Forrorrois replied.

"Maybe we should have waited a few more cycle," Thoren reflected.

"He'll be fine. By now Neeha knows he's returned back from the Plane of Deception, we can't wait any longer," she stated.

"Unfortunately, on that point, you're correct," Thoren replied.

"I hope that Neeha will allow us to negotiate for Celeste's release..." Forrorrois faltered when her thoughts fell to her little daughter.

"Forrorrois, you mustn't worry about Celeste. The others on the council will ensure that she is kept safe. You're her mother and that is a sacred bond that even Neeha wouldn't try to break."

"How can you say that, Commander? It was the council who were the ones that allowed Neeha to take Celeste from my family and give her to Bohata in the first place! They allowed their high guard to draw weapons on my parents and stun them. I don't trust any of them," Forrorrois replied.

"I would have to agree with Forrorrois," a voice replied from the doorway to the cargo hold.

Forrorrois and Thoren turned quickly to find Guruma standing behind them. The stomp of a hoof told Forrorrois that Nur had arrived with him.

"Guruma!" Thoren said, coming to his feet and straightening his forest-green tunic in respect.

"Relax, Thoren," Guruma said as he patted Thoren's shoulder. "Take your seat."

"No, please, Guruma, take my seat. I will stand," Thoren insisted.

"If you insist," Guruma replied, taking Thoren's place in the jump seat while Thoren moved to the doorway of the cargo hold.

"What brings you and Nur?" Forrorrois asked.

"I wanted to speak to you before you reached Elda and Nur was kind enough to bring me to your ship. He is curious to see other places before he returns to his world."

Forrorrois looked back into the cargo hold at Nur and smiled. *You are welcome to join us, Nur,* she thought to him.

Nur bobbed his head. *Thank you for allowing me to travel with you.*

"Forrorrois, I need to know what you intend to do and say when you reach Elda," Guruma stated.

Forrorrois turned back to Thoren and Guruma. "I'm not sure yet. When we arrive in orbit, I'll signal the council that I have returned with Trager. After that it all depends on what Neeha does once she sees Trager and if she will let Celeste go? Neeha obviously doesn't respect our joining. The thought of Celeste in the hands of that female makes my skin crawl…"

Guruma rested his hand on her shoulder. "I understand your concern more than you know, Forrorrois. The Council of Elda has made drastic decisions in the past, I know this personally…but you must stay strong. In the end, the universe has a way of correcting things."

Forrorrois studied him carefully as she sensed a pain that radiated from him was from a very old wound, but when he looked up at Thoren, the pain melted away. She moved to question him, but her ship's computer called for her attention.

"I have an incoming transmission," Forrorrois stated in surprised.

"Greetings from Elda, Forrorrois," a voice stated aloud over the ship's comm in Eldanese. "You and Haator are to proceed to the following coordinates where you will be met by Neeha. You are expected in one-quarter kel."

The transmission abruptly ended before Forrorrois could reply.

Guruma heaved a sigh. "Their informant didn't waste any time."

Forrorrois entered the coordinates and looked over at Thoren, sensing he was disturbed by Guruma's comment.

"Unfortunately, since the explosions in the supply wing of the hangar bay, I would have to agree that the council has a spy on my ship," Thoren replied.

Guruma looked up and nodded. "Yes, I've been watching the council's interaction with their spy network from the Plane of Deception. The majority are Eldanese females—second and third daughters that are hoping for a chance at increasing their stations in life since the first born daughter will inherit the family business and wealth."

"This foul underbelly that the council has created will destroy Elda," Thoren cursed. "How can they not see this?"

"Thoren, you've been isolated from the Eldatek culture too long," Guruma replied. You need to be more cautious of the machinations that drive each family to acquire power and political standing. You were lucky that you were allowed to escape at such a young age. Without a family to arrange for a joining, you were freed to make choices that other first born males would have only dreamed of. Personally, I was proud of the choices that you have made."

Thoren straightened at Guruma's unexpected praise. "I was fortunate that you allowed me to serve directly under your command."

Forrorrois glanced at Guruma as a shadow of a smile graced his lips. And then it was gone. *There is something the Dramudam founder isn't telling Thoren—but what?*

"And you've served me well while I was trapped in the Plane of Deception," Guruma stated as he came to his feet. "But for now my presence here on this scout ship needs to be kept to ourselves. I'm certain word of my return has been leaked, but my whereabouts remain unknown—thanks to Nur's kind assistance. Nur and I will be watching. You must both trust that the universe will set itself right when all seems to be wrong."

Forrorrois moved to object to his riddle but was astonished when Guruma touched Nur's wither and the two vanished.

"I hate it when he does that," she cursed under her breath.

"So do I," Thoren commented, unexpectedly.

Forrorrois looked over at her former commander in a new light.

"I'd better wake Trager and make certain he's ready for his meeting with Neeha," Thoren continued. "Where are the coordinates taking us?"

"An asteroid field—I need to get closer to determine the exact position," Forrorrois replied, studying the long-distance sensor readings.

"This doesn't make any sense," Thoren stated.

"I agree. Please get Trager and tell him what's happening. Hopefully, I'll have more information when you've return."

"Very good," Thoren replied. He then turned and headed for the rear cabin.

Forrorrois returned her attention back to her control panel and enhanced the long-range sensors. The space between her and the panel filled with a hologram of the approaching asteroid field. Her sensors detected a station on the surface of a large asteroid.

She didn't look up when Thoren returned with Trager.

"This station is located at the coordinates I was given," she announced.

Trager moved in closer and studied the image floating before her. She glanced at him, noting he was steadying himself with the arm of her command chair. A fleeting doubt crossed her that maybe she should have waited as few more days until he was stronger. She pushed the doubts from her mind when Trager spoke.

"There appears to be a small landing port, here," he said as he pointed to the right of the station. "The remainder of the station must be below the asteroid's surface."

"When we're closer, I can switch to short-range sensors," she offered. "Hopefully, I'll be able to get enough data to pull a floor plan together."

"That sounds good," Trager replied.

"Are there signs of any other ships?" Thoren asked from his position behind Forrorrois' chair.

"No, but they could be shielded from my sensors," Forrorrois replied. "I'm switching to short-range sensors…that's odd." Forrorrois made a few more adjustments, but she still only saw the enlarged surface of the asteroid and station.

"What seems to be the problem?" Thoren asked.

"The station is shielded. I'm unable to detect the schematics of the structure or penetrate below the asteroid's surface. It appears the composition of the asteroid may be part of the problem."

Trager leaned forward and studied the image. "Very clever."

A sudden signal from her ship's computer made Forrorrois pause. "We have another incoming transmission. I'll put it on the comm."

"Forrorrois and Haator please proceed to the landing pad," the female voice stated in Eldanese then the transmission ended.

Forrorrois looked at Trager. He nodded for her to proceed.

"This doesn't feel right," Forrorrois said as she maneuvered the ship towards the asteroid.

"I agree," Trager replied, "but until we know what Neeha is planning, we need to play along so we can get Celeste back."

"Trager's right, Forrorrois," Thoren agreed.

Forrorrois finished her maneuvering and landed. When she cut her engines, the ship suddenly lurched downward. She caught the arm of her command chair and watched as the pad her ship was on began to descend. Looking upward through the cockpit canopy, she saw the opening above them spiral closed. There was no way out without damaging her scout ship.

"They've established an atmosphere outside the scout," she announced when the pad came to a stop. Lights came on, illuminating the cylindrical room. A door slid open at the nose of the ship. A figure in turquoise robes stood at the opening and waited.

"Forrorrois and Haator please disembark your craft and follow your escort," the female voice stated in Eldanese over the scout's comm. "Leave all weapons on board. Commander Thoren, please remain on board."

Forrorrois glanced between Thoren and Trager. "Guruma was right, they know our every move," she whispered.

"Until we know where they have Celeste, we don't have a choice," Trager said. Forrorrois could sense the frustration that he kept from his exterior.

"I will remain here until you return," Thoren said.

"Hopefully, we won't be long," Forrorrois said as she stood from her chair and removed her stun weapon from her waist. She set it on her chair and walked to the cargo hatch. The hatch was already open and the ramp extended. Trager followed her without a word.

Forrorrois looked up at the observation plates of the cockpit and saw Thoren watching them walk towards the door. As they approached the Eldanese council guard in turquoise robes, the female motioned them to follow her. The door to the landing pad closed after Trager and she stepped through. Forrorrois' eyes widened when her zendra link to her ship was suddenly severed. She glanced at Trager, sensing he too was alarmed by the emptiness in his mind.

Forrorrois empathically reached out and was surprised when she didn't sense the Eldatek female in front of them. She quickened her pace and extended her hand towards the female before Trager could object—Forrorrois pulled back when her hand passed through the female's arm and robe. She was a holograph.

"What is this?!" Forrorrois cried out, stopping dead in her tracks.

"I'm not sure," Trager replied, "but we need to keep following her until we know."

Forrorrois gave him a hard stare then followed after him.

The holograph came to a stop in front of a door at the end of the corridor. As the door slide open the projection faded.

Forrorrois paused suspiciously at the opening.

Trager looked inside. Suddenly, Forrorrois felt his elation as he ran into the dimly lit room. Forrorrois followed him through and spotted their daughter, Celeste, standing in the center of a spot of light in a darken room. She was dressed in simple long orange robes. Forrorrois reached out with her mind and met with nothing. "Trager, it's not her!" she cried out as he dropped to his knees and wrapped his arms around thin air.

Forrorrois' heart sank as she felt Trager's wish to finally hold his daughter torn from him. She crossed over to him and fell to her knees beside him, enveloping him in her arms. He leaned into her embrace and fought back the tears. The moment was short lived when the lights came up in the circular room.

A single older female voice spoke from a platform three meters above them.

"Haator, so you truly are freed from the Plane of Deception."

Trager and Forrorrois jumped to their feet as the familiar voice said Trager's Eldanese name. Trager's angry gaze was already riveted on the clay-brown face and black eyes of the Eldanese female dressed in richly embossed golden-yellow robes. His mother stood haughtily over them—emboldened by her three symbolic council braids tracing down one side of her salt-n-pepper hair.

"Neeha, I should have known. I have left one deception only to be trapped by another," Trager accused. "Where is Celeste? Where is my daughter?"

A low chuckle emanated from Neeha. Forrorrois looked up at the Eldatek female standing above them like judge and jury, anger boiling inside her against this cruel being.

"Haator, have you forgotten the laws of Elda so quickly. No male has rights when it comes to a female child. Even the mother's rights can be superseded by the council's wishes if the need is great enough. And as part of the council, I can determine that need. Haator, you are hereby ordered by the council to return to Elda with me as a second to your late brother's joined one, Bohata, in order to satisfy her rightful claim of Slovak. Talman died before producing a female heir, leaving Bohata's family in a precarious position. If you refuse, Celeste will be given to Bohata to be raised as her daughter, replacing the heir you were to produce with her."

Forrorrois' jaw dropped at Neeha's condition. Trager turned to Forrorrois and moved to speak but no words came out. His shoulder's sagged as his gaze moved to the floor.

"You've won, Neeha. Give Celeste back to Forrorrois and I will go with you," he said in a hush voice.

Forrorrois collapsed to her knees, stunned. Before she could speak, a door slid open to her left and a small voice cried out.

"Momma! Momma!"

Forrorrois turned on her knees towards her daughter and was nearly bowled over by the force of the three-and-a-half year old, in yellow robes, crashing into her kneeling frame. Forrorrois buried her face into her little girl's fine black hair and sobbed as she held her. Trager dropped down beside her and enveloped them both with his arms.

"Poppa?" Celeste said as she pulled back to look at Trager.

"Yes, Celeste, it's Poppa," he replied, sniffing back tears.

"I can touch you," the little girl bubbled as she fell against his chest.

Forrorrois struggled to stop crying as she watched Trager hold his daughter for the first time—and his last.

"Haator, it's time to go," Neeha ordered.

Forrorrois could feel Trager's struggle as he tightened his hold on Celeste. She knew that Celeste could feel it too.

"Haator!" Neeha barked.

Trager stiffened then slowly released Celeste. "You be a good little girl and help your momma, OK?" he said in English.

Celeste looked at him and started to cry. "She's making you go, isn't she?" Celeste replied back in English.

Forrorrois followed her daughter's accusing finger towards Neeha. It was plain—Celeste knew.

"Please, Celeste, I have to go to keep you safe. I love you, always remember that," Trager replied, gently wiping the tears from Celeste's face.

Forrorrois trembled as he turned toward her.

"I will always love you as well, my ashwan," he said as he leaned forward and kissed her longingly. "Monomay, please hold and protect them in my absence," he whispered when he released her, and then kissed his daughter's forehead.

Forrorrois twisted when she heard the door slid open. Two female high guards in red robes, bearing weapons, entered the room.

"Haator! Now!" Neeha ordered. "I will not ask again."

"Poppa, No!" Celeste cried out as Trager stood up and faced the guards in red. Forrorrois sobbed clutching her daughter to her breast as Celeste struggled to go after her father. Trager had made his decision so that she could keep Celeste, but all Forrorrois could think was how she wanted to knock Neeha off the platform above her for being so cruel. She grabbed her daughter and threw her onto her hip as she charged after Trager. One of the high guards lowered her weapon at her.

"Forrorrois, no! Think of Celeste," Trager begged.

Forrorrois stopped in her tracks and watched as Trager was shoved by the second guard in red robes toward the door. Resignation filled Trager's eyes. He lowered his head and passed through the opening.

Celeste wriggled from her arms and charged the closed door, screaming for her poppa. Forrorrois caught her as she slammed her small fists on the door panel then crumpled to her knees and rocked her gently.

A voice spoke above her. "This is the only way."

Forrorrois looked up at Neeha in disgust. "It was the cruelest way," Forrorrois spat. "No wonder he left you to join the Dramudam. You don't love him. He's just a pawn to you, just like Celeste was nothing but a pawn."

"You're wrong, Forrorrois. I do love him, but he has a duty to his family that he must fulfill…"

Forrorrois seethed at her words. "We are his family! He has a duty to us!"

"That's where you are wrong, Forrorrois. You are nothing but an unsanctioned dalliance. I admit he would have been worth more to Bohata if he had been chaste, but the fact that he has proven that he can produce a female child restores his value to her since she is in need of an heir."

"All you are worried about is your own power and Trager is just a means for you to secure it. I will find a way to get Trager back, Neeha. He is my joined one and Celeste's father. No one can break that bond between us."

"His name is Haator and we shall see," Neeha replied. Then she turned and left the platform, leaving Forrorrois alone in the circular room with Celeste.

Forrorrois lifted the still sobbing Celeste in her arms. The door slid open as she rose. Forrorrois broke into a run and raced to the other end of the corridor. As she reached the second door, it slid open and revealed her scout ship waiting for her. Commander Thoren jumped to his feet as she ran for the ramp. He met her inside with questions in his eyes.

"We have to prepare for take-off," she announced as the hatch closed behind her and she stormed into the cockpit with Thoren trailing behind her—Celeste still on her hip.

"Where's Trager?" Thoren asked.

Before Forrorrois could answer, Celeste spoke angrily in Intergaltic. "The mean Eldatek female took him."

Thoren studied her. "What?"

"Neeha. Neeha forced Trager to go back to Elda or she was going to take Celeste back with her. She claimed something called Slovak because Trager's older brother died without producing an heir with Bohata!" Forrorrois spat.

Thoren paled at her words. "I'm sorry..."

"Not as sorry as Neeha is going to be if I ever catch up with her!" Forrorrois vowed. "What's taking this launch pad so long to reach the surface? Neeha is getting away!"

"Forrorrois, please, Neeha has won," Thoren said gently. "Take Celeste and go home back to your world."

Forrorrois turned and stared at Thoren, stunned. "How can you say that? Trager is my joined one, Celeste is his daughter! There has to be something in Eldatek law that I can use to stop this insanity."

"Unfortunately, there isn't," Thoren whispered sadly, but a voice from the cargo hold contradicted him.

"Not true. There is a way."

Forrorrois and Thoren turned to find Guruma and Nur standing in the cargo hold.

Forrorrois recovered first and ran toward Guruma with Celeste still in her arms. "Tell me!"

Guruma's eyes widened in delight as he spotted Celeste.

"Look at how big she is! Nur come see Celeste."

Forrorrois was stunned as Guruma reached out for her daughter.

Celeste's eyes grew round as she spotted Nur. "Momma, it's a horse with funny wings!" she cried out in English.

"Guruma, please, tell me what I have to do to get Trager back," she insisted in Intergaltic as Guruma took Celeste from her and set her on Nur's back.

"Celeste, why don't you talk with Nur? I'm certain that he can tell you some great stories," Guruma said.

"Momma, Nur talks in my head," Celeste bubbled in Intergaltic.

"That's great, peanut, why don't you practice talking with him in your head? Nur can teach you how," Forrorrois encouraged. Once she knew Celeste was occupied, she signaled Thoren and Guruma to join her in the cockpit. "Guruma, please, I can sense you know how I can get Trager back."

"I do, but you have to understand the present political climate on Elda," Guruma stated, lowering his voice. "These are the things that drive council members like Neeha into desperate acts."

"You mean like sanctioning the kidnapping of a child," Thoren stated in frustration.

"Yes, Thoren, but it's even more intertwined than just that single act. Who do you think helped Collinar escape from the rehabilitation station in the first place?" Guruma insisted.

Forrorrois watched as Thoren's eyes widened. "The council, because of Neeha," Thoren breathed. She almost smiled when he digested the information.

"Think about it, Commander," Forrorrois whispered. "The Council of Elda orchestrated Collinar's escape in order to divert me while they took my daughter. Neeha used the council because she wanted to maintain her power base. She didn't have to trust Collinar—she just had to know he would make a straight line for Earth given the right opportunities."

"I think it goes even deeper than that, Forrorrois," Thoren interjected. "There has been a growing rift between the Council of Elda and the Dramudam—a growing anger that overshadows the good that the Dramudam has done in providing peace in this galaxy. The council believes that the Dramudam is directly responsible for undermining the Eldatek cultural values. More and more second and third-born Eldatek males are leaving Elda for opportunities that can only be made available to them in the Dramudam. In fact, it is the only place where an Eldatek male is treated as an equal to their female counterparts."

"Thoren is correct, Forrorrois," Guruma stated. "When I founded the Dramudam, the council didn't object too loudly because they saw it as a place for their surplus male population to go without disrupting the balance of power. But now, more and more first-born males are asking for the opportunity to join the Dramudam. Then, after they've been allowed to become Dramudam, they resist when they are ordered to return to Elda to fulfill their duty and become joined with another house. Without these joinings, the power could shift to houses that were once not so prestigious. When Trager chose to join with you, Forrorrois, an off-worlder, the ripple effect was astonishing. Now that Trager has returned from the Plane of Deception, Neeha seeks to re-secure her standing in the council by forcing Trager to join with Bohata's house."

Forrorrois shook her head. "Guruma, this is all well and good, but how does this help me get Trager back and still keep Celeste safe from Neeha?"

"It's simple really," Guruma began. "You go to the Council of Elda and you demand your right of Penock—Right of First Joining. Even a simple examination will prove that you two are joined. Of course Neeha will then deny your claim because you didn't petition her for her son. The remaining councilors must then decide if the joining is legitimate—which more importantly would make Celeste legitimate. Since Neeha is on the council, I suspect that the other councilors will side with her against an off-worlder."

Forrorrois shook her head. "Guruma, how does that help? Neeha has still won."

"Patience, I haven't finished yet. Next, you will have to challenge Bohata regarding her right to Slovak—Right of Second Joining. This is a bit trickier since everyone will recognize Bohata's right as a widow without a female heir, but now you are also forcing her to prove her family's worth to Neeha."

"Doesn't Neeha already know her family's worth? That would have been established at Talman and Bohata's joining," Thoren jumped in.

Guruma gave a knowing smile. "Yes, but Neeha's status has increased several times since she has risen in the ranks of the council. Bohata's family on the other hand has not faired so well. There is a disparity between the families making Trager worth more.

"What do you mean, worth more?" Forrorrois questioned.

"His worth determines the Joining fee. It's paid whenever the female's family has a lower status than that of the male's family."

Forrorrois looked at the sly old Eldatek and nodded. "Which is now the case...I think I see where you're going with this. So if I can come up with a larger joining fee then it's conceivable that I could out bid Bohata!" Forrorrois exclaimed.

Guruma's eyes sparkled. "Exactly."

"But Guruma, the fee we're talking about here is a fortune," Thoren stated. "Where is Forrorrois going to find that kind of sum?"

Guruma smiled. "There are ways to earn the amounts we are talking about, but it will involve negotiations with less than savory clientele."

Forrorrois narrowed her eyes. "What do you mean less than savory?"

Thoren shook his head. "He means there are traders who are willing to travel into areas that are not normally patrolled by the Dramudam that are called the Environs. It's a lawless portion of space—any goods that are moved through them can bring a premium. Guruma, this is a bad idea."

"I would have to agree with Thoren, Guruma. I don't have the first idea how to negotiate trades in those regions," Forrorrois confessed.

"Ah, but we happen to know someone who does and might be willing to negotiate for his freedom in exchange for his assistance," Guruma replied.

Forrorrois' jaw dropped as she realized what Guruma was suggesting.

Thoren shook his head as he held up his hands. "No. I will not agree to this. Collinar is being transported back to the rehabilitation station where he belongs. He is still responsible for atrocities against countless worlds. To even consider releasing him is unthinkable."

"But Guruma, you already said that Trager is worth more now because of Neeha's standing in the council. Why would she have to re-secure her standing?"

Guruma smiled. "Because, my dear Forrorrois, Neeha could potentially lose her standing in the council if the joining of Trager to Bohata's house doesn't occur—now that the houses of Elda know that he's back. She was already publicly embarrassed once when Trager eloped with an off-worlder. To Neeha, the fee is a formality for Bohata's family, except that you still have a tenuous prior claim on Trager and of course there is your daughter. This complicates things. Now, if she had succeeded in having Collinar kill you during your encounter with him, then she would still have had Celeste to offer to Bohata. Once word got out that you succeeded in freeing Trager from the Plane of Deception, Neeha shifted tactics and used Celeste as an enticement to convince Trager to return to Elda."

Forrorrois pulled back in disgust. "I can't believe that Neeha would attempt to have me killed."

"Oh, I agree, she wouldn't have done it directly. And since Trager volunteered to return back to Elda, she no longer needs to eliminate you. Which also means that Collinar will no longer have an ally to keep him out of the Dramudam rehabilitation station," Guruma added. "Neeha thinks she has outwitted you, but you can still claim your right of Penock—Right of First Joining. A joining, I might add, that was legitimized by witnesses. The council will convene and set the fee that must be met by either party in order to assert their claim on Trager."

"But what about Neeha? She's part of the council!"

"In this matter, Neeha won't have a vote, since she is involved. Once the price has been set, Neeha will have to agree to the party who meets the price. There will be a period of time designated in which the two parties will be given in order to raise the fee. At the end of that period whoever meets the fee will have Trager released to them. If both parties raise the fee, then bidding will begin. Therefore it is imperative that you raise at least twice the fee to ensure that you succeed."

"Guruma, this is like slavery. How can a mother auction her son off that way?" Forrorrois scoffed.

"Forrorrois, it is the way of Elda. One cannot judge what is foreign to them. You must decide if you can do what is necessary."

Forrorrois looked down at the floor plates of her cargo hold. She had Celeste back, but her daughter still needed her father. When she looked up she gazed into Thoren's black eyes. "I must get Trager back. Help me."

Thoren looked away for a few moments before he replied. "Do you know what you are doing?"

Forrorrois nodded. "Yes…I'm making a deal with a monster."

Thoren studied her hard. "What about Celeste?"

"I don't know yet…" Forrorrois confessed.

"I'll take her back to your parents on Earth," Guruma replied.

"No…They'll know where to find her, I don't want my parents placed into danger again," Forrorrois said shaking her head.

"She'll be safe this time—Yononnon is there as well as Jack. And we are watching Earth more carefully now to prevent the council from approaching Earth again. Nur and I will also be keeping an eye on things. You have my word that Celeste will be kept safe."

Forrorrois studied Guruma for several heartbeats. "All right," she finally replied. But wait until I have petitioned the Council of Elda."

"Fair enough," Guruma agreed.

"Then it's settled. Commander Thoren, do I have your permission to take Collinar out of security?" Forrorrois pressed.

Thoren looked up at the ceiling plates. "I can't believe I'm agreeing to this. Yes, Forrorrois, I'll release Collinar into your custody on the condition that you bring him back alive to the Tollon once you have raised the fee for Trager's release. It will be your report that will determine if he has fulfilled his sentence to the review board at the rehabilitation station."

"Thank you, Commander," Forrorrois stated with a formal Dramudam salute and a deep bow.

"Thank me when you've returned in one piece," Thoren replied stiffly. "We'd better head back to Elda. The Tollon should be in orbit now. You have a petition to submit."

Forrorrois felt heaviness in her chest as she looked back into the cargo hold at her daughter laughing with Nur. She would have to leave Celeste once more to raise the fee. How can she explain this to her little one after she's already been through so much?

CHAPTER 14

The Tollon had caught up with Forrorrois' long-distance scout shortly after her encounter with Neeha on the planetoid. She was still numb at Trager's decision to go with his mother so that Celeste would be freed—a selfless act that Forrorrois was desperately trying to reconcile in her mind. Intellectually, she understood why he did it, but emotionally, she couldn't accept that he would willingly go back to Elda under Neeha's control. When she piloted her scout back to the Tollon, Forrorrois held Celeste on her lap. She didn't want another minute to pass for her little girl where she felt afraid. Thoren sat quietly beside her on the jump seat, lost in thought.

When she landed in the Tollon's hangar bay, there was a subdued welcome. Guruma had already informed Goren about what had happened. Forrorrois remained on her scout alone with Celeste while Thoren returned to his staging room off of the bridge and sent a message immediately to the Council of Elda requesting an audience for Forrorrois.

Patiently, the Tollon had orbited Elda for over a kel, before Forrorrois asked Perkins and Alham to stay with Celeste while she took a walk to Thoren's office. Forrorrois knew that the council's slow response was little more than a power game to assert their authority against the Dramudam, who had no jurisdiction inside Eldatek solar system. She waited in Thoren's office on the Tollon and marveled at Thoren's outward calm as they continued to wait, but inside she could sense his irritation at the delay.

Finally, a voice sounded over the comm in his office.

"Commander, we are being hailed by the Elda Council."

"Thank you, put it through to my office," Thoren replied.

Forrorrois sat up slightly as the audio message was relayed.

"The Council of Elda has granted Forrorrois' request for an audience. The council will convene at fourth kel."

The message ended as abruptly as it began. Forrorrois shook her head slowly.

"Short and sweet," she said as she looked up at Thoren.

"Do you need an escort?" Thoren asked.

"No, I will go alone."

"Do you think that's wise?"

Forrorrois gave him a wry smile. "I promise to keep my temper. I think my Eldanese is strong enough to follow their proceedings."

"I see. You do realize that if something happens down there I won't have the authority to assist you."

"I understand, Commander. Now, if you'll excuse me, I have to prepare myself. Guruma be with you, Commander," she said as she rose to her feet and saluted him.

"And also with you, Forrorrois," Thoren replied standing with her, returning the salute.

Forrorrois turned and left the room. Her stomach was in knots by the time she reached her ship in the hangar deck several decks below. She was surprised to find Leenon sitting in the cargo hold of her long-distance scout dressed in traditional orange Eldatek robes.

"Forrorrois, the commander told me that you were ready to go down to the surface," Leenon said as she stood up from the cargo container she had been sitting on.

"Yes, I am," Forrorrois said as she glanced at the bundle of forest green fabric still resting on the cargo container.

Leenon picked up the bundle and presented it to her with her head slightly bowed. "Forrorrois, I've prepared some formal Eldatek robes for you to wear during the audience. It is important that you present your petition as a joined one, not as a Dramudam. The other council members will listen more readily."

Forrorrois looked at the bundle in Leenon's hands, stunned at her offering.

"Thank you, I'll change into them immediately," she said humbly as she took the folded robes.

"Forrorrois, please, allow me to be with you in the council

chamber. I feel responsible for what has occurred and I wish to make amends," Leenon said with her head hung in shame.

Forrorrois pulled the bundle of clothes to her chest, uncertain. Then she reached out with her free hand and touched Leenon's forearm. "It's in the past. I would welcome your guidance and support, my adopted Eldatek mother," she replied formally. Forrorrois felt Leenon's humble relief as she used the respectful term of endearment. "If you could help me dress, I would be most grateful for your assistance."

"I would be honored," Leenon replied, in a hushed voice.

Forrorrois smiled as she subvocalized to her scout to prepare for take-off. She found it hard to remain angry at Leenon when she knew her actions were done for love—even if her love was for Trager.

****

Forrorrois and Leenon stood patiently before the ornately carved doors of the council chamber. Forrorrois wore the forest green robes that Leenon had prepared for her and Leenon was wearing orange robes. The pair was forced to wait well past the appointed time. As the doors opened whispers rose from the hundreds of Eldanese females dressed in a multitude of colored robes that were seated inside. They surrounded Leenon and her on either side of the aisle of the circular-domed room as they entered. Keeping her eyes forward, Forrorrois descended the aisle toward the base of the raised petitioner's stand in front of the council's dais. Leenon whispered to her that they were representatives from the major houses of Elda as they climbed the steep gray stone steps to the petitioner's stand. Forrorrois could feel Neeha's smugness as she stared down at her from her place at the councilors' dais.

"Forrorrois, the council has seen fit to grant you a brief audience. Please step forward and state your reason for this request," the Eldatek councilor to Neeha's right announced in Eldanese.

Forrorrois wet her lips subconsciously as she smoothed her green robes and approached the railing of the petitioners stand. With her ship so far away, she knew she wouldn't have any support from the computer's language banks.

"You can do it," Leenon whispered from behind her. "Trager taught you well."

Forrorrois straightened at Trager's name. "Wise females of the Council of Elda," she began in Eldanese. "I have come before you to petition for my right of Penock with Haator, son of Councilor Neeha."

The room exploded in a rippled of surprised whispers as Neeha stood to her feet. The other two members of the council moved to stop her.

"Who told you to do this? Me'Hal?" Neeha accused.

Forrorrois could feel Leenon's fear grow as Neeha addressed her informally by her Eldanese name in a calculated slight as the councilor pointed towards her, but Forrorrois stood her ground.

"No, Me'Hal ka Wil'Amay of Elda did not, but I am in my rights to demand my right of first joining with Trager," Forrorrois stated, emphasizing Leenon's formal title.

"His name is not Trager! It is Haator, he is Eldatek not Dramudam!" Neeha screamed.

Forrorrois kept her head with the distraught Eldatek female. The other councilors were uncertain what to do in the confusion. Finally, the eldest member took her staff and stuck the floor.

"Enough!"

The chamber fell into an expectant silence as all eyes turned to the elder councilor. The Eldatek female eyed everyone then her gaze fell onto Forrorrois.

"The demand for Penock has been made for Haator, son of Neeha, by Forrorrois of Earth. What proof do you have that this Joining occurred, Forrorrois?"

Forrorrois was surprised when Leenon stepped up beside her and placed her hands on the railing. "Councilor Kil'Treahaa, the Joining occurred—I witnessed it and it was strong," Leenon replied.

"You spiteful..." Neeha began but cut herself short when the elder councilor tightened her grip on her staff and warned her with a glance.

"Me'Hal ka Wil'Amay of Elda, second daughter of Wil'Amay of Elda," Councilor Kil'Treahaa began in a formal tone to restore order. "Why would you vouch for this off-worlder?" she asked.

"I vouch for her as her adopted mother," Leenon stated. Forrorrois looked up at Leenon, stunned at her public statement.

Once again the room began to roil in excited whispers.

"Me'Hal ka Wil'Amay...do you understand what you are saying?" Councilor Kil'Treahaa asked.

"Yes," Leenon stated, smoothing her orange robes to calm her nerves. "When Forrorrois came to the Tollon we had no records to tell us what planet she was from. I was given the responsibility to care for her when she chose to train as a Dramudam by Commander Thoren. Medically, I had determined that she was barely a young adult and Commander Thoren felt that it would be best if she was supervised instead of housed with the other recruits. Both Yononnon and I took this responsibility very seriously. She is a daughter to us and I sanctioned the Joining between Haator and her once she was of age."

"And yet, even with this supervision, she still engaged in a relationship with a senior officer," Councilor Kil'Treahaa pressed.

"Pardon your indulgence," Leenon continued, "but that relationship occurred after Forrorrois had completed her training. She was detached from the Tollon at that point and assigned to Earth to protect it. Trager was not her superior at the time of their joining. In fact, Forrorrois was of age in her culture and free to make the choice of a joining."

Forrorrois looked briefly down at her hands—Yononnon had never told Leenon what he had suspected about her and Trager before she had originally left for Earth. *Just as well,* she thought, nervously.

"I see," the elder councilor remarked. "Me'Hal ka Wil'Amay, I should remind you that even if Forrorrois was of a consensual age on her world, Haator was not free to make such a choice," Kil'Treahaa stated. When Leenon didn't answer, she continued. "Me'Hal ka Wil'Amay, as a second daughter I can understand a yearning for a family of your own, but this action is very unorthodox. What proof do you have, besides an adoptive mother's love, that this Joining occurred?" Councilor Kil'Treahaa continued.

Forrorrois could sense Leenon struggle for a moment as her claim was challenged, but she continued without missing a beat. "You can examine Haator's mind and find the joining signature, then examine Forrorrois' mind and you will find that they match," Leenon replied.

The whispers erupted once more.

"I am a trained Med Tech, I know that this can be done," Leenon insisted. "And there is the matter of Celeste, their daughter, proof that their Joining has been consummated."

"It does not matter! The Joining was not sanctioned by me!" Neeha began to argue. "Neither Forrorrois—nor you, Me'Hal—petitioned for my son…"

The elderly councilor banged the floor once more with her staff. "This matter must be discussed before a decision can be made. Neeha, I must ask you to abstain on this issue since you are directly involved. Further, the decision will impact Bohata's right to Slovak with Haator. This session is adjourned for one-quarter kel at which time a decision will be rendered. Forrorrois and Me'Hal ka Wil'Amay, you will be escorted to a waiting area while we deliberate. Neeha, you too must leave during these deliberations."

Forrorrois felt Neeha's rage at being excluded from the discussion, but she left without argument. Leenon touched Forrorrois' shoulder and motioned for her to follow the two high guards in red as they approached the petitioner's stand. Forrorrois looked at Leenon then climbed down the steep steps and followed them out of the chamber.

****

Forrorrois looked over at Leenon as the hour ended. The sound of the door opening to the chamber that they were waiting in made her stomach tighten. She grabbed Leenon's hand tightly.

"I'm scared," she whispered.

"The females of the council are wise, Forrorrois, all of Elda is watching them," Leenon whispered back.

Forrorrois narrowed her eyes. "What?"

"Your case is being scrutinized by more than the council. The Eldatek race is chaffing under the present archaic system. If the council's decision doesn't appear fair, then the debate will widen to the general population. There are those that sympathize with your situation, even though you are an off-worlder," Leenon stated in a hushed voice.

Forrorrois glanced at her, but she didn't have a chance to respond as two high guards in red robes entered the room and escorted them from the waiting area back to the council chamber. Together, they climbed the steep gray steps to the petitioner's stand.

The members of the council stared back at her. Forrorrois was surprised to see Neeha, back in her seat among them. The elder councilor tapped her staff onto the floor for the council chamber to become silent.

"A decision has been made," Councilor Kil'Treahaa announced.

All eyes turned to her in anticipation.

"In Forrorrois' petition of the right of Penock with regard to Haator, son of Neeha, the council agrees…"

Forrorrois closed her eyes briefly at the announcement in a quick silent prayer of thanks. When Neeha moved to object, she was silenced by a raised index finger from Councilor Kil'Treahaa as the elder councilor continued.

"The council also recognizes Celeste as Haator's legitimate child and heir to Forrorrois' line. She can remain with Forrorrois with no further threat of removal."

Forrorrois began to shake as she realized Celeste was safe. She tightened her grip on the railing to maintain her composure while the elder councilor continued.

"On the petition of Bohata's right to Slovak with Haator, the council also agrees. Haator, the second-born male of Neeha is expected to fulfill his duty to Bohata after the death of her joined one, Neeha's first-born male, Talman. Since these two legitimate claims conflict, the council is forced to resolve the claim by establishing a joining fee based on Haator's present worth. This joining fee will be based on the independent relationship of each petitioner's household to that of Haator's household. This is to preserve parity of status under the laws of Elda."

Forrorrois' stomach sank as she took Leenon's hand.

"The joining fees must be presented in two mol time in this chamber. If both petitioners present their assigned fee then bidding will commence starting at the amount of the higher fee. The joining fee for Bohata's family will be set at fifty thousand trups. The joining fee for Forrorrois' family is three hundred thousand trups. These values are set based on status and rank. This decision is final. This session is adjourned."

Forrorrois' heart stopped at the amount of the Joining fee. She gripped the railing tighter as the councilor's staff hit the stone floor. The chamber was abuzz with astonishment. The sheer weight of the emotions threatened to overwhelm her as she felt her knees begin to buckle.

"Say nothing," Leenon whispered, taking her arm.

"But Leenon…" Forrorrois whispered back.

"Say nothing," Leenon warned.

Forrorrois looked up at Neeha as she smiled smugly down at her from her place at the council table. Neeha had won this round, but Forrorrois had two mol to change the decision.

Leenon guided her down the steep steps from the petitioner's stand. The eyes of the prominent houses of Elda followed her and Leenon as they made their way up the ramped aisle to the large ornate doors. Waves of hope and uncertainty churned from the hundreds of female Eldatek that stood to either side of them as they passed. Forrorrois glanced back at the council dais once more and found Councilor Kil'Treahaa still watching her. She felt no animosity from the elderly female—the decision she handed down was well within the laws of Elda.

Forrorrois remained silent until they left the city and boarded her long-distance scout ship. As the hatch slide shut she stepped into the cockpit and sat down heavily into her command chair. Leenon took her seat beside her in the jump seat.

"Three hundred thousand trups...Leenon, how am I going to raise three hundred thousand trups in two mol?"

"It is a very steep sum," Leenon confessed.

"How did they come up with such different sums?" Forrorrois said as she blindly stared at her ship's controls.

"Simple—Bohata's family has status on Elda and you have none on your own or even combined with mine since I am also presently a Dramudam without any property. The joining fee is used to prevent the status of families from becoming too diluted."

"It's all about power!" Forrorrois spat.

"Unfortunately, yes," Leenon agreed.

Forrorrois shook her head as she went through the motions and prepared for lift-off. "Somehow, I'll find a way to raise this amount," she vowed. But her heart was heavy when she knew she would need to raise more than six hundred thousand trups to even hope to win the bidding.

✶✶✶✶✶✶✶✶✶✶

Forrorrois wasted no time when she had returned to the Tollon with Leenon. Her heart was breaking at the decision she had to make, but she knew where she was going, Celeste would be in danger. She would be safer on Earth under Yononnon and Jack's protection. Forrorrois knelt down on the floor panels of the Tollon's hangar deck as she looked at her daughter. Nur stood off to one side, with Guruma sitting on his back, quietly waiting while Forrorrois prepared to say her goodbyes. Forrorrois gathered Celeste in her arms and hugged her tightly, painfully aware that Goren was standing behind her.

Perkins and Alham had already said goodbye, since they had to go out on patrol.

"You be a good little girl and listen to Uncle Guruma and Nur. They are going to take you back home to Grandma and Grandpa," Forrorrois said in English. "And Uncle Yononnon and Uncle Jack are going to need your help while I'm away, so you need to be their special helper."

"Why can't you come with me, Momma?" Celeste replied, her fear of separation pressing in Forrorrois' mind.

"I have to help Poppa come home, peanut," Forrorrois said, pulling away slightly so she could see her daughter's face. "You want me to do that, don't you?"

"Yes," Celeste admitted. "Why did Poppa go with that mean lady?"

Forrorrois placed her hand gently on her daughter's cheek and shook her head. "Celeste, Neeha isn't a mean lady, she's just very sad. Poppa is her son and he wanted to help her be happy again. She didn't want to be mean to you. Neeha's your grandmother, just like my mother is your grandmother."

She empathically felt the three-and-a-half year old struggle with the concept.

"After Poppa makes Neeha happy again, he'll come home, right, Momma?"

Forrorrois smiled at her daughter's innocent black-and-white world. "Yes, Celeste, Poppa will come home again once Neeha is happy again. You'd better go with Uncle Guruma now. Nur's going to give you both a ride back home. And when you get there maybe Uncle Yononnon can tell you some stories."

"Does Unca Non tell funny stories?" Celeste asked, wide eyed.

"Yes, he does," Forrorrois replied, smoothing back her daughter's long black hair. "And Uncle George is there too. He can show you some magic."

"I like Unca George's magic tricks!" she squealed. "Maybe he can show Nur and Unca Guruma, too!"

"Of course he can. Now be a good girl," Forrorrois said as she scooped Celeste up in her arms and placed her on Nur's back in front of Guruma. "And tell everyone I love them!"

"I will, Momma," Celeste called out as Guruma placed a protective arm around her.

"You're doing the right thing, Forrorrois," Guruma whispered.

"I hope so," Forrorrois whispered back. She straightened and smiled at her daughter. "Be safe, Guruma," she said in Intergaltic as Guruma grabbed a handful of red mane. Nur turned and ran down the deck then vanished into thin air. "Please be safe," she whispered. She looked up when she felt a hand on her shoulder from behind. It was Goren.

"Yononnon and Jack will protect her and your family," he rasped.

Forrorrois reached up and collected his fingers in hers. "I know...I just worry about her...about everybody."

"For right now, you only have two beings to worry about—yourself and Trager. I can come with you, if you want me to?" Goren replied. "I'm certain that the Commander would give me leave from the Tollon."

Forrorrois looked up at her Silmanon friend and smiled. "That's all right, Goren. Where I'm heading there is only one other being I can take."

"Watch your back then," Goren replied.

"I will," Forrorrois replied. She released his hand with a sigh and headed out the hangar bay doors.

Her mind was spinning as she approached the security corridor. She was met by Thoren when she entered the secured area.

"Commander, is everything ready?"

Thoren nodded, but she could sense his reserve.

"If there was any other way, I would do it," Forrorrois reassured him.

"I know," Thoren replied. "I'll keep the corridors empty until you have him on your scout ship."

"Thank you, Commander."

She watched as he stepped aside. The force shield dropped,

letting her proceed down the corridor. Forrorrois stopped in front of Collinar's holding cell and found the Utahar lying on his bunk staring up at the ceiling plates.

"What do I owe the pleasure?" he stated, slowly looking over in her direction.

"A deal," she replied.

Collinar's aloofness shifted to curiosity as he rolled to face her. "A deal? What a tantalizing thought. What kind of a deal, my little Forrorrois?"

Forrorrois felt the words stick in her throat. "A deal for your release," she replied.

Collinar's eyes widened slightly then narrowed. "Oh, you are tempting me. And what do I need to do in order to receive this deal?"

"You need to help me raise some capital in a very short amount of time."

Collinar snorted a laugh and stood to his feet. "Are you offering to let me buy my freedom? I'm astonished a Dramudam would make such an offer."

Forrorrois narrowed her eyes. "I'm not making the offer as a Dramudam."

Collinar studied her for a moment with intrigue. "I see. What do I have to do to buy my freedom?"

"You have to help me get Trager back," she replied.

"Pardon me, but didn't I just give you information to free Trager from the Plane of Deception?"

"Yes, but he traded himself for our daughter, Celeste," Forrorrois admitted.

Collinar's surprise filtered into her mind. "What a selfless and absolutely foolish thing to do," he replied.

Forrorrois closed her hand in a fist. "Forget it, Collinar—coming to you with this offer was a mistake." As she turned to leave, Collinar jumped from his bunk and crossed over to the opening—a hairsbreadth from the purple hue of the force shield.

"Wait, Forrorrois, I was hasty in my choice of words," he recanted.

Forrorrois folded her arms as she turned back to look at him. "I said forget it. Not in a million revolution am I going to ask for your help. This was a stupid idea."

"Oh, Forrorrois, the fact that you even considered it makes me wonder even more," he purred. "Ah, yes, you said you were coming to me not as a Dramudam, but as what, Forrorrois? Why do you need a large amount of capital? Except for ransom, maybe? Perhaps, to get Trager back from Elda?"

Forrorrois knew she needed to play her hand now or Collinar would lose interest. "Yes."

"Hmmm, let me get this straight. You want me to help you raise a large sum of capital in a short amount of time to ransom Trager—from his mother. And, in exchange, you will guarantee my freedom?"

Forrorrois ignored his smugness and nodded. "Yes, that about sums it up."

"What kind of capital are we talking about?"

"At least six hundred thousand trups," she replied deadpanned.

Collinar's eyes widened. "Not the kind of capital the average Dramudam has lying about." Then he began to chuckle as he shook his head. "Wait this isn't a ransom…it's a joining fee! You got caught trying to scamper off with Neeha's second born son. And didn't I hear recently that Trager's brother, Neeha's first born, passed away? Ah, Forrorrois, you have gotten yourself into a mess," Collinar replied, sitting back down on his bunk, amused.

Forrorrois knew the Utahar commander well enough not to show the anger that was bubbling inside her. He was goading her. Instead, she sighed and turned to walk away. "I'm sorry you're not interested in my deal. The Tollon will be reaching the Rehabilitation Center in two more cycle. I doubt that Neeha will help you escape a second time—especially now that she has Trager."

She could sense Collinar's bravado shift to concern. "Now, Forrorrois, I never said I wasn't interested. And personally, I would like the opportunity to repay Neeha for her kind gesture. I could be persuaded—if there was some additional capital offered up beside my freedom. A being has to have something to restart his life with. You weren't thinking of just releasing me as a pauper, were you?"

"The thought had crossed my mind," she replied.

"I would have been disappointed in you if it hadn't," Collinar said with a sneer. "All right, I declare a truce between us until the funds are raised. I will expect the reasonable sum of fifty thousand trups for my troubles as well as my freedom," Collinar said.

Forrorrois nodded. "A truce then. You will receive fifty thousand trups for your assistance and your freedom—if we succeed to raise the capital. But to collect either, you must return with me to the Tollon so that I can vouch for your cooperation to the release board at the Rehabilitation Center. One false move and I will kill you."

Collinar's eyes sparkled at her threat. "But of course," he replied.

On Forrorrois' silent command the force shield of Collinar's holding cell dissipated.

She waved for him to come out.

"What? No shackles?" he said as he looked at the now deactivated opening.

"We're under a truce, and besides I think you'd enjoy them too much," she replied, waving him out once more.

Collinar began to chuckle as he stepped into the corridor and began to walk in front of her.

Forrorrois followed behind him as they made their way to the hangar bay. To Thoren's word the corridors were empty of all personnel. When they entered the cargo hold of her ship, she could feel Collinar's confidence increase.

"There is a change of clothes for you in the rear cabin. Come to the cockpit once you're changed. I'll be lifting off in a few moments, so don't take too long."

"Yes, my commander," Collinar replied.

Forrorrois glared at him then headed for the cockpit. She sat down in her command chair and began preflight preparations. It wasn't long before Collinar returned wearing dark baggy merchant pants and a gray top with a vest.

"Not very stylish," he commented.

"I don't want to stand out where we are going," Forrorrois replied.

"Then you'd better change out of that uniform and keep your Dramudam mark hidden. They get one whiff of what you are and they'll kill you on sight."

"I would be disappointed if they didn't try," she replied. "I'm glad that you're aware of where we're heading," she said, finishing her preflight.

"The Environs are the best place, if not the only place, to raise a large amount of capital—assuming you're willing to take some risks. With this fast, well equipped, long-distance scout of yours, we could move through some pretty dangerous areas. Depending on the type of cargo, we could see a reasonable profit within a mol. The full amount will be tricky, but possible in two mol time."

"Then we'll go for the highest risk jobs," Forrorrois said without looking at him.

"I may enjoy this after all," Collinar replied. "The idea of seeing you working the other side is enticing."

"Well, Collinar, don't get too enticed, I don't want to be forced to kill you before we even get started. The ship's on autopilot. I'll be back after I've change," Forrorrois stated, rising from her chair.

"Try to make it alluring, you'll get more…offers for jobs that way."

Forrorrois forced the nausea down from his suggestion. "I'll keep that in mind," Forrorrois replied then she headed for her rear cabin to change, but in her mind all she could think was that this was going to be a long two mol.

****

Jack stepped outside Forrorrois' base for some fresh air and a walk when he heard a noise on the edge of the clearing in front of the hangar opening. He stepped around and almost fell backwards when he came face-to-face with a large black horse with a fiery red mane, tail and eyes. As he looked up, he swallowed hard when he realized that the horse had equally large red bat-like wings.

A familiar giggle sounded from its back.

"Unca Jack!"

Jack warily looked between the horse's wings and spotted Celeste on it's back—behind her sat none other than Guruma himself! He'd seen him once or twice when he had come to visit with Forrorrois.

"Celeste! Guruma! Where did you come from? And who is your…friend?" Jack called out in Intergaltic, nodding towards the bat-winged horse.

"Our friend is Nur, and he was kind enough to bring Celeste home to her grandparents," Guruma replied, sliding off of Nur's back then lifting Celeste down to the ground.

Jack knelt to the ground as Celeste wiggled from Guruma's grip and catapulted into his waiting arms. He squeezed her tight, fighting the tears that threatened to fall as he felt her tiny beating heart against his chest. "I've missed you so much, peanut! Your mom told me you were safe, but she didn't tell me you were going to be home so soon!"

"Nur took us home, it was really fun. There were all these pretty colors, and it was a bit scary, but Nur told me it was all right," Celeste replied, squeezing him back.

"That's great Celeste. Could you tell Nur thank you for bringing you home for me?

"You can tell him, Unca Jack! All you got to do is think it," she replied.

Jack collected Celeste into his arms and stood up. He eyed Nur for a moment then nodded his head and thought, thank you. To his surprise the large horse creature bobbed his head and snorted.

The sound of Danielle's voice sounded behind him.

"Jack, are you out here?" her voice trailed off in English when she rounded the granite outcropping. "Oh my sweet Lord," she gasped, stepping back.

"It's all right, Danielle, this is Guruma and Nur, they've brought Celeste home," Jack said calmly back in English as he turned towards her, still holding Celeste in his arms.

Danielle gasped as she spotted Celeste and ran to her, ignoring Guruma and Nur. "Oh my goodness, Celeste! Thank you, Lord! My little granddaughter is home!"

"What is all this racket, Danielle?" Frank said as he came around the corner followed by Yononnon.

Jack smiled as they both stopped and gapped at Nur and Guruma.

"Give her here, Jack," Danielle pleaded. "Let me hold my little peanut."

With a broad grin, Jack handed Celeste over as Danielle smothered her granddaughter with hugs and kisses. Frank soon joined her.

Yononnon saluted Guruma, his fist over his heart with his thumb and small finger extended as he bowed his head. "Thank you, Guruma," he stated in Intergaltic.

"No, Yononnon, thank Nur. He gave us a ride back to Earth. He's a Beliespeir, he speaks by telepathy."

"A Beliespeir, I thought they were only legend," Yononnon gasped. "It is an honor to meet you, Nur. You do us all a great service by returning Celeste back to her grandparents," Yononnon said with a deep bow.

Nur bowed back to Yononnon.

Jack was startled when he heard a voice in his mind that wasn't the computer.

It is a great pleasure to see Celeste with her family. She has a joyful mind and I will miss her. Guruma, we must return to the Tollon, Nur replied.

"You're right, Nur," Guruma agreed. "Jack, Yononnon, Forrorrois has asked that you watch over Celeste until she can return in three mol. If it is Monomay's will, Trager will be with her."

Yononnon stepped forward to assist Guruma onto Nur's back.

"Where is Trager now?" Jack asked.

"On Elda," Guruma replied, settling in behind Nur's great wings.

Yononnon looked up at Guruma, stunned. "You don't mean that."

"Unfortunately, I do," Guruma replied, looking over at Jack. "Bohata has invoked her right of Slovak with Trager and Forrorrois has challenged her with Penock. Now the race begins to see who will raise the Joining fee."

"Monomay protect them both," Yononnon whispered. "What is Forrorrois' fee?"

"Three hundred thousand trups."

From the horrified look on Yononnon's face, Jack knew that the amount was a king's ransom.

"How will Forrorrois raise such a sum?" Yononnon gasped.

"She will, that's all that matters," Guruma replied. "Come, Nur, let us go back to the Tollon."

Before Yononnon or Jack could object, Nur leapt forward and vanished into thin air. Jack watched as Yononnon's shoulder's sagged. He shared his concern for Trager and Forrorrois. As he looked over at Celeste and the Jolans, he wished things were different.

"I don't understand, Jack," Frank said as he stepped away from Danielle and Celeste. "I heard Trager's name. What's going on?"

Jack heaved a sigh. "Trager is still on Elda," he explained switching from Intergaltic to English. "But I don't know exactly why."

Stunned, Frank looked at him then he shifted his gaze to the quiet subcommander beside him.

"Yononnon, you have to know something more. I can see it on your face," Frank urged.

Yononnon glanced at Jack then cleared his throat. "Trager is being held by the Council of Elda until Forrorrois can bargain for his release," the subcommander struggled in English.

"Why? What has he done?" Frank pressed.

"He is the second born son, and his first born brother has died. Custom states that he must join with Bohata, his brother's wife."

"But he's already married to my daughter. You're not telling me that you take multiple wives on Elda?"

Jack almost smiled as Yononnon glanced at him—confused by the odd suggestion.

"No Frank, the Eldatek are a matrilineal culture. It's the women who can take multiple husbands," Jack replied.

Frank looked at him stunned. "OK, but what about Danica?"

"She has claimed her right for Trager as well," Yononnon stated. "To settle the matter Danica and Bohata must each bid for the right to keep him."

"I still don't understand," Frank replied.

"Think of it as a dowry, Frank," Jack offered.

"I thought they were an advanced culture?" Frank insisted. "This is insane."

"I agree with you, Mr. Jolan, this practice is barbaric," Yononnon stated. "Please excuse me—I must attend to a few items on my ship. I'm glad to see that Celeste has been returned to your family."

Frank placed his hand on Yononnon's forearm, stopping him. "Please, forgive me for my rudeness. I realize that Trager is your friend. This news must be very hard for you as well."

Jack watched as Yononnon's shoulder's sagged slightly as he looked down at Frank's hand. He nodded.

"There is nothing to forgive, Mr. Jolan. Your daughter is strong. If anyone can find a way to bring Trager home, she will, if it is Monomay's will," Yononnon replied, lightly touching Frank's pale hand with his chestnut-brown fingers. Then he turned and headed for the hangar bay.

Frank watched after him then looked over at Jack. "I really stuck my foot in it that time," he swore under his breath.

"No, actually you didn't," Jack replied. "Yononnon really does believe that the practice is barbaric. Men on Elda are considered second-class citizens. What happened to Trager only reinforced that with Yononnon. He's rooting for Danica to succeed so that his friend will be free to return to Earth."

"Wow and I though my government was screwed up," Frank

replied. He heaved a sigh then shook his head. "Who was this Monomay that he mentioned?"

"Think of Monomay as another name for God," Jack answered. "He may not show it, but Yononnon is a very religious person."

"I didn't know that," Frank replied. "But I should have guessed from his demeanor."

Jack rested a hand on Frank's shoulder and smiled, glad that his friend was able to accept Yononnon in a different light. He wished that Trager and Forrorrois had come home with their daughter and they were a family once more. But for now, he must honor Forrorrois' wishes to protect her family here on Earth.

∗∗∗∗∗∗∗∗∗∗∗

Forrorrois returned to the cockpit dressed in boots, baggy cargo pants and a dark long sleeved top that clung to her figure. She had on a vest with pockets to camouflage her assets.

Collinar appraised her as she entered.

"Subtle, but intriguing. Are you certain you haven't done this before?" he said with a leer.

"No…that's why I have you along," Forrorrois replied.

Collinar smiled. "It's good to be needed. All right then you'll need to loose the braid, it's too Dramudam."

Forrorrois looked at him, and then she removed the clip that secured the end of her long braid and shook out her auburn hair.

"Very nice," Collinar said with a sparkle in his eye.

Forrorrois shook her head in disgust.

"Now, about your name—Forrorrois isn't going to work out there. Believe it or not, you do have a bit of a reputation. Utahar tend to talk."

Forrorrois looked at him in surprise. "You've got to be kidding me. And what do you suggest that I call myself?"

"Danica will work—it's not as notable as a Dramudam ship name like Forrorrois."

"And what are you going to call yourself?" Forrorrois asked as she took her seat.

"Trell," Collinar replied. "I've used it in the past while I've been in the Environs. It may prove useful to have some name recognition to get some of the bigger jobs."

"All right, Trell," Forrorrois replied. "Here are the ground rules. I refuse to take any job that involves trafficking in nonspacefaring beings or weapons. I rank mercy missions high on the list of 'yes, we can do it' and I don't allow anyone to touch me without an invitation."

Collinar sighed as he shook his head. "You've just ruled out the most profitable jobs."

"We'll cope," Forrorrois replied.

"All right, Danica. Let me punch in the coordinates for our first stop. Hopefully, we'll find someone still working that area that we can contact."

"Be my guest, Trell," Forrorrois said as she motioned towards the control panel.

CHAPTER 15

After two days of travel, Forrorrois finally guided her long-distance scout ship down to the landing pad of the nondescript trading post. She had engaged the hyperfold drive twice to cover the vast distance to the Environs from Elda. So far, Collinar had kept his word and the use of his trader name, Trell, seemed to carry some weight in getting them past the scrutiny of a few lone mercenaries. Forrorrois looked over at him as she cut her engines and sensed Collinar's adrenaline was engaged.

"Are you ready?" Collinar said as he released the harness and looked out at the dusty world beyond the cockpit.

"Yes," Forrorrois replied. "I'll wait at the top of the ramp while you meet with your contact. At the first sign of trouble, I come down and introduce myself with my hand resting on my weapon."

"Close enough," Collinar said as he rose from his seat. "Here he comes now."

Forrorrois looked out the cockpit canopy and spotted an approaching Gintzer that reminded her of Peldor. Collinar rose from his seat and headed to the back, Forrorrois followed and subvocalized to her ship to open the hatch and extend the ramp.

She was surprised when Collinar drew on a smile as he descended the ramp.

"Motan, old friend, it's been a long time," Collinar called out with a wave of his hand.

Forrorrois watched the Gintzer, sensing a bit of animosity from the boar-like creature. Without warning Motan swung at Collinar and caught him square in the jaw. The sight of Collinar being hit brought a smirk to her lips. Collinar stumbled backwards and touched his hand to his lip which was cut and bleeding yellow blood. Forrorrois slowly came down the ramp, keeping her eye on the Gintzer with her hand on her weapon. Motan glanced at her then looked again at her reaction. "What's so funny?" he demanded.

Collinar looked over at her, surprised.

"Nothing," she replied. "Nothing at all. You two just carry on. I like a good show."

Collinar narrowed his eyes at her, but Motan began to laugh. "Trell, you old space slug, where did you find this one?"

Collinar recovered his composure and nodded towards Forrorrois. "Motan, this is Danica, she's my new pilot. She flies a fast ship and is handy with weapons—as well as other things."

"I see," Motan replied. "A bit pale and small for my liking, but I can see the appeal."

Forrorrois nodded towards him and lowered her hand from her weapon.

"Quite a ship you've got there...Dramudam design," Motan continued. "Where did you find it?"

"I...salvaged it," Collinar replied, with a slight smile.

Motan grinned, showing his small chewing teeth spaced between his protruding tusks on his lower jaw. "I bet you did. Now, Trell, tell me what type of job were you looking for?"

"Something with a large payoff," Collinar replied.

Motan rub his tusk absently in thought. "I might have something, it's risky, possibly some weapons play. I've been having trouble finding a taker."

"Intriguing," Collinar replied. "Please tell me more."

"There's an item that needs to be moved from a certain royal house to another royal house. Unfortunately, there is a minor war that's waging between these two royal houses. Rumor has it that the return of this item might be the key to ending this minor war."

Forrorrois looked at Motan and shook her head. "Then why doesn't the one house just return the item to the second house?"

Motan looked at her and started to laugh. "Silly female, affairs of state are never that simple. By just returning the item, the first royal house would have to admit that they took the item in the first place, and then they would lose face. If the house that they stole the item from admits that they were unable to protect the item from their rival house, then they would lose face. If the item were returned without it being publicly known that it was ever stolen, then the incident never really happened."

Forrorrois looked at the Gintzer and then at Collinar. Her head spun from the convoluted logic.

"Don't worry your lovely little head about it, Danica," Collinar replied with a condescending smile. "I just need you to fly and shoot."

Forrorrois moved to speak but Collinar cut her off.

"Motan, this sounds perfect and profitable. When will you have the arrangements made for us?"

"I can have details for you in one half kel. In the meantime, please partake in the hospitality of the outpost," Motan replied then he hesitated and looked at Forrorrois. "Maybe not all the hospitality," he added with a leer.

"Thank you, Motan. I think this time I have some other distractions to keep me occupied," Collinar replied, lustfully following Motan's gaze to Forrorrois. "We'll meet you back here in a half a kel."

Forrorrois fought the revulsion in her stomach while she held his gaze and drew on a seductive smile. Without warning, she slinked her way down the ramp over to Collinar's side and slipped her arm around his waist then dropped her hand to his buttock and squeezed.

Collinar's eyes widened at her action. He quickly recovered and pulled her close.

Motan gave a lusty laugh. "Excellent."

Forrorrois watched the Gintzer turn and walk back toward the cluster of builds past the landing site. She moved to extract herself from Collinar's grip, but he tightened his hold.

"Not yet," Collinar whispered. "Get back on the ship first, we're still being watched."

Forrorrois reached out with her empathic senses and confirmed two minds just on the periphery of her range. "I agree," Forrorrois replied. "I count at least two." She let Collinar lead her back up the ramp into the cargo hold. Once inside, she gasped as he turned her suddenly towards him and kissed her fiercely, yet tenderly, on the lips. Her body reacted to his fire, but her mind cried out in disgust.

Forrorrois subvocalized for the hatch to close and the ramp to retract. As soon as the hatch shut, she drew her weapon and slammed Collinar into the reinforced metal.

Collinar licked his lips with a grin. "Very convincing," he said, straightening to his full two-meter height.

"Keep your distance," Forrorrois warned, punctuating her words with her stun weapon.

"You taste even sweeter than I thought you would," he continued, easing himself onto the crate next to the cockpit doorway while he nursed his jaw.

"Hope you enjoyed it, it's you're last," she replied, putting her weapon back on her waist. "I'm getting some rest—alone. Keep an eye out just incase someone decides my ship is worth more to them than us doing that job."

Collinar leaned back against the lockers behind the crate he was sitting on. "Yes, my commander."

Forrorrois narrowed her eyes at him then turned and stepped into the rear cabin. When the door slid shut, she walked over to the bunk and collapsed on the firm padding. "Trager, I'm trying really hard here. Please stay strong for me," she whispered.

✶✶✶✶✶✶✶✶✶✶✶

Collinar tasted his lips once more as he watched the door to the rear cabin of Forrorrois' long-distance scout. Her seductive act in front of Motan was very convincing. *Why are you taking this risk, Forrorrois?* Collinar thought as he continued his stare at the door panel. *Why are you willing to break all the rules to get Trager back?* There had been only one being Collinar ever felt that way about—Ma'Kelda. But his beautiful subcommander betrayed him, forcing him to kill her—just like he was forced to kill her treacherous adopted daughter, Ahzell. *Trager will betray you, just like Ma'Kelda betrayed me,* Collinar thought with a sneer toward the rear cabin's door. *You were better off with him trapped in the Plane of Deception. On Elda, he will revert back to his cultural boundaries and become a concubine—a pathetic second choice.*

Collinar came to his feet and stepped into the cockpit. He knew there wasn't much he could do there since Forrorrois had blocked all the controls from him, but he wanted to get some distance from her all the same.

****

'The ship is being approached,' the long-distance scout's computer sounded in Forrorrois' mind through her zendra link. She opened her eyes and she stared up at ceiling plates above her bunk in the rear cabin. "Time for act two," Forrorrois murmured as she climbed out of the bunk and looked in the mirror. Her auburn hair fell softly about her shoulders. Forrorrois resisted the urge to pull her tresses back into a loose braid. The traditional Dramudam single braid would only raise more suspicions. "You can do this," she told herself as she turned towards the door. When the panel slid open, she was surprised to find Collinar poised to knock.

"Ready to go?" she asked, stepping in front of the hatch.

"Yes," Collinar replied, falling into step beside her.

Forrorrois was glad that he resisted touching her—feeling instead his excitement for the upcoming job when the hatch slid open and the ramp extend to meet Motan.

"Let me do the talking," Collinar whispered to her.

"Of course," Forrorrois replied.

"Motan, please approach," Collinar called out.

The Gintzer showed his lower teeth in a grin and came up the ramp. "Trell, I'm glad that you and Danica are still here. I have the information crystal regarding the pickup. You get the drop-off information there. As for the item—I don't have any information except that it's at these coordinates, but only for the next three kel. After that it will be moved to another location."

"What about the fee?" Collinar asked before he touched the crystal.

Motan chuckled. "The fee will be triple standard rate plus hazard. You'll get 30 percent at the pickup and the remainder on successful delivery."

Forrorrois sensed Collinar's excitement at the amount, but his exterior remained calm.

"If this job is so dangerous, then why doesn't it pay more?" Collinar replied.

"Trell, as a comrade you know that if it paid more an unsavory element would want to take the job—instead, the powers that be want it kept in the strictest confidence. If you perform well, there may be more profitable jobs to follow."

Collinar smiled and took the crystal from Motan. "Well said."

"I thought you'd understand," Motan replied. "Hopefully, I'll see you in five cycle."

"Hopefully, sooner," Collinar said with a nod.

Forrorrois watched the Gintzer turn and walk away. When he was a respectful distance from the ship, she closed the hatch and retracted the ramp. "So what is fee?" she asked Collinar.

"One hundred thousand trups," Collinar said as he held up the clear crystal.

Forrorrois' eyes widened. "That's great!"

"No, it's not," Collinar replied. "We should have gotten twice that amount if the job's as dangerous as Motan is implying. Where's a data port?"

"Right here," Forrorrois said as she pointed to the narrow bench set into the wall next to the side hatch. "Why didn't you ask for more if you think it's more dangerous?"

"That's not how it's done here, besides this job's a test. Motan wants to be certain he can trust both of us before he offers the more lucrative jobs," Collinar stated as he inserted the crystal and waited.

Forrorrois smiled as the coordinates and information filtered into her mind.

"Where's the monitor?" Collinar demanded.

"What monitor? This ship uses zendra communications to uplink data," she replied.

"You're kidding me!"

"Actually, no, Collinar, I could inject you with zendra if you'd like?"

Collinar gave her a horrified look. "Don't even think about injecting some parasitic life form into me!"

"Oh, come now, Collinar, think of the advantages you would gain by such a modification? And besides, the zendra are symbiotic, not parasitic."

"You disgust me," Collinar replied.

"Thank you," Forrorrois said with a smile.

"Just shut up and get us out of here before Motan thinks we're having second thoughts," Collinar snapped. "Put in the coordinates so I can see where we're heading."

Forrorrois smirked to herself and walked past him to her command chair in the cockpit. Collinar flopped down beside her in the jump seat and stewed. "The coordinates are laid in," she said as she brought the long-range sensors on line. Collinar leaned forward to study the holographic star map that now floated between them and the canopy.

"That's the Intonius system," he announced. "Not a very friendly place."

Forrorrois was a few steps ahead of him and accessed her data files on the Intonius system. The star system was a virtual war zone—with all ships challenged the moment they approached. "Tell me about it," Forrorrois replied as she initiated her take-off sequence and eased the long-distance scout from the pad.

Collinar gave her a look then continued. "There are two habitable worlds in the system, each with a royal house: Sten and Pedra. Rumor has it that the beings both evolved on a single world that was destroyed by the power struggle between these two ruling houses over a thousand revolution ago."

Forrorrois shook her head. "Wonderful…What are the names of the royal families?"

"Stentous and Pedraco, respectively—they named their worlds after the families."

"Well, that simplifies things," Forrorrois said. "According to the coordinates Motan provided, we are heading straight for a moon orbiting Sten." She piloted her scout in a steep ascent. "What do you suppose the item is that we are looking for?"

"I'm not certain, yet," Collinar replied. "But I am certain that this is going to be interesting."

"Why is that?"

"Experience. I've never taken a job from Motan that wasn't interesting. He has a reputation for taking on the more difficult jobs. That's why they pay so well."

"Ah," Forrorrois replied. "Hmmm...I see from my files both worlds are fifty percent water and the remainder mostly marshlands. The inhabitants are Kohanian, an amphibious race. They trade a type of water lily that is dried and used as an additive in a variety of food supplements—including emergency rations. Oh, I hope that's not the reason they taste so nasty..."

Collinar snorted at her comment. "What? Are you saying that you find them offensive? Some beings find that flavor quite a treat."

Forrorrois wrinkled her nose. "Let's just say I'll pass," Forrorrois replied. "Anything else you can think of, that might be useful?"

"Actually, yes. The Kohanian find contact with warm-blooded beings very distasteful. You may find that they may make comments that will seem extremely rude..."

"Ruder than your comments?" Forrorrois interjected.

Collinar gave her a sideways look then sneered. "Possibly ruder. They do so to determine whether you're worthy of their time. You mustn't react to their comments, just smile and continue the discussion with them as if you've been given the greatest compliment."

"All right," Forrorrois replied, cautiously. "Since you'll be doing most of the talking, it shouldn't be a problem."

Collinar chuckled. "That's where you're wrong. Only the females speak vocally and they will only negotiate with another female. I doubt that I will pass muster on that small technicality."

Forrorrois looked at him in surprise. "You are kidding me?"

Collinar shook his head. "Check your protocol files."

Forrorrois accessed her files on the Kohanian and sighed. "Just wonderful," she murmured when she confirmed he was telling the truth.

"Before we enter the Intonius system, I strongly recommend that you shroud your ship to prevent any confrontations until we reach the moon."

I agree," Forrorrois replied. "Do you have a contact name?"

"Yes, Mo'onah, she's supposed to be the head horticulturalist to the royal family—rather an important position since their main export is the dried water lilies."

Forrorrois nodded her head. "Interesting contact, I'll have to brush-up on my botany."

"Good, you're catching on to the fine art of negotiation," Collinar said with a smile.

"Engaging shroud," Forrorrois announced, "entering the Intonius system in twenty-seven tol."

"Amazing," Collinar murmured. "I've often wondered what it was like inside your craft when the shroud was engaged."

Forrorrois shook her head. "Not very exciting, I'm afraid."

"If you're traveling with a second ship that's also shrouded, how do you see each other?" Collinar asked. His tone was nonchalant but Forrorrois could sense he was more than a bit interested.

"I could tell you, but then I'd have to kill you," Forrorrois replied back, keeping her eyes forward. His shock filtered into her mind then shifted to humor.

"So, what do you think the item is?" Collinar said as he changed the subject. "The royal family jewels, perhaps?"

Forrorrois tried not to smirk as his remark struck her. He was unaware of the English innuendo of his suggestion. "Who knows?" she replied. "Settle back, we've got some time before we reach the moon."

****

Trager lay on the hard bunk of the otherwise bare cell, clothed in simple tan robes, and studied the smooth gray granite walls and the heavy plank door of black imported wood. He tested the shackles that bound his wrists and ankles once more time, mindful of the pacifying jolt the restraints could inflict if he resisted too vigorously. From his time as the head of security on the Tollon he knew that they were designed to prevent him from slipping them over his hands and feet. Without Forrorrois' talent to reduce her mass, Trager knew he wasn't going anywhere without an escort.

He closed his eyes and took what little solace he could from the thought that Celeste was once again reunited with Forrorrois. Trager cherished the brief moment he had to actually hold his daughter before Neeha ordered him to choose—his freedom or his daughter's. In his mind, there was no choice—Celeste needed to be released back to her mother. But still, Neeha wouldn't take him at his word that he would submit to her will. To his indignity, she had him stripped of his uniform at weapon point to reinforce he was no longer under the protection of the Dramudam—that he was nothing but a simple Eldatek male bound by duty to fulfill his obligation to his mother's house.

Trager retraced the shuttle flight from the asteroid belt to Elda in his mind. He had recognized the main government building when he was taken to the prison located deep below the council chamber from the landing pad outside of Lor'Koria, the capital city of Elda. The grandly carved red stone building had seemed less oppressive when he was a child—innocent then of the machinations that drove the Eldatek society. His only surprise, as he descended down the gray stone corridors to his holding cell, was when he overheard his mother actually attempt to petition Councilor Kil'Treahaa that he be placed under house arrest at her home in Lor'Koria until everything was resolved. But her request was politely declined by the elder head councilor, who stated that it was imperative that no appearance of favoritism could be shown to a member of the council. He never heard Neeha's response as the door to his cell was closed—shutting him away from the politics that forced him back to his birth world.

He had lost count of time since he had entered the windowless cell. He could only guess that when the single light panel above him dimmed that darkness had fallen over the desert city. The brightness of the panel above him told him that it was still daylight in the city above him.

Trager knew in his head he had done the right thing, but the crushing pain in his heart belied that fact. Trager closed his eyes tighter. "Please forgive me, Forrorrois, for not telling you that this was the only way to get Celeste back safely," he whispered, clenching his eyelids tighter to hold back his tears. "Please, Monomay, ease my ashwan's sadness and give her comfort that Celeste is with her once more," he prayed.

The sudden sound of the small metal observation panel sliding to one side set in the door made him fall silent. He glanced cautiously toward the black wooden door. A pair of black almond-shaped eyes stared in at him. Abruptly, the panel slid shut and the door swung open. Trager was surprised when an Eldatek female wearing yellow robes entered the cell. Mechanically, he sat up and dropped his shackled bare chestnut-brown feet to the cool gray stone floor.

"I wish to speak with him alone," the female ordered, with the wave of her hand. The guard bowed and closed the door.

"Haator, do you know who I am?" she asked when they were alone together.

Without making eye contact, Trager surreptitiously studied her for a moment then realized that he did recognized her. "Yes, you are Bohata, my deceased brother's joined one," Trager replied, respectfully. "I am sorry for your loss."

"Thank you," Bohata replied.

Trager waited for her to continue, but she just stood quietly and studied him.

When she did speak, she stepped closer to him.

"You have complicated things with your off-worlder, Haator. The council has recognized Forrorrois' claim of Penock and her daughter has been recognized as legitimate."

Trager closed his eyes briefly. "Monomay be praised," he whispered.

"Yes, Monomay be praised, because the council has also recognizes my claim of Slovak," she continued.

Trager looked up in surprise. "How can they recognize both?"

"The council, in their wisdom, has decided to assign a joining fee to be presented in two mol. At that time, I expect that you will become my second and that you will provide me with an heir. You will forget that off-worlder and perform your duty to me."

Trager shook his head. "You and the council may force me to perform my duty, but I will never forget Forrorrois. She is my true ashwan and the mother of my child."

"You are so insolent to believe you have any claim to a female child," Bohata growled. "Your brother failed in his duty to me. Let's hope that your time in the Plane of Deception hasn't impaired you as well."

Trager moved to object, but Bohata turned away from him and signaled the door to be opened. When the guards opened the door she left quickly. The door closed once more, leaving him alone to his thoughts. Frustrated, Trager lay back on his bunk and stared at the ceiling panels. Then he smiled as he realized that Forrorrois still had the chance of coming up with the joining fee, freeing him from Elda once and for all.

****

Jack was sleeping in his room at Forrorrois' base when he started awake at the sound of his cellular phone. When it rang a second time, he fumbled in the dark on the bed stand for the intrusive object. He looked at the display and was surprised when he saw Agent Aster's number.

"Stern," he mumbled.

"Jack, its Aster. I apologize for the lateness of the hour," his friend began in his slight British accent, but Jack cut him off.

"Its all right Aster, I'm awake," Jack stated as he turned on the light. "What can I do for you?"

"Well, it's more like what can I do for you," Aster replied.

Jack shook his head in confusion. "Come again?"

"My director wants me to set up a meeting with you, himself, and

Forrorrois, to clear up this whole enemy combatant issue that General Caldwell seems to be driving."

Jack sat up and stared at his phone. "That's unexpected," Jack replied.

"I agree," Aster remarked. "But the request is coming from the President, himself."

"Really?"

"Yes, the President was quite troubled when he learned of the recent charges leveled against Forrorrois' family, Captain Perkins, and yourself. He wants you and Forrorrois to speak with my director so that he can understand if the charges are warranted or not."

Jack sighed. "There's a problem, Aster. Forrorrois isn't local at the moment."

"How not local?"

"Very not local, Aster, she's got some personal business she's dealing with at the moment."

"I see…that would explain why I haven't been able to reach her directly."

Jack took a breath and let it out slowly. "Look, if the President still wants me to speak with your director, without Forrorrois, I can make arrangements to come down to D.C. in the morning."

"I think it will still be helpful," Aster replied. "As I mentioned, the President was distressed when he was supplied the Enemy Combatant list during his regular security briefing. The list seems to be growing longer everyday—becoming filled with regular folks that don't seem to fit any particular profile."

"I agree, the Jolans are a perfect example of people being used to get at another target," Jack replied.

"Precisely. Between you and me, I don't care for the direction this country is moving in at the moment," Aster answered. "Now, Jack, I need you to come prepared to provide candid answers. I realize that you're taking a risk coming to a secure building like the Bureau, but I will guarantee your safe passage."

Jack sighed. "Aster, I know I can trust you, but I don't feel comfortable walking into any secure building right now. Can you make arrangements for me to meet with your director on more neutral ground?"

"It's a possibility—I'll confirm a location that's more satisfactory."

"Good, I'll meet you at your apartment first thing in the morning and you can drive me in, but the first sign of trouble, please know that I'll have backup."

"Backup? Is Captain Perkins with you? There's been a lot of concern over his disappearance from the base after he was arrested."

"No, Perkins is unavailable at the moment," Jack replied.

"He's safe though, right?"

"As far as I know," Jack stated, evasively. "We can talk in the morning, Aster. I'll see you bright and early. Oh, and Aster, Forrorrois not being local at the moment is between the two of us. As far as your director is concerned she's sending me instead, for security reasons."

"Understood. Thank you, Jack. I appreciate this," Aster said. "Good night."

Jack shut off his phone and heaved a sigh. He knew he could trust Aster, but could he trust Astor's director? Getting out of bed, Jack pulled on his pants and a shirt and headed out of his room down the hallway to the hangar bay when Danielle stepped out of Forrorrois' bedroom in her robe and slippers.

"Is everything all right, Jack?" she asked. "I thought I heard your phone."

"Yes, I think so," Jack said. "Aster called—he wants me to come down to Washington, D.C., for a meeting in the morning."

"Are you sure that's a good idea, Jack? I think the world of Aster, but he is F.B.I.," she replied.

"I agree, Danielle, that's why I want to talk to Yononnon about providing me with some back up—just to be certain."

He was surprised when Danielle smiled.

"Jack, Yononnon's not in the hangar bay, he's in the living room. It was so cute. Celeste pulled out a book that Danica reads to her in that language that Trager speaks and asked Yononnon if he could read her a bedtime story," Danielle began with a twinkle in her eye. "He was a bit nervous at first, but Celeste completely charmed him."

"Oh, really?" Jack said as she redirected him to the living room.

"Frank, George, and I left to go to bed since we couldn't understand a word he was saying, but Celeste was just tickled pink to listen to him read the story to her," Danielle continued, lowering her voice as they reached the living room.

They both paused as they spotted Yononnon—asleep in the chair with Celeste curled up in the crook of his arm—the book forgotten on his lap.

"Oh…how sweet," Danielle whispered.

Jack grinned as he pulled out his cell phone. He aimed the internal camera at Yononnon and quickly snapped a picture.

"You'll have to send me a copy of that," Danielle whispered as they both looked at the image on the small screen of his cell phone.

"Of course. It's a shame that I have to wake him," Jack said as he put his phone back in his pants' pocket.

Yononnon stirred awake as they approached his position.

Danielle motioned for him to stay still. "Shhh."

Yononnon's eyes widened as he looked down at Celeste curled against his chest.

"Thank you for reading to her, Yononnon," Danielle continued in a whisper. "I'll take her now, and put her to bed."

The large subcommander recovered his composure and lifted Celeste and handed her to Danielle. Celeste barely stirred awake. "It was an honor," he replied.

Jack grinned as Danielle draped Celeste over her shoulder and carried her back to Forrorrois' bedroom, where she, Frank, and George were now sleeping.

"You're a natural with children," Jack commented in Intergaltic as he took a seat on the couch next to Yononnon's chair.

Yononnon straightened in his chair. "It was a pleasure to read to her. On Elda, males are rarely given the privilege of sharing time with their children," Yononnon replied back in Intergaltic.

Jack's smile faded at Yononnon's unguarded comment on how

rigid the Eldatek culture was with their division of male and female roles. Yononnon cherished every moment with his niece and he didn't hide his joy as he watched Danielle carry her down the hallway.

"I'm glad that you're here. Celeste really has taken to you," Jack continued.

"She's been through a lot for a little one," Yononnon admitted. "While I was reading to her, she had several questions about Neeha. She asked me if I knew how long her poppa was going to have to stay on Elda. When I told her that I didn't know, she said the oddest thing. She said that she hoped that her poppa could help Neeha to feel happy again."

Jack was stunned. "She thought Neeha was sad?"

"Yes, when I asked her why she thought that Neeha was sad, Celeste said that when she had told her momma that Neeha was mean, that her momma had told her no, that Neeha was just sad because she missed her son," Yononnon replied, shaking his head. "Every time I assume I know how Forrorrois thinks, I'm surprised."

Jack nodded. "You'll have to thank Forrorrois' parents for that. Their belief system is based on forgiveness."

Yononnon looked over at him for a long moment in thought—then nodded. "The more I spend time with Danielle and Frank, the more I sense this about them. This helps me understand why Forrorrois has never killed Collinar even when there were multiple opportunities for her."

"I know," Jack replied. "Let's just hope that it doesn't get her killed some cycle."

Yononnon grew more serious. "I agree," he admitted, picking the forgotten Eldanese text off his lap and setting the book on the low table in front of him. "It's late, I shouldn't keep you up," he said, stifling a yawn.

"That's all right, Yononnon, I just got a call from a friend down in Washington, D.C.—the capital of this country," Jack began. "There has been a request that I speak with a senior official about reports he's received regarding my current status of being wanted by the government."

Yononnon gave him a hard stare—no longer tired. "Jack, you realize this could be a trap."

"Oh, I definitely agree, Yononnon. That's why I wanted to know if you could provide me with some backup—like you did at the base with the general."

"Of course I can provide you with backup," Yononnon replied, "but if you believe this might be a trap, then why are you going at all?"

"Because, if it's not a trap, then Forrorrois' family could be free to live their lives again and maybe so could Perkins and me."

"Ah, I understand. Do you trust the Human that called you?"

Jack nodded. "Yes, Aster has proven himself to me on more than one occasion as well as to Forrorrois and Trager. It's not him that I am worried about. It's the Humans that he works for that might double-cross me."

"I see. When do we leave?" Yononnon asked.

"In one kel," Jack replied. "I figure you might want to see the Capital before the sun rises. It's a sight to behold."

Yononnon smiled. "I would enjoy seeing that."

"Good, now get some sleep," Jack ordered as he turned and headed back to his room in the living quarters. "I'll get you in a kel."

CHAPTER 16

Jack arrived at Aster's apartment building, located in the outskirts of Washington, D.C., at the appointed time. Prior to leaving Yononnon's one-seat long-distance scout, he had the subcommander scan the building and surrounding area, to be certain that Aster was not being used to lure him into a trap. Satisfied the building wasn't being monitored, Jack buzzed Aster's apartment from the main door.

"Hello?" Aster's voice sounded on the speaker.

"Aster, its Jack."

"I'll be right down," Aster said.

Jack looked around—feeling a bit exposed—standing between two glass doors. He looked up at the stairwell, relieved to see the F.B.I agent coming down the stairs. Aster was tall and slim, but well built with short black hair, brown eyes, and a pale complexion. He rarely wore anything but a suit. Jack remembered how apprehensive he had been when Aster had figured out Forrorrois' identity, proving he was exceptionally good at his job. Then he had earned Jack's trust when he proved he could keep Forrorrois' secret—even when her secret almost cost Aster his closest friendship.

"I'm glad you could make it, Jack," Aster said as he opened the door. "My car's in the garage in back, come with me and I'll explain what we'll being doing this morning."

"OK," Jack replied and followed him down the hallway to the back exit. He didn't say another word until they exited out the door through a covered walkway to a three-story parking garage. Jack glanced around at the cars and confirmed that they were all empty.

"My car's right here," Aster said as he unlocked the door with his key fob a few meters away.

Jack walked up to the passenger side, opened the door and took a seat. He watched as Aster entered the driver's side and took his seat behind the wheel. He relaxed slightly when the long-distance scout ship's computer informed him that the vehicle was bug free.

"Are you carrying any weapons?" Aster asked as he turned the key in the ignition and began to back out of his spot.

"I thought about it," Jack confessed, "but I figured that I would be searched before the meeting."

"Yes, we both will. The meeting is at a hotel with a conference center. My director has secured a meeting room," Aster replied. "There will be two agents present standing guard outside the meeting location to make certain that we are not disturbed. We'll be coming into the hotel through the underground garage entrance. I'll stay with you the entire time and escort you to wherever you want me to take you after the meeting. If you want lunch, we can pick up some lunch on the way back."

"We'll see how it goes first," Jack replied as he watched Aster guide his small grey sedan through the morning traffic. "If something goes wrong, there's always plan B."

"True," Aster remarked. "By the way, what exactly happened to make General Caldwell put out a blanket arrest request for you, Captain Perkins, and Forrorrois parents and brother?"

Jack shook his head. "The general was contacted by Collinar."

He almost smiled when Aster's eyes widened. "He's not back on Earth, is he? I thought he was in some Dramudam prison."

"They prefer to call them Rehabilitation stations. Unfortunately, he had escaped recently," Jack replied dryly. "Luckily, Forrorrois intercepted the errant commander as he was coming into the atmosphere over Antarctica—needless to say, General Caldwell was furious," Jack replied.

"Amazing," Aster replied. "I want to hear the rest, but you'd better save it for the director. Ah, I'm glad I took the back route. We're here."

Jack glanced out the window as Aster turned down the ramp to the garage of the large conference-oriented hotel set on the outskirts of the city. He didn't spot any undo activity, but he did spot a surveillance camera that monitored their arrival. Aster parked in a space near the elevator and motioned for Jack to get out as he shut off the engine.

Jack nodded and reached out with his zendra link—relieved to sense Yononnon's scout computer was still within range. He opened his door and climbed out, then followed Aster to the elevator. The doors opened, revealing a posh brass interior with wooden panels. Aster pushed the button for the convention center and heaved a sigh as the doors slid closed.

'Two armed Human males are waiting just outside the lift,' the scout's computer reported to him through his zendra link in Intergaltic. Jack tensed.

"What's the matter, Jack?" Aster questioned as he glanced at him.

"There are two armed men waiting for us," Jack replied.

Aster gave him a bemused look then nodded. "I know, I told you that there would be two men with the director."

Jack looked at him carefully, wishing that he had Forrorrois' gift as an empath. "Aster, I'm trusting you to get me in and out of this meeting in one piece."

"I won't let you down, Jack. Besides, Forrorrois would hunt me down if I let anything happen to you!" Aster joked nervously as the elevator stopped at the appointed level.

"She would, too," Jack replied just as the doors slid open. He watched the two men waiting on the other side nod to Aster when they stepped out of the elevator.

"The director is waiting for you. Second door on your right," one of them stated.

"Thank you," Aster replied.

"One moment, Colonel Stern," the other agent said as he pulled out a handheld metal detector.

Jack stood still as the man passed the wand over him.

"He's clean," the agent stated.

"The director will see you both, now," the first agent said, pointing towards the conference room door.

Jack nodded to the agents and followed Aster through the

door. Inside was a narrow room with a long polished black metal conference table with four black-leatherette chairs—two on each side. The windows had been shuttered with thin gray metal vertical blinds. The room's lights were dimmed slightly to accommodate a ceiling-mounted projector that was pointed at a white screen positioned on the wall at the far end of the table. A blue square of light filled the screen as if prepared for a presentation. Glancing across the room from the door he had just entered, Jack spotted an emergency exit with an alarm on the crossbar—the only escape route besides the hallway. Jack turned his attention to an imposing man in a dark gray suit that sat at the far side of the conference table. He had a piercing stare and distinguished graying hair. Without a word, the lone man stood from the table and circled around to meet them. Jack was surprised when the man offered his hand.

"Colonel Stern, I'm Director Elliot Hayman of the F.B.I.," the intense tall man stated. "Your willingness to meet me here was a show of good faith on your part. I only wish that Forrorrois could have joined you."

"It's just Stern, now, Director Hayman. I've resigned my post after my last encounter with General Caldwell," Jack replied, taking the man's hand and shaking it.

"But you did so under duress, Colonel," Hayman countered as he pointed towards a chair at the table nearest to Jack. "Please take a seat and we can begin."

"Thank you, sir," Jack said as he followed him over to the table and took a seat across from him. Aster took the seat beside his director.

"I'd like to ask you to please describe the series of events that led up to General Caldwell's request to have you, Captain Perceval Perkins, George Jolan, Frank Jolan, Danielle Jolan and Forrorrois to be listed as Enemy Combatants?" Hayman began, picking up a pen and poising it above a yellow legal pad on the table in front of him.

Jack hesitated, uncertain. 'Computer, status?' he subvocalized.

'Two additional armed beings are positioned near the door to the outside of the building from your position. There is an alarm on the door. The room has a listening device that is transmitting audio and visual,' the ship's computer report through Jack's zendra link. Jack glanced around and saw a telecommunications phone on the table between him and Director Hayman. A small green light glowed innocently on its gray surface.

"Please, Colonel Stern," Director Hayman continued. "I assure you that I am aware of what continued positive relationships with Forrorrois means to this world. Her connections to the Dramudam are known to me."

Jack raised an eyebrow at the director's candid comments and glanced at Aster. Aster nodded for him to go on. Jack glanced down at the telecommunications device on the table. "May I ask who is also joining this conversation?"

Director Hayman smiled. "Very astute, Colonel. May I introduce your commander and chief?"

Jack turned toward the screen when the projector turned on and a face appeared. His eyes widened when he realized that the face belonged to the President of the United States. Reflexively, Jack stood at attention and saluted. The man on the screen saluted him back. Jack quickly glanced around the room and spotted the video camera strategically placed above the screen.

"At ease, Colonel Stern," the President ordered. "Please take a seat, I'm here as an observer. I'm very concerned with the events that have occurred over the past few weeks and I want to hear your side of the story to determine a plan of action. I must confess that I'm disappointed Forrorrois wasn't able to make it today, I was very impressed with her when we met a few years ago."

Jack relaxed slightly and resumed his seat across from Director Hayman and Aster. "That's kind of you to say, Mr. President. Forrorrois sends her apologies, but she has commitments that prevent her from attending this meeting," he replied.

"Nothing too dire, I hope," the President stated.

"Nothing that immediately endangers Earth," Jack replied.

There was an odd silence as his words sunk in.

"That's good to hear," the President finally answered. "Director Hayman, please begin your questions."

"Colonel, as I mentioned before, we would like you to describe to us—to the best of your ability—the events that led up to your being listed as an Enemy Combatant by your commanding officer," Director Hayman began.

Jack glanced at the President's image on the screen then back at Hayman and Aster.

"Yes, sir," Jack began. "A tornado touched down at the Air Force base where I was stationed. The hangar that I was in collapsed and trapped me in the debris. General Caldwell contacted Forrorrois and requested her assistance to extract me. Forrorrois agreed."

Director Hayman leaned forward. "So at this point, General Caldwell's relationship with Forrorrois seemed stable enough for the general to feel comfortable in requesting her assistance?"

"Yes, sir," Jack replied. "From what I was told later, he had ordered the area cleared so that Forrorrois could land without compromising her security. When she arrived, Forrorrois confirmed that the collapsed hangar was structurally unstable and that any attempt to extract me through conventional emergency equipment would have endangered the lives of rescue workers, as well as my own. She also determined that I was slipping into shock and they couldn't wait for a team to stabilize the debris."

"So, at this point—from what you were told—Forrorrois was acting in good faith providing assistance," Director Hayman replied, jotting down some notes on a yellow legal pad.

"Yes, sir," Jack said, curious as he glanced at the pad of paper.

"Please go on," Hayman said as he looked up from his notes.

Jack held the man's piercing gaze. "Forrorrois asked the general for a volunteer to help locate me. Captain Perkins agreed to help her since he had been the last person to see me in the hangar just before the tornado hit."

"Interesting, please go on," Hayman said as he jotted down a few more notes.

Jack averted his eyes from the notepad and continued. "At this point, all I know is that Forrorrois and Captain Perkins were successful in extracting me, but Forrorrois was injured by some falling debris and was taken along with me and Captain Perkins to the base hospital." Jack glanced over at Aster and could see he was bursting with questions, suddenly reminded that Aster hadn't been privy to these events.

"What injuries did you, Forrorrois, and Captain Perkins receive?" Hayman asked.

"As I mentioned before, I was suffering from shock, a mild concussion, a broken arm, and a bruised ankle. During the rescue, a part of the building above me shifted and Forrorrois shoved Perkins out of the way and shielded me from the falling debris with her body. Perkins received some minor cuts and bruises, but Forrorrois was struck by several pieces of metal—one of which punctured her lung. Amazingly enough, even with her injuries, she still managed to get both Perkins and me out of the building to the emergency vehicles outside. I was told that when she tried to return to her ship, she passed out. It was at this point, that she was taken to the base hospital by the ambulance crew where she was treated for a collapsed lung and broken ribs," Jack said. He glanced at Aster and could see his friend was increasingly alarmed by his report, but still he remained quiet as Director Hayman spoke.

"Do you know of anything else that occurred at the base hospital that would have caused General Caldwell to include yourself and Captain Perkins in his request for your enemy combatant status?"

Jack paused. What he said next could never be retracted. "Well, that evening, General Caldwell was contacted by Commander Collinar," he replied evasively.

Stunned, Hayman set down his pen.

"The Commander Collinar that attacked Earth a few years ago?" the President asked, breaking his silence.

Jack almost smiled. His evasion had worked. The mention of Collinar had deflected the questions from himself and Forrorrois. "Yes, Mr. President," Jack replied. "Collinar had escaped from the Dramudam rehabilitation station where he had been incarcerated for the past four years and was requesting asylum from General Caldwell."

"Interesting that the general didn't mention that in his report," Hayman scoffed, picking up his pen and resuming his notes.

"Yes," the President remarked, dryly.

"Colonel, please continue," Hayman requested, recovering his composure.

"Of course, sir," Jack replied. "It was at this point that General Caldwell attempted to hold Forrorrois on the base by force. He even threatened her family if she tried to resist. This betrayal forced Forrorrois to escape from the hospital—even though she was still badly injured. Concerned for my safety, Forrorrois also took me out of the hospital as well. How she did it, I have no idea since I was still foggy from the pain medication they had given me."

"What about Captain Perkins? Where was he during this period of time?" Hayman asked.

"As I said, I was on some pretty heavy pain meds. I was told later that Captain Perkins had been placed on inactive duty and was not on the base at the time of Forrorrois' escape. I do recall being on Forrorrois' scout ship after she escaped and that she stopped at her parents' house and took them and me back to her base to protect them against General Caldwell's threats."

"You stayed at her base? What was it like?" the President pressed.

Jack avoided looking at Aster, knowing his next statement was going to be a lie. "I can't really say, Mr. President. Forrorrois kept me in a room while she healed my broken arm and watched over me for a few days before returning me to my cabin. As a good faith gesture, she did let me keep my cell phone and allowed me to stay in contact with the air force base while I was there."

"But wasn't she still badly injured?" the President asked, much to the distraction of Director Hayman.

Jack suppressed a smile. "Yes, Mr. President. But once Forrorrois had access to her advanced medical equipment, she was able to heal her injuries and then mine."

"Amazing," the President mused.

Director Hayman cleared his throat and glanced at the screen.

"Director, please continue you questions," the President said, a bit sheepishly.

"Yes, Mr. President," Hayman replied. "Now, Colonel Stern, what about Captain Perkins? Can you shed anymore light on what caused General Caldwell to arrest him?"

Again, Jack paused, uncertain how much to say. "I'm not entirely certain what caused General Caldwell to have Captain Perkins arrested. This occurred while I was still recovering at Forrorrois' base so I wasn't aware this occurred until much later. My only thoughts are that the general was grasping at straws on how to bring Forrorrois back in and decided to use Captain Perkins as bait."

Hayman gave him an odd look. "And why would he think that would bring Forrorrois in?"

Jack took a deep breath and exhaled slowly. Then he looked into Hayman's piercing eyes. "Because, Director, Forrorrois has an established pattern of protecting those that have worked with her, and Captain Perkins helped her get me out of the collapsed hangar. General Caldwell tried to leverage that and force her to come back to the base once she heard of his arrest. Unfortunately, the general didn't anticipate that Captain Perkins would facilitate his own escape before the general could draw Forrorrois back onto the base."

"But why would Captain Perkins feel it was necessary to escape?" Hayman pressed.

Jack smiled and shook his head. "Director Hayman, you know as well as I do that being listed as an enemy combatant gives you fewer rights than a prisoner of war. Given the choice of having no representation to prove your innocence or going AWOL, what would you choose?"

Hayman dropped his gaze for a moment. "I see your point. Where was Captain Perkins arrested?"

"I was told that the MPs came to his apartment and requested that he return with them back to the base for questioning. It wasn't until they reached the base that they informed him that he was under arrest. At that point Captain Perkins managed to escape from custody and later contacted me on my cell phone. When I told Forrorrois what had happened, she picked Captain Perkins up and took him to a secure location to protect him."

Hayman paused for a moment. "Let me get this straight. This occurred when you were still recuperating at Forrorrois' base."

"Yes, sir," Jack replied.

"And you still were in possession of your cell phone?"

Jack nodded. "Yes, sir. Forrorrois left the cell phone with me as a sign on good faith that I was not a prisoner."

"But you were confined to a single room—wouldn't that suggest that you were a prisoner?" Hayman pressed.

"No, sir," Jack replied. "I was still healing and unable to move about."

"I'm sorry, Mr. Stern, but it still sounds like you were a prisoner."

"I beg to differ, Director Hayman. At all times while I was recuperating at her base, she treated me as respected guest," Jack insisted.

"But didn't you feel it was your duty to gain intelligence on her base?" Hayman persisted.

Jack sighed. "Director, please understand that just as there are classified areas that would be off-limits to nonmilitary personnel on the base I was assigned to, it is only natural that Forrorrois would have classified areas as well at her base. As a guest, I respected the protocol of her base."

"All right, I'll accept that," Hayman remarked, setting down his pen once more. "And I can understand Forrorrois wanting to remove a leverage point from the general. But Colonel, I still don't fully understand your relationship with Forrorrois? And why would she remove you from the air base in the first place? You were receiving medical care at the base hospital."

Again, Jack forced himself not to look at Aster. "Director Hayman, as I'm certain you are aware, I was the lead investigator for the OCU on the base. Since Forrorrois' arrival back on Earth I've had several encounters with her. After a few years Forrorrois grew to trust me and made a request to General Caldwell that I become her liaison to the base."

"Reasonable, but I sense there is more to this—especially after the reports that I've read four years ago regarding her husband—Trager, wasn't it?"

At the mention of Trager's name, Jack tensed. "I don't understand where you are going with this, sir?"

"Wasn't it at your cabin where Trager was originally picked up?"

Jack forced himself not to react. "Yes, sir."

"So you were also a friend of the family, not just a liaison to the base."

Jack nodded his head slowly. "Yes, sir, my relationship with Forrorrois and her family had grown into a mutual friendship."

"Colonel, do you think that you are capable of separating your feeling of friendship from your duty as an officer in the U.S. Air Force and the lead investigator for the OCU?"

Jack's eyes widened at Hayman's double-edged question. "Director Hayman, I can assure you, that my first and utmost loyalty is to the protection of this world and this country...."

"Please, Colonel, I didn't intend to imply that your loyalty is in question here," Hayman quickly retracted. "I just wanted to put into perspective why Forrorrois would make the choices she has made regarding yourself and Captain Perkins."

"Of course, sir, I apologize for my outburst, sir," Jack replied, composing himself.

"No apologies necessary, Colonel," Hayman stated, picking up his pen. "Now, what about Commander Collinar? Where was he during all of this?"

"He was approaching Earth in a ship he had stolen during his escape from the Dramudam rehabilitation station where he had been incarcerated. By the time he reached Earth's atmosphere, Forrorrois was fit enough to intercept his craft over Antarctica. It should reassure you to know that Collinar is now back in the custody of the Dramudam," Jack answered.

"Actually, yes," Hayman nodded. "Was General Caldwell aware of his recapture?"

"When Forrorrois returned from taking Collinar into custody, she told me that the general was aware. After that, she returned me back to my cabin," Jack replied, carefully.

"Let me understand this, she left you unattended at her base?" Hayman stated.

Jack pulled on his best poker face as he realized he had said too much. "She left me with provisions and assured me she wouldn't be longer than a few days," he said with a shrug.

"And you believed her?" Hayman scoffed.

"I didn't have a lot of choice," Jack answered.

He almost smiled when Aster averted his eyes.

Hayman stared at him and tapped his pencil slowly on the black metal tabletop before continuing. "OK, what happen when Forrorrois returned you to your cabin?"

"I contacted the general and he ordered me to report to the flight surgeon. He stated he wouldn't clear me for active duty until the flight surgeon cleared me," Jack reported. "It was when I reported to the base for the physical that General Caldwell attempted to have me arrested under the charges of collaboration. I suspected that he might treat me like he had treated Captain Perkins so I had a contingency plan and escaped before he could take me into custody."

Director Hayman shook his head with a sigh. "General Caldwell never gives up..." he commented under his breath.

"No, sir," Jack replied, relieved he didn't press for more details.

Hayman looked up. "Colonel Stern, if my records are correct... this occurred on the same day that Forrorrois' family members were listed by the F.B.I. as enemy combatants. In fact, George Jolan, Forrorrois' brother was scheduled to be arrest that afternoon in Las Vegas. An eyewitness in Las Vegas stated that a craft appeared on the roof of the hotel that George Jolan was staying in and fired some type of stun weapon, allowing Mr. Jolan to escape."

Jack stared straight ahead and nodded. "Yes, sir, that's correct."

"Colonel Stern, you seem to have a remarkable amount of knowledge on this whole affair. I appreciate your candor, especially regarding the circumstance."

"I also appreciate your candid answers, Colonel Stern," the President remarked over the speaker phone set on the table. "I asked Director Hayman to bring you here so that we could clear up this whole mess. General Caldwell has put this whole world in a dire strait by attempting to negotiate with a known enemy of the state. Now, I can't promise that I can clear this up immediately, but be assured this matter will be addressed. You took a great personal risk by agreeing to meet with us. I wish to now offer to place you into protective custody until we can resolve this..."

Jack glanced at Aster and saw his confusion. With a shake of his head, Jack slowly rose from his chair. "No, sir, I don't wish to accept your offer at this time," Jack replied.

"Colonel, I'm afraid that I must insist," the President stated.

"That was not part of the agreement," Jack stated, backing away from the table.

"I agree," Aster spoke up. "Colonel Stern was promised safe passage to and from this meeting."

"Colonel, please reconsider," the President appealed. "You have the information that we need to find out who in this government is working with General Caldwell."

Jack stared hard at the image of the president then at Director Hayman. "Are you telling me that this has nothing to do with Forrorrois' family and friends being listed as enemy combatants?"

"Yes and no," the President confessed. "Finding who is ultimately responsible will, in due course, free all of you of these charges. Be reasonable, Colonel—both you and Captain Perkins could have your lives and pensions back. Forrorrois' family would be protected from ever having to face these charges again. All of this can happen if you assist us in finding out who is pulling the strings for General Caldwell."

Jack felt the trap closing in on him. He glanced at Aster and could see that his friend was appalled at being used to bring him in. Diplomacy or force was his only way out. 'Computer, inform Yononnon to be prepared for an emergency extraction,' Jack subvocalized. "Mr. President," he said aloud, "I must state one more time that I cannot agree to being placed under protective custody. Believe me, Mr.

President—I'm as interested in finding out who General Caldwell is working with as you are."

"Then we have a common goal," the President pressed.

"Yes, but I can't find any answers if I am in your custody," Jack countered, backing towards the emergency exit. "I'm sorry, but this meeting is over."

Both Aster and Director Hayman jumped to their feet.

"Colonel, this isn't a request!" Hayman called out after him.

Suddenly, the hallway door to Jack's right swung open as the two armed agents burst into the room with their guns drawn. He didn't wait to find out if they were authorized to use deadly force as he turned to his left and hit the crossbar on the emergency door. The alarm howled loudly. Outside, Jack found two agents already unconscious on the ground. He looked up and spotted Yononnon waiting for him in his one-seat long-distance scout with his stun rifle poised on the emergency exit from which he had just emerged.

Jack ran toward the unshrouded craft that Yononnon had parked on the access road beside the hotel. Reflexively, he ducked his head when Yononnon fired twice more while the two agents from the hallway emerged from the door. Yononnon dropped them a few meters from the door. Jack quickly started up the ladder scrambled into the cockpit and behind Yononnon's command chair while the subcommander re-engaged the shroud and dropped the canopy back into place. Jack barely had time to grab the back of Yononnon's chair before the subcommander had the EM warping shield engaged and they were airborne once more.

"Well, that went well," Jack commented dryly in Intergaltic.

Yononnon looked back him and almost grinned. "I was monitoring the conversation. You handled yourself well, considering that they brought you there under false pretense. I'm sorry that your friend betrayed you."

"I'm not so sure that he did," Jack replied. "Don't leave yet. I want to hear the rest of their conversation."

Yononnon nodded, maintaining the scout's shrouded position just above the street.

Jack leaned forward and watched Aster emerge from the emergency exit and turn towards his director, clenching his fists—his gun still in his holster.

"Why did you and the President do that?!" Aster accused over the shrill of the door alarm. "Colonel Stern came in to speak to us under the condition that he would have immunity for this meeting! He gave us candid answers as a show of trust!"

Aster's director didn't answer him—instead he bent down and checked the pulse of one of the four agents that Yononnon had dropped just outside the door. "He's alive," Director Hayman stated.

"Of course he's alive!" Aster growled in frustration. "They're all alive. They used a stun weapon on them. The Dramudam don't kill, they're peace keepers—like a bloody galactic U.N.! Haven't you figured that out yet?"

Jack watched Hayman stand up and stare at Aster.

"Are you telling me that Colonel Stern is a Dramudam, Agent Aster?" Hayman asked in a measured voice.

Jack almost smiled as Aster narrowed his eyes at his superior. "No, but he's obviously under their protection," Aster replied. "You've broken their trust with your double-cross on Colonel Stern. They won't be willing to negotiate now."

Hayman glanced towards the place that Yononnon's ship had appeared—oblivious to the fact that Jack and Yononnon were still there just meters above them.

"You're right—trying to bring the colonel in by force was a miscalculation. Forrorrois didn't trust us enough to attend the meeting and sent the colonel instead. Then she pulled him out when we changed the rules," Hayman said as he looked back down at the four agents unconscious on the ground. "Help me get them inside before we attract any more attention. And let the hotel know that they can turn off that damn door alarm."

"Yes, sir," Aster replied, stiffly. Grabbing one of the unconscious agents by the scruff of his suit jacket, Aster dragged him through the door back into the conference room.

Jack nodded his head. "Aster didn't betray me and he didn't tell his superior that Forrorrois was not on Earth," Jack replied, turning to Yononnon. "His shock was genuine. For now, the F.B.I. will continue to think that Forrorrois is still on Earth and protecting me, Captain Perkins, and her family from these trumped up charges."

"That would be reasonable for them to assume," Yononnon said. "Where do you want to go now?"

Jack took a deep breath then let it out slowly. "Arlington. I'll give you directions. I have to visit my brother, I'm long overdue."

Yononnon gave him an uncertain look. "Forgive my ignorance, Jack, but isn't your brother dead?"

Jack nodded. "Yes, he's buried in Arlington."

He was surprised when Yononnon caught his breath and bowed his head briefly. "Monomay honors those who honor their family," the subcommander said in a hushed voice. "Point the way, Jack. I will take you where you wish to go."

Jack glanced at the somber Dramudam subcommander and patted his shoulder. "Thank you." Then he pointed west.

Yononnon raised the shrouded scout above the city streets and headed westward, following his silent direction. Inside, Jack struggled to understand what path his life was moving in. *Maybe a moment of reflection will help me,* he thought as they approached the sprawling national cemetery with its regimented rows of white marble markers.

"Pardon me for asking, Jack, but what do all the white stones represent?" Yononnon asked as they glided over the enormous site.

"They represent those who defended the right to freedom for all of the beings of this country," Jack whispered. "All those who served in the armed forces who served honorably can choose to be buried here under specific conditions."

He glanced over at Yononnon and was surprised to see his coal black eyes glistening. "It is a great honor for you to allow me to come here," Yononnon replied in a reverent voice.

Jack swallowed hard then cleared his throat. "The Dramudam fight for the same things that these Humans fought for. Your presence does them honor, Subcommander. Now, please, land over in that road and I will walk to my brother's grave."

Yononnon did as he asked without another word. Jack let the stillness embrace him as he waited for the canopy to rise then he climbed down the ladder that emerged from the side of the ship. The warm late summer breeze welcomed him as he made his way between the stones then stopped at his brother's marker—a single tear slipped down his cheek as he bowed his head in prayer.

★★★★★★★★★★★

Jack studied his brother's white cross marker set in the sea of neat rows that made up Arlington National Cemetery. The marble contrasted against the lush green grass—a stark reminder that so many had given so much to keep the country free. But times were strained by the paranoia that had infected the government. And there were those in power that wanted to erode the rights of the people, forgetting that their role was to serve the people—to serve like the men and women in the graves around him had served.

Jack didn't look up when he heard footsteps approaching. He just sighed when they stopped beside him.

"I wasn't sure you would be here—especially after the hotel," Aster's voice sounded.

Jack shook his head and looked over at his friend. "You're right, I almost didn't," Jack replied. "But then I went against my initial instinct and stayed a little longer to listen to what you said to Director Hayman. I decided I'd give plan B a chance."

"Then you know I wasn't fully informed of Director Hayman and the President's agenda," Aster said, uncertain.

"Yes," Jack replied. The relief on Aster's face was enough to tell him how horrified he was about the whole event.

"Thank you," Aster said. "Jack, if Forrorrois isn't on Earth, who was your backup?"

"Subcommander Yononnon, he's nearby, probably listening in on what we are saying," Jack replied. "He's a friend of Trager's."

"Really?" Aster said as he subconsciously glanced around.

Jack almost smiled. "Yes."

"Is there anything more I can do for you or Forrorrois' family?"

Jack shook his head and smiled. "No, we're good. I'll contact you if anything changes, but in the meantime, it might be wise to limit contacting me—just incase they are monitoring your calls. I think they would become suspicious if certain calls were repeatedly scrambled."

Aster nodded. "I agree. Next time you speak to Forrorrois, let her know that I send her my best."

"I'll do that," Jack replied.

"Thank you. Oh, and if I learn more about who the general is working with I'll let you know."

"Thanks, Aster, be safe," Jack replied.

Jack watched Aster turn and leave up the path. Finally, Jack sighed and lightly touched his brother's marker then he walked in the opposite direction—back to Yononnon's shrouded scout. He wished he had better news for Forrorrois' family, but for now they would need to continue to stay at Forrorrois' base.

****

Trager looked up from his bunk as he heard the door of his cell open. When he recognized Head Councilor Kil'Treahaa, in her golden yellow Eldatek Council robes, enter his cell, Trager respectfully came to his feet and dropped his gaze to the floor.

He could sense the elder female study him with her sharp coal-black eyes as she leaned on her staff. Her face was creased with wisdom and her long gray hair flowed about her shoulders in a mantle—only three thin braids entwined with gold cords shouted her elevated rank.

"It is a shame to see you chained and out of your Dramudam uniform, Haator," Kil'Treahaa remarked.

Stunned, Trager glanced up. "I don't understand," he remarked.

"And you shouldn't," the councilor replied. "May I sit down?"

Trager motioned to his bunk with his wrists shackled in front of him and backed away. "Forgive my manners, Councilor. Please take a seat."

From the corner of his eyes he could see the elderly female nod with approval as she crossed to the bunk and sat down. When she lowered herself, Trager arranged his tan robes and respectfully knelt on the floor, against the wall, ensuring his head was not higher than hers. The shackles cut into his bare ankles, but his dismissed the discomfort and arranged his shackled hands on his lap submissively.

Kil'Treahaa leaned forward, still holding her staff. "Haator, have you spoken with Neeha since you've been brought back to Elda?"

"No, Councilor, I have not," Trager replied, keeping his gaze indirect.

"Hmmm," the elder female remarked. "Have you heard of the council's decisions in this matter?"

"Yes, Councilor," Trager said, dipping his head slightly. "Thank you for allowing Celeste to be recognized as legitimate. And thank you for recognizing Forrorrois' right of Penock."

"But what of our decision to grant Bohata the right of Slovak?" Kil'Treahaa mused. "What have you to say about that?"

Trager struggled to remain calm. "Bohata's petition for Right of Slovak was expected."

"Well said," Kil'Treahaa commented. "Your time with the Dramudam hasn't dulled your mind after all—although your joining with an off-worlder would suggest otherwise."

Trager remained impassionate to her slight as he stared at the gray stone tile in front of him.

"Do you also know that Forrorrois has left the Tollon to try and raise the joining fee that she neglected to provide to Neeha when she joined with you?"

Trager almost smiled. "I suspected that she would."

"Did you also know that she took another with her?"

Uncertain, Trager shook his head. "How could I know this being held in this cell?"

"True. Although I do find it odd that she would choose to

ally herself with her sworn enemy for such a task," Kil'Treahaa continued.

Trager looked up briefly. "Who do you speak of?"

"I speak of the Utahar, Collinar."

Trager took a sharp breath as he dropped his gaze. "I hadn't heard this," he replied.

He could sense her amusement while he attempted to remain impassive.

"She must care for you a great deal to take such a risk," Kil'Treahaa added. "But then again, the sum of the joining fee has been set unusually high—partly as compensation to Neeha for being paid after the fact and partly because of the disparity of her station as a Dramudam to that of Neeha's present position as a member of council. Whatever the outcome, I must have your assurance that you will comply with the final decision."

Trager looked up for a moment. "I'm bound by the laws of Elda to comply, but my heart will always be with my first joined one."

Kil'Treahaa scoffed at his words. "You're as defiant as your father was," she remarked. "Haator, you should know that your brother was dutiful to Bohata. Talman's death was unfortunate. He was not lacking as other's might claim. This fact would become obvious if you were joined with Bohata as her second."

Trager studied the councilor's gnarled hand as she clutched her staff. He narrowed his eyes slightly as he considered her words. His mind began to race.

"But Councilor, then why must we go forward with this charade?" Trager stated. "Isn't there a better solution?"

"The original solution of giving Celeste to Bohata to nurture as her own heir was the better solution, but your clever off-worlder found a way to bring you back from the Plane of Deception," Kil'Treahaa replied.

Trager took a quick breath. "And by seeking my help to release Celeste from the obligation, Forrorrois unwittingly forced Neeha's hand to offer me as Talman's second. But Neeha wouldn't have forced me to trade places with Celeste if she had known of Bohata's condition.

Bohata's house and Neeha's house could both lose face and status if this becomes public!" he gasped.

"I thought that there was a spark of intelligence in those eyes of yours, Haator," Kil'Treahaa said while she pulled herself to a standing position, using her staff. "Think on my words, but say nothing—especially if you are seeking petty revenge against your mother. It will not be Neeha that suffers, but Forrorrois. If this becomes public knowledge, then there will be no other solution except to have Celeste forcibly given to Bohata to preserve the bond between Neeha and Bohata's houses and now that you are available Neeha could still have you joined with another house to broaden her powerbase. The universe will correct itself in time, Haator, Monomay will see to that, but only if you say nothing."

Shaken by her veiled threat, Trager struggled to his feet, encumbered by his shackles and bowed to her. "I will consider your words," he replied.

"Good," Kil'Treahaa said as she reached out and touched him lightly on his bowed head. "There are many houses that are licking old wounds and would be unwilling to look for new solutions if this became public. Perhaps you could use that intelligence of yours to come up with a resolution that will provide the parties involved with no further loss of status. Show me that your time as head of security on the Tollon has provided you with some wisdom. Who knows, you might even discover a way to return to your off-worlder."

Trager deepened his bow. "May Monomay provide wisdom to us all," he replied in a hushed voice. He didn't straighten until Kil'Treahaa had left his cell and he was alone once more. Trager shuffled back to his bunk and sat down—stunned. The councilor's words echoed in his mind—along with her threat. There must be a way to provide Bohata an heir without Celeste or himself being used as pawns. If Bohata's house was threatened so was his chance to reunite with Celeste and Forrorrois. Now, more than ever, he needed Forrorrois to succeed in raising the Joining fee—even if it meant that she had to recruit the assistance of the likes of Collinar.

CHAPTER 17

Forrorrois adjusted the scanners once more on her two-seat long-distance scout. There was no doubt in her mind that the coordinates they had been given for the pickup were heavily shielded. The only way to reach them was on foot through the swamp. She glanced over at Collinar who was sitting in the jump seat next to her command chair in the cockpit. He was chaffing impatiently for information.

"Well?" he demanded.

Forrorrois shook her head. "We head in on foot."

"No, you head in on foot," Collinar countered. "The Kohanian female won't deal with a male."

His obstinate response irritated her, but he was right. "All right," Forrorrois replied. "Just don't try anything foolish, the ship's computer—"

"—won't give me access," Collinar droned, finishing her sentence—much to her annoyance.

"Right," she said as she rose from her seat. "Let's hope that Mo'onah is at the meeting place."

"She will be. Just remember that Mo'onah will try to insult you to determine your worth. You mustn't react and don't insult her back," Collinar stated, coming to his feet as she passed him then followed her into the cargo hold.

Forrorrois nodded her head while the hatch opened and the ramp extended. "I'll remember."

"Good, I'll be waiting," Collinar replied with a sneer.

She ignored him and walked down the ramp. The weight of her stun weapon on her waist comforted her as she stepped onto the spongy ground. Reaching out with her mind, she didn't sense anyone in the immediate area.

'Computer, guide me to the coordinates,' she subvocalized.

'Proceed straight ahead for one bul,' the computer responded in her mind.

Forrorrois realized she could have reached the meeting place quicker if she had used a hovercycle, but the Kohanian's preferred to use minimal technology. An interesting deception since they were actually quite technologically advanced. The sun was quickly setting through the murky haze of the atmosphere. She began to hike to the site, ignoring the insects that swarmed her, and stumbled upon a timeworn footpath. A few steps in, Forrorrois felt her zendra link sever—she had entered the shielded zone. Forrorrois reached out empathically and didn't sense anyone near by. Cautiously, she continued on the path, hoping it would lead her to Mo'onah.

Forrorrois walked for nearly a half-a-hour before the path become steeper and firmer. The sound of something moving through the tall grass made her stop. She reached out empathically and felt a mind nearby. The tall grass parted and a svelte amphibious creature stepped forward. Forrorrois studied the broad mouth and expressive raised yellow eyes that reminded her of a brown frog. The creature wore a sheath like dress of slick material that mimicked layered lily pads.

"You are here to see Mo'onah?" the creature half-spoke, half-croaked.

"Yes," Forrorrois replied, studying the creature as it clasped its webbed hands.

"I am Mo'onah. Who are you?"

"I am Danica."

"Danica," the creature replied, "what a pale unappealing creature you are. Are you female?"

Forrorrois ignored her slight and nodded. "Yes."

Mo'onah stepped closer to her. "You smell of rotting flesh," she remarked, raising her webbed hand to her snout.

"Forgive my offensive smell, I've been trapped in a cargo ship with a male who doesn't bath," Forrorrois replied.

Mo'onah raised one of her amphibian eyes. "Yes, that can be most unpleasant, but one must endure. I sense you have an open mind."

Forrorrois steeled herself as Mo'onah stepped closer and reached out her webbed hand toward her temple.

"As distasteful as this will be for me, I must request that I touch your dry skin," Mo'onah stated.

Forrorrois felt panic over take her. If Mo'onah was telepathic, then her cover was blown. But if she said no, then the meeting would be over. Glancing around, Forrorrois spotted a puddle of water—her thoughts fell to fishing when she was a child and her father teaching her to wet her hands before touching a fish.

"Mo'onah, if you must touch my face, please let me make my dry skin more appealing," Forrorrois replied. Without waiting for Mo'onah to respond, Forrorrois knelt down and scooped the water from the puddle with her cupped hands and patted them against the skin of her face. She could feel the Kohanian's uncertainty turn to approval. Forrorrois stood up and waited as Mo'onah approached her. The Kohanian's slippery fingers felt cool against her left temple.

"You are a complicated creature, Danica," Mo'onah remarked. "You are not what you pose yourself to be."

Forrorrois stiffened as Mo'onah's left hand grasped at the top of her shirt. Before she could object, the Kohanian tore the fabric and exposed her Dramudam mark.

"You are far from home, Forrorrois."

Forrorrois' eyes widened as Mo'onah spoke her ship name. Without thinking, she raised her right hand and touched her fingers to Mo'onah's temple, completing the telepathic link.

Mo'onah gasped at the unexpected connection. "Intriguing," she whispered. "You are not here as Dramudam, but as a mother protecting her family. I judged you wrong."

Forrorrois lowered her hand. "I'm also here to help, Mo'onah."

The Kohanian lowered her webbed hand. "I believe you. You risk much to be here in the Environs. You are worthy to carry this back to Pedra."

Forrorrois was surprised when Mo'onah retrieved a small sphere from the folds of her garment and handed it to her. In the low light, Forrorrois could see movement in the liquid interior.

"You will contact my counterpart to the Pedraco royal house, Hel'ket. She is their head horticulturalist," Mo'onah continued.

"Protect this with your life. Inside this sphere is the proto-life of the next generation of Pedra water lilies mixed with Sten genetics. Our houses may be feuding but our race must survive. The lilies are the livelihood of both worlds. A mixing of the genetics every eighty revolution is necessary to prevent the inbreeding that would devastate both of our economies."

Forrorrois held the sphere protectively and bowed. "As a mother, I will protect this with my life," she vowed.

"The Houses of Stentous and Pedraco are in your hands, your reward will be great," Mo'onah replied with a slight nod. "For now, all I can give you is this small payment, the rest you will receive from Hel'ket."

Mo'onah retrieved a small pouch from her garment and handed the bag to Forrorrois.

"Thank you for your trust," Forrorrois whispered as she took the pouch.

"You must go now, Forrorrois. Your mind holds the coordinates— Hel'ket will be there in one kel," Mo'onah replied.

Forrorrois turned and hurried back down the path through the darkening gloom. She started when she suddenly made contact with her ship's computer through her zendra link. Mo'onah had lifted the shielding. Forrorrois fed the coordinates to her scout and quickened her pace.

When she finally reached the edge of the clearing, she spotted a light from her scout's cargo hold. Forrorrois ran up the ramp and spotted Collinar sitting on a crate with a pistol-like stun weapon. She sensed his relief when he realized it was her.

"I'm not going to ask how you got your hands on that," Forrorrois commented with a nod towards his weapon and headed into the cockpit.

Collinar put the small weapon onto his belt and shrugged. "I slipped it from Motan when we sealed the deal."

Forrorrois took her seat in her command chair. "I'll thank you not to use it on me while we are working together."

"I'll oblige if you do the same for me," Collinar replied. "What happened to your shirt?"

Forrorrois looked down at the torn fabric and her exposed Dramudam mark. "Let's just say next time, knowing that the customer is telepathic would be helpful," she replied.

"Obviously the customer wasn't too upset by this little discovery," Collinar said with a shrug. "You're still alive."

"Luckily," Forrorrois agreed. An odd amusement filtered into her mind from Collinar at her answer.

Collinar sat down on the jump seat next to her. "Where are we heading now?"

"One of the moons of Pedra. We're delivering this," she replied, holding up the small sphere with her left hand.

Curious, Collinar leaned forward and examined the sphere. "What is it?"

Forrorrois finished her preflight and glanced over at him. "A mix of the Pedra and Steno water lily genetics," she replied.

Collinar shook his head. "This is priceless. We are definitely being underpaid for this job," he sniffed.

Forrorrois rolled her eyes at his remark as she slipped the small globe protectively into the pocket of her vest. She called up the coordinates for Pedra that she had fed into the ship's computer then maneuvered her scout back into space, her only hope was that Motan's next job would bring her closer to the joining fee she needed for Trager' release.

∗∗∗∗∗∗∗∗∗∗∗

Jack walked into the hangar bay of Forrorrois' base and was surprised to find Frank and George sitting at the workbench with Yononnon. The three stared intently at a board game that was resting on the bench. He quietly studied the odd six-sided board made out of a tan colored cloth with a hexagon pattern printed on the material. At three of the alternating corners there were three darkened patches. Each darkened corner had a different set of colored stones that were staged, one color for each player. Jack smiled as he realized that it was Chole Chole, an Eldatek game of strategy.

"It's a good thing your sister isn't here, George, she's a tough Chole Chole player," Jack remarked in English as he looked over George's shoulder.

Yononnon glanced up. "Danica often had me rethink my strategy," he replied solemnly in English. "She must have inherited her talent from her father."

Jack studied the board carefully then he grinned. Frank had the red pieces and he was dominating the board. George was struggling to maintain a presence with his grey pieces, while Yononnon was poised for a decisive strike with his black pieces. Jack was about to comment when his cell phone rang in his pocket.

He walked away from the workbench and pulled his cell phone from his pants pocket. When he looked at the number, he was surprised to see it was Aster's.

"Stern, here," Jack said into the phone.

"Jack, its Aster. Am I glad that you answered," his friend gasped.

Jack grew concern from the distress in his friend's voice. "What's wrong?"

"I've been shot in the shoulder," Aster panted.

Jack gripped his phone tighter as the word 'shot' sunk in. "Where are you?" Jack pressed.

"I'm in an alley a few blocks from where I live. Two men in black suits jumped me as I entered my apartment. I don't know how much longer I can keep avoiding them. I've stopped most of the bleeding—I think the bullet went all the way through."

Jack's heart began to pound as he crossed back to the workbench.

"I'll come find you," Jack said, "just stay on the line so I can trace you."

"Jack, they might be triangulating my position from my phone," Aster objected.

Jack's mind raced. He barely noticed that the Chole Chole game had come to a halt as all eyes now gazed in his direction. "Hang in there, Aster. I'll find you. Contact me in twenty minutes. I should be over D.C. by then."

"All right," Aster replied. "I'll keep moving until then."

Jack looked over at the George, Frank, and Yononnon.

"Yononnon, we need to head out right now, Aster's been targeted and I need your help to extract him."

"I'll prepare my scout," Yononnon stated as he immediately crossed the hangar bay to his single-seat scout ship.

"I can help," George volunteered, but Jack shook his head.

"Sorry, George, but I need you to stay here and help your father hold down the base," Jack replied. "Aster's been shot in the shoulder and he's on the run. I don't know what kind of trouble we're going to run into when we find him."

"Jack, please," George insisted. "I've been studying to be an EMT in my spare time in Vegas."

Jack didn't have time to argue, he looked to George's father. "Frank?"

"It's all right—take him with you," Frank replied. "You might need another pair of hands."

"OK, move out!" Jack ordered.

Without a word, George scrambled to the scout ship and up the ladder. Jack followed after him.

"George, go down into the rear cabin, Yononnon, do you have…" he began, but Yononnon just handed him the emergency med kit. "Thank you," Jack replied as he took the pouch from him and tossed the shoulder bag to George in the cabin a few steps below his position.

"I've laid in a course to Aster's quarters," Yononnon stated. "Steady yourself."

Jack grabbed the back of Yononnon's command chair as the scout ship lurched forward into the night sky.

****

Jack studied the holographic display of the streets and buildings that hovered between Yononnon and the canopy of the one-seat scout's cockpit. Below them were the dimly lit streets a few blocks from Aster's apartment building. Fortunately, since it was late on a weekday, most people were home for the evening. He glanced back when George came up the steps behind him from the rear cabin.

"Do you see anything?" George asked.

"Nothing conclusive, yet," Jack replied. "Hopefully, Aster will turn on his phone soon so that we can get a fix on his position."

"I'm picking up some activity several streets over," Yononnon stated, pointing to the location on the street holograph that floated before them.

Jack nodded. "Check it out."

Yononnon maneuvered the shrouded craft towards the life signs. As they cleared the building, Jack spotted a car parked on the street near the light of a street lamp.

"Even if we find him, how will we get him out without people seeing us?" George gasped.

"I'll keep the scout shrouded," Yononnon replied, "but that means I won't be able to use the ship's weapons if we have to use force to extract Aster."

"I've got a few ideas," Jack stated while he opened the weapons locker beside Yononnon's command chair and pulled out a stun rifle and two oval handhelds. Then his gaze fell on a small familiar weapon. Jack grinned as he pulled it out as well. He turned and handed Yononnon the stun rifle and George one of the smaller oval stun weapons.

Yononnon remained seated as he took the rifle. Jack felt the large Eldatek male eye him as he placed the stun weapon and the second weapon onto his belt.

"Jack, in Aster's present state, he may not be strong enough to survive the effects of that weapon," the subcommander cautioned.

"It's not for him," Jack replied. Yononnon raised an eyebrow, but didn't object further as he readied his stun rifle.

George moved to speak, but Jack's cell phone rang in his pants pocket making him pause. Jack pulled the phone out and answered quickly, recognizing Aster's number.

"Stern, here," he stated.

He was stunned when he didn't hear Aster's voice on the other end of the line.

"I thought you would come," the familiar voice replied.

"General Caldwell," Jack hissed.

George and Yononnon looked over at him in shock.

"What have you done with Aster?!" Jack demanded.

"Nothing, I've got him right here. Although regrettably, he is worse for wear," the general calmly replied. "I assure you he's still alive."

"I want to hear his voice," Jack insisted.

"If you insist," the general sighed.

"It's a trap, Jack! Get out of here!" Aster's voice called out.

"That's enough," Caldwell stated. "He might actually make it if you trace this signal and meet us here ASAP."

"They're in the alley," Yononnon said, pointing at the coordinates fixed from the cell phone signal in the floating holographic map. "I see four life signs. One is weakening."

Jack covered the phone with his hand. "It must be Aster—the general's using his cell."

Before Jack could make the request, Yononnon maneuvered the scout over the alley. Jack grew alarmed when he spotted Aster flanked by two men slumped against a brick wall with his hand pressed against his wounded shoulder. General Caldwell stood over the wounded F.B.I. agent, wearing dark street clothes, as he spoke into Aster's cell phone.

"General, this is low even for you," Jack stated into the phone.

"Very rich, coming from you, Stern," Caldwell's voice sounded. "Agent Aster will be brought up on charges for withholding information on your whereabouts. His only chance is if you, Captain Perkins, and Forrorrois surrender immediately."

"No deal, General," Jack replied.

"I'm sorry to hear that, Jack. It's a shame that Agent Aster's body will be found in this alley—a victim of a random mugging," the general continued.

Jack's eyes widened as one of the men pulled out a pistol and leveled the barrel at Aster's head. He shook the fear from his mind and reminded himself that he still had the element of surprise from the vantage of the hovering scout ship's cockpit. Narrowing his eyes, Jack turned to Yononnon. "Stun everything in the alley but Aster."

He didn't have to state the order twice. Yononnon raised the cockpit canopy and surgically lanced the alley with the red beam of his stun rifle. The general and the two men in black suits dropped where they stood in the garbage strewn ally. Aster weakly glanced up as Yononnon resumed his command chair and maneuvered out towards the street. The subcommander landed the scout, still shrouded, half on the sidewalk and half on the street. The moment the scout was on the ground, Jack was down the ladder on the side of the craft and headed into the alley. George followed after him with the emergency kit slung over his shoulder. Jack dropped to Aster's side and checked his pulse—it was weak, but steady.

"Aster, can you walk?" he asked.

"I think so," Aster replied.

"George, help Aster back to the scout," Jack ordered.

"You got it," George replied. He eased Aster to his feet and supported him with his shoulder.

"What about them?" Aster growled.

Jack looked over at Caldwell and the two men in disgust.

"I'll handle them, you go ahead," Jacked replied. "George, Yononnon will help you get Aster into the rear cabin. I'll be right behind you."

"Sure thing, Jack," George said. "Come on, Agent Aster, it looks like your shoulder is bleeding again."

Jack turned his attention to Caldwell and the two men. An idea formed in his head as he pulled out the second weapon from his belt. Making a slight adjustment, he aimed the small oval weapon at Caldwell. A bluish-green beam lanced forth engulfing the general's unmoving form. Jack smiled while his former commanding officer shrank to less than nine centimeters in length. His smile grew into a grin as he stripped the two men in suits of their weapons and repeated his action. Scooping the three miniaturized men up, he deposited them into his jacket pocket and ran back to the street.

Jack felt for the side of the shrouded craft until he caught the rung of the ladder. Then he was up the ladder into the cockpit in a heartbeat. When he reached the rear cabin, he saw Aster already stripped to the waist, lying on the bunk, with George circling the bioknitter over his wound. Yononnon was by George's side providing instruction. "Subcommander, get us back to the base," Jack ordered.

Yononnon nodded his head and returned to the cockpit.

Jack crossed over to Aster and touched his forehead. His skin felt clammy to the touch.

"Hang in there, Aster," Jack stated.

"I'm doing fine, Jack. George is a natural, just like his sister," Aster said through clenched teeth. "The pain is starting to subside."

Jack patted the young man's shoulder and nodded his approval.

George smiled nervously as he continued to circle Aster's shoulder wound with the bioknitter.

"So what's your assessment, George?" Jack asked.

"Well, he's suffering from blood loss," George began. "There's some damage to the muscles and his shoulder blade was clipped when the bullet exited out his back, but the wound is responding to the bioknitter. Agent Aster, it looks like with some rehab, you'll be able to fire a pistol again in no time."

"Thanks, George. And please, just call me Aster."

"Sure..." George replied then he looked over at Jack and shook his head. "I still can't believe they did this to him. He's a federal agent!"

"Neither can I," Jack said with a shake of his head. "But I'm going to find out why," he added as he pulled the general and the two men from his jacket pocket.

George almost dropped his bioknitter when Jack laid the three miniaturized unconscious men on the bunk beside Aster's leg.

Aster struggled up on one elbow to see then swallowed hard. "You're kidding me..." he gasped.

"Nope," Jack replied. "I plan to get some answers."

Without another word, Jack subvocalized for the storage cabinet door to open and extracted a small fauna containment box out. He lifted the three unconscious men into the box and threw a cloth over the lid.

✸✸✸✸✸✸✸✸✸✸✸

Forrorrois was smiling when she left the surface of the Pedraco moon. Hel'ket had met her where Mo'onah had said she would be. This time, Forrorrois had been greeted warmly. Hel'ket gratefully paid her the remainder of the fee, plus she had handed Forrorrois an additional pouch, insisting it was a bonus to help her as a mother.

Collinar was visibly relieved when they headed back toward Motan's base.

"I've got the ship on autopilot," Forrorrois announced. "Let's get something to eat."

Collinar nodded and followed her back to the rear cabin. "So what do you have?" he asked taking a seat at the small table.

Forrorrois opened a cabinet and pulled out bottles of water. Opening a small container, she grabbed a couple of packages, then carried them back to the table and placed the items in front of Collinar.

He looked at her and sniffed. "Energy bars and water?"

"They're good for you," she replied. "Filled with vitamins and minerals."

"Wonderful," he said as he opened the wrapper and bit into the bar. He chewed slowly and washed the dry bar down with his water. "So, show me what we got," he said after he swallowed.

Forrorrois took the two pouches and set them on the table. Collinar reached over and opened them, spilling the contents out on the table between them. In the first pouch were several large gems of extreme clarity and the second were thin metallic rectangular high denomination currency. From the look in Collinar's eyes Forrorrois suddenly realized that they had been paid very well.

"So how did we do?" she asked, leaning forward.

376

"I don't know what you said to them, but this is twice the fee that Motan had promised us," Collinar replied.

Forrorrois smiled as she pulled the third pouch and added the contents to the other two. Collinar's eyes sparkled as she emptied the pouch.

"Those are Prophet stones—extremely rare," Collinar exclaimed as he picked up one of the teardrop shaped black stones that was about the size of the tip of her small finger and held the translucent stone up to the light.

Forrorrois followed what he was doing and gasped as she saw the rainbow reflected inside. "They're beautiful," she whispered. "Where do they come from?"

"They come from a volcanic planet near a black hole," he said as he continued to stare at the stone. "Soothsayers and shamans from around the galaxy would give their firstborn for stones such as these."

"What do they use them for?" she asked, still admiring the kaleidoscope of colors that sparkled inside the stone.

"It is said to allow the user to enter into a more intense trance. Some even say that they can use them to see the future," Collinar stated as he concentrated on the light through the stone. "You should try it some time. If my suspicions are right, you probably have hidden mental talents that you haven't even discovered yet."

Forrorrois glanced at him, sensing that he believed every word he had just told her. The thought sent a shiver down her spine. She looked back at the take from the job and slowly exhaled as she carefully divided the gems and currency into two equal piles and pushed one towards Collinar.

"Take your share," Forrorrois said as she placed her portion back into one of the pouches. "And you can keep that Prophet Stone as a bonus, but I'm keeping the rest of them."

He lowered the translucent stone to the table and looked at her cautiously. "This single stone alone is worth more than five times what you agreed to pay me. Aren't you worried that I'll run?" he asked.

Forrorrois shrugged her shoulders. "You want your freedom to return to the Utahar, you can't do that if you run," she replied.

Collinar snorted and placed his share in the other pouch. "True."

"Hopefully, the next job Motan finds us will be more profitable," she stated, rising from the table.

"Let's hope so," Collinar replied.

"I need to get some rest," Forrorrois said. "Let me know when we reach Motan's base.

"Yes, my commander," Collinar said as he rose to his feet.

Forrorrois gave him an irritated look and sensed his amusement while he left her alone in the rear cabin. After the door closed, Forrorrois crossed over to the bunk and triggered a hidden compartment at the base. She dropped the two pouches inside and closed the panel. Kicking off her boots, she lay back on the bunk, Collinar was satisfied for the moment, but she knew she wouldn't be able to keep him that way once she reached the amount she needed for the joining fee.

****

"Are you sure you want to do this?" Yononnon asked once more while Jack stood in the hallway just outside the communications room of Forrorrois' base.

Jack shook his head. "No, but I have to get answers."

"But Jack, he was your commander," Yononnon stated.

"Yes, and he tried to kill Aster," Jack replied. "He has threatened Forrorrois' family and collaborated with Collinar. This has to stop. I have to stop him."

Yononnon looked down at the floor and nodded. "All right, but you must understand, I can't go in there. I shouldn't even be here on the planet surface. Revealing my presence here will only complicate matters."

"I agree," Jack said as he put his hand on the door. "Go check on Aster and George. Aster lost a lot of blood and he's going to need fluids, make sure that he's getting plenty."

"Of course," Yononnon replied.

"Oh, and Yononnon," Jack added. "Whatever happens in this room—don't let anyone inside. I don't want anyone else implicated."

Yononnon studied him for a moment then nodded curtly. Without a word, the large Dramudam subcommander turned and headed for the hangar bay, leaving Jack alone in the hallway.

Jack took a deep breath then exhaled slowly before he pushed the door open and crossed over to the towel covered fauna containment unit on the counter. He reached out and drew the material from box to reveal General Caldwell and the two men in black suits, sitting inside.

Instinctively, the three miniaturized men looked up, shielding their eyes as light replaced darkness. They froze as Jack dominated their field of view—fear became visible on their faces when he looked down at them through the clear cover of the container. Until that moment, his captives hadn't realized the precariousness of their position. Jack kept his face passive as he gradually took a seat at the counter and let the incomprehensible reality of the moment sink into the minds of the three men. Caldwell had seen the reduction weapon used on Forrorrois so it didn't take him long to understand what had happened—the two men in suits that were with him didn't have that luxury. Remaining silent, Jack hinged back the cover of the sound proof box. His action made the three miniature men step back against the far clear plastic wall of the container.

Jack's apathetic stare continued for almost thirty seconds. He had turned the tables on his former commander and he wanted to savor the moment. Finally, Caldwell crossed the half-meter by quarter-meter box defiantly and called up to him.

"What are you planning on doing, Stern?"

Jack glanced down at the graying man that had once been his commanding officer and tried to keep the disdain from his voice. "I want answers, General," he replied.

"Where's Forrorrois?" Caldwell demanded.

"She's busy at the moment, sir," Jack answered. "General, what you and these two men did to Agent Aster wasn't necessary."

"He'll live," Caldwell scoffed. "Forrorrois can heal him."

Jack fought to keep his composure, relieved his ploy had worked. Caldwell continued to believe that Forrorrois was there. "General, your actions were rash and have drawn attention—attention that neither of us wants."

"You're a traitor to your own kind, Stern," Caldwell called up. "You've used your position for personal gain."

Jack shook his head. "I have to disagree, General. It is you that has abused your position. You've endangered this entire world. I don't know who these men are that you've associated yourself with, but from what I witnessed tonight, I'm appalled. They were willing to assault an F.B.I. agent—possibly even murder him—as if they would have full immunity." Jack watched the two men as he made his accusation. Unfortunately the two were still overwhelmed from the shock of being reduced to a mere nine centimeters in height—too overcome for him to read their reactions. He suddenly rose from his chair making all three men involuntarily step backwards inside the fauna containment unit. Then he turned his back on the container and made a step toward the door.

"Stern! Where are you going?" Caldwell demanded.

Jack glanced back at the general briefly then he lowered the lid on the containment unit. The soundproof lid silenced the general's tirade. Then he draped the cloth back over the box and left the room, closing the door between them. In the hallway, he leaned against the wall and exhaled as he cleared his mind. He glanced up when Frank approached him.

"How did it go?" Frank asked.

"I think the general needs to cool his heels for a while. I'll check in on them in a few hours," Jack replied.

"I see," Frank said.

"How's Aster doing?" Jack asked, changing the topic.

"Good, he's still on Yononnon's scout," Frank replied. "Yononnon insisted that he stay there while George watches him, but Aster's going to need to rest for a few days to recover from the blood loss."

Jack sighed. "I'm glad we reached him in time."

"Me too. Aster has been very good to us over the years. It wasn't until recently that I fully appreciated how much he did for Danica when we were sequestered on the air base."

Jack smiled. "He's been a true friend," he replied. Then he glanced back at the door to the communications room and his smile faded as trepidation filled him. "The general is extremely lucky Danica wasn't here to see what he did to Aster. I doubt very much she would have restrained herself."

Frank tensed. "At times my daughter has a darker side that worries me," he admitted.

Jack rested his hand on his friend's shoulder. "She struggles with it, but you've taught her right from wrong. If she hadn't learned these lessons from you then she wouldn't be seeking a diplomatic solution on Elda to free Trager."

"You're right. She's grown," Frank replied.

Jack pulled on a weary smile as he lowered his hand. "Yes, she has. Now, if you'll excuse me, I need a break. I'm going to my room for a bit. After that, I'm going talk with Aster when he's up to it. I need to ask him some questions about what happened. We've got some leverage now. If things go well, we might be able to use General Caldwell and the two men in a trade to gain a pardon for your family."

Frank's brown eyes brightened. "That would be a miracle if we could get our lives back." Then he looked down at the floor. "Although, I doubt I'd be able to return to work. They'd limit the projects that I could work on."

Jack studied his friend for a moment. Working for a defense contractor with a security clearance was a touchy thing. "Possibly," he replied, "but financially you would be taken care of, Danica has made provisions for you, Danielle, and George if you ever needed assistance."

Frank looked up, a bit surprised. "That's good to know, but I'm a bit young to retire just yet," Frank replied. "We'll probably have to move. Last time, it took a few years before the neighbors started talking to us again after Danica was cleared of the enemy combatant charges the first time. Even if we are cleared, I doubt that they'll be able to be so accepting this time. There will always be doubt."

Jack nodded. "The general has destroyed a lot of lives in his pursuit of power. But we mustn't give in."

"You're right. I've prayed on this a lot lately, Jack, and I realize now that what we've been asked to sacrifice is so small compared to what we're trying to protect. God gave me an extraordinary daughter. In the darkest hours, she has never given up. She puts my own faith to shame," Frank whispered, dropping his gaze to the floor once more.

"No, Frank. It's your faith that has given her strength."

His friend looked up at him in silent reflection. Jack placed a hand on Frank's shoulder and gave it a squeeze. "Now go and check on your extraordinary son. He kept his head today and probably saved Aster's life."

Frank pulled on a tired smile then turned and walk down the hall. Jack watched him then sighed as he headed for his room.

****

Trager woke up with a start at the clatter of hooves on stone in his darkened cell. He glanced around and saw a large shadow looming in the small room. As the shadow approached him, he scrambled to sit up.

"It's all right, Trager, it's me, Guruma. Nur's with me," the familiar voice whispered.

Trager's heart raced. "Are you here to free me?" he whispered back.

"Unfortunately, no," Guruma replied. "For now we have to let this play out. Otherwise, Celeste and you will never be safe from Neeha's plotting."

Trager sighed. "You're right. But why are you here? Do you have news from Forrorrois?" he asked with renewed hope.

"Some. She has left for the Environs to try and raise your joining fee."

"I heard," Trager confessed. "Is it true she took Collinar with her?"

Guruma hesitated, before he replied. "Yes, you should know she did so under my advice."

Stunned, Trager stared at the shadow before him. "Why would you do that? He's dangerous!" he replied, struggling to keep his voice down.

"Trager, she was only given two mol to raise the fee. Collinar knows the ways of the Environs. Forrorrois can use him. She needs to succeed to free you."

Trager shook his head. "I disagree, the risk is too great."

"Be patient, she can handle him. The universe will right itself. Nur and I must go now before we're discovered."

Trager's mind began to turn as his thoughts fell to Kil'Treahaa's words earlier that cycle. "Wait, Guruma, before you go, I must tell you something!"

"Tell me quick, someone is coming."

"I was told that if I join with Bohata that the result will be the same as it was with my brother."

"Who told you this?" Guruma whispered back.

"I can't say at the moment," Trager replied. "But if it's true, Bohata's family will still lose face unless Neeha reasserts her claim to Celeste. Neeha could still force me to join with another."

"This isn't good. It's even more critical that Forrorrois raises the joining fee. Be very careful what you say and do, Trager. Your life may be in the balance," Guruma warned.

Trager's eyes widened. "You don't think that Talman's death was more than just an illness…"

"At the moment, I can't say," Guruma replied. "But for now, stay cautious and be strong."

Trager moved to speak, but the sound of hooves was replaced with the sound of the door opening. The lights came up in his cell as two guards stepped inside and glanced around.

"Who were you speaking to?" one of the guards demanded.

"No one, I was having a bad dream," Trager replied, his gaze cast to the floor.

Both the female guards sneered at him then closed the door leaving him in the dark once more. Trager lay back down on his bunk and stared up at the ceiling. Guruma's unspoken words pressed on his mind. The thought that his brother's death might not have been natural shook his confidence. *I was never supposed to escape from the Plane of Deception! Neeha doesn't know about Bohata. If she suspected Bohata's condition she would never have exchanged Celeste for him.*

The revelations and suspicion rang in his head. *But did Bohata have his brother killed? Would Neeha have still offered her Celeste if she suspected that Talman's death was not natural?*

Trager's heart began to race. *How much does Kil'Treahaa or the other member of the council know and why haven't they told Neeha?* A deep seated unease spread inside him. There was no doubt in his mind—he was a liability to Bohata and her family. Guruma was right—his very survival was becoming increasingly dependant on Forrorrois' success in raising the exorbitant joining fee.

★★★★★★★★★★★

The sound of crickets in the hot late summer night air filled Jack's ears as he stepped through the camouflaged opening of hangar bay of Forrorrois' base. He smiled when he spotted Yononnon sitting on a rock outcropping staring out into the meadow of wispy grass. The large Eldatek male looked up when he approached.

"Beautiful night," he offered in English.

"Yes," Yononnon replied back in English.

"Mind if I join you?" Jack asked.

"Please do," Yononnon replied and shifted over on the rock to make room for Jack.

"Thank you," Jack said as he sat down. Then he looked up at the patch of sky over the clearing. The stars were peeking through the thin cirrus clouds high above.

"How is the interrogation going?" Yononnon asked, glancing up at the stars.

"Slow, they're not very talkative yet," Jack replied.

"It takes time," the subcommander replied. "I remember watching Trager work an interrogation. He would patiently wait until they would say the right word or signal that they were ready to talk. Sometimes it would take days. I was always amazed at his quiet determination."

"You must be glad that he's back from the Plane of Deception," Jack observed, glancing over at him.

Yononnon looked over at him and nodded. "I am. I've missed him."

Jack nodded back. "We've all missed him."

Together, they looked back at the stars and sat for a while listening to the crickets.

"Yononnon, I have a favor to ask," Jack said, still looking at the stars.

Yononnon paused then looked over at him. "Please ask, I will do what I can for you," he replied.

Jack shifted his gaze to the subcommander's chestnut-brown face. "The favor is more for Forrorrois' father."

Intrigue was written on the subcommander's face as he glanced over at Jack. "Please, go on."

"Frank Jolan is a hard worker. But because of all that has happened he may never be able to return to his job. This would be a difficult thing for him to face. Like Forrorrois, he is very good with his hands and he has the mind of a modification scientist. Would you be willing to let him work with you on the ships?"

Yononnon smiled. "Of course, Frank can also help me practice my English, George is welcome too."

Jack sighed. "Thank you, Yononnon—it will help them both feel more useful."

"Do you want me to prepare zendra as well?" Yononnon offered.

Jack shook his head. "Not yet, I think that would be rushing things. Just ask them for assistance and go from there."

"This will be good," Yononnon replied.

Jack smiled. "Thank you, now if you'll excuse me, I have to begin the next round of interrogation."

"Of course," Yononnon said as he returned his to gaze at the stars. "I'll come in shortly."

"Take your time," Jack replied. He rose from the rock and stretched slightly then headed back to the camouflaged mouth of the hangar bay of Forrorrois' base. His skin tingled slightly as he passed through the barrier into the vaulted area. Jack walked over to the extended ladder on the side of Yononnon's scout. When he moved to climb up, George peered over the side of the cockpit.

"Hey, Jack," George called down in a hushed voice.

"I was just going to see how Aster's doing," Jack called up.

"He's doing fine," George replied, climbing down the ladder. "I just gave him another pain killer and sedative. His shoulder blade is still causing him some discomfort."

"Oh...I was hoping to talk with him," Jack said as George dropped to the stone floor of the hangar bay.

"Maybe in a few hours," George said.

"I see. Well, I'll check in then," Jack said as he turned.

"Jack," George called out, making him turn back towards the young man.

"Yes?"

"Thanks for taking me along," George said with a glance down at the stone floor.

Jack softened his stance. "I'm glad that you were there, you did a great job with Aster's shoulder."

Looking back up, the young man beamed like a kid. "Thanks."

"Now, why don't you see if Yononnon needs some help around here—I'm certain he could use another pair of hands or maybe two pairs if you can pry your dad away from watching that granddaughter of his."

George hesitated. "Do you think he'd want us around?"

"Of course," Jack replied with a grin. "These ships don't perform maintenance on themselves—well, at least most of the maintenance," Jack continued with a grin as he turned and headed for the living quarters.

CHAPTER 18

Jack sat at the bench in the communications room of Forrorrois' base, staring at the three miniaturized men in the fauna containment box that sat on the counter before him. Two days had passed since he had taken General Caldwell and the two men in black suits. The two men had barely spoken, still dumbstruck by the insanity of their situation. General Caldwell was more prepared for what they were experiencing, but even so, the general had grown quiet by the second day and Jack was wondering if he was close to cooperating given the right situation.

With a sigh, Jack leaned forward and started his questions again, maintaining his bored indifference to demonstrate his willingness to continue the interrogation for as long as it took to get the answers.

"Why was Agent Aster targeted?"

General Caldwell stood up from the wooden chair Jack had miniaturized for him and paced the length of the clear plastic fauna containment unit then back again with his arms crossed. The strain of the bizarre captivity was beginning to show on his former commander's demeanor.

"General Caldwell, why did you and these two men target an F.B.I. Agent?" Jack pressed. "Especially when the act of harming him would draw negative attention to you from the Bureau."

Caldwell stopped in his tracks and glared up at him. Jack glanced at the two men in black and almost smiled when he read the uncertainty in their faces—almost fear—that the general might talk. Then his smile faded. As much as he loathed the general for what he had done, he already knew that these other two men were willing to do anything to reach their objective. If he pushed any further, he might provoke the two men to react. Keeping the three in the same containment unit was becoming risky.

Without warning, Jack reached into the containment unit and scooped up his former commanding officer then deposited him on the counter in front of him. While Caldwell quickly regained his footing and straightened to glare contemptuously at him, Jack hinged the cover shut on the containment unit.

"Who pulled the trigger?" Jack asked, resuming his questioning.

Caldwell stared at him then back at the clear plastic wall that separated him from the two men in black.

Jack took the towel that was lying on the counter and covered the container, blocking the view of the two men in black suits. Caldwell glanced up at him, uncertain.

"They can't hear you, the container is soundproof with the cover on—as you already know," Jack stated. "You have about fifteen minutes before you begin to feel a chill. Then hypothermia will begin to settle in."

Caldwell looked up at him alarm. "You wouldn't do that, Colonel! You can't treat a prisoner this way!"

Stunned, Jack looked down at the miniature general. "General, I'm treating you a lot better than you treated Agent Aster," he replied. "Besides, as you've pointed out in the past. I don't work for you anymore. I just need to know who pulled the trigger."

Caldwell glanced back at the thick terry covering that separated him from the wall of the containment unit.

"I assure you that they can't hear you," Jack said.

"They will kill me if they find out I've talked," Caldwell admitted.

Jack's eyes soften. "You're in pretty deep with a rough crowd."

The general looked down at the countertop he was standing on.

"General, the only way I can protect you is if I know who the players are," Jack encouraged.

Caldwell looked up, surprised.

Encouraged, Jack continued. "I know we've never been friends, General, but you did treated me fairly after my wife and daughter were killed. You could have advised me to muster out, but instead you offered me the opportunity to head up the OCU. Believe me—at the time I thought that it was joke—"

"You were the right man for the job," Caldwell replied briskly, unfolding his arms and dropping them to his sides.

Jack nodded. "It took me some time to realize that," he admitted. "General, that's why I want to give you this one chance to pull yourself out of this hole you've dug and salvage your career in the Air Force."

Caldwell looked up at him, uncertain. "What about your career?" he called up.

Jack shook his head. "It doesn't matter anymore—I'm on a different path now."

Caldwell gave him an odd look. "What about your pension?"

"Like I said, General, it doesn't matter anymore," Jack said with a shrug. "Protecting the Earth is more important than just protecting one country. Protecting Forrorrois' family is more important than any government pension that can obviously be taken away at a whim."

He watched as Caldwell shifted on his feet then the older man refolded his arms defiantly.

"We need the technology Forrorrois has to protect the Earth," Caldwell retorted.

"We're not ready for it," Jack stated.

"Who says so? The Dramudam?" Caldwell exclaimed. "They are not even here!"

Jack guarded his tongue. The general was clever. "They're here when we need them. They're not an occupying force."

"Oh and why is Forrorrois here then? Why does she have this base?"

"You know why," Jack replied. "As a Human, she has every right to be on Earth. As a Dramudam, she's our first line of defense until reinforcements arrive."

"You're beginning to sound as sanctimonious as she does," the general scoffed.

"And you're sounding as close-minded as ever," Jack stated, struggling to maintain his composure.

"When I get out of here, I'm going to—"

Jack looked at him, stunned. An incredulous laugh erupted from his lips as he cut him off in mid-sentence. "You are going to what, General? Court-martial me? Declare me an enemy combatant? Strip me of my pension? Drive me and my friends from our homes? No, wait—you've done that already," he replied, sarcastically.

His former commander stared up at him, speechless.

Jack took a deep breath and let it out slowly. "General, I'm asking you one last time. Who are you working with and who shot Agent Aster?"

"And if I don't tell you?" Caldwell asked, still defiant.

Jack sighed. "Then I will turn you and your two associates over to someone who will get the answers from you—people who may not have issues using methods that are out of line with the Geneva Convention. Methods possibly even more brutal than what an Utahar would utilize. Was it you that shot Agent Aster?"

Caldwell blanched at the name of the Utahar. "If it helps, Colonel, I didn't pull the trigger," he offered. "Is Agent Aster all right?"

Jack sat back in his chair and studied the general. "I already know that you didn't pull the trigger," Jack said with a sigh. "You should know Aster was provided medical assistance and survived the blood loss."

"Then why did you ask me who shot Aster?" the general pressed.

"Because I wanted to hear it from your lips," Jack replied. "And I'd like to know who did."

Caldwell furrowed his forehead as he scowled up at Jack. "I don't know who did it—he was shot by the time I arrived. Now what?"

Jack shrugged his shoulders. "That's up to you, General. You provide the names of who you've been working with and I'll help you cut a deal."

Caldwell's shoulders suddenly sagged. "I don't know who they are," the general confessed. "They contacted me when it came out that Forrorrois was actually Danica Jolan. The two men with me were the only ones I've ever met."

"And you never questioned who they were?" Jack asked, incredulously.

"At first I was suspicious and I told them I wasn't interested," Caldwell stated. "But then things started to happen, requisitions for equipment and supplies that had been turned down were suddenly filled. They called it a show of good faith on their part. After that, I didn't hear from them for a while. Then, a year or so back when the Base Realignment and Closure Committee was eyeing the base in Rome, I didn't know where to turn. The two men showed up and offered their assistance. I was desperate to keep the base open. When my base was removed from the closure list, I was ecstatic."

Jack softened his posture. "General, I understand that you didn't want to lose your base, but what did you promise them?"

Caldwell looked away and heaved a sigh. "I promised them alien technology."

Jack's eyes widened in surprise. "You don't even know if these people are part of the U. S. Government?!"

Caldwell looked up with a start. "Of course they are! How else would they have removed the base from the closure list so quickly?"

Jack rolled his eyes. "It could have been a coincidence that they took advantage of. General, they could be working for a foreign government."

"No. Look at how easily I was able to get you all listed as enemy combatants. They have power," Caldwell insisted.

"If this is true, then they've also made some powerful enemies in the government. Which means so have you, sir," Jack said as he rose from his chair.

The general stepped back as Jack loomed over him and moved to run, but Jack blocked him with his hand.

"There's no place to go, General, except back in the box," Jack stated. He scooped Caldwell up in his fingers and removed the towel from the container with his free hand. Then he lifted the lid and lowered Caldwell inside. He watched as the two men in black stared at the general, suspiciously.

Jack lifted a square of clear plastic material from the table and slipped it into slots in the walls of the fauna containment unit, separating the two men from the general. Jack smiled as he picked up a second square and slipped the plate into a second set of slots dividing the container into three equal areas. Without warning, he reached in and scooped up one of the men in black suits and deposited him on the table in front of him. The man stood frozen as Jack closed the lid to the containment unit and placed the towel over the box once more.

The man turned to run but Jack blocked him with his hand and shook his head.

"There's no place to go," Jack stated. "And if you did escape, you'd die from hypothermia within a few hours."

"You're insane," the man called up.

Jack smiled—it was the first time the man had spoken. "No, I'm just trying to get some answers," he replied.

"I'm not talking," the man stated, crossing his arms.

"I didn't think you would," Jack said with a shrug, "but your buddy doesn't know that and neither do the people you work for. Besides, who said that I need you to say a word?"

Jack's lips twitched with a grin as the man looked up at him in horror. He sat back and watched the man cast his gaze to the counter top.

Fifteen minutes passed before Jack scooped the man up and redeposited him back into the fauna containment unit. Then he scooped up the other man and repeated the process. When his fifteen minutes were up, Jack deposited him back into the clear plastic box. Each man was now separated by the dividers Jack had installed and now each man stared at the other two filled with suspicion. Jack draped the towel back over the fauna containment unit plunging the three into darkness and left the room.

Outside, he was surprised when he found Yononnon waiting for him.

"How did the interrogation go?" the subcommander asked in Intergaltic.

"Good," Jack replied in Intergaltic. "I think the general is almost ready to talk. The other two men aren't quite there yet."

"I see," Yononnon replied.

"You seem troubled," Jack observed.

"I just received a message from Commander Thoren," Yononnon replied.

"Any word on Forrorrois and Trager?"

"Yes, Trager is still being held on Elda and Forrorrois has headed for the Environs to raise the joining fee."

"I don't like sound of the Environs," Jack remarked.

"You shouldn't, it's not a good place," Yononnon replied. "Even the Dramudam won't patrol there."

Jack's eyes widened as he shook his head. "It's worse than I thought. Why would she go there?"

"Mercenaries can make large sums on high risk ventures in the Environs," Yononnon answered.

"I hate the thought that she's gone there by herself," Jack said, shaking his head.

Yononnon averted his gaze. "She didn't."

Jack's brief relief shifted to concern as he studied Yononnon's reaction. "Who's with her?"

"She took Collinar with her," Yononnon remarked in disdain.

"What?!" Jack exclaimed. "H—he's her worst enemy!"

"True, but he does know the ways of the Environs."

"But she can't trust him!" Jack insisted.

Yononnon sighed and shook his head. "She's cut a deal with him. He'll have the remaining portion of his sentence commuted to time served."

"What's that going to matter once they've left Dramudam space? He'll just run, or worse, try to kill her."

"No," Yononnon said. "If I've learned anything about Collinar, above all else, he wants power. The level of power that he held in the Utahar as a commander was quite impressive—and now he wants to regain it once more, but he can't if he's on the run from the Dramudam. The Utahar can't afford to have a high profile being with an outstanding warrant assuming the position of commander. That would mean that they would have to permit the Dramudam to board their ships and allow us to arrest him at any time or face a confrontation. The Utahar may engage in many illicit activities but they prefer to do so covertly, as do their customers. The deal Forrorrois is offering Collinar is his only chance to get back into the Utahar fold and have a chance to become a commander once more."

Jack snorted a laugh. "You're kidding me. This is almost poetic! I still don't like it, but at least I understand what motivates Collinar." He heaved a sigh. "Yononnon, don't say a word about this to her family, they'll only worry."

"I won't," Yononnon answered.

"Thank you," Jack replied. "Next cycle, we'll be traveling down to Washington. Aster is healthy enough now to speak with his superiors. We'll bring the prisoners as well. It's time to turn them over to the authorities."

Yononnon hesitated. "Did you learn anything from them?"

"Only that the two men preyed on General Caldwell's fear that his base was going to be closed and that he was going to lose his command."

"Ah, I understand," Yononnon replied. "He was faced with a difficult decision."

"Yes—unfortunately his solution has endangered this planet," Jack scoffed. "I wish Forrorrois was here, she could read their emotions and tell me what direction I should be going with my questions."

Yononnon hesitated for a moment before he answered. "What about Celeste? She's an empath like her mother."

Jack heaved a sigh. "Believe me, Yononnon, I've thought about it, but she's too young. Celeste's not ready to be exposed to the emotions she might feel from them—especially from those two with the general. Besides, the less other Humans know about her the better."

Yononnon nodded. "I agree. I'll have my scout ready at first kel."

"Thank you," Jack said with a nod. The next forty-eight hours were going to be interesting.

****

Forrorrois waited at the top of the ramp of her long-distance sc while Collinar negotiated a second job with Motan. Her empath senses told her that Motan was pleased with the success of their first mission and was eager to give them a more profitable assignment. From the satisfied look on Collinar's face she could tell that he was elated with their next mission.

Collinar strode up the ramp towards her as soon as Motan turned and walked away. When he reached the top, he tossed her the data crystal. Forrorrois caught the cube, curious at his excitement. She walked over to the data port and inserted the crystal. The information filtered into her mind. Stunned, she looked over at Collinar.

"Medical supplies?"

"Yes, I explained to Motan that I had turned over a new leaf and wouldn't engage in any slave traffic or weapon sales. Transporting medical supplies was the best he could offer."

"What was the rate?" she asked, suspiciously.

"About double what we made on the last job," he replied.

"For medical supplies?"

Collinar chuckled. "Did I forget to mention that the supplies were needed in a minor war zone in the Mur'troff system?"

Forrorrois quickly accessed the Mur'troff system from the data tanks and her jaw dropped. "Minor? They've been lobbing nukes at each other for the past two hundred revolution!"

Collinar shrugged. "The pay is good. There's just a tiny issue of getting the medical supplies to a small group that has been cut off from their main supply route. Better yet—if we could extract them from behind enemy lines you could save their lives."

Forrorrois stared at him then pulled the data crystal from the port and stormed into the cockpit.

"Think of it as a humanitarian act," Collinar continued. "Did I mention that there were children trapped with them?"

The word *children* froze Forrorrois to the very heart. She turned slowly and studied Collinar.

"What do you mean 'there are children trapped with them?'"

Collinar paused. "The troops that need the supplies just happen to have invaded a small independent agricultural community and are holding the families hostage. We could help both sides by removing the invaders and taking them back to their side. The invaders pay us for rescuing their soldiers and the families are saved from the invaders. Who knows, maybe the villagers will pay us as well."

Appalled, Forrorrois sensed, in his perverse little world, that Collinar believed what he was telling her. She turned back to the cockpit and threw herself into her command chair in frustration. "All right, we'll go in and extract them, but if they try anything on my ship, I'll space them," she swore.

Collinar chuckled. "Believe me—I would help you if they did."

She shook her head. "Prepare for lift-off."

Inside, Forrorrois felt sick as she laid in the course. Collinar had read her too well and had known exactly what to say to make her take the job. She hated him for his receptiveness and prayed that she really could make a difference to the families the invaders had descended on.

****

Jack stood behind the command chair of Yononnon's one-seat scout and watched as they approached Washington, D.C.. Behind him, Aster was sitting on the bunk in the rear cabin of the craft next to the towel covered fauna containment unit in which Jack had placed the miniaturized General Caldwell and the two men in black suits. Butterflies danced in Jack's stomach when Yononnon began to descend to the coordinates Aster had negotiated with Director Hayman—a park that wouldn't be open to the public for another hour. Aster had assured him that this time Hayman would not go back on his word. Still, Jack could only hope that this meeting wouldn't be a repeat of his last visit with the Bureau director.

Jack studied the lay of the land. There was a large pavilion that covered several rows of picnic tables on a cement slab. He spied a large

black SUV with darkened windows parked on one side of the pavilion on a patch of asphalt. The SUV could easily hold seven people, he suspected.

"Scans show only the black vehicle within the meeting site," Yononnon reported, in English. "Three Humans are inside. One I've identified as Director Hayman, the other two are males with small hand weapons."

"Good," Jack replied. "I want you to stun the occupants of the vehicle then land the scout on the other side of the pavilion. Make it real close, but keep the EM warping field in place. I don't want to give our position up—just yet."

"Understood," Yononnon replied.

"Aster, are you ready?" Jack called into the rear cabin.

"Yes," Aster answered, appearing behind him on the three small steps that led up from the cabin below holding the towel covered fauna containment unit. He handed Jack the box as he came up the steps. "Was it really necessary to stun my director?"

Jack nodded. "Yes, I want to re-enlarge the three prisoners before we turn them over to the Bureau. The less they see the better. And that includes anything they can see by satellite."

Aster started as the canopy rose above their heads. "OK, I see your point. They probably do have at least one satellite trained on these coordinates."

Yononnon rose to his feet and towered over Jack and Aster. "Let me go ahead and help you with the prisoners," the large Eldatek male said as he turned and climbed out of the cockpit, down the extended ladder on the side of the sleek bluish-black craft.

Jack followed after the Dramudam subcommander then leaned over the side of the cockpit and handed him the towel covered box. Yononnon took the box and headed into the shelter. Jack motioned for Aster to climb down the ladder. Aster did as he was told, favoring his left arm and shoulder. Jack followed after the two and joined them in the pavilion.

Yononnon pulled his stun weapon from his waist and fired at the towel covered box, before Aster could object. Then the

Eldatek commander pulled the towel off the box. Inside, the three miniaturized men were unconscious in their segregated portions of the fauna containment unit.

"You're a bit free with that stun weapon, Yononnon," Aster quipped, staring down at the unconscious men.

Yononnon glanced over at Jack, confused.

Jack shook his head for Yononnon to ignore the comment and hinged open the clear plastic lid of the containment unit. "Aster, Yononnon's just doing what I asked him to do. We have to minimize exposure. Now, help me place one man per table so we can enlarge them. Hayman and his men will be waking up soon. Here, take one, Aster," Jack said as he lifted out a man in a now rumpled black suit and handed him to Aster. "Careful, don't drop him."

Aster nervously held out his hands and let Jack place one of the men in his shaking palm. Then Jack watched him while he stepped over to one of the wooden picnic tables and placed his precious consignment in the center of the middle plank.

"Yononnon, here you go," Jack continued as he placed the other man in Yononnon's chestnut-brown cupped hands.

Jack reached into the containment unit one more time and pulled out the general. He gently curled his fingers around his former commanding officer's unconscious form and lifted him out. Jack placed the general at the center of the picnic table and studied him for a moment before he placed the towel inside the now empty fauna containment unit and closed the lid.

There was a flash of bluish-green light to his right that made him turn. He smiled when he realized that Yononnon had fired on the first man—returning him to full size. A second flash enveloped the second man. Jack picked up the box and stepped back from the general. Yononnon fired a third time, enlarging the general.

Yononnon slipped the weapon back on his waist and took the clear plastic box from Jack. "I'll be waiting for you on the scout."

"Thank you," Jack replied. He crossed back to his former commanding officer's side and placed his fingers against the general's throat to check his pulse. After a moment, he was satisfied that the general was fine. The sound of a car door opening made him look up over at the black SUV—Hayman and his men were awake. "Aster, are you ready?" he said in a low voice.

Aster nodded.

Together, Jack and Aster stood their ground as the three men approached—two with drawn handguns.

"Director Hayman, weapons won't be necessary," Aster said when the three entered the pavilion.

Hayman eyed the three unconscious men laying on the picnic tables. "Are they alive?"

"Yes, Director Hayman," Jack replied. "I apologize for stunning you and your men, but after our last encounter..." Jack paused then shrugged. "The headache will go away after an hour or so."

Hayman winced. "How long will they be out?"

"About five more minutes," Jack replied. "Do we still have a deal?"

Hayman paused. "Only if we get information from them," he stated.

Jack sighed and shook his head.

"That was not what we agreed on, Director," Aster stated, stepping in between Jack and Hayman.

"That's all right, Aster, they'll talk," Jack replied. He pulled out a cylinder from his pants pocket and moved to the table with one of the men. With a sigh, he placed a cylinder against the unconscious man's neck. The hiss of the hypo cut through the early morning air.

Hayman stepped forward, alarmed. "What did you just do?!" he cried out.

Jack ignored him and the agents with guns and walked over to the other unconscious man. Without a word, he placed the cylinder against his throat. Again the low hiss made everyone in the pavilion tense.

"Are you insane? What are you doing?" Hayman demanded. "Step away from them!"

The two men with pistols stepped forward to enforce the director's order. Jack slipped the hypo back into his pocket and backed away from the tables toward the shrouded scout ship with his hands raised.

"You'll find that the two men will be more cooperative, but I would begin questioning them the moment they wake up, which is in about two more minutes. The effects will only last about an hour, maybe two at best," Jack stated. "As for General Caldwell, I believe that he was being coerced by the two men. I wouldn't treat him too harshly."

Hayman stared over at the two men and then the general. Suddenly, one of the men in the black suits began to stir.

"Looks like they're waking up faster than I thought they would. Contact me when you have your answers," Jack stated when their attention was drawn toward the men on the tables. "And, Director Hayman, you're welcome for the safe return of Agent Aster," he added as he turned and walked toward the shrouded scout.

"What if I have more questions?" Hayman called out after him.

"You'll get them from the two men," Jack stated, without looking back. "Just remember that I gave you your answers. Now you owe me, Captain Perkins, and the Jolan family." Jack paused when he felt the tingle of the EM warping field that shrouded the ship just a hairsbreadth away from him. He turned to face Hayman once more. "Remember the promise that the President and you made to remove our names from the enemy combatant list. We're not the enemy, the people supporting those two men are."

Before Director Hayman could say another word, Jack reached through the EM warping field that shrouded the scout and caught the rung of the ladder. Hayman and his men gasped audibly as he vanished from their view.

Jack hurried up the ladder and climbed into the cockpit with Yononnon's assistance when he reached the top. He moved behind Yononnon's command chair and breathed.

"Subcommander, take us back to the base," Jack said in Intergaltic, placing his hand on the command chair to steady himself.

"Certainly, Jack," Yononnon replied in Intergaltic.

Jack fell silent as he watched the park below them grow smaller while the ship ascended under Yononnon's skilled guidance.

After a few minutes, Yononnon glanced back at him.

"Why did you protect the general?" Yononnon asked.

Jack looked at the Dramudam subcommander, uncertain how to answer. His last minute choice hadn't been rational. He glanced away and heaved a sigh. Then he looked back at Yononnon. "I protected him because he once was my commanding officer," Jack confessed.

He was surprised when Yononnon gave him an approving nod. "I would have done the same," the subcommander replied.

Jack was oddly relieved by Yononnon's confession. A comfortable silence blanketed them both while Yononnon piloted the scout back to Forrorrois' base. All that was left to do was to wait for Hayman's response.

****

Perkins was surprised when he walked into Goren's office in the hangar bay and found both Commander Thoren and Goren waiting for him inside. The door panel slid shut, allowing the three some privacy.

"Commander Thoren, sir," Perkins said, straightening to attention with a fluid salute—his right hand at a slight angle to his temple.

Commander Thoren smiled and returned his salute with the Dramudam variation then motioned Perkins to a chair. "Please, be at ease and sit, Captain Perkins."

Nervously, Perkins accepted the chair beside the Dramudam commander, then he glanced over at Goren in his chair behind his desk, but the Silmanon's impassive velvety black furred face gave him nothing.

"Captain Perkins, I have a few matters I need to discuss with you," Thoren continued.

Perkins tensed. "Certainly, sir," he replied.

"I was pleased to hear that you have successfully completed the training that Forrorrois and Colonel Jack Stern sent you here to obtain from Master Pilot Instructor Goren. In fact, a long-distance scout and a pursuit ship have been equipped for your use in supporting

Forrorrois' effort to protect the Earth. You are scheduled to leave next cycle after first kel."

Perkins looked into the Dramudam commander's almond-shaped black eyes and studied the slight wrinkles that marked his chestnut-brown face. "It will be good to return home," Perkins confessed.

Thoren smiled then unexpectedly reached out and patted Perkins on the shoulder.

"Forrorrois trained you well. I would have been proud to have you as a member of my crew, but like Forrorrois, your destiny lies with Earth," Thoren remarked before he lowered his hand. "In time, if you decide to join the Dramudam and become marked, you will be welcomed aboard the Tollon."

Perkins was surprised when he felt a lump form in his throat. In the short time he had been on board the Tollon, he never thought it would be possible that a part of him would want to stay.

"Commander Thoren, if ever I decide to join the Dramudam, I would be honored to serve under you," Perkins replied.

Thoren rose from his chair and saluted him. "May Guruma be with you, Captain Perkins."

Perkins and Goren promptly rose from their chairs.

"And also with you," Perkins replied, with his right hand at a slight angle to his temple. He waited until Thoren lowered his hand before he finished his salute, but remained at attention.

"Now, you must excuse me, Captain Perkins. Goren will provide you with the details of your departure."

"Yes, sir," Perkins replied. He watched the Dramudam commander turn and head back out from Goren's office into the hangar bay. As the door panel slid shut, Perkins heaved a sigh of relief and looked towards Goren.

Goren's black eyes sparkled. "The commander can be quite an imposing presence. His offer for you to join the Dramudam was a genuine one. I agree with his assessment. You're skilled as a pilot and hold the qualities of honor and duty that are necessary in the Dramudam. When Colonel Jack Stern requested that you stay on the Tollon, you didn't disobey him even though it was sudden decision.

Goren just rasped a gruff chuckle. "Get out of here," he scoffed and headed back to his office.

Perkins watched him go then patted the nose of his scout.

"Goren doesn't care for beings saluting him," a female voice stated behind him.

Perkins turned, surprised to see an Eldatek female standing behind him. She was wearing a green and black pilot's uniform just like he was wearing, except her black pant's had the black strip instead of the grey strip he had on his.

"You're right, he doesn't," Perkins replied, studying her red clay-brown face and almond-shaped eyes. "Do I know you?"

The Eldatek female pilot shook her head. "Probably not, I'm usually not in the hangar at this time. I was performing some maintenance on my pursuit in the hangar wing, just down there," she said, pointing down the long archway filled with pursuit ships.

"I see," Perkins replied. "It was nice to meet you," he added, suddenly uncomfortable when he didn't see anyone else close by.

The female smiled and stepped closer. "I was wondering. I could use a hand with a stubborn access panel. Do you have a moment?"

Perkins glanced around, nervously. "I really must be going, I have to meet Alham and some of the other pilots in the Recreational center and I'm running a bit late."

"I'm certain she would understand if you took a moment to help another pilot," she purred.

Perkins shook his head. "I'm really sorry, but I must go," he stated as he stepped backwards towards the main hangar bay. He drew a sharp breath when she slipped her hand under her tunic at her waist. Concentrating, Perkins reached out to the Tollon's computer. 'Computer, urgent message for Goren. I've found the spy!' he subvocalized.

"Oh no, you don't," she hissed, pulling out her weapon.

"Ah crap!" Perkins cursed in English. He dove for the skids of his one-seat scout, reducing his size as he rolled. The Eldatek female's shot barely missed him.

"Where are you?!" the female spy hissed in Intergaltic.

In miniature, Perkins ran behind the skid to the rear of the scout. The floor plates shook from several approaching footfalls, but help was still too far away. Perkins started when the female appeared out of nowhere and towered over him.

"I don't know how you did that, but you're dead now!" the spy cried out.

Perkins glanced back at the skid then jumped upward with his enhanced reflexes and strength and caught the top edge. He swung his leg up then rolled over the flat top surface. Misjudging the width of the surface, Perkins swore as he tumbled off the far edge. A flash of red exploded behind him from the full concussive force of the spy's weapon. Perkins hit the metal floor plate hard. There was a sickening sound in his ears as he felt a couple of his ribs crack from the force—knocking the wind out of his lungs. The spy was on him before he could recover.

"Forget the weapon," she hissed, slipping the oval back onto her waist, "I'm going to squash you like an insect!"

Perkins eyes widened as the Eldatek female raised her boot over him with a sadistic grin. He moved to roll, but a blur of green and black tackled the spy. The weapon flew from the female's waist and nearly hit Perkins as the two bodies careened under the belly of his scout. Holding his side, Perkins caught his breath and sat up. He concentrated and resumed his full size. When his head cleared, he spotted the spy still under his scout—she was struggling under the fury of Alham's pounding fists.

"Are you all right?" Goren rasped, helping Perkins to his feet.

"Yes...kind of," Perkins replied, still holding his ribs. "But Alham—ah, don't you think you should stop them?" he asked, noticing the crowd of pilots and hangar crew that had encircled his ship.

Goren looked over at the two female Eldatek fighting below the scout and sighed. "I suppose so. Break them up," he finally ordered to the on looking pilots.

Alham's long black hair was free of the traditional Dramudam braid and her eyes were wild with anger when a couple of fellow pilots finally pulled her off the spy. She kicked the offending Eldatek female one last time while they dragged her backwards.

"Compose yourself, Master Pilot!" Goren ordered.

Perkins watched Alham glare at the moaning semiconscious assailant that still lay between the skids under his scout and made a mental note never to tick off Alham. He started when the large boar-like Gintzer, Peldor, moved in with his security contingency.

The burly subcommander paused for a moment as he glanced between Alham and the spy, then he began to chuckle. "I'll take over from here," he replied gruffly to Goren. "I'll have a med tech meet us in the security wing."

"She's High Guard," Alham hissed.

Peldor hesitated for a moment. "How do you know?"

"She has the mark on the back of her neck," Alham replied. Before anyone could stop her, Alham shook off her two fellow pilots that were holding her arms and vaulted back under Perkins' scout ship. She grabbed the semi-conscious Eldatek female by the hair and rolled her onto her stomach.

Peldor crouched down and stepped under the belly of the craft. "Show me!"

"There!" Alham spat, lifting the wad of black hair. A bright red inverted triangle, traced in black, marked the base of the female's skull—just below her hairline. "There's no doubt in my mind that she was sent by the council."

Perkins was surprised when a gasp arose from the Eldatek crew members as they reflexively took three steps backwards.

Peldor growled. "Take her to security."

A lemur-like Bevitch male stepped forward. "But, sir, if she's High Guard, she has immunity!"

The Gintzer stared the Bevitch security guard down. "This female just assaulted a guest on this ship and may have been responsible for planting explosives in the storage wing that nearly caused casualties—not to mention several acts of espionage and possibly kidnapping and the violation of the Isolation Treaty. Until I have definitive proof that she's High Guard, then she will be treated as a spy. Now, take her to security and put her in a holding cell with restraints. Have Kela meet us there, I want a med tech I can trust."

The Bevitch's pale blue eyes widened against his gray fur covered face. "Yes, sir!"

Perkins' straightened the best he could when the Gintzer turned his attention towards him.

"Are you injured, Captain Perkins?" Peldor asked.

"I think I cracked some ribs," Perkins replied. "It would have been worse if Alham hadn't showed up when she did."

Peldor showed his lower teeth between his tusks in an odd grin as he glanced over at Alham. "She did well," he snorted. "Alham, escort Captain Perkins to Bio Med," he ordered.

Alham brushed back the hair from her face and straightened. "Yes, Subcommander," she replied.

Goren nodded to Peldor and stepped back as Alham took Perkins by the arm.

Perkins smiled at her while she escorted him through the hangar bay into the corridor of the Tollon. When the double doors closed behind them, Alham looked at him with concern.

"Are you all right? When I saw her ready to step on you, all I saw was red," she gasped.

"I'm glad you did, my life flashed before my eyes as I was staring up at the bottom of her boot," Perkins confessed, stopping in front of the lift door. "You saved my life."

"I guess we're even now," Alham replied as she glanced at the floor while the lift door slid open and stepped inside. Perkins followed her in and waited as the doors closed. Before he could say another word, Alham pinned him against the wall and kissed him hard on the mouth. He winced when her hand pressed against his side.

Alham pulled back—distress darkened her face. "I'm sorry, I thought…" she stammered.

Perkins shook his head. "It's just my ribs," he whispered then he looked at her and tasted her on his lips. "Forget the ribs," he gasped, grabbing her forcefully and kissing her back. He wanted her. Alham didn't need any coaxing as she pressed her body against his. He breathed in her spicy scent and wished the lift would jam between the decks so they could stay intertwined, but the lift didn't cooperate as it slowed to a stop. Alham released him and stepped away, tasting her lips.

Perkins held his side while he exhaled. He needed to return to Earth, but he wanted Alham.

He glanced down as she took him by the arm and guided him down the corridor into Bio Med. Perkins moved to speak, but the moment was broken when Leenon intercepted them as they came through the door.

"Goren told me you were coming. Alham, tell me what happened!" Leenon ordered pulling out a bioscanner and passing it over Perkins.

"The spy attacked Captain Perkins while he was in the hangar bay," Alham spat.

"A few cuts and bruises…what's this…three broken ribs!?" Leenon said to herself as she finished scanning him. "Captain Perkins, please come into this examination room and remove your tunic."

Perkins followed the head med tech with Alham right behind him. He did as he was told and unfastened the diagonal flap of his green tunic. When he moved to slip it off, his broken ribs objected.

"Alham, assist him," Leenon ordered while she busied herself with the tray of instruments beside the examination table. "Captain Perkins, I'll need you on the examination table."

Perkins let Alham pull the tunic off his shoulders exposing his well toned lightly tanned upper torso and arms marred only by the darkening bruise across his ribs. He suddenly felt self-conscious when he realized that both Alham and Leenon were studying him—each for different reasons. Sitting on the edge of the table, he shifted onto the padded surface.

"Lie back, I want to make certain that those ribs are aligned before I set them," Leenon ordered.

Perkins gasped and supported his ribs with his hand while he laid back. He started when Leenon pressed a cylinder against his arm. His body relaxed as the pain killer hissed against his skin.

"That's better," Leenon said, circling his ribs with a bioknitter. "So did the spy hit you with something?"

Perkins glanced away for a moment, uncertain what to say. "No."

Leenon paused for a moment. "Then how did you break your ribs?"

"Well, I kind of fell off the skid of my scout," he confessed.

Leenon set down the bioknitter and gave him a hard stare. "Excuse me, I know I'm not a pilot, but a skid isn't that high. Do you mean you fell against the skid?"

Alham began to giggle as Perkins shook his head a bit embarrassed. "No, I fell off the skid," he admitted.

Leenon looked over at Alham, annoyed. "What's so funny?"

"Captain Perkins wasn't full-sized when he fell off the skid," Alham replied, still giggling. "He's like Forrorrois—he can contract his mass at will."

Leenon looked at the ceiling and heaved a sigh. "I'd forgotten that little piece of information. You're lucky you didn't break your neck, Captain Perkins," she replied, retrieving the bioknitter and passing the cylinder over his ribs once more.

Perkins watched in amazement while the fresh black-and-blue bruise began to ease into a light shade of yellow then back to his normal slightly tanned skin.

"Well, it might have been worse than that if the spy had stomped on me. Luckily, Alham tackled her before she could squash me," Perkins said.

Leenon set the bioknitter down once more with a look of horror and stared at Alham. "Yes, you were lucky," Leenon whispered. "Captain Perkins, you should be all set, now. You can put your tunic back on."

Perkins took a test breath and was relieved that he could breathe deeply once more. He sensed a tension forming in the room as he sat up and pulled on his tunic.

"Captain Perkins, could you step outside please. I'd like to examine Alham, now," Leenon requested.

"Of course," Perkins replied, slipping from the table and refastening the diagonal flap of his forest green tunic as he walked out into the main room of Bio Med. The door barely closed when he heard the raised voices. He glanced around at the two other female Eldatek in beige med tech uniforms and nodded nervously toward them. They nodded curtly back and resumed their duties. Perkins heaved a sigh and waited for nearly ten minutes before the examination room door slid open once more.

"Alham, you don't have a choice!" Leenon called after her as Alham stormed out of the examination room.

"I won't go back there!" Alham replied. "Come on, Perkins, it's time for you to head back to the hangar bay."

Before Perkins could react Alham grabbed his arm and dragged him out of Bio Med. "Ah...All right," he stammered.

He was surprised when they turned in the opposite direction from the lift and headed down the corridor. They stopped in front of a door panel which hissed open at Alham's silent command. Perkins was taken aback when he realized they were in Alham's quarters.

"Have a seat," she said, pointing to a black couch.

"Ahhh...sure," Perkins replied then he crossed the room and sat down. He looked around the Spartan room and noted a small kitchenette near the door to the corridor. Opposite the entrance was a second door that Alham went through. The door panel hadn't closed, allowing him to peer inside. He was surprised to see Alham pulling items out of a dresser and putting them into a medium-sized duffle bag that was set on her bed.

In less than five minutes, Alham closed the bag and slung the duffel over her shoulder.

"I'm ready to go," she stated.

Stunned, Perkins got to his feet and followed her back out into the corridor. She led him to a different lift.

"What are you doing?" Perkins asked when the lift doors closed.

"I've got to leave the Tollon, immediately," Alham stated without looking at him.

"I don't understand?" Perkins replied.

The lift doors open before Alham answered. Instead she grabbed his arm and half dragged him to the hangar bay. "I've got to get a ship before I'm arrested," she stated as they reached the double doors of the hangar bay.

Perkins moved to speak as they stepped through the double doors, but stopped when he spotted Goren coming out of his office. His heart skipped a beat when the Master Pilot instructor motioned Alham to come over. Alham hesitated then obeyed—her shoulders slightly slumped. Uncertain, Perkins moved to follow her inside then stopped dead in his tracks at the doorway. Inside was Commander Thoren.

"I see you're packed," Thoren observed.

"Yes," Alham replied, looking straight ahead.

"You were correct that the spy was High Guard," Thoren continued. "This puts the Tollon in a bad position."

"Yes, sir," Alham answered.

"You can't remain on the ship," Thoren stated.

"I understand, sir," Alham said, glancing toward Thoren. "I only ask for a scout and some supplies."

"I can't do that, Alham. If I do, I will bring the Tollon under the scrutiny of the council," Thoren replied.

"Commander, permission to speak, sir," Perkins uttered as he stepped through the doorway.

Goren inserted himself between Thoren and Perkins. "Captain Perkins, this is an internal matter. Please go to your scout and prepare to leave immediately for Earth."

"But, sir, Alham was only trying to protect me!" Perkins interjected.

Goren shook his head and took him firmly by the arm. "Please go now, Captain Perkins. Subcommander Yononnon will return to the Tollon upon your arrival."

Perkins glanced at Alham and then back at the commander and Goren.

"Go, Perkins," Alham said without looking at him.

With a heavy heart, Perkins turned, feeling Goren's grip lighten as he headed out of the office for his scout. He looked towards the enormous doors of the hangar bay as they began to slide open, beyond was the shimmering atmospheric barrier that separated the hangar bay from the vacuum of space. Perkins ordered the ladder to extend and the canopy to rise above the cockpit of his scout. This wasn't the way he wanted to leave. He pulled himself up the rungs of the ladder and stood for a moment to look one last time out at the hangar bay. With a sigh, he descended the three steps into the ship's rear quarters. Inside, he stopped when he spotted a miniaturized one-seat scout, just like his own, sitting on his bunk. There was also a fresh pilot's uniform. Perkins picked up the black pants and swallowed hard when he saw that the gray stripe of the student pilot had been replaced with the black. He had no doubt that Goren had left him the uniform.

He turned at the sound of someone hurrying up the ladder into the cockpit. Before Perkins could make his way up the three steps, a large cloth item flew down the steps and hit him square in the face—nearly knocking him off his feet. Stunned, he realized that it was a duffle bag. He tossed the bag to the floor and charged up the steps into the cockpit to confront the intruder. To his surprise, he spotted Alham in his command chair beginning an emergency lift-off. The canopy had dropped into place, forcing Perkins to cling to the back of Alham's seat when the scout began to lift upward.

The comm came alive. "The hangar doors are open and ready, Captain Perkins," Goren stated.

Alham put her finger to her lips and motioned for Perkins to reply. Perkins looked at her, confused, but she motioned to him once more. "Ah, I appreciate that, sir," he stammered.

"Captain Perkins, you are cleared to depart. Safe journey," Goren stated.

"Thank you, Goren," Perkins answered, looking over at Alham. "Thank you for everything."

He was surprised when Alham tinted the canopy so that no one could see in and then she maneuvered the scout from its parking slot. In moments, she had the craft in front of the shimmering atmospheric barrier. When they catapulted out into open space, Perkins tightened his grip on the back of her chair. Perkins regained his footing while Alham set a course. He moved to speak but she rose from the command chair and motioned him to sit. Without a word Perkins took a seat, bewildered.

"What just happened?" he finally asked.

"I assaulted a member of the High Guard," Alham stated. "If I stayed aboard the Tollon, Commander Thoren would be forced to take me back to Elda to face trial."

"But you did that because she was trying to kill me?!" Perkins stammered.

"And I would do it again to protect you," Alham replied, defiantly. Then she softened her voice as she continued. "Unfortunately, that doesn't change Eldatek law. Thank you for not telling Goren that I was on board."

Suddenly, Perkins realized that the miniature scout ship on his bunk wasn't meant for him. "I think he already knew," he replied.

"How would he know? Commander Thoren was ordering Peldor to report to the hangar bay with security to take me into custody. I panicked and ran from Goren's office. When I saw your canopy still open, I took a chance and climbed aboard," Alham confessed. "I don't understand."

"Just look in the rear cabin," Perkins said with the nod toward the opening.

Alham gave him a strange look and climbed down the three steps.

Perkins smiled when she began to scream excitedly in Eldanese. Then she ran back up the steps into the cockpit. He subvocalized to the scout's computer to prepare to engage the hyperfold and looked up at her from his commander chair.

"So, do you have any plans?" he asked.

Alham looked over at him as she stood at the top of the step. Her shoulders drooped. "No…I just knew I had to get off the Tollon. Now that I have a long-distance scout, I could go anywhere."

"Well, if you want, you could come with me to Earth?" Perkins suggested, nervously, glancing up at her.

Alham caught her breath. "Do you mean that?" she whispered.

Perkins stood from his commander chair and nodded.

He staggered backwards as Alham fell into his arms in a fierce hug and began to sob.

Stunned at the sudden flood of tears, Perkins held her tightly and laid her head against his shoulder. Without a second thought, he kissed her forehead and smoothed her hair. "Shh, it's all right," he cooed.

"I just wasn't sure if you wanted me enough to let me come with you to Earth," she sobbed.

"Hush," he chuckled. "Of course I want you to come with me."

"I don't know the first thing about Earth except for what you and Forrorrois have told me—I can't even speak your language," she continued to sob.

"You'll learn. We'll figure this out together," he whispered.

Alham lifted her head and looked him in the eyes, sniffing back her tears. "Together?"

"Yes," Perkins replied, pulling on his best smile. He was surprised when she leaned forward and kissed him. The warmth of her lips invited him. Perkins melted into her arms and pulled her firmly against him, savoring the taste of her mouth as he returned her kiss. His heart raced at her passion. Perkins didn't care what came next—he only cared that he didn't have to be without her. But his rational mind reminded him that they were still too close to the Tollon. "Let's begin the hyperfold before they send pursuits after us," he gasped between kisses.

"Good idea," Alham whispered her lips just a hairsbreadth from his. "We can continue this discussion after we're in hyperfold."

Perkins caught his breath when Alham's eyes flirted with him. "Oh, definitely," Perkins grinned as she slipped from his hold and took a seat on the top step to the rear cabin. "Hold that thought."

He resumed his command chair and made the finally corrections. Perkins never thought this would be the way he would spend his time heading back to Earth. Exhaling, he glanced over at Alham and smiled. "Computer, initiate hyperfold," he said. The ship shuddered then the stars blurred, but all he could focus on was Alham's beautiful black almond-shaped eyes.

CHAPTER 19

Aster stepped into the interrogation room of the F.B.I. offices in DC carrying a manila envelope. He studied General Caldwell cautiously before he took a seat across from him at the metal table. The older man's dark street clothes were now rumpled and his gray eyes were bloodshot from lack of sleep. Barely a week had passed since two men wearing black suits had ambushed Aster in his apartment and shot him—some how Caldwell was involved with them and had used him to try to get to Jack Stern and Forrorrois. Aster didn't feel as forgiving as Jack had been toward the Air Force general. He dropped the manila envelope he was carrying onto the top of the metal table top.

General Caldwell's gray eyes flicked down towards the package, then back at Aster.

"You're free to go," Aster stated. "You'll find your wallet and other personal items inside."

Caldwell reached out and picked up the envelope, then examined the contents. He pulled out his wallet and slipped the black leather billfold into the back pocket of his slacks. Then he drew out a set of keys and some change. "So, Agent Aster, what's the catch?"

Aster crossed his arms and leaned back in his chair. "No catch, we don't have anything to hold you on."

Caldwell shook his head. "No, I walk out of that door and I'll be dead in the hour."

Aster shrugged. "Not my problem. You don't have anything we want. Besides, those two men that jumped me in my apartment and shot me, they've been very cooperative."

"I was with them, you saw me in the alley," Caldwell countered.

"Your word against mine," Aster replied with a bemused grin.

"Surely those two men aren't telling you that I ordered them to shoot you?" the general grappled.

"I'm not at liberty to say," Aster replied. "That's need-to-know, you understand."

The general's jaw dropped open like a large mouth bass. "You can't be serious..."

"Like I said, General, I've got nothing to hold you on, so I have to cut you loose. I wouldn't want to be accused of violating your civil liberties."

"Stern can testify that I was there in the alley," the older man insisted.

"Oh, I don't know," Aster replied. "At the moment he wouldn't be considered a credible witness...being on the Enemy Combatant's list and all. But, from what Jack Stern told me, it did sound like you were coerced."

The general's gray eyes widened. "Jack was right, I was coerced. I need protection. The people who sent those two men after you will send more after me."

"Like I said, at the moment being on the Enemy Combatant list doesn't bolster Jack's credibility," Aster sighed. "Now, of course, if he wasn't on the list any longer that might change things, but... nawww."

"We could talk about this," the general pressed.

"General, personally, I don't like you," Aster replied with a shrug. "And as long as Jack Stern, Captain Perkins, Forrorrois and her family are listed as enemy combatants, I'm not going to change my mind on how I feel."

"But I signed the original orders, Agent Aster," the general blurted out. "I could rescind them. But I expect protection in return."

Aster smiled. He reached inside his dark gray suit jacket and pulled out a thick envelope, then dropped it on the table.

General Caldwell eyes widened as he stared at the envelope then back at Aster.

Aster slowly nudged the envelope with his fingers toward Caldwell then sat back in his chair.

General Caldwell glared at him.

Aster just tilted his head and smiled as he waited.

The older man finally harrumphed in disgust then reached out and took the envelope. He opened the flap and pulled out a legal document with several pages. Caldwell fingered the pages as he scanned through them. On the edges of several pages were colored tabs which caused him to pause.

"I just need your signatures where I've flagged the pages," Aster stated as he slid a pen towards the general.

Caldwell drummed the table with his fingers. "I'll want my lawyer to review these before I sign them."

Aster shrugged his shoulders and slid the document back to his side of the table. "I understand, but I'll have to release you in the meantime, since legally I can't hold you any longer..."

Caldwell narrowed his steel-gray eyes at him. "Bastard," he growled under his breath. "You leave me no choice then," he snarled as he reached across the table and dragged the document back towards him.

"Very good," Aster replied, his face deadpan. "As soon as you're done, I'll make the arrangements for your protection and a lawyer if you'd like—unless you have one in mind."

Caldwell tapped the table with his fingers once more then he took the pen and began to sign the flagged pages. With a snort, he set the pen on the papers and shoved them back toward Aster.

"Thank you, General," Aster said as he gathered the papers and neatly placed them back into the envelope. Then he slipped the packet back into the interior breast pocket of his dark gray suit jacket. "I'll make arrangements for you to have your phone call. As far as I am concerned, General, you are here as our guest."

General Caldwell sat back in his chair with his arms folded across his chest. "Of course," he replied, nodding his head. "Agent Aster, you've always impressed me with your ability to step in at just the right moment. Let's just hope that you are a man of your word."

"And I hope you are as well," Aster replied. "I'll send someone in with some coffee."

"Thank you, I'd appreciate that," the general snapped back.

Aster stood from his chair and nodded as he left the room. When the door closed behind him, Aster breathed. His director was waiting for him in the hallway.

"Good work, Agent Aster," Hayman said. "Get that paperwork

processed and alert Forrorrois that she, her family and friends are no longer on the enemy combatant list."

"Right away, sir," Aster replied. "Thank you, sir."

"After that, I'm certain that the President may want a word with Forrorrois," Hayman continued.

Aster hesitated. "Of course, sir, I'll see if she or Jack is available." He turned quickly and headed down the hallway before his director could question him. His head was tumbling with thoughts of how he was going to continue to hide the fact that Forrorrois wasn't on Earth.

⁎⁎⁎⁎⁎⁎⁎⁎⁎⁎⁎

Forrorrois felt the tension in her shoulders from the long tedious flight to the outpost where the invading soldiers had been cut-off from their support troops. Two hundred revolution of bad blood had rendered the Mur'troff system nearly impossible to navigate without great risk to any ships friendly—or otherwise. The quadrant had been littered with space mines which forced her to run with her shields at full strength—in addition to using her EM warping field to prevent detection from the hostile forces from either side. She didn't doubt one moment that if either side found out that she was a Dramudam, being a mother wouldn't save her life this time.

Collinar sat quietly next to her, studying the holographic display that floated between her command chair and the control panel. He sighed and pointed towards a small planetoid with an artificial atmosphere held in place by several generators strategically placed around the surface.

Forrorrois studied the planetoid's surface. There were a few places where the generators had failed—marked by patches of brown against the verdant areas still under a hazy shimmer—a paradise being eaten away by the endless war.

"Since you never told me where to pickup the medical supplies, I can only assume you think this extraction would be more profitable," she said, dryly.

"You wound me," Collinar replied. "Actually, the medical supplies are on here. The soldiers were coming here to take them when they experienced trouble with their engines and ended up stranded on the surface."

"An interesting fact, conveniently omitted from the info cube," Forrorrois scoffed.

"The most interesting fact that was omitted is that the family that the soldiers are stranded with happens to be sympathizers who provide medical supplies to the soldiers in exchange for food," Collinar remarked.

Forrorrois rolled her eyes. "Fine, let's just get these soldiers and their ship out of here before the family secret is revealed."

"Ah, you are learning," Collinar purred. "I recommend landing in an area with no atmosphere nearest to the coordinates we were provided. We'll walk in from there to prevent detection. When we get there, let me do the talking. If you sense anyone is lying, let me know immediately by tapping your leg lightly three times with your non-weapon hand. Any movement from you weapon hand will be considered an act of aggression."

"Sounds like you've been here before," she quipped.

"I have, the family here knows me," Collinar replied.

Forrorrois looked over at him in surprise. He wasn't lying. "Who do they know you as?"

"Trell, of course," Collinar said with a shrug.

"Do they like you?"

Collinar snorted a laugh. "I've been known to assist them with moving medical supplies to both sides of the war. Profiteering can be lucrative. When I had a subcommander that I could trust, I frequently made trips into the Environs to raise revenue for my less-than-approved endeavors."

Forrorrois found herself chuckling. "You're telling me that the Utahar have standards?"

Collinar looked over at her slightly annoyed. "We're not as barbaric as you'd like to think," he retorted. "It's just a few Utahar have stretched the envelope."

"Like you?" she snorted.

Collinar looked forward. "I'm a visionary."

"That's choice," she muttered under her breath.

"Oh and the Dramudam are any better?" Collinar exclaimed. "They should be on your side trying to get one of their own back from a hostile force that's taken your joined one—the father of your child. Yet they sit on the sidelines, conveniently calling your situation an 'internal matter,' and hide behind their Isolation Treaty to justify their non-action. All because it's the *Council of Elda*—the pathetic Eldatek males that make up the majority of the Dramudam quake in their boots when the council's name is invoked. Now who's barbaric?"

Forrorrois dropped her gaze as her hands tightened on the arms of her command chair. "It's not like that," she whispered, trying to keep her emotions in check.

"Stop deluding yourself, Forrorrois," Collinar shot back.

Anger rose inside of her. She wanted to reach over and knock the smirk off of Collinar's face, but she couldn't because what he was saying was exactly what she had been thinking. The Dramudam's non-action when she needed them the most, when Trager needed them the most, cut her deep. Even Guruma was nowhere to be seen, just when she desperately needed his guidance. She closed her eyes for a brief moment as she tried to calm herself. When she opened them again she stared forward.

"There are things driving all these events that have not been revealed. When they are, the universe will right itself," she whispered.

She could feel Collinar's golden feline eyes stare at her. "What drivel have they indoctrinated you with? Sounds like something that the great Guruma would say," he answered, sarcastically.

Forrorrois refused to react. "Make sure you secure your seat harness, I'm preparing to land."

Collinar snorted at her then fastened his harness. "The only Eldatek male that I felt had any promise was Trager and that was only after he joined with you," he muttered, sitting back in his seat.

Stunned at Collinar's unsolicited remark, Forrorrois glanced at him.

Collinar shifted uncomfortably in his seat from her stare and looked straight ahead.

Forrorrois reached out empathically and sensed embarrassment. As much as she wanted him to explain his last comment, she let his off-handed approval of Trager drop. She re-focused on bringing her long-distance scout a short distance from the atmospheric shield where Collinar had suggested.

"There are environmental suits in the cargo hold," she stated, bringing the ship down to the surface. "I've opened the locker for you."

"Good," Collinar replied, unfastening his harness. "Leave your helmet, the design might be recognized as Dramudam."

Forrorrois glanced down at her helmet in the holder on the right side of her command chair and nodded. Collinar wasn't stupid. She finished powering down the engines and paused for a moment before she followed him into the cargo hold. Collinar was already suited up when she arrived.

"The moment we pass through the atmospheric boundary, we'll be detected," Collinar stated, while Forrorrois pulled on her silvery environmental suit. She pulled the hood up from the collar of the suit. The clear curved plastic face plate slipped into place when she finished.

From the corner of her eyes she noticed that Collinar already had secured his weapon to the waist of his silvery suit. His face plate was already in place when he spoke.

"How much air do we have without external tanks?"

"The carbon dioxide filters will keep the air breathable for about one kel," she replied.

"How about communications?" he asked.

"The audible comm link will keep us in contact through the ship's computer well into the meeting location inside the atmospheric enclosure. They would need very sophisticated technology to block our signal," Forrorrois replied, turning toward the cargo hatch.

"I guess we're lucky they are too busy trying to kill each other that they have let their technology slip," Collinar quipped. "Still, we should be prepared for any surprises."

"Understood," Forrorrois agreed fastening her stun weapon to her waist and slipping her reduction weapon into the pocket at her knee. She ordered the atmospheric barrier to engage across the mouth of the cargo hatch as she opened it. Once the ramp extended she waved for Collinar to take lead. He nodded and strode down the incline.

****

Trager stared at the four gray walls of his cell annoyed at the shackles that still bound his wrists and ankles. They were unnecessary, while he was in the cell, but he knew the Council of Elda guards had left them on him to underscore the fact that he was no longer free. The council wanted to ensure his spirit was broken to rehabilitate him back to the ways of a subservient Eldatek male. He glanced at the doorway when the lock clicked and the door swung open. To his surprise, Bohata stepped into the cell. Trager dropped his gaze to the floor out of deference to her having been his deceased brother's joined one. Inside, he was in turmoil, uncertain whether or not she was capable of having had murdered his brother. Or if Talman's death really was just an untimely illness and Bohata was an unfortunate female left without her joined one before a child was produced.

He glanced up when the door closed, leaving the two alone. Bohata watched him for a few moments before she spoke.

"You still have defiance in your eyes," she scoffed. "Some of it is from your time in the Plane of Deception, but the rest is from your clinging hope that Forrorrois will manage to raise the joining fee and rescue you from your duty to me."

Trager looked to the floor once more and calmed himself. *Giving her something to gloat about wouldn't help,* he conceded.

"I've heard that Forrorrois has chosen a very dangerous path to raise the funds. You should have told her that you have your duty to perform and that she aught to be satisfied that she still has Celeste. What a horrible tragedy if she were to be harmed while taking such risks. Poor little Celeste could be left without her mother or her father."

Trager stiffened at her words, uncertain if Bohata meant them as a veiled threat.

"Think long and hard on what I'm saying, Trager," Bohata continued. "One word from you and we could send a message to Forrorrois to tell her to end her reckless pursuit. You could save her and allow her to move on with her life. She could join with one of her own kind and find a happiness that would elude her with you."

Trager took a measured breath and exhaled slowly in an attempt to cleanse the seed of doubt from his mind that Bohata was trying to plant. Her clever words twisted inside him to take root, but he ripped them out. Boldly, he raised his gaze to meet hers.

"Forrorrois is my heart and Celeste is my soul. I will wait for them even if it means waiting for the rest of my life, Bohata. Even if Forrorrois is unable to raise the prohibitive fee that the council has set for her, I will never be yours. If we are forced to join, it will never bear fruit," he warned in a low growl.

Bohata paled at his words then recovered her composure. "There are ways to ensure that even the most unwilling male performs his duties," she scoffed. "You will return to the ways of Elda as soon as Forrorrois fails."

Trager didn't lower his eyes as she turned and waved the door open. For the first time in his life he allowed himself the satisfaction of publicly defying a female on Elda—and it felt good. Not because of the defiance, but because he knew he was right. The bond between Forrorrois and him was strong and could not be broken by the sheer will of another—several millennium of evolution had intertwined them mind, body, and soul through the joining ceremony. The link had developed over time to ensure a couples union would remain strong throughout their lives. Bohata should know this. *As long as Forrorrois was alive…*Trager froze at the thought. *What if Bohata's earlier comment about Forrorrois taking* *risks really was a threat?* The shackles weighed heavily on his ankles and wrists. He glanced around the cell and wished there was a way he could escape.

He dropped his head in his hands in frustration. The unexpected sound of a throat clearing made him look up. Trager's eyes widened when he saw Guruma standing before him.

"Guruma!" he gasped in a low voice. "How did you get in here?"

The old Dramudam founder smiled and shook his head. "Look closer, Trager."

Trager studied him and realized that there was a shimmer that outlined Guruma's form. "You're in the Plane of Deception," he gasped.

"For now," Guruma replied. "Nur and I have discussed many things recently, and even with the danger, it is safer for me here."

"But there's a war starting there!" Trager gasped.

Guruma shrugged. "The Aethereals are too busy to care that I'm back—besides the Plane of Deception allows me to keep an eye on things. Like your conversation just now with Bohata."

Trager caught his breath. "Then you know that Forrorrois may be in grave danger."

"I suspected something when I was plotting some new foci into the Environs. Nur has been very helpful with this. He can sense places where beings that he's met have been—a very useful talent. It seems your suspicion may reinforce a new piece of information I've gathered. There is a very sizable bounty out for two beings in the Environs. Their descriptions match Forrorrois and Collinar. I was on my way to see you when Bohata arrived in your cell."

"Then it's true, Bohata will stop at nothing to keep Forrorrois from raising the Joining Fee," Trager replied, shaking his head. "But I don't understand why? She could save face if Forrorrois raises the Joining fee."

Guruma shook his head. "No, she needs to reinforce her power base with a second joining. With Neeha's elevated status as a council member, Bohata and her family will increase their status. A child would only enhance it."

"But if she can't carry a child, then my life will be in jeopardy and Neeha will suffer the doubt that she produced two males that were unable to produce an heir, but that doesn't make sense, what about Celeste?" Trager said, dropping his voice to a barely audible whisper.

"I've given that some thought," Guruma replied. "I'm certain that rumors would be circulated that Celeste couldn't be your daughter, casting further doubt on Forrorrois' claim of first joining and masking Bohata as the actual source of the problem. And I'm still trying to figure out what Bohata's plan is for continuing her fight to maintain Penock with you since that would openly reveal her inadequacy. I'm sorry, Trager, but my time here is limited. The energy levels are recovering much slower due to the increased activity by the Aethereals."

"Guruma, I can't stay here any longer and do nothing—Forrorrois' life is in danger! Send for Nur and get me out of here!" Trager insisted, glancing at the door.

Guruma shook his head. "No, you must be patient, Trager."

Trager came to his feet and stepped closer to Guruma's shimmering image. "I can't risk Forrorrois' life! I need to get out of here and warn her about the bounty!"

Guruma's eyes softened. "And once you warned her, what would you do next? The council would only send more High Guard to track you down. And Celeste will become Bohata's target once more."

Trager caught his breath. "I'll be there to protect her this time," he persisted.

"And where would you go?" Guruma questioned. "The council has the coordinates of your base on Earth now. The Dramudam won't be able to protect you without the repercussions of interfering with the internal affairs of Elda even if the Elda Council sends more High Guard to Earth violating the Isolation Treaty. You'll be on the run for the rest of your lives. No, the risk is too high, Trager. You'll not only be endangering your daughter, Trager, but you'll be endangering Forrorrois' family as well," he cautioned.

Trager clenched and unclenched his fists, frustrated by Guruma's logic. "I can't stand it any longer staying here doing nothing, Guruma," he bemoaned. "Every cycle Forrorrois spends in the Environs with Collinar…" Trager looked away, sickened by the thought. "The risk is too great even without Bohata's bounty."

"Up to now it's been a calculated risk," Guruma observed, "but you must let this play out so that you can remain free with Celeste and Forrorrois without having to look over your shoulder for the rest of your lives. I must go now, my focus is fading…"

"Please Guruma! If you won't free me, then you must find Forrorrois for me and warn her about the bounty!" Trager pressed.

"I will, I promise," Guruma replied. Then he faded to nothing.

Alone once more, Trager lay back on his bunk and brooded. His worse fears were beginning to unfold. *Please find her in time, Guruma,* Trager prayed.

****

Forrorrois felt restricted in her silver environmental suit as Collinar and she walked across the desolate plain. She glanced at Collinar when they reached the atmospheric barrier that surrounded the small compound that the Mur'troff family was living in—the same family that was profiteering from the war. If she believed Collinar, they were the same family that was harboring the enemy soldiers who needed to be extracted. A bad taste formed in her mouth as she thought of the convoluted lie that Collinar had told her to get her to take the job. The family didn't need to be rescued—they were profiteers, who provided the medical supplies to both sides without either side knowing. And now the other side had regained the territory the family's compound was in and unknowingly trapped the enemy as they came for their supplies. The whole situation was incredibly delicate. All she wanted was for the extraction to go swiftly and the pay to be good.

"Forrorrois, I need you to follow my lead very carefully. They shoot strangers before they ask questions," Collinar cautioned as they stood before the atmospheric barrier. "So make no sudden moves. And for your own safety play a simpleton or they'll make advances. They don't get many females out here that they're not related to."

"What?" she exclaimed. "You're kidding me, right?"

Collinar shook his head. "You're not going to pull this off acting like that. And I can't have you disabling the customer because some being touched you. We need this job," he scoffed. "Play it my way and we'll get out of here in one piece."

Forrorrois took a deep breath then let it out slowly. "All right, I'll follow your lead, but at the first sign of trouble I'm back to the ship."

"Fair enough," Collinar replied. He stepped forward through the atmospheric barrier and she followed after him.

Her empathic senses bristled the moment they emerged on the other side. An audible alarm sounded and several humanoid beings ran out of the buildings armed with laser rifles. She tensed for her weapon, but was surprised when Collinar stopped in his tracks and pushed the hood of his silver environmental suit from his face. He motioned her to do the same.

"Smile like a child," Collinar whispered to her through clenched teeth.

Forrorrois glanced around at the growing circle of beings and slowly retracted the visor of her suit then pushed back her hood as well. Uncertain, she pulled on an innocent childlike smile as six beings approached them with their weapons ready.

The emotions around her shifted from anger and distrust to recognition and excitement. The circle of four males and two females lowered their weapons.

"Trell!" a comely female exclaimed. She rushed toward Collinar and literally flung her body into his frame with such force that Collinar had to take a step backwards.

Forrorrois sensed he didn't mind the female's forwardness, returning her lingering kiss as he squeezed her tight to his body. The lewdness that flowed from his mind made her stomach turn. Forrorrois struggled to keep the nausea down when the female turned a jealous eye towards her.

"Who's she?"

Forrorrois glanced at Collinar to determine what he wanted her to do.

Collinar chuckled as he squeezed the female's waist. "Breen, this is my pilot, Danica. She means nothing to me."

The female sneered at her then returned her gaze to Collinar and pouted. Forrorrois continued to smile.

"Trell, I've missed you. Look at your hair—it's all shaggy and unkempt. It's been too many revolution since you've visited us," Breen replied.

"I came as soon as I heard that you had a problem," Collinar purred while Breen ruffled his medium length blond-hair.

A large male stepped forward and nodded to Collinar. "We're glad you've arrived, Trell. The cargo is inside. We need it removed—before it's detected," he stated with a glance towards Forrorrois. His hesitance tempered his interest.

"You can speak in front of Danica. She's a bit slowwitted but she can fly a ship and handle a weapon," Collinar replied. "Danica, stay here while I make arrangements for the cargo," he continued in a slower meter, emphasizing each word.

Forrorrois restrained herself and drew on a simple smile. "I'll wait here," she replied with a doe-eyed look. Collinar's amusement filtered into her mind.

The large male's lusty interest shifted to pity as he gave Forrorrois a sympathetic look and motioned for Collinar to follow him. Forrorrois stood where Collinar told her to stay while Breen sashayed with Collinar into the large round building at the center of the compound. The others lost interest in her and left her alone as they went into the building after them.

Forrorrois sighed and relaxed slightly while she reached out with her mind. Collinar knew what he was doing. As long as they thought she was mentally lacking, she was safe.

****

Forrorrois shifted on her feet while she stood in her environmental suit watching the door of the round building. She hadn't moved from where Collinar had left her for the past two hours. None of the members of the compound approached her, but occasionally one would pass her, giving her a sympathetic look as they walked by. She hated to admit it, but Collinar's statement to the family that she was simpleton had protected her from a possibly hazardous situation. The Mur'troff, despite all their gruffness, was actually charitable to the mentally challenged, but at the same time they gave them a wide berth, leaving her on her own, undisturbed.

The sun was beginning to set when Collinar finally emerged from the building. Four unfamiliar large males in worn black uniforms followed him out of the building. Forrorrois recognized their uniforms from the data files. They were the enemy soldiers. Each carried a heavy bag slung over their shoulder. Collinar approached her. She could feel his amusement at seeing her still standing where he had told her to wait.

"You listened very well, Danica," Collinar stated as he stopped in front of her. "These beings are coming with us on a trip. Go now and get the ship and land it here."

Forrorrois ignored his condescending tone and gave him a simple smile. "I like trips," Forrorrois replied. "I'll be right back."

She turned and walked away with almost a skip to her step. They started to talk before she was out of earshot.

"What a shame," one of the soldiers commented. "She's actually quite pretty."

"Yes, but not much of a conversationalist," Collinar replied. "She does love to fly and she's actually very good under pressure."

"Anything else she's good at?" one of the soldiers said, lustfully.

"Please, it would be like forcing yourself on a child," Collinar stated distastefully, his voice almost lost from the distance between them.

Forrorrois pulled up her hood of her environmental suit and engaged her visor, relieved to finally be out of earshot. She reached out to the ship on the other side of the atmospheric barrier and ordered the craft to approach her position when she reached the edge. Her shrouded long-distance scout responded in her mind. In moments, the craft landed near her. She approached its eerie red form and walked up the ramp. Her skin tingled as she passed through the EM warping field into the cargo hold. Forrorrois retracted the visor and pushed back the silver hood.

'Computer, drop the shroud and move to Collinar's position,' she subvocalized. "As soon as everyone is onboard prepare for an immediate return to orbit. Re-engage shroud as soon as the scout is out of visual range."

'Understood,' the computer responded.

Forrorrois took her seat in the cockpit and glanced over the sensors. She tensed when a blip showed up on her medium-range sensors. Her sensor deflectors were still up, but the approaching craft would have a visual on her within moments on its present trajectory.

The scout settled in the middle of the compound and extended the cargo hold ramp. Forrorrois could hear the footfalls running up the ramp.

"A ship's coming, Danica," Collinar stated, stepping into the cockpit, "get us out of here and make certain that they don't detect us."

"Hide-and-go-seek?" Forrorrois asked.

Collinar almost looked irritated at her then glanced back at the four soldiers in the cargo hold. "Hide-and-go-seek," he agreed, sitting down in the jump seat beside her command seat.

"I like hide-and-go-seek," she said with child-like glee. "I hope everyone is sitting."

Before Collinar could fasten his harness, the scout lunged forward just clearing the buildings. Forrorrois grinned when she heard one of the soldiers tumble to the floor plates.

"Oopsie," she uttered mischievously when she heard the soldier swearing in the cargo hold.

Collinar gripped the edges of his jump seat in response to her erratic flying.

'Computer, re-engage shroud and head for the closest magnetic pole,' she subvocalized.

'Shroud engaged,' the computer replied in her mind.

Forrorrois turned to Collinar and grinned. "Where to, Trell?" she chirped.

Collinar gave her a stare then shook his head while he handed her the information cube. "I think I left you standing in the sun too long," he quipped.

"You're funny," she replied, maintaining her simpleton persona for the soldiers in the back while he dropped the cube into the data port. The Mur'troff system appeared. A marker flashed on an asteroid halfway across the system. Forrorrois plotted a course and released the controls to the scout's computer.

"We're going to talk after this," Collinar muttered.

"I like our talks," Forrorrois answered. "The ship knows where to go now."

"Good," Collinar said with a glance back towards the soldiers.

Forrorrois leaned over and looked him in the eyes. "I can smell her on you," she said in a low voice.

"Does it make you jealous?" he whispered back with a leer.

"No, I'm just glad you got some. Now, maybe you'll leave me alone. Just take a shower before you lay down in the rear cabin. I just changed the sheets," she replied with a straight face.

Collinar narrowed his golden feline eyes and folded his arms as he shifted his stare forward.

Forrorrois moved to speak, but stopped when one of the soldiers approached the cockpit.

"Trell, looks like we lost them," the soldier said as he entered the doorway and looked at the sensors. "You're right—Danica certainly can pilot a ship. Thanks for getting us out of there with the medical supplies. If you'd been a quarter-kel later we would have all been discovered and our contact would have been exposed."

Collinar shrugged his shoulders. "You can thank me with a bonus when we reach the drop-off coordinates," he replied.

"I'm sure that can be arranged," the soldier replied. "And maybe something pretty for Danica," he added.

Forrorrois beamed a child-like grin. "That would be really nice," she exclaimed. "I like pretty things."

She was surprised when she sensed gentleness from the soldier. He smiled at her and nodded.

"Trell, we'll talk after we land," the soldier said. Then he turned and returned to the cargo hold.

Forrorrois glanced over at Collinar. "I had him all wrong, he's a pretty decent being," she whispered.

Collinar nodded his head slowly. "That's good to know. It'll make negotiating the bonus a bit simpler."

Forrorrois shook her head and returned her stare forward. She chastised herself for not staying focused on the goal of earning as much as she could from each job. Forrorrois wanted to make every being in the Environs be a villain, but, like her, they were just trying to survive. For once, she wished she had Collinar's talent for getting the most out of each deal.

CHAPTER 20

The Mur'troff soldiers had paid Collinar well for the extraction and medical supplies. He smiled to himself at Forrorrois' amazement when he actually gave her the entire sum without a word—including the bonus. He was even more stunned when Forrorrois actually told him to keep the bonus for himself. Forrorrois' balance was now well over three hundred thousand, excluding the unknown value of the prophet stones. His share of the profits was well above the amount she had originally agreed. This venture definitely exceeded his expectations—he knew he would never have been so generous if their roles were reversed. Once he won his freedom from the rehabilitation center, he would be well on his way to buying back his command in the Utahar.

Collinar continued to marvel over Forrorrois' act with the soldier. Her childlike grin at receiving 'the pretty' from the soldier was absolute brilliance. 'The pretty' turned out to be a large crystal orb, about the size of her fist, with swirls of green inside—the value was minimal at best. But the goodwill that Collinar gained from her simpleton performance would be invaluable the next time he was through the Mur'troff system.

Collinar was even more pleased when they stopped back at Motan's. The next job he had for them was worth over four hundred thousand trups. More than enough to help Forrorrois reach her goal of six hundred thousand trups for the joining fee and to let him get back to settling his score with Neeha. Unfortunately, the location was in the Horgoth system on the planet Roca, known for every vice imaginable, all wrapped up in an air of civility. This time he didn't tell Forrorrois to act simple. They would need their wits about them to receive the item that needed transporting and get off world to the delivery point before one of the local crime lords discovered their presence.

Forrorrois had baulked at first, since they were not informed about what exactly they were retrieving, but time was growing short for her to raise the funds. The amount would put Forrorrois well above the amount needed to free her impotent joined one, Trager, from the clutches of his conniving mother. What Forrorrois ever saw in that Eldatek male was beyond him! Her fire was smothered by his presence. Collinar watched her eyes brighten as they landed and began their reconnaissance—together he and Forrorrois could be such a team! He licked his lips at the thought. But for now he needed to wait until the job was finished. Once he was free from the rehabilitation station then could he even the playing field.

Forrorrois and he traversed the poorly lit alleyway to the coordinates Motan had provided, glancing sideways at every sound. Even with the enumerable variables, his confidence was high that they would be given the item and swiftly be on their way. Collinar's eyes shifted to Forrorrois and noticed that she had grown increasingly cautious.

"Relax, they'll be here soon," Collinar chided.

"It doesn't feel right," Forrorrois replied.

Collinar reminded himself that she was an empath and increased his vigilance.

"Someone's coming," she whispered.

Before Collinar could respond, he heard footfalls in the meandering alleyway. "Let me do the talking," he said as he signaled for her to stop.

Forrorrois nodded and took a step back.

A few moments passed while they listened to the approaching footfalls. Finally, the being became visible. Collinar was puzzled when he saw that the being that they were going to meet turned out to be an Utahar male. The contact was wearing a short dark cloak with the hood pulled forward so his face was partially covered. On closer inspection, Collinar thought he recognized him, but he couldn't place from where.

"So you're Trell," the contact said, "and your associate?"

"Danica," Collinar replied.

"So…the rumors are true then," the fellow Utahar commented.

Collinar stared at the Utahar male more cautiously, now certain he'd never seen him before or he would probably have killed him for trying his patience. "Rumors?"

"Yes, there is a rumor that an Utahar is traveling with a small pale female and they are raising a large amount of capital in a short period of time," the cloaked Utahar replied.

Collinar exhaled slowly through his nose. *This wasn't going to end well,* he thought. He was not surprised to hear two more sets of footfalls coming in their direction. He glanced at Forrorrois and noted that she was already tensing.

"You have us at a disadvantage," he stated. "We don't know your name."

"I didn't give it," the Utahar replied with almost a sneer.

"Well, if you're not going to be sociable, we'll be on our way," Collinar stated, with a glance towards Forrorrois. She nodded and stepped out beside him.

"I'm afraid that you're not going anywhere until you hand over your currency," the Utahar stated, emphasizing his point by pulling the weapon from his waist.

Collinar shook his head calmly. "I'm afraid that you are confused. We don't have any currency. We are here for a job to earn currency," he replied slowly, as if to a child.

"Bad answer," the Utahar replied as he stepped closer—his weapon poised.

Collinar surreptitiously took the large knife he had secreted in a sheath at the small of his back from under his shirt, and threw the blade in a single fluid motion. Astonishment clouded the Utahar's face then melted into disbelief as he dropped to his knees and fell forward on his side. A gratifying hollow thud echoed in the alleyway when his head impacted the pavement.

Forrorrois looked at Collinar and rolled her eyes. "He's got company..."

Collinar followed her gaze as two more Utahar turned the corner of the alleyway and spotted them. Forrorrois fired her stun weapon and dropped both of them in their tracks.

Voices called out and more beings began to advance on their position. Collinar reached down and tore his knife out of the assailant's chest, then wiped the yellow blood from it's blade onto the dead Utahar's cloak in satisfaction.

Forrorrois grabbed his arm and pulled him down the alleyway. "You can savor the moment later," she scoffed.

Collinar's bloodlust had been awakened, but she was right, this was not the place. Together, they ran, following the twisting and turning alleyway, then, to Collinar's dismay, the passage stopped abruptly in a dead end. The meeting point had been a more thorough trap than he had initially given them credit. Forrorrois and he looked around frantically, in unison their gaze fell to a small grate set low to the pavement on the side of a building. Unfortunately, the opening would only provide refuge to a small rodent.

Voices from the alleyway reminded him that there were too many of them to be able to defend against. He looked at Forrorrois and crouched with his knife ready.

"Looks like our streak of good fortune has come to an end," he stated. "Reduce yourself and head into the grate—they won't expect weapon's fire from there. I'll draw their attention while you get into position," he ordered.

Forrorrois shook her head. "That's a suicidal maneuver. We can get out of here together," she replied, reaching into a small pocket of her vest with her free hand while she stood ready with her stun weapon in her right.

"Don't be so deluded, Forrorrois," Collinar scoffed.

"Just shut up, I've got an idea," Forrorrois answered. "Back up closer to the wall and don't resist me."

Collinar narrowed his eyes at her then growled to himself as he did as she asked. When his heel touched the wall, he spotted four more beings: two very large Gintzers and two more Utahar males. They came around the corner firing, affirming Collinar's suspicion that this was a trap.

Forrorrois sprayed the alleyway with her stun weapon and

dropped the two Gintzers, but the two Utahar managed to duck behind a column.

"I thought that was you, Collinar," one of them called out.

Forrorrois gave him a look. "A friend?" she asked, sarcastically.

Collinar shook his head, recognizing the voice. "No, a former subcommander," he growled. "Turban," he called out, backing closer to the wall nearer the grate. "I should have killed you when I had the chance, you mangy coward."

"And you should have remained in that rehabilitation cell with the Dramudam," Turban taunted back. "But I'm glad that you didn't, because now I can kill you and collect the bounty on both your heads."

Collinar's eyes widened. "Bounty? What bounty?"

Turban laughed. "This is too choice. You don't know!!! Four hundred thousand trups for the two of you alive and two hundred thousand trups for both of you dead, but personally, I'll take the two hundred thousand," his former subcommander cackled.

Collinar glanced at Forrorrois. "Whatever you're going to do you'd better do fast," he growled under his breath.

"Not yet," Forrorrois whispered back. "We need to know who put up the bounty or we won't know who we can trust!"

Collinar hated to admit she was right. His relationship with Motan had been compromised and now they needed facts.

"As much as it pains me to say, I can't believe a Roca crime lord would care enough about me to put two hundred trups on my head. Although there was an incident involving a couple of their daughters honor..." Collinar called out.

"The local crime syndicate has nothing to do with this," Turban replied. "It's bigger than this backwater planet."

"Oh really..." Collinar dismissed, "I think you're just a go-between. You were never that important. I doubt that you'll ever even see a single trup once you've turned us over."

"I've done well for myself over the past four revolution while you rotted in rehabilitation," Turban boasted.

"In the Environs? That's not hard," Collinar scoffed.

"Show's how much you know, I've got connections!"

"Oh then who put the bounty on my head?"

Turban hesitated. Collinar's lips curled into a smirk. "You don't know, do you?"

"It's hush hush," Turban replied. "That's the way things are done now, the rules have changed."

"No, it's the way it's done with a lackey," Collinar sneered.

"Careful, Collinar, you're pushing him too hard," Forrorrois warned in a low voice.

Collinar shot her an annoyed look. "Just be ready to move," he hissed.

"I know who my client is, she's an Eldatek," Turban retorted, "obviously very wealthy and very well connected politically."

Forrorrois gave Collinar a sideways glance. Inside, his anger rose at the word Eldatek.

"Old or young," Forrorrois called back.

"Young," his former subcommander laughed.

"Bohata…" Forrorrois hissed under her breath. "I'll pay you three hundred thousand trups, if you'll let us go," she called back.

Collinar glanced at Forrorrois then shook his head, but she gave him a look that kept him quiet.

"Believe me, Forrorrois, I'd rather kill Collinar for the pleasure of it and take just one hundred thousand trups for his carcass," Turban replied. "But they'll give me two hundred thousand trups for you alive. Lower your weapons and we can cut a deal."

"No deal," Forrorrois replied. "I give you Collinar and I go free."

Collinar stiffened when Forrorrois grabbed his arm and aimed her stun weapon at him.

Turban laughed. "Less bounty, but to tell you the truth, I rather like the idea of just killing Collinar. Deal," Turban replied.

"What are you doing, Forrorrois? He's going to kill you," Collinar whispered.

"Keep quiet and be ready. I still need you," Forrorrois whispered back. "Now, drop your knife," she stated, nudging him in the ribs for show.

Collinar slowly loosened the grip on his knife and let metal blade drop to the pavement with a clatter.

Turban peered around the column at them and laughed when he spotted Forrorrois holding her weapon on Collinar. The second Utahar followed him out with his weapon ready. "I've been saving this for the next time we met, Collinar," he stated, pulling a knife from the waist of his pants.

Collinar looked at the blade and grew angry. "That's my knife, you scum!" he growled.

"Yes, and now I'm going to have the pleasure of killing you with the very weapon that you've used on so many others," Turban replied with delight flashing in his feline golden eyes as he stepped closer.

Collinar tensed to pounce on the insubordinate former subcommander, mindful of the glint of his cherished blade held ineptly in the imbecile's hand, but Forrorrois' grip on his arm tightened. Without a word, she threw something to the ground. He threw up his hand as a blinding flash and smoke filled the poorly lit alleyway. Collinar felt Forrorrois turn him as Turban lunged blindly with Collinar's own cherished ceremonial blade. Her hand slipped to his waist and held him tight.

"Don't resist," she whispered through clenched teeth.

Collinar suddenly felt disoriented. A red flash from the second Utahar's weapon made him flinch, but the shot went wild over their heads. He stumbled backwards, but Forrorrois held onto him tightly.

"Don't resist," he heard Forrorrois whisper once more.

A flash of red from Forrorrois' stun weapon blanketed the smoke filled alleyway. Then Collinar felt everything go black as he fell to his knees. The last thing he remembered was being dragged by the scruff of his collar—then nothing.

∗∗∗∗∗∗∗∗∗∗∗

Collinar slowly opened his eyes. A dim light from a distant source defined the shadows around him. The smell of stagnant water and decay filled his nostrils. He suddenly realized his head was resting on something soft. When he moved to lift his head, he stopped from the sharp pain in his temples.

"Remain still while your head clears," Forrorrois' voice whispered.

Collinar glanced up, surprised to see her face just above his. He was even more startled when he realized his head was resting on her lap. Uncertain, he rolled onto his side and breathed in the scent of her thigh.

"What happened?" he whispered. "Where are we?"

He tensed when he felt her hand on the side of his face. She brushed his disheveled blond-hair gently away from his eyes.

"We escaped into the grate in the wall," she whispered.

Startled, Collinar glanced around then rolled onto his back once more and stared up at her.

"I didn't see you bring a reduction weapon with you," he stated.

"I didn't use one," she replied.

"What? That's impossible!" he exclaimed, forcing past the headache to sit up and look her in the eye.

"No, just improbable," she replied.

"But how?" Collinar insisted.

Forrorrois hesitated. "Ma'Kelda," was all she finally said.

Collinar froze at the name. His heart began to pound in his chest as he pulled away from Forrorrois. He tried to get to his feet, but the throbbing pain in his head forced him to his knees.

"The headache will pass," Forrorrois whispered.

Collinar stared at her in the dim light, unnerved by the name of his former subcommander—his former lover—dead by his own hands.

"She did love you," Forrorrois continued. "Even when she helped me escape—she knew full well the act would cost her life—but she still loved you."

Collinar looked away. "Enough," he replied.

"Don't fight it, Collinar," Forrorrois whispered.

"I said enough!" he growled, lunging forward and grabbing her arms. He felt wetness on his left hand and gasped, releasing her. He was surprised when he saw her red blood on his fingers. He looked at her again—confused that she had done nothing to defend herself. "You're bleeding!"

"Yes," Forrorrois replied, dully.

"Did Turban cut you with that blade?" he persisted.

"Yes," she answered.

Collinar raised his fingers to his nostrils and sniffed. An odd sweetness mixed with the metallic scent of her blood. The familiar odor made his heart stop. He touched his tongue to the smear of blood on his fingers then quickly spat it out. The hint of bittersweet told him everything. "That mangy imbecile, he put poison on the blade. It's slow acting, but even a miniscule amount in your blood stream will slowly paralyze you then eventually kill you."

"I was afraid of that," Forrorrois replied. "I'm sorry, Collinar, but I won't be able to make it back to the scout. Already, I can barely walk. At this size, we wouldn't make it far."

"Then reenlarge us before you're too weak," he ordered.

"I'm sorry, I already don't have enough energy," she stated.

Panic crept into his mind. "You just need some fresh air. You must go outside," he said, grabbing her arm and pulling her to her feet. She stumbled as she rose and leaned heavily against him.

"Nur, I hear you," she mumbled. "We're in the wall grate…"

"Wonderful, she's delirious," Collinar cursed. Abruptly, she fell limp against his side. He struggled to keep her deadweight from slipping back to the floor. "Forrorrois…Forrorrois," he stammered,

Collinar froze when an oversized boot scraped the paving stones just outside the grate opening. The light dimmed as a shadow fell across him. He struggled to drag Forrorrois backwards when a large figure crouched down and peered inside.

"Nur, you're correct, they're inside," a voice stated.

"Nur?" Collinar muttered, remembering Forrorrois' words just before she'd passed out. He strained to see the face. Recognition left him dumbfounded. "Guruma?"

"Yes, Collinar," Guruma replied. "Hurry, we don't have much

time. Hand me Forrorrois, then climb onto my hand. We need to leave this place before your assailants wake up from the effects of Forrorrois' stun weapon."

Speechless, Collinar did as he was told and guided Forrorrois' unconscious form though the slats of the grate to Guruma waiting fingers. Then he crawled out and stared up at the ancient Dramudam founder, towering above his miniature form.

"What happened to her?" Guruma asked, still crouching as he held her close to examine her.

"Poisoned—we have to get back to the scout immediately so that I can make an antidote!" Collinar insisted. He looked passed Guruma and stepped back in alarm when he spotted the enormous four-legged black-furred creature with flapping leathery red wings standing behind the Dramudam.

Guruma glanced back, and then nodded. "Collinar, this is Nur. He'll take us back to your ship. You can tell me the rest once we've stabilized Forrorrois. Now come, we must hurry."

Before Collinar could object, Guruma scooped him up and slipped him inside his breast pocket, and then he lowered Forrorrois into Collinar's waiting arms.

"Try and keep Forrorrois comfortable while Nur takes us back to the scout," Guruma whispered.

Collinar slid to his knees and cradled Forrorrois in the tight space of the pocket. Her breathing had become shallow.

****

In miniature, Collinar paced on the counter in the cargo hold of Forrorrois' long-distance scout. Anger rose inside him at the thought that Forrorrois had taken a knife thrust that Turban had meant for him. "I will find you, Turban, and make you wish for a swift death," he swore while he waited for her ship's computer to synthesize the antidote for the poison in Forrorrois' bloodstream. Guruma towered above him, full-sized, and passed the bioscanner over Forrorrois' miniature body once more, as she lay still on the counter near him.

Collinar had wrapped her in several silver thermal blankets that Guruma had miniaturized with a reduction weapon. He glanced over at Nur, irritated when he felt the creature telepathically brush his mind with his.

"She's slipped into a coma," Guruma whispered.

"I don't understand," Collinar cursed. "The poison Turban used normally takes a full cycle to reach this stage."

"Perhaps the timing of her reduction and her weakened state amplified the poison's effect," Guruma offered.

"Perhaps," Collinar replied.

"It's ready," the Dramudam founder stated, stepping over to the port set in the wall panel above Collinar's head, and slipped a cylindrical hypo inside.

"Miniaturize the hypo and I'll begin administering the first dose," Collinar ordered.

Guruma didn't say a word as he set the cylinder beside Collinar and took aim. In a flash of bluish-green, the cylinder contracted down. Collinar scooped up the hypo with one hand and looked at the readout then adjusted the dosage. He raced over to Forrorrois and knelt down beside her small vulnerable body. Pulling back the thermal blanket, Collinar pressed the hypo against her throat. The cylinder hissed slowly. He closed his eyes for a moment then rocked back on his heals at he sat down on the counter and watched her.

Guruma pulled a chair up to the counter and took a seat without a word.

He glanced up at the creased reddish-brown face of the Eldatek male and heaved a sigh.

"I'll need to give her an injection every hur for five dosages," he explained for no other reason then to break the tense silence. "We probably won't see any improvement for at least a kel."

When Guruma remained silent, Collinar looked away and rubbed his arms suddenly aware that a chill was setting into his bones.

Without a word, Guruma rose from his chair and opened a locker. There was a greenish-blue flash then he returned and laid a miniaturized silver environmental suit beside Collinar. Collinar stared at the metallic material for a moment then nodded and pulled on the suit, silently grateful to feel warm again. He resumed his place next to Forrorrois' still form and studied her shallow breathing.

"Your skill around medical equipment is apparent," Guruma finally spoke. "Did you study before you joined the Utahar forces?"

Collinar looked up, annoyed at the perceptive question. "As a matter-of-fact, yes," he replied.

"I see," Guruma said with a nod.

An uncomfortable silence fell between them as Collinar refocused his attention back on Forrorrois.

"No, Nur, I can't feel her mind. I wish I could right now. We're doing everything we can," Guruma replied, glancing back toward the large four-legged creature. Even with the large red wings now folded compactly in the cramped space of the small cargo hold, the large creature looked fearsome.

Collinar studied the creature carefully. "So, Nur is a Beliespeir," he stated.

Guruma nodded. "Yes."

"Intriguing, I always wanted to meet one," Collinar said, still watching the creature.

Nur shifted on his feet, nervously.

"It's not polite to stare, Collinar," Guruma stated as he continued his watchful vigil over Forrorrois.

"My apologies, Nur," Collinar sneered as he shifted his gaze back at Forrorrois.

"Yes, Nur, I'll be fine," Guruma said with a glance at the creature.

Collinar's eyes widened when Nur took a step forward and vanished. "Where did he go?"

"He was feeling a bit claustrophobic and decided to take a walk," Guruma said as he sat back in his chair, towering over Collinar.

"Take a walk? We're in orbit around the planet!" Collinar exclaimed.

"Nur went to another dimension to stretch his legs and find something to eat," he clarified.

Collinar snorted, amused at the concept of moving so easily between dimensions.

"You should rest, Collinar. I'll wake you in time for the next dose," Guruma offered.

"I'm fine," Collinar shot back.

"Suit your self," Guruma replied with an annoying calm. "Oh, before I forget, I thought you might like this back."

Collinar's eyes grew large when Guruma set his full-scale ceremonial knife on the counter, not far from where he was sitting.

"I've cleansed the blade to prevent anyone else from becoming poisoned," Guruma added.

Collinar narrowed his golden feline eyes as he stared over at the Dramudam founder. "Why would you give this back to me?"

Guruma sighed. "Because I saw the look on your face when Turban pulled the blade out in the alley—I could see that it meant something to you."

"It's just a blade," Collinar scoffed, denying his feelings as he remained seated next to Forrorrois.

"No, it represents your past," Guruma insisted.

Collinar gave him an irritated look. "You sound like the guards at the rehabilitation center."

"Pardon me for the observation."

An awkward silence fell between them. Collinar rolled onto his knees and checked Forrorrois' pulse with his fingertips. It was thready at best. He placed the cylinder against her throat and gave her the second dose then he rolled back on his heels to a sitting position to wait once more with his arms crossed on the tops of his knees.

"Thank you," Collinar suddenly said, without looking at Guruma.

Guruma gave him an odd look. "For what?"

Collinar closed his eyes impatiently and exhaled. "Thank you for returning the knife to me. I never thought I would see it again."

"You're welcome," Guruma replied. "It's beautifully designed and well balanced. May I ask where you got it from?"

Collinar looked over at the enormous blade for a moment. "It was a gift from one of the worlds that I plundered."

"A gift?"

"Don't act so surprised," Collinar scoffed.

"May I ask from whom?"

Collinar took a deep breath and looked away. "It was from Ma'Kelda."

"I see," Guruma replied. "She was very thoughtful."

"She's also very dead," Collinar growled.

"I'm sorry, I didn't mean to pry."

Collinar looked away, irked at the enormous Eldatek leaning over him. He masked his irritation as he reached out and touched Forrorrois' throat once more to check her pulse. "She seems to be responding to the treatment, her heart rate seems a bit stronger, but it's still thready," he stated. "Her temperature is beginning to rise, though. That's not a good sign."

Guruma closed his eyes. "Monomay hold your children close."

Collinar studied the elder being, surprised at the unexpected prayer. He was distracted when Forrorrois suddenly gasped. Her eyes flew open—unseeing—as her body arched. Collinar leaned forward and grabbed her shoulders to prevent her from hurting herself during the convulsion.

Alarmed, Guruma leapt from him chair. "What's happening?!"

"I don't know, scan her!" Collinar called out.

Guruma passed the large bioscanner over Collinar and Forrorrois. "Her body is reacting to the release of toxins as it fights the poison."

Collinar's eyes widened, there was no time to waste. His mind raced for a solution. In an instant an idea hit him. "Guruma, I need you to get some dry caya leaves and crush them. Then mixed them with just a touch of hot water to make a hot poultice," he ordered as he began to strip the thermal blankets away from Forrorrois' seizing body and then began to pull off her vest and top. "I need enough to cover her body."

"What are you doing?" Guruma stammered while Collinar pulled off her boots and pants.

"I'll explain in a moment, just make that poultice!"

Guruma finally left the counter and pulled down the tin where Collinar had seen Forrorrois keep her ya.

Collinar threw her clothes and the thermal blankets to one side. He couldn't help but run his hands across her warm pale skin—tempted by her body's accessibility. Collinar moved to take off her scant undergarments, but refrained when Guruma returned with a square plate steaming with hot crushed caya leaves. He reached over and grabbed a handful, only to pull back abruptly with a growl when he burned his fingers.

"I'm sorry, you said hot," Guruma apologized.

Collinar blew on his fingers then reached over and grabbed two handfuls pushing past the burn. "Don't be. The hot poultice will draw the toxins from her body through her skin," he replied, smearing the dark greenish pulp over her stomach and chest. His fingers lingered as he traced her Dramudam mark, reminding him of her choice to reject him. Setting his jaw, he raced back to the plate and gathered more of the caya paste then he repeated the process until he had covered her, front and back, from the neck down.

Forrorrois arched again in pain, her eyes wild as if seeing something horrifying. Collinar knelt down and pulled her head and shoulders onto his lap and placed both hands against her temples. "Forrorrois, I know at some level you can hear me, I made you tougher than this, fight!" he urged.

Forrorrois arched once more. Collinar gasped when her mind invaded his, drawing him into the horror that reflected in her eyes. Abruptly, he was in her body, looking up at faces covered with masks—the agony of transformation from human to modified soldier that he had forced upon her, she now thrusted into him without mercy. His veins seared as the acidic solutions washed through them. His very molecules twisted as they deformed under his skin. His eyes widened in abhorrence as he experienced firsthand the torture that he had inflicted.

Collinar screamed at the unimaginable torment. As suddenly as her convulsions had started, they stopped and she fell limp in his arms. He collapsed forward as she released his mind. His head swirled from the images—Collinar forced himself to draw a breath when he realized his lungs were burning for air. In the distance he heard his name, but his mind refused to focus.

"Collinar!" Guruma shouted once more.

Collinar started when he felt his shoulder being nudged and looked up at the elder being—still cradling Forrorrois' head on his lap.

"Scan her again," he called up weakly.

Guruma passed the large cylinder over both of them. "It's working," Guruma exclaimed. "Her temperature is coming down and the toxin levels are dropping."

"Excellent," Collinar whispered as he wiped the drying poultice from Forrorrois' neck then pressed the hypo against her throat for a third dose. "After her next dose, we'll need to wash the poultice from her skin with cool water then bundle her with thermal blankets to keep her warm," Collinar stated aloud, slowly recovering from Forrorrois' unexpected psychic assault.

"Remarkable. How did you know that would work?" Guruma asked.

"It's simple," Collinar remarked, recovering his overabundant self-confidence. "The caya that you Eldatek drink also cleanses the body of low level toxins. As a poultice, the effects are magnified and caya is capable of drawing out lethal toxins through the skin. In Forrorrois' miniaturized size, the effect is even more intensified." He was surprised when Guruma sat back and shook his head.

"You should have remained a healer."

Exasperated, Collinar looked up at the Eldatek male. "There's no power as a healer in the eyes of the Utahar," Collinar snarled. "I took the path of command, instead."

"A pity," Guruma said as he rose from his chair. "I'll prepare a bowl of water for cleansing the poultice."

Collinar watched the elderly founder move back to the basin where he had retrieved the caya. "How do you suffer that old fool, Forrorrois?" he muttered, brushing some crusted poultice from her pale cheek. He looked up when Guruma returned with a shallow bowl and a hand towel then the elder being sat down once more next to the counter.

"She seems to be more peaceful," Guruma observed.

"Her coma's not so deep," Collinar briskly replied. He pressed the hypo against her throat for the fourth dose. His body was still weak from Forrorrois' earlier psychic battering. He glanced up at Guruma and sighed. "She's ready, lift her up and place her in the water."

"Certainly," Guruma said.

Collinar struggled to his feet and climbed over the edge of the shallow bowl into the calf-deep water. His environmental suit kept him from getting wet, while he knelt beside her and washed the poultice from her body. Her pale skin aroused him, but he felt Guruma's watchful gaze and didn't allow his hands to linger in any one place too long. He wished she were conscious so that he could justify his lusty thoughts—instead, he repeatedly scooped water onto her body until the crusted poultice was finally rinsed away. He felt her body begin to shiver from heat loss. With a sigh, he looked up.

"Dry her off and then wrap her back up in the thermal blankets," he called up.

He watched as Guruma scooped up Forrorrois' unconscious pale form from the shallow bowl and placed her gently on the towel. Closing his eyes, Collinar caught his breath then he grabbed the edge of the bowl and climbed out. He stumbled to his knees with exhaustion onto the countertop. To his surprise, Guruma steadied him gently with his chestnut-brown fingers. "I'm fine," he growled, waving him off. "How are Forrorrois' vital signs?"

"She's improving."

"Excellent," Collinar said, regaining his balance. He got back on his feet and walked back over to Forrorrois. By the time he reached her, Guruma had already wrapped her back up in thermal blankets. Collinar pulled the silvery material of the thermal blankets back from her throat and pressed the hypo against her throat for the fifth and final dosage.

"Now we wait," he stated, sitting back down on the counter next to Forrorrois.

"Get some rest, I'll watch for any signs of change," Guruma stated, handing him a miniaturized thermal blanket.

Too exhausted to argue, Collinar accepted the silvery blanket—he stretched out next to Forrorrois and fell promptly asleep.

****

Forrorrois stirred awake, suddenly aware that she couldn't move her arms or legs. Remembering the poisoned knife, she panicked until she realized her limbs were only pinned by the tightly wrapped thermal blankets. With a glance upward, she was surprised to spot Guruma's enormous form leaning over her. The fog of her mind began to clear when she remembered reducing herself, along with Collinar, during the escape from the bounty hunters. Guruma passed a bioscanner over her and smiled. Looking past Guruma, Forrorrois was relieved to see that she was in the cargo hold of her long-distance scout.

"How is she?" Collinar's voice sounded.

She started, glancing over towards his voice and saw him kneeling next to her, also in miniature, wearing a silver environmental suit.

"She'll be fine with a bit more rest," Guruma replied.

"How long have I been out?" she asked, struggling to pull her arm out of the tight blankets.

Collinar loosened the top blanket to let her move. "A little over a cycle," he replied.

Forrorrois finally freed her arm then froze when she didn't see a shirt sleeve. Panicked, she lifted the blankets up and peered inside. "Where are my clothes?!" she demanded, pulling the blankets tightly up to her chin.

"Don't be such a prude," Collinar scoffed. "Nothing happened—Guruma was here the whole time to make certain of that."

Forrorrois shifted her glance toward Guruma's gentle gaze.

"Yes, I was here," Guruma confirmed. "You should thank Collinar for saving your life. He's surprisingly skilled as a healer. I doubt even Leenon's abilities would have been enough."

Forrorrois glanced over at Collinar's smug look and struggled for the words. "Thank you," she finally whispered.

"Now we're even," Collinar remarked.

Forrorrois gave him a puzzled look. "For what?"

"You took the knife thrust that was meant for me," Collinar replied. "Here are your clothes," he said, tossing the bundle on her chest as he got up. Before she could say anything else he stalked away to the far end of the counter.

"What's with him?" she muttered.

"The treatment was very difficult, he's exhausted," Guruma said with a gentle smile. "If you're able, get dressed and I'll see about making both of you some mawya."

"You'd better make his vaya," she replied, sitting up carefully while keeping herself covered.

Guruma chuckled. "I'll see what I can find."

After he left, Forrorrois quickly pulled on her shirt and vest, then her pants and boots, uncertain how long her brief moment of privacy would last. She felt something scratchy in her bra and pulled out a piece of caya leaf. "What the Hell?" she puzzled.

Collinar approached her, smirking. "I would have removed your undergarments for the treatment, but Guruma didn't seem to approve."

"Then I'm glad he was here," she shot back, tossing the leaf fragment aside.

"You still have a good figure for a female who's had a child," he jested.

Forrorrois moved to object, but stopped when she sensed he was just baiting her. Guruma approached with three full-sized mugs and set them to one side on the counter.

"I'll reduce them in a moment," he said, pulling the reduction weapon from his waist.

Forrorrois looked over at Collinar and shook her head. "No, I think it's time for me to return Collinar back to full-size," she replied.

She felt Collinar's excitement grow.

"Are you certain that you're strong enough?" Guruma asked.

"Of course she is," Collinar eagerly answered for her.

Irritated, she glanced over towards the Utahar. "I'm pretty certain," she answered.

Guruma's concern flowed unchecked into her mind, but finally he relented. "All right, both of you, up onto my hands," he offered.

Forrorrois was surprised when Collinar assisted her to her feet, but she didn't object. Guruma's hands were warm to the touch as she climbed up onto his palm. Collinar followed after her. She continued to feel Guruma's concern as he curled his fingers around them and gently lowered them to the floor panel.

Collinar hopped down, then turned unexpectedly and lifted her by the waist to the floor. She hesitated at his uncharacteristic manners before she pointed to the floor.

"Cut the crap and sit down with your back to me," she snapped.

Collinar smirked then did as she asked without a word.

"Now, close your eyes and relax," she ordered while she sat snuggly behind him with her legs on either side of his thighs.

"If you wanted to be intimate, you only needed to ask," he purred in a low voice.

"Don't be so foul," she warned. "Now, clear your thoughts—all your thoughts!" she added when she felt his lewdness filter into her mind. Abruptly, his mind calmed—much to her surprise. "Very good." She reached up and lightly placed her fingertips against his temples. "Exhale slowly and relax," she whispered. "Relax and let my mind guide your body."

She felt Collinar's body tense slightly as she pushed into his thoughts. A flash of Ma'Kelda's face flicked in her mind. She smiled when she realized that it was Ma'Kelda who had taught Collinar how to meditate. A tear suddenly rolled down her cheek when she felt his sudden grief. "Shhh…let it go as you fall deeper. Feel the cells of your body resonate with mine, feel our energies become one," she continued to whisper. The power surged through her into Collinar. He gasped as she began to enlarge them both—her hands shook from absorbing the energy of her surroundings and channeling it into the energy-mass exchange. All around her the room shifted back to normal scale. As the energy ebbed, she collapsed against Collinar's back, exhausted. She was amazed that he was still conscious, heaving in unison with her. Guruma grabbed her shoulders when she began to slide to the floor panels.

Collinar crumpled to the floor, panting. "That was incredible," he gasped. "No wonder Trager gave up everything to join with you. The intensity of a union with you…"

"Collinar, why must you reduce everything to such a base level," she replied, cutting him off.

"Must be the company," he rasped.

"Let me help you into the rear cabin, Forrorrois," Guruma offered.

"Thank you," she replied as she struggled to her feet. "I think I'll have that mawya now."

She was surprised when Collinar remained curled on the floor panels while Guruma guided her to her bunk in the rear cabin. Each time she caught a glimpse of his mind, Forrorrois struggled even more with his duality—the choices he could have made that would have made him a different being. She pushed the thought from her mind and accepted the red stone mug of mawya from Guruma. He left her alone in the rear cabin without a word, immersed in her thoughts.

****

Collinar finally pulled himself off the cargo hold's floor panels of Forrorrois' long-distance scout onto a crate. The last cycle had drained his reserves in the struggle to cure Forrorrois from the poison that had been meant for him. He looked up with surprise when Guruma handed him a red stone mug and sat down on a second storage crate beside him. Sniffing the steam wafting from the mug, he pulled on an odd grin.

"Vaya?" he remarked.

Guruma smiled as he lowered his mug from his lips. "Forrorrois thought it might be helpful."

454

He snorted a laugh then sipped the tart liquid. His throat relaxed as the vaya soothed the dryness. "Good choice," he replied.

"There are many choices in this universe, Collinar," Guruma remarked.

Collinar tensed, sensing another lecture, but he was stunned when the elder being didn't continue, he just took a sip of his mawya. Confused, Collinar stared down at his mug of vaya.

"So where's Nur?" Collinar asked to change the subject.

"Oh, he's around," Guruma replied. "He's probably still checking on a few things for me."

Collinar snorted at the evasive answer. Then he narrowed his golden feline eyes. "So what brought you and Nur to the Horgoth system, in particular, the planet Roca?" he asked, studying the Dramudam founder.

"Trager warned me that there was a bounty on both your heads," Guruma replied.

Intrigued, Collinar leaned forward. "Trager warned you? How could he know that? He's stuck in a cell on Elda."

"Beings talk when they think they have the upper hand. Trager just listened," Guruma said with a shrug.

"You're cunning, I like that in a being," Collinar remarked. He took a sip of his tart vaya and grinned. "So who put the bounty on our heads?"

"I suspect, Bohata," Guruma replied. "But her motives are confusing."

Collinar rolled his eyes as he shook his head. "So, Forrorrois was right about her," he scoffed. "No, Bohata's motives are obvious. She's on a path that she can't change, so she's ensuring her success—right, wrong, or indifferent."

"Maybe you are right," Guruma replied. "How close are you to raising the joining fee?"

Collinar shook his head. "Not close enough. After this mess, I can only assume that Motan knows who Forrorrois and I really are. I doubt that he'll give me any serious work from this point forward. Knowing him, he'd turn me in himself for such a large reward."

Concerned, Guruma leaned forward. "Is there anyone else?"

"No, not for the sums that we need to raise in the time we have left. I'm afraid that Bohata's bold move has paid off handsomely," he admitted.

"I see," Guruma replied. "I guess there is only one other way."

Collinar raised an eyebrow in surprise. "Steal it?"

Guruma shook his head and chuckled. "Not exactly, more like fabricate it."

Collinar's eyes widened. "And how do you intend to do that?"

Guruma shook his head slightly. "I'm afraid you'll have to trust me on this one."

"You are a sly being," Collinar purred, his golden feline eyes flashing. "It's hard not to like you."

Guruma shook his head. "I'll try to take that as a compliment."

Collinar chuckled as he leaned back and sipped his vaya. His freedom was drawing nearer.

CHAPTER 21

Nervous excitement grew inside Perkins as he piloted his Dramudam one-seat long-distance scout past the orbit of Mars. As a little boy he had dreamed like many other children of being an astronaut. He would sit with rapt attention whenever a shuttle launch took place. When he entered the Air Force he still secretly wished he would be picked as a shuttle pilot. Then, when he discovered the adreneline rush of piloting an attack helicopter, his childhood dream was all but forgotten. Now, he had come full circle. But he wasn't just a pilot for NASA or the Air Force, he was now facing an even higher purpose, he was a pilot assigned to help protect the entire Earth. He could only imagine that this was what Forrorrois must have felt when Commander Thoren had first sent her back.

Perkins glanced behind him and smiled when he heard footfalls on the three steps that lead up to the cockpit from the rear cabin. Alham was finally awake.

"Glad to see you are awake, sleepyhead," he commented in English.

"We're almost to Earth! You should have woken me up sooner," she scolded in Intergaltic, when she looked at the holographic display that floated between Perkins command chair and the canopy.

"Ah, English," he reminded her. "And we still have another hour before we see the Earth in all its glory."

"You still should have told me," she said, this time in English. "Did I say that right?"

"Yes," Perkins said back in English. "And you are doing fine—I can tell you've been practicing."

Alham smiled. "Thank you, I know the ship's computer will help me through my zendra link, but I want to be ready when I meet Forrorrois' mother."

"And her father and brother," Perkins reminded. "It's a patriarchal society, so please don't exclude them."

"Right," she replied. "I keep forgetting."

"You'll do fine, just relax," Perkins said with a smile.

Panic crossed Alham's face. "I can't relax! How am I going to explain this to my Uncle Yononnon?"

"How are 'we' going to explain it, this was my idea too," he countered gently. "I could just hide you until he leaves to go back to the Tollon," Perkins offered.

"Believe me, I have given this a great deal of thought," she replied. "The less he knows, the less he will have to deny later. I just want to be able see him, he is my family."

Perkins nodded. "I know, and from what I've heard about Yononnon, I think he would be all right on why you left. But you need to consider his position in the Dramudam."

"All right, maybe remaining hidden until Yononnon leaves is a better solution," she admitted.

Perkins pulled up the long-distance sensors. A small blue speck began to grown in the center. "We'll reach Earth, soon," he said, trying to distract her. "Think of it as your new home."

"I can't wait to see it from the surface," Alham said wistfully. "From the stories I've heard it's very different from my desert homeworld, Elda."

"Earth has deserts if you get homesick," Perkins offered.

He was surprised when she leaned over and kissed him on the cheek.

"Thank you for being so considerate," she whispered.

Perkins smiled to himself as she fell silent beside him. Together, they watched the blue speck grow as they drew closer to Earth.

****

Jack grinned when Celeste wrinkled her nose at him at the dinner table. Danielle and George had prepared a lovely Sunday supper and they had all just sat down. He was especially pleased that Yononnon had finally elected to join them, accepting a seat between him and Celeste. The large Dramudam subcommander had become less reclusive, especially since he had taken on teaching Frank and George how to repair the numerous ships that now filled Forrorrois' hangar bay.

George brought out the last dish from the kitchen, while Danielle glanced around the table. She finally nodded and took her seat on the other side of Celeste.

"Frank, if you would like to say grace," she offered, reaching over to Celeste and taking her small hand.

Jack's grin widened as little Celeste looked up at Yononnon and offered her hand.

Yononnon glanced around, uncertain as everyone took the hand of the person next to them.

"It's OK, Unca Non," Celeste whispered.

Yononnon gave her a gentle smile then took her small hand in his much larger one.

Jack took his other hand with an approving nod then took Frank's. George completed the circle by taking his mother's free hand.

"Dear Lord, thank you for providing us this food and protecting those who shelter in this home," Frank began. "We ask of you, oh Lord, to watch over Danica, Trager, and Captain Perkins who are unable to be with us so that they may return safely to our family. Amen."

"Monomay, hold your children close," Yononnon whispered, in English, as he released Jack's hand.

Everyone paused as they glanced in the subcommander's direction.

"Thank you, Yononnon, that was beautiful," Danielle said quickly, breaking the silence.

Jack watched the tension in Yononnon's shoulders relax from Danielle's kind words.

"Yes, it was, thank you," Frank added. "Now, please, let's all eat, George and Danielle have worked hard preparing this wonderful meal. Let's enjoy it while it's still hot!"

Jack picked up the bowl of orange squash in from of him and took a scoop before passing it to Yononnon. Yononnon glanced around, uncertain at first then he did the same. Danielle took the bowl from him then scooped a small amount onto Celeste's plate.

Celeste grinned. "I like squash," she announced, "you're going to like it too, Unca Non."

Jack took the mashed potatoes from George and took a scoop and gave them to Yononnon before he could comment. Soon everyone's plates were filled and they began to eat.

After sampling everything, Yononnon looked over at Danielle. "This meal is delicious, Mrs. Jolan, thank you for asking me to share it with your family."

Danielle flushed with pleasure. "I'm glad that you finally agreed to join us, Yononnon. And please, call me Danielle. We consider you a part of our family as well. From what I understand, you and your sister Leenon acted as foster parents to Danica while she was training on the Tollon."

Yononnon glanced over at Jack then he nodded. "Yes, she was assigned to us by Commander Thoren. Danica filled a place in our hearts that my sister and I hadn't realized was empty."

"I'm certain that she also provided you with challenges as well," Jack teased.

Yononnon sighed. "Yes, she did."

Both Danielle and Frank began to chuckle. Soon, Jack and George joined in, leaving Celeste looking around the table with four year old confusion.

"What's so funny?" she demanded.

Danielle leaned over and shook her head. "Nothing, Peanut, eat your dinner."

"Oh, is this one of your, 'when I'm older' things?" Celeste pouted.

"Yes, dear, now eat your squash," Danielle insisted.

"You're wiser than your years, Celeste," Yononnon chortled as he gazed down at her adoringly.

Jack smiled as he looked around the table. He turned when Frank leaned forward.

"Yononnon, at the end of the prayer you added 'Monomay, hold your children close'. Can you help us understand?"

Jack watched as Yononnon shifted in his seat, uncertain. When he moved to speak, Celeste spoke up.

"I know, Grandpa," she chirped. "Poppa taught me."

Frank glanced at Yononnon then at Celeste.

Jack pulled on a smile. "Of course you can, Celeste. Wouldn't it be nice to hear what Trager has taught his daughter, Frank?" Jack stated.

"Ah, certainly," Frank replied.

Celeste grinned at the sudden attention. "Monomay, the patient, is mother of the Eldatek. She watches over them and reminds them that when things seem difficult, that if they are patient like she is, the universe will correct itself."

To Jack's amazement, Yononnon reached out to Celeste and stroked her long black hair.

"I couldn't have said it better myself," the large subcommander replied. "Your father has taught you well."

Celeste beamed at his praise.

Frank and Danielle's continued silence caused Yononnon to look up. Jack moved to speak but Yononnon smiled gently at Frank, then Danielle.

"It should comfort you that many cultures across the galaxy hold similar beliefs to your own—a nurturing being who comforts us in difficult times and provides us with an understanding of right and wrong. Without this knowledge, we would all fall into despair."

Frank paused then nodded. "You're right, Yononnon. Celeste, your father has taught you well."

Jack sat back in his chair, relieved. The peaceful moment was shattered when the base's computer sounded in his mind. He looked over at Yononnon who was already on his feet.

"What's the matter?" Danielle gasped, when Jack was out of his chair moments after Yononnon.

"A ship has just crossed the defense net," Jack announced. "It's Dramudam."

"Please stay here until we've confirm who's onboard," Yononnon urged.

Together, Jack and Yononnon raced down the hallway to the Communications room. Jack pulled stun weapons out of the weapons cabinet and tossed one to Yononnon. Yononnon caught it with one hand and slipped it onto his waist in one fluid motion.

"Computer, establish a comms link with the approaching Dramudam craft," he ordered in Intergaltic.

"Communications established," the computer announced aloud.

"Approaching Dramudam scout ship, please identify yourself," Jack stated aloud in Intergaltic.

"Alpha Charlie One requesting permission to land, Colonel," a familiar voice replied in English.

Jack's heart caught in his throat as he heard the voice. "Alpha Charlie one, you are cleared for landing! Perkins, you young pup! What brings you back?" he called back in English.

"I've finished my training and I'm here to relieve Subcommander Yononnon," Perkins replied.

"We'll be waiting for you in the hangar bay. I'll have a cold beer waiting for you, Stern out."

Jack couldn't help but grin as he pulled the stun weapon from his waist and placed it back into the weapons cabinet. "I can't believe he's back."

"It's good to hear he's completed his training, Jack. As much as I've enjoyed being here, my presence has been a violation of the Isolation Treaty," Yononnon confessed.

Jack looked over at the large Eldatek male. "Not so fast, Subcommander, we have a tradition whenever we change out personnel. You have to have a drink with us. Perkins must be thirsty after travelling so far and we have to catch up on the news from the Tollon."

Yononnon's black eyes sparkled at his suggestion. "I can't go against a tradition—I will stay until first kel to help celebrate Perkins completing his training."

"Excellent! Now, let's tell the others about the great news," Jack replied. His mind was spinning at the prospect of seeing his friend, Perkins, again. He hated to admit how much he'd missed him.

****

Perkins landed his Dramudam long-distance one-seat scout inside of the hangar of Forrorrois' covert base on Earth. He never thought he would be so happy to be home again. Still, he was nervous as he glanced back toward the steps that led down to the rear cabin. Alham decided to remained below until he decided whether or not to tell Yononnon that she had arrived with him to avoid arrest for assaulting a council high guard—even though she had done it to protect him.

"I'll let you know when it's safe to come out," Perkins called back.

"I'll wait," Alham called back up the steps.

He spotted Jack, Yononnon, and Forrorrois' family waiting for him to emerge.

"Here it goes," Perkins whispered to himself as he raised the canopy and extended the cockpit ladder. He pulled off his helmet and grinned, brushing back his blond-hair from his eyes, suddenly aware at how long it had grown over the past few months compared to his regulation buzz cut. Jack met him as he climbed down the ladder. Perkins snapped to attention and saluted him.

"Perkins, reporting for duty, Colonel," he stated.

Jack inspected him, then straightened and returned the salute. "It's good to have you back. And it's just Jack, now."

Perkins remained at attention. "You'll always be colonel to me, sir."

Jack nodded with approval. "At ease, Airman."

"Thank you, sir!" Perkins replied with a grin as he finally dropped his hand to his side.

"Look at you in your Dramudam pilot uniform," Jack remarked. "Very sharp!"

"Master Pilot," Yononnon observed. "He no longer has a grey novice strip on his pant leg."

"I stand corrected, Master Pilot," Jack replied.

"Unca Perkins! You're dressed like Poppa," she squealed.

Perkins crouched down and caught her as she ran into his arms. He hugged her tight, grinning. "I've missed you, Peanut," he whispered.

"I've missed you, too," she whispered back.

Perkins looked up as Frank, Danielle, and George approached and let Celeste go.

"You look so handsome," Danielle commented as he stood up to greet her.

"Thank you, ma'am," he replied.

"So do you have any word on Danica?" Frank asked.

Perkins paused, glancing toward Jack. "She is still working on a way to free Trager from Elda," he answered.

"Celeste?" Danielle suddenly said, glancing around. "George, did you see where she went?"

Perkins looked around. His heart stopped when he spotted her at the top of the ladder climbing into the cockpit of his single-seat long-distance.

"I'll get her, Mrs. Jolan," Yononnon stated.

Before Perkins could stop him, Yononnon was up the ladder extended from the side of his scout after Celeste. By the time Perkins climbed up after him, Yononnon was staring back down at him.

"Do you have something to tell me, Master Pilot?" Yononnon asked in a quiet but stern voice.

"Grandma! There's a pretty lady in the ship!" Celeste announced, peering over the edge of the cockpit.

Perkins slowly climbed back down the ladder, keeping his eyes on the large Eldatek male looming over him. "Yes, sir! I—I can explain, sir," Perkins began.

Alham appeared behind Yononnon and quietly slipped from behind him then climbed down the ladder and stood beside Perkins.

"Yononnon, isn't that Alham, your niece?" Jack observed.

Perkins glanced over at Jack then Yononnon and swallowed.

The large subcommander scooped up Celeste and carried her down the ladder. "Celeste, please go to your grandmother," he said, pointing the little girl toward Danielle. "Yes, Jack, this is my niece, Alham," Yononnon replied.

"Frank, I think we need to give them a moment to discuss this in private," Jack urged, watching Celeste run over to Danielle with an uncertain look on her face.

"Of course, George, Danielle, let's give them a moment," Frank replied, gently taking his wife's arm and Celeste's hand.

When Jack turned to follow them out, Perkins called out in Intergaltic. "Jack, stay, please?"

Jack glanced over at Yononnon. The large Eldatek male gave him a brisk nod.

After Forrorrois' family had left the hangar, Perkins looked back at Yononnon. He knew he'd better start talking and fast.

"Explain why Alham is here!" Yononnon ordered in Intergaltic.

"It's not what you think, Subcommander," Perkins began.

"It better not be," Yononnon replied darkly.

Perkins swallowed hard. "I brought Alham here to prevent her from being arrested and taken back to Elda."

"I cannot believe that my niece would do anything that would result in her being arrested under Eldatek law," Yononnon stated incredulously.

Perkins glanced at Alham beside him then over at Yononnon—uncertain what to say.

Yononnon's eyes widened when the silence in the hangar bay deepened. He threw a startled glance at Alham. "Is this true?"

"Yes, Subcommander," Alham replied, holding the large subcommander's gaze. "I didn't want to involve you, so I was going to hide on Perkins' scout until you left for the Tollon."

"What are the charges?" Yononnon pressed.

Alham dropped her gaze to the floor. "Assaulting a member of the Council High Guard," she confessed.

Perkins was surprised when Yononnon gasped and took a step back—the color draining from his chestnut-brown face.

"Please, sir, Alham was defending me from a spy on the Tollon. This spy ambushed me in the hangar bay when I was preparing to leave the Tollon," Perkins insisted. "She would have killed me except Alham stopped her."

"You are certain she was High Guard?" Yononnon asked Alham.

"Yes, sir. I saw the inverted red triangle mark at the base of her skull," Alham answered, her gaze still cast to the ground.

"This is serious. I apologize, Perkins," Yononnon replied, his shoulders sagging slightly. "You were right to take Alham off the Tollon, but she can't stay on Earth. Like my presence here, it's a violation of the Isolation Treaty."

"Please, Yononnon, there is a way I can stay," Alham whispered, taking Perkins arm.

Reflexively, Perkins placed a comforting hand on Alham's. His action wasn't lost on Yononnon, who took a deep breath as her suggestion sunk in. The large subcommander cautiously closed the distance between them and gently rested his hand on his niece's shoulder.

"Alham, what you are suggesting will only allow you to stay on Earth and not violate the Isolation Treaty," Yononnon whispered back in concern. "But it won't prevent the council from hunting you down and taking you back to Elda for trial."

"Please, Uncle, I care for him!" she pleaded. "I know I don't need it from you, but as my only relative present, please give me your blessing!"

Slowly, Yononnon turned to Jack. "Do you vouch for the character of this subordinate?"

Jack glanced at Perkins and Alham then smiled. He looked back over at Yononnon and nodded. "Yes, I would trust him with my life—and have on multiple occasions—he's been a loyal friend."

Perkins felt his heart begin to pound when Yononnon studied

him hard. "Is this what you want, Master Pilot Perkins?" the subcommander finally asked him.

Perkins nodded his head. "Yes, sir, I care for Alham and wish for her to remain here on Earth with me."

Perkins watched as Yononnon weighed his words while Alham tightened her grip on his arm.

Yononnon looked at his niece. "Alham, as Aasha ka Felia, second daughter of Felia ka Wil'Amay of Elda, you are free to make your choice with no expectations or support from your family," Yononnon replied formally. "But know that your joining will be witnessed."

Perkins was surprised when tears began to stream down Alham's face. "Thank you, Uncle," she cried as she released Perkins arm and hugged Yononnon fiercely.

Jack walked over to Perkins and slapped him on the back. "I guess there's going to be a wedding," he stated in English.

Perkins' nodded. "I guess so," he replied back in English, suddenly feeling a bit shaky.

"Do you love her?" Jack asked.

Stunned, Perkins stared at Jack, surprised at his question. Then he spotted Alham's beautiful clay-brown face. An excitement filled him as she glanced back at him and smiled. "Yes, I do love her," he confessed.

"Good, that's all I need to know," Jack replied. "We'd better tell the Jolans," he continued in a louder voice, switching back to Intergaltic. "I'm certain that Danielle will enjoy having another female to talk to and help with Celeste after being stuck with all of us males."

Yononnon crossed over to Perkins and bowed to him. "Please, Perkins, come with me," Yononnon said in Intergaltic. "I need to explain the Joining ceremony to you."

Perkins looked nervously at Yononnon with his formal request, uncertain whether he should bow back then he decided he should. "All right," he replied with a quick bow.

Yononnon nodded with approval then motioned to Jack. "Jack, if you could take Alham to Danielle, there are preparations that must be made. As the head female, Danielle will need to be informed of the ceremony."

"Of course," Jack replied, offering his arm to Alham.

Alham glanced down at Jack's arm, uncertain, and then she encircled his forearm with hers. Sniffing back the tears, she smiled and wiped them from her face.

Perkins watched as Jack led Alham away then swallowed hard as Yononnon placed his hand on his shoulder and guided him back to his scout, uncertain what was going to happen in the next few hours.

****

Jack glanced back as he left Perkins with Yononnon, curious what the large Eldatek male had in store for him. All he was certain of was that Yononnon wasn't going to kill his friend for announcing his intent to marry the subcommander's niece. Although, when Alham's grip tightened on his arm, Jack hesitated for a moment then looked back at her as they stepped from the hangar bay into the passage that led into the living quarters of Forrorrois' base.

"You're trembling," Jack remarked in English.

"I'm nervous, Colonel Jack Stern," Alham confessed back in English, glancing at him with her black almond-shaped eyes. "I'm intruding on Forrorrois' family unannounced. What must her mother think of me?"

Jack patted her hand. "You will find that Danielle is a gracious hostess, who will be overjoyed to accommodate a friend of her daughter while she is away. And please, call me Jack."

"Thank you, Jack, you are very kind," Alham replied. "I can see why Perkins thinks so highly of you."

"Are you ready to meet them?" Jack asked.

Alham smoothed her uniform then nodded. "Yes."

"Good."

Jack escorted Alham into the living area and found Danielle and George sitting around the kitchen table. The table had been cleared and he could smell coffee brewing in the kitchen. Danielle stood from her chair and pulled Celeste close to her.

"Danielle, I'd like to introduce Alham, Yononnon's niece," Jack announced.

Celeste grinned and broke from Danielle's hold and ran to Alham. "See, Grandma? I told you she was pretty!"

Alham crouched down and beamed as she traced her fingers on he child's face. "So are you, Celeste, Forrorrois' daughter. You have your mother's lips and cheekbones," she whispered.

"Really? Everyone says I look like my father," the little girl squealed.

"Yes, really," Alham replied in a hushed voice as she stood.

Jack was surprised when Alham suddenly bowed deeply toward Danielle.

"I am honored to be received in your home, Danielle, mother of Danica, Forrorrois to the Dramudam," she stated formally.

Jack watched as Danielle glanced at him, uncertain, then back at Alham. Then he was amazed as she pulled on one her warmest calm smiles as she reached out and clasped Alham's hand in both of hers.

"I'm honored to have the niece of Yononnon here in this home," Danielle replied, guiding her to a chair. "Please sit, Alham," she said as she released her hand, and then turned briefly to her son. "George, could you help your father in the kitchen and bring us some coffee, please? Or do you prefer mawya, Alham?" she asked, turning her attention back to the young Eldatek woman.

Jack marveled at Danielle's gracious skill at setting Alham at ease.

A tentative smile spread across Alham's lips as she nodded her head. "If it isn't too much trouble, I would enjoy some mawya."

Danielle sat then motioned towards the chair next to her. "Of course it's no trouble. George, tell your dad to put on some water. Now, please sit, Alham, you must be exhausted from your long trip."

"Thank you, Danielle, mother of Danica, you are most kind," Alham replied, taking her seat.

"Please, Alham, it's just Danielle," she insisted with a gentle smile.

Alham shyly smiled back.

Jack waited for Danielle to take her seat before he took his own chair beside Alham. "Danielle, Alham trained as a pilot with Danica on the Tollon. They are friends," Jack offered.

Danielle relaxed slightly at his revelation. "It's good to meet a friend of Danica's. Please tell me, do you have news?"

Alham glanced nervously towards Jack.

"Danielle is aware that Trager is awaiting Forrorrois' petition of Penock," Jack explained.

"Oh, that is good she knows," Alham commented. "Danielle, your daughter is my dearest friend. We all pray for her success in raising the joining fee so that she can bring Trager back home to Earth."

Danielle looked down at her hands. "I see."

"You mustn't doubt, Danielle, Danica will succeed," Alham insisted. "I have seen your daughter do amazing things—overcome incredible odds. She is strong and resourceful. She will return with Trager, of that I have no doubt."

Danielle looked up with tears in her eyes. She reached out and took Alham's hands in hers. "Thank you, Alham," she whispered.

Jack looked up when Frank and George came into the room with mugs of coffee and mawya and quickly cleared his throat. Danielle pulled on a strong front and nodded to George as he set the mug of mawya in front of Alham. Jack smiled to himself as George then retreated to the other side of the table and took a seat next to his father.

"Alham, I'd like to introduce you to my husband, Frank, and my son, George," Danielle said with a warm smile as she released Alham's hands.

"I'm pleased to meet you both," Alham replied as she stood from her chair and bowed to them.

Jack stifled a smile when Frank and George stood quickly and bowed back, before resuming their seats.

"She's Yononnon's niece," Danielle added. "And she served with Danica on the Tollon. They were in pilot training together."

"Oh?" Frank remarked. "It's a pleasure to meet you, Alham. Are you staying long?"

Jack sensed Alham's panic at the question and touched her arm to reassure her. "Frank, Danielle, Alham is here with Perkins. She and Perkins are going to be married."

Danielle's eyes widened, then she began to smile. "Well, I'll be! I never thought I would see the day!"

Alham gave Danielle a confused look then glanced at Jack.

"She means she thought Perkins was never going to find the right woman," Jack explained.

"Oh?" Alham replied.

"Don't worry, Alham, Perkins is a wonderful young man. Congratulations!" Danielle inserted quickly. "Jack, why did you keep us all in suspense?! When's the wedding?"

Jack grinned. "Tonight—Yononnon is preparing Perkins for the ceremony as we speak."

"That doesn't leave us anytime for a bachelor party," George scoffed.

"I don't understand," Alham stammered.

"Never mind them," Danielle replied. "There are a million things we need to do! What are you going to wear?"

"Ah…I haven't really thought about it," Alham confessed. "I have a robe from Elda that I could wear."

"That sounds perfect," Danielle replied. "Is there anything else you might need? I'm not familiar with your customs."

"Well, the joining ceremony is performed in silence," Alham said carefully. "All that is truly necessary is a meditation sphere, a ceremonial knife, and a special ya all of which I have in my bag on Perkins' ship."

Jack kept his face impassive when Danielle's eyes flickered towards his at the mention of a ceremonial knife.

"Oh, that's good, you'll have to explain the ceremony to me as we make the preparations," Danielle replied, regaining her composure.

"Danielle," Alham asked, hesitantly, "I must ask you a great request, though. As the head female of this household, would you do me the honor of witnessing our joining?"

Danielle's eyes softened. "Of course I would. It would be my great honor."

"Thank you," Alham breathed in relief. Then she glanced toward Jack. "There is another matter, that I must ask you about—in private," Alham remarked.

Danielle's eyes widened slightly. Then she rose from her chair and took Alham's elbow. "I understand, come with me. Celeste, please stay here with your Uncle Jack."

Jack took Celeste's little hand in his and smiled when she resisted as they left down the hallway for some privacy.

"Why can't I go with them?" Celeste pouted.

"Because they have to talk about big girl stuff," Jack replied. "Someday your mom will have the same talk with you."

He tried not to smile when Celeste pulled her hand from his then heaved a sigh as she crossed her arms without a word.

"I can't believe it, Perkins is taking the plunge—and with Yononnon's niece! Does the guy have a death wish, or what?" George asked with a shake of his head. "Did you see the look on Yononnon's face when he found her on Perkins' ship? He didn't look too happy."

"He's right, you know," Frank replied. "Maybe we should check on Perkins to make certain Yononnon didn't hurt him."

"Perkins is fine," Jack laughed. "I wouldn't have left him with the subcommander if I thought otherwise. Besides, they're going to be in-laws—they need to get to know one another."

"Ah, you don't think it's a shotgun wedding, do you?" George blurted out.

Jack's eyes opened wide then he glanced down at Celeste. "No, I seriously doubt that, George."

"Tone it down, George, we've got some tender ears in the room," Frank added.

"Sorry," George replied. "I was just thinking that they spent a lot of time alone, travelling back to Earth…"

"George…" Frank warned.

"OK," George apologized.

"Frank, can you watch Celeste while I check on Perkins and Yononnon and see if they need anything for the joining ceremony?"

"Sure. Come here, Peanut," Frank replied.

Jack let Celeste cross over to Frank, then rose from the table and headed for the hangar bay. He couldn't bear to tell the Jolans that Alham was hiding on Earth from the same people that had taken Celeste. For now, he wanted this to be a joyous occasion.

CHAPTER 22

Forrorrois maneuvered her shrouded two-seat long-distance scout into orbit over Elda. The day had arrived for her to bid for Trager's freedom against Bohata in front of the Council of Elda. Smoothing the forest-green Eldanese robes that Leenon had given her to wear, Forrorrois glanced at Collinar when he shifted in the jump seat beside her.

"What's on your mind?" she asked.

Collinar glanced back at her—the arrogant flash in his golden feline eyes was absent. "After this cycle, you'll have Trager back—Guruma's contribution to the remaining balance of your joining fee has ensured that. All that's left is for you to speak on my behalf so that my remaining sentence at the Dramudam Rehabilitation station will be commuted."

"That's true," she replied. "Are you having second thoughts?" she asked.

Collinar gave her an odd look. "Why would you say that?" he replied. "Why wouldn't I want to be free?"

"No reason," Forrorrois replied, with a shrug. "You've just been pretty quiet since we reached the Eldatek solar system."

"I'm just bored," he deflected. "Although, I do wish I could see Neeha's face when you outbid Bohata," he remarked with a renewed flash in his eyes.

Forrorrois looked at her sensors and nodded. "I'm looking forward to seeing that look myself," she admitted. She looked over at her sensors and sighed. "Here comes the Tollon, we'll meet Leenon and Commander Thoren on the surface."

With a few adjustments, Forrorrois dropped the EM warping shield that shrouded her ship from Elda's sensors and smiled to herself when an urgent message was transmitted from the surface.

"Forrorrois, hold your position until the council has approved your clearance to approach Elda."

Collinar chuckled as he rose from his chair. "You still have a lot to learn about diplomacy…I'd better go to the cargo hold. My presence may cause further irritation."

"Probably a good idea," she replied. The Tollon approached her position and settled into orbit. She watched as two Dramudam scouts left the hangar bay from the underside of the large Peace ship and headed for the space port near the capital city that sprawled in the desert below her position.

Shortly after they landed a second transmission came from Elda.

"Forrorrois, you are clear to approach the terminal. Remain on your craft after you have landed. The council guard will escort you to the council chamber."

"Understood," Forrorrois replied.

She set the coordinates for the terminal and guided her scout in. When she landed, she was surprised to see Subcommander Peldor emerge from one of the Dramudam scouts and approach her craft. She rose from her command chair and went into the cargo hold. Collinar was already on his feet.

"I think Peldor is here to take you back to the Tollon during the proceedings," Forrorrois stated.

Collinar rolled his eyes. "I assumed this would happen."

"Do you have everything?" she asked, sensing his internal hesitation.

Collinar straightened. "Yes," he said as he with drew the small sack from his vest pocket. "I want to thank you for the profitable venture."

Forrorrois nodded. "The next time we meet will be at the Rehabilitation center. I'm certain that Peldor will think more kindly of you if you give me the stun weapon you lifted from Motan." She punctuated her words with a glance at the weapon strapped visibly to his thigh.

Collinar sighed as he loosened the holster from his leg and handed her the weapon still sheathed inside.

Forrorrois took the bundled, patiently. "Anything else?"

Collinar hesitated, and then sighed once more. "Yes." He drew the ceremonial blade that he had concealed in his vest in a fluid motion.

Forrorrois eyed him for a moment as he turned the blade over in his hand then he paused in reflection. With a sigh he reversed the blade and handed her the knife, handle first.

"Forrorrois...please accept this small token," Collinar said.

She glanced down at the blade, surprised when he offered her the knife as a gift rather than as a forced disarmament. As she touched the blade, an image of Ma'Kelda giving him the blade filled her mind. His reluctance to relinquish the cherished relic seeped into her mind.

"Of course, but only on the condition that you'll accept it back when you are free," she replied, gently taking the blade from him and placing both the blade and the holstered stun weapon inside the weapons cabinet.

Collinar gave her a hard stare as the door panel slid shut. Then he snorted. "I'll believe that when I see open space again."

She shook her head as she turned towards the side hatch and silently ordered the panel open. Forrorrois knew his bravado masked his moment of melancholy and allowed him his arrogant front. Shifting her gaze through the opening, she saw Peldor salute her from the deck of the terminal when the ramp extended.

"It does this old Gintzer's heart good to see you in one piece, Forrorrois," Peldor stated after she saluted him back.

"It's good to see you too, Subcommander," Forrorrois said with a grin.

Peldor came up the ramp and cautiously eyed Collinar. "Are you ready to return to the Tollon, Collinar?" he asked.

"No," Collinar replied, holding out his wrists to the Gintzer. "But I doubt that you will take no for an answer."

Peldor grinned, showing his small chewing teeth between his curved lower tusks. "I see your time with Forrorrois has improved your sense of humor," he replied gruffly while he secured Collinar's wrist with restraints. "I half expected you would run before you made it back to my custody."

Collinar shrugged. "I gave it some thought, but Forrorrois charmed me into staying."

Peldor snorted a laugh. "I will see you back on the Tollon, Forrorrois. Good fortune with your negotiations."

"Thank you, Peldor," Forrorrois said with a halfhearted smile. She watched them walk down the ramp. Alone, her thoughts weighed heavily on the insanity she was about to faced within the hours ahead of her. She looked up at the sound of footfalls approaching her scout. Four red-robed Council High Guards had arrived.

"Forrorrois, we are here by the order of the Elda Council to escort you to the council chamber," one of the Eldatek females announced.

"I'm ready," Forrorrois replied, raising her head high. The multiple pouches of currency weighed heavily in the folds of her forest green robes as she descended the ramp towards the guards.

✸✸✸✸✸✸✸✸✸✸✸

Trager was amazed when the shackles were removed from his ankles and he was given brown slippers for his feet. He smoothed his simple tan robes and didn't say a word as he was escorted from his cell to the council chamber—his hands still restrained at the wrists. The red-robed council guards led him through a door to a balcony that was equidistant between the petitioner's stand and the council's dais. As he looked around, he soon realized that the chamber was packed by female representatives from all the most influential houses of Elda. The council's actions this cycle were going to be watched and analyzed to the nth degree. Guruma was right, change was coming.

His heart pounded in his chest when he spied Forrorrois being led down the center aisle to the petitioner's stand to his left. Leenon was beside her. Forrorrois kept her head high as she ascended the steep steps to her place at the railing. She glanced around the chamber until she spotted him. Trager's heart leapt as her lips parted without a word when their eyes met. Trager moved to rise from his chair, but his guards prevented him. Forrorrois strained against the railing

477

until Leenon touched her arm and shook her head. Her actions were enough to let him know that she was there for him.

A second petitioner's stand suddenly rose from the floor to the right of the center aisle before the council dais and the murmur in the chamber increased while Bohata ascended the steps wearing turquoise robes.

Suddenly, all attention focused on the door at the rear of the council dais when the council members entered the chamber. Everyone rose to their feet until the council members took their seats at the long table on the front edge of the platform. Trager spotted his mother, Neeha, seated at the far end from where he stood. Kil'Treahaa, the senior member of the council, struck her staff on the floor three times to silence the room. Everyone took their seats and strained forward to listen. The time had arrived.

Kil'Treahaa rose from her chair and leaned heavily on her staff. Then she straightened and spoke in a clear voice. "Forrorrois also know as Danica Jolan, daughter of Danielle Jolan of Earth, adopted daughter of Me'Halka Wil'Amay of Elda, second daughter of Wil'Amay of Elda, presently serving in the Dramudam aboard the Tollon: you have been summoned this cycle to pursue your petition of Penock for Haator ka Neeha, second and only living son of Councilor Neeha. Your petition for Penock has been accepted by the Elda Council."

Trager stood silently and watched as Kil'Treahaa turned to face the second petitioner's stand and continued to speak.

"Bohata ka Frolan, first-born daughter of Frolan of Elda, you have been summoned here this cycle to pursue your petition of Slovak for Haator ka Neeha, second and only living son of Councilor Neeha. Your petition of Slovak has been accepted by the Elda Council. Since both claims are legitimate in the eyes of the council, a joining fee was established for each party according to her present rank and the status that they will gain from a recognized joining with Haator ka Neeha, second and only living son of Councilor Neeha. Bohata, was your family able to raise the joining fee of fifty thousand trups?"

Trager watched as all eyes focused on Bohata standing alone on the petitioner stand to his right.

"Yes, Councilor Kil'Treahaa," Bohata replied, pulling a small pouch from the folds of her turquoise robes.

One of the council guards ascended the steps and took the pouch from Bohata. Then she opened the pouch and nodded toward Councilor Kil'Treahaa.

A murmur of approval rippled through the crowed. Trager glanced toward Forrorrois, but she looked straight ahead stoically.

The ancient councilor turned from Bohata to the second petitioner stand. "Forrorrois, was your family able to raise the joining fee of three hundred thousand trups?"

A hush fell across the chamber as the representatives of the houses of Elda turned as one—all eyes focused on his dear sweet ashwan. Forrorrois straightened then nodded.

"Yes, Councilor Kil'Treahaa," Forrorrois replied, pulling a larger pouch from the folds of her deep-green robes.

Trager's heart began to beat faster as the council guard ascended the steps and took the pouch from Forrorrois. Then she opened the pouch and nodded toward Councilor Kil'Treahaa.

To Trager's surprise, a second murmur of approval rippled through the crowed. Trager glanced toward Forrorrois, but she continued to look stoically ahead.

The anticipation in the chamber increased as Councilor Kil'Treahaa looked back at Bohata.

"Both joining fees have been met. Bohata, do you understand what this means?"

"Yes, Councilor," Bohata replied. "I wish to bid for my right of Slovak against Forrorrois' right of Penock. Therefore I raise my original fee to three hundred thousand trups with an additional one hundred thousand trups to open my bid," she stated, pulling a larger pouch from the folds of her robe.

Trager's eyes widened as several members of the crowd gasped at the bold first bid. He looked to Forrorrois and found her conferring with Leenon.

"Forrorrois," Councilor Kil'Treahaa said as she turned to face her. "Are you prepared to counter?"

Forrorrois nodded her head and pulled out two medium sized pouches from her robes. "Yes, Councilor Kil'Treahaa. I will match Bohata's one hundred thousand trups and increase the bid by another one hundred thousand trups."

The chamber began to murmur at Forrorrois' counter bid. Trager's head swam as he realized that the bid was now at five hundred thousand trups.

Kil'Treahaa waited for the council guard to ascend the petitioner's stand and examine the contents of the two pouches. When the guard verified the contents the chamber erupted in excited whispers. Annoyed, Kil'Treahaa struck the floor of the dais multiple times until the chamber grew silent once more.

Trager gazed at Forrorrois in wonder when she glanced at him with a fleeting smile. Then her face became impassive as she stared once again forward.

Kil'Treahaa glanced towards Bohata. "Do you wish to counter, Bohata?"

Bohata straightened then nodded. "Yes, Councilor," she replied. The room grew tense with anticipation as she drew out another pouch from her turquoise robes.

"I raise my bid by another one hundred thousand trups to match Forrorrois' and then increase my bid by another one hundred thousand trups," Bohata announced.

The chamber vibrated from the restrained crowd. Trager had never heard of such a joining fee. Bohata was bankrupting her family to secure her right of Slovak with him. Again the council guard verified the announced bid. The hushed crowd in the chamber turned all eyes to Forrorrois leaning in their seats to hear her response.

"Forrorrois, the amount of the joining fee stands at six hundred thousand trups. Do you wish to counter?" Councilor Kil'Treahaa asked.

Forrorrois paused for a moment, causing the room to tense. Then she pulled out two pouches from her robes. "Councilor Kil'Treahaa, I do counter. I will match Bohata's six hundred thousand trups and raise it with five Prophet Stones."

The crowd in the chamber gasped at the unorthodox bid even before the amount was verified. Trager studied the stunned council as they began to confer with each other. Bohata staggered as she caught the railing. A council guard steadied her.

Kil'Treahaa struck the floor several times with her staff. "Silence! Silence or I will clear this chamber," she ordered.

Finally, the crowd in the chamber grew quiet. Trager looked around room and shared in the amazement of all the females of the prominent houses of Elda as the guard nodded confirmation to Kil'Treahaa that Forrorrois' bid was legitimate.

"Forrorrois, where may I ask did you ever come into possession of Prophet Stones?" Neeha demanded.

Trager stared at his mother, surprised to hear her voice for the first time since the hearing began.

Forrorrois turned toward Neeha and nodded. "They were a gift from a mother to another mother," Forrorrois replied.

Murmurs rippled once more through the chamber, but were quickly silenced at the stare of Councilor Kil'Treahaa. Trager struggled not to smile at Forrorrois' deft answer. No Eldatek female would argue such a statement.

"There is no known value assigned to a single Prophet Stone, let alone five," Councilor Kil'Treahaa stated. "Without a consensus on a value, this bid will have to be suspended."

Trager's heart began to pound at the councilor's words—he looked toward Forrorrois and saw her hands grip the railing tightly in front of her.

"The council needs time to confer," Kil'Treahaa continued. "Clear the chamber."

The room exploded in protest at her order as the females of the prominent houses were taken aback by the unexpected turn of events.

"Clear the chamber!" Kil'Treahaa demanded. "Forrorrois, Me'Hal, and Bohata stay. Guards remove Haator."

Trager jumped to his feet and rushed the railing towards the petition stand that Forrorrois was standing on. "Forrorrois!" he cried out.

"Trager!" Forrorrois cried back, straining against the railing of the petitioner's stand.

The council guards pulled Trager backwards from the railing and pointed a stun weapon at him. Trager broke from their grasp and rushed the railing once more. He was stopped short as the whine of the stun weapon sounded behind him. "Forrorrois," he cried out once more as he crumpled to the floor.

"Trager!" Forrorrois screamed.

Then Trager heard nothing.

*★★★★★★★★★★

Forrorrois strained against Leenon's hold as she saw the council guard fire the stun weapon on her ashwan. "Trager!" she screamed, leaning against the railing, then she fell to her knees as they dragged his unconscious body from the balcony set to one side of the councilor dais in the Council of Elda chamber.

"Leenon, I've done what they asked, what have I done wrong?" she moaned as the door shut at the back of the balcony separating her from Trager once more.

"Get back on your feet," Leenon urged in a hushed whisper. "You must remain strong."

Forrorrois struggled to her feet and leaned heavily against the railing of the petitioner's stand where she and Leenon stood. The chamber had been cleared of everyone except the council members on the council dais, Bohata on the second petitioner's stand to her left and the council guards at all the doors.

"Stand straighter!" Leenon whispered.

Forrorrois stepped from the railing and calmed the anger that washed through her veins. Leenon was right, she thought as she smoothed her forest-green robes. She glanced at Bohata in her turquoise robes and felt her chilling glare. As she looked over at the council, she felt a mix of emotions—several of them surprisingly positive.

"Well played…" Councilor Kil'Treahaa commented as she stepped back to her chair and took her seat.

"Well played?" Neeha exclaimed. "Councilor Kil'Treahaa I must protest!"

Forrorrois was surprised when Neeha fell silent as the elder councilor turned in her seat to face her.

"Protest? Councilor Neeha, what is there to protest?" Kil'Treahaa queried. "Forrorrois has obviously outbid Bohata, and you are about to have your status raised by recognizing the joining between Forrorrois and your second born to an obviously very wealthy and powerful off-world family. And the offer of Prophet Stones—who would have thought that a lowly Dramudam would possess five of them, let alone even one."

"But she is an off-worlder!" Neeha moaned.

"Who's provided a female child—an empath—a rarity here on Elda," Kil'Treahaa countered.

Forrorrois straightened as she listened to the elder. *I haven't lost!* But then she felt heaviness in her heart and looked over at Bohata. Her sorrow tugged at her as the female leaned heavily against the railing of her petitioner's stand. Tears welled in her eyes as she sensed Bohata's loss.

"I don't have to accept the joining fee!" Neeha spat. "It is my right! Bohata was my first born son's joined one. I will not throw her into the street. Talman's name will not be disgraced in whispers that he was unable to provide Bohata a female heir. Haator will redeem his brother's name. He will provide Bohata with an heir."

Kil'Treahaa sighed and glanced to Bohata. "Is this what you really want, Bohata? Do you really believe that joining with Haator will give you this heir?"

Bohata looked up at Kil'Treahaa and tightened her grip on the railing. Forrorrois studied her as she sensed fear radiating from her— instead of the hope that should have been there.

"It was my hope," Bohata replied, looking away from Kil'Treahaa's prying eyes.

"Bohata, please," Kil'Treahaa whispered. "It's time for the truth."

Bohata's eyes grew wide. "It's past time for the truth," she wailed as she clutched the railing.

Kil'Treahaa rose from her chair and stepped to the railing of the council dais. "Bohata, it's never too late for the truth."

Bohata bit her lip and gazed up at the vaulted ceiling. Then her shoulder's sagged. "It wasn't Talman's fault," Bohata stated in a hushed voice.

Forrorrois looked at Leenon, confused, but Leenon placed her hand on her arm and shook her head for her to remain silent.

"What?" Neeha whispered, her full attention now on Bohata.

"Talman was able to sire a child," Bohata whispered. "I was the one who was unable to carry one."

The chamber fell into a deathly silence as Bohata slid to her knees. Forrorrois gasped at the overwhelming shame that washed towards her from the other petitioner's stand.

"Talman never told anyone, he loved me. When he died, my heart broke," the Eldatek female sobbed, crumpled in her turquoise robes. "But I soon realized that without him or an heir, my ties to Neeha were dissolved. Forgive me, Forrorrois, but Celeste was my only hope. With her I would have an heir that would have still bound my family to Neeha's. When Neeha gave her back to you in exchange for Haator, I was still faced with the same dilemma."

Stunned, Forrorrois stared at Bohata.

"Why didn't you tell me," Neeha whispered. "I love you like my own daughter. If I had known, I would never have sent Celeste away."

Forrorrois moved to object, but again Leenon stayed her.

"I would have brought disgrace to your family and my own, Neeha," Bohata replied. "At least now you are free of my charade."

"But your family! You're Frolan's only daughter, there isn't another to carry on your family's name," Neeha stammered.

To Forrorrois' surprise Neeha turned to her and Leenon and dropped to her knees.

"Forrorrois, have pity on this female and her family!" Neeha wept. "There must be a way."

Shook by the sudden plea, tears spilled onto Forrorrois' cheeks as the once proud Neeha was reduced to begging for her assistance. She moved to speak, but the sound of hooves on the gray stone tiles of the chamber made her turn to the center aisle. She gasped as Nur stepped forward with Guruma on his back—his red bat-like wings presented in their full splendor as he tossed his fiery red mane and tail. Several guards rushed from their posts at the doorways with their staffs poised, but Kil'Treahaa waved them back.

"This meeting is a closed one, Guruma," she stated.

"I beg your permission to address the council, Councilor Kil'Treahaa, I have information that may be of value," Guruma requested as he slid from Nur's back and straightened his forest-green Dramudam tunic.

"What information would this lowly male have in this matter?" Neeha spat.

"Please, Councilor Kil'Treahaa, I know that the council does not recognize the authority of the Dramudam and my presence means nothing. But both Forrorrois and Haator are under the authority of their commander, Thoren ka Loh'Haa. I beg in the name of Loh'Haa ka Zelle'Fah, please hear what I have to say," Guruma pleaded, falling to his knees and averting his eyes.

Stunned, Forrorrois looked down from her petitioner's stand at Guruma and then over to Leenon in confusion, but Leenon cautioned her to remain quiet.

Neeha froze when Guruma invoked Loh'Haa ka Zelle'Fah's name.

Kil'Treahaa's jaw dropped at his words then dismissed Neeha with a glance and studied Guruma for a moment. With a sigh, she nodded. "In honor of my aunt, Loh'Haa ka Zelle'Fah, may she slumber in Monomay's arms, I will allow it. Rise and face the council, Guruma."

Forrorrois glanced at Leenon, uncertain.

"Kil'Treahaa is Commander Thoren's cousin," Leenon whispered.

"Loh'Haa ka Zelle'Fah was Thoren's mother, but he was orphaned when she died shortly after he was born because the joining was unsanctioned."

"Oh?" Forrorrois whispered back with a raised eyebrow.

"Thank you, Councilor Kil'Treahaa," Guruma said with a deep bow, touching his head to the stone floor. Then he stood and looked upward at the dais.

Forrorrois hid her amusement as Neeha sat back in her chair and glowered.

"There seems to be several matters here, spoken and unspoken," Guruma began. "Me'Hal, are you aware of the situation that your niece, Aasha ka Felia, is in?"

Forrorrois turned to Leenon, surprised. "What situation? What's happened with Alham?"

Before Leenon was able to answer, Neeha began to chuckle. "Assaulting a member of the Council High Guard and then running instead of facing justice? I would call that more than a situation, Me'Hal, I would call that a scandal."

Forrorrois touched Leenon's arm. "Is this true?"

Leenon nodded, her gaze cast to the ground. "Yes, it's true."

"Tell Forrorrois where the incident occurred," Guruma pressed.

Leenon looked up. "It happened on the hangar deck of the Tollon."

At loss for words, Forrorrois stared at Leenon.

"Very odd," Guruma replied. "Now why would a council high guard even be on a Dramudam ship…wearing the uniform of a Dramudam master pilot?"

"This is all very amusing," Neeha broke in hastily, "but I don't see the relevance to what we are discussing."

Kil'Treahaa glanced toward Neeha, then Guruma and shrugged. "I'll allow it for the moment. Please proceed Guruma, but don't take too long in getting to your point."

"Thank you, Councilor," Guruma said with a nod. "My point is that a council high guard was planted on the Tollon as a spy and saboteur…"

"Careful, Guruma," Kil'Treahaa interjected. "What you are suggesting is highly inflammatory."

"Understood," Guruma replied. "Aasha ka Felia was performing her duty as a Master pilot of the Dramudam, and as a friend to Forrorrois, when she intervened on an assault on Captain Perkins, a human whom Forrorrois had sent to the Tollon to complete his pilot training. Aasha's actions were honorable, as she defended Captain Perkins from an assailant who later was identified as a member of the Council High Guard."

"I see," Kil'Treahaa remarked, glancing towards Neeha. "I was unaware that any high guard was assigned to a Dramudam ship. This is highly irregular."

Forrorrois studied Neeha as she shifting nervously in her seat without another word.

"Yes, it is," Guruma replied.

"Is Perkins all right, Guruma?" Forrorrois called down to him.

Guruma smiled up at her. "Yes, Forrorrois, Leenon patched him up before he headed back to Earth. Unfortunately, Aasha ka Felia disappeared shortly before she could be taken into custody. Her whereabouts are still unknown."

Forrorrois stared back at Leenon. "Why didn't you tell me?"

"There wasn't time before the petition," Leenon whispered.

Kil'Treahaa heaved a sigh. "Guruma, your point?"

"Yes, Councilor," Guruma replied. "My point is that Aasha ka Felia is facing charges that, if all the facts were revealed, would prove to be an embarrassment to the council. Bohata has an equally embarrassing situation that could cause the end of her family line if it were revealed. I would like to suggest a possible solution that may allow all to save face."

Forrorrois sensed Bohata's interest peak as she stared down at Guruma from her petitioner's stand. Leenon gripped Forrorrois' hand as she too stood at rapt attention.

Kil'Treahaa leaned forward. "I'm listening."

"I suggest that Neeha accept the original joining fee from Bohata for the opportunity that she may have a female child from Neeha's line through Haator," Guruma began.

Forrorrois trembled at his suggestion as Neeha sat up in her chair.

"Are you suggesting that Haator remain on Elda?" Neeha questioned.

"No," Guruma replied. "But I am suggesting that Bohata still needs the opportunity to keep her ties with your family through a female heir."

"But Guruma, there is a fact that you are missing," Kil'Treahaa stated.

"Ah, yes, a rather delicate matter," Guruma replied, glancing toward Bohata.

Forrorrois felt shame radiate from Bohata at the wordless fault. Her heart ached for the Eldatek female. "What about a surrogate?" Forrorrois blurted out.

"A surrogate?" Kil'Treahaa questioned.

"Yes, a surrogate to carry the child," Forrorrois replied. "Bohata said she was able to conceive, she just wasn't able to carry full term. All she would need is someone to carry the child for her."

"This is extremely irregular," Neeha spat.

"No more irregular than you kidnapping Celeste from my home and giving her to Bohata," Forrorrois spat back.

They both froze when Kil'Treahaa rapped the floor with her staff. "Enough! This is not the time to reopen old wounds. Forrorrois, are you offering to carry this child?"

Forrorrois felt all eyes focused on her. She turned and faced Bohata then nodded. "Yes, for Bohata, I would carry this child."

Bohata's eyes glistened as she gripped the railing.

Leenon shook her head. "No, this won't work. I'm sorry," she stated. "Forrorrois' body would reject the child—she would never carry to full term."

"Why not, Leenon, I carried Celeste?" Forrorrois countered.

"Yes, but she was part human, this child will be full Eldatek—from Bohata and Haator—the chance for complications would be extremely high," Leenon replied. "I'm sorry, Bohata. Without a willing Eldatek female this will never happen."

Neeha shook her head in defeat. "No Eldatek female would offer. It's just not done."

Forrorrois stared at the council in disbelief. Anger welled up inside her. "How can you say that?"

"It is the way of Elda," Bohata sobbed. "To be a surrogate would be to give up ones power."

"This is true," Kil'Treahaa admitted.

"But there might be one who is willing," Guruma insisted. "One who would gain much and no one would need to know the details of the actual birth. A genetic test after the birth would erase all doubt that the child was Bohata's and Haator's. And all of Elda would be enriched by the compassion that was shown by the council and Neeha for Bohata's family."

Kil'Treahaa leaned forward in her chair. "I'm listening, Guruma."

"I suggest Aasha ka Felia—she is a second born female, with an older sister that has already produced an heir. I suspect that she would find the terms acceptable, if the charges of assaulting a member of the council's high guard were dropped, and that she was free to pursue her own life and to be joined with whom ever she chooses without interference from her family or the council."

Kil'Treahaa tapped her fingers against her staff as she sat back. "You ask much, Guruma."

"I could monitor the pregnancy personally," Leenon offered. "No one else would know, Bohata's privacy would be ensured."

Kil'Treahaa glanced to Neeha. "Would you agree to this? Haator is your only living son."

Forrorrois felt Neeha's gaze and looked up at her. The animosity had dissolved. Forrorrois nodded to her. Neeha turned to Bohata. "Is this what you want, Bohata?" she asked.

Bohata bit her lip and nodded. "Yes, Neeha, I want to reestablish the bond between our families. A female child from Haator will be enough and satisfy our laws. After that, Haator should be free to return to Forrorrois...their joining is strong...no one should divide them."

Forrorrois began to shake as the tears pressed for release. She gripped the railing tightly as Leenon slipped her arm around her waist to steady her.

Neeha turned to face Kil'Treahaa. Forrorrois held her breath.

"Councilor Kil'Treahaa, if Aasha ka Felia agrees to act as a surrogate for a female child between Bohata and Haator, then I will allow it. I will also agree to allow Haator to remain with Forrorrois," Neeha stated.

Forrorrois covered her mouth as the tears streamed down her cheeks. "Thank you, honored mother—praise will be raised in your name to Monomay for your grace and justice," she said as she bowed deeply to Neeha.

As she looked up she saw Neeha was visibly shaken by her unexpected words.

Councilor Kil'Treahaa smiled at her reaction. "Then the council has decided," she announced. "A statement will be released that it is the council's decision to allow Bohata a female child from Haator to secure the family ties with Neeha, after which Haator will return to his joining with Forrorrois. Bohata will provide a joining fee of fifty thousand trups to Neeha for this service. Forrorrois will provide three hundred thousand trups plus three of the five Prophet Stones to Neeha to compensate her for the joining fee that was not originally paid when she initially joined with Haator. Also, it is my insistence that Neeha publicly acknowledge Celeste as her granddaughter and Forrorrois' heir. Forrorrois, you will make more of an effort to bring Celeste to Elda to visit with Neeha. Haator should come as well. As retribution for her crime against the Council High Guard, Aasha ka Felia must provide community service for a period of one revolution at the discretion of the council. Bohata will go into seclusion for a period of one revolution with both Me'Hal and Aasha attending her, the expense of this seclusion shall be provided by Forrorrois at the cost of one hundred thousand trups. Is this satisfactory, to all parties?"

Forrorrois nodded. "Yes, Councilor Kil'Treahaa."

"Bohata?" the councilor asked.

"Yes, yes I agree!" Bohata called out.

"Neeha?" the councilor asked turning to face her. Forrorrois held her breath as Neeha hesitated.

"Yes," Neeha finally replied. "It is satisfactory."

"Good," Kil'Treahaa said as she rose to her feet with the help of her staff. "Forrorrois, the remaining balance that you bid today will be returned to you as compensation for your separation from Haator since his return from the Plane of Deception. Guruma, I suggest that you bring Aasha ka Felia to me personally so that I can hear her agree to the terms. As soon as we have her commitment, I will have the statement released to the Houses of Elda. After that, Me'Hal will be provided access to Haator to prepare him."

Guruma bowed toward the council. "I will return shortly, Councilor Kil'Treahaa." To everyone's surprise, Guruma mounted Nur and galloped back up the center aisle with Nur's wings unfolding. Then the two vanished as they before they reached the great doors. Forrorrois grinned at Guruma's exit and turned back to the council dais. She was surprised at the sly smile that graced Councilor Kil'Treahaa's lips.

Forrorrois watched as Neeha and the second councilor rose from their table and followed Kil'Treahaa out of the chamber. Then Bohata was lead away. Forrorrois turned when the council guard ascended the steps towards her and Leenon. The guard paused then pulled three pouches from the folds of her red robes and handed them to her. As Forrorrois took them, the guard bowed toward her and motioned toward the stairs. Up to this point she had never felt more than contempt from the Council High Guards, this sudden sign of respect took her by surprise. Forrorrois nodded back and then Leenon and she descended the steps. Her head was swimming from the decision. Now, all she could hope was that Alham and Trager would agree to the terms as well.

****

Perkins stood in the living room of Forrorrois' base in front of the makeshift altar Yononnon had helped him prepare for the joining ceremony. He glanced over at the large Dramudam subcommander and tried to smile when he nodded to him with encouragement. Then he glanced over towards Jack, Frank and George and felt his stomach summersault nervously. Suddenly, his eyes were drawn to the hallway as Alham entered the room with Danielle dressed in her flowing burnt orange Eldanese robes. His nerves vanished as he stared into her large almond-shaped black eyes. He had never seen her with her glossy black hair free of her traditional loose braid—except after the fight with the member of the High Guard—his eyes traced the single raven lock entwined with a turquoise cord similar to the one Yononnon had placed in his short blond-hair. Perkins moved to speak but hesitated when Yononnon shook his head. Desperately, he ran the subcommander's instructions over in his mind.

Alham smiled demurely at him as he lifted the bowl of ya from the table and sipped from it then he handed the ya to her. She took the bowl from him and raised it to her lips, but stopped when the sound of footsteps came from the hall. Everyone followed her gaze.

Perkins was shocked to see Guruma standing, in the flesh, before him.

"Guruma!" Alham gasped.

Perkins glanced at Jack and Forrorrois' family as they nervously held their positions—uncertainty plain on their faces.

"Alham, please forgive me for my timing," Guruma apologized in Intergaltic, "but I must speak to you before you drink that ya."

"Forgive me, honored founder, but I'm about to be joined," Alham replied back in Intergaltic.

"Please, indulge me, Alham. Perkins, I must speak with Alham alone," Guruma insisted.

Perkins was shocked when Alham handed him back the bowl of ya.

"I'm sorry, Perkins, I'll be right back," she whispered.

Forrorrois: Tears of Many Mothers

Perkins watched her leave with Guruma down the hallway. Jack crossed over to Perkins with Yononnon. "What's going on?" Jack whispered in Intergaltic.

Perkins shook his head. "I don't know. Yononnon, is this part of the ceremony?"

Yononnon shrugged. "No, but it's an honor to have Guruma appear."

"Is everything all right?" Danielle asked in English.

"I don't know," Jack replied in English. "Alham said she would be right back after she speaks with Guruma."

"I see," Danielle said, glancing back toward the hallway.

The sound of returning footsteps made everyone turn. Guruma stopped at the entrance of the room while Alham came inside and took her place besides Perkins. She reached out and took the bowl from his hands, but to his surprise she set it back down on the makeshift altar with a sigh. Perkins caught his breath as he saw the sadness in her eyes. "Are you all right?" he whispered in Intergaltic.

"No..." she whispered back in Intergaltic. "Perkins, I'm so sorry. I must return to Elda, immediately."

Perkins searched her black eyes as the tears began to stream down her clay-brown cheeks. "Why?" he whispered.

"I've been offered a chance to clear my name," she replied. "After a revolution I will be free to return. Then we can be joined...if you will still have me?"

Confused, Perkins touched her arms lightly. "Of course I would still want you! Why wouldn't I?"

Alham lowered her head. "I must carry a child for another who is unable. I will not be chaste for you."

Perkins lifted his hand and dried the tears from her face with his fingers. "If this is what you must do to clear your name then I understand. Alham, I love you and I still want to be joined with you."

"Oh, Perkins," she sobbed, "I wanted to be joined with you now."

Perkins pulled her tight and rocked her. "I'll come with you, if you want."

"If only you could," she whispered. "I love you so much, Perkins."

"It's time," Guruma gently stated from the hallway.

Perkins tightened his grip as Alham moved to pull away. Then he kissed her forehead as he lightened his hold. Alham touched his face with her fingers as she struggled to smile. Before he could say a word she turned and rushed from the room. Guruma bowed deeply towards Perkins then followed Alham down the hall. Perkins hardly looked up as Jack rested a hand on his shoulder.

"Are you going to be all right?" Jack asked in English.

"No," Perkins replied. "I need to be alone right now."

"Of course," Jack said as he patted his shoulder.

Perkins nodded and walked down the hall to the hangar bay. He half-hoped he would find Alham waiting there for him, but all he saw were the menagerie of Dramudam scout and pursuit ships that stood waiting for the next mission. He climbed the ladder of his one-seat scout and into the cockpit. The tears pressed for release by the time he flopped himself into the command chair. Covering his face he let them flow, his heart breaking as he thought of Alham. Perkins understood duty, but he'd always been the one who had left. Suddenly he understood how hard it was to be the one left behind.

****

Shocked, Trager stared hard at Leenon before him, resplendent in her yellow Eldanese robes, as they stood alone in his gray cell. Her request was completely unheard of. He shook his head in shock.

"Let me get this clear in my head," he began. "You want me to father a child with Bohata and you are telling me that Forrorrois has agreed to this?"

"Yes," Leenon replied. "Once a girl child is conceived you will be free to return with Forrorrois back to Earth."

"I'm sorry, Leenon, but I refuse to join with Bohata," Trager stated. "My brother may have found some part of her that he could be compassionate to, but she repulses me."

"Trager, please, I'm not asking you to physically lay with her. Medical science has other methods to ensure that a female child is conceived. You only need to provide the basic genetic material. As a Med Tech, I would do the rest."

Trager looked at her warily. "And how may I ask are you asking me to provide the genetic material?"

Leenon gave him a wry smile. "I'll leave that up to you."

Trager winced. "All right, if this is the only way Forrorrois and I can finally be together again, I'll do it. But after this, I'm done with Bohata."

Leenon shrugged. "The child will be your daughter too and Celeste's half-sister, it will be hard to completely severe your ties. And think how happy you will be making Neeha."

"Neeha! She's the one who started this mess in the first place," Trager scoffed.

"And believe it or not your mother does love you," Leenon replied.

Trager sighed. "Fine, when can I see Forrorrois again?"

"As soon as the procedure is completed," Leenon said as she turned towards the door. "We will be leaving within the hur. I'll be back for you then."

Trager watched her leave his holding cell then he sat back on his bunk. *Patience,* he reminded himself. The thought of being home again with Forrorrois and Celeste suddenly made him smile.

CHAPTER 23

Forrorrois stood outside the Dramudam Rehabilitation station's hearing chamber awaiting the final decision on Collinar's sentence. She started when she felt Collinar's emotions approach the door from the other side. His pleasure told her that her testimony had swayed the panel.

As the doors opened she could see his pleasure shift to surprise at seeing her standing there.

"Forrorrois, they told me that I was going to be transported to the nearest travel hub. I didn't expect it was going to be by you," Collinar stated with a leer.

Forrorrois knew his words were just bravado and shook them off. "Don't flatter yourself, Collinar—they assigned me since I was the only available Dramudam."

Collinar snorted a laugh. "So when can we leave?"

"Now, if you like," she replied. "I have your things already onboard my long-distance scout."

"Lead the way, my commander," he joked.

Forrorrois sensed an odd stare from a few of the Dramudam leaving the hearing chamber at Collinar's comment. "Let's go," she said as she rolled her eyes.

They walked in silence as they made their way to the hangar deck of the Rehabilitation station. She led Collinar up the ramp and closed the hatch then waved him toward the jump seat beside her command chair. He flopped himself down beside her filled with his self-confident air.

After they had been cleared for take-off, Forrorrois guided her scout away from the station into deep space.

"You can change out of those incarceration overalls. I've put a change of clothes on the bunk for you in the rear cabin."

"Thank you," Collinar replied as he rose from the jump seat.

Forrorrois glanced at him, surprised at his civility. He returned a few minutes later wearing the black mercenary pants and pullover shirt and tan vest with multiple pockets that he seemed to enjoy wearing while he was in the Environs.

"So, what travel hub are you taking me to?" Collinar asked, stepping into the cockpit.

She set the scout on autopilot and rose from her command chair. "I'm not taking you to a travel hub," she replied.

Collinar gave her an odd look. "What do you mean?"

"Excuse me," she said as she brushed past him into the cargo hold.

"Forrorrois, I distinctly heard them say that I was going to be taken to a travel hub where I was free to go wherever I pleased!" Collinar insisted.

His irritation filtered into her mind. Forrorrois struggled to keep the amusement from her face as she opened a metal container in the cargo hold and pulled out a half-meter long object wrapped in a cloth. When she removed the covering, Collinar eyed her cautiously.

"I thought you would rather start your journey sooner," she said as she held out the miniaturized craft to Collinar.

Collinar took the ship from her and examined it with an appraising eye. "This is an Utahar long-distance scout. How did you get it?"

Forrorrois masked the smile from her face. "Let's say I didn't give back all the ships that I shot down a few revolution ago," Forrorrois said with a shrug. "I figured it would be better if I gave it to you once we had some distance between us and the rehabilitation station."

"Does it have weapons?" Collinar asked, glancing up from the scout.

"Yes and few extra fuel cells to get you a couple of hyperfolds from here. I've also made certain that there are supplies to hold you for a few mol," Forrorrois replied, sensing his suspicion.

"Well, this is overly generous," Collinar quipped. "Do you assume I am still in your debt?"

"No, consider all our accounts settled," she answered. "The next time we meet it will be a fresh start. Neither will owe the other."

Collinar narrowed his eyes for a moment then he began to laugh at her veiled threat. "Of course."

Forrorrois turned to the weapons cabinet and pulled out a few items. Collinar's eyes widened as he recognized them.

"I can't send you out there unarmed," Forrorrois said as she handed Collinar the stun pistol still in the holster he had lifted from Motan.

Collinar took the holster and strapped it onto his waist with a gleam in his golden-feline eyes.

"I also want you to take this," Forrorrois said as she handed him his ceremonial blade—handle first.

Collinar looked down at the micro-thin blade then back at her—his lips parted in surprise.

"I made a promise to you that I would return it once you served your time in the Rehabilitation Center," she replied. "Besides, Ma'Kelda would have wanted you to have it back."

Collinar took the ceremonial blade without a word and turned the knife over in his hands. He looked away as he slipped it into the sheath on his holster just behind the stun pistol.

Silently, Forrorrois reached up and lightly touched his golden-tan face with her fingertips—amused by his confusion. Then she stepped up on her tiptoes and leaned in as if to kiss him. As his confusion deepened, she pulled away just as he leaned into the kiss and drew her reduction weapon, firing before his lips met hers.

With a sigh, Forrorrois looked down at his tiny crumpled form and tasted her lips. "Sorry, Collinar, not in this lifetime," she said as she couched down to scoop him up.

✸✸✸✸✸✸✸✸✸✸✸

Collinar started awake in the cockpit of the Utahar long-distance scout that Forrorrois had shown him in her cargo hold. He glanced around and suddenly realized he was in space.

"Have a good nap?" Forrorrois' voice sounded in his cockpit.

Collinar twisted in his seat and spotted Forrorrois' long-distance scout through the canopy of his ship—a chuckled rumbled deep from his chest as he stared at her watching him from her cockpit. "Forrorrois, you never cease to entice me."

"I aim to please," Forrorrois replied. "Have a good flight to wherever you're heading, Collinar. Let's hope we don't meet again soon."

"A shame if we don't, Forrorrois," Collinar replied. "You would have made a superior Utahar."

"From you, I'll take that as a compliment," Forrorrois replied.

Collinar grinned as he set a course and tested the engines. They responded to his controls and the craft began to roll as he veered away from her scout. "The intensity that we could have had together—Give Trager my regards."

"I will," Forrorrois replied, turning her craft in the opposite direction.

Collinar watched her scout blink from his sensors as the distance between them grew. Her generosity still bothered him as he headed back to Utahar space. The slate between them was clean he reminded himself. He owed her nothing. *But still*, he thought as he tasted his lips. Collinar pushed the fantasy from his mind. Forrorrois had given him the opportunity to take back his position in the Utahar—it was time to reassert his power.

✶✶✶✶✶✶✶✶✶✶✶

As Forrorrois arrived at the space terminal of Lor'Koria, the capital of Elda, she was surprised when she was met by a red robed member of the Council High Guard. The Eldatek female stood a good head taller than her when Forrorrois descended the cargo hold ramp of her long-distance two-seat scout. Forrorrois was even more surprised when the guard bowed her head to her before she spoke. Contrition emanated for the female as she met Forrorrois' gaze with her almond-shaped black eyes. Forrorrois studied her clay-brown face and high cheekbones when she spoke.

"Master Pilot Forrorrois, joined one of Haator ka Neeha, Councilor

Neeha has requested an audience with you in her home," the high guard female requested in Intergaltic.

Forrorrois suddenly felt self-conscious that she was wearing her modified black Dramudam uniform and not the green robes that Leenon had given her for the hearings. "Councilor Neeha's request is very gracious," Forrorrois began in Intergaltic, "but I think it would be better if I just retrieved Haator from the detention center and relieve Elda of my presence, besides I am not dressed for an audience with a member of the council."

The high guard bowed once more, this time from the waist, and remained there as she made her request again. "Honorable Forrorrois, of the Earth house Jolan, please reconsider. Councilor Neeha humbly extends this request. Haator has been transferred to her home to save you the inconvenience of a trip to the detention center. What you are wearing is the honored uniform of your position in the Dramudam and will be met with respect."

Forrorrois studied the guard's long loose black hair as it nearly touched the deck of the landing pad from the depth of her bow. She sensed no deception. "All right, since Haator is there, I will agree to meet with Councilor Neeha at her home."

Relief emanated from the red robed guard as she straightened. "Councilor Neeha will be honored that you have accepted an audience with her. Please allow me to provide escort."

Forrorrois nodded. "Thank you," she replied and followed after the high guard from the hangar bay into the streets of the Elda capital. Her mind was tumbling as she tried to decipher Neeha's motives for the unexpected audience.

✶✶✶✶✶✶✶✶✶✶✶

Trager paced impatiently in the room off of the elegant reception hall of Neeha's home. He had left for the Dramudam before his mother had acquired this opulent residence, complete with a dominant use of the expensive red stone on the walls and floors found only in the most exclusive homes on Elda. The glossy stone floors were carpeted

500

with thick hand woven rugs patterned with traditional desert bird and animal designs—each richly colored in tans, reds and turquoise. His mother had positioned herself well in her political rise to the Council of Elda.

He was still uncertain why Neeha had him released into her custody from the detention center or why she had even returned his modified all-black Dramudam uniform—cleaned and pressed. Trager hadn't had any contact with his mother since Forrorrois' final petition for Penock, being told to wait in the room by the council guard that had escorted him there from the council building. He looked up when a servant door opened at the far end of the room. His eyes widened as he saw Guruma enter with Celeste in tow.

When their eyes met, Celeste squealed in delight and broke free of Guruma's hand and ran to him.

"Poppa!" she cried out.

Trager dropped to his knee and scooped her into his arms in a tight hug. Tears streamed down his cheeks as he rocked her. "My sweet little Celeste," he whispered to her.

"Poppa! Unca Guruma said we were going home soon!" Celeste chattered. "Is this true?"

Trager looked over at Guruma and searched his wise eyes. Guruma smiled and nodded. Trager's heart soared as he held Celeste at arms length to take her all in. "I think so, Celeste. Let me look at you. You've grown so big!"

His little daughter grinned up at him with her round clay brown face and sparkling black eyes. "I'm a big girl!" she chimed mixing English with Intergaltic.

"Yes, you are," Trager grinned back.

"Are you going to stay with me and Momma, now?"

"That's what they've told me," Trager replied. "How did you get here?"

"Nur gave me and Unca Guruma a ride," Celeste said, glancing back at Guruma.

Trager looked over at his wise old friend and nodded. "Tell Nur, thank you."

Guruma gave him an impish smile. "I will—I'd better go before they find me here."

Trager glanced down at Celeste in a panic, pulling her closer to him.

"Don't worry, I'm not taking her, I thought that Celeste could ride back with you and Forrorrois after Forrorrois has her audience with Neeha," Guruma assured him.

Trager glanced towards the door to the reception hall and rose to his feet, still holding Celeste's hand. "Forrorrois is here?"

"Yes, she's just arriving now. Neeha requested an audience with her," Guruma replied.

"Here in Neeha's home?" Trager stated incredulously.

"Yes," Guruma said with a twinkle in his eye. "Politically, Neeha has gained significant approval from the other houses from her recognition of your joining with Forrorrois—as well as recognizing Celeste as Forrorrois' heir. Plus, her compassion towards Bohata in allowing her to conceive a female heir from you, for a reasonable fee, and maintain ties with her family was also well received. The public view of the wisdom of the council has risen significantly. And you mustn't discount Neeha's new found wealth from the substantial joining fee she received from Forrorrois, including the coup of gaining possession of three Prophet Stones. I'd say, politically, Neeha has done exceptionally well in this transaction."

Trager shook his head and sighed. "And the houses of Elda are at peace once more."

"Exactly," Guruma replied.

"Thank you, Guruma," Trager replied. "Somehow I think you had more than a little influence of the outcome of this whole thing."

Guruma shrugged. "I'd have to say Forrorrois played a big role introducing us to Nur."

"Yes, without Nur, I might not have survived that Aethereal attack and we wouldn't have escaped the Plane of Deception," Trager reflected. "Please tell Nur that my home is his home if he wishes to come and visit. I'm deeply in his debt."

"I will," Guruma replied. "I'll check up on you when you get back to Earth."

"I will look forward to seeing you, good journey," Trager answered as he watched the elder Dramudam founder turn and leave the room. He glanced down and smoothed his daughter's long black hair.

"Poppa, I feel Momma in the next room," Celeste whispered. "Let's go see her."

Trager glanced toward the door to the reception hall. "We have to be patient—your momma needs to speak to your grandmother first before we can see her. Now, come and sit with me on the couch. You can tell me what has happened on Earth since your momma and I have been away."

He could see the disappointment in her almond-shaped black eyes as she heaved a sigh.

"All right," she replied.

Trager smiled at her, then picked her up and took her over to the couch. His heart swelled as she began to tell about the last several mol with Yononnon, Jack, Forrorrois' parents and her uncle George at Forrorrois' base.

★★★★★★★★★★★

Forrorrois was escorted by the red-robed high guard that had met her at the space terminal into the vaulted reception hall. She looked down to the far end of the long room and spied a cluster of chairs and couches arranged for intimate conversation. The walls were covered in tiles of the same glossy red stone as the ya mugs that Yononnon and Leenon had in their quarters on the Tollon. The floors were scattered with intricately patterned rugs of tans, reds, and blues. The walls were also hung with tapestries woven in similar pattern motifs depicting desert animals and birds indigenous to Elda. The female took her to the middle of the hall then backed out when Neeha rose from a chair and walked toward her. Forrorrois felt underdressed in her black modified Dramudam uniform as she took in the opulent flowing gold and white robes that Neeha was wearing.

"Master Pilot Forrorrois, it is good of you to accept my invitation to my humble home," Neeha said in Eldanese as she approached her.

Forrorrois glanced around the hall and reminded herself not to be rude. "Thank you for your gracious invitation, Councilor Neeha, it is honor to be here in your lovely home," she replied carefully in Eldanese.

"My complements on your Eldanese, you speak it quite well," Neeha said graciously. "Please, I have refreshments for us."

"Thank you, I admit I'm not used to Elda's climate," Forrorrois said as she let Neeha take her arm and guide her to two couches that faced each other with a low stone table between them.

"Yes, I'm told you make your home in a much more temperate climate. I hear it even precipitates ice crystals in the cooler season," Neeha said with a slight nod.

Forrorrois took a seat on the couch, surreptitiously brushing her hand against the opulent burnt orange brocade fabric. Her feet barely touched the floor from the height of the seat. She was surprised when Neeha pulled out a low footrest from under the couch and placed a pillow behind her back to accommodate her shorter stature.

"Thank you," Forrorrois said as she watched Neeha take her seat across from her.

"Mawya?" Neeha offered.

"Yes, please," Forrorrois said as she took the carved red mug from Neeha and let it warm her hands. "Councilor Neeha, pardon my confusion, but I don't understand why you invited me here."

Neeha nodded pleasantly toward her. "Please call me Neeha ah," she offered. "It is more appropriate, now that our families are united with your formally recognized joining with Haator."

Forrorrois was stunned at Neeha request. Dropping a formal title and adding ah to a name was a familiar acknowledgement. Neeha was requesting that she greet her as her joined one's mother. "Of course Neeha ah. Please call me Forrorrois ah."

Neeha smiled at her indulgently. "Of course, Forrorrois ah, it is well now that you are publicly acknowledged as my extended daughter. What does your mother call you?"

Forrorrois glanced at her mawya then took a sip. As she lowered her mug she cleared her throat. "She calls me Danica," Forrorrois replied.

"What a beautiful name, so much more refined than your ship name Forrorrois," Neeha replied, then she paused. "But I understand why you choose to use your Dramudam name—I understand that it was given to you by Guruma himself."

Forrorrois allowed Neeha to recover from her faux pas and nodded. "Yes, Guruma did mark me himself. It was quite an honor."

"I'm told it is," Neeha replied. "Would you like some bread and towan paste...I also have sliced yahwa fruit to help cool your pallet."

"Thank you, Neeha ah," Forrorrois said as she took a triangle of flat bread with the red paste spread thinly across its surface then took a bite and munched it slowly. The burn of the paste flowed across her tongue and filtered into her nose. From years of practice she paced herself before she picked up a slice of yahwa and took a bite of the soothing fruit. She sensed a renewed respect from the Eldatek female across from her. "It's been some time since I've had such fresh towan paste," Forrorrois commented with a smile after she swallowed.

"Thank you, my family started its fortune with towan root processing," Neeha replied. "What does your family do?"

Forrorrois was uncertain how to answer—things had changed drastically over the past year. "My father, Mr. Frank Jolan, is a modification scientist. My mother, Mrs. Danielle Jolan, works with charity groups that help those less fortunate. My brother, George Jolan, is a travelling performer of illusions."

Neeha studied her for a moment. "Charity work is a very honorable profession. From the size of the final bid you offered for Haator, your family must hold considerable wealth. Forgive my initial impression of your family's stature on your world."

Forrorrois tried not to smile at Neeha's assumption. "Neeha ah, it's understandable if you measured it against the austerity of my base. My parents' measure wealth by the good one can do for others. They believe in a more spiritual existence than a material one. My mother taught me compassion to even those I first perceive as my enemy—for only through understanding their circumstances can I reach a state of forgiveness."

Neeha glanced down at her hands. Shame washed from her toward Forrorrois. "I can see now why Haator was attracted to you. He is my only living son now and he has honored his brother's memory by providing the means to allow Bohata to have an heir in his brother's stead. This would only be possible through your mother's upbringing. I must admit that I have judged you wrongly, Forrorrois ah."

"Please, Neeha ah, there were mistakes on both sides," Forrorrois whispered.

Neeha glanced up—a tear tracing down her cheek. "You are most gracious."

Forrorrois let her own tears fall as she smiled toward Neeha. "Can we start fresh?"

Relief smoothed Neeha's face. "Yes," she said with a nod. "I believe there is someone who has been waiting anxiously to see you," she stated, signaling to a servant standing out of earshot at the far end of the hall.

Forrorrois turned to see the servant open a door. She jumped to her feet when she saw Trager come, out carrying Celeste. She didn't expect her daughter to be in Neeha's home—and from Neeha's confusion neither did she.

"Take care of my granddaughter, Forrorrois ah, she carries my blood," Neeha stated as she stood to her feet.

Stunned, Forrorrois glanced at Neeha and nodded. "I will, Neeha ah." Then she ran to meet Trager and Celeste and pulled them into a hug. She shook with tears of joy knowing her family was finally whole.

EPILOGUE

Forrorrois smiled over at Trager and Celeste in the jump seat beside her command seat of her long-distance two-seat scout. She was relieved to finally be returning back home to her base on Earth as she landed her scout in the hangar bay. The sight of her family, Jack, and Perkins waiting for them made her heart beat faster. Wordlessly, she subvocalized to the ship's computer to open the cargo hatch and extend the ramp. She barely had her harness unfastened before she heard feet running up the ramp.

Celeste vaulted from Trager's lap. "Grandma! Grandpa! Unca George! Unca Jack! Unca Perkins!" she cried out in English as she ran into the cargo hold of the scout.

Trager grinned as he watched Celeste.

Forrorrois rose from her command chair. "Are you ready?" she asked in English.

"Yes," Trager replied in English.

Forrorrois hesitated as he caught her arm and kissed her.

As he pulled away he smiled at her and whispered, "Have I told you today that I love you?"

"Yes, but I don't mind hearing it again," she whispered, "I love you too."

His eyes sparkled as he rose from the jump seat.

Together, they entered the scout's small cargo hold crowded with everyone.

"It's great to have you back, son," Forrorrois' father said as he extended his hand toward Trager.

Stunned, Trager took his hand. Forrorrois grinned as Trager's eyes widened as her father pulled him into a bear hug. George and Jack slapped Trager on the back as they greeted him warmly. Forrorrois turned to her mother and gave her a hug.

"Thank you, Mom, for watching Celeste for me while I was gone. All these men in the house must have been a handful," she whispered.

"I wouldn't have wanted it any other way," her mother whispered back. "But I'm so glad you're home with Trager."

"Me too, Mom."

Forrorrois glanced over at Perkins and smiled when she saw him in a proper Master pilot uniform. She was surprised when she sensed a melancholy from him.

"Perkins' seems sad," Forrorrois asked as she glanced over at her mother.

"He's pining over Alham," her mother whispered. "They were just about to be married when Guruma took Alham back to Elda."

Forrorrois gasped as she looked back at Perkins. "I didn't know," she whispered.

Perkins glanced at her and tried to smile. Forrorrois walked over to him and pulled him into a gentle hug.

"I'm so sorry, Perkins," she whispered.

"It's OK," Perkins said as he pulled away slowly, averting his eyes. "Guruma told me that she could come back in a year. I just hope she does."

"She'll be back, Perkins, I know she will. She loves you."

Perkins looked at her in surprise. "She told you?"

"Yes," Forrorrois replied, "she told me when I asked her what her intentions were toward you the last time I was on the Tollon."

Perkins shook his head as he looked up at the ceiling, embarrassed. "Was it that obvious?"

"Only to an empath," Forrorrois assured him. "Now, pull on a smile and let's get this welcome home party started."

"I'll try," Perkins replied.

Suddenly, she spun around as Jack hugged her from behind.

"You did it!" Jack cried out, hugging her tightly.

"I did, didn't I!" she beamed.

"As much as I've enjoyed having Yononnon here, I'm definitely glad to have Trager back," Jack said as he let her go.

"I bet you have some stories to tell," Forrorrois laughed.

"A few," Jack grinned.

"What about the general?" Forrorrois asked a bit more seriously.

Jack sobered. "He's in protective custody with the F.B.I.—Aster's keeping an eye on him. Aster had him sign papers to rescind the enemy combatant charges against you, your family, Perkins, and myself as a condition of providing him protection. We'll talk about it later."

Forrorrois sighed. "That's a relief. Who is the general being protected from?"

"We're still working on that," Jack said with a nod. "Aster's been following some leads in Washington. We can see him tomorrow. Right now, we'd better head into the living quarters. Ever since your mother heard you were on your way back with Trager and Celeste she's has been a slave driver having us make preparations."

"I can just imagine," Forrorrois laughed. Suddenly, she felt her pant leg being tugged and looked down at Celeste.

"Momma, don't forget Grandma Neeha sent presents," Celeste called up to her, grabbing her hand.

"You're right, Peanut," Forrorrois said as she smiled down at her little daughter. "Trager, could you and Perkins grab that crate that Neeha sent and bring it into the living room?"

"Of course," Trager replied, signally to Perkins.

"Oh my goodness, what in the world did Neeha send!?" her mother gasped when Trager and Perkins each grabbed a handle of the large square metal crate and grunted slightly from the weight.

"It's traditional on Elda for the mother of the male who has entered into a recognized joining to offer welcome gifts to the female's family as a token that the families are now united," Trager replied.

"But we didn't send her anything," her mother stammered.

Trager shook his head. "Danielle, my mother has been well compensated, you needn't be concerned," he replied as he and Perkins struggled with the crate down the ramp into the cargo hold.

Forrorrois watched her parents' glance at each other, still uncertain. "I paid a significant joining fee to Neeha. Believe me, Mom, we're covered," she insisted.

"Danica, I'll want to hear more about this joining fee business when we have a moment," her father replied quietly then followed Trager and Perkins down the ramp.

Forrorrois glanced over at Jack, uncertain.

"I think you'd better leave out the details on exactly how you got the joining fee. I don't know if they would approve," Jack whispered.

"I'll definitely do some editing," Forrorrois whispered back.

She grinned when George put his arm around her and gave her a hug.

"Good to have you back, sis."

"It's great to be back, brother o'mine," she replied, hugging him tightly.

Forrorrois followed everyone down the ramp and into the living quarters. Her mind wandered to Jack's comment about the general being in protective custody, but she pushed it out of her mind. Tonight, she only wanted to think about having her family whole again.

★★★★★★★★★★★

Reluctantly, Forrorrois headed for Washington, D.C. with Jack in her two-seat long-distance scout, leaving Trager at the base to be with Celeste, her family, and Perkins. The matters on Earth had been left unattended for far too long. Her family and friends needed to be safe again, but they couldn't until she knew who was using the general. She guided her craft into a park and landed next to a parking lot with a single gray four-door sedan sitting in the neat rows of painted parking spots. Her brief scan confirmed that Aster was sitting inside. Forrorrois wished she was meeting with him under more social circumstances.

Jack and she stepped down the ramp and into the early morning daylight as they passed through the EM warping shield. Aster smiled when he spotted them and got out of his car.

"It's good to see you again, Aster," she called out as they approached.

"Yes," Aster replied. "It's been too long. You're looking well."

Forrorrois smiled at him. "Thank you, you're looking well yourself considering a recent gunshot wound to the shoulder."

Aster grinned. "Your brother, George, patched me up good as new."

"Yes, I hear George has become quite the EMT," Forrorrois replied and waved towards the direction of her shrouded ship. "Let's take a seat in my cargo hold. I'd like to hear about how your investigation is going."

"Yes, he has," Aster said as he stepped forward and gingerly felt for the ramp with his foot.

Forrorrois and Jack followed him up the ramp and took seats on the crates inside the cargo hold. Aster sat down next to Jack and glance around.

"It's been a while since I've had the pleasure of being invited onto your scout ship," Aster continued. "I'm also glad to hear that Trager is back with you again."

Forrorrois nodded, sensing he really meant what he said. "Yes, four years is a long time."

"You'll have to give me the details of how you reached him," he said.

"Yes, I'd like to hear about that as well," Jack chimed in.

"Well, the story is a bit lengthy, but if Collinar hadn't pointed me to the Beliespeir I never would have reached Trager in time," Forrorrois replied.

Forrorrois smiled when both Jack and Aster gave her a double take.

"Collinar helped you?" Aster stammered. "Why would he do that?"

Forrorrois shrugged. "He offered me information so that I would consider helping him shorten his sentence at the Dramudam Rehabilitation station," she replied.

"I see," Aster answered, definitely intrigued.

Jack took a deep breath, but kept silent.

"Enough small talk," Forrorrois said as she ducked the unasked questions. "Jack filled me in on your holding General Caldwell and the two men. I really appreciate you getting him to rescind the enemy combatant charges against my family, Jack, Perkins, and myself."

Aster drew on a self-satisfied smile and shrugged. "Having the charges dropped wasn't that difficult once I had the right motivator. And Jack did soften them up for me."

Forrorrois glanced over at Jack and felt a guilty pleasure emanate from him. "I want to hear about this later, Jack. What have you learned about the two men that were with the general when you were shot?" Forrorrois pressed.

Aster sobered before he continued. "Unfortunately, I've run into a wall with the two men. Shortly after I brought them in, they were ordered released. My director wasn't pleased, but he wouldn't say exactly who ordered their release. They disappeared shortly afterwards. The general wouldn't talk after that, but I doubt he knew much more than what he had already told me."

"So for now it's over, do we just wait until they strike again?" Forrorrois asked.

"I'm afraid so," Aster answered.

"Why would I think that it would be easy," Forrorrois moaned. "What about my parents, do you think it's safe for them to return home?"

Aster nodded. "I think so. I spoke with Jennings and he said that he would personally coordinate surveillance on their home for a while to be certain. "We've even spoke with your father's employer and explained that he was on special assignment with us and that being declared an enemy combatant was just part of his cover. He can start back to work next week or whenever he's ready."

"Thank you, Aster, that's the best news my parents could have right now," Forrorrois replied.

"Oh, and I was asked by the President to personally deliver this to your brother," Aster said, pulling an envelope from his suit jacket and handed her it.

Forrorrois took the envelope and turned it over to see George's name on the front. "What is it?"

Aster grinned. "It's an invitation to perform for the President and his family at the White House."

Forrorrois' jaw dropped. "You're kidding me!"

"No, in fact I have invitations for your parents, Jack, Perkins and you plus one, just incase Trager would like to come along," Aster continued pulling several envelopes from his jacket. "He promises no press. It's just the President's way of extending his apologies for everything that has happened. He considers you an ally and wants to put this unfortunate situation behind you."

Forrorrois smiled. "Tell the President that I'll deliver the invitations and see if my brother is available for a command performance. In this election year it must be difficult for him to be thinking about mending fences with me since his two terms are up in a few more months. I'm kind of sorry to see him go."

Jack started to chuckle when Aster moved to speak. "She's joking, Aster, of course we'll be there. George has been working on a few new illusions and he'd love the opportunity to have a private audience to test them out on."

"That's a relief," Aster replied. "The President seems to be fairly strong in the popularity polls at the moment."

Forrorrois glanced down at the envelopes—each individually addressed in beautiful calligraphy. Maybe things were changing. "Aster, thank you for everything."

"My pleasure," Aster replied. "Now go home and tell your family. I'm sure that you and Trager would like to have your privacy back."

Forrorrois' eyes twinkled. "As much as I love everybody, my little base has been bursting at the seams for the past several months. And Trager and I do have some catching up to do."

"I've already got that covered," Jack replied. "I've asked Perkins to come and stay at my cabin. The Air Force has reinstated me as the lead investigator for the OCU and Perkins has been put on special assignment with me. It'll help Perkins keep his mind off of Alham until she returns in a year."

Aster leaned forward. "Alham?"

"Perkins' engaged," Jack replied.

"It's complicated," Forrorrois added.

Aster hesitated. "Is she from out of town?"

"Very out of town," Jack replied. "She's Yononnon's niece."

"Why do I ask?" Aster said, shaking his head.

"We should be going, Jack," Forrorrois stated as she rose from the crate she'd been sitting on. "It was great seeing you again, Aster."

"Yes, it was," Aster replied standing with Jack. "Next time don't make it so long."

Forrorrois gave him a hug. "Keep me and Jack posted on the general."

"I will," Aster said with a nod. "I have a feeling the general will be back at the base before you know it—keeping Jack on his toes."

Jack winced as he offered Aster his hand. "You sure you couldn't keep him in protective custody a little longer?"

Aster laughed, shaking Jack's hand. "Sorry old boy, I can't keep him indefinitely. Besides, I think you and Perkins will do a better job of protecting him than my people can on that base, now that you are aware of the situation."

Forrorrois watched as Aster nodded to her once more then walked down the ramp into the sunlight toward his car. She glanced toward Jack and smiled.

"Ready to head back?" she asked.

"Actually, yes," Jack replied. "No offense, but I'm looking forward to sleeping in my own bed again."

Forrorrois grinned. "I know exactly how you feel," she said as the hatch slid shut.

GLOSSARY OF NAMES AND TERMS

Aasha ka Felia:
See Alham.

Aethereal:
A race of beings that live in the Plane of Deception—a dimension that intersects this dimension at high energy foci. This dimension may be influenced by the hyperfold dimension that ships from this dimension travel through during hyperfold travel. Height 7.04 pol (1.9 meters) with a hunched posture. They generally have pale gray or mottled skin with web-like elastic wings that stretch along their side from their ankles to their wrists. When they fly their wings make a slight sound akin to the rustle of dried leaves. Their hands are clawed and are used in battles for territory and winning a mate. Their eyes glow like red embers and they have fine needlelike teeth that protrude from their mouths and drip with a silver saliva. They derive sustenance from the shifting colored mist that composes the Plane of Deception. Aethereal have a very low tolerance for intruders into their territory, but are also very ritualistic and will announce their war declaration prior to the attack with banshee-like wailing. The actual attack will occur at a later date, without notice or sound, as an ambush and the intended victim will be rent with the razor-sharp claws of the attacking Aethereal.

Alham:
Dramudam, master pilot on the peace ship Tollon, of the Eldatek race. Eldatek name is Aasha ka Felia. Second-born daughter of Felia ka Wil'Amay. Niece to Subcommander Yononnon (Eldatek name: Vu'Rel ka Wil'Amay) and Lead Med Tech Leenon (Eldatek name: Me'Hal ka Wil'Amay), both also assigned to the Tollon. Older sister, first-born daughter Li'Kur ka Felia, remained on Elda to study the

family textile business. Height 6.85 pol (1.85 meters), black almond-shaped eyes, red clay-brown skin.

Ashwan:
An Eldanese word meaning "lover."

Aster, Ken:
Special Agent in the Federal Bureau of Investigation in the U.S. government, of the Human race. Previous career in the U.S. Air Force Special Operations: Specialized in explosives, mainly briefcase-sized Weapons of Mass Destruction (WMDs). Height is 6.85 pol (1.85 meters), medium athletic build, black hair, brown eyes. From the ages of twelve to sixteen he went to school in England while his parents were stationed there with the U.S. military. He picked up a slight British accent, slang, and mannerisms which color his speech when he is in tense situations.

Beliespeir:
Beliespeir translates loosely to "wings of time". Equine in form with various colored fur, mane and tail. Leathery bat-like wings and glossy hoofs. They communicate telepathically and are able to travel through time and space. Average height as withers 5.64 pol (1.524 meters). Considered a mythical being by most members of the galaxy due to the fact that they keep to themselves. The race never developed the need for space travel since they were able to travel to any location and dimension that they can create a mental picture of and can move to any time given enough reference information.

Bennett, Carl:
Assistant Director in the F.B.I., of the Human race. Immediate supervisor of Special Agent Ken Aster. Height is 6.7 pol (1.80 meters), medium build, brown eyes, salt-n-pepper hair. Middle aged.

Bohata ka Frolan:
Of the Eldatek race. First-born daughter (and only daughter) of Frolan

of Elda. Joined one to Talman ka Neeha. Height 6.85 pol (1.85 meters), black almond-shaped eyes, red clay brown skin.

Braheen ka Wil'Amay:
Of the Eldatek race, resides on Elda. First-born son of Wil'Amay of Elda. Presently not joined. Height 6.85 pol (1.85 meters), black almond-shaped eyes, red clay brown skin. His older sister, first-born daughter, Felia ka Wil'Amay, studies the family textile business run by their mother. His younger sister, second-born daughter, Me'Hal ka Wil'Amay (ship name Leenon) and his younger brother, second-born son, Vu'Rel ka Wil'Amay (ship name Yononnon), both serve in the Dramudam.

Caldwell, Samuel:
General in the U.S. Air Force, of the Human race. Ranking officer at the Air Force base north of Rome, New York. Height 7.04 pol (1.9 meters), square build, gray hair, gray eyes.

Caya:
An herbal tea with the scent of rose hips and lemon grass, made from the ca plant found wild on the first moon that orbits the planet Elda. It is consumed by Eldatek Dramudam members to strengthen their autoimmune system.

Collinar:
Utahar, commander of the fleet ship Sheetal. Responsible for ordering cruel experimentation on supposedly low-level life forms. Extremely cunning and brutal in his efforts to gain more power within the Utahar. Mortal enemy of Forrorrois. Height over 7.4 pol (2.0 meters), athletic-supple build, golden feline eyes, shoulder-length blond hair, golden-tan complexion.

Cycle:
A period of time equivalent to approximately twenty Earth hours. It is divided into five equal periods called kel.

Defense net:
A network of beacons set up in a grid-like pattern around a large area, possibly a planet, to sense unauthorized travel in that given area. It is capable of transmitting a warning to the intruder and also a distress signal if the warning is ignored

Deflector shield:
A defense shield that absorbs and disperses the force of enemy fire.

Dramudam:
Translate to "Seekers of Peace." A strict organization of beings who give up their allegiance to their home worlds to protect all worlds equally without bias. Formed by Guruma (originally of Elda) and later ratified by the known free worlds in the galaxy upon the signing of the Isolation Treaty. Traditionally each Dramudam is "marked" with the symbol of a golden comet passing a red four-pointed star located on the upper left of the chest. The beings also wear their hair (if they have it) long, in a single loose braid down their backs. The traditional salute consists of the right hand clenched with the thumb and pinkie extended, over their Dramudam mark, symbolizing the comet passing the four pointed star. This is usually accompanied by a bow toward the senior officer.

Danica:
See Forrorrois.

Eldatek:
A race of beings born on the planet Elda. They can be distinguished by their reddish brown skin, black almond-shaped eyes, and long, thick black hair. Most males on average stand 7.4 pol (2.0 meters), while the average females stand approximately 6.3 pol (1.8 meters). The race is matrilineal in structure. Although both the males and females may equally hold leadership positions in lower-level offices, the positions of the ruling council are strictly held by elder females. Arranged joinings are commonly used to secure wealth and power

among the more elite families when the males reach the age of forty. Females generally wait until they are fifty before entering a joining. Males are restricted in the accumulation of wealth, property and selection of their joined one. The males and females are raised separately beginning age five. The males are commonly cloistered in a monastery for their schooling until they are twenty-five, while the females remain with their mothers to be instructed in the family trade. The average life span is two hundred revolution. Duty and honor are highly prized qualities in their culture.

Empath:
A being which can mentally sense another being's emotional state.

Environs:
A fringe lawless portion of space not patrolled by the Dramudam. Environ traders who are willing to accept the higher risks associated with travelling in this portion of space generally are able to raise large amounts of capital in a short period of time.

EM warping shield:
A light-bending, passive defense shield that camouflages a ship from being detected visually. It has a limited amount of scrambling capacity on other frequencies, assisting in detection prevention.

Felia ka Wil'Amay:
Of the Eldatek race. Mother of first-born daughter Li'Kur ka Felia and second-born daughter Aasha ka Felia. Heir to the family textile business. Height 6.85 pol (1.85 meters), black almond-shaped eyes, red clay brown skin.

Forrorrois (Fôr rôr rəs):
Dramudam, trained as a pilot on the peace ship Tollon, of the Human race. Earth name is Danica Jolan. At age seventeen, she was rescued from an Utahar experimental research station where she had endured several modifications at the molecular level. Modifications include

heightened empathic abilities, increased reaction time, increased muscular strength and bone density, photographic memory, and the ability to reduce her molecular mass to 5 percent of the original mass. She stands 5.9 pol (1.6 meters) tall, has auburn hair, brown eyes, and pale skin.

Frolan of Elda:
Of the Eldatek race. Mother of Bohata ka Frolan. Runs family ya import/export business. Height 6.85 pol (1.85 meters), black almond-shaped eyes, red clay brown skin.

Gintzer:
A race of beings originating from the planet Gint. Racial traits include a boar-like head with a set of curved prominent lower tusks, large square frame and short bristle-like brown fur, with a tendency for aggressive behavior. Average height is 7.04 pol (1.9 meters), for both males and females. Both males and females hold equal positions in society and government.

Goren:
Dramudam, master pilot instructor of the peace ship Tollon, of the Silmanon race. Noted as one of the best pilot instructors in the Dramudam fleet. Joined the Dramudam after his family was killed in a raid by the Utahar on an outpost fringe world. Height 7.04 pol (1.9 meters), medium athletic build, liquid black eyes (no whites surrounding the iris), short black-velvety fur that covers his face and body, small round ears, face resembles a pug-nose mule. Gravelly voice.

Guruma:
Original leader of the Dramudam, of the Eldatek race. He led by example, living a very simple life that stressed duty, honor, ship, and ceremony as key elements of a proper Dramudam. Many elements of his traditional upbringing on Elda were incorporated in his leadership and in the original foundation of the Dramudam traditions. Since the

original formation, many traditions from other races have also been introduced, giving the Dramudam a rich heritage. Almost all group Dramudam ceremonies involve dance as a form of expression. This can be directly attributed to Guruma and the Eldatek. Guruma was presumed dead after an Utahar attack destroyed his ship in a savage battle five revolution after the signing of the Isolation Treaty. There are rumors that he still lives in another plane of existence and may appear at critical moments to guide the Dramudam. This is difficult to document since only a limited number of beings have reported witnessing this occurrence. Height 7.04 pol (1.9 meters), medium build, almond-shaped black eyes, long straight gray hair, chestnut-brown complexion.

Haator ka Neeha:
See Trager.

Hartcourt, Karen:
Secret leader of the emerging terrorist organization World of Armageddon Federation (WAF) positioned as a police detective for a small Upstate, NY, police department, of the Human race. Height 6.3 pol (1.7 meters). Brown eyes, black hair. Fair complexion. Genius level intelligence but suffers from an inferiority complex that drives her ambitions. Not above killing to attain her goals.

Hayman, Elliot:
Director of the Federal Bureau of the Investigation, of the Human race. Height 7.04 pol (1.9 meters). An imposing man, with a piercing stare, and distinguished graying hair.

Hel'ket:
Head horticulturalist to the royal family of Pedraco, of the Kohanian race. She possessed strong telepathic abilities that allowed her to communicate with empaths. Height 6.85 pol (1.85 meters), broad mouth, no hair and yellow raised amphibian eyes.

Hovercycle:
A small personal transport that hovers above the ground and can carry one to two passengers. Extremely maneuverable and can travel at high speeds at various altitudes.

Hyperfold drive:

A propulsion system used by spacecraft to cover large distances between star systems. It allows the craft to travel close to the speed of light while distorting space to the point of folding it on itself, reducing the travel time between the two points to a fraction of the time through the hyperfold dimension. Calculations using fractional dimensional analysis allow this process to be successful.

Intergaltic:
The common language used for trade and communication between worlds in the galaxy.

Isolation Treaty:
The treaty signed by the free worlds of the galaxy, which states that all planets have the right to govern themselves without outside interference within the bounds of their solar system. All underdeveloped worlds are protected from contamination of advanced technology so that they may develop at their own pace. Any travel between solar systems will be done in good faith of the treaty. Any violators of the treaty will be dealt with by the Dramudam in accordance to the treaty. The Dramudam are overseen by a council of representatives of the free worlds if a dispute is brought against the Dramudam in their handling of an incident.

Jennings, Trenton:
Special Agent in the Federal Bureau of Investigation in the U.S. government, of the Human race. He specializes in linguistics: English, Spanish, French, Japanese, Russian, Mandarin, and several dialects of Arabic. Height is 6.85 pol (1.85 meters), medium athletic build,

blond hair, blue eyes. Has a biting sense of humor. Likes to charm the ladies, and is extremely confident in his abilities. He's a rising star in the bureau, enjoys field work, but still not comfortable with the bureaucracy. He prefers to be called by his last name: Jennings.

Jolan, Danica:
See Forrorrois.

Jolan, Danielle:
Danica Jolan/Forrorrois' mother, of the Human race. Nickname Danny. Height 6.1 pol (1.65 meters). Hazel eyes, auburn hair. Fair complexion.

Jolan, Frank:
Danica Jolan/Forrorrois' father. Height 6.6 pol (1.78 meters), of the Human race. Brown eyes, dark brown hair with evidence of gray near the temples. Medium complexion.

Jolan, George:
Danica Jolan/Forrorrois' older brother, of the Human race. Height 6.7 pol (1.80 meters). Dark brown eyes, medium brown hair. Medium complexion.

Kil'Treahaa:
Of the Eldatek race. Head of the Council of Elda. Mother of first-born daughter, Tete ka Kil'Treahaa. No other living children.

Kel:
A time period equivalent to approximately four Earth hours. Also used when describing meal intervals: i.e., first kel = breakfast, second kel = lunch, third kel = dinner, fourth kel = late evening, and fifth kel is the middle of the night shift.

Kohanian:
An amphibious race of beings from the Intonius system which is

located in the Environs. The race is divided between two planets, Sten and Pedra, each ruled by a royal family, Stentous and Pedraco, respectively named after the royal families. Both worlds are approximately 50% water with the remainder being marshland. They can be distinguished by their brown hairless skin which is usually wet and slick, yellow raised eyes, and broad mouths that do not contain teeth. Most males on average stand 6.3 pol (1.8 meters), while the average females stand approximately 7.4 pol (2.0 meters). The race is matrilineal in structure with males generally relegated to simple menial tasks while the females hold all positions of power. The race generally has a disdain for warm-blooded beings and will only negotiate with females of any race. They generally are extremely rude during initial encounters with other beings to determine their reaction to decide if they are worthy of their time. The major export from their system is a type of dried water lily that is used as an additive in a variety of food supplements including emergency rations. The average life span is one hundred revolution. The two royal houses are presently in a thousand revolution war with each other making entering the Intonius system, without an escort, extremely dangerous.

Leenon:
Dramudam, lead med tech on the peace ship Tollon, of the Eldatek race. Eldatek name: Me'Hal ka Wil'Amay of Elda, second-born daughter of Wil'Amay of Elda. Second-oldest sister to Subcommander Yononnon (Eldatek name: Vu'Rel ka Wil'Amay). Older sister, Felia ka Wil'Amay, remained on Elda to study the family textile business. Height 6.85 pol (1.85 meters), black almond-shaped eyes, red clay brown skin.

Li'Kur ka Felia:
Of the Eldatek race. First-born daughter of Felia ka Wil'Amay. Sister to second-born daughter, Aasha ka Felia. Heir to the family textile business on Elda. Height 6.85 pol (1.85 meters), black almond-shaped eyes, red clay-brown skin.

Lor'Koria:
Seat of government and capital city of the planet Elda. Location of the Council of Elda.

Mawya:
A hot drink with a strong scent and taste of lemon and mint that is frequently drunk at first kel by the Eldatek Dramudam members. The leaves of the maw bush dissolve in hot water to form a ya or tea. The maw bush is found growing on the second moon that orbits the planet Elda. Mawya is noted for its calming, yet sharpening, effect on the mind.

Ma'Kelda:
Was the subcommander on the Utahar fleet ship Sheetal under Commander Collinar, of the Utahar race. She stood nearly 7.4 pol (2.0 meters) in height, had a curvaceous svelte figure, waist-length blond hair and feline golden eyes. She possessed strong telepathic abilities that allow her to communicate with empaths and was adept at altering another being's emotional state when she is within two meters. She died at Collinar's hands when he suspected her of treason.

Me'Hal ka Wil'Amay:
See Leenon.

Monomay:
Monomay the Patient, Mother Provider of the Eldatek people. A religious symbol normally in the form of a female or desert bird, often a mask carved of a glossy red stone, or in rare cases, wood. She embodies the virtues that all Eldatek strive for: patience, duty, honor, humility and servitude. Homage to her is generally performed through silent individual prayer and meditation. Ritualistic public displays are frowned upon. Meditation is normally performed with the aid of a meditation sphere that allows individuals to focus their thoughts. Cleansing rituals are performed by individuals twice a revolution: once on the second cycle after the cycle of their birth

and then ten mol later. The ritual involves fasting and seclusion in a meditation chamber for six kel. As with many religions, these practices are performed more rigidly by the very young and the elderly, while those in the prime of their lives tend to forgo these observances except in times of uncertainty.

Mo'onah:
Head horticulturalist to the royal family of Stentous, of the Kohanian race. She possessed strong telepathic abilities that allowed her to communicate with empaths. Height 7.4 pol (2.0 meters), broad mouth, no hair and yellow raised amphibian eyes.

Motan:
Mercenary broker in the Environs, of the Gintzer race. Has a reputation for lining up mercenary jobs that pay extremely well, but tend to be high risk. Height 7.04 pol (1.9 meters).

Mo'yuto:
A process sanctioned by Eldatek law of removing a female child from a second born male who is in an unsanctioned joining—if the Elda Council agrees that it is in the best interest of the child—and placed with the childless Joined one of a first born son, if that first born son has passed without providing a female heir.

Neeha:
Member of the Council of Elda, of the Eldatek race. Mother of Ralana (first-born daughter), Talman (first-born son) joined to Bohata and Haator (second-born son) who is presently serving in the Dramudam. She runs the family business with her daughter and is the major producer and exporter of towan root products, which include towan paste and towan juice, on the planet of Elda. Her husband, Telcore, died of a fever shortly after Haator's twentieth birthday. Neeha was bitter when Haator left Elda to join the Dramudam and assumed the Dramudam ship name Trager. Height 6.85 pol (1.85 meters), medium

Forrorrois: Tears of Many Mothers

build, almond-shaped black eyes, long straight salt-n-pepper hair, reddish clay-brown complexion.

Nin'Te ka Vel'Una:
Of the Eldatek race. First-born (and only) daughter of Counselor Vel'Una of Elda. Heir to the family masonry business on Elda. Height 6.85 pol (1.85 meters), black almond-shaped eyes, red clay-brown skin.

Nur:
Member of the Beliespeir race. Equine in form with black fur, and a fiery red mane and tail. Red leathery bat-like wings and glossy black hoofs. Telepathic and able to travel through time and space. 5.64 pol (1.524 meters) at the withers.

Peldor:
Dramudam, a squadron leader and security officer on the peace ship Tollon, of the Gintzer race. Height 6.96 pol (1.88 meters), muscular build, boar-like features.

Perkins, Perceval:
Captain in the U. S. Air Force, of the Human race. Expert Apache helicopter pilot. Close friend of Colonel Jack Stern. Prefers to be called Perkins. Height 6.96 pol (1.88 meters), slim muscular build, blue eyes, blond hair.

Penock (Right of):
Right of First Joining.

Pintra:
Of the Eldatek race, now deceased. Mother of first-born daughter Seralan ka Pintra (deceased with no heir) and second-born daughter Kil'Treahaa (now Head Councilor of Elda).

Plane of Deception:
A dimension that intersects this dimension at high energy foci. This dimension may be influenced by the hyperfold dimension that ships from this dimension travel through during hyperfold travel. The entire dimension consists of a disorienting mist that swirls in ever-changing color patterns. Inhabited by the Aethereal race.

Reduction weapon:
A handheld weapon that reduces an object's mass to 5-percent of its original mass. Emits a bluish-green beam. It also can be set to reverse the process and restore an object to its original mass. If the object is living, the subject may experience loss of consciousness for up to twenty minutes. Living subjects also experience a greater amount of physical heat loss from the body, which, if left unchecked, can lead to hypothermia in less than a half a kel and death within a full kel.

Ralana ka Neeha:
Of the Eldatek race. First-born (and only) daughter of Councilor Neeha. Her two brothers are Talman, who is joined to Bohata, and her youngest brother Haator ka Neeha who now serves the Dramudam as a Master pilot [ship name Trager]. Presently, she runs the prominent family towan root products processing and export business with her mother, Neeha. She presently is unmarried and without children. Height 6.85 pol (1.85 meters), medium build, almond-shaped black eyes, long straight black hair, reddish clay-brown complexion.

Sensor deflector array:
A defensive array that alters an incoming signal slightly, making it look like the ship is in another, random position. This randomization process prevents triangulation on the original position.

Seralan ka Pintra:
Of the Eldatek race, died of the fever before becoming joined. First-born daughter of Pintra of Elda, sister of Kil'Treahaa (Head Councilor of Elda).

Sheetal:
An Utahar ship under Commander Collinar.

Ship Name:
The name that a Dramudam receives after they have completed their training during their marking ceremony. It is symbolic of shedding all ties to their homeworld and accepting the Dramudam as their family. This tradition is to allow the individual to act impartial when in a mediation situation where claiming allegiance to an individual world might cause a conflict of interest.

Silmanon:
A race of beings originating on the planet Frayhee. Racial traits include a fine, black velvety fur that covers the entire body, long mulish facial features, slightly pug nose, liquid black eyes with no visible whites, and small round, highly sensitive ears. Their voices tend to have a gravelly coarseness that often gives the mistaken impression of a harsh, gruff manner. Few ventured from their home planet, so little is known about their social habits.

Slovak (Right of):
Right of Second Joining.

Stern, Jack:
Colonel in the U.S. Air Force, of the Human race. Served for twenty-four Earth years as a helicopter pilot before becoming grounded due to a mild heart condition. He was later reinstated to co-pilot status and eventually pilot when his health improved. He was reassigned as the officer in charge of the Observables Classification Unit (OCU). Height 7.2 pol (1.95 meters), salt-and-pepper hair, steel gray eyes, medium build. After his wife and daughter were killed in a car accident by a drunk driver, he became reclusive and focused on his work in the OCU. When he met Frank and Danielle Jolan he found a new focus in his life helping them reunite with their daughter, Danica.

Stun weapon:
A small, oval, handheld weapon that renders its intended victim unconscious for approximately twenty-five tol (fifteen minutes), depending on the individual recovery rate of the subject. The weapon emits a reddish beam.

Subvocalization:
A method of communicating with the ship's computer, in which words are formed in the throat but never audibly vocalized.

Talman ka Neeha:
Of the Eldatek race, left hand of Commander Thoren. First born son of Neeha, member of the Council of Elda. Talman is joined to Bohata. His older sister is Ralana ka Neeha (who studies the family Towan business) and younger brother is Haator ka Neeha (who now serves the Dramudam as a Master pilot (ship name Trager)). Height 7.4 pol (2.0 meters), medium athletic build, almond-shaped black eyes, long straight black hair, chestnut-brown complexion.

Telepath:
A being who can communicate by thought alone to another being. Two telepaths can have two-way communication, whereas a nontelepath may receive nothing, images, or words from the telepath. Depending on the strength of the telepath's ability, they may receive images to entire thoughts from a nontelepath. An adept telepath may establish two-way communication with a strong empath if they are within close proximity of one another.

Trell:
Cover name used by Collinar when working in the Environs as a mercenary.

Tete ka Kil'Treahaa:
Of the Eldatek race. First-born daughter (only living child) of

Kil'Treahaa of Elda—Head of the Council of Elda. Tete heads family red stone quarry business.

Thoren:
Dramudam, commander of the peace ship Tollon, of the Eldatek race. A fair but stern leader. Trained under Guruma, Thoren was said to be the first Dramudam to have a vision of Guruma after Guruma's ship was destroyed in an Utahar attack. During the first vision he received his Dramudam mark. Since that time all fully trained Dramudam are marked with the comet passing the star in the Ceremony of the Beginning. Entered into service in the Dramudam before the signing of the Isolation Treaty amid rumors that he was born illegitimate: both parents are listed unknown. Rumored to be the nephew of Counselor Kil'Treahaa. Height 7.04 pol (1.9 meters), medium athletic build, almond-shaped black eyes, long straight salt-n-pepper hair, chestnut-brown complexion.

Tollon:
A Dramudam peace ship under Commander Thoren.

Trager:
Dramudam, subcommander of the peace ship Tollon, of the Eldatek race, left hand of Commander Thoren. Master pilot, squadron leader and head of security, he is known for his easy smile and intense devotion to duty and ship. Eldatek name: Haator ka Neeha. Mother: Neeha of the Council of Elda, Elder sister: Ralana, who runs the prominent family towan product processing and export business, and Elder brother Talman who is joined to Bohata. Height 7.4 pol (2.0 meters), medium athletic build, almond-shaped black eyes, long straight black hair, chestnut-brown complexion. Mustache and goatee in a Van Dyke that frames his mouth.

Utahar:
A race of beings born on the planet Uta. Distinguished by their golden tan skin, golden feline eyes, and full blond hair. Males on

average stand 7.0 pol (1.9 meters), while females stand approximately 6.8 pol (1.83 meters) on average. Both males and females equally hold leadership positions. The average life span is one hundred fifty revolution. Cunning and racial purity are highly prized qualities in their culture. They view all other races as inferior to themselves and eagerly promote black market trade of slaves and technology to worlds that turn a blind eye to the Isolation Treaty. Telepathy is rare but does occur.

Vaya:
A tart, fruity hot drink that has a slightly viscous texture, which soothes the throat. It is made from a fungus that grows in the shade of rock outcroppings in the deserts of the planet of Elda. A small pinch of the powdered red fungus dissolves quickly in near-boiling water, usually drunk after third kel or just before sleeping. It has a slight sedative effect and is also reported to suppress the libido.

Vel'Una of Elda:
Of the Eldatek race. Heads the family masonry business on Elda and is a member of the Elda Council. Mother of Nin'Te ka Vel'Una her first-born, and only, daughter. Height 6.85 pol (1.85 meters), black almond-shaped eyes, red clay brown skin.

Vu'Rel ka Wil'Amay:
See Yononnon.

Wil'Amay:
Of the Eldatek race. Heads the family textile business on Elda. Mother of Felia ka Wil'Amay (her first-born daughter), Me'Hal ka Wil'Amay (her second-born daughter–Dramudam ship name: Leenon), Braheen ka Wil'Amay her first-born son, and Vu'Rel ka Wil'Amay (Dramudam ship name: Yononnon). Height 6.85 pol (1.85 meters), black almond-shaped eyes, red clay brown skin.

Ya:

The Eldatek word for a hot tea or drink. It is made by steeping various plant parts in hot (near boiling) water. Various ya may be steeped with varying effects. Most ya blends fall into the category of medicinal. They may affect the digestive system, nervous system, and libido.

Yononnon:

Dramudam, subcommander of the peace ship Tollon, of the Eldatek race, right hand of Commander Thoren. Master pilot, squadron leader and general ship coordinator. Younger brother to Me'Hal ka Wil'Amay (Dramudam ship name Leenon). His oldest sister, Felia ka Wil'Amay, and older brother, Braheen ka Wil'Amay both still reside on Elda. Height 7.4 pol (2.0 meters), large athletic build, almond-shaped black eyes, long straight black hair, chestnut-brown complexion. Mustache that frames his mouth. Eldatek name: Vu'Rel ka Wil'Amay of Elda, second-born son of Wil'Amay of Elda.

Zendra:

Symbiotic artificial organic life forms injected into beings for the purpose of facilitating communications between individuals and a variety of computer systems. A side effect of the zendra is overall improved health of the host being and more rapid healing times, since zendra prefer to live in a healthy environment.

GALACTIC TIME AND LENGTH CONVERSIONS

The following is reference information regarding time and galactic length. It is for reference only and to assist in general conversions and not for precise time or distance/length calculations. It should also be noted that with the exception of arcs, there is no difference between the singular and plural forms of the time or distance units.

Time Measurements

The following is the approximate conversions from galactic arcs (arcs) to Earth time frames. Uses the assumption 365.25 days in an Earth year:

Earth reference 360 degrees = 1 period
1 Earth year = 350,640,000 (galactic) arcs
1 Earth month = 29,220,000 arcs
1 Earth week = 6,743,076.923 arcs
1 Earth day = 960,000 arcs
1 Earth hour = 40,000 arcs
1 Earth minute = 666.667 arcs
1 Earth second = 11.111 arcs

The following is the standard vincamol, mol, kel, hur and tol equivalents of galactic time (arcs) related to Earth time frame, where vinca = 20, benta = 10, geno = 5, fol = 1:

1 vincamol = 320,000,000 arcs = 0.913 Earth years = 1 revolution
1 vincamol = 20 mol
1 mol = 16,000,000 arcs = 16.667 Earth days = 0.548 Earth months
1 mol = 20 genokel = 5 bentagenokel
1 bentagenokel = 4,000,000 arcs = 4.167 Earth days = 0.593 Earth weeks
1 bentagenokel = 5 genokel
1 genokel = 800,000 arcs = 1 cycle = 20 Earth hours = 0.833 Earth days
1 genokel = 5 kel
1 kel = 160,000 arcs = 4.00 Earth hours
1 kel = 20 hur

1 hur = 8,000 arcs = 0.20 Earth hours
1 hur = 20 tol
1 tol = 400 arcs = 0.60 Earth minutes
1 tol = 20 vincafol
1vincafol = 20 arcs = 1.8 Earth seconds
1vincafol = 20 fol
1 fol = 1 arc = 0.090 Earth seconds

Length Measurements
The following are conversions to facilitate approximate calculations of length between the galactic length (tran/pol/vel) and the Earth measurements of length (meter/miles/feet/inches), where vinca = 20, benta = 10, geno = 5, pol = 1:

1 bul = 5 vincatran = 2,700 m = 1.678 miles
1 vincatran = 20 tran = 540 m
1 bentatran = 10 tran = 270 m
1 genotran = 5 tran = 135 m
1 tran = 27 m
1 tran = 5 vincapol = 27 m = 88.583 ft
1 vincapol = 20 pol = 5.4 m = 17.717 ft
1 bentapol = 10 pol = 2.7 m = 8.86 ft
1 genopol = 5 pol = 1.35 m = 4.43 ft = 53.150 inches
1 pol = 0.27 m = 0.886 ft = 10.632 inches
1 vel = 1/20th pol = 0.0135 m = 0.0443 ft = 0.531 inches

Common Reference Lengths
1 tran = 1/100 bul = 1/20 vincatran = 5 vincapol = 100 pol = 2000 vel
1 meter = 3.703 pol = 3.281 ft = 39.37 inches = 100 cm
2 meter = 7.407 pol = 6.562 ft = 78.740 inches = 200 cm
1 cm = 0.657 vel = 0.394 inches
1 inch = 1.669 vel = 2.54 cm
3 inch = 5.007 vel (5.0 vel)
3.937 inches = 6.571 vel (6.6 vel)
30 meters = 111.09 pol = 2221.8 vel = 1.111 tran

Common Reference for Speed of Light in a Vacuum:
Speed of light = 1.0 x 10^6 tran/fol = 3.0 x 10^8 meters/second
Distance traveled by light in 1 vincamol = 3.2 x 10^{14} tran

Angular Measurements

The following are conversions to facilitate approximate calculations of angular measurements between the Galactic unit (von) and the Earth/Terran measurement (degree), where vinca = 20, benta = 10, geno = 5, von = 1:

1 von = 18 degrees
1 genovon = 5 vons = 90 degrees
(May also be used to express the direction right or east in Intergaltic)
1 bentavon = 10 vons = 180 degrees
(May also be used to express something is behind someone or the direction south in Intergaltic)
1 betageno = 15 vons = 270 degrees
(May also be used to express the direction left or west in Intergaltic)
1 vincavon = 20 vons = 360 degrees
(May also be used to express that someone has come full-circle, the direction straight ahead, or the direction north in Intergaltic)

Note: 15 vons = 270 degrees. It can also be referred to as negative genovon (-90 degrees). The more common variation is bentageno with the von dropped (loosely translated as ten and five von in Intergaltic or in English 180 plus 90 degrees).

KEY FAMILIES OF ELDA:

Kil'Treahaa of Elda (Mother) – Head of the Elda Council (Sister to deceased First-Born Seralan ka Pintra)
(1) Tete ka Kil'Treahaa: First-Born Daughter
    i. Head of family red stone quarry business
    ii. Only living child of Kil'Treahaa
    iii. Has a living first-born adult daughter: Lah'na

Zelle'Fah of Elda (Mother) – Previous head of family masonry business (now deceased)
(1) Pintra ka Zelle'Fah: First-Born Daughter
    i. Inherited family masonry business
    ii. Joined
    iii. First-born daughter: Seralan ka Pintra & Second-Born daughter Kil'Treahaa ka Pintra
(2) Loh'Haa ka Zelle'Fah: Second-Born Daughter
    i. Untimely death from fever shortly after childbirth
    ii. Not Joined
    iii. First-born Son—illegitimate: Thoren ka Zelle'Fah (now Commander in the Dramudam)

Pintra of Elda (Mother) – Previous head of family masonry business (now deceased)
(1) Seralan ka Pintra: First-Born Daughter
    i. Was Heir to family masonry business until untimely death from fever
    ii. Not joined
    iii. No children
(2) Kil'Treahaa ka Pintra: Second-Born Daughter
    i. Inherited head of family masonry business until becoming head of Elda Council
    ii. Joined

iii. First-born daughter: Tete ka Kil'Treahaa (who now heads family Masonry business)

Wil'Amay of Elda (Mother) – Head of family textile business
(1) Felia ka Wil'Amay: First-Born Daughter
   i. Heir to family textile business
   ii. First-born daughter: Li'Kur ka Felia
   iii. Second-born daughter: Aasha ka Felia (Dramudam ship name: Alham)
(2) Braheen ka Wil'Amay: First-Born Son
   i. Not joined
(3) Me'Hal ka Wil'Amay: Second-Born Daughter
   i. Serving as a med tech in the Dramudam – ship name: Leenon
   ii. Not joined
   iii. No children
(4) Vu'Rel ka Wil'Amay: Second-Born Son
   i. Serving as a pilot in the Dramudam – ship name: Yononnon
   ii. Not joined
   iii. No children

Neeha of Elda (Mother) – Member of the Elda council, Head of family towan root products processing and export business
(1) Ralana ka Neeha: First-Born Daughter
   i. Heir to family towan root products processing and export business
   ii. Joined
   iii. Has a living first-born daughter: Hesthra ka Ralana
(2) Talman ka Neeha: First-Born Son
   i. Joined one to Bohata ka Frolan
   ii. No children
(3) Haator ka Neeha: Second-Born Son
   i. Serving as a pilot in the Dramudam – ship name: Trager

ii. Unsanctioned joining to off-worlder Danica Jolan (Dramudam ship name: Forrorrois)

iii. Illegitimate daughter: Celeste

Frolan of Elda (Mother) – Head of family ya import/export business

(1) Bohata ka Frolan: First-Born Daughter

   i. Heir to family ya import/export business

   ii. Joined one to Talman ka Neeha of Elda

   iii. Only living child of Frolan

   iv. No children

Vel'Una of Elda (Mother) – Member of the Elda Council, Head of family masonry business (sister by joining to Wil'Amay of Elda)

(1) Nin'Te ka Vel'Una: First-Born Daughter

   i. Heir to family masonry business

   ii. Joined

   iii. Has a living first-born daughter: Ki'ahway